The Collected Supernatural and Weird Fiction of Richard Marsh Volume 5

The Collected Supernatural and Weird Fiction of Richard Marsh Volume 5

Including Two Novels
'The Death Whistle' and
'The Chase of the Ruby' and Four Short Stories
of the Strange and Unusual

Richard Marsh

LEONAUR

The Collected
Supernatural and Weird
Fiction of
Richard Marsh
Volume 5
Including Two Novels 'The Death Whistle' and 'The Chase of the Ruby'
and Four Short Stories of the Strange and Unusual
by Richard Marsh

FIRST EDITION

Leonaur is an imprint
of Oakpast Ltd

ISBN: 978-0-85706-852-1 (hardcover)
ISBN: 978-0-85706-853-8 (softcover)

http://www.leonaur.com

Contents

The Death Whistle

Chapter 1
Appointing An Heir

"If you like you'll be able to live upon the interest;—many a man who is thought well off lives on less. Or, if you prefer to aim at the big things and you're that kind of man—you'll have enough capital in hand to enable you to bring off successfully some of those greater villainies which make men millionaires."

The listener laughed; the situation appealed to his peculiar sense of humour. The man in the bed looked at him.

"I like to hear you laugh, lying here. If I were out of this, and we were alone together, and had had a little difference of opinion, I shouldn't like it quite so much. The devil's strongest in you when you laugh."

"You're so funny."

"I am. I've been a funny man my whole life long; an unconscious humorist. The mischief is, I've found it out too late. If I'd suspected the truth a dozen years ago I shouldn't be dying in jail."

"If s not a pretty place to die in. And yet I don't know; it's as good as any other."

"You didn't think so once."

"Once!—Once I thought jam the concentrated essence of happiness."

"So did I. I thought it so strongly that I held it worthwhile to swallow a few bitters to get it. That's where it is, and why I'm here, Bruce." The other nodded. "I've a feeling you don't believe half that I've been telling you; that you regard my story about the fortune which is lying ready for your hand as a convict's fairy tale."

"My dear chap, I always believe everything I'm told. I've been the confidant of a large number of veracious histories since I've been inside this place. The silent system is not so rigidly enforced as to prevent one's being that. My powers of credulity are boundless."

"Yes, I know. If I thought you were setting down among the rest of the prison lies what I've told you, I should lie in my grave and scorch."

"Don't do that. And don't talk about it either. It presents unpleasant *vistas* to the imagination."

"Perhaps if I were to tell you my history you might bring yourself to believe that I am leaving you a fortune. I grant that under the circumstances the notion does want swallowing."

"My dear Edney, I give my confidence to no one."

"So I've noticed."

"But if you choose to give me yours, I am entirely at your service. I agree with you that when a man who has been sentenced to ten years' penal servitude observes that he proposes to make you his heir, you are inclined to ask yourself what to. It is easy enough to bequeath any number of castles in Spain, to anyone; but one hardly expects to have to pay legacy duty on bequests of the kind."

"You won't pay legacy duty on what I'm leaving you."

The man in the bed grinned. He lay back on his pillow and coughed. Coughed badly and long. So long that one wondered if he would stop before he was broken to pieces. Blood issued from his mouth. He was not a pleasant spectacle. His companion rendered him such assistance as he could, showing gentleness and patience which contrasted oddly with his stalwart form. After the paroxysms were over, the man in the bed lay motionless, scarcely seeming to breathe. Words came thinly from his lips. "I'll go off in one of those bouts, please God."

"You mustn't talk."

"But I must talk. That's just what I must do. Perkins won't be back yet. I ought to be able to tell you all that's needful before he comes. I mayn't have another chance." Perkins was dispenser and warder combined. Canterstone was but a small jail. There were seldom many prisoners in the infirmary. At present there were but three: George Edney, dying; Sam Swire, a 'traveller,' 'doing a drag,' the victim of too much drink and too little food; and Andrew Bruce, recovering from a sprain, a good-conduct man, whose term of two years' hard labour was nearly at an end, and who was quite capable of looking after the two sick men who were in bed. Therefore, since the prison was not over-staffed, when Perkins went to dinner he simply locked the outer door of the infirmary and left Andrew Bruce in charge. Which explains how it was that George Edney and he were able to discuss their private affairs so freely; even proposing to enter into more delicate matters still. In Edney's opinion there was only one drawback.

"Go and see what that brute in the next room is doing."

Bruce did as he was told; passing for the purpose into the adjacent apartment, which was merely divided from its neighbour by a brief partition wall. Presently he returned.

"Swire's asleep; fast as a top."

"Good thing too; not that I can talk loud enough to give him much chance of overhearing."

"I tell you again that you oughtn't to talk at all."

"Chuck all that! Sit as close as you can, so as to spare my breath."

Bruce drew a chair as close to the bedside as possible, leaning forward, his elbows on his knees, so that his head was within a few inches of the other's face. He kept his eyes fixed upon the narrator's countenance, not only as if desirous of reading what was transpiring in his brain and behind his actual words, but also as if struck—and amused—by the singularity of his appearance. Normally small, weak-legged, loose-limbed, blear-eyed, he now seemed nothing but skin and bone. His lips were bloodless; patches of sandy stubble concealed his cheeks and chin; every now and then he gave a gasp, recalling the sounds made by a 'roaring' horse. As he proceeded, Bruce realised more and more clearly how entirely he looked the part of chief actor in such a tale as that which he was telling.

"I'm a solicitor by profession. Never on my own account;—hadn't the money to start with. I was managing clerk to a man who had. His name was Glasspoole,—Frederick Glasspoole, of Birchester. Connect anything with the name?"

"With the name of Frederick Glasspoole?—Nothing, at present."

"I thought you might have heard something of the story—read about it in the newspapers, perhaps—and so have saved me trouble."

"I'm willing to save you all trouble."

"I don't want to be saved that way.—He was a good fellow—young, and a fool. His father had left him a fine practice. Not only did he act for most of the townsfolk, but he was agent for some of the chief estates in the neighbourhood. But he had two faults—he wasn't fond of work, and he trusted me. The latter in particular was a grave mistake."

The grin which accompanied the words seemed to lend to the speaker's corpse-like features something of the grotesque horror which we associate with a gargoyle.

I was not an immoral character—not, that is, in any unusual degree. But I am, and always was, non-moral. Morality, that is, didn't enter into my scheme of creation at all. I hated work; though no one could work harder than I could when I chose, and had an end in view; and I liked a good time—my notion of a good time. I realised, quite early in life, that my good time meant money. Not in small sums. I didn't want to do the prodigal for, say, six months, and then have to live on husks for an indefinite period. That wasn't my idea; not a little bit. What I wanted was fifty or sixty thousand pounds. Then I would invest it in something gilt-edged, live on the interest, and get every farthing's worth of fun out of it that could be got.

"The point was how to procure the fifty or sixty thousand

pounds. It wasn't likely to be obtained out of the savings of a managing clerk. Glasspoole himself hadn't anything like that amount of ready money. His father's estate was sworn at something over ten thousand pounds. I happened to know that each year's income was spent during the same twelvemonth. So it seemed that even if, by some process of hanky-panky, I diddled him out of his business—which I perhaps mightn't have found an impossible feat—I should still have had to work for the rest of my life. Which was exactly what I didn't want to do. I tried betting—on horses and on the Stock Exchange. But that didn't make me appreciably richer. I dabbled in one or two other directions. Still the money wouldn't come. So, at last, I made up my mind what I would do.

"Instead of a profit, my little ventures had resulted in a pecuniary loss—which was what I hadn't intended. To meet it, I had had to make free with other people's property. Not to a large amount. Still it was more than I was ever likely to be able to replace. Worrying about it put me on the track of my great idea.

"In Glasspoole's charge there were all sorts of securities—bonds, shares, insurance policies, mortgage and title deeds; all sorts of things. Large sums of money—or money's worth—passed through his hands on behalf of his clients. And his hands meant mine. There was one estate in particular—the Dene Park estate, belonging to the Foster family—the fee-simple of which was practically inside the walls of Glasspoole's office. Nothing would be easier than to obtain the money I wanted—by turning thief.

"Why shouldn't I? I did my best to sum up the pros and cons, and give a judicial decision as to which side had the best of it. I argued in this way.

"On the one hand, I should be found out. I never deceived myself as to there being any room for doubt upon that point. On the other, I should have the money. I did not propose to spend it. My idea was to put it away in a safe place, where I alone should know of its existence, and to which I only should have access. I should be sentenced, probably, to between five and ten years' penal servitude. I doubted if I should object to prison much more than I did to Glasspoole's office. When I had served my term I should be a man of means. In other words, by doing—at the outside—ten years' imprisonment I should have earned a fortune; which I certainly never should be able to do by any other means whatever. You catch the notion?"

"I perceive that you're a pretty sort of a scoundrel."

"I'm one sort, you're another. I understand that you're here for something very much like murder."

Bruce laughed. Stretching out his hands he placed the other in a more comfortable position on his pillow. The sick man gave a little sigh of satisfaction.

"Your touch is as soft as a woman's, when you like.—Well, my scheme went on rollers up to a certain point. I stripped the office bare, laying hands on everything within reach; turning things into cash as I went on,—often, I am sorry to say, at a shocking loss. It's astonishing how certain kinds of property depreciate when you're in a hurry to realise. I put the money away as fast as I got it. By the time the crash came I had the satisfaction of knowing that I was comfortably off. They arrested Glasspoole and me on the same day."

"Glasspoole?—Was he your accomplice?"

"Neglect, my dear sir, neglect. I should never have been able to collar everything in the way I did do if his neglect of his clients' interests had not been really culpable. However, they were able to prove nothing against him actually criminal; and he was acquitted—a ruined man. I got ten years; which was three more than I expected, because I had hoped to get off with seven. But the judge happened to be Quince, who has a special prejudice against solicitors who misappropriate."

"You deserved the ten years; every day of it."

"I fancy that most of us in this establishment do deserve all we've got,—you as well as the rest."

"I'm not denying it."

"That's just as well.—The mischief is that I didn't get on in prison so well as I desired. Somehow it didn't agree with me at all. I haven't done six years, yet in about six hours I'll be dead."

Bruce, noticing the difficulty he had in speaking, in breathing, in living, thought it probable that he was right.

"I always understood that before a man got to your condition they gave him his discharge."

"So they do. They told me, a month ago, that I was a dead man. And they offered to let me out."

"Offered?—what do you mean?"

"They don't turn a man out to die in the streets, or even in a workhouse. They ask him if he has anywhere to go to; if he has any friends."

"And haven't you any?"

"After what I've been telling you, do I strike you as being the kind of man who is likely to have friends? Like you, I've none."

"How do you know I've none? You know nothing about me."

"I'll stake my fortune that there's not one creature living who'd stretch out a hand to save you from hell-fire. That's one reason why I'm making you my heir."

"One reason—what's another?"

"Just now you called me a pretty sort of a scoundrel. I attempted no contradiction. But, as a scoundrel, compared to you I'm a pigmy, in you there's the making of a criminal Colossus. You've no principles; no scruples; no attachments; nothing to cause you to stay your hand. You're handsome—you look like a Greek god; but I don't know if you're aware that those blue eyes of yours are of the shade and kind which are found in the heads of many gentlemen who finish at the end of a rope. You've nerve; courage enough for anything; for assurance, a countenance of triple brass. You're a giant in stature; you've the strength of a Hercules; and the sort of constitution which has never known what it is to be ill.

"You know the world; and, I fancy, you've seen—and done—a few things in it. You're a man of education; possibly a scholar; certainly a public school and university man. Given the chance, you should go far. And I'm going to give you the chance. Put these things together and you've another reason why I'm making you my heir."

"You flatter me; ascribing to me qualities which I was not aware that I possessed."

"I think that's possible. But you'll discover their existence as occasion arises for you to use them. I imagine that the fact that you've had the temper of a fiend is responsible for your being here."

"Well, there may be something in that."

"You must get that under, or it'll land you again. A man of your type, who, when he's raging hot inside, can seem as cold as ice, is the most dangerous creature on God's earth.—Go out in about a fortnight, don't you?"

"To be exact, in ten days."

"I'll be underground before then. Seems odd that I should have done it all to make you rich."

"It does—extremely. If this money exists, as you assert, why didn't you avail yourself of the discharge which was offered you, and make use of it yourself?"

"What use could I have made of it had I got it? I'm doomed to die; I may as well die here as anywhere. I've got beyond the stage when money could buy me anything which I could enjoy. Also—a big 'also'—the key to it all happens to be in a place where, in my then condition, I couldn't have got at it. I'd have had to take a partner, who'd have robbed me. It'll give me more satisfaction to know that it's being used by a man like you."

"Do you seriously suggest that, masquerading as George Edney, I should lay claim to moneys which are deposited somewhere in your name? Not only would the counterfeit be detected in an instant, but, I take it, there are associations which I should find it difficult to explain away.':

"I'm suggesting nothing so foolish. The money is not in any way connected with my name, or with me. It's deposited in the name of Smithers—Francis Smithers. And he is nothing but a name—and a signature. You'll have to get the signature right; but I credit you with the capacity for doing that. Unto this hour, no one has ever seen him in the flesh. When you come on the scene it will be his first appearance on any stage."

"I don't understand."

"I thought it would be better that no one with a memory for faces should be able to associate George Edney with Francis Smithers, so I took care that none of the depositing should be done by me in person."

"Then how am I to get at it?"

"You know Richmond Park, near London ?

"Very well."

"I was born at Richmond. I know every inch of it. When, down at Birchester, I was casting about for a hiding-place which no one could suspect, the Park struck me as being just the thing. Entering from the Richmond Gate, do you know what they used to call the drive towards the White House?"

"I do."

"Going towards the house, when you have passed the plantations, the ground dips,—with the Penn Ponds on your right."

Bruce nodded.

"A dozen yards due west of the north-western corner of the smaller pond—which is the one you first approach—among uneven ground, three feet deep, there is a tin box, which contains everything necessary to place you in immediate possession of the fortune of which I am now appointing you the heir. You will have no difficulty in finding it; but to further mark the spot, I broke a piece of bamboo off the cane which I was carrying and stuck it into the turf. So few people penetrate into that part of the park—partly because it is out of the way, and partly because the unevenness of the ground makes walking unpleasant—that, unless the deer have trampled it under foot, I shouldn't be surprised to find that piece of bamboo still thrusting up its nose amidst the tussocky grass."

Chapter 2
In Richmond Park

The conversation was interrupted by the return of the dispenser, Perkins. Three days afterwards George Edney lay dead. Before the end actually arrived he was reduced to such a condition that—for him—talking was impossible. Only once did he again mention the subject to Bruce. Then he merely mumbled the directions which he had given him as to the alleged whereabouts of the tin box.

"Remember, twelve yards due west of the north-west corner of Little Penn Pond, three feet underground."

The day before Bruce left jail, something occurred which was destined to stick in his memory. The prisoners were walking round and round the circular path which did duty as exercise ground. The time for exercise was nearly up when he heard someone say behind him, in those low, clear tones which the jail bird uses who desires to evade the observant warder's eyes and ears, "Mind you don't forget Richmond Park."

Bruce waited for a second or two, as was the desirable etiquette on such occasions, then glanced behind. The words had not come from the man immediately at his back, but from the next but one. Bruce recognised in him the 'traveller,' Swire, who had been the sole occupant of the other half of the infirmary when Edney had been relieving his mind. At Edney's request he had gone, before the tale began, to see how Mr Swire was engaged, and had found him, to all appearances, fast asleep. He remembered that Perkins, on his entrance, had found him still sleeping. Had the ingenuous Mr Swire been feigning slumber, for purposes of his own? Edney had spoken in such a subdued voice—he could not have spoken loudly had he tried—that Swire could scarcely have heard much, even if he had been listening. Still, Bruce was curious.

"What do you mean?"

"Don't go and take the blooming lot; just leave a bit for someone else."

It seemed as if Mr Swire's hearing had been at least sufficiently keen. Presently Bruce asked another question.

"When do you go out?"

"Oh, I've lots to do yet; when they do get me into a place of this sort they like to keep me just as long as ever they can."

The warder's voice rang out.

"Now then. No. 37, do you want to get reported for talking the day before you leave?"

Bruce was No. 37. He did not wish to be reported. During the remainder of exercise he held his peace. But he was free to hope that for a considerable period Mr Swire might continue an inmate of Canterstone Jail.

The following day—the great day on which he was to return to the world—was Saturday. His sentence expired on the Sunday. Since that was a day of rest in the prison, as among men outside, those prisoners whose terms expired on a Sunday were discharged the day before. Bruce had asked and received permission to leave at an earlier hour than was usual, as he was desirous of catching the first train up to town. Soon after six o'clock on the Saturday morning he passed through the prison gates,—for the first time for two years. He was dressed in his own clothes; carried a Gladstone bag—of somewhat attenuated appearance; and had in his pocket the gratuity of ten shillings which he had earned, and £2. 13s. 6d. which he had brought with him into jail.

When he reached the station he found that there was still some minutes before the ticket office would be open. Since he had the place to himself he spent the interval in examining his countenance in the looking-glass which was over the fireplace,—it was two years since he had seen a mirror. The change in his appearance amused him. His beard had grown; he had been clean-shaven when he went in; his moustache had attained to huge dimensions. He thought of how Edney had likened him to a Greek god. It struck him that a Viking would have been an apter comparison. His many inches—he was nearly six feet three; his fair hair and beard, both showing a tendency to curl; his pink and white skin; his bright blue eyes,—all these things were attributes of the old sea rovers.

He recalled Edney's association of blue eyes, like his, with murderers', and smiled; revealing, as he did so, two rows of beautiful teeth. Physically, prison regimen had had no injurious effect on him; he presented a perfect picture of bodily health. The suggestion of a continual smile seemed to irradiate his features, conveying the impression that he had not a care in the world. Wherever he went eyes were turned to look at him—especially when the eyes were in feminine beads.

When he reached London he breakfasted at a modest Swiss-Italian restaurant, which was close to the terminus. Then, walking to Waterloo, he took train to Putney. There he started to look for lodgings. Possibly his taste was fastidious. He called at at least a dozen houses before lighting on anything which seemed to suit him. He had seen four in the road in which he then was—Dulverton Road it was stated to be on a tablet at the corner. At No. 25 there was again a card promising 'apartments' in the window. It was a modern forty to fifty pounds a year 'villa,' with electric bells, tiled doorstep, and all the latest improvements. He pressed the white china knob which was at the side of the stained-glass-windowed door.

His ring was answered by a girl—a dark girl, apparently somewhere in her twenties; not a servant, but looking like a lady in her plain indigo serge dress. She appealed to him then and there; something in her appearance differentiated her from the females who had presented themselves to him at the other houses. He was not so struck by the rooms, but they would serve. They were on the ground floor. The girl spoke of them as the 'dining-rooms'—the sitting-room being in the front and the bedroom at the back. The furniture was not substantial in kind, nor liberal in quantity. About everything there was a gimcrack air, which suggested the jerry-builder.

"And what is the rent you are asking?"

The girl looked at him with what he was conscious were inquiring eyes—as if she were desirous of ascertaining how much he was willing to pay.

"Is it for a permanency?"

"I'm afraid that at present I cannot say. I may be gone in a week; or I may stay"—there was a flash of laughter in his eyes—

"I may stay forever."

Her countenance remained unmoved.

"Of course it makes a difference if it's for a permanency. Mother has generally had five and twenty shillings."

"Five and twenty shillings!" Twelve and sixpence was the maximum price he had proposed to himself to pay. He had seen rooms at that rent a few doors down the street. But there there was a blowsy woman, with a baby in her arms; not this girl, with the sweet, soft voice. "Is that inclusive?"

"That would be inclusive."

"Then I'll take the rooms."

Later he saw her mother, who had returned from shopping. She was a Mrs Ludlow a widow. A little woman, with trouble written large on her face. Bruce, whose keen blue eyes saw everything, said to himself," She worries."

Still later, in his bedroom, he considered the position; incidentally taking an inventory of his belongings.

"Frock-coat and waistcoat; two pairs of trousers; two shirts; two pairs of socks; one necktie; one pair of boots,—except what I stand up in, that completes my wardrobe. Gold links, studs, watch and chain,—these things represent my jewellery; and £2. 14s. 9d. my entire fortune. Considering that the rent is twenty-five shillings a week, that won't go far." He paced up and down the tiny room. "She asked if I was going to be a permanency. It looks like it! I've about enough money to see me through the week. And then? I don't want to return to Canterstone Jail for obtaining food and lodging under false pretences—especially from Miss Ludlow and her mother. It'll have to be George Edney's fortune or—or something else."

He arranged his clothes in the chest of drawers, then went out into the passage.

"I'm going out, Mrs Ludnow, and perhaps may not be back till late."

"Would you like a latchkey? Mr Rodway, who has the drawing-rooms, and who is often out late, always uses one. I have two."

Bruce went out with one of them in his waistcoat pocket.

"That woman has never been deceived, or she would scarcely be so trustful,—unless it's her nature to be deceived and come again. In the atmosphere to which I had lately been accustomed such simplicity would be regarded as suggestive either of a lunatic asylum or a fairy tale."

He strode across Barnes Common, up Clarence Lane, into Richmond Park, as one who knew the way. It was then about three o'clock in the afternoon. Although the weather was fine, a strong breeze blowing from the north-west hinted at approaching rain. When he got inside the park he stretched out his arms, raising himself on his toes, like a man who wakes from sleep.

"This is something like. It's worthwhile doing two years' hard labour if only for the sake of regaining one's capacity for enjoyment. I feel as if my school days had returned, and as if the world lay in front of me—my oyster-shell, filled with priceless gems, which it only needs a touch of my knife to open. Perhaps it does!"

He took off his hat and marched across the turf, laughing as he went. It was all he could do to keep himself from breaking into a run. As he neared the lakes his pace grew slower. Although it was Saturday afternoon not many people were about. He scanned closely those who came within scanning distance. When he had crossed the road leading from the Sheen Gate he seemed to have the whole park in front of him to himself. Reaching the edge of the smaller pond he paused, observing the lie of the ground.

"How did Edney put it?—A dozen yards due west of the north-western corner;—that will be the corner on the opposite side, straight ahead." He walked to the point in question. "West?—As I stand here I am looking south; the west is on my right. Now for your dozen yards." He took a dozen paces, then stooped to examine the turf. "As he said, the ground's uneven enough. That precious tin box of his may be here or hereabouts, or it mayn't. Very much it mayn't. I was never on quite such a wild-goose chase since the days when l used to dream of going in search of hidden treasure. If the man was gammoning me all the time? I doubt it; and yet—perhaps I'm the only man who would—What's that?"

Something caught his eye a foot or two from where he was standing; something which might very easily have escaped his notice had not his glance been such a keenly observant one. It looked like a splinter of wood amid the coarse grasses.

"Edney's piece of bamboo, as I'm a sinner! Then, on that occasion, at any rate, the man was not a liar."

Gripping the scrap, which was all that was visible, he endeavoured to drag it out of the earth. It was not an easy task. The turf had grown so close about it that it was held as in a vice. He cut away the fibrous roots with his penknife. Presently he held it in his hand. It was part of a slender bamboo cane, about ten inches in length. A ferrule, nearly eaten away by rust, was still at one end. The wood itself was rotten. It was only by careful handling that he had succeeded in drawing it out intact.

"To think of that having been here all this time—half a sixpenny cane! How many years is it? I suppose it must be seven. He had served six; and the presumption is that he paid his last visit here some time before what he called 'the crash' came. It shows that he chose his place with knowledge—it has even gone unmolested by the deer. Then am I to take it that the tin box is underneath, containing the key to the fortune—my fortune? One thing's obvious, that since I've lit on this, which, in its way, is 'confirmation strong as holy writ,' it's worthwhile examining a little farther." He stood up, considering; turning the piece of cane over and over in his fingers.

"Three feet deep, he said. I can't get down to that with a penknife, not to mention that to excavate a hole that size in Richmond Park in broad daylight might attract attention. Although there are not many people about, still there's the risk. I require no audience and I want to be asked no questions. I'll go on to Richmond; there I'll buy something to dig with; after dusk I'll return. In the meantime I'll replace this piece of cane; it'll serve as a landmark a second time. I may want it after the shadows have fallen."

He carried out his programme; walked over to the town; purchased in George Street a mason's trowel and a small digging fork. As the day was drawing to a close he strolled back towards the Penn Ponds with the two tools in his jacket pockets.

He returned by the route which Edney had described,— along the drive leading to the While House. This necessitated a sharp turn to the right as soon as the plantation was passed. Almost immediately afterwards the lake came into full sight. The month was April, when the night comes quickly, especially on a grey day such as that was. It was distinctly chilly. The wind had risen still higher. Heavy clouds tore across the sky. He had not seen a creature since entering the park—until the lake came in sight. Then he saw that someone—something—was by the water's edge. Was it a man? a deer? a bush?—what?

He stopped instantly, drawing back into the shadow of the tree which he was passing. The light was bad, as he had desired it should be. As the object he was eyeing was at a distance of over a hundred yards, the prevailing obscurity made it difficult to determine what it was. However, his powers of vision happened to be unusually acute.

"It's a man; that's what it is. He's kneeling down, and is leaning so far forward that his nose almost touches the grass. Unless I err, he's very close to Edney's piece of cane. What's he doing there, at this time of day? Is it accident or intention?"

Presently from the crouching figure proceeded a sort of chuckling sound.

"He's found it. It's intention. He seems to be so wrapped up in what he's looking for, and so unsuspicious of anyone being hereabouts, that I ought to be able to get at him before he scents my neighbourhood. The wind's coming from him. I used to be a bit of a hand at a deer-stalk; let's see if I've forgotten the trick."

It seemed that he had not. Aided by the configuration of the ground, by the darkness, by the noise the wind was making—it was fast blowing up a storm—by his own dexterity and deftness of movement, he came within nine or ten feet of the now nearly

22

recumbent figure—obviously still unnoticed.

"He's digging!—the dear man!"

Leaping through the air like some huge wild creature, Bruce sprang upon the unheeding man, and, gripping him by the shoulder, swung him round upon his feet; meeting with no more resistance than might have been offered by an automaton.

The man he held helpless in front of him was Sam Swire.

CHAPTER 3
THE BOX

Beyond doubt Mr Swire had, in his time, been in some curious situations. He was a man with a history, so the thing was certain. The probability is, therefore, that he was not an easy man to take by surprise. That on that occasion he was surprised is undeniable. He had all the outward marks and signs of amazement in the superlative degree. The muscles of his face were twitching as if he were suffering from St Vitus' dance; his mouth seemed to be opening and shutting of its own accord.

"So you weren't asleep?"

The fact that, under the circumstances, he should have regained the faculty of speech so quickly as he did was creditable to his presence of mind, and showed how wide his experience must have been. True, his voice was a little tremulous, and he showed a tendency to stutter. Still, what he said was understandable.

"It's—it's His Highness!"

'His Highness' was the nickname by which Bruce had been known in jail, and had reference to his appearance, deportment, and such fragments of his story as were known or guessed at.

"And you were lying when you told me that you had still some time to serve?"

"Never said it. What I said was that I still had lots to do. So I had,—pretty nearly four and twenty hours. I came away from home this morning—same as you did. Only it seems that they let you out extra early. But we aren't all persons of importance, and that's where it is."

Bruce returned to his original position.

"So you weren't asleep?"

Swire grinned. He was rapidly becoming his normal self.

"Well, I can't say I was—exactly. When the cove told you to see what I was up to, I thought that there might be going to be some interesting conversation. So when you came and had a look, of course I was as sound as a baby. Bound to be when I knew it would oblige."

"And you heard?"

"Not all;—bits here and there;—about enough."

There was silence. They looked each other in the face. Swire spoke next.

"You take your hands from off me. Perhaps you don't know your scrunching up my shoulder-blades."

"What are you doing here?"

"Now that's just the question I was going to put to you."

"You know what I am doing."

"And you know what I am doing, so we're even."

"I see—that's it. The further question arises—what shall I do with you?"

"You take your hands off—that's what you'll do with me."

Instead of answering Bruce transferred one hand to the other's throat; gripping it in such fashion that the man's jaw dropped open and continued motionless, as if suddenly paralysed. Apparently he made an effort to remonstrate, but his utterance was choked; to struggle, but his limbs merely twitched, as if they belonged to some lay figure. The grip became firmer and firmer, until Mr Swire's countenance assumed a very unpleasant appearance indeed. When it was relaxed he fell backwards on to the ground like a log, remaining motionless as one. Bruce stopped to look at him.

"He's not dead, but he's as near to death as it would be wise to bring him."

From about the neck, which he had just been holding in such a close embrace, he look a coloured handkerchief. With it he tied its owner's legs together. From a jacket pocket he took a

24

second, using it to tie his hands behind his back.

Then he turned his attention to other matters.

"So he did find the landmark, and he's started digging with a pocket knife. If Edney's box of treasures is any size, it would have taken him some time to dig it out with that. Yet with such a blade it ought to be a useful knife. He might have tried it upon me if I had given him a chance." Something touched him on the face. It was a drop of rain. "It's coming, is it? I thought it wasn't far off." All at once the rain descended with torrential violence. "It begins to occur to me that I'm going to get wet. There's one comfort—it's likely to save me from further disturbance."

He laughed beneath his breath, as if the whole business was a joke.

"In a matter of this sort method's desirable. The first thing to do is to cut out a square of turf, which can be replaced so as to show as little sign of disturbance as possible. And for that purpose Swire's knife will come in handy."

Working rapidly, cutting out a thick slab of turf, he laid it. intact, upon one side. With his trowel he loosened the earth which its removal had made accessible, using his hands to shovel it out. The pelting rain, seeming to drain it into the hole, turned it into mud as he went on.

"I ought to have got down nearly three feet. Let's hope Edney's three didn't mean four; this is becoming awkward." The depth to which he had attained, and the nature of the tools with which he was working, necessitated his lying flat on his stomach on the soaking grass. "I'll probe for it." Using Swire's knife as a probe he thrust it into the ground nearly as far as it would go—until its further ingress was prevented by some hard substance.

"That feels like metal. We will trust it is. It oughtn't to take me long to get as far as that." As he was resuming work Swire evinced signs of returning consciousness. He lay five or six feet from the open hole. Even at that short distance only his outline was visible in the prevailing darkness. Odd sounds came from him; then groans; then words, and with words, bad language.

"Where am I?—What are you playing at?—What's

happened?—Who the?"

Then came the torrent of bad language. Without saying a word, with the man's own knife Bruce cut off a thick tuft of grass. Moving towards him, just as he was in the very midst of a flood of expletives, Bruce crammed the grass into his mouth. It served as an effective gag. The man might writhe and twist, and he did, but he could not rise to his feet; his own handkerchiefs bound him too adroitly; nor could he make himself heard. Picking him up indifferently, as if he were some inanimate log, Bruce bore him back into the drive, a distance of perhaps two hundred yards. Depositing him by the fence of one of the plantations, his face against the woodwork, he left him, still without a word.

Then he returned to his labour. A few seconds later he was lifting out of the hole which he had made what seemed to be a metal box.

"Then Edney wasn't lying—which seems to show that the ruling passion is not always strong in death,—unless the point of the jest is still to come, and his treasure box contains nothing worth the finding."

He crammed back into the hole as much of the soil as he could. Replacing the slab of turf, he strode off with the box in his hand;—apparently oblivious of Mr Sam Swire, lying on the sodden ground, bound and speechless, in the darkness, the wind, and the pelting rain. He glanced at his watch.

"Nearly ten. Clarence Gate will be closed. It will have to be Sheen."

He passed through Sheen Gate unobserved. Covering the ground at the rate of a good five miles an hour, he returned to Dulverton Road. On the lonely road, at that time, in that weather, he did not meet a soul. The downpour never slackened. As he neared his destination he thought of the condition he was in.

If they see me they'll wonder what sort of lodger they've got hold of; what I've been doing, where I've been. Which little matters I might find it difficult to explain. Perhaps Miss Ludlow's latchkey will enable me to get to cover before I'm scented;—they won't see me."

The latchkey did him the service he desired. By its aid he slipped into the house and into his bedroom before anyone was conscious of his presence. Hardly was he in his room when someone rapped at the panel. Mrs Ludlow's voice was heard.

"Would you like any supper, sir? You didn't say before you went out, so I left something on the table in case you might."

"Thank you, but I've had all that I require. I'm wet and rather tired, so I think I'll tumble in."

He did not "tumble in" quite so soon as his words—spoken from behind the cover of the locked door—suggested. First of all he placed himself before the looking-glass. The figure he presented seemed to afford him amusement,—though it was probably as well that he had not been seen on his entrance, and that the road along which he had come was a lonely one. No one could have encountered him unawares without being struck by his appearance; and wondering; and asking questions. It was not unlikely that food for cogitation would have been provided by the answers received.

He was soaked to the skin, his clothes being glued to his person as if he had just emerged from a long sojourn in the water. They were in an indescribable state of dirt. He wore a dark grey suit of Harris tweed, which served as an excellent foil to the stains of the reeking sandy turf on which he had been lying. His hands were caked with mud; it grimed his face, matted his beard. As he regarded himself in the mirror he laughed beneath his breath—which seemed to be a trick to which he was addicted.

"It's eminently desirable that there should be something worth having in Edney's treasure box; because this suit is clearly done for, and I've only a frocker to take its place; and with a frock-coat one can hardly wear a bowler, even if this bowler can ever be worn again."

He undressed himself; washed; scrubbed himself with towels. It was an indifferent substitute for a bath, yet luxury compared to the methods of ablution to which he had become accustomed at Canterstone. Then, in nondescript garb, he tackled his find.

It was a box, about nine inches by six, apparently made of

thin sheets of rolled iron. Probably originally it was japanned; there were traces here and there of what might have been japan; but now it was so eaten by rust that, save where the metal was still obscured by fragments of dirt, it was all a dull red.

"The key would be no use even if I had it; the lock's a wreck. And rust has riveted the lid to the body of the thing."

He shook it. No sound proceeded from within.

"If it were empty!—that would be the crowning jest. The question is, how to prise it open?"

It was a work of time, but he did get it open at last—with the aid of Mr Swire's knife, his own digging fork and trowel, and, it should be added, Mrs Ludlow's fire-irons, which served as levers. When it was open the reason why nothing had been audible when the box was shaken became obvious; the interstices left by the contents had been packed with cotton-wool,—which had become rusty, like the receptacle in which it was contained. Mr Edney had meant that nothing should be heard.

"A thorough-going man, that benefactor of mine. May his dishonest bones rest in peace! He evidently did his best to keep his treasures in condition."

The contents proved to be of a varied kind. Turning them out upon the bed, disentangling them from the rusty cotton-wool in which they were enveloped, Bruce examined them one by one. The first article on which he lighted had on him somewhat the effect of a cold douche. It was a portrait; a woman's photograph;" cabinet" size; a half-length. She was seemingly between thirty and forty years of age, and was in evening-dress;—as is the custom of a certain type of woman, who loves to attire herself in her splendours, merely for the sake of photographic reproduction. She wore a 'picture' hat; had two necklaces round her throat; ornaments in her hair; an anchor-shaped brooch in the bosom of her dress. Not a bad-looking woman; a trifle thin-lipped; and with some peculiarity in the shape of her nose which seemed almost to amount to a twist.

"Who is it, I wonder?—wife or sweetheart? or somebody else's sweetheart? It's an unexpected find, and unwelcome—

suggesting complications. From what I saw of him, one would hardly have associated Edney with a woman;—but one never knows. I hope, for your sake, madam, and for mine, that we shall never meet, or there may be trouble. More trouble.—What's this at the back?—The photographer's name 'Rayner, Birchester.'— Birchester? That's where it all took place. So it would seem that if I want to know something about you, madam, I have only to inquire at that address. But, as it chances, I do not want to know anything. I prefer to know nothing. Still, I'll keep your photograph, lest, some day, it may be required for reference. And yet—all sorts of unexpected disagreeables might arise from a trifle of this sort. Anyhow, for the present we'll put you by."

He next picked up a cheque-book, containing a hundred blank cheques—"to order"—drawn on the Strand branch of the National Bank.

"Cheques are all very well, given a balance; but without a balance, dangerous—in certain hands. As one or two gentlemen in Canterstone Jail seem to have found. Is there a balance in our favour at the Strand branch of the National Bank?"

It appeared that there was, if one might judge from the evidence of a pass-book, which was his third discovery. It was indorsed, on the plain parchment cover, in a hold round hand,—"Francis Smithers, Esq."

"Smithers?—Francis Smithers?—I don't care for the name myself; but still, if there is a solid balance at the back of it—a balance, if you're credited with it under any name, is sweet, especially when it finds you with a fortune of less than three pounds sterling."

The pass-book contained but a single entry. That was on the credit side—"By cash, £1000." It was attached to a date nearly seven years old. Bruce stared. After such a preface the blank pages seemed to have a singular eloquence.

"Mr Edney was really not such a liar as one might have supposed,—£1000, bearing no interest, not drawn upon for seven years,—the National Bank must feel that it has got rather a good thing. That's the sort of account that any bank would like to have.—What have we here?"

In the flap were two papers. One was a printed form on which the same institution acknowledged the receipt of £5000 on deposit, to bear interest at the rate of 2½% until further notice. The date was the same as that on which the drawing account had been opened. The second was a half-sheet of note-paper, on which was written, in a crabbed legal hand, "Address given, Cosmopolitan Hotel, Charing Cross."

"I see. So at the Strand branch of the National Bank, Francis Smithers, Esquire, has a thousand pounds, on which he can draw at sight; and five thousand pounds, on which he can draw at seven days' notice. The latter sum has been bearing interest. I presume the rate has varied with the bank rate. Assuming it to have averaged two and a half *per cent*, then there should be standing to his credit, in the shape of interest, something like another thousand pounds. Very pretty indeed.—And at the time these two accounts were opened he was residing at the Cosmopolitan Hotel.

"A highly respectable address. I had his word for it that he did not put in a personal appearance in the matter—yet it seems unnatural to have arranged a transaction of this sort through the post. I wonder. The bank people must have imagined that they had an oddity in the way of a client. So they had. One hears a good deal about bankers' unclaimed balances. Do they fancy they've got a haul in this little lot? If so, they'll be disillusioned when I appear upon the scene. And yet—it's not all plain sailing.—Next, please."

The next was a blank envelope. In it was a document issued by the Shoe Lane Safe Deposit Company, by which, in consideration of a certain sum of money received on a date this time nearly eight years old, they conveyed to Francis Smithers, Esquire, for a term of 99 years, one of their safes, to wit, No. 226. Accompanying this document was a tiny key of ingenious construction, to which was attached a tag inscribed, "Key of safe." There was also another half-sheet of note-paper on which was written, in a plain flowing hand, "Francis Smithers." Above it was the superscription, "My signature."

"The key at last; the Open Sesame which is, or is not, to unlock the door to all these riches. As the dear man correctly said, the signature's the essential thing. With it, one's sufficiently in the dark. Without it, where would one be? He vowed that I should find it easy; it doesn't look difficult, the sort of running hand they teach at school. As he was good enough to hint, I'm tolerably deft with a pen. Its presence here suggests that this is not his usual calligraphy; and that it was therefore the part of wisdom to keep a copy, to jog his memory, in ease he himself should forget how he wrote his name.

"He seems to have had an eye for all eventualities, save one—a prison death-bed. I wonder what's in safe No. 226. That, at any rate, I should have no difficulty in learning. I've the receipt—the key; they can hardly refuse me access to my very own safe, mine own for 99 years. He was a far-sighted man; did he expect to live to enjoy his possession for the whole of his term? Now what remains?"

There remained a letter-case in which there were twenty five-pound notes, not numbered consecutively, and many of them well worn, and a wash—leather bag containing fifty sovereigns.

"Something tangible at last. It is highly possible that this may be worth more to me than all the rest put together. I have this. I haven't that, and never may have. A man may keep himself alive for some time on £150; while, although Open Sesame does open the door, it may be that it is only to find destruction awaiting one on the other side."

Collecting the various articles, he contemplated them in the mass. Then, taking up the woman's photograph, he subjected it to a further examination.

"I like this least of Mr Edney's treasures. I should have been obliged to him if he hadn't put it in the box. It's too suggestive. Who is she? What's she doing in this galley? Has she a right to be here? He said he had no friends, and preferred to die in prison rather than trust himself to their tender mercies if he had any; that's a fact. She mightn't have been his friend although—theoretically—'a nearer one still, and a dearer one.' That sort of thing depends upon circumstances, and upon one's point of view. But in that case, where do I come in? I think I should like to know something about the lady; and yet—perhaps not. Confound the woman! I've a mind to burn her. But before I proceed to that extremity I'll sleep on it. Anyhow, don't let me blink at the situation. Let me look it straight in the face. These are the fruits of felony; the spoils of a sneaking swindler and a constitutional thief. If I avail myself of them, I sink to his level. I've been in trouble, but am I prepared to do that?"

Picking up the wash-leather bag he jingled its contents.

"That's eloquent music to a man who has less than three sovereigns between him and a return to jail. I'm afraid that I may not prove altogether impervious to temptation. Men refuse to act as trustees; but I'm not sure that I shall refuse to act as heir, even to a swindler of the very first water. But I'll sleep upon it all."

And he did, soundly, as if conscience did not trouble him. He was asleep almost as soon as he was between the sheets. But possibly that was because such a bed as Mrs Ludlow's was a luxury to which he had been strange for a considerable space of time.

CHAPTER 4
THE FIRST CHEQUE

The following day was Sunday. It rained unceasingly. For that reason and others—some of them connected with the condition of his wardrobe—he remained indoors, considering. On Monday the sun shone. When he had finished breakfast Mrs Ludlow appeared in person to clear the table, and to receive his orders for the day. Then she lingered, having evidently something on her mind. Presently it appeared that she was not quite so trustful as he had supposed. Possibly an inspection of his luggage had not inspired her with confidence.

"I am sure that you will understand, Mr Smithers"—he had given the name of Smithers on his arrival, and so had taken at least a preliminary step— "that no offence is intended, but might I ask if you're in business?"

"In business?—I'm afraid not."

"Are you—are you looking for a situation?"

"I wasn't thinking of doing so, just at present."

"Because, sir, you're a perfect stranger to me, and—and"

"You'd like your rent in advance?"

"Perhaps you would give me a reference."

"I'd sooner pay you; it will save us both trouble."

"I hope that no offence will be taken where none is meant; but the truth is, money is an object to me just now, and I dare not take any risks."

"Money is an object to most of us, and only foolish people do take unnecessary risks. I assure you, Mrs Ludlow, I am not in the least offended, and am quite willing to pay you weekly in advance."

He gave her two sovereigns; his own. When she had gone he turned the change she had given him over and over in his hand.

"That almost settles it. Less than a pound represents my all. What's a pound to a man of my pretensions? I fear I shall have to trench upon that fortune."

Arrayed in his frock-coat and incongruous headgear in the shape of that relic of a bowler, he sallied forth to take the air. In the High Street he bought another bowler and a silk hat. Glorified by the latter, he journeyed on top of a 'bus to town. He had never enjoyed a ride so much in his life. It is some distance from Putney to Regent Circus. But it was not one whit too far for him. The whole thing was a continuous delight. Given fine weather and no need for haste, one could hardly choose a pleasanter method of progression through the London streets than the top of an omnibus. And in his case there were special circumstances which made the occasion memorable;—it was so much better to be there than in Canterstone Jail.

In Regent Street he was measured for two or three suits, and made sundry other purchases, for which he paid with Mr

Edney's banknotes. Then he strolled along the Strand, where he surveyed the outside of the National Bank. Thence to Shoe Lane, to inspect the Safe Deposit Company. He was impressed by the idea of solidity conveyed by the plain stone frontage.

"If a man has a safe in a place like that it must have something in it; it's bound to. It can't be empty." He twiddled a tiny key which he took from his waistcoat pocket. "I wonder what's in my safe, No. 226. I'm half disposed to investigate it right away. But perhaps I'd better postpone that pleasure till—till I'm in a more settled state of mind."

He lunched at the Cosmopolitan Hotel, an idea having occurred to him. Mr Smithers had opened his two banking accounts while a resident of that palatial hostelry. If he were to draw his first cheque at the same address it might tend to allay any tendency to unhealthy suspicion. Suppose he were to enter his name in the books, and make it his headquarters? There was something in the notion; a good deal perhaps. But Miss Ludlow lived at Putney. There was plenty of time to turn the matter over in his mind.

At Dulverton Road that evening his coal-scuttle happened to be empty. He rang for it to be refilled. Miss Ludlow appeared. The idea that that graceful, dainty-looking girl should perform for him offices of that sort did not appeal to him at all.

"Allow me to take the scuttle. If you'll show me where the coals are, I'll fill it in no time."

But the girl showed so plainly by her manner that she would rather he did not, that he had to yield. She went out with the scuttle in her hand leaving him to fume upon the hearthrug.

"I can't stand this. I'm not going to have a girl like that wait upon me hand and foot as if she were some dirty drudge. Don't they keep a servant?—Then who cleans the boots?"

The question suggested disagreeable possibilities—especially when he reflected on how much his boots had stood in need of cleaning the preceding Saturday night, and how beautifully polished he had found them in the morning. On her return—with the refilled scuttle—she answered the inquiry which he had addressed to himself.

"We don't keep a servant. Mother and I do the work between us."

"But isn't that hard on you?"

"Oh, I don't know. Things are hard. Not that it matters. One gets used to them."

She showed a disposition to linger—with which he was entirely in sympathy, very much preferring her company, just then, to his own.

"If you will allow me, I shall be happy to engage a boy to do the rougher work,—boots, and that sort of thing."

"It's very good of you, but I'm afraid we couldn't afford it."

"I'd pay him."

"But we should have to deduct the amount from your rent—we should have to charge you less—and that's what we couldn't afford."

"You need do nothing of the kind."

"But attendance is included in what you are paying mother;—we couldn't allow you to pay for what you don't have."

"That's rubbish. If I choose to supply myself with a myrmidon in the form of a boy, I don't see what that has to do with you. Am I a slave that I should not be suffered to provide myself with a dozen grown-up serving-men?"

'There's that way of putting it, no doubt. You are not a slave."

She looked at him with dancing eyes. He noticed what pleasant eyes they were; big—brown—open—sunny. She stood observing him—with apparent unconsciousness of the fact—as if something in his personality struck her and gave her courage.

"I hope you didn't mind what mother said to you this morning?"

"Do you mean about my being a stranger?"

"Yes. She has a good many troubles just now, and she's anxious."

"She's quite right; I am a stranger—and not one to inspire confidence either."

"I'm not so sure of that."

"I am—or if I do it's confidence misplaced."

"Mother didn't mean anything."

"Then she ought to have meant something. But I believe she did. I do her more justice than her daughter. I came here with an ancient Gladstone and two suits of old clothes—one on and t'other off; there wouldn't have been much there to fall back upon in case of unpaid rent."

"Believe me, Mr Smithers, neither mother nor I had any fear that there would be that."

She spoke with sudden gravity, as if fearful that his lightness of tone was on the surface only. But he laughed at her.

"Then you ought to have had;—always suspect everyone. That's business. By the way—question for question!—I'll put to you the inquiry your mother put to me, so you mustn't take offence;—aren't you in business?"

"I've tried all sorts of things. Typewriting was the last; but there doesn't seem much money in that. So I'm looking for something else in which there is some money. If I find it, mother will have to get a servant. She can't do everything herself."

Mr Smithers, recently Bruce, immediately began to cast about in his mind as to whether he could not find for her something more congenial than—horrid notion!—cleaning a strong man's dirty boots. But he did not put this fact into words.

"You have another lodger?

"Oh yes, Mr Rodway has the drawing-rooms. He's been here ever since we came. Not that we've been here very long, but perhaps we shouldn't have come at all if it hadn't been for him. He's in my brother's bank."

"Your brother's bank?"

"Well, the bank in which he is employed. He's in the Strand branch of the National Bank."

"In the Strand branch of the National Bank? How very odd!"

He felt that it was odd;—so odd that it nearly took his breath away.

"He's much older than I am—he has a wife and family—he's been there for years—he's one of the cashiers. Why is it odd?"

"Its oddity consists in the fact that I have an account at that particular bank."

Whether or not he had intended to utter the words, he could not, at the moment, have said. But they were uttered-beyond recall. She spoke with a little air of malice.

"I believe that several people have accounts there. Where's the oddity of your having one?"

He turned his side face to her, resting a foot on the kerb and an elbow on the mantel. Should he answer? And if so, what? He had no time to think—it seemed easier to answer.

"There is something peculiar about the matter, and it's this. Seven years ago I opened two accounts there—a drawing and a deposit account. Up to the present I have not drawn a cheque upon the one or the interest from the other. I am thinking of doing so now."

"Seven years! I wish that mother or I could afford to open an account at a bank and leave it untouched for seven years! I'm going to see my brother at the bank tomorrow morning."

"Are you? Then perhaps you wouldn't mind taking a cheque for me and cashing it."

"I shall be delighted."

When she had left him he was not in two but a dozen minds. In the first place, what had he done? He had certainly done one thing—he had burnt his boats. He had taken a step which would lead him—where? Could it be called an open question? If so, time alone could supply the answer—he might have to wait for it till the end of his life.

Even if he did not entrust her with the cheque of which he had spoken, she would tell her brother what he had said. Unless he forbade her. On what grounds could he do that? It would be to arouse suspicion there and then If she told him, the probability was that inquiries would be immediately made; the whole business would be stirred up. Suppose he allowed her to present the cheque and there was trouble—a consequence which he esteemed extremely possible. Would he not be in the position of the cowardly scamp who, lacking courage to offer his own forgery across the bank counter, passes on the risk to any unconscious substitute? How would she be placed in case anything did happen? At the very least, she would have to bear witness against him The notion tickled him. He laughed.

The result of his cogitations was that he took out of a brand new despatch box, which had been one of the day's purchases, Mr Smithers' pass and cheque books and his signature. Producing also pens, ink, and paper, he set himself to imitate the latter.

"Let me see how close I can get to it. I'm out of practice. It's some time since I wrote anything—even a copy." Before he set to work he scrutinised the deposit note and the entry in the pass-book. "I suppose it is all right—that nothing has been drawn—that there's no hanky-panky about it anywhere. I'm in such a curious position that my naturally unsuspicious nature sees deception everywhere. Like a child who has to find its way about a strange room in pitch darkness, I'm a little timid—and awkward—the whole thing seems to be so pat that I'm convinced there's a flaw somewhere—and that will floor me."

He covered a sheet of paper with the two words—"Francis Smithers"— written in a hand which was so exactly like the original that it would have needed an expert to detect the difference. For a man who was 'out of practice,' he did it with surprising ease.

"I haven't lost the knack—fortunately. Or is it unfortunately? I wonder. If only a man standing where I stand could see into the future!—It's a convenient but a dangerous gift, that of penmanship—on these lines. We can only trust that, on this in occasion, the danger is reduced to a vanishing point.—For how much shall I draw my first cheque? It should not be for too much—at the same time it ought to be enough to make it worthwhile."

He wrote a cheque for £50, signing and endorsing it "Francis Smithers." Then he went to bed—in thoughtful mood.

In the morning repentance came. His rest had been broken—for him an unwonted experience. Visions of a girl's face and a pair of big brown eyes had disturbed his slumbers. When he rose he had changed his mind.

"She shan't take the cheque, and cover me. I shouldn't forgive myself if anything happened to her. Whatever risk's about, I fancy I'm equal to taking it. I'll not screen myself behind a woman's petticoats;—I'm not such a cur. I've not got down to that level yet,—though I'm promising fair. I'll take the cheque to the bank myself."

But in so deciding he was reckoning without the lady. While he was at breakfast she came in in her hat and jacket.

"Will you give me the cheque of which you spoke last night, Mr Smithers?"

"Cheque?"

He looked up at her—as if feigning forgetfulness.

"You said you would like me to change a cheque for you at the National Bank."

"So I did,—yes,—just so. But I don't think I'll trouble you. Miss Ludlow. There may be some formalities, which you might find a nuisance."

"I'm sure I shouldn't;—it will be a pleasure. In fact, by letting me change it you'll be doing me a service."

"Doing you a service?—How so?"

"I want to see my brother, but I'm not so sure that he will want to see me,—and your cheque will serve as an excuse."

"I see." He did not see; but that was by the way. "If, by getting you to do me a service I shall be doing you one,—if you put it in that way,—I will trespass on your kindness." He passed her the cheque, which he took from his pocket. "It's for £50;—tell them to make it three tens and four fives. You understand that you're responsible for whatever happens—in the way of worry."

She smiled and nodded.

"I'm used to responsibility;—in this case I'll take all there is about."

"Will you?" he said to himself, grimly, when she had gone. "If you only knew the peculiar nature of the responsibility you are incurring, your eagerness would be less.—After all. I am a cur; I've let her do it. Now I shall be on tenterhooks till she returns, imagining all sorts of delightful possibilities. If any of them do come off, I'll—I'll what? What can I do if any trouble comes to her because of her connection with a blackguard of my type? Cut my throat? Hang myself? Much benefit she would receive from that. I can do nothing.—So, at this point, let me arrive at one decision, and stick to it.

"I'll do all that has to be done myself; I'll drag no one with me into the mire in which I choose to run the risk of drowning.— How long ought it to take her to get to the Strand and back? Goodness alone can tell. She may have to do a dozen errands of which I know nothing—there may be a hundred and one delays. Suppose—oh, confound supposing! One thing's sure—I'm a haunted man until she does return. Why on earth did I let her take that cheque!"

CHAPTER 5
A VISITOR

Mr Smithers had a little conversation with his landlady while she removed his breakfast things, in the course of which she gave utterance to some candid opinions on the subject of her son and daughter.

"Theodore—that's my son's name—is a very clever man. Sometimes I'm almost afraid that he's too clever."

"In what sense? How can a man be too clever?"

He knew very well, from personal experience. But he chose to ask.

"It doesn't become me, his mother, to say anything; especially considering what a position he's gained, and he's done it all himself, for it's little enough I've been able to do for him, and his father died when he was a little lad. I only hope he'll get all that he thinks he will, and that it'll bring him happiness."

"I presume that he's a shrewd man of business? "

"Wonderfully shrewd—and hard. I won't say that he's hard as the nether millstone, because a man can't be expected to think of nothing but his mother all his life especially when he has a wife and family. Not like Netta."

"Netta? Is that your daughter's name?"

"It is, sir I wish there were more like her in the world. What it would be to me without her I don't know. But then I always do think that a woman has got more of the milk of human kindness in her than a man. There are some of the contrary opinion. I only speak as I've found. It seems to me that women know more of the pains and troubles of life, and perhaps this softens them. So many men only want a woman to make use of her. It isn't fair." "My landlady's a philosopher," mused her lodger, she having departed. "That last shaft might have been meant for me. I'm making use of a woman at this very moment and wish I wasn't.—Netta? Odd name! Yet it suits her.

"I'm of her mother's opinion that there's more in her than meets the eye; and what one sees is sufficiently prepossessing.— Curious that I should give a second thought to a woman after my experience of the sex—which doesn't tally with Mrs Ludlow's. Man's a composite creature." He referred to his watch. "Not eleven yet. How the time does drag. With comfort I can't go out, and I can't stay in until that girl returns—very possibly with a policeman. Suppose she is accompanied by a man in blue? What a very short holiday I shall have had."

Liking up the day's *Telegraph* he began to read—starting with the outside advertisement page and going straight on. To him a newspaper was still a luxury. It was some time before he came on anything in which he seemed to find a particular interest. When he did it took the form of a short paragraph in one of the columns headed "London Day by Day"—though what association it had with the headline was not quite clear.

The Marchioness of Skye gave birth to a son and heir on Sunday evening at Gairloch Castle, the family seat. Gairloch Castle, which stands on the edge of a precipitous cliff, is one of the most remarkable ancestral homes in Britain. It is also one of the most ancient. If tradition goes for anything, the castle possesses a well-authenticated ghost. The

Gairloch piper is famous. It is stated, however, that the wild wail of his weird pipes is only audible when a gale is blowing from the north-west, so that the gale may have something to do with the music. We understand that the Prince of Scotland has consented to act as sponsor. The Marquis of Skye, who has been staying in Paris, returned to the castle yesterday morning, to find that both mother and child are progressing favourably.

When he had finished the paragraph Mr Smithers, laying down the paper, stared into vacancy, as if his mental eye saw a picture before him in the air.

"That's a relief! That's a weight off my mind! What a weight—and what a relief! Bravo Alec—and bravo Sarah; well done! My only regret is that it isn't twins. But let's hope it will be twins next time, and the time after, and then again, until there are it a baker's dozen. You mayn't believe it, my good people, but the farther I'm off from Gairloch the better I'll be pleased. Indeed, my only hope of happiness lies there—if I've any hope at all.—So Alec's been to Paris—may Paris have meant propriety.—And Shon's pipes are only heard in a northwest wind? And, inferentially, only at Gairloch? Two little errors. I've heard them in all winds and in all places. I've grown used to them, so that I've begun to fancy that I know just when they may be expected."

The fashion of his countenance changed—growing grim and stark; more obviously reminiscent of the Viking's, to which he had himself compared it. He remained for, possibly, half an hour as rigid as if he had been carved in stone. With a start he returned to life, casting quick inquiring glances round the little room, like a man who had been dreaming. It was with a conscious effort that he took the paper again between his fingers, reading on mechanically until, for the second time, he came on something which roused him to unmistakable attention.

This time it was a paragraph in the body of the paper, the headline being, "Mysterious Occurrence In Richmond Park." It seemed that on the preceding Sunday afternoon—a few hours before an heir had been born to the Marquisate of Skye—a man was found in Richmond Park bound hand and foot, and gagged. He was in a wretched plight, having been exposed to the elements during the pitiless rains of the night and morning. His state of exhaustion was so complete that for some time after his arrival at the hospital, to which he had been taken as soon as possible after his discovery, fears were entertained for his life. Sympathetic treatment, however, had worked such a change that there was now little doubt of his eventual recovery. He had been too far gone to be able to talk much, yet it seemed that he had managed to tell a strange story.

He had been attacked in the darkness by a gang of ruffians, who, having used him with brutal violence, had, with the probable intention of avoiding pursuit, left him in the helpless condition in which he had been found. That robbery had been the object there seemed no doubt, as the victim of the outrage, who was a man in humble circumstances, had had upon him at the time, secured in a canvas bag, nearly five pounds in gold and silver coins; while, when he was found, the bag had vanished, and in his pockets were only a few coppers. The paragraph concluded by stating that at present nothing had been heard of the cowardly assailants; and while it was believed that the police had a clue, the whole affair was wrapped in mystery.

"Mr Swire means to make five pounds out of it, even if he loses the box of treasures. An ingenious man, and ready-witted. He won't blab. First of all, because of his constitutional objection to telling the truth; and second, because, in the course of the inquiries which would inevitably ensue, some damaging little discoveries might be made affecting him. He'd get nothing out of it anyhow. As it is, he probably thinks that he has a pull over me;—a double, if not a treble, pull. It will be one of the chief objects of his life to light on me again. When he does, then there'll be another tug of war.—Mem.: look out for Swire."

Miss Ludlow did not return till late in the afternoon. Before then Mr Smithers had made up his mind half a dozen times to rush off to the bank to see what had become of her. He was picturing her in all sorts of disagreeable positions. When she did appear he was standing at the window watching for her arrival with more anxiety than he would have cared to admit even to himself. So desirous was he to quickly hear the worst—feeling sure that there was a worst—that he had the door open for her before she had had time to ring, offering a somewhat lame explanation of his reasons for doing so.

"Excuse me for acting as door-opener, but I didn't want you to be kept waiting. I thought you were lost."

"I?—or the money?"

"You! Hang the money!"

He held the door open for her to enter his sitting-room. The lightness of her tone had caused his heart to jump in his bosom; for he perceived that nothing very dreadful had happened to her after all, or there would not be that smile in her voice—and in her eyes, and on her lips.

"Thank you; but you need never be afraid of my being lost; I'm not worth losing. The truth is, I thought they would never let me out of that horrid bank. I might have gone to rob it, instead of merely to change a cheque."

"I was afraid that there might be some formalities. You know I warned you."

"Formalities, you call them! They asked me enough questions to fill a book; wanting to know how old you were, how short you were, how black you were. I quite expected them to insist on my drawing a likeness of you on the spot. I might have managed a caricature of you; farther than that I don't think I could have gone."

"You do draw caricatures?"

"Oh yes, at times.—They seemed to think that I knew everything about you; and that if I didn't, then I ought to."

"It is fortunate for me you don't."

"Perhaps. One never knows. Men are—men." She looked at him with laughing glances "However, they did give me the money at last. At least, my brother did. Here it is, three tens, four fives, as requested. If I might be allowed to offer my advice, were I in your place, I should not again leave money untouched at a bank quite so long. I fancy they get so used to having it on the premises that they resent your asking for it back again almost as much as if it really were their own."

"I understand the feeling, and will bear the advice in mind.—I hope your interview with your brother was pleasanter?"

Her face clouded.

"No. it wasn't pleasant at all. But then, I didn't expect it would be. Only I'm afraid mother will be disappointed.—The great thing is that I got your money. But you mustn't suppose that their curiosity's appeased. I shouldn't be surprised if a director, or the manager, or somebody came and asked you some of the questions which they asked me. They don't want to give you your own money if they can help it, I feel sure."

After she had left him he remained some moments fingering the banknotes she had brought.

"I wonder what it was she went to see her brother about, which made him so unpleasant. It's not my business, but I'm a trifle curious.—Poor little girl! I expect they teased her. What a brute I was to let her go. Nice thoughts she'll think of me of me if she ever does find out. No doubt she's right; I may expect to be interviewed. It's not to be supposed that they'll disgorge dumbly to an unseen stranger. I'll go to them myself tomorrow and have it over."

But the expected interview took place before the morrow.

An hour or two later there was a tapping at his sitting-room door. Miss Ludlow entered.

"My brother from the bank wishes to see you. Mr Smithers, if you are not engaged. Do you mind his coming in?"

There was a twinkle in her eyes as she spoke, which he understood, or thought he did. "My brother" did not wait to hear if Mr Smithers minded. He entered before that gentleman had a chance of speaking. Whereon Miss Ludlow withdrew, leaving the two men alone together.

Mr Smithers found himself confronted by an individual whom he certainly should not have recognised as the lady's brother. His erectness of bearing lent to him an adventitious appearance of height; he looked as if he could not bend. His black hair, parted with rigid precision in the centre, was turning grey at the edges. His face was square and broad. One was struck by the thinness of his lips, and their length—details which were thrown into greater prominence by the fact that his upper lip and jaw were clean-shaven. The austerity of his appearance was accentuated by the primness of his attire. Mr Smithers thought that he had never seen a more unclubbable-looking man—even in Canterstone Jail.

That this was a person who had considerable control over his feelings—and who was quite capable of concealing the fact that he had any at all—was obvious. Which made it the more surprising that he was so evidently and singularly moved, staring at Mr Smithers—as if he were unable to take his eyes from off him—as if he were some uncanny creature. That gentleman's keen observation was hardly likely to allow the peculiarity of the other's manner to escape his notice. He asked himself some questions.

"Has he seen me before? or have I seen him? I don't remember his face; and it's not a face one would be likely to forget. Yet one never knows. Is there going to be trouble? He looks like the sort of man who could make it."

Chapter 6
Mr Ludlow Requires Some Information

Mr Theodore Ludlow spoke first, Mr Smithers waiting almost ostentatiously for him to do so. But he only got as far as two words—half a question.

"Are you?"

"Francis Smithers.—Don't you recognise me?"

"I do not."

"No? And yet you look at me as if we had met before. Have we?"

"Never."

"Then allow me to introduce myself. You, I believe, are Mr Ludlow, of the Strand branch of the National Bank?"

46

"I am."

"Pray take a seat."

"Thank you; I prefer to stand."

"Allow me to offer you a cigar."

"I don't smoke."

"A little whiskey?"

"I never drink intoxicating liquors."

"Then what may I offer you?"

"Thank you; nothing. I am here on business, though informally." Hitherto he had remained standing by the door where he had entered. Now, coming a little forward, he rested the knuckles of one hand upon the table—the stare with which he had been favouring the other becoming, if anything, still more inquisitorial. "Am I to understand that you are Mr Francis Smithers?"

"You are, since I am."

"The Mr Francis Smithers who has an account with us?"

"Who has two accounts with you—that is, with the bank of which you are a servant."

The words were chosen with malice—which Mr Ludlow possibly observed. His tone became resentful.

"A cheque for £50, signed Francis Smithers, was presented today."

"That is so."

"You sent my sister with it."

"Pardon me; that is hardly the correct way of putting it. Miss Ludlow informed me that she was going to call on you, and I asked her to cash a cheque for me at the same time."

"You asked her to cash a cheque for you."

"Certainly. Was there anything objectionable or strange in that?"

The two men's glances met, as if they were measuring swords. For an appreciable period they regarded each other in perfect silence. Then Mr Ludlow started a little back, almost as if he had been struck a blow. His eyes fell. When he spoke again it was without raising them.

"The accounts were opened under peculiar circumstances?"

"I am probably better acquainted with the circumstances under which they were opened than you are."

"I doubt it."

"Mr Ludlow—the accounts are mine; not yours."

"They were placed in my hands at the time they were opened, and it was I who was instructed to make inquiries. I made them."

"Are you aware, Mr Ludlow, that your manner is a little singular? May I ask what is the purport of your presence here, and who has sent you? I am not accustomed, at this hour to receive visits from my bankers' clerks, especially when their bearing is so—unusual."

Mr Ludlow looked up. Something seemed trembling in his eyes and on his lips—which, however, died away in front of the other's calm imperturbability. His glance sank again.

"Possibly you may find it convenient to call at the bank in the course of tomorrow. There are one or two matters into which we should like to enter with you."

"Possibly I may not find it convenient—and very probably."

"I think you had better."

"Why?" Once more the cashier's glance went up and down—apparently he found the other's eyes unpleasant to encounter. "I should be sorry, Mr Ludlow, to have to be the cause of you losing your situation."

This time the bank clerk looked up with surprise, which was unmistakably genuine.

"You be the cause of my losing my situation—you!"

"Yes, I. I am unwilling to suppose that your discourtesy is intentional—as I can conceive of no reason why you should desire to be rude." He paused, regarding Mr Ludlow with an intent, smiling scrutiny, before which that gentleman seemed to quail. "I am content to attribute it to your naturally unfortunate manner. It would occasion me genuine distress to have to intimate to your manager that while you continue in the employ of the National Bank, my account must be transferred to an establishment whose officials have been trained to treat its customers with civility. The fact seems to be, Mr Ludlow, that because I have allowed considerable sums to continue idle in the hands of your employers through a term of years, you imagine yourself entitled to regard them as the owners of my moneys. I will comment on that position when I see your principals. In the meantime, I have the pleasure of wishing you good-evening."

Crossing the room, Mr Smithers himself turned the handle of the door and held it open. After a moment's hesitation, Mr Ludlow went through it without a word; without, for instance, troubling himself to say goodnight Not only did he leave the room, but he left the house, shutting the street door behind him with a bang. Scarcely had he departed than Miss Ludlow came hurrying in to Mr Smithers.

"Has Theodore gone?"

"I believe so—he went out into the street."

"But mother begged him to see her after he had seen you, and he said he would. What can he be thinking of? Has anything happened?"

"Happened? In that form the question's rather difficult to answer. I am inclined to think. Miss Ludlow, that your brother's manner is a little unfortunate sometimes."

"Sometimes! It too often is." Miss Ludlow's brown eyes—obviously anxious—were searching Mr Smithers' smiling face. "Has there been any unpleasantness?"

"I didn't like his manner, and I told him so."

"You told him so? Then there has been unpleasantness. Because he certainly would not like to be told that.—Was he very rude?"

"Middling—though I suppose he thought it was all in the way of business."

"This comes of leaving your money untouched for all those years—it is just as though they had taken it for granted you were dead, and had spent it. I told you they wouldn't want to let you have it back again."

"I daresay not—though what particular concern it is of your brother's I fail to understand. I imagine he's a character."

49

Mr Ludlow appeared to have the same opinion of Mr Smithers. He found himself in the street with his hat in his hand. Before putting it on his head he summed up his feelings with sufficient terseness.

"I thought I'd seen all sorts, but he's unique." At this point on went the hat, he settling it, with both hands, at the proper angle, as became a careful man. "I can't he mistaken. Anyhow, of that I will make sure."

His residence was at Brixton. Instead of going there, however, he paid a visit at the Universal Hotel. The Universal is one of that group of huge *caravansaries* to which the Cosmopolitan belongs. He was about to inquire for the manager, Mr Hibbert, but was saved the trouble by perceiving the man himself standing in the great hall, engaged apparently in doing nothing. It is odd how frequently gentlemen in Mr Hibbert's position are found similarly occupied, especially when one considers the machine like accuracy with which the establishments they superintend are run.

The two men shook hands. They spoke about the weather. A few remarks were exchanged on a subject about which it chanced that Mr Hibbert had been in correspondence with the National Bank—where the Universal Hotel had an account. Some platitudes were uttered. Then, just as he was going, and had even turned on his heels. Mr Ludlow bethought himself of a question—which, although he did not say so, he had come very much out of his way to ask.

"Oh, by the—way, do you remember that when you were in the reception-room at the Cosmopolitan a man used to come there named Smithers!"

"Smithers?—Francis Smithers?"

"That's the man."

"Let me see,—that must be nearly seven years ago."

"All that."

"You called one day and asked me to point him out to you?"

"I did. Can you remember what he looked like?"

"It's part of my business to remember that kind of thing. At one time he was in and out a good deal. I remember him very well."

"What did he look like?"

Mr Hibbert half closed his eyes, as if he were looking for a photograph among the tablets of his brain.

He was a short, slight, sandy-haired man, with washed-out eyes. He always looked to me as if he were short sighted, but I don't fancy he was, because he never wore glasses. Overdressed, half-bred; lavish with his money—he always tipped everyone he ran across each time he came. It must have cost him something. Used to enter his address as Newcastle-on-Tyne, but he was certainly a South countryman."

Mr Luidlow had been listening attentively, as if weighing each word the other spoke.

"At the time you pointed him out to me he was occupying Nos. 121 and 122."

"That I couldn't say. You'll find it in the books. They keep them. He always had two rooms—that I do know. He flung his cash about in style, as if he hadn't yet got used to the feel of it."

"And you recognise him if you saw him again?"

"I should anywhere. What's the trouble?"

"At present there's none, and there never may be any. Only I thought I'd just ask you—Thanks!—Goodnight!"

This time Mr Ludlow did not forget his manners. He ruminated as he went his homeward way.

"I thought I couldn't be mistaken; not to that extent, at any rate. I remember Hibbert pointing him out to me as he sat at dinner in the *a-la-carte* saloon, and thinking what an ugly little brute he looked. This man's a berserk. He's unique—unique! After my experience, it's something to come upon a new variety."

Possibly Mr Ludlow's experience was not so large as he supposed. Some men are apt to overestimate their knowledge of their fellows.

Soon after his arrival at the bank on the following morning the manager came up to him and made certain inquiries as he stood at his desk preparing for the work of the day.

"Well, did you see Mr Smithers?"

"I did."

"And is it all right?"

"If you mean—did Mr Smithers proffer any evidence which would identify him with our Mr Smithers, he did not. He showed me the door."

"Showed you the door?"

"And intimated that if I continued an employee of this establishment, he might deem it advisable to transfer his account to another."

"What did you say to him?"

"I said nothing. He didn't give me a chance. I fancy that this Mr Smithers is a person to whom most people would find it difficult to say anything he didn't wish them to. He's unique."

"He must be a character—to leave his money in our hands in the way he has done."

"It is unusual."

"Unusual! I should think it was. What do you think of him?"

"I think nothing."

The manager kept his eyes upon the speaker's face, which, for expression, was like a blank page.

"The signature's all right."

"It seems all right."

The manager drummed his fingers on the polished counter. He was aware, from occasionally painful experience, that his head-cashier was caution personified.

"Did you tell him I should like to see him?"

"I did. And he informed me, in reply, that when he did condescend to come your way, he would give you to understand that you were making a mistake in attempting to treat his moneys as if they were your own, merely because they had been in your hands so long."

His superior officer showed signs of being disconcerted.

"That's just it—it's exactly that kind of feeling which I don't wish to provoke. Of course, if he's the man, there's nothing more to be said. But is he the man?"

"That, I am afraid, I must leave you to decide."

The manager went off grumbling. Mr Ludlow continued his work. He had said nothing which was not true; only, in view of his chiefs evident uneasiness, it seemed odd that he should have omitted all mention of the interview which he had had with Mr Hibbert.

CHAPTER 7
SAFE No. 226.

During the next few days, in his own fashion, Mr Smithers seemed to enjoy himself. He and his landlady's daughter bade fair to become close friends. The gentleman had leisure; the lady's household duties did not occupy all her time; it was not unnatural that they should have been occasionally in each other's society—especially as it appeared that they had so many tastes in common. He liked rowing; she liked being rowed; and though the river at Putney is not an—oarsman's paradise, as something on which to float a boat they seemed to find it better than nothing at all. Then they both were fond of walking. And it is impossible to deny that walking is good exercise, and that the neighbourhood of Putney offers some agreeable opportunities of proving it. There is Wimbledon Common, which, in its way, is charming. There is Barnes Common, which also has attractions. And there is the towing-path, which is not bad. While for those who choose to go farther afield, there is Richmond Park.

These two did not choose to go farther afield. Not only did the gentleman take the lady into Richmond Park, but he sat down with her on the turf beside Penn Ponds, almost on the identical spot where Mr Edney's treasure box had been found There they talked about all sorts of things—wandering over that wide range of subjects over which men and women do wander when, at a certain stage of their acquaintance, they are alone together, and are feeling very much at their ease.

Mr Smithers looked in at the Strand branch of the National

Bank when it suited him, as he had told Mr Ludlow that he would do, showing no sort of hurry to gratify the not wholly unjustifiable curiosity of the chief officials of that establishment. When he did put in an appearance those officials had rather a bad quarter of an hour. The manager, Mr Barnett, found himself one day alone in his private office with a radiant individual, who somehow or other did not at all fit in with his preconceived notions of the bank's eccentric client. He had looked for something abnormal, but not in this direction.

This handsome, bearded, blue-eyed giant, with charming manners and air of perfect breeding, was not what he had expected. He was so faultlessly attired, there was in his bearing such a suggestion of a man born to command, that Mr Barnett was conscious of feeling himself at a distinct disadvantage. That this man was 'a swell'—as he would himself have phrased it; and, in fact, afterwards did—and 'a swell of the first water,' he had no doubt whatever. The discovery threw a new light upon the matter. His experience had taught him that 'swells' might be expected to develop eccentricities in financial matters.

"If Ludlow had told me," he said to himself, " that the man was a duke, a marquis, or an earl,—I'll swear he's hobnobbed with the lot of them—I should have known whereabouts I was. But with all his cleverness, Ludlow's a mole." Aloud he observed, "I trust that your coming here has subjected you to no inconvenience, Mr Smithers."

"Not at all. I was passing and dropped in. I allow no one and nothing to subject me to inconvenience."

"You see, in the matter of your account"

"Accounts," amended the visitor. Mr Barnett accepted the amendment.

"I beg your pardon—in the matter of your accounts there has been, from our point of view—technically, that is—a certain amount of irregularity. You, of course, remember the circumstances under which they were opened." Mr Smithers nodded. "It was all done through the post, in itself an unusual proceeding. There was no personal interview, no introduction, no reference offered."

"Before you go any farther, Mr Barnett, be so good as to understand me. I am a peculiar man." The manager had realised that already. He did so still more clearly when he perceived the very odd something which had come into the speaker's eyes. It is my habit to do as I like with my own. Sometimes I open accounts at certain banks for reasons of my own—with the intention of leaving them intact for considerable periods of time."

"Pleasant for the banks, but dangerous sometimes for you."

"Comments are not invited. This is the first instance of the kind in which I have had any trouble."

"Pardon me, there is no trouble now—not the least, not the slightest. We are only anxious for your own protection."

"I am capable of protecting myself." There was that in his manner which lent to his words a singular significance, and filled his hearer with vague discomfort. Interest has been accruing on the £5000 which you hold for me upon deposit. Have the goodness to transfer that interest to my current account, and advise me of its exact amount."

"I can let you know at once if you like."

"Advise me through the post. Use that medium for all your communications, and don't send any of your clerks to call on me except at my request. I have lately returned to England, and have taken rooms at Putney. I find that my landlady is the mother of one of your clerks, a person named Ludlow. Some days ago he came to me, acting, I gathered, in accordance with your instructions, and—was offensive."

"I feel certain that it was far from his intention to be anything of the kind."

"I am not dealing with intentions, but with facts. Recommend him not to take advantage of his connection with his mother to offend again. I am a man of action." He rose from his chair as he spoke and stood straight up; Mr Barnett was emphatically conscious that he looked it. "I have lived in parts of the world where the point of view is not that of the London commercial man. Mr Ludlow came within an ace of discovering that the other evening. Good-day, Mr Barnett."

Mr Smithers left the manager in a condition which might almost have been described as one of fluster.

"I wonder what part of the globe he has lived in?" inquired the official of himself, he's not the sort of individual I should like to quarrel with. I can conceive of circumstances under which I wouldn't contradict him for—for a good round sum. In spite of his smile, his soft voice, his pleasant manners, a look came into his face just then which—upon my honour—which was scarcely human. I take it that his name's no more Smithers than mine is. He's somebody, or he has been. I'll refer to headquarters , but I don't see myself what concern it is of ours under what name he chooses to masquerade—so long as he doesn't attempt to overdraw. We've done pretty well out of his account—so far."

When he appeared in the public office the head-cashier put to him a question.

"Well—is he the man?" The reply was enigmatic.

"With reference to Mr Francis Smithers' account—pay all cheques which are in order unless you hear from me to the contrary."

This time it was the manager's face which was expressionless—a fact which Mr Ludlow resented in his turn.

"What's in the wind now?" he wondered. "There's always something at the back of his head when he talks like that."

After leaving the bank Mr Smithers journeyed to the stronghold of the Shoe Lane Safe-Deposit Company. He handed in his visiting-card at the Inquiry Office.

"I want access to my safe—No. 226."

The clerk glanced at the piece of pasteboard.

"Mr Francis Smithers! You have your key?"

"I have."

"Please sign your name here."

Mr Smithers did as he was told—in a volume which resembled the visitors-book of an hotel. The clerk disappeared with the volume and the card into an inner office, presently returning with a little book of what looked like coupons, one of which he began to fill up.

"It is some time since you were here?"

"It may be some time before I am here again."

The clerk glanced at the visitor, as if inquiring if the intention was to snub. Mr Smithers found himself in possession of a slip of paper authorising someone to give him admission to safe No. 226. Presently he was walking along a corridor which reminded him unpleasantly of an establishment under whose too hospitable roof he had recently spent two years. There were heavy doors on either side. Even the bunch of keys which his companion wore chained round his waist was disagreeably suggestive. The custodian's manners, however, were affability itself. He threw open one of the doors.

"There, sir—there's your safe." Mr Smithers found that his safe was one of those which the door had shrouded. "Would you like a room?" Mr Smithers thought he would. "You can have No. 14, that's disengaged at present; at the end of the passage, on your right. Anything heavy to carry?"

Mr Smithers thought not. The porter left him—strolling to the other end. The owner of the safe proceeded to unlock.

"Let's hope there's no trick about the key, or the lock, or anything—I shall look like an idiot if I've forgotten how it goes."

There was nothing of the kind. The door swung back upon its bright steel hinges as easily and noiselessly as if it had been accustomed to constant opening and shutting. The whole inner space was filled by what looked like a deed box. A drop handle in front was evidently intended to be used to draw it out. Mr Smithers drew it out. He carried it to where the porter stood at the end of the passage. The official waved his hand towards an open door.

"No. 14, sir—you'll find it empty."

Mr Smithers found it empty. Its proportions suggested rather a cupboard than a room. But there were two chairs, a table, and materials for writing. He shut the door and slipped the bolt.

On this, the occasion of the first examination of the contents of my safe, the strictest privacy may be advisable. Anyhow, we'll have it. What's inside Mr Edney's second treasure box?"

There was a good deal inside—of a very varied character. There were bonds, share certificates, securities of different kinds. Mr Smithers favoured them with but a cursory inspection. His actual knowledge of such matters was but slight. But he saw and understood enough to realise that in the aggregate they represented a considerable sum—probably over £50,000. What struck him as odd was that they were examples of so many different investments. There were consols, foreign government stocks, railways, waterworks, gas companies, mines, industrial undertakings—apparently every kind of security in which money could be invested was illustrated there. There was not a large amount in any of them. In not one more than a thousand pounds. In some less than a hundred. Together, however, they stood for a very comfortable sum.

"Mr Edney appears to have been a man of discretion. The precept about not putting all your eggs into one basket must have been continually before his eyes. Possibly he had made up his mind that whatever panic overtook the commercial world, something he held should go scot-free. I seem to have an interest in eighty or ninety different undertakings. It will take me all my time to collect my income. And then the arrears,—the arrears for seven years on all these things. I shall have to educate myself commercially at once, or some of them will do me, that's certain. And no man likes to be done, even when he unexpectedly finds himself, shall we say, a millionaire.—What's in all these things? They look like jewel-cases. They are!"

They were.—well filled jewel-cases too. When he saw their contents their owner stared. On jewels he had been a recognised authority once upon a time. Here he recognised fine examples of the rarest gems—in rings, bracelets, brooches, earrings, necklaces, tiaras.

Where did the man get them? Did he plunder all the jewellers' shops in town? There's no name on any of the cases—which is odd, since, as a rule, a jeweller's so fond of his own name—and ladies are so desirous of having the names of certain jewellers upon their cases. The names of just those houses who deal in these kinds of things. What's it mean? Does it suggest the wholesale trade? Or was the fellow a fence upon a generous scale? It looks as if I were entering into even muddier waters than I expected. With such an eye for the share market as he had, he can hardly have been reduced to such investments as this—which are sometimes so difficult to turn into cash—as experience happens to have taught me.—Great Caesar's ghost!"

The exclamation was induced by the contents of a small leather case which he had initially overlooked. It was filled with unmounted diamonds—cut stones—looking like drops of light.

"The interest grows. Here are some of the finest stones I have ever seen,—from Africa. South America, India. That's Brazil. I wonder how many carats it is? And what light! what colour! It's worth—I don't care to think how much it is worth.—But what's the explanation of the mystery? Where did the fellow get them? A half-educated solicitor's clerk, buried in the heart of the country? These alone are worth a nice little fortune. If I didn't know, I should say it was impossible that they could be genuine. But I do know. These are not only—as the phrase goes—'real' diamonds, but there's not an indifferent stone among them.—It begins to occur to me that there was a good deal more in Mr Edney than I imagined, or than he hinted at in his last dying speech and confession."

How much more there really was, his heir had still to learn. The proofs lay before him in that box—as yet unnoticed and untouched.

CHAPTER 8
THE WHISTLER

Among the remaining contents four things in particular arrested the inquirer's attention—for this reason. They were among the somewhat heterogeneous collection of what looked like odds and ends which still awaited examination at the bottom of the box. Two were contained in coarse brown paper, tied with string and sealed. Taking one of them up, Mr Smithers weighed it in his hand.

"What's in here? Seems light enough. This isn't jewels. What's on the seal? Nome sort of hieroglyphic. More mysteries; I've suddenly been precipitated into their atmosphere. I didn't expect to find the contents of my safe quite so interesting."

When, having cut the string to avoid breaking the seals, the packet was unfastened, for a moment or two he regarded what was within as the greatest mystery of all. There was nothing inside but small blank sheets of different coloured papers. Then he began to understand—comprehension coming on him with an uncomfortable sense of shock.

He drew out one of the sheets of white paper, felt it with his fingers, held it up to the light, examined it with curious minuteness, as one might peer into a doubtful work of art.

"That's banknote paper, unless I err, or an uncommonly good imitation.—That's no imitation; that's the genuine thing. I've reason to doubt if any outsider could get as near to it as that. What are we coming to now? As in the children's game, I'm beginning to get warm."

The other packets held banknotes of nearly all countries— English, French, German, Russian, American. They were arranged in bundles, each in a rubber band. There were four packets of English notes—fives, tens, twenties, fifties. The paper being so thin, it was difficult to estimate their number, but there were possibly three or four hundred of each value. Mr Smithers examined them first in the mass, then a specimen from each bundle.

"If they're not genuine they'd deceive Old Nick; I can detect no flaw. If it weren't that those blank sheets are so suggestive, I should pronounce them unhesitatingly as genuine. Supposing them to be forgeries, then they're the work of an artist who, in this line of business, I should imagine has never yet been equalled—luckily for the police and for the world at large. Yet it's against reason to suppose that they are real, unless my respectable benefactor was a millionaire. Taking all the countries together, there are presumably over a hundred thousand. Look at this pile of Americans—enough greenbacks to buy an English title.—Hullo!"

Running through the bundle of English five-pound notes, something struck him—a peculiarity in the numeration. He referred back to the one on top.

"The same number twice over—that settles it."

He glanced quickly through some of the other bundles, to find that the same peculiarity recurred again and again.

"They're numbered in hundreds—starting all right, and running on all right until the hundred is reached, and then beginning all over again. No bank of issue does that kind of thing. I'm the heritor of the largest—and finest—collection of forged banknotes I ever heard of, or, I imagine, the police either. The position is becoming much more delightful than I ever supposed it would be. Can Mr Edney have been a man of infinite jest?—What have we here?"

He picked up a dark-green leather box—the largest and most conspicuous article still unexamined. Round it were half a dozen seals.

"Judging from its appearance this should hold the key to the situation. There is something odd about those seals. What is it that the die is supposed to represent? Looks as if someone has been playing tricks with Masonic symbols. To open the box, I am afraid you will have to be broken. Sorry, but it can't be helped."

As it would have been a work of time and difficulty to have removed them intact from the grained leather, he cut through them with his penknife. A boss on the front suggested a spring. He pressed it.

"Now for the secret of the mystic casket. This is heavy enough. What is it going to be this time?—Imitation gold, for a change?"

The guess—if it was intended for one was wide of the mark. The case was crammed with metal plates, each in an envelope of oiled paper. He inspected them one after the other, more and more grimly as he went on.

"Very pretty—very pretty, indeed. Idyllic—nothing less. I think, Mr Edney, that if I had understood what kind of man you really were, 1 should have shed upon your expiring brow a tribute of admiration. I cannot but regret a wasted opportunity. Evidently these are the plates from which those works of financial art have been produced. I find myself in possession of something really superior in the way of forgers' outfits. Apparently little is wanting to enable me to set up in the trade on my own account to-morrow. I wonder what the police would give for this little lot—and the banks.

"I gathered from Mr Edney's last dying speech and confession that his little capital was the fruit of the use he had made of the contents of his employer's office, one Frederic Glasspoole; being indebted for the lion's share of it to the unwitting generosity of a certain Foster family, of Dene Park. I cannot but think that it came also from other sources, to which he omitted to refer, and so failed to do himself justice; for he must have been a really high-class scoundrel on a first-rate scale—a professional felon, in short. I am sorry, because it introduces an element into the mailer of which I am at present indisposed to take advantage."

He closed the boxful of plates; returned the banknotes to their brown-paper cover.

"The notes are false, and I'm not prepared to give a definite opinion on the bonds and the shares, but I'll swear to the jewels. The only point is, who and where are those who still, at the present moment, bewail their loss? Are they fair ladies whose soft cheeks have been seamed by scalding tears, or are they mere tradesmen who've been ruined? In either case, the position's not a pretty one. The yarn about the solicitor's office and Frederic Glasspoole, and the Foster family, and Dene Park, and all the rest of it—can the whole thing have been a myth? We'll institute inquiries. I'm disposed to dedicate my life, or a portion of it, to vicarious restitution. Is salvation to be reached along that road? Are the cleansing fires there?"

Only one thing that remained received much notice from Mr Smithers—a memorandum pocket-book, in a limp cover—a waistcoat-pocket affair. It was crowded with memoranda, few of which conveyed much meaning to him, at least after the hasty inspection which, at the moment, was all he was disposed to vouchsafe. There were notes in what looked to him like short-hand; masses of figures, with which were apparently associated observations in the same cryptic characters; and a number of what seemed to be chemical formulae.

Only on one page was there an entry which he who can might read. Presumably it was a list of men's names. There were six of them Augustus Chaffinch, Bob Hammic, Samuel Water-son, Gustav Kronberg. Philip Fenturn, Sam Brown. After the last name there was a note of interrogation in parentheses—thus '(?)'. At the bottom of the page, by itself, was what might have been a pseudonym—"The Linkman."

"Friends of the late Mr Edney's, I presume. It is possible that one day I may meet these gentlemen, or some of them. It is also possible—extremely!—that this little volume may contain matter which was intended for Mr Edney's own private and personal information, and which, therefore, may be of interest to me as his heir. My education in certain useful directions was unfortunately neglected, and I don't understand shorthand—if this is shorthand, which has yet to be shown. But it is within the range of possibility that I may light on someone who does, and who will be willing to impart instruction to me."

He slipped the memorandum-book into the pistol-pocket of his trousers, withdrawing a pistol to give it precedence.

When, at last, he emerged from the Safe Deposit Company's premises, and had gone some little distance towards Fleet Street, he was accosted by an individual who, he had been conscious, had observed his appearance from the other side of the road. He was a short, burly individual, in build and get-up suggesting the pugilist, or the racecourse hanger-on. He wore a shabby suit of tweeds of a rather conspicuous check; what was intended to represent a mighty pearl adorned his greasy scarlet necktie; and his brown billycock hat, dented, was a good deal on one side of his head. It would be to compliment his voice to call it husky.

"Excuse me, guvnor, but is your name Smithers?"

Mr Smithers looked at him—not liking what he saw.

"It is."

"Francis Smithers?"

"The same."

The stranger's next remark was a trifle unexpected. It look the form of a volley of expletives.

"Well, I am something well somethinged!"

"Are you? I'm sorry. But I don't see how it interests me."

"Do you mean to tell me that you're the Francis Smithers as owns safe 226 up yonder?"

"May I ask why you inquire?"

"Why I inquire! May you ask why I inquire! Well, you have got a face! Who the something are you?"

The man spoke with a ferocity which was, in its way—its very ugly way—impressive and suggestive.

Mr Smithers only smiled.

"My man, I am going in that direction." He pointed with his cane. "You go in the other, and don't speak to me again."

"Not speak to you again! Me not speak to you again! I'll say what I've got to say to you if you skin me alive; and there's more than me as'll have their say too."

"It is possible that you—and they—may have that pleasure on some other occasion. You certainly won't this afternoon."

Mr Smithers moved forward, tranquilly. The other followed.

"Hearken here, guvnor."

"You heard what I said. If you take another step in this direction, or speak another word, I'll summon a policeman."

"A policeman! You'll summon a policeman! That tops it! Blimey if I don't feel I must be going off my dot! Why, I'll follow you to the other side of the world, and keep talking to you all the time!"

Mr Smithers laughed, as if he found the other's exaggeration amusing. Lower down the road there happened to be a constable, and at that instant he chanced to be looking in their direction. Mr Smithers beckoned to him with his stick. After momentary hesitation, in evident response to the signal, he advanced in their direction. The stranger beheld his advance with an evident mingling of suspicion, fury, and trepidation, looking as, if he could screw his courage to the sticking point, he would—but he couldn't. He began to bluster.

"All right, my ikey bloke, then it's knife, is it?—and, mind you, it will be knife!"

Turning on his heels he went striding up towards Holborn at a pace which wanted very little to make it degenerate into a run. Mr Smithers moved smilingly towards the approaching policeman.

"It's all right, officer. Sorry to have troubled you; only that individual seemed disposed to be offensive. Although an entire stranger, he seems to think that he knows me, so I thought that you might know him. Judging from the pace at which he's travelling, it seems probable that you do."

The man in blue treated the matter in the stolid, take-it-for-granted official manner.

"Shouldn't be surprised. There are one or two that I know round here, and they know me."

Mr Smithers went his way. The policeman, standing in the road, followed with his eyes the retreating stranger.

That night, towards ten o'clock, Mr Smithers, taking his ease in his sitting-room at Putney, heard all at once someone whistling, someone who could whistle, possessed of a correct ear and a tuneful pipe. In the prevailing silence—it was very still at Putney—the sound, though not a loud one, was oddly audible. Mr Smithers. who was reading at the time, was at first under the impression that the whistling was in the house. The pipe was so sound and true, the air such a quaint one, the whole thing so unexpected, that he could not help but pay attention.

The tune was gone through to an apparent end; then there was silence, lasting, perhaps, for five or six minutes. Then the performance was repeated. This time Mr Smithers was disposed to think that the performer was in the street, close to his own window; so close indeed as to make it seem that he was actually in the room itself. The illusion was so strong that it had on the solitary reader a curious effect. Had his eyes been closed he could have declared that the performance was within a foot or two of the chair on which he was sitting; but whether behind, before, or above him, he could not have positively said. Again the tune was whistled to an end; again there was an interval of silence; then again it was recommenced;—always conveying to the listener the impression of the performer's acute proximity.

Is it a street musician, whistling for coppers? If so, it's queer that I shouldn't have heard him coming down the street in this stillness. Then, why should he have singled out this house? He does it uncommonly well; those upper notes are as clear as a bird's, and the tune's quaint."

Once more an interval of silence; another repetition.

"Why doesn't he vary his theme? Is it the case of a composer who's in love with Ins own melody, or what's the notion?"

That time the interval was prolonged. The minutes passed and nothing was heard.

"Had enough of it, I suppose; or perhaps the appreciation shown was not sufficiently material. I might have sent him out some coppers if he'd waited, if only for the sake of asking him to treat us to another tune."

Probably more than half an hour had gone when the whistler returned, to whistle the same tune.

"Is there any meaning in it? Or is it merely some idle lounger, who's whistling for want of thought, and who's a lover of only one thing at a time? Whoever it is, he must have his lips glued to the window, unless he's availing himself of a crack in the pane."

As he was rising from his chair, with the intention of crossing to the window to make inquiries, Miss Ludlow came into the room. These two had reached a stage of intimacy where want of ceremony went unnoticed.

"So it is in here; I wondered where it was. But—why! it isn't you?"

"What isn't me?"

"It isn't you who's whistling? Mother and I were wondering

who it was. It sounds in here—is it in the street?"

"You come with me and we'll ask the performer to explain his partiality for my window-pane; his face must be close against it. Step softly; we'll catch him in the act."

They went quietly along the passage. Noiselessly Mr Smithers drew back the latch, opened the door, stepped out—to find that nothing and no one was in sight. They had been so confident of discovering the performer within a foot or two of the sitting-room window, that it was some seconds before they were able to understand that there could be no one there. They looked at each other with startled faces.

"Well," exclaimed the lady, "of all the extraordinary things! Why, he was whistling while you were opening the door. I could have declared then that he was on the doorstep. Where can he have gone?"

"That's the question. If he hadn't gone, I should have said it was impossible he could go before we had a peep at him. There's not a creature in the street."

"There doesn't seem to be." The lady was standing by the gentleman on the pavement. Nothing was visible in either direction except the gas-lamps and the shadows. "If anyone was about, we should be sure to see them. And yet, can anyone have been playing you a trick?"

"What kind of trick? It would be a novelty in tricks which would satisfactorily account, under the circumstances, for the instantaneous disappearance of a whistling man."

Nothing more was heard of the mysterious performer, and nothing at all was seen, until the household had retired to bed. Mr Smithers, as his wont was, was soon asleep, which made it all the stranger that he should suddenly have found himself lying wide awake in the darkened room. For a moment he could not imagine what had aroused him. Then he understood.

The whistler had returned. Through the blackness came the sound of his clear, musical pipe, piping the same tune. Mr Smithers sat up in bed and struck a match. A reference to his watch showed him that it was a quarter to four. "This is a trifle too much—worse than the waits. One doesn't want to be woke up in the silent watches of the night to listen to any gentleman whistling, even though he's a master of the art. It sounds as if he were outside this window now. What does it mean?"

CHAPTER 9
BENJAMIN RODWAY

Late one evening Mr Smithers, alighting from a hansom at the door of No. 25 Dulverton Road, perceived that somebody else was entering the house in front of him. Mr Smithers addressed him, jumping to conclusions.

"You are Mr Rodway?"

"I am. And you are Mr Smithers?"

"The same. Come into my room and have a smoke. As everybody's gone to bed, we shan't be keeping them up." Mr Rodway accepted the invitation. "Since we're fellow-lodgers, it's odd that you and I shouldn't have met before; I've been here some time now."

"As I'm out all day and night, it's not so odd as it seems."

"If you put it that way, I suppose it isn't. But are your hours so irregular? I thought you were at the bank. I believe I've seen you there."

"I was."

"Was? Have you left?"

"Sacked—kicked out. Told to consider myself lucky that I'm not in jail, and, so far as I can understand, sentenced to penal servitude for the term of my natural life."

There was a quality in the speaker's voice which commended itself to Mr Smithers' ear. He remembered him very well, having particularly noticed him perched on a high stool, with his legs bunched under him, nibbling at the end of a pen and staring into vacancy. Not a typical-looking clerk—too careless in his attire, too restless, too self-assertive, possibly too dreamy. He was short and squarely built, with a big head and a bull neck. His hair stood badly in need of brushing; his tie was crooked; there were stains on his waistcoat. He looked like a man who would be unhappy in a new suit of clothes. His face suggested power; there was a sympathetic twinkle in his eyes; he had a humorous mouth. There were few things Mr Smithers loved better than humour, forgiving much to those who had it, for he found them rare.

"What was the penal servitude to be for?"

"For messing up the books. Hang the books! They said they wouldn't balance. I wasn't denying it, so I chucked them across the office—just shaving Barnett's head—and went. I've been wrestling with those books for fourteen years. I've had enough of it. I once knew a chap who was a booking-clerk on a railway. Booking-clerks have to make up out of their own pockets any shortage in their change. That chap was great at shortage—though he never understood how it was—so great that at the end of the month, instead of being paid for the work he'd done, he had to pay for the privilege of doing it. He'd always handed over to delighted passengers more than his earnings. He concluded to try and earn his living somewhere, where trying didn't cost so much. I'm like that chap when it comes to balancing books. They unbalance me. I hate 'em. Mr Smithers, you have the pleasure of entertaining the most miserable man in England. I congratulate you."

"No hope?"

"None. At least, except at intervals, and that's only because I'm built that way. It's really hopeless. Yet I've the greatest fortune the world has ever seen—just beyond my reach."

"It's like that with many of us."

"I daresay. Only you speak sarcastic, and I'm dealing with a fact. It's there in plain sight, though I can't get at it; and the probability is I never shall."

"Again your case is not an uncommon one."

"I'm not suggesting that it is. Everything about me is common. A discharged bank clerk! I am no more fitted to be a bank clerk than I am to be the Pope of Rome, and I should make a bad fit in his shoes. I'm that most unfortunate of all God's creatures—an inventor."

Mr Smithers had surmised it before he had spoken, from certain signs.

"I thought you were something of the kind; I mean, that is, that you had some such hobby."

"You did? It's come to that, has it? I carry about with me the marks of the beast. Have they been talking to you about me here?"

"Do you mean the Ludlows?—Not a word."

"I thought I could rely on Mrs Ludlow not giving me away, and I was dead sure of Netta. But I must have sunk pretty low if I bear my shame on my face."

"What's the particular trouble?"

"He guesses that there's a particular trouble, though I'm a man of many troubles, This is a person to be feared. I am not prepared to enter into my particular trouble. I know too much about you."

If Mr Smithers was startled he did not show it.

"Do you? In what sense?"

"I've heard about you at the bank. It seems that you nearly punched Ludlow' nose. I wish you had quite; I shall have to kick him some day. It might have prepared his mind. You're the office mystery. Barnett's of opinion that you're the *Czar* of all the Russias, slightly disguised. I'm not going to be laughed at by a possible emperor.

"You should only judge people from your own experience of them, not from hearsay. I'm not so bad as Mr Barnett appears to suppose. Tell me about your invention."

"You will only say that I am mad, as all the others have done. As a matter of fact it is they who are mad and I who am sane. I wish I could get a chance of proving it."

"Pay me the compliment of imagining that I also am sane, unless you have particular reasons for keeping silence. I am no gossip."

"I care nothing if you've a tongue which blabs everything to everyone; it will do me no harm. I'll tell you in half a *dozen* words—now prepare to laugh! I have discovered perpetual motion."

"That is rather a large order, and suggests a fairy tale, unless you're joking."

"Nowadays it is the fairy tales which are proved to be true. Rontgen rays, the phonograph, the telephone, wireless telegraphy—weren't those fairy tales till the right man came along? Now they're solid facts.—What's that?"

It was the sound of someone whistling a quaint little air. The two men were silent Rodway seeming the more surprised of the two. Mr Smithers only smiled.

"It's someone whistling."

"I can hear that. But who, at this hour of the night? It's after one. Is it ventriloquial effect, or a trick of a phonograph? It seems in the room. Is it someone whistling to you?"

"Not that I am aware of. What form does perpetual motion take with you?"

"A very practical one—electricity.—I shall have to see who that chap is. He gets on my nerves."

"It's all right. Possibly some belated roisterer. How do you mean—electricity?"

"Why aren't electric motors so popular as they might be? Because they're only able to carry with them an insufficient supply of motive power. When that's exhausted they come to a standstill, until they're provided with a fresh supply. I'll turn you out a motor which shall be provided with an initial charge. Fresh power shall be generated by the mere forward movement of the machine, which shall be adequate to supply the place of that which is being used; so that, given enough power to drive you ten miles, it will automatically generate enough to drive you a hundred, or a thousand, if it pleases you."

"Incredible!"

"So they all say. So they always have said of every new thing. When it comes, old men ask themselves how they came to be such blockheads as not to have seen it before—its simplicity's so patent. That's one of life's little ironies. Find me the capital and I'll put a motor on the road inside six weeks which shall do what I've told you. But the capital's what I can't find, except on terms to which I decline to listen. I'm not going to sell my birthright for a mess of pottage."

Rising from his chair he began striding about the room, swinging his arms with ungainly movements which were apparently intended to give emphasis to his words. One perceived how it was that his attire became disarranged.

"I've been pressing hot-foot after the thing ever since motors came into being. It's been a monomania—an obsession. I saw it from the first, but only, as it were, obliquely. I couldn't get at it quite all round. I've thought I had, once and once again, but I've just missed it by a scarcely appreciable fraction. It's occupied my thoughts night and day, and I've been working at it night and day. I've done everything with my own two hands, for want of funds, and because I was afraid of letting anyone get a glimpse at what I was after. All the while, all day long, I've been sitting on a stool at that confounded bank, the thing getting between the figures and me. I had a little capital, but that's all gone, and now I just owe everyone; it's a wonder I didn't take to robbery and murder.

"I've lost my situation—that doesn't matter; but I've got a bum bailiff in at my workshop—that does matter. He might collar my whole idea. Luckily— it's my one stroke of luck—he happens to be such a dunderheaded idiot that he couldn't see a thing even if you hit him in the eye with it. The Ludlows came here at my suggestion. I said to Netta, 'Get your mother to take a house and furnish it. I'll take the drawing-rooms. What I pay for them will more than provide for the rent.' It looks like it! My goodness gracious! Do you know I owe them more than six months' rent? Aren't I a pretty scoundrel? Every penny I've had has been spent upon that motor. I'm nothing but a swindler and a thief. Imagination fails to picture what would have happened if you hadn't come upon the scene. They'd have been turned into the street for sure, and I should have cut my throat. That precious Theodore wouldn't help his mother with so much as change for a farthing."

Mr Smithers thought of Mrs Ludlow's anxiety about his own rent, and excused her again. Mr Rodway's frankness threw a lurid light on many things which had puzzled him. He told himself he was an ass.

"Are you sure you've got this thing of yours at last?"

"Certain—as sure as I am that you and I are in this room. But what's the use now? With bums to the left and bums to the right, credit *nil,* and not a rag of reputation left to cover me! It's too late—I'm a wrong "'un!"

He stopped to listen.

"That beggar's back again, with the same tune. What is his little game? If he's not trying to attract the attention of someone in this house I'm a Dutchman. Why, he must be close to your window. Sure I'm not in the way, and that it's not a friend of yours?"

"Certain. How much would it cost to put this scheme of yours on a working footing?"

"I've only been working from models. To build a full-sized motor might possibly cost a thousand pounds. You see, I should have to get everything at the start. When the proper plant was set up they could be turned out at a profit for a quarter, for a tenth of the sum; for less than that. It would depend on the style of thing that was wanted. To put the whole thing on a proper footing might cost anything from ten to twenty thousand pounds."

"If you can prove to me that the idea is a practical, workable reality, and not an hallucination of your brain—and, mind you, I should require proof!—I will provide a thousand for the first car, and if that is successful, a further twenty."

"Mr Smithers! Are—are you joking?"

"I am not. I have capital which I am desirous of diverting from the channels in which it at present rests. If—it's a very big 'if'—if your scheme satisfies me that it's feasible and ripe, and that sort of thing, I am ready and willing to give it financial support."

"There's one of the greatest fortunes in it that the world has ever seen; one of the greatest—the greatest! Only I've—I've been disappointed so many times that I've got a bit heartsick. What terms would you make? I'm not to be bought out, and I'm not to be staved off with an invisible royalty. I'm going to manage the whole concern."

"I'd have no desire to oust you. My proposal would be halves—share and share alike."

"Then—then it's done. I—I've got a pain in my side, or something; you—you've made me feel quite queer. Do you—do you think it would be too late to go to my workshop now? If s only a mile off, along the Wandsworth Road. I'd have a sack over the bum bailiff's head, and you could sit on him. Then, when we'd got him nice and quiet he's a dear old soul, somewhere in the nineties—I'd set my model in motion and prove to you the truth of all I've said inside of half an hour."

"Don't you think it is a little late for an expedition of the kind? Won't the morning suit, especially as it seems that you will have the whole day free?"

"It isn't that; only—you won't change your mind before the morning comes? I've known it happen."

"Not I. I'm not that kind of person, as you will learn."

"Because, anyhow, so far as sleeping's concerned, it won't make any difference to me whether I go or whether I don't. I never am much of a hand between the sheets, and tonight I shan't close my eyes for thinking. Why, there's that whistling chap come back again, and the same old tune! He must be trying to put his nose through your window. You are sure he's not a friend of yours?"

"I have already told you."

"Then in that case I'll go and speak a quiet word or two to him, as if he were a friend of mine, and ask him if he doesn't think if s time he went to bed. I must do something to relieve my feelings."

Mr Rodway quitted the room. When he had gone Mr Smithers observed to himself:

"You will have to find him first, which may be difficult."

He stood on the hearthrug, stroking his beard, in an attitude of expectation. Presently Rodway's voice was heard calling to him from without.

"Mr Smithers! Mr Smithers!"

"I thought so."

He strolled to the front door, to find Rodway standing on the doorstep with a queer look on his face and in his eyes. His voice seemed to be a little unmanageable.

"Have—have we taken to hearing things, like some chaps take to seeing them?"

"I don't follow you."

"Was—wasn't there somebody whistling?"

"There seemed to be."

"Seemed to be! What do you mean by seemed? Was there or wasn't there?"

"There was."

"Wasn't he jammed close up against your window?"

"Since you came out to make his acquaintance, you ought to be able to give me information on that point."

"I ought, but I can't. He was whistling even as I was opening the door, so I thought I'd pounce upon him in a friendly way and take him by the collar. But when I got outside I didn't see so much as the whisk of a cat's tail. Where he's hidden himself beats me, unless there are ghosts about, in which case I shan't be happy. I'm not afraid of many things, but spooks I bar. I'd sooner have a *tête-à-tête* with a roaring, raving, hungry lion than with the mildest mannered ghost that ever breathed."

"Come in and have a little more whiskey."

Mr Rodway went in.

CHAPTER 10
THE RODWAY POWER

Me Rodway's workshop took the form of a shed which seemed a little out of the perpendicular. There certainly was more of it on one side than the other. It had once been covered with tar; which fact, however, was rather of the nature of a reminiscence, since there was so little of it left. The building stood in the centre of an uneven plot of ground, which was a sort of interlude in an otherwise unbroken line of shops and houses. With scant regard to the feelings of the shed and its tenant, the spot seemed to have been treated as a place where rubbish might be shot. Miscellaneous examples of household refuse were everywhere—empty tins in endless variety, broken crockery, old boots and shoes. A disreputable board—also crooked—announced that "This Eligible Property Is To Be Sold For Building Purposes."

"The reason why it hasn't been sold ages ago," explained Rodway, as he arrived upon the scene with Mr Smithers, and perceived that that gentleman was struck by its appearance of rurality," is because it belongs to five sisters, and they can't agree how much they want for it, so they keep on getting nothing."

"And are you the tenant of the five?"

"Well, I suppose I am. But I pay my rent, or rather I don't pay my rent, to a scoundrel of an auctioneer who earns a dishonest living by putting executions into peaceful homes. He's the ruffian who's harrying me. And here's his hireling assistant."

Mr Rodway opened his workshop door. The hireling referred to was a venerable and very dirty old man, who was bent almost double on a backless wooden chair, which he had propped up against the side of the shed for the sake of additional support. Mr Rodway regarded him with critical consideration.

"Now the question is, what's to be done with you? Chloroforming you would cost more than you're worth, and killing you might make a mess—besides my not wanting to have any more rubbish than I can help about the place. If I give you a shilling, you could go out and get some beer."

"I could that, and some grub too. It's little enough I've had since I've been in the place. I never see one like it."

"You mean that you never saw a place in which the arrangements for bailiffs were so handsome?"

"'Andsome? I don't know what you call 'andsome, considering there's only two or three old sacks for a bed, and the 'ard ground's made my old bones ache all over."

"Wouldn't the shortest way be to pay the debt?" suggested

Mr Smithers. "What's the amount?"

"With costs, seven-four-six. And glad I'll be to get it. Rather than have much more of this kind of thing, I'd go into the 'ouse. They do give you a bed."

Mr Smithers handed over eight sovereigns, declining to receive any change. As he departed, the old man's face was lit up by senile joy.

"This won't do for a beginning," declared Rodway. "You're here to do business, not to show charity. For all you know, that motor of mine may turn out to be a first-rate fraud; then I'll owe you eight pounds, and you'll be putting in an execution."

"Then let's come to business."

"As fast as you like. Do you know anything about electricity?"

"Not a particle."

"Then—this doesn't sound like business; but unless you want to receive a course of elementary instruction on the spot, you'll have to take a good deal for granted."

"I may be disposed for the instruction later on. At present I want to see what you have to show. What's this?"

He was looking at a double row of thin rusty rails which performed a complete circuit round the building, suggesting a miniature railway track.

"That's the road on which I do my trials. You see, I say that one of my motors, of any size, will go for any time and any distance. There isn't much space in here; so, to obviate that, I've built this oval track. My motors will run on road or rails; they're indifferent which it is. They'll go round and round a thing like this forever."

"Literally, forever ?"

"Now, there you have me. 'Ever' was meant for a figure of speech. For the process of generation, certain conditions and certain constituents are required. When those are exhausted they have to be resupplied."

"Then you only claim that your motor will go farther than the one at present in use?"

"Only! It's a good big 'only.' Give me a motor charged for ten miles; if it's one of mine, that ten-mile charge will take it right round the world, perhaps twice round. I haven't worked it right out, but before very long I guarantee that the wastage shall be so slight that it shall go on practically forever!'

"Once round the world on a ten-mile charge should be good enough."

"Should be! It is. You wait and I'll show you."

From a cupboard which he unlocked, Mr Rodway took what looked like a metal box on wheels, handling it with as much care as if it had been a piece of priceless china. He regarded it as a parent might a favourite child, enlarging on its virtues with an enthusiasm which was infectious.

"It's primitive, but it's practical, as you're going to see. No pretty paint, no dainty finish, nothing to please the eye; that has all to come. Its children will be things of beauty; all the resources of civilisation will be drawn upon for their adornment. Their sire's an ugly, shapeless monster. Yet, before very long, it will be the world's greatest curiosity, and people will come from all the far corners of the globe to have a squint at it. This is Benjamin Rodway's Power Motor—his first; and you'll be the first person to see it in motion. It contains sufficient power to run about a mile—say ten minutes. It'll run sixty miles an hour easy if it's wanted to; but round this track we're bound to let it go slow, or it runs off". I'll start it, and it shall keep on running just as long as you want it to."

The box on wheels began to move forward along the rusty rails.

"It's nearly noiseless."

"Compared to the present things, it is quite, and runs smoother. For any bumping, the road's responsible."

"Will it carry passengers?"

"What do you think! It will carry anything! Before many years are past it will be drawing trains along all the railroads of the world, and driving ships through all its oceans. But to begin with, mind you, it's for the road; you're not going to induce railway companies to transform all their rolling stock in four and twenty hours. When they see perpetual-motion cars covering all the roads, then they'll start thinking. That motor's one horse-power."

"You don't mean it!"

"It'll carry me. I'll show you."

He balanced a short length of board upon the little engine, which looked so like a clockwork toy. On this he perched himself. The motor went steadily forward, apparently heedless of the burden which had been imposed upon it.

"It's not easy to keep your balance upon a thing of this sort—if I move, the thing's upset—but, bar moving, this ugly little monster will carry me a thousand miles without beginning to be tired."

"For how long a time do you say the thing will keep on running without your touching it?"

"At this rate of progression, until your hair turns grey."

"Then, if we go and have some lunch and then return, we shall find it still running when we come back?"

"We shall; very much we shall. It had been running day and night unceasingly for very nearly a fortnight when that bum's arrival on the scene yesterday put a stop to the proceedings."

"You and I will call together on Messrs Magruder & Barnes, a firm of electrical engineers, of whom you may have heard."

"Leading men in the profession."

"I will put to them certain questions. If their answers are satisfactory, and if, on our return, we find your child still running, all that will remain will be to put the matter on a regular business footing, and I will come in as your partner."

Rodway stared.

"I say! You've a way of moving! There are all sorts of matters to be gone into which you haven't touched; questions of validity of patent, and all that sort of thing. For all you know, the whole thing may be a gigantic swindle. You admit that you know nothing; for all you can tell, I may be sending this little beauty along by clockwork."

"Don't be afraid. As we go on, I shall make all the inquiries you can desire, and possibly more. The agreement will contain clauses to the effect that if your invention fails in any respect to come up to your description, then I shall be at liberty to at once withdraw my capital, and to hold you responsible for the return of any moneys which may already have been expended."

"I hope you're not going to be a Rhadamanthus, or whatever was the name of the party who couldn't bend. There is such a thing as a middle course."

They proceeded to the offices of that firm of eminent electricians. They did not see either of the principals, but they interviewed one of their chief understudies—who seemed amused by the simplicity of the inquiries which Mr Smithers put to him.

"I am going to ask you for information on a point on which you may possibly think that none should be required, since the whole matter should be at the finger-ends of Macaulay's schoolboy; but since I am willing to pay your own terms for information, I trust that you will have no objection to offer on that head." The understudy bowed. "Suppose a box twelve inches square, on wheels. How much electric motive power could be packed into it? That is, to carry it what distance?"

"You want a precise answer, or an approximate one?"

"An approximate one will do."

"For me to be precise I should require certain particulars which you might not be disposed to furnish.—I believe you are the Mr Rodway who I have been given to understand is at present engaged in the production of something revolutionary in motors."

The gentleman thus suddenly referred to flushed up to the roots of his hair.

"I am."

The understudy smiled.

"Then in that case I think it extremely probable that the particulars would not be rendered. I may say roughly, Mr Smithers, that such a motor as you describe could be constructed to carry sufficient power to drive it any distance between one and five miles. The exact distance would depend upon a variety of circumstances."

"It would then stand still?"

"Certainly, until recharged."

"Is there any process by which such a motor could be driven five hundred miles instead of five?"

"I know of none—no self-contained power, that is. If you do, we shall be very glad if you will let us hear of it. You would find it very well worth your while."

When they again found themselves in the street Mr Rodway's manner was contemptuous.

"I should like to see him build a twelve-inch motor to run five miles, giving him his own conditions!"

On their return, after lunch, to the Wandsworth Road, they found the box on wheels still going round and round on its treadmill way. Mr Smithers referred to his watch.

"We have been gone nearly three hours. If it is going at the rate of six miles an hour, which I suppose is about the mark, then it has already journeyed eighteen miles. In the light of our friend the expert's dictum, that seems almost good enough. Give me some notion of how it's done, enough to show that it's neither clockwork nor trickery, and I'm your partner."

The desired information was soon supplied. Before long Mr Smithers recognised that he was in the presence of a new illustration of the working of certain laws of nature which bade fair to do all that its discoverer claimed for it. As steam superseded hand and horse labour, so the Rodway Power promised to take the place of steam. Beyond doubt, a new commercial and industrial revolution was impending. On only one point did there seem to be any uncertainty.

"Can the whole process—idea and all—be patented?"

"It's patenting it at every possible point, before the intervention of the capitalist, that has brought me to my last shilling. I'm an authority on patent law—I ought to be; I've studied it hard and long enough, and am prepared to prove to you that it's protected at every point at which the law can protect it. But, at the same time, I don't want you to misunderstand. It will be impossible to keep the secret of how the generation's brought about—there are bound to be infringements.

"But I propose to grant licences to people both at home and abroad to use our processes on royalty terms. They'll find it less troublesome and cheaper than infringement. As for the little pettifogging buccaneers, they'll find our metal a trifle too heavy; and anyhow, we can afford to laugh at them. If you will supply the initial capital, and make it as much as you can, we're face to face with the most colossal fortune the world has ever seen."

Before he left that tumbledown workshop, in which the little box on wheels, representing such mighty possibilities, still continued its apparently ceaseless gyrations, it was understood that Mr Francis Smithers was to be a joint owner of the Rodway Power.

Arriving at Dulverton Road, he was greeted by his landlady's daughter, interrogation written large all over her.

"Well, are you going to make his fortune?"

Mr Smithers laughed. It was noticeable that this girl seemed to have a knack of reaching down to a spring which was inside him, which at her touch bubbled up into pleasant, honest laughter.

"I like your way of putting it. The fortune which is going to be made is mine."

"That's what you say. For my part I believe that you're one of those fairy godfathers one reads about, who go about the world shedding kindnesses."

"You think so?"

"I feel sure of it. I've been watching you—well, for some time now—and I've noticed that when people want things very badly, you can't help letting them have them."

"Always?"

"So far as I've observed. It's a sort of a kind of a peculiarity you have."

He was turning over in his fingers an unopened letter which

had been awaiting him upon the table.

"In this case it is I who will get the best of it. I am not the philanthropist you suppose. Mr Rodway has invented something which will transform the existing conditions of trade and locomotion. Those fortunate individuals who may have a proprietary interest in it will find themselves masters of the world in a much more real sense than any king or emperor, and the quite possible possessors of wealth exceeding that dreamed of by any of the fabulists. It is by a happy chance that I am one of them. But then, I'm a lucky man."

"Do you mean it, or are you only talking like that as a cover to your generosity?"

"My generosity is a figment of that very active imagination of yours, young lady. I have none."

"That's all stuff and nonsense; because, you see, I know better."

"Rodway's a gold mine of incredible richness, which I propose to work for my own particular benefit."

"Why haven't others seen it if that's the case? He's tried and tried to get them to."

"Because they were so unhappy as not to be able to see what lay right in front of them. Or perhaps they weren't on the ground at the mathematical moment when it was there to see. I tell you I'm a lucky man."

He opened the envelope with which he had been trifling.

"You are, in having such a temperament. And you ought to be a happy one, if happiness consists in making others happy; because I'll be bound you've made Ben Rodway the happiest man the world contains this day."

Mr Smithers was regarding a small square of pasteboard which he had taken from the envelope he had opened. On it was nothing but a blot of scarlet sealing-wax, impressed with a seal. It was this impression at which he was glancing. It was a replica of the curious hieroglyphic, suggestive of a Masonic symbol, which had been impressed on the seals which had secured certain packages which he had found in safe No. 226. After a momentary examination he looked up at the lady.

"It's something to have made someone happy, isn't it?"

"I believe it's your mission in life to go about doing that sort of thing—a Bayard knight, without fear and without reproach, righting wrongs, and setting the crooked places straight."

"I would that your picture were an accurate one."

"It's not so far out, I believe, as you choose to pretend."

But he shook his head, and she shook hers back again, with malicious intent, as she left the room.

He returned to an examination of the seal upon the square of pasteboard, commencing to whistle the opening bars of the quaint melody which the persistence of the unseen whistler caused to assail his ears at moments when they least expected it. It was done, it seemed, without intention; because as soon as he realised what sounds were proceeding from his lips, they ceased.

"No, thank you. No echo, please. We've enough of the original. First that; then this; what next? May the next act take place in the open! I dislike an unseen enemy, and am quite prepared to fight for my inheritance. It's lucky I've no nerves; much of this sort of thing might wear them to fiddle-strings. If there's to be much more of it, even I shall be all agog to get to grips."

Chapter 11
Mr Ludlow Visits His Mother

One evening Mr Smithers took Miss Ludlow to the theatre. During their absence Mrs Ludlow had a visitor—no less a person than her son. He did not seem to be in very good humour on his arrival; not in that pleasant humour in which a son should be who only pays an occasional visit to his widowed mother. What little he came with vanished when he heard of his sister's absence.

"Where's Netta?"

"She's gone with Mr Smithers to the theatre."

He could not have seemed more startled if his mother had struck him.

"What!"

Mrs Ludlow repeated her observation, a little tremulously. She stood in awe of her son, who had always domineered over her, as if he had been the parent and she the child.

"Do you mean to say that you've allowed Netta to go with that—that man alone to the theatre?"

"Why not? She's been with him two or three times before. She's always enjoyed herself. He's very nice to her."

"Mother, you're a fool!"

"Theodore!"

"As for Netta, when I see her I shall take the liberty of making a few remarks to her which she won't forget."

"It's no business of yours what Netta does. She is old enough to look after herself you've left her to do it for a good many years. Now she's quite capable of doing it. I'm sure she wouldn't do anything she thought was wrong, and I'd trust Netta to know the difference between right and wrong as well as you do. Mr Smithers is a perfect gentleman; he always behaves to her like one."

"I say again, mother, that you're a fool!"

"You ought not to speak to me like that; you shall not do it! You forget that I am your mother. You won't hold out a finger to help me, and yet you want to ride roughshod over us as if we were slaves."

"Don't talk nonsense, if you can help it. I merely decline to allow my sister to disgrace me. I owe all I am to my own exertions. I might, I should, be in the gutter for all the help I have received from either parents or friends. I don't intend to allow myself to be ruined by the folly of those with whom I am connected."

"You are more likely to disgrace your sister than she is to disgrace you, in spite of all your boasting!"

"That is a question of opinion. Anyhow, I've the most to lose."

"How dare you say such a thing of your own sister?"

"Because it happens to be true; and I always make it a rule

to look the truth straight in the face. What is Rodway thinking about to allow this kind of thing?"

"There is nothing between Netta and Mr Rodway. You yourself forbade it."

'And Rodway went out of his way to inform me that he didn't care one snap of his fingers what I forbade, as you are very well aware. He's as much set on her as ever he was."

"I don't believe she thinks of him at all—not in that way."

"You're not suggesting that there's anything between her and that scoundrel with whom she has gone out tonight?"

"Why do you call him a scoundrel? He's not behaved like a scoundrel to us. I don't believe he is one. I don't know what we should have done without him."

"You object to my calling you a fool, so I'll do my best to refrain. Only don't behave as if you were one. I tell you that if you allow your daughter to associate with Mr Smithers, before long you'll be wishing that she had never been born."

"What do you mean? Why do you say such dreadful things? What do you know about him, or what do you think you know, that you are hiding from us?"

Theodore regarded her with the hard-set stare from which, from his boyhood upward, she had shrunk. The expression of his face suggested unspeakable contempt.

"As matters are at present, it doesn't suit me to tell you all I do mean. Only understand that rather than Netta should be connected in any way with—Mr Smithers, I'd cut her throat."

"Some sons are a comfort to their mother, but it seems to me that you have always gone out of your way to make me miserable. You won't answer my letters, and when you do come you talk like this. I can only hope that you have come because you do mean to give me a little assistance; if you don't, we shall be in the streets before long."

"I am not in a position to help you, even were I so disposed; I myself am pressed for money."

"Is that true?"

"I should not say it if it were not. I have had losses which have placed me in a situation of considerable difficulty."

"I can only say that every week I am afraid that Mr Judson will enforce the bill of sale he holds. I give him nearly all Mr Smithers pays, for fines. When Mr Rodway paid up his back rent it all went, for what Judson calls arrears of interest. The more I keep on paying, the more I seem to owe; the debt grows larger instead of less."

"You shouldn't have gone, in the first place, to a moneylender of Judson's type."

"Where was I to go? You wouldn't help. I had to get the money from somewhere."

"Then you must take the consequences of your own act. You can't expect the man to release you from a contract into which you entered with your eyes open."

"Theodore, you can have no natural feeling. You know that this man is squeezing the life-blood out of your mother's heart, and you talk as if it were no concern of yours."

"I am a man of business first of all. My standard of commercial honesty is a high one. A contract once entered into must be carried out to the letter, at whatever cost. I wish my feeling on that subject were yours. You would have been saved from your present position."

Mrs Ludlow put her hand up to her face and cried, her son watching her as he might have done some mechanical toy. Presently he proffered a suggestion.

"Why don't you get Rodway to help you? I hear that there's something in that crack-brained scheme of his after all, and that he's likely to coin money."

"I will not ask Mr Rodway for what my son declines to give me, especially after the way in which you yourself have behaved to him."

"What's my treatment of Ben Rodway got to do with you? I'm not going to ask him for assistance. You have cried 'Wolf! wolf!' so often and so long that I've my doubts as to the imminence of the danger; but if you're in anything like the danger you say you are, you'll be glad to accept help from whatever quarter it may come. There's Smithers; why not try him?"

"You hint at such a thing!—after what you have been saying!"

"Don't confuse the issues. There's no reason why you shouldn't get out of him whatever may be got. There's no reason, but very much the contrary, why you should wish him to associate with your daughter."

"Theodore, you're a wicked man—to want your mother to play such a part!"

They were sitting in the kitchen, which, since it was the only living-room she had, Mrs Ludlow had, perforce, to use as a parlour. Theodore stood up.

"It's no use my attempting to argue with you. Our points of view are different. I recognised that fact many years ago. It seems you never will.—Stay here. I will return to you shortly."

"Where are you going?"

He had moved to the door.

"I am going to take advantage of Mr Smithers' absence to look through his rooms."

"Theodore!—You have no right to go into his rooms at all."

"I have reasons of my own for wishing to make certain inquiries, and I must ask you to take it for granted that those reasons are a sufficient justification for what I propose to do. Do as I tell you—stay here till I return."

He shut the door behind him as he went out, leaving his mother to disobey him at her peril She showed genuine concern.

"He has no right to go into Mr Smithers' rooms when he's not there! What does he mean by it? What can he want? He is so headstrong, so sure that he is right and that everyone else is wrong, that I'm sometimes afraid that he supposes that, just because he chooses to do a thing, no one has a right to say a word against it. What will Mr Smithers think if he finds out?"

On that point, at least, Mr Theodore Ludlow seemed to be indifferent Had the entire contents of 'the dining rooms' been his own personal property, he could scarcely have treated them with less ceremony. He examined, hurriedly yet systematically, everything that could be examined. The bedroom first, beginning with the chest of drawers, which he overhauled as thoroughly as any custom-house officer could have done. He commented on the voluminous nature of his wardrobe.

Clothes are a weakness of his, evidently;—he's that type of man—a walking clothes-horse. The place is crammed with them;—seems to have the tailor's entire stock."

He felt in pockets; looked through letter-cases; studied old envelopes, inside and out; turned out portfolios; pried into books; opened everything that could be opened. Resenting, indeed, the fact that there should be anything which could not be opened;—without, that is, resorting to measures at which even he seemed disposed to draw the line.

In particular, there was a despatch-box to which he objected strongly because it refused to let him see what was inside. It was a first-rate article of its kind, and provided with an excellent lock. None of his keys—he had an extensive assortment -would fit it. Being a persevering man, and having the very best causes for not wishing to be baffled, he tried the persuasive power of the thin blade of his pocket-knife when inserted in the interstice of the lid. In vain. That despatch-box was so very well made that it was with difficulty he could induce even the point to enter; and when he had succeeded in getting it so far, without giving him the slightest warning it snapped clean off.

"That's awkward—very. I doubt if I shall be able to get that out again. If he opens his desk and finds the point of my blade just inside the lid, he'll wonder how it got there. Let him. It's possible, even if he's able to make a shrewd guess, that he may consider it desirable not to push his curiosity too far. Men in his position must occasionally find it prudent to know as little as they conveniently can. The mischief is that I've learnt nothing that I don't know already, and there are one or two things I want to learn. It is possible that they're inside that despatch-box. I'm disposed to gel at the inside of it somehow—and anyhow. If they are there he won't be able to object; I'll be holding him between my finger and my thumb. If they're not (here, it won't matter much either. Should he wish to know why I thought it my duty to examine what he pleases to call his property, I should have no objection to explain, if necessary, in the presence of a policeman. How am I going to get at the thing? I am not anxious to smash it into pieces with a poker. A chisel ought to do it—What's that?"

'That' was a ring at the front-door bell. He was on the point of quitting the room in search of the requisite tool when it rang through the house. Considering his indifference to Mr Smithers' feelings on certain matters of which he had just been speaking, it was odd that the mere tinkling of the electric bell should cause him to show such distinct signs of discomposure. He referred to his watch.

"It's not he. He can't be back already from the theatre. It's only just after nine."

His mother's troubled face looked at him from the kitchen door.

"There's someone ringing, Theodore. Hadn't you better come into the kitchen?"

"I'll go and see who it is," he said.

And he went.

Chapter 12
Bob Hammick

On the doorstep stood the man who had accosted Mr Smithers on the occasion of his first visit to safe No. 226. He looked rather shabbier than he had done then; his hat was a little more on one side, and there was that about his general appearance which was more than ever suggestive of the prize-ring. Perhaps this peculiarity was accentuated by the fact that he had been drinking.

The two men confronted each other in silence, until the stranger broke the ice in his own fashion.

"Well? Know me? Or are you only trying to know me next time we meet again?"

It was then that Mr Ludlow perceived that the stranger had been ministering to his thirst. Being himself a person of such rigid teetotal principles, it is possible that the discovery did not lend to prejudice him in the other's favour. His manner was sufficiently brusque.

"What do you want?"

"What do I want? A good many things; so don't you, or anybody else, make any blooming error. And I'm going to have 'em."

Apparently Mr Ludlow had already arrived at a conclusion that this was not an acquaintance which it was desirable to encourage further. He made as if to shut the door in the stranger's face, a manoeuvre which that individual frustrated by the sudden advancement of his foot.

"I want to see Smithers—Francis Smithers—Mr Francis Smithers."

At the mention of this name Mr Ludlow reopened the door, a proceeding on which the stranger remarked.

"That's right, guv'nor; you open it before you're sorry, and you keep it open, unless you want to get yourself knocked out."

"Can I give Mr Smithers any message?"

"Can you give him any message? No, you can't. I'll give him my own messages, if it's the same to you, or if it ain't."

"He's not in."

"Then I'll wait till he is in. I've come to have it out with him, and I'm going to have it out with him if I wait a fortnight."

Mr Ludlow reflected. This was obviously an extremely objectionable person, and he was in a most unpleasant state. All the bank clerk's instincts cried out against the creature's neighbourhood. But, at the same time, Theodore was so very anxious to be posted up in Mr Smithers' private affairs that he felt—strongly—that he should allow no opportunity of acquiring information to escape him. Here, for all he could tell, was such an one close to his hand. The fellow was drunk enough to be talkative; distinctly the sort of character with whom no respectable character would allow himself to be even remotely connected. Yet the man's manner pointed to a close association between himself and Mr Smithers. Perhaps, under the influence of a little judicious handling, his blabbing tongue might place Mr Smithers even more at Mr Ludlow's mercy than he was already.

So, for reasons, Theodore did what he would rather not have done; he asked the intoxicated rascal into Mr Smithers' sitting-room, and there he kept him company.

"Come inside and wait."

Apparently the suggestion took the stranger by surprise.

"I don't mind if I do; I'd just as soon wait inside as I would out. You use me as a gentleman, and you'll find I'm all right."

Mrs Ludlow had been listening to the conversation from the vantage of the kitchen door. When the stranger staggered into the hall she remonstrated.

"It's no use that person waiting for Mr Smithers, Theodore. He won't be home till ever so late."

But Theodore declined to be advised; he preferred to order.

"You go into the kitchen, and stop there. This is my affair, not yours."

When the stranger was in the sitting-room, and stood—with his hat still on the side of his head—bucking up against the dining-table, Mr Ludlow felt, as he regarded him, that he had never found himself in less congenial company.

"Is Mr Smithers a friend of yours?"

"Friend of mine! Him! He's my enemy—that's what he is. Knife's the word between him and me."

"What's your name?"

"Hammick, Bob Hammick's my name. I've not been ashamed of it even when I've been standing in the dock."

Mr Ludlow pricked up his ears at this. So this was the sort of company Mr Smithers kept—that of the denizens of the dock. Precisely what he had expected.

"And pray, Mr Hammick, how has Mr Smithers offended you?"

"How!—Hasn't he robbed me?—Isn't he standing between

me and millions?"

"You are joking. He can hardly have robbed you to that extent."

"Of course, if you know more about me than I know about myself, there's an end of it. You're a fly cove, you are, but maybe you're a bit too fly. I tell you he's holding me out of a hundred thousand pound—perhaps more."

Mr Ludlow perceived that Mr Hammick's mood was argumentative; and as he himself was indisposed in that direction, he resolved to violate his principles still further, and ply the visitor with drink until—if luck would have it so—the power of loquacity was all that was left to him.

"Will you have some whiskey?"

"Will I have some whiskey? Do I look as if I were a chap that won't have whiskey? So help me, I'd like to drown in it! Give me whiskey all day long and all night through, and I'd still keep wanting it."

These were shocking sentiments. But Mr Ludlow concealed the feelings of disgust they must have roused in him. He took a glass and a decanter of whiskey out of Mr Smithers' cupboard. Mr Hammick at once commented on the single turn bier.

"Ain't you going to have nothing? Is the one glass to do for both of us?"

"Thank you. I do not drink."

"Blimey, but I thought you didn't. You look that kind of bloke. Well, I do—and I hate them that don't. They're poison. I never do business with a man who won't take his fair whack. The odds are that while you're drinking he's watching; waiting for you to turn yourself inside out for his amusement—when you don't know what you are doing! I know! I've been there!— Hang me if I don't believe that's your little game! That's what you've brought me in here for! Shouldn't be surprised but what you think that when I've lowered enough—and you've lowered nothing—you'll get a few pickings off me. Then that's where you're wrong, d—d wrong. I'll keep on mopping it up as long as there's any to mop up, but you'll get nothing out of Bob Hammick, not if I swallowed a barrelful."

So it proved. Mr Hammick's perspicacity was unexpected. Rather than have aroused his suspicions, Mr Ludlow almost wished that he had simulated a taste for what he held in abhorrence. But it was now too late. Hammick was not to be beguiled. Although he made rapid inroads into the decanter, the only effect of his potations was to make him scurrilous to the verge of combativeness. He delivered himself of a continuous flow of language on the subject of teetotallers.

Indeed, when Mr Ludlow did manage to slip in a question edgeways, it was received with so much animosity that, since he was far from desiring a set-to with the intoxicated ruffian then and there, he judged it the better part of wisdom to cease from his inquiries. Foiled in one direction, his agile brain moved in another, hitting on something in which the vagabond might still be made of use. Bringing forward the despatch-box which he had found intractable, he placed it on the table.

"Can you open a desk?"

"Can I open a desk? There isn't a desk in England I couldn't open, nor a safe neither."

"I mean without a key."

"And I mean without a key. Do you think I want a key to let me inside a thing? What kind of a softy are you taking me for?"

"Suppose you try your hand on this."

"This? A bramah lock, that's what this has got. They think them bramah locks clever.—I'll show you!"

He took from his pocket what looked like a piece of twisted wire. A portion of this he endeavoured to insinuate into the tiny keyhole. He was, however, more drunk than he supposed. His hand shook so that the wire would not go in. It is possible, also, that his eyes saw two locks instead of one; he certainly made jabs where the lock was not.

While he was still contending with this unfortunate difficulty, someone addressed him from behind.

"What tricks are you up to?" The speaker was Mr Rodway; the pair had been so engrossed in other matters that they had not observed his entrance. He came forward to find an answer to his own inquiry—"Trying to pick the lock!"

Taking Mr Hammick by the collar of his coat, he swung him across the room with so much goodwill that it was only coming in contact with the wall that saved him from the floor. Then he looked at Ludlow.

"And you're aiding and abetting him !

Mr Ludlow greeted his whilom colleague with no enthusiastic welcome; he held his peace—which Mr Hammick declined to do.

"Who done that?" he demanded. "Who done that? You let me get hold of the man who laid his hand on me and you'll see me kill him."

Mr Rodway showed no alarm. On the contrary, he regarded his would-be destroyer, who evidently found it difficult to keep upon his feet in spite of the near neighbourhood of the wall, with some appearance of contempt.

"So you're drunk, are you? Apparently your blue-ribbon friend has been dosing you with Mr Smithers' whiskey. I've seen you before. I've noticed you hanging about two or three times lately, and have wondered what mischief a blackguard of your stamp was after. Now I begin to understand." He turned to Ludlow. "He's a friend of yours, is he?"

"He's nothing of the kind. I never saw him till half an hour ago. He's a friend of your friend Smithers."

This charge Mr Hammick hastily denied.

"I'm no friend of Smithers! He's the greatest enemy I have! I'll put my knife into him yet before I've done with him." He steadied himself, with the seeming intention of getting his recent assailant into focus—an attempt in which he succeeded, at least to some extent. "So it was you who laid your hand on me, was it? Darn your impudent face! I'll smash it!"

He made what was in more senses than one a blind rush at Mr Rodway. Had he reached him he might possibly have carried out his threat. But that gentleman did not let him get so far. Stepping aside as the other came on, he dealt him a swinging blow on the jaw. In Mr Hammick's then state but little was needed to carry him off his feet. That blow laid him out for good. He went crashing down among the chairs, lying still where he had fallen, in a manner which suggested that he must have made a mistake as to the person who was to be killed. Mrs Ludlow came rushing into the room.

"Theodore! Mr Rodway! What is the matter?"

Rodway explained.

"The matter is, Mrs Ludlow, that Theodore has been making this man drunk on Mr Smithers' whiskey, and has then been inciting him to break open Mr Smithers' despatch-box."

"It is false!"

"It is not false, as anyone has only to look at your face to see." Indeed, Mr Ludlow did not look happy. Possibly he was conscious that for a man of his high character he was in a somewhat invidious position. "As for your drunken friend."

"I tell you again that he is not my friend."

Mr Rodway went unheeding on—"and associate, I'll make short work of him."

He did. Possibly the blow he had received had had the effect of bringing the results of the whiskey Mr Hammick had imbibed to a sudden head. When Mr Rodway, gripping him by the shoulders, proceeded to drag him along, very much as if he had been a sack of potatoes, all he did by way of protest was to give utterance to some inarticulate grumblings. Hauling him along the passage, through the front door, across the pavement, Mr Rodway deposited him in the gutter and left him there. Presently, reviving to a dim consciousness of where he was, scrambling to his feet, mumbling threatenings and slaughters, he staggered along the pavement in search of haunts where he was better known and appreciated.

On Mr Rodway's return to the sitting-room, Mrs Ludlow assailed him with her prayers for peace.

"Mr Rodway, I hope there'll be no trouble. I warned Theodore not to let the man in."

"No doubt he had good reasons of his own for ignoring your

warning."

"Nothing of the kind. The man wanted to see Smithers—I let him wait."

"You let him wait—that scoundrel? You innocent dear!"

"Now don't quarrel! don't quarrel! You know, Mr Rodway, that I've trouble enough to bear already. I hope you are not going to add to it."

"Not on this occasion, at least, Mrs Ludlow. But as I have something to say to Theodore in private, I would ask you to leave us alone."

"You promised me."

Her son interposed.

"Go! don't you hear what you are told? Are we a couple of children that you should try to tell us how to conduct our own affairs?"

The obedient mother went. Rodway eyed her offspring with what were not looks of admiration.

You're a pretty dear; a charming son. A comfort to your mother, and the prop of her age. If mothers were endowed with the prophetic instinct, they would strangle such babies as you at their birth."

"Is that kind of thing all you have to say to me?"

"Oh dear no, I've other kinds of things to say as well. You've been dropping hints lately that there is something dark and dreadful about Frank Smithers."

"Frank Smithers? It has got to that, has it? I suppose it will soon be Frank."

"I hope so. The day on which I am admitted to so much intimacy will be the proudest of my life. I'm something of a judge of a man; he is one. Straight as a die; grit all through; incapable of a mean or dirty action; a gentleman born and bred. With nothing of the strain of the cur in him which is so strong in you."

"Is that the reason why you have lent him your sweetheart?"

"Lent him my sweetheart? What do you mean?"

"I thought you were going to make Netta your wife. Yet you've sent her off with him to the theatre. Is that the result of the bargain? some small return for the cash he has given."

"Ludlow, your mother and sister are ladies. Can you have got the blackguard strain from your father, because you are a blackguard through and through? I want to keep my hands off you in this house, if I can help it. So I will merely say that if you again spit out slanderous insinuations of the kind against Netta or Smithers or me. I will wait till you leave this house; I will go with you; and when we are clear of it, we will try conclusions as to who is the better man."

Do you suppose that I allow myself to be influenced by threats in doing what I think is right? I have warned you; if you neglect my warnings, the responsibility is yours."

"It is."

"Do you intend to tell Smithers what has taken place to-night?"

"Certainly. Every blessed thing—including your slanders."

"Then you'll be sorry for it afterwards. As to Mr Smithers, in the future I will deal with him."

"I should. And for your own sake, put it as far forward into the future as you can. You'll find it safer."

CHAPTER 13
THE LEADING LADY

In the meantime Miss Ludlow and Mr Smithers were enjoying the play at the Pandora Theatre. Or rather, perhaps, it should be written that Miss Ludlow was, while Mr Smithers sunned himself in her society. It is probable that the lady's capacity for enjoyment was greater than the gentleman's. She was possessed of an unspoiled appetite for pleasure which found delight in everything. To her a theatre was an abode of romance; the mimic traffic of the stage a perpetual joy. She had not arrived at that period when one sits in judgement.

Unfortunately, the gentleman had. His experience of the contemporary drama was so extensive that it required unusual fare to titillate his palate. He found his companion's satisfaction with what she saw much more charming than the thing which pleased her, and was content to watch the light come into her eyes, her lips part as the interest grew, the fleeting colour paint her pretty cheeks. He found in her, indeed, something which he had not expected to find again in any woman. She held him to her with bonds of whose nature she did not dream.

That night there seemed some special reason why he took even less interest than usual in what was transpiring on the stage. The play was a successful one, the house crowded. The acting could hardly have been better. Yet there was one character the rendition of which seemed to have an odd effect on Mr Smithers. What made it still more singular was that it was the principal part in the piece, and that, by the evident common consent of the audience, it could not have been more worthily rendered.

The *rôle* was a feminine one—that of the heroine. It was played by an actress whose name, according to the programme, was Papillon—Miss Esme Papillon. She was a tall, graceful woman, possessed of a voice to whose musical tones it was a delight to listen. Possibly Mr Smithers was the only person in the crowded theatre who did not find them pleasant. On her first appearance he was covertly observing his companion—who, unconscious of his scrutiny, herself had eyes for nothing but the stage—thinking what a pretty ear she had.

At the first sound of the actress' voice he looked round with a start. When he saw her, an indefinable change took place in his countenance. It was not so much that the smile in his eyes and about his lips vanished, as that its expression altered. He looked at his programme, as if searching on the list for a familiar name, and failing to find it.

"Papillon? Esme Papillon? Is that meant for her? Then in that case she must be the actress who has suddenly taken the town by storm. It would be quite in keeping if she were. She does everything suddenly." He watched her, something singular in his blue eyes. "She can act—she always could. But then the stage was different. Is she also to be a sword of Damocles? This is another ease of grasp your nettle."

Murmuring an excuse to his companion, much to the scandal of the audience he quitted his seat during the progress of an act. Fortunately his was the last seat in a row. Marching straight out of the theatre, he went round to the stage door. At the moment the office was empty. Cerberus had gone on an errand. Mr Smithers took advantage of the doorkeeper's absence to walk straight past his den into the dim recesses beyond. He met a youth carrying something in a jug, of whom he made inquiries.

"Which is Miss Papillon's room?"

Without hesitation the youth replied, plainly unconscious of there being anything irregular in the other's presence where he was.

"Papillon? Straight on; second door to the right."

Mr Smithers did not find the way quite so straight as the youth implied; but he groped along until he reached a door on which was tacked a visiting-card, inscribed with a lady's name. He stood on no ceremony, but then and there, turning the handle, opened the door.

"Who's there?" exclaimed a voice as he was entering.

He did not answer till he was inside and had his back against the door.

The first act had just concluded, the curtain having fallen almost immediately on his leaving the auditorium. Possibly the consciousness that it was drawing to a close had prompted him to rapid movement. The last plaudits of the audience were still echoing in the theatre. It had been a great personal success for Miss Papillon. Flushed with victory, flattered by the compliments which the audience had showered on her. she had hurried to her dressing-room: a light-hearted woman, without a care in the world. Humming a lively tune beneath her breath, with her dresser's assistance she was commencing to change her costume for the second act, when she was startled by the sudden opening of the door.

When she saw who it was had entered, she stood staring for a moment or two with rigid eyes; then underwent, all in an instant, so complete a metamorphosis, that it almost seemed that the woman who was, could not be the woman who had just been. She dropped so limply on to a chair, that one might have been excused for wondering if the bones had dropped clean out of her. Behind her make-up, the muscles of her face began to twitch as if she were suddenly seized with an attack of St Vitus' dance. Grease paint was incapable of concealing the appearance of sudden age. The tall, graceful, happy, triumphant woman of a moment back had become, all at once, a sort of gibbering lay figure.

He was the first to speak, and then it was to the dresser, who had remained motionless, looking from one to the other.

"You can go."

The dresser turned to the actress:

"Excuse me, Miss, but do you want this gentleman in here? You know there isn't much time to change."

The actress was still. Mr Smithers, moving forward, laid his hand upon the dresser's shoulder.

"Did you hear me tell you, you could go?"

The dresser showed those signs of resentment of which her mistress seemed incapable.

"Take your hand off my shoulder; don't you touch me. I don't know who you are or what you want; I don't believe you've any right to be in here, so the sooner you take yourself away from here the better. Anyhow, I'm not going to take my orders from you, and I'll have you know it."

Mr Smithers turned to Miss Papillon.

"Tell her to go."

The actress obeyed.

"Go," she muttered.

This time the dresser consented.

"I'll go fast enough; I'm sure I'm willing. It's no business of mine, only you know what the rules are, and how much time there is to change; and if the stage is kept waiting, don't let me be blamed."

She went out grumbling. Mr Smithers turned the key and shot the bolt.

"Don't kill me," moaned the woman on the chair. "For God's sake, don't kill me."

"You ruined my life; branded me with ignominy; brought me to open shame. If you propose to attempt to play that part again I shall kill you. If you don't, so far as I am concerned, you may go scot-free. I want to come to an understanding with you, that is all. So try to be as open, as candid, as truthful with me as you can, for both our sakes. What are you doing here?"

"I'm acting. Don't you know?—I've made a great success."

"I know about the acting and the success, but why are you here at all?"

"What was I to do?—where could I go? I always had a natural bent towards the stage."

"I'm aware of it. I ought to be."

"So—so I tried acting; and—and I'm married."

"Married!"

He uttered the word in a tone of voice which induced Miss Papillon to draw herself together on her chair, cover her lace with her hands, and repeat her former petition.

"Don't kill me!—For God's sake, don't kill me!"

"Kill you! What for? For doing me the greatest service in your power? To hear that you are married is almost as good news as to hear that you are dead. May I ask who is the happy man?"

"Bellamy."

"The actor?"

"He—he worried me till I married him."

"Did he? What a man of discernment the fellow must be. And you've rewarded him."

"I—I've made the hit of the piece! All London's coming to see me act in it! "

"And shows its taste in so doing. To know that your efforts are properly appreciated must be delightful for you—and Bellamy." Someone rapped at the panel of the door in peremptory fashion. "There's really no reason why these good people should be any longer kept out, as matters stand."

A little man was standing without, made up as the character he enacted in the play—a choleric, and comic, red-headed Irishman. At that moment he appeared to be the person he represented. His questions tumbled over each other as they came from his lips.

"Who are you? What's the meaning of your extraordinary behaviour? What business have you behind the scenes? Who admitted you? How dare you intrude yourself into my wife's apartment?"

Mr Smithers' placidity was in striking contrast to the other's excitement.

"Mr Bellamy?—I have only just heard of your matrimonial good fortune. Allow me to offer you my congratulations."

"Who wants your congratulations? Who asked for them? How dare you offer them at this time of day? Do you suppose you're in a barn? Are you aware you are in a respectable theatre?"—Mr Bellamy addressed himself to his wife, the lady's dresser standing with an aggrieved air at his elbow: "My darling Esme, I cannot tell you how concerned I feel. Mrs Jones assures me that this person positively forced himself into your room. If he has offered you any impertinence, even the slightest, I shall call him to a personal account. My dearest, I do beg that you will not allow yourself to be distressed—the whole house will be prostrated."

The lady gave unmistakable symptoms of having achieved a rapid recovery.

"It's all right, Freddy!—don't be a fool!—and for gracious' sake don't let's have any fuss!—Now, Jones, move yourself, and get me into my change as fast as you can."

When Mr Smithers returned to his stall he found Miss Ludlow quick to notice that there was something new in his demeanour.

"Where have you been? I thought you'd gone for good and forgotten me. And what is the matter with you? you look all smile."

"I feel like that perhaps its the effect of the play."

"Isn't it a lovely play? And isn't Miss Papillon splendid?"

"She seems to have some notion of acting."

"Seems to have some notion of acting! Is that all you can say? Why, she acts magnificently. And isn't she beautiful?"

"I have seen worse-looking women."

"Surely you are not blind?"

"Blind?—Me?—What do you mean?"

"That's the one thing I don't like about you—your pretending to be so cynical;—at least, not exactly cynical, but you never will admit that things are half so splendid as I think they are."

"That's my misfortune."

As he looked at her radiant face, lighted with the joy which only comes of innocence, he felt that it was.

He enjoyed the second act amazingly—for him; finding rare delight in observing Mr Bellamy, whose part was not so prominent an one as it might have been, and even greater pleasure in studying his charming wife. She represented a type of person who was a theatrical fashion of the hour—a woman with a past. That past she seemed to find an inconvenient possession, especially when the other characters began to make themselves disagreeable to her on account of it. She made a sweet sinner in that hour of her penitence. Her genuine distress touched the audience even in the stalls and boxes. The curtain had to be raised twice at the end of the act, and then she had to come in front of it alone.

"How cruel they are to her!—how cruel!" Miss Ludlow's reference was to the characters on the stage. The audience could scarcely have been kinder. Mr Smithers was still. Presently the young lady delivered herself of a scrap of proverbial philosophy—"How dreadful it must be to have done something of which you are ashamed!"

"Horrible!"

"You must go in fear and trembling lest someone should find out what it is you have done, and then when it is found out it's worst of all."

"Sometimes one does a thing of which one doesn't know whether one ought or ought not to be ashamed."

"I can't see how that can be. We all have an inward monitor which points out to us the difference between right and wrong."

"I'm not sure that it's so simple as you suppose. The strands are apt to cross each other; then life becomes a complicated thing.—Suppose that someone for whom you cared turned out to be not all that one ought to be—what would be your own personal attitude in such a case?"

"I should forgive the sinner, but hate the sin."

The words were spoken with a smile. Mr Smithers, leaning back in his stall, looked up at the crimson velvet curtains as if he saw something in—or at the back of—them, which moved him to contemplation.

CHAPTER 14
BROKERS AND THE MARRIAGE QUESTION

One afternoon Mr Smithers, returning to Dulverton Road, saw what looked like a furniture van standing outside the door of No. 23. As he came along the pavement he observed it with surprise. Men were taking things out of the house and placing them in the van, in a manner which suggested that a removal was taking place. As he had only quitted the house a few hours before, and had then heard nothing to lead him to suppose that such a move was intended, he could but wonder what the thing might mean. As he reached the door a man came out with a couch on his head, which he recognised as being part of the furniture of his own sitting-room. To this man he put a question.

"What's the meaning of this? And what are you doing with that couch?"

"The meaning of it is, governor, that this is a bust-up, and I'd thank you to stand out of my way."

"A bust-up! What are you talking about?"

"A bill of sale is what I'm talking about. We're taking away what's scheduled. If you ask inside there, perhaps they'll be able to tell you more about it than I can. If you're a friend of the family, at a delicate moment like this the old lady may be glad to see you. Only, as this couch isn't exactly a featherweight. I'll ask you to move aside and let me put it in the van."

"Put that couch down."

"Put it down? May I ask who you might be?"

"Put that couch down. Or, better, take it back where it came from. I'll talk to you in there."

"Look here, governor, don't you be silly, and don't you make no mistake. I don't know who you are, and I don't care; but you can take it from me that it's all regular, and that it's either the money or the things."

"You shall have the money. Do as I tell you—take that couch back to the sitting-room."

"I'll be very glad to do it if it is going to be the money; but as it ain't easy to turn a couch this size in a passage this width, my male being outside there in the van, I'll just ask you to lend me a hand."

Mr Smithers lent a hand. As they were carrying the couch between them Mrs Ludlow emerged from the kitchen, crying and wringing her hands.

"Oh, Mr Smithers, it has come at last! I've done my best to prevent it, but it has been more than I could manage."

"I am afraid, Mrs Ludlow, that I don't understand what it all means."

"Mr Judson has distrained upon a bill of sale. I borrowed seventy-five pounds from him when we came here. He's had it all back again, and yet he makes out that, with arrears of interest and what he calls fines, I still owe him more than I borrowed."

"The amount is one hundred and twenty-seven pound ten and five, and you may be sure its owing. Mr Judson is a sharp man of business, but he don't make mistakes when it comes to figures in a case like this. He'd find it too expensive."

"You shall have the money. Bring those things back out of the cart."

"Excuse me, sir, I'm not doubting your word; but me and my mate have had the job of taking out them things, and we don't want to have the trouble of bringing them back for nothing. I'd like to see the money before we start."

Mr Smithers produced a roll of banknotes from his despatch-box.

"Here it is. Return those things exactly as you found them, and there will be something for yourselves."

Soon everything was as it had been, and the van had gone. Mrs Ludlow was rendered almost inarticulate by a combination of gratitude and shame.

"Oh, Mr Smithers, I don't know how to thank you—I was in despair when you first came—you've been my guardian angel all along; I don't know how I ever shall repay you."

"We will discuss that together later on. In the meantime, if you don't mind, I should like to speak a word or two to Netta."

Mrs Ludlow retired tearfully to her own quarters. Her daughter would have gone with her had not Mr Smithers interposed.

"Stop. I wish to speak to you." The girl confronted him with white cheeks and big eyes. "I don't think you have used me very well."

"I know I haven't. My only excuse is that I have always had some faint hope that Theodore would do something to help us, rather than let the worst come to the worst, and that that odious usurer would be staved off. I didn't realise till Mr Judson's van was actually at the door that the hour of reckoning was upon us."

"That is not what I mean. You ought, long ago, to have given me an opportunity to remove this burden off your shoulders, and your mother's."

"Why? My own brother refused to help. Why should I come to you, a stranger?"

"I deny that I am a stranger."

"You're the best of friends, but you're a stranger."

"It is in your refusal to admit that I am not a stranger that my grievance lies."

"You've been too generous to me already. I've been conscious all along that I ought not to have allowed it, but you have such a way that I've not known how to refuse. But what kind of girl you take me for to suppose that I should be willing to encroach still further upon your generosity I am unable to imagine."

"It's not a question of generosity. Is it possible that you're not aware what you have been to me almost since the moment I first saw you?"

"Mr Smithers!"

"Don't call me by that odious name."

"Odious?—But it is your name."

"It has a prefix."

"A prefix? Really, I don't know what you mean. Mister is a prefix."

"Netta, you are honest with everybody else; be honest with me.—Don't you know I love you?"

"I know you like me; or at least I suppose you like me, or you wouldn't be so kind."

"'Like!' 'kind!'—don't use such words! I didn't mean to speak so soon, but events have moved more quickly than I expected. Netta—answer me!—will you be my wife?"

She looked up at him with eyes which did not flinch, although her cheeks were flaming.

"You ask the question as if you were demanding my money or my life."

"Perhaps I am—or at least their equivalent.—Will you be my wife?"

"Please be calm. I don't know you when your eyes blaze like that. Let us consider."

"I'll consider nothing."

"Then, since somebody must consider, I will. In the first place, I'm nobody and nothing; a beggar; indebted to your charity for a roof to cover me; while you are a great gentleman and a rich man."

"As for the great gentleman—fiddle! But it's true I'm a rich man. Rodway and I have received an offer of a million sterling for the Power."

"A million sterling!"

"Which we've refused. Soon we shall be offered fifty millions. We shall refuse that also. We're running for a record in the way of wealth. And I owe it all to you."

"To me?—Really you can say things!"

"If you only knew what it meant to me when you gave me shelter in your home."

"Let you lodgings, I suppose you mean?"

"Shelter, I said; shelter is what I meant. Perhaps you never will know; if you ever do, you'll understand. By so doing you gave me an opportunity of meeting Rodway."

"You were not the only person Mr Rodway had met. He had met heaps of people. None of them could see anything in his great invention. You alone had the seeing eye."

"Anyhow, you afforded me an opportunity of proving that I was not such an idiot as the rest of them. It began with a little thing—with my ringing the bell, and your appearance at the front door."

"You call that a little thing?"

"At least it was one for which you were directly responsible—as you have continued to be directly responsible for everything that has taken place throughout. Now it promises to end with such great things—for both of us."

"I don't see how I am concerned in all this greatness."

"Not as my wife?—Netta, play with me some other time. Just now I'm in such deadly earnest. Tell me that you will be my wife."

"I should like to, very much."

"Then, as I should like it still more, that's settled."

"You've chosen such an odd moment—when the sound of the broker's cart is still in the street."

"That broker's cart brought me to my senses. It showed me in one flash in what an unsatisfactory state affairs must be between us if you could wait for such a crisis before hinting that you were in trouble. It made it imperative on me not to leave you with any excuse for similar conduct in the future."

"I'm afraid you're going to be the dominant partner."

Shortly afterwards she said :

"I've always wondered what it felt like to be kissed by a man with a beard."

"And now, what's your candid opinion?"

"Well—it's odd to feel all that hair so close. With a beard you look poetic; but then, in every sense, you're unusual. I don't like bearded men as a rule-—I prefer them shaven and shorn."

'Shall I shave?"

"Certainly not. The idea! I've fallen in love with you as you are, and if any alteration's made—that's a catastrophe which 1 wish to avoid.—Do you know I've not the slightest right to marry a rich man, because I've never had a five-pound note of my very own—to do with just as I liked—in my life."

"You'll like five-pound notes all the better now."

"I suppose you've always been rich?"

"Not I. It'll be as novel an experience to me as to you."

"But you must have been rich to leave all that money untouched in the bank for so many years?"

"That was different. Now we are about to deal with millions." He looked down at his foot.

"I see. Then in your opinion one is only rich when one deals with millions. What a lot of poor folks there must be. What will Theodore say?"

"Who cares?"

"But he is my brother."

"Even the best of brothers have little to say in matters of this sort, and he's the worst."

"And then" she paused, as someone was heard opening the front door with a latchkey. "There's Mr Rodway—what will he say?"

"You don't mean?"

She nodded.

A light dawned on him. "What an ass I must be not to have seen!—Now I understand.—I hope he won't take it—hardly." When Mr Rodway appeared at the open door his partner had his arm about the lady's waist. "Ben, you've come in the nick of time. Netta has just promised to be my wife."

Mr Rodway dropped on to a chair.

"You call that the nick of time!—And I was hurrying home to ask her to be mine."

"My dear chap!—I hadn't a notion!—If you had only dropped a hint, I would have yielded you the precedence."

"It would have made no difference if you had." This was the lady.

Mr Rodway groaned.

"That's a nice thing to say! And I daresay I've asked that girl a dozen times!—sometimes when I hadn't a sovereign in my pocket."

"I should think you must have asked me quite twenty times, and frequently when you hadn't a shilling."

"It's a theory of mine that marriage, like everything else, is a matter of perseverance. No girl says 'yes' till you've asked her about fifty times."

"That isn't always the case."

And Miss Ludlow looked up at Mr Smithers. He drew her closer to him.

"I'm glad I've won, Ben; but I'm awfully sorry you've lost."

"Don't allow your satisfaction to be lessened by any little consideration of that kind. It's true you've dashed the cup of happiness from my lips, but that's a matter of not the slightest consequence. There are only about half a dozen girls I really care for; and as I've lost sight of the other five, in capturing this one you've robbed me of the entire six. After what I've gone through in proposing to her, off and on, shut goodness alone knows when, it does seem hard."

"I am grieved," observed the lady, "that all that labour should have been wasted. But if you put the matter into the hands of a competent private detective, I cannot help thinking that you will light on traces of at least some of the five."

"It's to be hoped so—and before very long. An unmarried millionaire is such a waste; especially as an aunt, three cousins, a niece, a friend of my boyhood's days, and a lady who knew my mother have all expressed their willingness to come and keep house for me. I didn't know I had so many relatives and friends—I loathe 'em all.—When's it going to be?"

"When's what going to be?"

"The marriage."

"What a ridiculous question to ask, when it's only just this moment that we've begun to think about anything of the kind. Indeed I haven't begun yet. In a year or two it will be quite time to talk about that."

"The marriage, my dear Ben, will take place next week."

"Next week!" This the lady.

"Or, at the outside, within a month. There is no reason why there should be any delay. Indeed, very much the contrary."

"I suppose I'm to have no voice in the matter?"

"Decidedly you are. I will say to you, 'That is the day on which we are going to be married'; and your voice will reply, 'Yes, it is.'"

"I appear to have come across an original kind of person."

"You'd much better have had me," groaned Mr Rodway. "I know you'll be sorry you didn't. You can twist me round your finger. But he'll twist you."

"He'd better try. At the eleventh hour I may change my mind."

"Do. Then I'll persuade you to change it back again.—By the way, I'm thinking about buying a place in the country."

"What do you call a place in the country?"

"I've been making inquiries, and I've heard of a place called Dene Park—belonged to some people named Foster—near Birchester, in Sussex. Seems rather a nice house, good grounds, and all that sort of thing."

"Hark at him! I hope that by a 'place' you do not mean a palace. Be so good as to remember that I am used to No. 23 Dulverton Road, which is not a 'place.'"

Rodway, who seemed to have been ruminating, delivered himself of the results.

"Dene Park? Foster family? Birchester? I've an idea that I've heard the name before. Wasn't it mixed up with a case in the law courts some years ago? I can't quite hit on the connection, but I believe it was—rather imagine it was associated in some way with a case of a fraudulent solicitor."

"I fancy you're right, and that there was something of the kind. Anyhow, it's on the market now, and, from what I hear, should be just the place for us."

"You've paid no attention to my modestly expressed hope that the place is not a palace."

"If it were, aren't you fit to be its queen ?"

"There's one thing," she said, "which may be urged in favour of your beard—that in moments of intense provocation it's a very convenient thing to have to pull."

By that time the daylight had come to an end. The evening had closed in. The gas having remained unlighted, the room was all in shadow. The silence which followed Netta's laughing words was followed by the sound of someone whistling. The three faces turned towards the window. Rodway was the first to speak.

"There's that whistling chap come back again! and the same old tune! Do you know, Smithers, I've heard him two or three times since that first night, and I've never been able to drop on him."

"I've heard him too."

"And I," echoed Netta.

"It's uncommonly queer. Always the same tune, and always whistled close up to the window; and yet it's not dark enough to prevent our seeing anyone if anyone were there, with the blind drawn up like that. Upon my word, I'm beginning to wonder if the thing's uncanny. I suppose, Smithers, that it's not a ghostly signal, intended to convey a special significance to you."

"Not that I'm aware. Allow me, my dear Ben, to direct the same inquiry to your address."

"It can't be meant for me. There isn't a ghost who takes sufficient interest in my proceedings to pay me a visit from the shades. There; he's finished. Where can the beggar have got to?"

A suggestion came from Netta,

"I've wondered if it mightn't be a bird, trained to whistle only that one tune. There is something bird-like about the tone."

"The same idea struck me," admitted Mr Rodway. "You can train a piping bullfinch to do anything. And yet I don't know how you're going to make the explanation fit, unless it's in one of the houses next to us."

"I've asked them. There isn't a bird in either."

"There you are then. That explanation's off. I am inclined to suspect a phonographic trick."

CHAPTER 15
THE MAN IN GREY

Mr Smithers journeyed down to Birchester to view that "handsome residential property" known as Dene Park. On the way down he read a newspaper. This paper contained an item of news in which he seemed to take considerable interest. It was an account of the christening of the Marquis of Skye's infant son and heir—Lord Alec Bruce of Gairloch. An imposing ceremony it seemed to have been, with a royal godfather and a brave show of friends. The paper observed that the baptismal rite had been postponed beyond the usual time owing to the delicate health of both the child and its mother. Mr Smithers knit his brow when he saw this.

"Sarah used to be as strong as a horse. She ought to be, considering the constitution with which she was endowed and the training she received; a type of your modern woman, practised in everything that makes for health; an athlete to her finger-tips. She's never known a day's illness. I wonder if what the thing says is true. I'd give a nice little sum to be sure it wasn't. Lord Alec Bruce of Gairloch! How odd it sounds. Is he a bonny bairn, I wonder, with the Skye blue eye? I warrant his father'll be making much of him. Alec and a bairn! Somehow I cannot get the two in focus."

The newspaper went on to state that the event was of special import to the ancient family, owing to romantic circumstances with which the world was more or less familiar. Taking, possibly, this supposititious familiarity for granted, the paper did not explain what these circumstances were. The allusion served to divert Mr Smithers' thoughts into another channel.

"'Romantic circumstances'? That's a pretty way of putting it. 'With which the world is more or less familiar.' Indeed. I'm laying odds that the gentleman who wrote that paragraph is ignorant of them himself. It'll be a drop of bitterness in the cup of Alec's happiness when he sees it—if he ever does. Gairloch! How the old storm-beaten place haunts me asleep and waking. Strange that I cannot get it out of my sight. That life is dead—buried. I've been born anew into another world. And yet, though I never fail to be conscious of the grave in which it is contained, all the time I see its ancient battlements, seeming to bid me walk on them again beside the sea. What's the scientific name for the capacity of seeing several things at once the things that are and the things that have been?"

As he turned this little problem over in his mind, looking, with scarcely seeing eyes, through the carriage window at the country they were traversing, he began to whistle. The act suggested obliviousness of the fact that he was not alone in the compartment. In the opposite corner, at the other end, was another passenger, whose presence Mr Smithers seemed, for the moment, to be ignoring. It is possible that this person had been taking as little notice of his companion as his companion had been taking of him. He also had been engrossed in his newspaper's version of the day's story, until his companion began to whistle. The instant the sound, which, under the circumstances, some would have regarded as a solecism, commenced, he seemed to prick up his ears. His eyes ceased to travel along the lines of his newspaper. He conveyed the impression of being all at once keenly on the alert.

After momentary hesitation, his hands which held the paper fell on to his knees. He glanced round with what almost amounted to a start.

His appearance was singular. Although probably rather over than under the average height, his enormous girth lent him the air of being short. Not only was he noticeable for breadth of chest, but his stoutness amounted to deformity. His neck was suggested by a single layer of fat. On it was perched a head which was small out of all proportion to the rest of him. It was bullet-shaped. The face was clean-shaven. A pair of round black eyes twinkled under overhanging eyebrows. The mouth was small and whimsical; the nose a comical little pug.

The man was about fifty years of age. He was attired in a loosely fitting suit of light-grey tweed, which served, if anything, to accentuate the contours of his massive figure; a soft hat, of the same shade of grey as his clothes, was in the rack above his head. The small portion of his waistcoat open in front was ornamented by a narrow strip of scarlet ribbon tied in a sailor's knot; a slender gold chain passed from pocket to pocket; he wore grey suede gloves and brown boots.

Probably, since his thoughts were far away, without realising what it was that he was doing, Mr Smithers whistled the little tune with which, owing to the persistence of the mysterious whistler, habit had made familiar. It was evidently this accident which attracted the attention of his travelling companion, the man in grey. He followed it, note for note, as if the sound of it filled him with so much surprise that he found it hard to believe his ears; then stared at the whistler as if he experienced a similar difficulty in crediting the evidence of his eyes.

He looked at the handsome giant in the opposite corner as he might have regarded a ghost; noting the air of distinction, the indefinable something which signified birth and breeding. Whether or not the other was conscious of his scrutiny he could not say. At least he showed no sign of it, keeping his eyes turned towards his own window. After an interval the whistling recommenced; the tune was gone through a second time. The man in grey, resuming his paper, observed the printed page with a glance which probably saw little and cared less for what was on it. The tune was gone through a third time. Another interval—this time broken by the man in grey.

In his turn he whistled; in the same soft, modulated tones

which had characterised Mr Smithers' probably unconscious little performance The air which he essayed bore a curious resemblance to the one to which he had been listening; a resemblance which the first performer could scarcely fail to notice. Effectually roused from his reverie, Mr Smithers woke to distinct perception that he was not alone. His glance journeyed to the other end of the carriage, observing his fellow-traveller with unmistakable amusement.

The man in grey ceased. Mr Smithers spoke.

"Your tune might almost be an echo of mine."

"It is an echo, and an answer."

"Indeed? Is that so? You are acquainted with the tune?"

"Very well indeed."

"It's only part of an air, isn't it? What is it called, and who is the composer?"

The man in grey pursed up into a sort of button the small mouth which went so strangely with his huge frame.

"It is entitled, to give a title to what never had one, 'The Death Whistle,' and was composed by Francis Smithers."

If the answer occasioned Mr Smithers any surprise, he showed no sign of it. He merely continued to regard the other with his characteristic air of languid entertainment.

"'The Death Whistle'? Rather a peculiar title with which to brand so quaint a melody. Is it an allusion to some incident with which it has been associated, or what?"

"It is an allusion to the Seal of the Eight Men, which was not to be broken by any one of them save in the presence of the other seven, under penalty of death."

The man in grey spoke in rather wheezy tones, which suggested asthma. Mr Smithers looked at him for a moment or two before he answered.

"Is that so?"

Taking up his newspaper, he recommenced to study its columns as if, for him, all interest in the conversation was at an end. The man in grey was also still continuing to eye the blue cloth cushion which was immediately in front of him as if it had been something unusual. Then his whole face broke up into a number of wrinkles, each one seeming to represent a separate smile. He turned towards Mr Smithers, beaming at him in a fashion which could hardly be described as pleasant.

"You're fond of the newspaper?"

"I beg your pardon?"

"You're fond of the newspaper!"

"One reads it."

"You find something in it of particular interest?"

Mr Smithers gave a slight movement which might have meant anything, but which did not seem to hint at his being disposed to enter into conversation. The man in grey wailed a second or so, as if for a reply; then, when none came, he went deliberately up to the other end of the carriage and placed himself in the seat directly opposite Mr Smithers.

"Permit me to offer you my card."

Lowering his paper Mr Smithers took the proffered piece of pasteboard, reading aloud the name which was engraved upon it.

"'Mr Augustus Chaffinch.' I'm afraid I have not the pleasure?"

"Oh yes, you have the pleasure. May I ask you for your card?"

"You're very good; but I'm afraid it's not my rule to exchange cards with strangers—thank you all the same."

"My name is not strange to you, although yours is to me. We've been calling to you—how long?"

"Calling to me?—How?"

"You were whistling just now what no one ever does whistle unless he is one of the Eight."

"Are you referring to the air you spoke of as 'The Death Whistle'?"

"I am, as you're aware. How often have we called to you? Take care that we don't have to call once too often."

"Who are you, Mr Chaffinch?"

"You know who I am; you've a retentive memory. I'm the

man who heads the list of seven names which is in the little book which you found in safe No. 226. I will give you the other six:—Bob Hammick; Samuel Waterson; Gustav Kronberg; Philip Fenturn; Sam Brown,—queried; and The Linkman. That is the order in which they stand."

"This is an unexpected pleasure!"

Mr Smithers laughed. Mr Chaffinch's face became the mass of wrinkles which lent to it such an uncomfortable resemblance to an india-rubber doll.

"On both sides. But you will find that where the Eight are concerned it is the unexpected which generally happens. Now tell me who you are."

"I'm Francis Smithers."

"That's a lie. You don't look like the sort who'd resort to the shelter of a dirty lie. The higher flights are in your line, so I wouldn't descend from them."

"How do you know that I'm not Francis Smithers, as much as you're Augustus Chaffinch?"

"How do I know that you're not Francis Smithers? Because I know that he lies in the pauper's burial-ground at Canterstone."

A sudden change took place in the expression of Mr Smithers' eyes, the pupils dilating till a speck of light seemed to glow in the centre of each. That Mr Chaffinch noticed it was proved by his commenting on its appearance.

"And after seeing the thing come into your eyes which has come into them now, I should have said you'd murdered him had I not been sure you didn't—for it's murder which is looking out at me. You're the homicidal type, which thinks as little of killing a man—or woman—as of wringing a chicken's neck. But if you try close quarters with me, you'll find that I'm not all fat, and that I'm almost as much possessed of the devil as you are."

Mr Smithers was still; content to regard the other smilingly. Mr Chaffinch leaned back in his seat, placing a suede-gloved hand on each fat leg. He cocked his small round head on one side, in a fashion which was grotesquely reminiscent of some unwieldy bird.

"I'll tell you something. I'm one of two persons now living who is aware of the connection which existed between George Edney and Francis Smithers. George Edney died in prison. As you appeared shortly afterwards as Francis Smithers, the presumption is that you were with him in Canterstone Jail—like him, a convicted felon.—Ah! you were?"

Mr Smithers sat rather forward on his seat. In an instant Mr Chaffinch's hand—popping in and out of the pocket of his shooting-jacket—held what looked like a toy revolver.

"If you touch me—or move more forward—I'll shoot you like a rat. I know enough of your history to make it easy to convince a jury that killing you would be justifiable homicide."

Mr Smithers looked from the man to the revolver, and from the revolver back to the man.

"It isn't your pretty popgun which would prevent my killing you, Mr Chaffinch, but the consideration of the mess you'd make, and other things."

"You keep those other things well to the front; you'll find it the part of wisdom. If you'd done so always, you'd have been wiser still."

"May I ask, Mr Chaffinch, why you take so keen an interest in me? "

Mr Chaffinch did not at once reply. He sat well back—as if with the intention of keeping himself as far from his companion as the width of the compartment permitted, his diminutive weapon pointing somewhat ostentatiously across the way. He eyed Mr Smithers as if reflectively. Presently his face again became a mass of wrinkles.

"I think it's possible that you actually don't know."

"You think correctly; I don't."

"George Edney was a man who would hardly give his entire confidence to anyone. Complete candour was with him a physical impossibility. He had his concealments even from me, as I have since discovered. It is scarcely probable that he told you everything; it is possible that you haven't found it all out since."

Mr Smithers only smiled, the quality of his smile seeming to strike Mr Chaffinch.

"As regards secretiveness, you're a man of Edney's kidney. The average human being might live with you on terms of intimacy your whole life long, and yet not know what kind of man you really are. I think it possible that you're such a bundle of contradictions that at more than one cross road you discover a stranger in yourself. Under certain conceivable circumstances, that sort of thing is not only a misfortune, it's a dangerous error;—as, before very long, you will possibly find. On this occasion you shall not be able to reproach me with want of candour. Before we part you shall understand me, however much I may remain in the dark concerning you.—Briefly: safe No. 226, to which you have had, and still have, access, is not—and was not—the property of George Edney, *alias* Francis Smithers, but of the Eight."

"The Eight! What Eight?" Seven of the names you have found in the little book to which I have already referred; Francis Smithers was the eighth. One other has in it an interest of a peculiar kind; but for your own sake it is to be hoped that with that other you will never come into contact."

"Making the joint stock company to consist of nine?"

"Making it consist of nine. But for the present we need only concern ourselves with eight. In that safe was a quantity of jewellery, representing a large sum of money. That jewellery is our joint properly. Smithers was merely its custodian. There were also plates for the production of the banknotes of most of the countries which circulate banknotes; genuine plates, you understand, procured, at the cost of much labour and money, from the issuing banks themselves. There was a large supply of paper, also genuine. Last, but not least, there were a large number of what were, to all intents and purposes, *bona fide* notes, representing, in the main, a comfortable fortune, even when divided by eight.

"Had not Francis Smithers taken us in, all this wealth would not have remained inactive on the premises of the Shoe Lane Deposit Company. As I have told you, only I and one other were aware of his identity with George Edney; we only hit on the discovery by chance, after he had been sentenced to penal servitude, on a charge which came to us as an entire surprise. So while the rest of the society has been awaiting the reappearance of Francis Smithers, and keeping an unsleeping eye on safe No. 226, to the best of my ability I have been following the movements of a certain inmate of His Majesty's jails; intending, on his emerging from them, to call the attention of the remainder of the company to the deception which he had practised on his faithful colleagues."

"Quite a romantic little story of yours, Mr Chaffinch!"

"You think so.—Let me continue the romance by pointing out the line we shall probably follow in your case. In the first place, we have got you."

"Have you indeed?"

"We know where you live. For that we're indebted to Bob Hammick; who, if he would only sign the pledge, would be a discreeter man."

"Is Mr Bob Hammick a gentleman who recalls a broken-down prize-fighter?"

"You flatter him by the description, but probably it's the man.—We are already in possession of certain details which intimately concern you. Very soon we shall be acquainted with the entire story of your life. You will find that we shall be able to make an awkward use of it."

"You really are of that opinion?"

"I really am.—We shall of course require you to return to us intact the property which was never yours, and shall call you to serious account for any part of it which may be missing."

"That will be very good of you."

"After that, we shall have to consider that you have obtained our confidence in a wholly unjustifiable manner, and shall have to decide whether it will be advisable to put an end to you at once, or to rest content with satisfactory hostages for your future good behaviour."

"In whichever direction it may incline, the decision of your charming society will be agreeable to me.'

"The Eight do not reside within a stone's throw of each other. They are scattered over different countries; engaged in various avocations. To communicate the facts to all of them takes time. When they have those facts they will commence to move. You will be at once advised of the form which their movement may take."

"It is really very good of you, Mr Chaffinch, to give me all these hints on behalf of your friends."

"In the meantime, I would advise you to meet us halfway. To volunteer the information which, otherwise, we shall obtain without your assistance; to hand to us, inviolate, our property "

"Your property?"

"Our property. Then, and then only, we may be disposed to treat your conduct leniently."

"And that you call meeting you halfway? Your notions of half-measures are your own."

"Should you, as time goes on, feel disposed to act on my suggestion, as I think is probable, you had better communicate with me at my private address—The Firs, Birchester; when I will personally undertake to do for you all that can be done."

"The Firs, Birchester? You live at Birchester? We shall not be far from each other. I am thinking of taking up my residence at Dene Park."

"Dene Park!—You?"

"In which case I suppose we shall be neighbours, in a sort of a way, and be able to keep an eye upon each other's movements. This, I think, is Birchester Station. Good morning, Mr Chaffinch. I have to thank you for making the journey seem so short an one."

"You're a cool hand."

Mr Smithers laughingly nodded towards the revolver which Mr Chaffinch still was holding.

"Were I you I should return that plaything to your pocket. To be seen carrying a toy of that kind makes one look so foolish."

Mr Chaffinch, standing at the carriage door, watched the other's tall figure as he strolled down the platform.

"He is a cool hand. Or is it only ignorance? It is easy for a man not to be afraid when he's ignorant of the danger he is running. If he knew that, to all intents and purposes, he is already a dead man, he might look at the world out of different eyes."

Chapter 16
Dene Park

Mr Smithers was delighted with Dene Park. Unfortunately the auctioneer and estate agent, Mr R. W. Felkin, with whom he had been in correspondence, not having been advised of his coming, was out at the time he called. He therefore had to be content with the society of one of that gentleman's clerks, who accompanied him on the visit of inspection.

Dene Park was distant three or four miles from the town of Birchester. They drove to it in a dogcart, the clerk taking the reins. It was a pleasant drive, through the rich, undulating, well-wooded Sussex country. He told himself that a man could hardly desire a more agreeable approach to his home. He noticed how well the youngster from Mr Felkin's office drove.

"You're used to horses?"

"Rather." Then the clerk added, as by way of an afterthought,—"At least, I was once."

Mr Smithers noted, too, what a good looking lad the speaker was, with an air about him which one scarcely expected to find in a country-auctioneer's assistant. He sat very upright; his well-shaped head was nicely poised; his cheeks had that healthy pallor which goes well with black hair. Occasionally his face was lighted up by an irresistible smile, half sweet, half roguish. His straw hat, with its broad ribbon, and his plain suit of navy serge, became him well. Mr Smithers, who was quick both in his likes and his dislikes, had taken a fancy to his driver before he drew up before some closed lodge gates.

An old woman came out of a stone lodge, which stood very much in need of repairs. She seemed to know his companion very well.

"Good morning, Mr Sidney. And how be you, sir?"

"Thank you, Mrs Brazier, I am going strong. And how are you—and Sam?"

"There's nothing much the matter with me except old bones. Sam, he ain't nothing to complain of neither, though that don't keep him from grumbling, none the more for that."

The youngster laughed.

"Sam wouldn't be happy if he didn't grumble. Would you mind opening the gates, Mrs Brazier? We've come to see the house."

"Is this the gentleman?"

Planting herself by the side of the cart, she stared up with her old eyes at Mr Smithers. The clerk regarded him with a quizzical glance. "That's the gentleman."

The old lady finished her inspection. Then, without a word, she swung the gates back on their hinges, standing grimly silent while the cart drove through. When they were past, Mr Smithers remarked to the driver—

"She seems to know you?"

"She knows me very well."

They entered an avenue of beech trees. Autumn's lingers were beginning to fleck their glories with russet gold.

"This is a fine drive."

"I have been told that this is the finest avenue of beech trees in England; I can well believe it. In this country we are famous for our beeches."

They continued between the two rows of giant trees for probably half a mile. Then the clerk drew up.

"This is the house."

He could hardly have chosen a more effective point of view. Emerging from the shadow of the beeches, an expanse of open park land stretched in front. The ground ascended gently from where they were. The house crowned the slope—at a distance of perhaps another half mile. Mr Smithers had not expected anything so striking. It conveyed the impression not only of size, but of stability, and even grandeur.

"It looks very well from here."

"It looks well from anywhere."

"Those trailing vines and creeping plants mayn't benefit the walls, but they soften the lines."

The youngster shook his head.

"The pruning knife is wanted badly. You'll find them over-run with the nests of all sorts of feathered things. I shouldn't be surprised if they'd got into the house itself. In an empty house a bird treats a broken window as an invitation."

"Is the place quite uninhabited?—No caretaker or any-thing?"

"I shall have to be your cicerone; there's not a living creature on the premises—except rats and mice, and similar small deer."

An excellent guide the speaker proved; threading his way in and out of the multitudinous passages with an instinct for direc-tion which seemed never at fault; passing from room to room with the sure step of one who knows them well. Splendid apart-ments some of them were. Mr Smithers laughed to himself as he pictured Netta's face of amazement on her first discovering herself to be the mistress of all this amplitude; her big, wide-open eyes as she set herself to explore the intricacies of her new domain.

They were in a spacious chamber on the first floor, which looked out over a series of Italian terraces on to a lake.

"This," explained his guide, "is the picture gallery; or, rather, it was. The walls were papered with family portraits, which were sold off by the yard."

A note of bitterness in the speaker's voice struck Mr Smith-ers' ear—not for the first time.

"You seem to know the house very well?"

"I ought to; I was born here."

"Indeed. How came that about?"

"It was my father's house; and his father's, and his father's before him, in a long line of right descent."

"Then you are?"

"My name is Foster—Sidney Foster."

Mr Smithers was still. He had suspected that the young

man might have some association with the house, but had not guessed that the connection was so close as it appeared it was. As he stood looking through the window on to the fair scene without, he was tickled by the irony of the position—that this man should be introducing him, as a possible purchaser, to the home of his fathers.

"How came your father to sell the place?"

"He didn't sell it;—he'd have died first."

The answer came with a strength of bitterness for which Mr Smithers was unprepared. He touched the other lightly on the shoulder. "It was not my intention to hurt you."

The youth laughed; a little wryly, perhaps, but still he laughed.

"Oh, you didn't hurt me. I got used to the situation long enough ago. The story's common property; it's known to everyone."

"Wasn't there something about a fraudulent solicitor?"

Mr Smithers was poking at the wall with the end of his cane. His companion indulged in a repetition of the former mirthless laughter.

"There was a good deal about a fraudulent solicitor;—a good deal too much. My father was one of the best fellows in the world, but in some matters simple as a child. He knew nothing about business, and cared less; and worst of all, he trusted everyone. His affairs were managed by a solicitor named Glasspoole, over at Birchester. To his keeping my father entrusted all that he had,—title-deeds, securities, everything. In his turn Glasspoole confided in his head-clerk—a man named Edney; George Edney—a scoundrel of the very finest water. Mr Edney merely applied the entire contents of his employer's office to his own private uses;—one day my father woke to find himself robbed of all he had—a beggar."

"But surely at least part of the property was recoverable?"

"I was only fifteen at the time, so I didn't know much about details; but I believe Edney juggled my father into doing all sorts of things he didn't know that he was doing. He did recover the title-deeds, but that was only after a large expenditure both of time and money, and then they were practically worthless. You can't keep up a place like this on the income it produces. He was in debt; his money and my mother's had slipped through the holes in Edney's pockets. Anyhow, he wasn't the man to pull things out of the mire. He died instead. Within the year my mother followed him. Then the mortgagees foreclosed—and now the property's in the market."

"Are you the only child?"

"I have a sister—Margaret. She's what she calls 'writing for the press.' She says that one of these days she's going to make a great name and a big fortune. In the meantime, thank God, she has enough to live upon."

"And you?"

"Felkin's been very good in giving me a berth in his office; but what I want is to be a land surveyor, or a bailiff, or a steward, or something of that kind. I ought to understand the work. If it weren't for Meg I'd emigrate, but I can't leave her in England all alone."

"What became of Edney?"

"He's in jail; and let's hope he'll die there—for my sake as well as his own."

"Why do you say that?"

"He turned the happiest home in England into a hell; he robbed me of my birthright; he killed my mother and father—he's as much a murderer as any that's gone to the gallows. If ever I have the misfortune to meet him face to face I'll treat him as one—I'll kill him as he killed them."

"You shouldn't talk like that."

"If he had used you as he has used me how would you talk? Wouldn't you want to have something in exchange?"

Mr Smithers was still describing patterns on the wall with the point of his stick. Instead of replying to the question he countered with another. "And Glasspoole—what's become of him?"

"He's a waiter at the Gaiety Restaurant in the Strand."

Mr Smithers wheeled round, genuinely surprised. "A waiter!"

"So I'm told. Edney ruined him as well as us—but he'd done more to deserve his fate than we had. It seems that he was one of those fools who like to leave undone the things they ought to do—a pretty common type. He wrote to me some time ago telling me just how he was built, and imploring my forgiveness. It seemed he hadn't been a knave, so I did forgive him. It doesn't appear to have done much good up to now."

Turning to one of the windows, the youngster stood in silence. Possibly he was endeavouring to dissipate some of his superfluous heat. Presently Mr Smithers asked still another question.

"Foster, have you heard of the Rodway Power?"

"You mean the new invention for generating motive force which is to turn the whole world topsy-turvy? Rather. I've a bit of a mechanical twist myself. Had things been different, I might have qualified as a full-blown C. E."

"I am one of the proprietors. We are getting together a large staff. Would you like a position on it?"

"Would I? Wouldn't I!"

"Then you shall have one. More—you shall have an opportunity to earn enough money to buy Dene Park back again."

"Buy Dene Park back again?—But I thought you were going to make an offer for it yourself?"

"I intend to buy it. That fact, however, will not alter the case. In the Rodway Power there are fortunes for all sorts of people. Show yourself the vertebrate animal I take you for, and there's one in it for you. Come to me with the money in your hand and say, 'I want my home,' and you shall have it."

"But it—it sounds like a dream! What am I to you? What interest can you take in me? Are you an angel descended out of heaven, or are you—are you jesting?"

"Neither. I'm a practical man, meaning every word I say. Only—I've a weakness. I've myself such a fondness for the house in which my father was born that when I meet a man whose heart sings to the same tune, a fellow-feeling makes me wondrous kind. I tell you that you shall be afforded an opportunity to re-gain your father's home.—I am about to be married, Mr Foster. I think my wife would like to meet your sister—if she will let us have that pleasure."

"Let you have the pleasure! Why—why, Meg's the most ex-citable girl in the world; and when I tell her what you've said, she'll be wanting to rush across the world to thank you."

"We won't trouble her to rush so far; we'll meet her at least half-way. Now, is there anything more I ought to see?"

Young Foster had no chance of tendering his own personal thanks. There was something in Mr Smithers' quiet, matter-of-fact air which forbade his doing so—which was perhaps as well. The lad seemed in a mood in which he might have found it difficult to put his feelings into words—that is, with any sort of dignity. His pale cheeks were flushed; every now and then his lips would twitch; there was a suspicious moisture about his eyes. He appeared to be altogether in a state of tremblement, which suggested that it needed but a very little more to make him show that in taking on manhood he had not put his boyishness behind him.

Their talk for a while was on the most ordinary topics. They were clear of the lodge gates, and were bowling along the road to Birchester before Mr Smithers put another question.

"By the way, you're an old inhabitant, and probably know something about everyone—do you know anything about a man named Chaffinch?"

"Of The Firs?—Well, I believe he's got lots of money."

"Where did he get it?"

"Did you ever hear of Chaffinch's Counters?"

"Can't say I have."

"I don't know much about them, but I've heard that he had some bars in different parts of London—luncheon bars, where they sold food as well as drink, which he called Chaffinch's Counters. He made a pile out of them, they say—then he turned them into a company. I understand he still has an interest in London public-house property—goes regularly to town. He's built himself a nice enough house—after a fashion. I believe he has some uncommonly queer visitors."

"How do you mean?"

"It's common talk that some very odd characters are to be seen about The Firs—male and female; and that some funny things take place there. But then I suppose chaps connected with public-houses have their own ideas. He's not a bad sort—in his way. Subscribes to everything; presides at smokers; offers special prizes at the flower show—and all that kind of thing. Is there anything particular you want to know about him?"

"No, nothing particular. I only asked."

CHAPTER 17
THE WAITER

Mr Felkin was in when they returned to Birchester—full of apologies for his previous absence.

"I hope that you were pleased with Dene Park, Mr Smithers. It is one of our finest local seats."

"So pleased that I have decided to buy it."

Mr Felkin beamed.

"At the—at the price quoted?" Mr Smithers nodded. Mr Felkin beamed still more. "This will be regarded by the neighbourhood as very good news, Mr Smithers. Dene Park has been too long unoccupied. Birchester will be delighted to hear that it is to be tenanted again."

The new tenant's smile seemed to hint that Mr Felkin's words might be a little premature.

"I was shown over the place by the son of the late owner."

"Young Foster! His is a sad story. You may possibly have heard something of it." Mr Smithers signified that he had. "A fine young fellow, the son—one of nature's gentlemen. And, of course, also a gentleman by birth and education. I was indebted to his father for many kindnesses. Indeed, it was owing to his encouragement that I first set up in business on my own account. I have endeavoured to show my gratitude in my attitude towards his son—though you will understand that I am perfectly aware that his qualifications are far beyond anything I can do."

"I have offered him a position in a commercial undertaking in which I am interested, which he has accepted."

"More good news, Mr Smithers; though I shall be sorry to part with Mr Sidney. I presume that you were acquainted with his family?"

"I cannot say that I was." He glanced at his watch. "My train leaves in a few minutes. Before I go"— he repeated the question he had put to Sydney Foster—"there's a man named Chaffinch who lives in these parts. Do you know anything about him?"

"Mr Augustus Chaffinch, of The Firs. Well, I do, and I don't. In a sense, all Birchester knows about him; as, indeed, does a considerable part of London. You are probably aware that he was the proprietor of Chaffinch's Counters."

"Is he married?"

Mr Felkin scratched his cheek.

"That I cannot tell you. I make bold to say that he ought to be, if he isn't."

"How long has he been here?"

"Between four and five years."

"Then he came after the Glasspoole fiasco?"

"Certainly. Sometime after. Fred Glasspoole had vanished from the neighbourhood entirely before he came; and George Edney had been for a considerable period in jail. May I ask why you inquire?"

"I journeyed down with him from town—he introduced himself to me in the train—I wondered what sort of person he was."

"Distinctly a character, Mr Smithers—an eccentric character. One with whom you are not likely to have much in common. They tell some very strange stories indeed about him—but a man in my position pays as little attention to scandal as he can possibly help."

"Just so, Mr Felkin.—With reference, then, to Dene Park, you shall hear from my solicitors in the course of tomorrow."

As he travelled back to London he went over the events of

the day in his mind.

"It's a pretty coil on which I'm entering. One man against how many?—What's the betting that the one man doesn't win?"

When the train entered Victoria he cast a rapid glance along the line of passengers as they alighted from the different carriage doors.

"I suppose I'm being followed, but by which of them among so many? What does it matter? Only when we come to grips will the band begin to play. By that time I may have a little orchestra of my own."

He drove straight to the Gaiety Restaurant. When the food he had ordered had been placed before him, he observed to the man who was attending to his wants :

"You have a waiter here named Glasspoole?"

The man was placing a cruet-stand within convenient reach of Mr Smithers. For some reason the words seemed to so take him by surprise that the cruet slipped from his hand. It was only by good fortune that the contents of the bottles were not distributed over the table. He repaired the mischief with a hand which obviously shook, muttering glibly as he did so.

"No, sir; no one of the name of Glasspoole here."

Mr Smithers looked at him—the man avoiding his eyes.

"Are you sure?"

"Quite sure, sir."

Without waiting to be questioned further, the man shuffled off down the room. Mr Smithers eyed him as he went. He was a short man, with a stoop. Indeed, his most prominent characteristic might have been summed up in that one word—stoop. His ill-fitting dress suit, a size too large, shone with grease and wear.

His face was pinched and thin. His hair was of a lustrous black, which went so ill with his general appearance that one suspected the source from which its blackness came, he was so long up at the other end of the room as almost to suggest unwillingness to return to the immediate neighbourhood of his duties. A customer appeared at the table adjoining that occupied by Mr Smithers. He tapped a fork against a wineglass.

"Waiter!" he cried.

Another attendant came to him.

"I'll send your waiter to you, sir."

Presently the little man reappeared, studiously avoiding a glance in Mr Smithers' direction as he came. That gentleman bided his time. When the newcomer had been served he re-summoned his attendant. For a waiter the little man was singularly inattentive, appearing not to notice Mr Smithers' signal. But the customer persisted. Then the little man approached with a rush.

"Anything more, sir?"

"Your name is Glasspoole," said Mr Smithers.

"Mine, sir? No, sir. My name is Frederick Emmett."

"Frederick Glasspoole, you mean."

"Excuse me, sir, but I do not mean that. I ought to know my own name, sir."

"You need not be so anxious to conceal your identity from me. I bring you good news, not bad."

"It's a long time since any good news came my way."

"The more reason why you should welcome that of which I am a bearer."

"May I ask your name, sir!"

"Francis Smithers. I am purchasing the Dene Park estate, near Birchester."

During this brief colloquy the little man had been gathering together the empty plates and dishes. When Mr Smithers said that, he replaced them on the table with something of a clatter.

"Are you indeed, sir? I—I used to know that part of the world."

"I thought so. Now be a sensible man, Mr Glasspoole. I have a proposition which I wish to make to you. Tell me where I can make it."

"A proposition which you wish to make to me, sir? Of what nature?"

"Of a nature which I believe you will find entirely satisfactory. But I cannot enter into details here. Where can we talk together at our ease?"

"Well, sir, I'm here till after one in the morning."

"In that case the matter must be settled in another way." He beckoned to an official in a frock-coat, who had been observing their proceedings with curiosity. "You are the manager?" The frock-coated individual bowed.

"I have discovered in this waiter a person in whom I take an interest; to whom I have a communication to make of some importance. You must let him come away with me at once."

The frock-coated individual seemed dubious.

"Emmett is on the staff. If he leaves now, he will not only subject us to inconvenience, but lose a day's pay, and run the risk of dismissal."

"I will make all that up to him. That's for you." He slipped a sovereign into the manager's palm, whereat the manager smiled. Mr Smithers turned to the waiter. "Go and put on your hat. I will wait for you here."

The little man still seemed disposed to hesitate; he regarded the manager—as if looking for a sign.

"Excuse me, sir, but"

The manager was brusque.

"Don't you hear the gentleman tell you to go and put your hat on, and say he'll wait for you here?"

The little man fled. The manager and Mr Smithers had some desultory conversation on the subject of rules and regulations as they affected waiters, the official evincing some mild curiosity as to the nature of the customer's acquaintance with this particular member of the staff, until the little man returned, disguised in an ancient overcoat and the ruins of a bowler hat.

Soon the pair were standing together outside the door of the establishment on the Strand pavement— the little man showing unlooked-for signs of a resolute spirit.

Now, sir, before I move another step, let me understand you. You've probably lost me my situation. It's the first regular situation I've had for—I don't care to think how long. Anyhow, you've lost me a day's wage. I can't afford to do without that."

"My dear Mr Glasspoole, let me beg you to regard that as compensation."

Mr Smithers handed him a piece of paper. The little man regarded it with incredulous eyes.

"A five-pound note? For me? What for? Why should you give me a five-pound note? What's—the game?"

"I tell you again that I wish to make to you a proposition which I believe you will find of a satisfactory nature. But I can't enter into details out in the street here, any more than in that grill-room downstairs. Where do you live?"

"Live? I live—if you can call it living—in a room—or what the landlord calls a room—in a court off Bow Street."

"If you will take me there I will come to the point without delay."

"Take you there! My wife and two girls are there—working."

"If it is not an unpardonable intrusion, I should prefer to make my proposition in the presence of your wife and daughters; it is one which they are entitled to hear."

"It's not a trick?"

"Mr Glasspoole, you are as suspicious as if you feared that I might be an ogre, desirous to make a meal off you."

"I am suspicious—I'm suspicious of everything and everyone—and with reason. If you'd gone through what I have, you'd know what the feeling was."

"Perhaps I have gone through what you have."

"You? You've never been on your beam-ends—never in this world! I don't know who you are, or what you are, and I don't know about trusting you—but I've got hold of what looks like a five-pound note—and you talked about Birchester—and—and sent my heart—what's left of it—up into my mouth—so I'll take you home. Come!"

The little man started off at a pace which was a near relation to a run.

"This is my home."

They had come up three flights of broken stairs. The little man pushed a door open at the top. A voice inquired from within—

"Who's there?"

"It's I—and Mr Smithers.—Go in."

Mr Smithers went in. He found himself in a small, barely furnished room, which stood badly in need of re-papering and re-painting. Seated at a table before the open window was a woman, who had once been pretty. She was still probably not more than thirty four or five, and not so much ill-looking as prematurely worn-out. She looked half starved; exhausted—not only for want of rest, but still more for want of peace of mind. A tragedy was in her anxious eyes; in her nervous, shrinking attitude; in her apparent constant expectation of another lash from misfortune's whip. A sewing-machine was on the table, which was piled up with what looked like partly-made garments. More were on the floor at her side.

Two girls, evidently sisters, had been assisting her in her work. In one pitiful respect they resembled their mother. As Mr Smithers entered they started to their feet, as if fearful that he would strike them a blow. The elder was perhaps fourteen years old. The three stood looking at him as though he had been some unknown, and therefore terrible, creature—the sure harbinger of fresh disaster. Their evident distress so affected Mr Smithers that for the moment he was without words.

"Fred," cried the woman, "what has happened? Who is this?"

"He says he's Mr Smithers. He's lost me my situation, and he's given me this instead."

He threw on the table the piece of paper which had been given him.

"It's a five-pound note. Is—is it real?—Lost you your situation? Fred!"

"Father!"

The two girls drew together with an instinctive gesture, which in itself was eloquent.

"At least he made me come away with him—though I don't know who he is or what he wants, and didn't want to come. Mr Nixon let me off, but when I go back again he'll say my place is filled. And so it will be, I know!"

"Fred, what will you do?"

"Father!" the two girls cried again.

"Mrs Glasspoole," began Mr Smithers.

But he had only got so far when the woman broke into half-tearful, half-frightened exclamations.

"Glasspoole! That's not my name! My—my name's Emmett."

Her husband offered tremulous corroboration.

"I told him so, but he wouldn't listen to me—he didn't care for what I said."

"But is your name not Glasspoole? If it was once, what business is that of yours? If it's Emmett now, how does that harm anyone? If you'd a name which was a curse to you, which was like a great weight under which you couldn't even stagger, which barred your path whichever way you turned, which kept you from earning your daily bread, wouldn't you want to put it behind you, so that you needn't go in hourly terror of being asked if you're that fool who was worse than any knave, since the pyramid of his colossal folly brought him, and all who had to do with him, to ruin and to shame? Wouldn't you try to keep your wife and children and yourself alive, under cover of some patronymic which didn't smell quite so strong in all men's noses? "

"Besides," chimed in his wife, "all sorts of people change their names. Why shouldn't we call ourselves Emmett if we choose?"

"I do not dispute your right to do so for a single instant. You wholly misconceive the purport of my presence here. I bring what I hope and believe you will think good news. But before I come to it, it is essential that I should clearly understand that you are Mr Frederick Glasspoole, of Birchester."

"Well, I am Frederick Glasspoole, late of Birchester. What then? What have you to say to Frederick Glasspoole?"

"As I told you, I am purchasing the Dene Park estate."

"Dene Park!" interposed the woman. "But—what has become of Mr and Mrs Foster?"

"They are dead."

"Dead?—Both of them? But where is Mr Sidney—and Miss Margaret?"

"At the death of their parents the estate was found to be so heavily encumbered that it was thrown upon the market."

"Fred!—did you know this?"

"Yes, I knew it; but what was the use of telling you? What was the use of letting you know that the ruin I had brought about was even greater than you supposed? The knowledge wouldn't have made you happier."

"I'm—I'm not blaming you, Fred; only I—I didn't know it was so bad as that."

"Bad!—I've acted as a general blight. For everyone with whom I have ever been brought into contact, the best thing that could have happened would have been that I had never been born."

"You mustn't say that—you mustn't say it! You're my husband—all that I've got—and I love you—and you've been very good to me."

"Carrie!—Good to you?"

"You have—you know you have! A woman never had a better husband than you have been to me. All that happened wasn't your fault; I was to blame as well as you. I was young, and frivolous, and empty-headed, and fond of pleasure, and didn't know life was so serious as it is. And you spoilt me because you loved me, and listened to my persuasions to neglect—for the sake of my silly pleasures—what never ought to have been neglected."

"I didn't need much persuading."

"Fred, a wife's duty is towards her husband, as much as a husband's is towards his wife. Inasmuch as I induced you to leave undone what you should have done, the fault—for what has come on us and others—was mine. I will not have you say—or think—that you were alone to blame."

"Come, Carrie—dry your eyes. You and I have shed enough tears to drown all our sorrows. Don't let us show Mr Smithers that our lachrymal ducts are as a perpetual spring. Well, sir; you say you have bought Dene Park. What has that to do with us?"

"Shortly, this:—I want you to be my steward."

"What!"

"I want you to be my steward. The house wants repairing; it has to be furnished; the whole property requires immediate attention from one who knows it. I am about to be married. I want the necessary works to be put immediately in hand, and pressed forward as expeditiously as possible, so that, when my wife and I return from our honeymoon, the place may be ready for our occupation."

"You want me to be your steward?"

"You know the property?"

"I ought to."

"Then you're just the man I want."

"Are you—are you jesting? Or—are you mad? Do you know my record?—what sort of an account I gave of my stewardship once upon a time?"

"It's because I know your story better than you suppose that I offer you this position. Men make mistakes which are of the nature of debts. When they have paid them in full they may claim quittance. The harder they have found the payment, the less likely they are to incur them again. You have paid for the mistake you made—dearly."

"God knows it."

"And are therefore entitled to a receipt, and to fresh credit. That credit I am prepared to offer you, in the full persuasion that trust will not be abused a second time. I understand that there is a tolerable house on the estate, which shall be at once prepared for your occupation. The formalities of purchase are not yet concluded, but they will be in the course of the next few days. By then I shall expect you to be ready to go down at once to take possession in my name. You will be furnished with instructions, which I shall look to you to sec are carried out in their entirety. I am sure that I shall not look in vain."

Mrs Glasspoole, on a broken-backed chair, was crying quietly. Her husband—his old overcoat unbuttoned, revealing the incongruous clothes beneath—was looking about him with bewildered eyes.

"To hear you talking, it's—it's as though one had risen from the dead."

"Look on me as one risen from the dead. It's not a bad idea of yours. Regard me as someone come out of the grave of your dead past to point out the way to better things."

"You—you're not jesting, sir ?

"I'm as fond of a jest as most men, but I'm in earnest now. To prove it, I will come to business.—As regards salary, I am prepared to pay you five hundred pounds a year and the house."

"Five hundred pounds a year—and the house?"

"In the meantime, you will clear out of this at once;—and by at once I mean inside twenty minutes."

"Inside twenty minutes?"

"Or less, if you can manage it. I will give you a hundred pounds—here they are, five tens and ten fives—which you will regard as a loan, to be paid back as I will afterwards explain. You will replenish your wardrobe and find yourself better quarters at any rate, before the night comes."

"But, sir—you—you must let me speak. How can I—show my face—in Birchester; a man with my story?"

"I trust you are not going to talk nonsense, Mr Glasspoole. There is one crime I find it difficult to forgive—the crime of cowardice. If you are the man I take you to be, you will go back to Birchester ready to show that the weakling they knew was a creature born of delusion; and resolute to prove to them what kind of man you really are. That will be a thing worth doing, Mr Glasspoole."

"But you forget that the whole countryside is covered with men and women who suffered because of me."

"Is that so?—Have you all their names?"

"Have I all their names!—Shall I ever be without them ?"

"Later, you and I will look into the matter together, and we will see what can be done."

"See what can be done!—What do you mean?"

"Money lost may be refunded;—if it's a question of money only."

"Do you mean that you'll refund it?"

"It's within the range of possibility. I imagine it's not a question of a large amount."

"But why should you pay anything at all? or even dream of such a thing? What has my shame to do with you? You speak of such things as if they were trifles; as if it were nothing that you, a stranger, should dig me out of the dirt into which I've sunk, cleanse me, and rehabilitate me in the eyes of men, at a serious expenditure not only of time but of money. What has Frederick Glasspoole to do with you? Or are you Don Quixote materialised out of realms of fancy?"

"Nonsense. No high faluting, Mr Glasspoole, if you please. I'm a man who, under curious circumstances, has come into what promises to be a monstrous fortune; monstrous altogether beyond the requirements of one man. There's no reason whatever why a little good shouldn't be done with some of it. Come, Mrs Glasspoole, don't cry. Put that sort of thing behind you forever and a day. The good time's come.—There's money on the table;—you have all sorts of things to buy;—the shops will soon be closed.—You girls, I have not the pleasure of knowing your names, but there's a fiver each for you;—girls want all sorts of things for their very own.—Mr Glasspoole, that is where I live. You understand that in the morning I shall expect you to report yourself at an address better suited to the man who occupies the responsible position of my steward."

There was silence when he had gone. Then they cried—each alone, and all together. Then they laughed and talked, words and thoughts tumbling over each other in their strange excitement. At their mother's suggestion, they thanked God for the great mercy which, it seemed, He was about to show to them. Then they went out, a happy *quartette*, to buy the things of which they stood so much in need. And before the night had closed, that court off Bow Street knew them no more.

Mr Smithers returned to Dulverton Road to find a certain young lady awaiting him, to whom, after his own fashion, he rendered a report of his adventures of the day.

"There's no longer any excuse for further attempts to postpone the evil hour on the ground that I haven't a house to take you to. I've purchased one this very day."

"You've bought Dene Park?"

"I have, with the appurtenances and stabling."

"What sort of a place is it?"

"Enormous—a palace on a small scale—about a hundred rooms and ten thousand acres."

"Are you laughing at me?"

"Not a bit—serious as a judge. I should say it's as fine a place as there is in Sussex, in every respect."

"What do you suppose I'm going to do in a place like that?"

"Oh, stroll round, and pick the flowers, and shoot the game, and dig the fields, and scrub and cook for the establishment, and that kind of thing."

She was moving about the room in the fidgety way she had when excited, which amused him mightily. In his case, excitement seemed to make him calmer, as though it needed a sudden demand on all his faculties to bring him to a state of complete quiescence.

I'm not at all fitted for such a place—not in the very least scrap. The height of my ambition has always been a twelve-roomed detached villa residence,—rent £90 a year. There's the very red-bricked edifice on the Barnes Road, with the loveliest bow windows and the front door painted green. I shouldn't be surprised if they want a hundred for it, but I shouldn't pay them more than ninety—on principle. I know I shall only disgrace you in your Sussex splendiferousness. Hadn't you better go carefully over the matter while there still is time, and request me to consider your offer, as made, withdrawn?"

"Oh no, I don't think so. That sort of thing would be a horrid worry. Better bear the ills I have. Besides, I have a sort of feeling that when a man gets in a scrape, it's only the part of decency that he should see it through."

"So that's your point of view. Very well. Then I have to request you to consider it off."

"That's all right. Then what we have to consider now is how to get it on again.—Netta!"

"Well ?"

"I'm beginning to have a glimmering of a notion that in you there's the germ of something rather good-looking."

"I know I'm beautiful, under all conditions. That's no news.—What a lot of letters you do have. What's that you've got there?"

He was holding a square white card, in the centre of which was a blot of scarlet sealing-wax. Above it was written, in a delicate running hand;

A reminder of our conversation;—*the first.*-A. C.

"How did this get there? Apparently it hasn't come through the post."

"Someone slipped it into the letter-box, I suppose. It was there with the rest of the letters.—What is it?" He passed it to her. "The seal looks like a pair of triangles. Who's 'A. C'? And what's the mysterious conversation he wishes to remind you of?"

"My dear person, I'm beginning to discover that all sorts of people wish to remind me of mysterious conversations. It looks as if I were going to be a mark for everyone possessed of a postage stamp and an envelope.—By the way, I want to come to an understanding with you. When is this marriage of ours to be?"

"Oh—in about a year."

"It will take place this day month."

"This day month? It can't!"

"It can, and will. So kindly make a note of the fact that this day month you are to be married—to me. After we are married we will go to Italy till Christmas."

"To Italy, till Christmas?"

"By that time the Park should be ready for our reception. So we will spend our first Christmas at home."

"Frank"—she was sitting on his knee, which was a convenient position for putting her arm round his neck—"Frank, you're like a fairy tale."

"The wicked fairy, I suppose. Don't spare my feelings. Call me an ogre right away. You may as well do it now as afterwards. I'll get reconciled."

"When I was quite a little child I used to have a fairy tale of my very own. I was the heroine. In it I was to have a husband—who was just like you; and whom I loved—just as I love you. And who gave me everything that my heart could desire."

"Do you think I'm going to give you everything that your heart can desire?"

"Everything, and—and more.—Frank, do you think that a girl can be too happy? I mean that I've heard people say that when a person's too happy, it's a sign that the happiness won't last.—Do you believe that's true?"

He tore the card bearing the scarlet seal into little pieces, dropping them into the waste-paper basket. And he laughed.

Chapter 19
Coming Events

The coming wedding began to cast its shadows before. To Netta those were astounding days. She moved in a continuous atmosphere of miracles or dreams. She did not know which it was, but it was all very wonderful. Had she been the favourite godchild of half-a-dozen fairy godmothers, she could hardly have borne promise of being a better dowered bride. Her future lord seemed to have made up his mind that she should go without no good thing. Jewels he showered upon her, at whose value she could only guess, but before whose beauty she stood amazed. She had not realised that such things really were, outside the fairy tales. He opened a banking account in her name—but not at the National Bank—against the magnitude of which she vainly cried. Her trousseau was in itself a dream. Amid that wealth of lovely raiment her soul was uplifted, half ashamed of herself though she was. She rejoiced over it as a mother over her child. But then pretty clothes never before had come her way; and the heart of nearly every woman craves for them.

"Do you think," she asked," that I'm a princess, that I need to be re-dressed from top to toe every time I'm seen in public? And do you propose to travel about with me and a great wilderness of trunks?"

"It's a mistake to suppose that it's much more bother to travel with twenty trunks than with one, especially abroad. You place them in charge of the railway company, and there's an end of them until you find them awaiting you in the bedroom of your hotel. Besides, you'll have a maid; she'll do all the looking after them that's needed."

"A maid!"

"Certainly, my wife must have a personal attendant. Who's to do your hair?"

"My hair!"

"And see that your hat is put on properly?"

"My hat put on properly! Do you think I would trust anyone to put my hat on except myself?"

"And do everything that's required? You'll find your maid waiting for you at the station when we start upon our honeymoon. Leave the task of finding her to me. I'll undertake to provide you with as satisfactory an article as the market can supply."

She made a small grimace and sighed.

"I know I'm marrying into royalty, and I'm sure I didn't ought."

The purchase of the Dene Park estate was completed with a decree of expedition to which not improbably the legal gentlemen on both sides were unaccustomed in matters of such importance. The works necessary to render the house inhabitable were at once commenced. Great firms were charged to see that it was duly furnished and ready for the reception of its master and mistress by the approaching Christmas season. Mr Glasspoole was installed in the steward's house, and endowed with the necessary authority to see that everything required was properly and promptly done.

The attitude of the Glasspoole family in their new position was both curious and pathetic. To begin with, they appeared to find it difficult to realise that their position had really and truly changed, which perhaps was not surprising. They suffered from self-consciousness to a degree which Mr Smithers seemed to find positively painful. He was at Dene Park when they arrived to take up their residence in their new quarters. When he looked in at the steward's house to bid them welcome he found the whole family dissolved in tears. His attitude on that occasion could hardly have been described as sympathetic.

"Excuse me, Mr Glasspoole, but I didn't request you to come down here to indulge in that kind of thing."

"I—I know it's weak of me, sir. But you don't know what it means to us to return to Birchester, and what our feelings are."

"Yes, I do; and if I didn't, I could see. I can see too much; too much feeling, Mr Glasspoole. Less water if you please. I want you to be regarded as an autocrat upon this properly; and how do you suppose you're going to be that if you go about with tears trickling down the side of your nose?"

"I'll—I'll see it doesn't occur again."

"Do. The Dene Park steward is a person of importance and dignity, which things don't accord with blubbering."

Sidney Foster, who had already left Birchester to take up a position on the staff of the Rodway Power, was duly informed of what had taken place.

"I'm delighted to hear of the poor chap's good luck; I always felt that he was more sinned against than sinning. Edney was the scoundrel; it was out of him that no good thing could come. But then, if you don't mind my saying so, Mr Smithers, I'm so off my head at my own good-luck that I can't help rejoicing at anybody else's."

Margaret Foster had been duly introduced to Netta Ludlow, with whom she had struck up an instant friendship, based on a difference of opinion on almost every conceivable subject. But then Miss Foster's views were her own.

"Of course, marriage ruins a woman's career," she observed, on one occasion.

Netta promptly cut her short.

"Marriage ruins a woman's career! What nonsense are you talking? Why, marriage is a woman's career. Wait till it's on the point of ruining yours, then you'll change your tone."

"Perhaps. I'll wait. When that time comes I hope it will be ruined by the same sort of person who is ruining yours. You have such an uncertain temper, and you do so bite one's nose off, directly one opens one's mouth."

"I never!"

"That I hardly dare to speak to you. So I can only hope that you'll not be offended if I say that Mr Smithers—I'm not fond of the name."

"Who cares what you're fond of?"

"Is just my ideal of what a man should be; big, and strong, and handsome; a gentleman to his fingertips; who has never done a thing in all his life of which he has cause to be ashamed, but who has done hundreds of which he has every right to be proud—and isn't."

"Thank you," observed Miss Ludlow, with exemplary meekness. "Now, if you don't mind, I'll kiss you."

And she did.

Already the Rodway Power was proving to be the gold mine its owners had expected. The experimental motors which had been built had realised to the full their inventor's anticipations. Their fame had travelled round the world. Everywhere men had awoke to the truth that that revolution in mechanical force for whose advent engineers had so long been looking, had at last become an accomplished fact. Electricity, that mystery of mysteries, had in a certain sense been bridled; constrained to do man's will in a degree which, but the other day, had been but an enthusiast's dream. It had been proved, beyond the suggestion of doubt, that not only was it possible, but easy, lo call it into inexhaustible being. The problem of the wastage of coal was solved. Steam, as a motive power, was doomed.

The Rodway Power, or some analogous substitute, had the commercial and locomotive future of the world at its feet. Orders from all parts of the globe were pouring in. It was obvious that no firm, however huge, could cope with them single-handed. Arrangements were being pressed forward, in virtue of which the process of manufacture could be carried on in various countries on terms which would produce for Messrs Smithers & Rodway an income which in its immensity would be altogether beyond anything of which adventurous financial magnates hitherto had dreamed. It seemed that the time might not be far distant when they would be able to draw cheques for millions with the same equanimity with which other rich men wrote thousands.

In the meanwhile they commenced to be fellow-lodgers in that little house at Putney.

Thither, one evening, repaired the brother of the expectant bride—Mr Theodore Ludlow. It chanced, when he arrived, that his sister was out, having gone to spend an hour with Miss Margaret Foster, at what that young lady called her 'digs.' Which euphonious word in this case represented three tiny rooms in some 'Ladies' Mansions' at the foot of Sloane Square.

Theodore inquired for her when he appeared. On learning where she was he frowned.

"Where's Mr Smithers?" He was told that Mr Smithers was in his sitting-room. "Then I'll see him."

His mother, who, even under altered circumstances, found it difficult not to regard her son with something like timidity, looked at him with anxious eyes. She liked neither his looks, his manner, nor his tone. She herself conveyed his request to the gentleman in question. Soon Mr Theodore was ushering himself into the lodger's presence.

Directly he saw him Mr Smithers perceived, by certain signs, that there was trouble coming.

Chapter 20
The Attack Which Failed

Mr Smithers opened the interview by ignoring the singularity of his visitor's bearing.

"I believe, Mr Ludlow, that it is no use my offering you anything. You expressed your views on tobacco and what you called 'alcohol' on a previous occasion."

"I did. And in any case, were I the most bibulous of men, I should decline to drink with you, as you are well aware!"

"Why should I be aware of it?"

"Men in my position do not hobnob with a thief."

"I fancy, Mr Ludlow, that men in your position do and say rather funny things."

"They have to, when they are brought into contact with such a character as you. When I look at you, and observe the air of brazen assurance which clothes you as with a garment, I am lost in wonder as to the hidden purpose which actuates the Almighty in allowing such reptiles as you to cumber the ground."

"Gently, Mr Ludlow, gently! Don't force the note too soon."

"Do you suppose that, however it may be with the rest of the world, you have deceived me for a single instant?—that I don't know who you are, and all about you?"

"I am not supposing anything." Do you suppose that I am not conscious that your name is no more Francis Smithers than mine is?"

"Is that so, really?"

"Do you suppose that I have not throughout been cognisant of the fact that you have been masquerading under another man's name, in order to obtain possession of property to which you have not the slightest claim?"

"You appear to be cognisant of a good many things, Mr Ludlow."

"You brazen it out, as I expected. It is your hide-bound impudence which makes you in an especial degree a danger to society. Yours is the countenance of the indurated criminal type, which is impervious to the blush of shame."

"Your choice of epithets is good."

"Not content with ordinary rascality, you have proceeded to the extraordinary, by endeavouring to entangle the affections of an innocent girl."

"You allude to Netta?"

"Don't you speak of her by her Christian name in my presence. I am her brother."

"A fact on which she has reason to congratulate herself, since you are so exemplary a son and generous a brother."

"It is easy for the rogue who has plunged his hand into another man's till to squander money on improvident women. I can but do my duty according to my lights, which are not of a kind which you are likely to appreciate."

"That is so."

"You may sneer, and sneer, and sneer; but you know, as I know, that I hold you in the hollow of my hand"—to illustrate his meaning, Mr Ludlow held out the hand in question—"and that I've but to move my fingers to crush you. In other words, I have but to speak to the constable in the street, and you'll be on the road to penal servitude."

"Shall I ring and give them instructions to communicate with the gentleman in question?"

"You may laugh as well as sneer, but you'll not find a prolonged sojourn in one of His Majesty's jails amusing. I came here with the express intention of speaking plainly, of calling a spade a spade, and of making myself understood. I have carried out that intention. Now you understand me."

"I am not sure that I do; but that is by the way. If those are all the remarks you have to make, I am afraid I have no right to detain you."

"They are not; I wish they were."

"I also."

"My instincts, natural and acquired, are on the side of society. My standard of honour is high. Rigid honesty is to me as the breath of my nostrils. For the double-dealer I have no sufficient words of scorn. My strenuous impulse would be to deliver you, on the instant, bound and helpless, to the vengeance of the law. But first—"

"First 'but'!"

"By the exercise of insidious arts you have insinuated yourself into my family circle."

"Hear, hear!—Very well put."

"You have inveigled both my mother and sister into an invidious position."

"That's a lie."

"I am therefore placed in the distressing situation of having to choose between doing violence to their feelings and my simple duty. Under these circumstances I have arrived at a decision which I fear does more credit to my heart than to my head. I have resolved to conceal—at least temporarily—my knowledge of certain actions of which I know you to have been guilty;—to put it into another form, to show mercy."

"Then you have arrived at a decision which does you credit."

"I am not so sure of that. I can only say that I have arrived at it after careful and profound consideration of the matter from every point of view. However, for the moment we will let that pass. To my resolution to show mercy, conditions are attached. In the first place, due and proper penitence must be shown— practical penitence. The account standing in the name of Francis Smithers must be restored to its original proportions—with interest up to date. So that when Mr Smithers does appear it may be found intact."

"And in the second place?"

"In the second place, the sum of ten thousand pounds must be placed in my hands as a guarantee of future good conduct."

Mr Smithers looked at Mr Ludlow as if suspecting a jest, but the cashier's expression continued to be of wooden severity.

"You were good enough to say that you wished to make yourself clearly understood. May I ask you to explain the exact meaning of that second condition?"

"You have used another man's money in speculations which—so far—have turned out successfully. It is therefore important that I should avail myself of your present position to secure the bank—of which I am a servant—against further fraud upon your part."

"Then in that case a guarantee policy for that amount, taken out in some sound company, would serve your purpose equally well?"

"It would not"

"The money must be placed in your hands in cash?"

"It must."

"And you would render an account weekly, or day by day?"

"I should not undertake to render any account."

"Then what security should I have against fraud on your part?"

"I have told you my conditions. I do not intend to haggle, to alter them in one jot or tittle. Still less do I propose to honour with my notice any impertinence which may I proceed from you."

Mr Smithers regarded him in silence. Then, going to a box which was on the sideboard, he chose a cigar, prepared it with fastidious care, lit it, and seemed disposed in enjoy it with complete disregard to Mr Ludlow's presence. The cashier eyed his proceedings grimly.

"I await your answer"

Mr Smithers took his cigar from between his lips, as if surprised.

"I beg your pardon?"

"I say that I await your answer."

"My answer I—To what?"

"Do you intend to accept my conditions, or to go to penal servitude?"

"Unfortunately I don't understand your conditions."

153

"I will repeat them. You are to restore the account at the bank to its original proportions, with interest added; and you are to deposit in my hands the sum often thousand pounds in cash as a guarantee of your future good conduct."

"It is that last condition which I don't understand. Shall I tell you why?"

"Certainly."

"Because I happen to know that you yourself are in a rather tight place; and I therefore fail to see how the depositing of such a sum of money in your hands would act as a guarantee of your future good conduct."

"What do you mean?—What are you daring to insinuate?"

"Nothing. I am no dealer in insinuations. I am merely wishful to remind you that you have been using other people's money in speculations which, so far, have turned out unsuccessfully. I do so, although I am conscious that the fact has no more escaped your recollection than it has mine. On the contrary, I am afraid it has cost you many wakeful nights, Mr Ludlow."

The cashier's complexion assumed a curious hue. His expression became, if possible, harder and more rigid than before.

"What nonsense are you talking? Do you suppose that any insolent innuendoes which come from you will make the slightest impression upon me?"

Mr Smithers laughed—the quiet laugh which was apt to come from him at unexpected moments; suggesting that, as regards the humorous, he had a point of view which was peculiarly his own.

"Very good. Then we'll let it rest."

"We will not let it rest; don't make any mistake about it. It's either going to be my conditions or penal servitude."

Mr Smithers said nothing. He only enjoyed his cigar.

"Which is it going to be?"

"Whichever you like."

"Then it shall be penal servitude."

"For you?—Then when do you think they're likely to discover the feats of legerdemain you've been performing with your books and cash?"

"You're—I believe you're the direct spawn of the devil!"

"Do you? I'm so sorry! That sort of belief can't be nice to hold."

"You understand that if you decline to take advantage of the offer of mercy which I am extending to you, before I leave this house you will be in the custody of a policeman."

"Oh no, I shan't."

"Be under no delusion—I mean what I say."

"Not you."

"You will find out when it is too late."

"Mr Ludlow, you really are more foolish than I supposed; while the extent of my folly you appear to have overestimated."

"What do you mean by that?"

"Is it possible that you fail to perceive that by your conduct since the occasion of our first meeting, crowned by the altitude you have taken up this evening, you have delivered yourself—to use your own figure of speech—into the hollow of my hand?"

"What good do you suppose you will do yourself by talking such nonsense?"

"You say you knew from the first that I was defrauding the bank."

"I did. You never deceived me for a moment."

"Then it was your duty to at once communicate the fact to your employers. By concealing your knowledge, you were conniving at a fraud on them."

"I had my reasons for keeping silence."

"Not a doubt of it. You will find that your employers will appreciate those reasons. I do. You allowed the fraud to be continued; you allowed me to finance your mother; to become engaged to your sister."

"I had no voice in either of those matters."

"You take care not to have—you were duly advised of what was occurring. It is only when you yourself are in pecuniary straits and in imminent danger of ruinous exposure that you endeavour, by means of threats, to levy black mail."

"Blackmail!—You insolent—"

"Steady! Let me advise you, Mr Ludlow, not to apply any more injurious threats to me, or—you may regret it. The alternative you offer—penal servitude or £10,000—is blackmail in its worst form."

"I only require that that sum shall be deposited."

"Deposited! With a man who is worse than penniless! Your choice of words is more than odd. However, we will not pursue that matter any further. You are, of course, at liberty to take any steps you like. On one point I should like to clear your mind of misconception—whatever you may think, I am the only person who is entitled to draw on that account of Francis Smithers."

"That I know to be false. I know that you are not the Francis Smithers by whom it was opened."

"The intention was to conceal the identity of the person by whom it was opened, and that identity you have not penetrated. I know what you think, and what inquiries you have made. But you are quite at sea. I repeat that I am the only person who is entitled to draw upon the account of Francis Smithers."

"I can but say—"

"Say nothing. You had better make any statement you have to make elsewhere. You see I know the facts; you only guess at them, and your guess is all abroad. On a single point I should like to have an understanding before requesting you to be kind enough to leave me. I am about to marry your sister. Do not imagine that I am marrying you. As you at present appear to me, you are a type of man for whom I have no use. You seem to be a bully; a hypocrite; something closely approximating to a knave; and, I also fear, a coward. You have been a bad brother, and a worse son. You have devoted your whole life to self-seeking—with results which, as you are yourself aware, are only too likely to be disastrous. With a person of such a character, understand once, and once for all, that I decline to have intercourse of any kind. Now I must ask you to relieve me of your society, Mr Ludlow."

"One—one more word."

"What is it?"

Mr Ludlow seemed to find some difficulty in answering. His fluency seemed to have deserted him. His attitude had undergone a marked change during the last few minutes. From dogmatic assertiveness, he had passed to doubt and hesitation. Anxiety had taken the place of sternness. Something had come into his face—a shifty, nervous, deprecating something—which lent to it a new expression. When he spoke it was almost as if he stammered. All at once his voice had become husky. "We—we look at life from different standpoints."

"I hope so."

"You—you judge me with undue severity."

"I doubt it."

"My—my standard of duty."

"No hypocrisy, if you please."

In the front of the other's interposition Mr Ludlow seemed to collapse more and more—as if some sustaining bone had been taken clean out of him. His tone descended nearly to a whine.

"I—I'm afraid there's a certain amount of truth in what you say. I—I have been the victim of some unfortunate speculations. At the time I entered into them I had every reason to believe that they were sound, and that the result would be blessed by Providence"

"Would be what?"

"Would be—would be all that could be desired."

"By you?"

"By me. Instead of which, owing to circumstances over which I had no control, I found myself confronted by a loss for which I—I was unprepared; and—and I'm sorry to say—"

"I know. You needn't go on. What was the amount?"

"It's—it's not a large amount. About—about £3000."

"You don't call that a large amount. May I inquire what your salary is?"

"Of course, in proportion to my salary, it is a large amount. I—I was comparing it in—in my mind's eye with the immense fortune with the accumulation of which you are credited."

"What right have you to make such a comparison?"

"None—absolutely none. I—I beg your pardon for making it. It—it was a most unfortunate phrase. Of course the amount is a large one; a very large—a painfully large one."

"You're a pretty sort of creature to attempt to measure swords with me. On my word, Mr Ludlow, you are a much more insignificant creature than I imagined." He paused, as if to listen. Someone was entering the front door. "I fancy that's Netta. If so, I will request her to do me the favour of witnessing the remainder of our little interview."

"I—I would much rather she did not come in here, at least for a minute or two, if—if you don't mind."

"I do mind; I had much rather she did come." He opened the door. "It is Netta.—Netta, would you mind obliging me with your company for a few moments?"

Netta's voice was heard replying.

"As a rule I do object, very strongly, to come anywhere where you are; but by way of an exception, for once in a while."

The young lady came into the room, all radiant with smiles—and impertinence. At the sight of her brother the smiles—and impertinence—vanished. Her face fell.

"Theodore!" she said. Adding, when she perceived the singularity of his appearance, "What—what is wrong?"

CHAPTER 21
THE BITER BITTEN

Mr Ludlow did not look happy. Especially to one who was accustomed to see in him a dominant, autocratic, self-righteous, insensitive personality, his present attitude came as a shock. To Netta this was a new Theodore. This hangdog, nerveless, frightened, anxious creature was not the family tyrant with whom she was only too familiar. That Theodore had looked a whole world in the face, bidding it contradict his smallest utterance if it dare; this, cringed as if in doubt whether to plead for pity or to shun it.

The singularity of his demeanour was rendered more conspicuous by his companion's perfect ease. Mr Smithers, taking Netta's two hands in his, regarded her wondering face with smiling eyes.

"Netta, I have to tell you something which will pain you; but for your own sake, for your mother's, and for mine, I think that you had better be told.—Your brother has more than once dropped you hints that he is acquainted with something to the detriment of my character?"

"You know that I never believed him."

"Of course I know it.—He came tonight to inform me that he intended to publish this knowledge—I don't quite know to whom, but we will say the world."

"He never dared!"

"He did dare. He was kind enough, however, to inform me that he would still continue to conceal the mysterious and wondrous things he knows if I would place in his hands £10,000."

"He must be mad."

"On the contrary, I fancy that he is singularly sane. But it appears that he is not actuated so much by a wish to hurt me as by a desire to save himself. He has been speculating beyond his means, and to make good his losses has resorted to irregularities which may imperil his position at the bank in more ways than one."

"Theodore!"

"You mentioned, Mr Ludlow, that the sum of which you stand in need is about £3000. Is that the exact amount?"

"The exact amount is £4250."

"Four thousand two hundred and fifty?—You use the word 'about' in a generous sense. Is that all? Will that cover everything?"

"Everything."

"Then if I give you a cheque for £5000, that will be sufficient?"

The cashier's eyes glistened. His figure grew suddenly straighten

"More than sufficient!—And—and you will have earned my

undying gratitude."

"I will place on paper the remarks you have heard me address to your sister: how you have endeavoured to blackmail me; how you have been guilty of serious defalcations. It will take the form of a confession, to which you will affix your signature. When you have signed it I will give you a cheque for £5000, because I am unwilling that the commencement of your sister's married life should be darkened by the shadow of her brother's shame. But you will understand, Mr Ludlow, that this is the only assistance you will ever have from me. Are you prepared to sign a document of the nature I have described?"

During Mr Smithers' observations his former dejected air had returned to Mr Ludlow with almost more than its original force. Apparently the proposition did not commend itself to him at all.

"I—I would rather not."

"I daresay!"

"What—what use would you make of such a paper?"

"No use at all, so long as you continue of good behaviour, and refrain from further slander. Should I have cause to complain of you, I should make what use of it I pleased."

"I—I don't think you ought to ask me to place myself in your power to the extent which you suggest. It would convey the impression that my—my attitude has been more—more regrettable than it has."

"You are, of course, entitled to hold such an opinion. Only if you do, I must ask you to leave my room."

"I'll—I'll sign."

Mr Smithers, sitting down to his desk, wrote something on a sheet of letter-paper. Netta, turning her back on her brother—with the intention possibly of seeing as little of his humiliation as she could help—leaned against the mantelshelf, on which there was a mirror. Until Mr Smithers sat down to write, Mr Ludlow's glance had been fixed upon the ground. During the silence which followed he looked up—to observe the writer. As he did so, there came on to his face a look of malevolence and vindictive hatred which scarcely suggested the undying gratitude of which he had spoken. Netta saw that look before her in the mirror. She started. Twirling round, she met her brother's eyes. He perceived that she had seen and understood.

As if alarmed at the use she might make of the knowledge, back went his glance upon the ground. When Mr Smithers had ceased to write, he had resumed his bearing of detected and dejected wretch, while from the other side of the room his sister regarded him with flaming eyes.

"Be so good as to read that through, Mr Ludlow; and if it correctly describes your conduct, sign it."

Mr Ludlow read it through, with a face which was a study in certain unusual forms of expression. Then, with compressed lips, he signed it.

"I will not ask your sister to act as a formal witness, but you will not fail to remember that she has seen what you have done." Taking up the paper, Mr Smithers carefully examined it. "Is this your usual signature? It is rather hieroglyphic for a bank cashier."

"Yes."

"You see, Netta?"

"It is not his usual signature—it is not in the least like it."

"So I suspected. You hear, Mr Ludlow. I am afraid I must ask you to sign it again. Leave this hieroglyph untouched, and under it place your usual signature, if you please." As he did as he was bidden, the set of Mr Ludlow's mouth and lips suggested the grin of a wild-cat. "That, at least, seems more in order. Is it, Netta?" The girl nodded. "Here is a cheque for £5000, payable to your order on presentation. And now, goodnight."

Mr Ludlow left the room, with the cheque unfolded in his hand, without deigning to go through any form of thanks or farewell either. Nothing could be less suggestive of undying gratitude than his proceedings when he found himself out in the street. He shook his fist at the window of the room which he had just quitted—which was not a kindly gesture. And as he proceeded on his way, he rained down curses on the head of the man whose cheque he was pocketing.

"He's cleverer than I thought, and carries heavier metal. I was a fool to go so unprepared; he had me at a disadvantage. But next time I'll know better—and that there will be a next time is as sure as that he's alive. If he thinks he has succeeded in throwing dust in my eyes he's mistaken—I know he isn't Francis Smithers; who and what he is I'll know before I pay him another call. That there is something really wrong about him I need no telling. Only let me hit upon the proof of what it is, and it'll be his turn to sign confessions. So this is to be the only assistance I'm to receive from him. Is it? We shall see. Before I've done with him I'll be as rich as he is. As for Netta, she looks on him as a demigod, and on me as so much dirt. I'll pay her! If I show her, beyond the possibility of contradiction, that he's a scoundrel, it'll be like dealing her her deathblow. I know her. It'll break her heart. And I'll break it—yet."

Within, Mr Smithers discussed the brother with his sister. "Nice fellow, Theodore!"

"I didn't think he was so bad as that."

"Nor I. But I begin to perceive all sorts of possibilities."

"Frank, do you really think he's grateful?"

"Grateful!" Mr Smithers laughed. "If he could do it with safety, he'd cut me up into little pieces here and now."

"I hope he wouldn't go quite so far as that, but—I'm afraid he will try to do you a mischief."

"Not a doubt of it."

"Frank, what shall you do?"

"Do? How?"

"You don't seem to realise in the very least the dreadful situation into which you are drifting. Why will you persist in having anything to do with such a family as mine—in which such unpleasant things take place, and in which there are such horrid people?"

"Sweetheart, in this life one has to take the sweets with the bitters. In taking you I take a measure of the sweets which is altogether out of proportion with one man's proper share. Would you have me altogether avoid a flavour of the bitters?"

"I'm afraid that one day you'll be sorry."

"For making you my wife? I've much more cause to be fearful that one day you'll regret the generous impulse which made of me your husband."

"Generous impulse—Frank—never! never! never! '*Till the sun grows cold, and the stars grow old*'—and never then! I wonder if there ever was such another man as you are!" Again Mr Smithers laughed. "You're not to laugh—you're always laughing—it's your one fault. Can't you be serious, even on the solemn subject of your own perfections?"

Mr Smithers tried to be serious—and failed.

CHAPTER 22
ON PUTNEY HEATH

It was the night before the wedding. The bride of the morrow and her mother had retired to rest. A restless fit possessed the expectant bridegroom.

"I'd not sleep if I went to bed, so what's the use of going? If Rodway were here we might find something to say to each other. The last few days he seems to have had a troubled conscience. Possibly his duties of tomorrow weigh heavy on his soul." Mr Rodway was to give the bride away. It was not strange if, at close quarters, he found the prospect hard to contemplate. "But he's not here. And in the house, alone with my own company, I seem to stifle. The night is line. A tramp across the Heath may perhaps brush away the cobwebs."

He went out. A clock struck one. Through the still, clear air the sound went swiftly. Other chimes pressed on the first. For a few seconds clock called to clock. He strode up towards Putney Heath. A tardy clock asserted its independence by striking the time some minutes after all the rest had finished, on a cracked bell, which shrieked.

"That clock's behind the times," announcing the fact with dissonant pride.—What mood has got me? Like that *beldam* in Macbeth. '*By the twinkling of my thumbs, something evil this way comes.'* I've a premonition strong upon me that fate's about to play me some scurvy trick. I wish tomorrow's ceremony were well over. Perhaps then I'd have a mind at peace,—if I'm ever again to know what it is to have a mind at peace. I seem to have murdered, not sleep, but peace. My thoughts keep reverting to that crime-stained Thane.—Who's that?'"

Turning quickly, he looked behind him. Nothing living was in sight. In the bright starlight he could see to the bottom of the hill.

"I thought someone was running after me—or was it that someone ran across the road? I heard footsteps. It couldn't have been a cat."

He resumed his walk.

"Perhaps Netta's nervousness has affected me. I suppose the eve of her wedding's a solemn moment to a girl. Certainly Netta seemed to find it solemn. To think that she should have cried when she said goodnight. Excitement—every nerve in her body is on end. There are a few great days in the average woman's life; the one on which she's married ought to be the greatest of them all. I fancy that's how it's going to be with Netta. And so—in another sense—it's going to be with me. Now, who's that?"

He again swung quickly round—again to find nothing to be seen. The appearance of solitude seemed to puzzle him.

"I'll swear that that time I heard someone running—and if they weren't a man's steps, my fancy's playing me tricks to which I'm unaccustomed. Where can he have vanished? There's plenty of cover. He may have slipped behind a bush or a tree, or thrown himself flat down on the uneven ground. Wherever he is he's not far away. I'm betting that he's within fifty feet of where I stand."

He had reached the Heath. Although there were houses within a stone's throw, immediately on either side of him was open country, broken by trees, gorse, blackberry bushes. The turf rose and fell. In that light it would have been easy for a dozen men to have remained concealed within the fifty feet of which he spoke.

"There are fellows who'd say that it were folly in a man in my position to trust himself alone up here at this romantic hour—especially upon his wedding eve. And it's certain that if any of my threatening friends are disposed to show that they mean business, now's their time to do it. I presume there are police-men hereabouts; but if the moment is well chosen, it's doubtful if they would be likely to come my way in time. It were the part of discretion to turn back, and turn soon; but discretion is a virtue to which I never was attached. For an argument—of sorts!—I'm just in the mood. It's a prescription, properly applied, of which I stand in need. Life's gone too easily of late."

Selecting a cigar from his case, he remained stationary till he had lit it, then strolled on.

"If the hounds are after me, they'll have the scent of my cigar to guide them. In a place like this, at this hour, the scent of a cigar should be perceptible to the dullest nose within a radius of half a mile."

He had proceeded, perhaps, another hundred yards, when for the first time he performed an instantaneous right about face. He had noticed something which might have escaped a less keen ear.

"That was someone stumbling over a bush—I've heard a gentleman do it in a covert before tonight. Where is he? I'd like to have someone with me here, so that we might have a little bet as to his exact location. He's a seasoned hand. Although he must have been taken unawares, he's gone to earth in a flash. I say he's inside that clump of what looks like gorse, and I'm ready to sup-port my opinion to the extent of a pony. Hullo!—more sport!"

He had been contemplating a group of brambles which were at a little distance on his right. All at once his glance travelled across the road to the more wooded ground upon his left.

"There's someone among those hawthorns, or whatever they are, and more than one. Two at least—I'll be easily convinced that there are three. I saw what looked uncommonly like heads against the sky-line;—I'm sure that there were two. There is going to be an argument—of sorts! It would be impossible to avoid them now, even if I so desired. The only result of any attempt to retrace my steps would probably be that the matter would be brought to a more rapid issue.—I'm inquisitive as to how it is they got where they are.

"There was only one man running—of that I'm positive. Yet there are probably four about me now. He could hardly have carried the others on his back. It's just as unlikely that they were awaiting my arrival—on the off-chance of my doing such an extremely improbable thing as take a solitary walk, at this hour, in this direction. There really seems to be something uncanny about the situation.—Shall I let them know I've spotted them, and provoke an attack at the moment which suits me? They must have realised that my suspicions have been aroused.—Not I. The element of uncertainty is half the fun; let them come when it suits them."

As he neared Wimbledon Common he became conscious that someone was approaching—"*with measured tread and slow.*"

"A policeman!—as I'm a sinner!—Nothing could be better. If I don't have a little amusement at the expense of my unseen friends, I'm only a relic of the man I used to be. The position is developing latent possibilities. Gentlemen of the Eight!—you're in for a bad five minutes. If I were only sure that Mr Augustus Chaffinch is among you!"

On came the policeman—on went Mr Smithers. They arrived within a yard of one another. Then Mr Smithers stopped. He addressed the constable in a tone of voice which must have been audible, say, within fifty yards or so.

"A fine night, officer."

"Yes—but it's a little late."

The remark might almost have been intended as a hint. The constable was a big, burly fellow, with a heavy black moustache. He eyed Mr Smithers with official suspicion, which was presently lulled when he perceived what manner of man he was.

"It is a trifle early. But I presume that in this part of the world one is not likely to meet with an adventure even at this hour of the morning."

"Well—it's pretty lonely."

"But there are no bad characters hereabouts."

"I shouldn't care to say as much as that myself. I've seen some uncommonly queer characters hereabouts."

"Surely not footpads, and that kind of thing?"

"Yes—I daresay what you'd call footpads Anyhow, parties who'd do a good deal for half a sovereign—and who've done a good deal, some of them."

"Your words make me think. I've come up Putney Hill, and do you know that I've more than once had an odd impression that I was being followed."

"Then if I was you I should go straight back down Putney Hill. You'll be safer there than here."

"You see those brambles to the left of that tree—only a second or two before you came up I fancied that I saw a man dodge down behind them."

"I'll go and see if you like."

"No—I wouldn't trouble you. It was only my fancy;—you know the sort of fancies one does get in a place like this."

"You'd better let me go and see. Such things have happened, and will happen again."

"Nonsense. You make me think of the ancient spinster who makes it a nightly rule to look for the burglar under the bed. Goodnight—have a cigar."

The policeman had a cigar. Each pursued his individual way. When he had gone a little distance, glancing over his shoulder, Mr Smithers perceived that what he had anticipated had taken place—the constable had quitted the highroad to stroll towards the patch of brushwood towards which his attention had been directed.

"I fear that you are just a trifle late—I fancy the birds were alarmed in time. They were alarmed; that's something." The constable, after wandering in and out among the bushes, was returning to the road. "I thought so. Not a feather to be found."

He walked on till, as he moved round the bend in the road, the policeman passed from sight.

"Now, will they come, or will they wait till he is out of hearing too? A shout would reach him. Perhaps their instructions
are to take no risks. I, on the other hand, am taking all there are
around. But the truth is, I'm curious to know what sort of gen-
try these are with whom I have to deal. Mr Chaffinch's mysterious jargon has inspired me with a desire to bring the matter of
the Right—a blessed word is Mesopotamia!—to something like
a test. I'll give them to the windmill. If, by the time I reach it,
they've still done nothing, I'll act on Robert's advice, and walk
back again down Putney Hill.—Who the deuce are you?"

The inquiry was addressed to a figure which seemed to rise
up out of the ground itself in front of him. Almost at the same
instant two other figures appeared on either side. Making no
attempt to answer his question they came at him with a rush.
Laughing, he drew back.

"So there's going to be an argument—welcome, gentlemen
of the Eight!"

When the first man came within his reach he dealt him a
blow on the face which hurled him back on to the ground from
which he so recently had risen.

"I hope I haven't hurt your nose, sir; I fear it's broken."

He met one of the others with his right. But the force of
the blow was broken by his companion; who, flinging himself
on Mr Smithers, twined his arms about his neck. The man staggered backwards, but, recovering himself, again came rushing
on. Cumbered by the fellow who had hung himself about him
with monkey-like agility, Mr Smithers was ill-prepared to encounter his fresh antagonist.

"Hold on!" muttered the newcomer. "I'll down him."

"Will you? I think you are mistaken."

Springing on one side, with a sudden twist Mr Smithers
wrenched himself free of the fellow who clung to him. Taking
him about the body he thrust him against his onrushing com-
rade with so much vigour that both were borne off their feet.
The man on whom he had first bestowed his favours having
regained his perpendicular, was returning to the attack; but on

seeing the fate which had befallen his friends, showed signs of hesitation—an attitude on which Mr Smithers was prompt to comment.

"I trust, sir, your nose is not seriously injured—you put your hand up to it as if it were. False noses, as you are possibly aware, are among the latest creations of science;—if your own is utterly destroyed, I recommend the fact to your attention. It's cool standing still; won't you try another little game of rough and tumble? You do the tumbling parts so very well.—Ah, there are your companions ready to rejoin you. Now all of you can come on together. For you, that must be so much more agreeable than one at a time."

The hearers, however, finding themselves once more in the enjoyment of an upright posture, did not show themselves so eager to renew the onslaught as might have been expected. They muttered together, keeping themselves at a prudent distance from where their antagonist stood contemptuously regarding them.

"Come! come! Aren't you going to down me? I'm waiting to be downed. On a chilly night like this I do beg you to believe that I do not wish to have to wait too long."

For a moment or two the trio evinced no marked signs of a pressing desire to accept his invitation. It seemed, indeed, to be doubtful if they would not rather retreat than advance. But on a sudden their tactics changed; they came flying at him with an impetuosity and a disregard of consequences which did them credit. Out went his arms, like metal rods. Over went the first man; his companions—without being knocked actually down—receiving probably as much of his attention as they quite cared for. Not one of them succeeded in getting within reach of him.

"Why don't you down me?" he cried. "You haven't downed me yet!"

While he was still speaking something was thrown over his head from behind—something wet and sticky. He found himself struggling in sudden darkness with an unseen assailant, his head and face enveloped in what was either a bag or a sack. It was jerked violently backwards. He felt that he was being borne off his feet—was conscious of a suffocating sensation, of a sickly odour which oppressed his nostrils—and then he became unconscious of everything.

CHAPTER 23
MR RODWAY DOUBTS

"Coming to, are you? Now then, what are you up to? Don't do that."

When Mr Smithers returned to consciousness, the first thing he even dimly realised was that a constable was in front of him, kneeling on one knee, and that it was from him the words proceeded. It was several seconds before he realised anything else; as, for instance, that he was sitting up upon the grass; that his hat was off; that the fresh, damp air felt grateful about his throbbing brow; that it was still dark; and that he was feeling, both mentally and physically, very queer indeed.

"Better have gone straight back, as I told you."

"I beg your pardon?" Mr Smithers had not caught the allusion conveyed in the other's words. Then it dawned upon him that this was the constable with whom—in a mischievous mood—he had had that little conversation. "I think I've seen you before?"

"You have, and not so very long ago either. When I saw you again, I thought you were dead. Do what I might, you wouldn't show any signs of life; and then, just as I was thinking of going off for help, you came to."

"Thank you; I'm very much obliged for the interest you took in me. Where was I lying?"

"On the grass here?"

"On the grass, just where you're sitting; on your back, looking up to the sky. You looked like a corpse, if ever I saw one. How are you feeling now?"

"Better, thank you; practically well, indeed. Only my head throbs."

"So it wasn't only your fancy about them chaps behind the

brambles. I saw nothing of them; they must have nipped off before I got there."

"Chaps behind the brambles?"

"Wasn't it them that did for you?"

"Did for me? It seems as if I must have had some sort of a fit. I feel like it."

"Fit? Do you mean to tell me that you haven't been robbed and assaulted?"

"Robbed?" Mr Smithers was standing up by now, seeming a little tottery. He was going through the contents of his pockets with apparent method. "Money, watch, chain, pocket-book intact; there's nothing missing of intrinsic value. That doesn't look like robbery. It must have been a fit."

"Didn't you see anyone?"

"See anyone '? I saw you. A fit's the explanation. Thank you, officer, again, for your assistance; there's a five-pound note to mark my sense of it. The presence of that note upon my person is sufficient testimony that I have not been robbed."

The policeman was looking from the note to its donor with doubtful eyes.

"I'm sure I'm much obliged to you, sir, especially as this is altogether beyond anything I've done for you; but I'm afraid I shall have to trouble you for your name and address. I shall have to report what's happened."

"By all means; here's my card. And now, for the second time, goodnight. I don't think I'm likely to meet with any more adventures on my homeward way. I am in no danger of another fit tonight."

The policeman watched him as he moved along the road, leaning a little on his stick, his limping, uncertain gait bearing but little resemblance to the buoyant ease which had marked his movements on their first meeting. Slightly opening the shutter of his lantern, he scrutinised by the aid of its light the banknote he was holding.

"Seems all right; yet if it is, what did he give it me for—a lump of money like that? Not for what I did, but for what 1 didn't do, that's about the size of it. There's a mystery somewhere which I haven't got the hang of. He's no more had a fit than I have. 'Francis Smithers'—that's his name, is it—according to the card he gave me. Well, Mr Francis Smithers, if you choose to let yourself be killed as near as a toucher, and don't choose to say anything about it, I suppose it's no business of mine; especially when there's a five-pound note to be earned by making it no business of mine. But if I was you, I wouldn't walk about alone in the dark any more than you can help. I should say, by the look of things, that someone had a down against you, and that you'd sooner they downed you than own up what it's for."

Mr Smithers communed with himself as he wended his homeward way.

"What was it they were after? It wasn't money, and apparently it wasn't me. It's now half-past two. I must have lain there a good hour—on the turf, with my face to the stars; a dignified position for a man who's to be married at noon. As during that time I was wholly at their mercy, they might have done anything. What did they do? It's not likely that their sole object was just to lay me there and leave me. They don't seem to have subjected the contents of my pockets to a very rigorous examination, if they touched them at all. They must have been after some particular thing—and found it pretty nearly right away."

An idea suddenly occurred to him. He stopped. Taking out the sovereign-purse which was attached to one end of his watch-chain, he stared at it with all his eyes.

"The key of the safe—as I'm a sinner! The key of safe No. 226 on the premises of the Shoe Lane Deposit Company. That was their objective—and they've got it at once. It was attached to my sovereign-purse, and now it isn't. Unmistakably now it isn't."

He resumed his walk.

"What do they think they're going to do with it? They can do what they please.—The idea isn't a bad one, though if I chose they'd be no nearer safe No. 226 than they were before. It doesn't follow, because they have the key, that they have the *entrée*. I suppose they'll try various little tricks of hanky-panky to get the *entrée,* having got the key; but I've only to lift my little finger to checkmate them. But I won't lift my little finger. I would give something to see the look on Mr Chaffinch's face when he learns what are the present contents of Mr Smithers' strong-box."

He laughed, as if in the enjoyment of a first- rate joke. He had reached the top of Putney Hill. Turning, stretching out his hand towards the Heath, with a mocking assumption of melodramatic earnestness, he said—as if addressing an unseen audience:

"This time you score, and you're welcome to your winnings, gentlemen of the Eight!"

A voice exclaimed, almost at his elbow.

"Smithers—by all that's holy! Man alive, what are you talking about?—What's the matter with you?—What are you doing here?"

Mr Smithers found himself confronted by Mr Rodway. If the encounter surprised him disagreeably, he concealed the fact with considerable skill.

"Ben!—Where have you sprung from? I never heard you coming. It's for me to ask what you are doing here, at this hour, when all good boys should be in bed."

"I'm known to the police. It's no new thing for me to be here at any hour. Many a time have I tramped the Heath and the Common all through the night, wrestling with a screw that wouldn't fit or a wheel that wouldn't turn. It's here and hereabouts that, in the silence, sometimes amid rain and wind and blackness, I've groped my way, through failure after failure, to the power. But with you it's different. You're to be married in an hour or two. You ought to be in bed, like a decent creature. What's happened to you? What nonsense were you spouting?"

Mr Smithers was conscious that the other's shrewd eyes were noting certain singularities in his appearance.

"I've had a fall."

"You look as if you had had a row."

"Do I?—It seems to have shaken me."

They went on down the hill together. Presently Mr Rodway made a remark which recalled what the policeman had said as he examined his five-pound note.

"If I were you, I'd bar lonely walks in lonely places in lonely hours."

Mr Smithers glanced quickly towards him.

"That's a cryptographic utterance; what's it mean?"

"Just what it says."

When they were back in Mr Smithers' sitting-room, *by* the light of the gas, Mr Rodway looked his companion carefully up and down.

"You have been in a row. Someone has been taking liberties with your collar and necktie; you've been rolled on the grass, and there's a scratch on your cheek two inches long. That's not the sort of ornament with which a bridegroom ought to go to the altar."

Mr Smithers was examining himself before the looking-glass.

"It does look pretty bad. I shall have to say you did it."

"You can say that to others; you can't to me.—Frank, own up!"

"Own up—what?"

"Who are you?"

"My dear Ben, isn't it rather late in the day to ask me such a question?"

"It is, but better late than never."

"No; sometimes better never."

"This isn't one of those times. Theodore Ludlow goes about singing a song which is nearly all bunkum, but not quite all. That he's got hold of the wrong end of the stick I've no doubt whatever, but I've just as little doubt that there is a stick to be got hold of. I'm a judge of a man; and you are a man, or you wouldn't be my partner. I was pretty stuck for money when I came across you. But it wasn't only money I wanted. I wanted a man—and I've got him. I'd trust you with my life, and with more than my life. But you're a man of mystery for all that. And

I want to ask you, right here and now, almost within sound of your wedding-bells, if you don't think you'll be doing the square thing by putting an end to the mystery, at least so far as I'm concerned."

"Ben, have you had this sort of feeling upon your mind some time?"

"Ever since the day on which Netta Ludlow consented to be your wife, when it became my business."

"How?"

"Because I love her better than my life—better than the power. All the time that I was struggling to get there, I kept saying to myself that when I did I'd get her too. Then you came along, and snapped her from underneath my nose."

"But she'd refused you?"

"Oh yes, she'd refused me, but she wouldn't have kept on refusing me forever if you hadn't come along. But that's all over. You're going to try to make her the happiest wife that ever lived, and I shouldn't be surprised if you succeeded. But do you know what sort of a girl she is?"

"I fancy so."

"She's made of you a hero. She's set you up on a pinnacle in her hall of heroes. If she finds out anything about you which is not in consonance with the heroic character, you'll come tumbling down with a rush, and your fall will kill her."

"And therefore?"

"This: Don't regard me as a partner only in mailers £. s. d. If you can't tell her what the mystery is—it you can, do, I earnestly entreat you to do!—but if you can't, tell me. As a brother sinner, you'll find me tolerant. And let me help you in guarding her from the discovery of what you had rather she didn't know."

"Why should you imagine there is a mystery?"

"Because I've common-sense. What's the meaning of this uncanny whistling that's always going on, and always the same tune? I daresay you don't know how it's done, or even who does it, but I do believe you know that it's meant for you. Then, you're the best spied-on man I ever heard of. I've reasons for knowing that a constant watch is kept upon your goings and comings, your risings-up and sittings-down, upon everything you do. For instance, someone dogged your footsteps up to the Heath just now. Who was it? You won't tell, but you've got their mark upon you. I'll lay odds that there is someone watching the house at this very moment, that there are eyes on the light in your window, possibly an ear glued to the pane."

"I should like to get it between my finger and thumb."

"I daresay! Probably you've tried to do so more than once and failed, because the thing is too well done. If you won't do anything else, and I can. see that you won't by the look of you, at least answer two questions: Have you ever been mixed up in any secret society, or political conspiracy with the Mafia, or Nihilists, or Anarchists, or any rubbish of that kind?"

"I assure you, never!"

"Do you go in peril of your life?—I know you don't care a twopenny d—if you do, and that you probably enjoy the mere notion of such a thing; you're that sort of man. But you'll soon have a wife to be considered. Remember that your danger will be hers. Think of what her feelings will be if she suddenly, without warning, discovers the position you are in. Is it fair to subject her to such a risk?"

"My dear Ben, I've just one remark which I should like to make."

"You haven't answered my second question."

"My remark will be my answer; it's this. I'm a tolerably strong man, with a confident belief in my capacity to take good care of myself and all that I hold dear."

"Is that all you intend to say?"

"Except that we both of us have onerous tasks to perform in the course of the next few hours, and that I do think that we ought to have at least half-an-hour in bed."

"I'm ready. Only, Frank, do remember, if ever the place you're in gets very tight, that two heads are better than one."

When he found himself in his own bedroom, Mr Rodway delivered himself of a curious observation.

"If all the facts were known, there's not an insurance company in England which would accept his life, even as an extraordinary risk, and for twelvemonths only. And he's going to marry Netta! All I can do is to remember what He said—'*Greater love hath no man than this, that a man lay down his life for his friend,*' and to hope that I may have a chance."

CHAPTER 24
HASTE TO THE WEDDING

It was a 'pretty' wedding. The number of persons actually concerned in it was six. There was the bride, who looked a 'picture,' in a dress which would have sat well upon a queen. No expense had been spared upon that costume.

"You're only going to be married once in your life," Mr Smithers had declared. "At least, that's the average expectation in cases of this kind; and you're going to come to me like a dressmaker's dream."

And she did. Netta was more than perplexed by the glorious shape which, before it was finished, that dream assumed.

"You know it's positively wicked to wear a dress like this only once. I ought to be married again in it, and before the fashions change; and however shall I manage that?"

"Oh, wear it to go to court in."

"To go where?"

"To court. I take it that my wife will make her obeisance to her sovereign among the other ladies of the land."

A comical expression came on Netta's face.

"I'm going to court now. Pray how long ago is it really since I was blackleading the kitchen grate?"

The 'ornaments' which the bride wore were of unusual beauty.

"I've never had a moment's peace," she asserted, "since these diamonds came into the house. I suppose the entire premises are worth about five hundred pounds, and this diamond necklace alone about fifty thousand. It does seem incongruous. I've slept with it underneath my pillow, and yet I haven't been happy.

The other night I dreamt that a horrid monkey-like-looking creature was insinuating its fingers under my pillow-case—oh dear! And then there are this tiara, and pins, and brooches, and bracelets—I ought to go about guarded—I know I ought. If we are going to take these things abroad with us, I shouldn't be one bit surprised if I came back grey."

"I think grey would rather suit you."

"Do you? Then, if the idea is that you shall be afforded an opportunity of judging at the earliest possible moment, then I don't like it. You don't want my jewels to turn me grey?"

"No, not particularly."

"What an agreeable way you have of putting things!" She sighed. "There's one thing: it would be rather romantic if I were to go prematurely grey because my jewels are of such extreme beauty that the mere fact of their possession affects the colour of my hair." She sighed. "Before I met you, the only jewellery I had was a silver brooch, which cost three and nine at an all-sorts shop in the Fulham Road."

The bride's mother was in tears—genuine tears. She was attired in a grey silk dress, fashioned with such cunning that it endowed her with an amazing appearance of juvenility.

"It makes you look not a day over thirty!" So Netta had assured her—to her distress; as if in her case juvenescence was synonymous with indecorum.

"I hope, Netta, that it doesn't make me look so young as you say it does."

"But it does—it makes you look a positive child—my sister, mother dear."

Solemnly, Mrs Ludlow shook her head. "I don't hold with people at my time of life looking so much younger than they are; it's nothing but flightiness."

And then there was the wrench of parting. The proverbial saying has it that "*my daughter's my daughter the whole of my life.*" But the girl was going into such a different world to that to which her mother was accustomed, and Mrs Ludlow, conscious of her manifold deficiencies, was so unwilling to venture into it herself, that the saying in this case was hardly likely to be verified. When Netta Ludlow became Mrs Francis Smithers, with the best will in the world to remain unchanged, it was impossible that she could continue to be to her mother the daughter that was.

So, although in her nervous, hesitant fashion, she gloried in her child's good fortune and in her prospects of boundless happiness, she herself could not but be conscious that she would be left alone. Residence with her son was out of the question; she had not been so foolish as to dream of it. She was a town-bred woman, and had expressed her unwillingness to occupy a house on the Dene Park estate.

"I don't mind the country now and then, *I'm* as fond of it as most, but I couldn't live in it all the time. I was born in Paddington, and Putney's the farthest I've lived from Charing Cross."

She did consent to go a little farther afield—to Wimbledon Common. There Mr Rodway had taken to himself a dwelling-place, and Mrs Ludlow had agreed to keep house for him.

"I understand him, and he understands me, and that's something. He says he's never going to be married, but marriage is a subject on which no man ever knew his own mind yet; anyhow, he won't be bringing a wife home before I've had time to look about me."

Margaret Foster was the solitary bridesmaid—rather troublesome an attendant Netta found her.

"Do you know, it sounds incredible nowadays, when lots of people live at weddings, but I've never seen one in my life. What did a bridesmaid ought to do? Ought I to carry you into the church, or merely drag you along by the hair of your head, and soothe you with something out of a bottle at regular intervals?"

"You've to do nothing whatever except look nice."

"That'll be easy—especially as Mr Smithers declares that it's the bridegroom's duly to provide the bridesmaid with her dress. That man's ideas are grand! But he's a mass of deception."

"Meg! how dare you say such things?"

He says the bridegroom ought to give the bridesmaid presents.

I can't help thinking he's mistaking me for someone of multitude. I'm becoming the possessor of a shopful. I say—excuse curiosity!—but why didn't you give the other man a try?"

"What do you mean?"

"Why didn't you marry Mr Rodway? Although you've neither of you breathed a word, I know he asked you—I can see it in his eyes. You might have bullied him; you're under a complete misapprehension if you think that you'll ever be able to bully Mr Smithers."

"Meg, you say you've never been to a wedding;—you're the first girl friend I've had."

"You're fortunate in being able to make so excellent a beginning."

"And I'm commencing to wonder if all girls talk like you do? I used to have quite a high opinion of my own sex till I made your acquaintance. Now I'm growing to have none at all."

"Thank you; that's meant to be cutting. But I suppose you must expect to be sat upon by some people when they're going to be married. But perhaps I shan't remain a spinster the whole of my life, and then it'll be my turn.—I had a proposal the other day."

"Meg!—No!—Who was it?"

"Oh—somebody who knows my value. He said 'Let's be married.' I said, 'Shan't!' But I don't suppose I shall be able to keep on saying 'Shan't' to everyone. I'm bound to be overwhelmed in the rush that's coming. Then I'll be able to do some trampling on my unprotected sisters."

Sidney Foster was best man. The idea of his occupying a position of such importance amused him—as he explained to Mr Smithers.

"It seems tremendous cheek on my part—to set up as your best man! You being such a swell, and all the rest of it; and I owing everything to you—though why you are so good to me is beyond me altogether. But of course, if you'd like me to do it, I should be only too proud and delighted."

"I should like you to do it," said Mr Smithers.

Mr Rodway, whose duty it was to give away the bride, appeared to find his role a little arduous. For one thing he was treated by the bridesmaid in a manner which he found embarrassing. On that young lady's shapely head the bump of reverence was extremely small. Upon previous occasions Mr Rodway, whose knowledge of women was practically limited to Netta, had found in Miss Foster a type of femininity which was altogether beyond his understanding. The bride and her mother drove to church in one carriage, while her bridesmaid and temporary father were together in another. This arrangement was to Mr Rodway the cause of some confusion. The lady—whose glories occupied the entire seat facing the horses—surveyed him, as he screwed himself into the smallest possible compass in an opposite seat, critically.

"It doesn't suit you?"

The gentleman started; he was already painfully conscious of being in apparel which his soul loathed.

"What doesn't suit me?"

"None of it suits you. And you've no notion of how to tie a bow."

"I never had. But they said I ought to wear one."

"It's meant for a bow?"

"Meant for a bow!" He put up his fingers in alarm. "Is it—is it very bad?"

"In an ordinary case I should advise no rumpling, but in your case it can make no difference. It couldn't possibly be worse.—I don't like your frock-coat."

"I loathe it. I feel that if I were to stretch my arms something would burst."

"I should let it burst. It might give you relief and make you happier. I've generally seen you in a short blue arrangement, with about thirteen pockets, every one of them filled to overflowing. In that you seemed comfortable."

"I am. I've practically lived in that jacket ever since I had it."

"It looks as though you had. A high collar doesn't suit you."

"It doesn't, and I don't suit it. Damn the thing! I—I beg ten thousand pardons. I assure you I didn't mean it."

The gentleman's complexion had suddenly assumed a vermilion hue. The lady was affable.

"Pray don't apologise. And I'm sure you did mean it. Isn't that waistcoat a little—striking?"

"Do you think so?"

"I always feel that half-a-dozen colours brought together within the narrow compass of a single garment do make it stand out."

"There aren't half-a-dozen colours in this."

"There are more. There are the primary colours in the form of stripes; and then they are arranged in innumerable combinations to form that very curious background."

"They said I ought to wear something in the fancy way."

"You have certainly succeeded in doing that."

"Do you think there'd be time for me to go and change it?—I don't want to turn the affair into a sort of Guy Faux show."

"No; I'm afraid there wouldn't be time. You might take it off and stuff it under the seat, or you might button your coat well over it.—Why do you nurse your hat? Won't it go on your head?"

"I'd rather do anything with it than put it there."

"You don't look—taking you together—as if *you* were expecting much enjoyment."

"I abominate the whole thing."

"Do you mean that you abominate driving alone with me?"

"Not only that."

"Not only that—but partly that. I see. You have an agreeable way of expressing yourself!"

"I—I assure you, Miss Foster, that I didn't mean anything of the kind."

"That is the second assurance of yours on which I feel compelled to cast doubts Do you object to my society because I also look a sight?—By the way, how do I look?"

"You—you look—you look like a dream of beauty."

"More so than Netta?"

"Of course that's different. She looks nice."

"Really!—Mr Rodway!—Then I am to understand that she looks nice, while I merely look like a dream of beauty. Pray what sort of a rag, tag, and bobtail kind of an affair is that? Don't you wish that you were master of the art of expressing yourself differently? Then you might be able to hint that it was my intention to turn the whole affair into a sort of Guy Faux show."

Mr Rodway looked about him in search of the help which was not forthcoming. Incidentally, he rubbed the nap of his hat the wrong way. Then an expression of something like resolution settled on his countenance. His tone was a little savage

"It was far from my intention to hint at anything of the kind, as you are perfectly well aware."

The lady looked at him with mischievous eves. The carriage drew up.

"I believe this is the church. You will now, for the present, be relieved of the too near abomination of my society."

CHAPTER 25

THE BRIDESMAID INTERVENES

In the church was that miscellaneous collection of persons— mostly women—which haunts such occasions, regarding a wedding—anybody's wedding—as a public show of a distinctly attractive kind. It was the general opinion that the bridegroom did credit to the proceedings. This view was given audible utterance to by more than one of the onlookers.

"'Andsome I call him," remarked one lady, who carried a baby, to a friend who led by the hand a toddling child. "A regular picture. 'Ow tall he is, and 'ow straight he do 'old himself. And don't that beard become him, and them blue eyes! And ain't his clothes something like a fit!"

"Ah!" rejoined her friend, "there isn't many of his sort about; I wish there was more."

"There's not enough to go round, that's certain sure. She's in luck, she is. He's something like a man."

As the bridegroom led his bride down the aisle, the common

183

feeling, expressed in more or less homely fashion, was with this lady—that he was "something like a man." He looked so proud and happy; he held himself with so much grace of bearing; such a glad light was in his eyes; he carried himself as if he had not a care upon his mind; as if he could look the whole world in the face, knowing no cause for shame in what was past, or for doubt or fear in what the future had in store for him; in short, he did seem, in such ideal fashion, to be all that a man should be, that it was not strange that among those present were some who esteemed themselves the more because of the knowledge that he was of the same clay as they were. In his person he did so much honour to the whole family of men !

The ceremony went without a hitch. Mrs Ludlow cried. Others cried—perfect strangers—they alone knew why. No marriage service could have been more successfully performed. Another pair was launched upon that matrimonial sea which knows, theoretically, but one point of parting—death; one resting-place—the grave. All went as merrily as marriage bells.

Curiously enough, it was while those bells were chiming, in an eager, frolicsome peal, that an incident occurred which might be said, in some degree, to have marred the perfect harmony.

One person at least was present in that building who was not in festive mood. Why he was there at all he himself could have hardly said; unless it was to make sure, by the evidence of his own eyesight, that the marriage did take place. This was the brother of the bride. He had been invited to the wedding—by his sister's wish; which invitation—possibly because he suspected it might not be warmly seconded by the groom—he had refused. He had told himself, more than once, that on no account should the occasion be illumined by the light of his countenance.

Yet, at the last moment, he had excused himself for an hour from the bank, in order that he might see all that was to be seen—as it were, *incognito*. He only had one sister; it may be that, on this great occasion in her life, his heart went out to her such might have been the case; but his conduct hardly suggested it. On the opposite side of the road, nearly fronting the church, was a tavern. In this he took refuge, consuming a sandwich and a bottle of lemonade, until such time as the wedding party had entered the building.

Then he followed; modestly declining the verger's offer to lead him to a front seat, preferring to place himself in close proximity to the door. The ceremony concluded, he availed himself of his position to be among the first of those who went. Finding himself in the street, he joined himself to the little crowd of loiterers which waited for the wedding party to emerge.

Immediately in front of him was an individual who one would scarcely have thought, from his appearance, could have been interested in such a function as a marriage. Although not an old man, he yet conveyed the impression of being, generally speaking, in the last stage of decay. He was clad in a nondescript array of rags, which held together he alone knew how. Strips of rag were wound round his feet in lieu of boots. An ancient peakless cap was crammed upon his head. His hair and beard had been untrimmed and unwashed much longer than was desirable. There was no doubt whatever that misery and he had long been bedfellows.

Presently there was a stir at the church door. The crowd woke up. All turned to see.

"Here they come!—Here's the bride and bridegroom!"

Mr and Mrs Smithers came along the winding churchyard path—the groom all radiance, the bride all blushes. Immediately behind them came Mr Rodway, with the bridesmaid on his arm; the best man, with Mrs Ludlow, bringing up the rear. Whether that is the legitimate order in which the procession ought to have been formed is by the way; that is how they chose to come. So soon as he perceived the newly married man, the dilapidated creature in front of Mr Ludlow began to behave in an extremely singular fashion.

"My gawd!" he exclaimed, "it's him!—You don't mean to say that"—he turned on Mr Ludlow with sudden ferocity of inquiry—"that that's the bloke who's been married?"

Mr Ludlow regarded him with barely concealed aversion,

while plainly struck by the peculiarity of his manner.

"Certainly. Why shouldn't he be?—Do you know him?"

"Know him!—Do I knowhim!—Him!—I'll show you if I know him—and I'll show him too!"

The fellow moved forward as if to thrust himself in the way of the little procession. Mr Ludlow caught him by the shoulder.

"If you have anything to show, show me."

"Show you!—You!—Who are you? Why should I show you?"

"I am the brother of the lady he has married. For any information about him worth having I am willing to pay handsomely."

"You're willing to pay for information?—You are?—How am I to know it?"

"By putting me to the test."

While these questions and answers had been hurriedly exchanged, the wedding party had reached the pavement. The bridegroom had handed the bride into the carriage which was waiting; had followed himself; the door had been closed; the coachman had driven off. The ragged stranger woke to the fact with sudden fury. If Mr Ludlow had not kept tight hold of him he would have rushed after the departing vehicle. As it was, he began shouting at the top of his voice.

"Let me get at him!—Let me get at him!—You see that bloke? He was in quod with me. Now look where he is and where I am! If I had my rights it'd be the other way round!—First he tried to murder me, then he robbed me after! If I was to speak a word he'd get a lifer!"

The better sort among the spectators, not knowing what to make of the man, drew back. Others pressed forward. The inevitable constable moved towards him.

"Now then—none of that! Off you go!"

"So help me, guv'nor," shrieked the man, in evident awe of the official eye and voice and hand," it's him you ought to be after, not me!"

Mr Rodway, perceiving Theodore Ludlow, taking in something of the situation at a glance, motioned to Sidney Foster; who, following Mrs Ludlow into the carriage which was waiting, immediately drove off. Into the next vehicle Mr Rodway ushered Miss Foster, speaking to her through the window.

"You go on. I'll follow."

She replied to him, an odd look in her eyes and on her face—

"Don't let there be a scene."

He nodded. Off drove the bridesmaid in solitary state.

Mr Rodway thrust his way through the knot of people towards the excited ragamuffin, addressing him as if he were some inferior animal whose one business it was to obey. A hansom was standing by the kerb. He pointed to it.

"Now, my man, get into that cab. I want to speak to you."

Ludlow interposed.

"None of that, Rodway. He's my find. I've been juggled with enough. I'm going to have no more of it."

Mr Rodway's mannier was stern; his words to the point.

"Don't be a fool! Do you want to have a disturbance here? You can come with us if you like. I'll see to this man, constable. Thank you very much."

He slipped a coin into the policeman's hand. The vagabond entered the cab, with a tell-tale readiness to yield implicit, unquestioning obedience in the presence of a representative of the law. The vehicle started; containing as curiously assorted a trio as, probably, even a hansom ever held.

It had been arranged that after the wedding the small party should return to the Cosmopolitan Hotel. There dresses were to be changed; breakfast—or what passed as such—was to be eaten; last greetings were to be uttered; bride and bridegroom were to be despatched upon their duplicate way. No programme could have been better arranged, only, unfortunately, when it came to the point, the whole fell flat. This was owing to the unaccountable absence of the bridegroom's partner. The meal was ready, the guests were ready, but this one was missing. Miss Foster alone was able to furnish an explanation of his non-appearance, and her account was principally remarkable for its vagueness.

"There was some sort of disturbance among the crowd outside the church, in which a man and a policeman seemed to be figuring largely. Mr Rodway would stop to see what it was about. He said he'd come on afterwards. That's all I know."

At least that was all she would tell. Nor, judging from her manner, was there any reason to suppose that she could have told more, even if she. Mr Rodway was known to have his eccentric moods. It seemed that he had been indulging in one quite recently. So, since time was of importance, boat trains refusing to wait for anyone, the five sat down to table; hopeful, every moment, that the absentee would come.

Before he did appear the meal was nearly concluded, the moment being close at hand when the honeymooning couple would have to start. As he came hurrying along the corridor, looking not at all as if he were about to take a prominent part in a marriage festivity, a waiter stopped him, having an envelope in his hand.

"Mr Rodway? I was told to give you this letter, sir, and to request you to read it before you joined the company."

Mr Rodway tore the envelope open with a finger which seemed tremulous. It contained a note written in a small, clear, almost masculine hand.

Dear Mr Rodway,—Whatever you may have heard, say nothing to anyone; let them go in peace. If you have the slightest regard for Netta, you will not turn the happiest day of her life into the most miserable. I don't suppose it will have any weight, but I beg you to behave as if nothing out of the ordinary had taken place, as a special favour to me. I will give you all the explanations you can possibly require afterwards.—Sincerely yours,

Margaret Foster.

Although the words were plain enough, Mr Rodway read them through again, as if, on the first reading, their meaning had escaped him. He turned to the waiter.

"Bring me some whiskey. Is there any place near where I can

have it?"

"I think this sitting-room is disengaged. I will bring you the whiskey in a moment, sir."

When it came he scarcely touched it. It seemed that all he wanted was an opportunity for a moment's solitary reflection.

"Say nothing! Let them go in peace! That means that I'm to be this man's confederate in still another crime. If I've any regard for Netta! Turn the happiest day of her life into the most miserable! God knows I've no desire to do that, and it's because she is what she is to me that I'm in agony. One woman should understand another woman's feelings better than I can. If she thinks that it would be better for Netta that for the present I should hold my tongue, I daresay that she knows best."

Netta was leaving the room to put on her coat and hat as he entered. She greeted him with a reproachful smile.

"I thought you weren't even coming to say goodbye. Where have you been?"

The sight of her seemed to tie his tongue into knots. He blundered in his speech.

"I've been—I've been—"

Miss Foster, the ever-ready, took the words out of his halting lips. Do you know where he's been? Shall I tell you? There was a noisy person outside the church. I'm convinced that Mr Rodway was simply burning to interview him. Now I expect he's had that interview. Don't you know that he's extremely inquisitive to any crumpled leaf which may affect your couch of roses?"

"I know that he's a way of doing things—which is particularly his own."

Netta went out, laughing. Miss Foster, following through the door which he left open favoured him with a meaning glance, murmuring a classic phrase.

"Mind! *Mum's the word!*"

Mr Smithers' voice addressed him from behind.

"Why, Ben, you're a pretty sort of deserter. I was afraid you wouldn't even come in time to drink us God-speed."

"There is always time for that."

There was something unusual in the speaker' voice, in the manner in which he sought to avoid the other's face. Mr Smithers commented on the peculiarity of the other's demeanour, in words which seemed to be a little touched with scorn.

"What's happened, Ben? I hope nothing unpleasant? On such a day as this nothing unpleasant must happen. In case of such a mishap, you just take the untoward event, twist it round, and you'll find that on the obverse side there's laughter.—Come, Ben, I recommend this wine; drink to this toast:—May our honeymoon be cloudless, and our married life like an April shower; with—at worst!—the sun close at hand behind the cloud."

Mr Rodway raised the brimming glass, steadily regarding Mr Smithers before he put it to his lips.

"I drink to Netta's happiness."

"Ah, Ben, that's a better toast than mine! No heeltaps, sir, to a toast like that."

Mr Rodway, draining his glass, placed it upside down upon the table, turning away without another word.

Shortly the bride returned, equipped for travelling. Goodbyes were said. The married couple had an escort down into the hall. When the carriage bearing them to the station had started, Mr Rodway turned to Miss Foster, who stood a little apart.

"I've allowed her to go off alone, unprotected, at the absolute mercy of a man who, if the half of what I've just been listening to is true, must be one of the biggest scoundrels in Europe; and this I've done—from the bottom of my heart, I believe foolishly!—all owing to you."

The girl contemplated him with laughing eyes, not one whit abashed by his black looks.

"My dear Mr Rodway, please make that bow of yours a little more presentable. Would you like me to tie it for you? It's a little public on the steps here, but I don't mind." While the gentleman—with every outward symptom of unwillingness—grappled with his refractory necktie, the lady continued:—"If what you say is correct—I rather doubt the quarter from which your information comes!—I can only give you the assurance of my personal conviction that sometimes in one scoundrel there is more good than in twelve just men."

CHAPTER 26
THE MAN IN THE MUSTARD-COLOURED SUIT

Mrs Smithers sipped her chocolate. She regarded her husband, who reclined—in a state of considerable undress—on a couch in front of her. She herself was attired in a nondescript garment, which, to a masculine eye, appeared to consist principally of lace and ribbons, and which was pretending to assist in the concealment of the fact that she had just stepped out of bed.

"I should think that I must be the laziest person in the world!"

"So long as you've an inward persuasion that you've cut the record, it's all right. This is a record-breaking age."

"How long have we been married?"

"Do you want an answer in seconds or in years?"

"This is the third of December."

"Since the second was yesterday, it's within the range of possibility that you are right."

"We've been married nearly three months."

"And you still live?"

"Still live!" She laughed as she stirred her chocolate. "It's only during those three months that I have begun to live."

"It's odd, but I've a somewhat similar—unreasonable—feeling about myself."

"Really?"

"Absolutely!"

"But it can't be quite the same to you. I'm coming to the conclusion that there's nowhere you haven't been; nothing you haven't seen and done. You seem equally at home in every country, with every language. You knew the whole world well before I came into your life at all; while I—I've only just begun to know there is a world. And you are teaching me—showing me its greatness and its glory, its marvel and its mystery. It's such a pleasant thing to be taught by one who knows, and whom one loves. It's that which makes it different for me."

The big man laughed. The lady looked across at him and smiled.

"I'm even beginning not to mind your laughter; to understand that where your heart is most concerned your laugh is nearest. It's a way you have. You hide the tender nature which is in that great big chest of yours—and I do believe that you've the tenderest soul that ever was!—under a cloak of perpetual—shall I call it mockery? See you with that little child which had lost itself in the *piazza* the other day. Laughing at its sorrows, you take ever so much trouble to make it happier than ever it was in its life before. It's a way you have. You'll be like that to me, and more, when my day of sorrow comes; and when you fold me in your arms and I hear your laughter, I shall know that with me all will be well."

They were at the Hotel du Quirinal in Rome, after a journeying hither and thither which had been to the young wife a continual rapture. It is so good a thing to have seen nothing when, in the springtime of your life, an opportunity comes to see all; especially if you are a woman who has just been married to a man to whom money is no object, and whose love for you is only equalled by yours for him. A girl's first big drink at her woman's cup of happiness, how sweet it is!

Netta Smithers had arrived at the conclusion that life was a fairy tale, in which there were nothing but good fairies; and that for a husband she had found the Admirable Crichton. Not in one jot or tittle had he hitherto fallen away from her high ideal. He is a remarkable man, who lives with a woman three months without doing that. Love is blind, but it has its seeing; moments; and in the course of three months those moments have an uncomfortable knack of developing into minutes; and even—too often—into hours. Until then the wife had seen nothing in her husband but what she was glad to see.

That afternoon an incident occurred which might have brought the first crumpling of a rose-leaf, if it had not been for him.

They were in a lazy mood; had stayed indoors throughout the morning, both attending to their correspondence. Letters with her took the form of endless paeans of laudation. They were delightful things to write; but—conceivably!—only a saving sense of humour, which lighted them here and there, kept them from being a trifle wearisome to read. Afterwards they decided to do some shopping. The amount of shopping which already had been done was not a little surprising. A perpetual stream of packages had been kept flowing towards their native land for which they were responsible.

They had finished lunch in their private apartment; the table had been cleared; they were just discussing the advisability of Netta's preparing for out of doors, when the door opened and someone entered. It was a large room. Mr Smithers' back was towards the door. Netta, supposing it was the waiter who had returned, having forgotten some part of his necessary duty, did not look up. So that, as it chanced, both were taken by surprise when they found standing between them a stranger. And not a prepossessing looking stranger either.

He was a man of medium height, slightly built, who carried himself with a rigidity which spoke of military training. His long yellow moustache, turned up in German fashion at the ends, served to accentuate the impression of aggressiveness which his whole bearing conveyed. He wore a "ditto suit" of mustard-yellow smooth-faced cloth, the waistcoat being cut very high in front, so as to give but a glimpse of the narrow band of black ribbon which encircled the stiff shirt collar, which fitted so closely that it seemed Smithers as if he imagined himself to be addressing some creature of the gutter, whom he could lash with his tongue as with a whip. His evident intention of being disagreeable had, however, no apparent effect upon his listener.

"I hold myself too straight for you?—Really?"

"You can grin. I am told that you are good at grinning. But you will not grin for long. We know all about you. You have just come out of jail. You went into jail as Andrew Bruce, you came out of jail as Francis Smithers. As Francis Smithers you at once proceeded to qualify for jail again by laying your hands upon our property."

"You refer to the contents of the safe in Shoe Lane?"

"You know what I refer to. No fool talk for me."

"I asked because I rather fancied that it was your friends who relieved me of the key of safe No. 226. In which ease they have possibly themselves gained access to its contents."

"Oh yes, it was my friends who relieved you of the key, and we have had a look at the safe. We also can do a thing or two. But for us, you are altogether too clever. In the safe there was nothing; you have put it all somewhere else. You think that smart? If, my smart chap, you have spent it, or turned any of it into money, or touched it in any way whatever, you will be sorry. You will find you have been too smart. For we will strip you to the buff, and we will crucify you, and while you are hanging there we will baste you with boiling oil—after we have torn your tongue out by the roots."

"You are evidently a man of humour, Mr Kronberg."

"You also—for the present. You will not be so humorous later. As for your pretty girl, we will tell her what sort of an animal she got hold of—that will please her! If it turns out that she stands in with you, then we will string her up at your side—that, too, you will find humorous! As you helped yourself to what is ours, in our turn we will help ourselves to what you think is yours—we will each of us have from her a kiss or two."

"Have the kindness, Mr Kronberg, to keep my wife's name out of any remarks which you may desire to address to me."

"Your wife! Your—!"

Mr Kronberg gave utterance to an opprobrious epithet. Mr Smithers moved towards him. In a moment the Austrian, falling back, was presenting a revolver at the other's head.

"Don't you try any of that!"

He possibly underrated the Englishman's agility and presence of mind. Before the words were out of his mouth his antagonist had gripped his wrist, and, with a dexterous movement, had wrenched the weapon out of his hand. There was a flash, a report—on a sudden Mr Kronberg descended on a heap to the floor. As Mr Smithers stood looking clown at him, not a muscle of his countenance changed. The occurrence apparently served to recall to his mind an ancient saw.

"Every bullet has its billet" He laughed, as if the application, in the present case, was comical. "During the single moment in which the muzzle looked his way—it discharged itself. For which of us set the trigger in action I have not a notion. The predicament is an awkward one!"

He bent over the prostrate man, who was bunched up in that very ugly fashion which is only seen in cases of serious trouble.

"Mr Kronberg!—No answer, no movement. It would seem that these gentlemen of the Eight are a little unfortunate." Lifting the Austrian's head, he placed him in a less ungainly attitude upon his back. "A rascal face, though saintly features do not make saints. His moustache gives to him an unnecessary touch of the grotesque. So that's where the bullet entered, within an inch of his heart. And only that small stain upon his beautiful yellow waistcoat if so small a show of blood is in itself suspicious. No pulsation. Did it kill him instantly? It's very odd how easily that sort of thing is done."

His wife's voice was heard speaking to him from behind the door which led into tin- bedroom.

"Frank!—Are you alone? May I come in?"

He looked up, smiling, his face turned towards the door.

"Patience! I'm coming to you in half a second." He glanced back at Mr Kronberg. "What shall I do—with this? Time's pressing.'

A large couch stood against a wall, on which was a huge bearskin carriage rug—one of his gifts to his wife. He picked up Mr Kronberg, and he placed him on this couch, with his brown hat and his revolver. Over the whole he spread the bearskin rug hurriedly. Just as he had finished giving the couch as neat an appearance as the circumstances of the case permitted, Netta came into the room

Chapter 27
Netta Cries

She was ready for their shopping expedition, looking charming in her long fur coat mill small hat, which was perched, *coquettishly*, a little on one side of her dainty head. She regarded her husband with a smile; which he returned—he was just moving away from the couch on which was the bearskin rug.

"What was that noise?"

"Noise? Like a pistol shot? Wasn't that overhead?"

It sounded"—she glanced about her—"it sounded as if it were in here. I wondered if that agreeable visitor and you were beginning to shoot each other." She sniffed "And what's the smell? It smells"—another sniff—"like fireworks."

"You've the great gift of imagination, which extends even to your nose."

"There is a smell"—sniff—"of something unusual. You're not to laugh at me. I'm sure my nose has no more imagination than yours has. Well, have you got rid of your visitor?"

"Yes; I've got rid of him."

"Who was he, and what did he want?"

"I'm afraid I can't give you a satisfactory answer to either question. I didn't wait for him to come to an end of his explanations. Are you ready?"

"Of course I am. Don't ever accuse me of keeping you waiting. I've been kept waiting—nearly!—thirty seconds."

"I want you to do me a favour; a great one. Get me a hat. You'll find a row of them hanging on the pegs in my dressing-room."

"Do you want any gloves?—and a stick?"

"I shall be exceedingly obliged by your providing me with both, if I may impose on you so serious a task."

When she had gone to do his errand he continued to stare at the bearskin rug.

"It looks odd, as if there were—something underneath. I must arrange it better than that. I don't wish to convey the impression to any uninvited person who may chance to stray into the room that we are using that rug for an improper purpose; as, for instance, to conceal something which ought not to be hidden. In all delicate matters one should avoid attracting the attention of the inquisitive."

He went to the couch and drew one end of the bearskin over the head, so that, descending in an even slope to the foot, it presented no marked inequality of surface. He contemplated this result with seeming satisfaction.

"I don't fancy that that looks as if there were anything remarkable underneath. If only someone doesn't sit down on it. If they do they may he startled. The risk of leaving it here *is* not inconsiderable—in an hotel one never knows who may take it into his head to come prying into one's sitting-room while one is out of it, but the risk of attempting to place it somewhere else before Netta brings that hat of mine would be still greater. It is when we return from our tour round the shops that complications will commence. Netta likes to recline upon this couch. While we are out I shall have to think of something."

The lady, re-appearing, found the gentleman transferring some cigars from a box upon a sideboard to his cigar-case. He was humming to himself an air which had caught his fancy in a new opera which they had seen at the Argentina a night or two before.

"You didn't tell me which hat you wanted, so, as there are about twenty, I had to guess. Don't blame me if I've brought the wrong one."

"You're sure to have done that. It is the wrong one. Thank you, that will do very well."

They had a delightful walk. The afternoon was fine. All Rome was out of doors. They wandered hither and thither, in the haphazard fashion which commended itself to Netta.

"I should like to lose myself," she would sometimes declare. "It would be something of an adventure, and in this world adventures are so few. But it's quite impossible to do it when one's out with you;—even in Rome, where I should have thought nothing could be easier. I'm sure three-quarters of the time I haven't the very faintest notion where I am. But your bump of locality is positively uncanny. Just as you're sure that you've never been near this place before. And that you'll never find your way out again, you just say, 'Oh, you take the third turning on your left, and the fourth on your right, and the seventh on your left again, and you go straight on till you come to a pump at the corner, and you twist round twice, and in front of you is the Strada Something-or-other, and there you are!' When you've been persuaded that you really are lost after all, and that you're doomed to tramp those ancient lanes and alleys till you die, I call that sort of thing provoking."

"Attribute it to my misfortune rather than my fault."

"I shall attribute it to precisely what I please. And it's lovely to go about with someone who always knows exactly where he is. It gives you such a feeling of safety."

They bought things, of various kinds, in various places. As a purchaser, Netta was omnivorous. Whatever caught her eye that she thought she would like to buy, she mostly bought. If it was not likely to be of use to her, then it would be just the thing for someone else. And people liked to receive presents from their friends who happened to be travelling; it showed that they were not forgotten. Her husband laughed at her.

"I suppose you're not aware that you can buy these very same things in town at about half the price?"

The lady puckered her brow. The suggestion troubled her.

"Can you? I suppose you can. But then you couldn't say that they were bought in Rome."

"No; you couldn't claim the credit of having been so foolish."

The lady drew herself up—offended—for about the twinkling of an eye.

"Now I shan't buy another thing,—at least, unless I see something I really want. Oh, isn't that glass vase pretty? Wouldn't it look lovely filled with roses?"

You have already invested in about twenty glass vases, which would all look lovely filled with roses!"

"Have I? So many as that? But it would be the very thing for mother."

"How? You've sent her five, to my certain knowledge. Have you any reason to suppose that she intends to set up as a collector of glass vases?"

"I know I've sent her one or two. I daresay she wouldn't know what to do with it. No; I don't think I truly want it."

But when the dealer beguiled her into holding the vase in her own two hands, and she perceived how pretty it really was, she melted—as did the money in her husband's pockets.

Finally they found themselves again in the Corso, with the lady a little tired, and disposed, since the weather was still warm, to take her ease outside a cafe." She loved, as she put it, to see the crowd go by. As they were about to take their seats at one of the little tables, she exclaimed—

"Why, Frank, there's your friend of the moustaches and the yellow suit."

Although the words could scarcely have failed to have startled him—for he had had the problem of how to dispose of what was underneath the bearskin present in his mind throughout the afternoon—he showed no sign of any feeling of the kind, but looked round leisurely in the direction in which she was glancing.

"Do you mean the man in the mustard-coloured suit ?"

"Yes—there he is, crossing the road behind that team—now—he's vanished."

"I certainly do not see him."

"You weren't quick enough—he was going at a tremendous rate. It certainly was he As he passed I noticed how he stared."

"Do you mean that he passed close to us?"

"Right behind us—as if he were coming from the Via Nazionale—perhaps from our hotel. When he saw you he quickened his pace; as if, remembering the result of his first interview, he was not anxious to risk another."

By now they were seated. Mr Smithers, having given his order, was lighting a cigar.

"There is probably more than one man in Rome who wears a mustard-coloured suit."

"But let's hope, not such another one as he. I'm sure it was your friend. I saw him too recently to be able to mistake his face for someone else's—with his ridiculous moustaches and insolent stare."

Her husband was silent. When he spoke again it was to call her attention to the fact that the evening was drawing in, and that it was growing colder.

On their return to the hotel he cast a curious glance at the porter who swung open the door. In the hall he paused for a moment, looking about him as if in search of someone, or in expectation of something happening. Declining to patronise the lift, they walked up the stairs to their rooms, which were on the first floor. Netta's maid met her on the threshold of her bedroom. She was a pleasant-faced woman, perhaps nearly forty years of age, whose services the young wife was beginning to consider indispensable, and to whom she had already grown attached. She greeted her mistress.

"I have a good fire for you, madam. It is growing cold."

"It certainly is chillier. Directly the sun goes in, the temperature goes down with a rush." She spoke to her husband. "Are you going into the sitting-room?" He nodded. "I'll be with you in half a minute."

With her maid she retreated into the bedroom.

Outside the sitting-room Mr Smithers for a moment stayed, as if listening. Then, opening the door, he took a step into the room and paused again; seeming—as he had done in the hall—to search the apartment for something unusual. Nothing unwonted was to be seen. He glanced at the couch. The bearskin descended—as he had left it—in an even slope from the head to the foot. He placed his hat, stick, and gloves upon a table; then moved to the couch.

"Could it have been him she saw? As she said, she was hardly likely to be mistaken. And yet" He drew the bearskin aside. There was nothing underneath. For the space of several minutes he remained, a corner of the rug in his hand, staring at the empty couch—considering. He was still there when his wife came out of the bedroom. Something in his attitude seemed to strike her.

"Frank, whatever are you standing there like that for? What are you looking at?"

He dropped the rug and turned.

"I fancy I was dreaming."

She went towards him, then stopped as if to listen. Indeed, she did listen. They both did—to the sound of someone whistling—whistling clearly and truly—the air they knew by heart. If they could trust the evidence of their ears, the performer was in the room; if the evidence of their eyes, except themselves the room was empty. Netta's lips parted, her eyes opened wider, her cheeks went a little pale.

"Frank!—it's the whistler!—the same tune—where can he be? What does it mean?"

He regarded her with his smiling eyes.

"It's odd—it is the tune."

Going to her putting his arm about her, he led her to the fireplace. The sound stopped—the air was finished. As it ceased, she burst into sudden tears. It was an unprecedented thing for her to do; he had never known her cry before. Sitting on an armchair which was at the side of the hearth he lifted her on to his knee, soothing her as if she were a little child.

"I know it's silly of me, but—Frank!—what does it mean?"

As he laughed, and folding his arms about her drew her closer to him, the sound of the whistling began again.

CHAPTER 28

A WOMAN ELOQUENT

The room which Miss Foster called her 'den,' and in which she, presumably, spent a considerable portion of her life, was an apartment about ten feet square, which was so encumbered with furniture of a peculiar kind that there was no room in it for anything else. She had acquired the knack of finding space in it for herself somehow, but her friends, less accustomed to the exigencies of the situation, were apt to show by their demeanour that their sense of comfort was to seek. The more familiar were the terms of friendship on which they stood, the more emphatic was the expression of their discontent.

"If you'd only let me drop three-quarters of this rubbish out of the window," her brother would observe, "one might be able to move about."

"My dear Sidney," his sister would retort, "in a room one is not supposed to move about."

This reading of the law, on the subject of deportment in certain places, did not seem to commend itself in Mr Rodway. He had called to see her, at the lady's special invitation, and to show by the manner in which he bore himself, must have been continually inspired by the wish that he had shown more wisdom. The subject of conversation interested him deeply, and when that was the case it was impossible for him to keep still. Let the rules as to the deportment which was proper in a room be what they may, he had to move about. In the present instance the consequences were that he had already knocked over a fair proportion of the articles which the room contained, and nearly knocked over all the rest—having just succeeded in upsetting a flimsy cane construction which was supposed to represent a table, and which was crowded with photographs, some of them in glass-fronted frames.

"I'm afraid," he explained, as he stooped to pick up what was left, "that some of the glasses are cracked."

"Shivered to splinters, you mean. I heard them smash. But it doesn't matter. They're only friends of mine.—You were saying?"

Mr Rodway picked some of the pieces of glass out of his fingers. He found that these interruptions diverted the even current of his thoughts.

"I—I was saying that it is wholly inconsistent with my ideas of duty to allow Netta to live with a man of whose real character she is so frightfully ignorant."

"But she has lived with him. You should have thought of that before."

"It isn't fair of you to say that. She would never have gone away with him upon her honeymoon in ignorance if it hadn't been for you."

"How intensely grateful she would be to me if she were acquainted with that fact. For she appears to have had a perfectly delightful time. 'Roses, roses, all the way!'—Oh, if we could all of us be certain of idyllic bliss for at least one period in our lives!"

Mr Rodway favoured the speaker with a sidelong glance, as if he suspected her of some esoteric meaning.

"But the awakening must come, and then it will be all the more bitter for what has gone before."

"But why must what you call 'the awakening' come? That's what I don't understand."

"Do you suppose that I could allow her to continue in ignorance—even if there were not others who will take advantage of the first opportunity to open her eyes?"

"To what?"

"To his record!—To the type of man he is!"

"What type of man is he?"

"You ask me that!"

"I can only say that, so far as I know, he's the type of man I should like to many."

"Miss Foster!"

"Mr Rodway!—I wish you weren't quite, so excitable. Heat doesn't impress me in the least. You say he's been in prison."

"I say!—Swire says. He ought to know, since he was there with him."

"That must have been a disadvantage to have had Mr Swire as a companion. And yet I don't know. I think I should rather like to meet Mr Swire."

"I'll take care you do nothing of the kind."

"You'll take care? Indeed. Nothing is more sure than that many reputable persons do go to prison. You don't know what he was there for."

"I can soon find out. I should have done it before if it hadn't been for you."

"Always me! How fortunate that you are acquainted with one person who's possessed of commonsense. I'm prepared to bet—and pay if I lose—that he was there for nothing discreditable."

"Your code of ethics is your own. A jailbird is a jailbird. What do you suppose your brother would say if he were acquainted with the facts, which you have forbidden me to communicate to him?"

"I have, for the present."

"Do you think he'd associate with him?"

"My brother is not a cur, or he wouldn't be my brother."

"I'm not suggesting he is a cur. On the contrary, he is one of the finest all-round fellows I ever met."

"And therefore the less likely to forget that, for all he has, and hopes to be, he is indebted—to the same person as you are."

"Don't you understand?"

"Please don't hammer that screen with your list. It wasn't built to resist a battering-ram."

"Don't you understand that that's the most hideous feature of the whole position?"

"What's the most hideous feature?—Now, you're about to renew the assault!"

"That, involuntarily, unconsciously, I should have played receiver to a thief! That the prosperity of the Rodway Power should have been built upon dishonesty!"

"There is that way of looking at it."

"There's only that way! One rogue points out to another where he has hidden the fruits of his rascality, and the second uses them to finance an honest man."

"Well, and why not?"

"Why not?—When, by so doing, he tars the unconscious wretch with his own brush. You don't understand what all this means to me; how it threatens to make of my whole life a grotesque wreck."

"Oh yes, I do understand. I understand that we are getting there."

"Getting where?"

"To the point; that your grievance is a personal one; which makes you so—robustious.'

"Miss Foster, I am perhaps old-fashioned. I was brought up on simple lines; being taught that there was a fundamental difference between right and wrong, and that the two could not be blended. If then, this man—"

"I decline to allow you, in my presence, to speak of him as a man; unless, that is, you mean that he is as much a man as you are, and probably more."

"If, then, my partner is a thief, and used a thief's money to place me where I am, then all I have has sprung from roguery; and if I wish to free myself from the taint of roguery, I must put it all from me and begin again."

"Don't you believe he's honest?"

"I did!"

"Don't you know even now, deep down in your heart, that you'd trust him before any other man you ever met?"

"In the face of what Swire says!"

"In the face of what Mr Swire says.—Mr Swire! You compare him to Mr Swire?"

"I don't. I feel that he ought to be confronted with Swire, and heard in his own defence."

"Shall I tell you what I feel? Listen to me, Mr Rodway; and please don't— merely because you're getting the worst of the argument—destroy all my furniture. That's the third time you've knocked down that flower-stand."

"Really, Miss Foster, I—I beg ten thousand pardons, but it— it's so fragile."

"It will be worse than fragile by the time you've done with it. It's not meant to be used like that. There is no reason why you should take advantage of the fact that it has no legs to stand upon worth mentioning."

The article in question was an elongated tripod, of too anaemic a constitution to stand up in the teeth of a healthy draught. Awed by its owner's severity, Mr Rodway replaced it as best he could.

"Now, if you will be so good as to attend to a few remarks I have to make, and to keep still. You say that the name of the man who died in prison was Edney—George Edney."

"Swire says it was."

"George Edney ruined my father; robbed us of our home; of all that, in those days, made life worth living; and drove Sidney and me out into the world to earn our daily bread."

"Miss Foster!—You don't mean it!"

Coming into unexpected contact with an unnoticed chair, Mr Rodway plunged down on it with a sudden vigour which caused it to emit a sinister sound of unmistakable resentment.

"I do mean it. I also mean that that chair is intended for sylph-like persons, weighing not more than six stone, and that you appear to weigh sixteen. I'm not sure that there is a chair in the room which is capable of bearing you; but if there is, it's that."

She pointed to a wooden chair which stood against the wall, of a singularly aggravating design. It had a very small, triangular scat, and a very straight, high, and narrow back. Mr Rodway perched himself upon it with something of the air of a humiliated schoolboy.

"I will tell you the story."—She told him the tale—so far as it was known to her—of Glasspoole's folly and Edney's knavery; he listening, open-eyed and open-mouthed. "Since the probability is that the money which Edney left to Netta's husband is part of that of which he robbed us, I think you will admit that I have almost as much right to judge him as you have."

"I'd no idea!—This is awful!"

"Of course you'd no idea. And in what sense do you use the word 'awful'? I suppose you must have something in you, or you wouldn't have invented the Rodway Power, but of your judgement in ordinary matters I have no opinion whatever. If accident hadn't brought you into contact with a profoundly honest, clear headed man, you'd have been the best plundered inventor that ever lived—such is my solemn conviction."

Mr Rodway only gasped—partly, perhaps, because the young lady expressed her views with such perfect frankness; and, possibly, partly because, while her flashing eyes continued to regard him with such accusatory sternness, he dared not move from die seat on which he was enduring the acme of discomfort. She went on, with an eloquent fluency which visibly impressed him:

"Let me state the case as it appears to me. Mr Smithers—or Mr Bruce, as you say he is—though I shall continue to call him Mr Smithers till he tells me not to sinned—that's the presumption. I don't know how or why. But I'm sure he did nothing dishonest; nothing mean; nothing unworthy; nothing which was in disaccord with an ideal code of honour. Yet he must have offended in a legal sense, or he would scarcely have found himself in Canterstone Jail. There he met George Edney. He listened to him, as he lay upon his deathbed—probably not believing one *per cent*, of what he said. When he found himself again outside the prison gates, with everything apparently—lost; with nothing to hope for; with the consciousness strong upon him of what men of your stamp say—and think—about jailbirds, he perhaps thought that he would at least see what amount of truth there was in Edney's statements.

"He learned that there was more than he expected—than anyone would have expected. He found himself in possession of a considerable sum of money. You may be sure that the problem which presented itself to him was the same problem which would have presented itself to you—what should he do with it? And I think he found a saner solution than you might have done. I believe that the decision at which he arrived was this—that he would use it to repair the mischief which George Edney had wrought. That he would leave no stone unturned to discover whom Edney had wronged, and how; and that then he would make it his especial care that the atonement should be greater than the injury."

"You believe that really?"

"With all the strength of belief that is in me. Doesn't everything point to it? His encounter with you was a stroke of fortune in this sense. Probably the fund on which he had chanced was insufficient for the purpose for which it would have to be employed. He recognised instantly the value of your invention; perceived that—for your own safety's sake—you stood in urgent need of a competent, honest associate; and straightway resolved to do a triple service—to you; to the world; to Edney's victims. He immediately saw that here was an opportunity to provide himself with ample funds to alleviate—so far as money could— the suffering which had been caused. So he became your partner; picking you out of the ditch—according to your own confession—and setting you on the highroad to wealth beyond the dreams of avarice.

"What was the first thing he did when success was assured? He went down and bought my old home—which had been the special object of Edney's wickedness discovered Sidney—who was all that was left of the Fosters; put him there and then in the way to fortune; assuring him that when he was possessed of sufficient means which he himself was placing in his hands he should reign again in the home of his fathers. He is not the type of man to make open overtures of pecuniary assistance to a high minded, high thinking, and tolerably respectable young woman; but I'm persuaded that he is putting into Netta's hand—without her knowing it—schemes for making a millionairess of me, even against my will. I'm beginning to perceive the cloven hoof peeping out of her letters. You wait and see. He's routed out Mr Glasspoole."

"Glasspoole! Is that the steward at Dene Park?"

"It is—also George Edney's employer, and dupe. I have it from Mr and Mrs Glasspoole's own lips that they were in the direst straits—discredited, despairing, at misery's last fence— when he hunted them out—and now see where they are.

"Sometime back I heard from an acquaintance that her husband had received a letter from a firm of solicitors advising him that they were instructed by some person or persons unnamed to hand him the amount enclosed as compensation for the loss he had suffered by Edney's criminality. The amount in question represented the original sum, at something more than compound interest. Since then I have heard of other similar cases. Your partner instructed Mr Glasspoole to draw up a list of his clients whom Edney caused to suffer wrong, and those one-time victims are now finding themselves in clover.

"And this is the man whom you, from the impregnable heights of your superiority in virtue and sapience, propose to brand as—I don't quite know what, but as something unspeakable. Why, Mr Rodway, if you were to do as you suggest, and were to attempt to disillusionise Netta, you would yourself be guilty of a shameful, unforgiveable crime."

The lady, becoming enamoured of her theme, had risen from her seat, and stood confronting him, with outstretched hands, as an eloquent counsel might have stood before a jury. He seemed to be at least as much impressed by her earnestness as would have been the average juryman. Having deserted his position on the chair against the wall, he fidgeted about from place to place, as if in search of words with which to express his meaning.

"You—you present a view of the case which is entirely novel to me; and—and no doubt there's a great deal to be said for it."

"A great deal to be said for it!—There's everything to be said for it!—everything!"

"Even granting that, you must bear in mind that it is not from me only—or even principally—that danger is to be feared. There are Theodore Ludlow and the man Swire. They have both of them objects to gain; to obtain them they'll stick at nothing."

"You and I will be a match for them."

"You and I? Really—I'm afraid I don't quite see how. I don't see, for instance, how you are going to prevent Ludlow from telling his sister what he knows, and Swire from making himself disagreeable."

"You are excessively dense. I'll show you how it can be done.

Will you sign a treaty of alliance?"

She held out her hand—of which he promptly took advantage.

"I shall be charmed."

"You promise to do everything I tell you?"

An expression of dubiety came over his features, as if he regretted the haste with which he had placed his palm in hers.

"I will certainly undertake to give any suggestion you may make my most serious consideration."

"That won't do at all—not in the least. In dealing with such creatures as the two you've named, I've methods of my own. To ensure success for those methods, it is necessary that I should have an ally on whom I can implicitly depend. The question therefore is—can I, or can I not, depend on you?—are you with me, or against me?"

"If you put it that way, I am with you—certainly—all the way."

"Then mind you are." They solemnly shook hands. "Don't sit there; that's your chair against the wall."

He looked at it and sighed.

CHAPTER 29
FRIENDS IN COUNCIL

It was not an announcement which was likely to appeal to the sympathies of Mr Swire, as the expression which was on that gentleman's countenance plainly showed.

> In connection with the Juvenile Branch
> of the Sons of Water,
> Mr Theodore Ludlow
> has kindly consented to give an Address,
> entitled
> Temperance: Whence It Comes, What It is,
> WHERE IT GOES.

Mr Swire glared at the placard on which the words were printed as if it were a personal enemy. Then, withdrawing a step or two, he surveyed the building with which it was associated.

"So this is Ebenezer Chapel, is it? and this is where he comes and gives his addresses? Very good; when he comes I'll take the liberty of addressing him."

Mr Ludlow was probably not gratified when he discovered who was awaiting his arrival outside the edifice within whose walls he was to deliver his acute and well-chosen observations. A more disreputable figure than Mr Swire presented would have been hard to find, or one more suited to illustrate at least a certain side of the forthcoming remarks. At the very gates of the chapel, in full view of the already assembling audience, this disgraceful-looking person addressed him with a degree of freedom which could not have been agreeable.

"So there you are, are you? Found you, have I? Perhaps you don't know I've been looking for you this month and more; daresay you've never guessed that I've found out how you've been kidding me."

Mr Ludlow endeavoured to pass off the obvious fact of Mr Swire's existence with an air of carelessness which scarcely suited him.

"Ah, Swire—still in the flesh? And what has brought you here?"

"The same thing that's brought you. You're going to give an address, and I'm going to give an address—to you."

Mr Ludlow glanced about him. Undoubtedly his encounter with this dreadful creature was becoming the subject of comment. Persons passing up towards the entrance turned to look. At the private door someone stood and watched. Perhaps it was an office-bearer; even a deacon. The lecturer on temperance felt that it would be advisable to rid himself of this fellow at the earliest possible moment. He spoke to him in low, peremptory tones.

"If you wish to speak to me, you can do so in an hour and a half."

"If it's all the same to you I'd sooner speak to you now."

"You cannot. I have a lecture to deliver. I will speak to you afterwards.—Now go. Let me pass."

Mr Swire had placed himself in front of him in a manner which was suggestive.

"Hand over a sovereign and I'll think about it"

"A sovereign!—What do you mean?"

"For gargle—that's what I mean. Do you think that I'm going to wait for you dry-mouthed?"

Mr Ludlow eyed Mr Swire with what might be described as scorn leavened with uneasiness.

"Are you aware that I am just going to deliver a lecture on temperance?—And you ask me to encourage you in your habits of drunkenness!"

"I don't want no encouragement. Money's what I want, that's all."

"Then you'll get no money for that purpose out of me.— Now, my man, stand aside."

"I'll stand aside when I've said my say to you, not before. You get your sister married to the biggest scoundrel in England—"

Mr Swire had commenced his observations in a tone of voice which was so audible that Mr Ludlow became immediately conscious of the extreme desirability of inducing him to cut them short, at least for the present. He produced a coin.

"Here's a shilling for you. While you are waiting, you can get something to eat."

In reply the other's language was full-flavoured.

"I don't want none of your shillings, and I don't want nothing to eat. Drink's what I'm after. Make it half a quid—its dry work waiting."

I will make it half-a-crown, but not another farthing. Will you take it and go, or shall i call a policeman?"

"Call a policeman!—You'll call a policeman!"

"I certainly will. I don't intend to allow myself to be annoyed by you. Be under no misapprehension."

Either Mr Ludlow's show of firmness, or the coin temptingly displayed between his finger and thumb, affected Mr Swire. He condescended to pocket the half-crown.

"When you've given that address of yours on temperance,

you'll find me waiting for you here; so don't you flatter yourself you won't."

Possibly this was an occasion an which Mr Ludlow would have been willing that the other should stray from the strict paths of truth, but Mr Swire evinced a fondness for veracity to which he was perhaps occasionally a stranger. When, at last, the lecturer appeared there, on the pavement was his friend. He remained in the building to the very last moment, so that as few of his audience should witness the meeting as might be. Before he left he thought it advisable to tell a falsehood to such persons in authority as were with him in the vestry—by way, perhaps, of exhibiting his zeal for the cause for which he had just been speaking.

"There's a sad case in which I am much interested—of a man who has given himself body and soul to the demon. I rather fancy he's waiting for me outside now. I still trust to be able to snatch him as a brand from the burning."

If such was the case he displayed his trust in rather a singular fashion. So soon as he was in the street, he marched off at the top of his speed, and had already, at the corner of the street, reached a region where cabs and omnibuses were procurable, before the sad case in question had him—literally—by the shoulder.

"That's the game, is it?—Thought that half-dollar of yours had done the trick?—Then you're wrong; it ain't."

Mr Ludlow professed surprise at seeing the speaker at his elbow.

"So you've not gone. I suppose it was owing to the darkness that I didn't see you.—Now what have you to say to me?"

"I've a good deal to say to you. Do you want me to say it here?"

Mr Ludlow considered—or pretended to.

"I'm afraid I'm rather pressed for time just now. I think I would rather make an appointment with you for tomorrow, and then we can go into everything together thoroughly and at our leisure."

"You made an appointment with me once before and didn't

keep it. What kind of a fool do you think I am? Before I lose sight of you, you and me's going to have an understanding."

"But I can't talk to you here."

"You live somewhere I suppose. You take me home; I'll talk to you there."

The suggestion did not commend itself to Mr Ludlow.

"Isn't there some place near here where we can be private?"

"There's a little crib I know of."

"Is it respectable?"

"For respectability it's equal In Buckingham Palace any day."

"Is it far?"

"Just round the corner"

"Then I'll give you ten minutes—not longer. You lead the way and I'll follow you."

"No, you don't. You might do your following in the wrong direction, once my back was turned. If I'm not good enough for you to walk with, you'll have to make believe I am, and that's all about it."

Again Mr Ludlow reflected. There were reasons—substantial ones—why he did not wish to have too of much Mr Swire's society. Still, on several accounts, he did not wish to have an open rupture with him then and there. Moreover, there was something which he really desired to say to him. So, summing up the matter, he arrived at a hasty decision to give the fellow the interview he desired, on his own terms.

"If you'll show me the way, I'll come with you. Only move yourself, and be quick about it."

In a few moments he became conscious that they were entering a neighbourhood which was not exactly savoury.

"Where are you taking me? You told me that the place of which you spoke was just round the corner."

"That was a figure of speech, that was; don't you know what a figure of speech is? It's under a quarter of a mile from where we're standing, and that's the gospel truth."

Mr Ludlow hesitated. There was something in the man's manner which he did not like, yet which he hardly knew how to deal with.

"I don't want any of your nonsense, you understand, and I'll have none. I'm not going with you to any thieves' kennel, nor to any place of the kind. I'd rather listen to what you have to say to me here."

"The idea! just as though I'd take you to such as them. I tell you there ain't a more decenter house in London." Mr Swire's tone suddenly changed, passing from what he intended for the persuasive to the avowedly bellicose. "I've had enough of your humbug. You won't let me come to your place; you won't let me talk to you in the street; nothing will suit but that you should go to my place, and now you're going, so don't let me hear no more about it"

Mr Ludlow concluded that probably the lesser evil would be to let Mr Swire have his own way, so he went. The quarter mile was proved to consist of a good deal more than 440 yards; nor did the character of the neighbourhood gel better as they advanced. At last, in a very narrow alley, Mr Swire paused before what was apparently a bird shop, on a very small scale. The little window was filled with birds in cages. More birds and cages decorated the doorway. Although it was long past the hour when they ought to have been asleep, some of them were still indulging in vocal exercises. Mr Swire waved his hand.

"Here you are! Ain't this good enough? No one ain't likely to come to much harm where there's all these birds about."

Some such thought was passing through his companion's mind. The place promised better than he had feared. A man appeared at the doorway, short, square-built, with a pipe in his mouth. He eyed Mr Swire and his companion, addressing the former. "So it's you, is it? Now what's the game?"

Mr Swire replied:

"I've got a little business with a friend of mine. Want to go up to the Cave, so that we can be alone together."

The man said nothing. The pair entered, not the shop, but a sort of covered entry which ran beside it, ending in what was rather a flight of steps than stairs.

"Where are you taking me?"

"To the Cave of Harmony."

"The Cave of Harmony? What do you mean?"

"The Cave of Harmony is where they hold the singing matches. I've known more than a hundred birds enter for a really big prize. There ain't no better room of the kind in town, nor one what's better thought of. Let me go up first and open the door."

Mr Swire went up first. Mr Ludlow followed, not with the best grace; there was a remoteness about the place which, in his present company, he did not appreciate. The apartment to which he was introduced seemed to be rather a loft than a room. There was no ceiling. The open raftered roof was whitewashed like the walls. A board on trestles represented a table. Ancient forms stood against the walls. Nails were everywhere; intended, the visitor surmised, to sustain the cages of the contestants when a 'singing match' was on. A musty smell made the air of the place offensive, though it was unwarmed and the night was cold. Gas flamed from a solitary bracket. As Mr Ludlow entered, not too willingly, Swire, pulling the door to behind him, turned the key, an action which his companion instantly resented.

"What do you mean by that?—I insist upon your unlocking that door at once."

"You insist!—How are you going to insist?—That's what I want to know."

The eyes of the two men met—for half-a-dozen seconds only. But it was long enough for Mr Ludlow to learn that in courage, of a kind, he had met more than his match. He himself was possessed of the sort of hardihood which, while it sticks at nothing, shuns physical violence even in the uttermost extremity. Against a rough-and-tumble encounter with a man of this type, in a place of this sort, every nerve in his body protested. Yet too late he realised that nothing short of that might enable him to successfully resist the fellow's demands. To get himself out of the difficulty by which he suddenly found himself confronted, he was prepared to promise anything.

"I don't understand you, Swire. What quarrel have you with me "

"We'll come to that presently. To begin with, I want you to answer one or two questions. The first is—What's the address of the bloke your sister married?—Where am I going to find him?"

"He's abroad."

"You told me that before, and I ain't saying he isn't. But what I want to know is, where shall I find him when he isn't abroad?—And, for the matter of that, where do you find him when he is?"

"I'll be frank with you."

"Perhaps you'd better."

"You gave me certain information as to the person with whom my sister has been ill-advised enough to associate herself in marriage. I have inquired into that information, and regret to say that, in the main, I have found it to be accurate."

"You have, have you?"

"I have not only ascertained that he is a convicted felon, but I have also learned of what crime he was guilty."

"What was it?"

"A dreadful, an atrocious, an unspeakable crime."

"What was it?"

"Murder."

"Murder?—Why, he only got two years."

"Owing to a technical flaw the jury returned it as manslaughter. But it was murder none the less—hideous murder. The story is a dreadful one;—the man's whole record frightful. He is one of those creatures whose existence is a reproach to civilisation."

"What price what he done after he came out?"

"There is that again. So far from punishment inducing him to halt in his career of crime, with unparalleled effrontery he continues in it to the present hour. And this is the man who has my sister for his wife."

"You wouldn't have known nothing about him if it hadn't been for me."

"That is scarcely correct. I had some knowledge of his character before I was aware of your existence."

"Are you denying that I put you on his track?"

Mr Swire spoke with a degree of warmth which induced Mr Ludlow to draw a little back.

"I am denying nothing. I am conscious of my obligations to you in that matter."

"What I want to know is, what I'm going to get out of it. Up to now I ain't got much."

"You must understand that I've many things to consider."

"I've only got two: one is to be even with him for what he done to me; the other is, to get as much out of him as ever I can."

Mr Swire presented with such admirable candour, and, it may be added, completeness, the only two motives which were really actuating Mr Ludlow, that for a moment that gentleman was silent. Mr Swire went on.

"We've got him between our finger and thumb, that's where we've got him. It seems that he's passing himself off as someone else. Well, we've only got to say the word and he'll be a good deal less than no one."

"He's no common villain, I assure you; nor is he so easy to deal with as you appear to imagine."

"Do you think I don't know him? Do you think that I don't know he'd make nothing of putting away either you or me? Ain't I had his hand upon me?—Is he fond of your sister?"

"So I've been given to understand—in his way."

"Then we've got him."

"How do you mean?"

"Through her. Putting the screw on her'll be putting the screw on him. If he's fond of her, he won't want her to know about him. It might break her heart. Some women's hearts break easy."

"I believe it would break hers."

"Then we'll start breaking it right away, which'll do the trick at once. That is, if he's fond of her. What I want you to do is, to tell me all about him that I don't know—who he is, what he is, and where he is. Then we'll talk about the terms on which you and I are going to work together."

"You must clearly understand that my chief anxiety is to guard my sister from all unpleasantness."

"Stow that! I know what your chief anxiety is. You don't care for your sister no more than for this deal board. You don't care for nothing and no one except yourself. You and I are birds of a feather; only you're a humbug, and I ain't." Mr Ludlow looked as if he did not relish the notion of being coupled quite so closely with Mr Swire. But he said nothing; he merely pressed together the fingers of his black kid gloves. "You let me know exactly how the land lies, and let's understand each other; then we'll set about that sister of yours together, and after we've said a few words to her, you'll find that husband of hers will turn out to be the most generous man alive. We needn't be afraid of her laying a finger upon us; and when we've had our say, she won't let him do it either."

"There's something in your notion."

"There's about as much money in it as he's got himself. I've played this game before, though I've never had so big a chance as I hope this is going to be. If you want to get at a man's pockets—a man what you've got between your finger and your thumb—find out the girl lie's fond of—really fond of, mind!— and if she's got a soft heart, so soon as you start breaking it, he'll open his pockets as wide as ever you want."

Mr Swire winked. Mr Ludlow sighed.

"I am bound to admit that in certain respects my sister has not treated me well."

"I shouldn't be surprised! And in certain respects we won't treat her well neither. In dealing with a woman, you'll find that I'm the equal of any man alive."

Chapter 30
The Vultures Gather

Christmas drew near. The preparations which were being

made at Dene Park for the return of the bride and bridegroom had been the talk of all the countryside. The old house had been glorified. For, while it was understood that no money was to be spared, instructions had been given that there should be no display of truculent taste—that there should be nothing to suggest the mushroom millionaire.

"I want the house to be a gentleman's, not merely an illustration of the power of moneybags."

So Mr Smithers had said; and he had been careful to place matters in the hands of persons by whom he knew his wishes would be observed. Mr Glasspoole, looking on, was a little mystified by some of the things which were being done.

"There isn't a bit of new furniture being put in the dining-room. I'm told that it's all of it two hundred years old at least, some of it more. And yet I'll be bound that it's costing as much as if it had been made on purpose."

This remark was addressed to an individual who had become quite a close acquaintance—no less a person than Mr Augustus Chaffinch. He favoured the steward with a quick glance out of his small, bright eyes, as if suspecting him of a joke. But Mr Glasspoole's face was gravity itself.

"I shouldn't be surprised if you were right about its costing nearly as much as if it had been made on purpose. I happen to know that £4000 was paid for the sideboard alone."

"Four thousand pounds! for the sideboard! Why, it's only old oak."

"That's all; but some old oak costs money."

Mr Chaffinch's tone was dry; a fact of which the steward seemed unconscious.

Exactly how it had come about, Mr Glasspoole himself was not quite clear; but it had been made plain to him that he could count on at least one friend at the scene of his former misadventures. Whatever might be the attitude of Birchester in general, there could be no doubt about the attitude of one of its inhabitants in particular. Mr Augustus Chaffinch was pleasantness itself.

A more agreeable neighbour—though, after all, he could be hardly called a neighbour—it would have been difficult to find. He placed himself and all that he had entirely at the disposition of the Glasspooles, showering attentions on the ladies of the family in a fashion which was the more delightful, since they were entirely unaccustomed to anything of the kind. And, in return, he required so little. Indeed, nothing at all. He merely showed a friendly interest in everything that concerned them— in their history, and their employer's history, and so on.

Possibly because, with natural delicacy, he perceived that there were points in their own story on which they were a little loath to dwell, he confined his inquiries—and they came from him continually, in an accidental sort of way—principally to their employer. Concerning him, he displayed an interest which was boundless—as, perhaps, was not surprising—as he himself put it, with his air of beaming good-nature, his fat face all wrinkled with smiles.

"Your governor, Glasspoole, is already one of the most re-markable men of the age. Before he's finished he may be even more remarkable still; if I were a sporting man, I should say that's the betting. Everything connected with the life story of such a man ought to be public property—especially if he's a self-made man. I'm a self-made man myself."

Mr Chaffinch displayed his rotund figure in a style which suggested a pouter pigeon. He hinted, in his casual way, at lines on which information would be valued.

"For instance, there's his behaviour towards you. I gather, my dear Glasspoole, from what you have said, that you were not in the most flourishing circumstances when you made his ac-quaintance."

Mr Glasspoole shook his head, gloomily.

"In the depths."

"And there he comes to you, a perfect stranger—I believe he was a perfect stranger?"

"Never heard of him before. Can't make out how he ever heard of me."

"That's it—how did he? Doesn't it seem to you, my dear Glasspoole, that he must have had a motive in what he did?"

"How do you mean?"

The thin man looked at the fat one in a hesitating, doubtful fashion, which superficially was perhaps his most prominent characteristic The 'sea of troubles' in which he had struggled for so many years seemed to have impressed on him an air as of continual indecision, as if he were always ready, at a moment's notice, to retreat from any position which he might appear to have taken up. Whether, however, this attitude was not more apparent than real, was a question on which his friend Mr Augustus Chaffinch had his serious doubts.

On more than one occasion he had found that Mr Glasspoole had a sticking-point, from which, although he might wriggle and writhe and display abject humility, it was difficult to dislodge him. When, for example, he asked some haphazard questions on a matter which was becoming the subject of common talk, for all practical intents and purposes the steward's mouth shut up like a rat-trap.

"Have you got a private fortune of your own, Mr Glasspoole, or are you making a fortune out of Mr Smithers?"

The question was asked with that appearance of genial unconcern which marked so many of Mr Chaffinch's inquiries. The other looked at him askance.

"I don't understand?"

"You're behaving uncommonly well, whichever way it is. I know you don't like allusions to old times, my dear Glasspoole, but when a man atones for his little mistakes of the past in the handsome way you are doing, I say that he's a credit to all of us. I hear that old Markwell, of Forest Lodge, received the other day a cheque for £9000, as compensation for what he lost through your misfortune. That's handsome, Glasspoole, really handsome—especially as I understand that the original sum was under five. No wonder the old gentleman's half off his head with joy."

"The money didn't come from me."

"No? Then from whom did it come? You know that this isn't the first payment of the kind which has been made." The steward was silent. "Does it come from Mr Smithers?"

"I am afraid I can give you no information, Mr Chaffinch."

"Everybody is saying it comes from him, but what I say is, why should it? He had nothing to do with what happened to you all those years ago—since he's a perfect stranger, how could he have?"

"He certainly had nothing to do with what happened to me."

"That's what I say. Then why should this money come from him?—why should it? A man doesn't hand over large sums of his own money to other men for nothing at all unless he has a motive."

"Mr Smithers is the most generous man that ever lived."

"Yes—I shouldn't be surprised. His generosity takes such peculiar forms that one wonders. Don't you?"

"I used to. I'm beginning to do so no longer."

"No?—Because you know—or have guessed—what's spurring him on?"

"I tell you again that Mr Smithers is the most generous man that ever lived. Look at his conduct to me."

"Just so. Look at his conduct to you, that's the point. It's odd that he, a perfect stranger, should take such an interest in you, and in what you did, and in Dene Park, and the Fosters, and all the rest of it—localising his generosity, as it were."

Mr Chaffinch might drop hints, suggest suspicions, indulge in dark allusions—on this particular subject he made no outward impression on Mr Glasspoole. As to the extent of the steward's knowledge, he was as much at a loss as ever. If the little man had only known it, more than once he moved his friend almost to anger.

But on other points the steward was much more complaisant. He allowed his friend not only the free run of the grounds, but also, practically, of his employer's house. This, possibly, was owing to the fact that Mr Chaffinch showed so frank an interest in questions of decoration, and furniture, and old houses. He followed the process of reincarnation which Dene Park was undergoing with almost as much delight as if the place had been his own. He was in and out of it continually, on good terms with the representatives of the firms by which the work was being carried on, hail-fellow-well-met with their workmen. And yet, either by accident or design, it happened that he was never on the premises when either Miss Margaret Foster or Mr Rodway was about—until one day. So it chanced that that was the first hint they received of the intimacy which existed between the Dene Park steward and the rotund proprietor of Chaffinch's Counters.

It was on the twenty-fourth of December—on Christmas Eve—the bride and bridegroom were expected home. Everything was in readiness for their arrival. Mr Chaffinch came over from Birchester in his buggy for the express purpose, as it seemed, of congratulating the steward on the fact.

It does you credit, Glasspoole—the highest credit—the way things have been done."

The steward shook his head, in his deprecatory way.

"I've had very little to do with it except in looking on."

"Nonsense!—that's your modesty!—I know better. If it hadn't been for you nothing would have been ready—nothing. You've worked like a slave. And I've no doubt whatever that, by such an employer, you'll find your services appreciated at their proper value."

Mr Chaffinch said this with a little grin, which seemed to endow his words with an odd significance.

"Though I hope to number Mr and Mrs Smithers among my most intimate friends"—Mr Chaffinch said this with a positive chuckle—"it's hardly likely that I shall be able to go in and out of their beautiful home exactly as I please, so before they do come home I should like to go over it once more—with you, if you don't mind."

Mr Glasspoole seemed a little loath, almost as if he thought that on the eve of the owner's return such a suggestion smacked of the indelicate. But he yielded.

"I am intending to go over the house myself, to see that everything is as it ought to be—you can come with me if you like."

Mr Chaffinch did like. He was loud in his praises of everything—and, indeed, there was much to praise. With singular expedition the place had been transformed from a tumbledown, rat-haunted building, into one of those ideally beautiful houses which are among the greater glories of rural England. Mr Chaffinch actually sighed with satisfaction.

"One ought to be happy, Glasspoole, in a home like this."

"And they will he happy."

"Of course they will—not a doubt of it; flawlessly happy. With everything that the heart can desire, how could it be otherwise? Lucky woman to have been dowered by providence with such a husband—a man with heaps of money, troops of friends, a noble, candid nature, and a character which will bear the strictest inquiry."

Mr Chaffinch evinced a disposition to linger here and there, which seemed to cause his companion some annoyance. Mr Glasspoole seemed nervous almost to the point of irritability. His friend commented on the fact.

"You're anxious?"

"I am. Who wouldn't be?"

"But you're over-anxious—there's such a thing as that."

"In my position how can I help it? Think of how much depends—to me—upon whether everything is exactly as he would wish it to be. Until he expresses himself as satisfied I shall be—I shall be on hot irons."

The little man was trembling. His friend patted him on the shoulder. Don't worry, Glasspoole—don't you worry. There's a time coming of which you've no notion."

The steward did not find the words so reassuring as they were perhaps meant to be—and that in spite of the amused laugh by which they were accompanied. Mr Glasspoole stayed for a moment to speak a last word to the housekeeper and the butler.

When Mr Chaffinch entered the hall he found that a man was standing at the open door, who, without ceremony, addressed himself to him.

"Is Mr Smithers in?"

Mr Chaffinch beamed.

"I believe that Mr Smithers is expected to return tomorrow."

"Are you the—the—?"

The stranger hesitated, as if in doubt how to conclude his sentence. No whit disconcerted, Mr Chaffinch turned to his friend, who was now at his heels.

"This is Mr Glasspoole—the steward."

"Oh, you are the man Glasspoole."

Not only were the words peculiar, but they were rendered more so by the manner in which they were uttered. They seemed to strike the steward as if they had been a blow. He drew back with a show of timidity which was not agreeable to witness.

The speaker, apparently perceiving the effect he had produced, was not slow in endeavouring to add to it. Nothing could have been more gratuitously offensive than his manner.

"I know your history, Glasspoole, and all about you, so don't attempt to put on any airs of stewardship with me. It won't do. I am the brother of Mrs Smithers. My name is Ludlow—Theodore Ludlow." Mr Chaffinch seemed to prick up his ears on hearing this. The bird-like scrutiny with which he had been regarding the stranger became intensified. "You will see that accommodation is provided for me here until my sister returns; for me and for—for this person."

Again he seemed to be in doubt as to the exact words to select. The person alluded in, who had hitherto remained, modestly, halfway down the noble flight of steps which led to the entrance, in obedience to a gesture from the speaker, now advanced. He presented a curious appearance; seeming ill at ease in a brand-new suit of clothes, and generally spick and span attire, which accorded badly with his slouching air and ruffian countenance. Nor did he seem to grow more comfortable when he became conscious of the interest with which Mr Chaffinch was regarding him. The steward, on the other hand, surveyed him with undisguised concern. He stammered a reply.

"I—I'm afraid I have no instructions—Mr Ludlow."

"You have my instructions, they are sufficient." He came into the hall. "There are some of the servants—I will instruct them. In my sister's house, where I am concerned, instructions from you are not required."

While, suddenly unnerved, the little man seemed lost in a maze of indecision, someone else came into the hall—no other than Miss Foster. Her appearance the steward hailed with open relief; while she, on her side, looked about her with curious eyes.

"Good-day, Mr Glasspoole. Who are these—gentlemen?"

"This gentleman says that he is Mr Ludlow, the brother of Mrs Smithers."

"So you are Mr Ludlow! Pray, Mr Ludlow, what are you doing here?"

The gentleman met the young lady's somewhat haughty gaze of inquiry with a truculent stare.

"To whom do I speak?"

"I am Margaret Foster."

"Oh, I understand. May I ask, Miss Foster, why you should express curiosity as to the cause of my presence in my sister's house?"

"You know very well, Mr Ludlow, why I should be surprised at finding you in the house of your sister's husband. Hadn't you better go?"

"At your command?"

"At my suggestion."

"I regret that, in such a matter, I am unable to regard the suggestion of a complete stranger with the attention to which—for some reason which I am at a loss to understand—you appear to think it entitled."

"You refuse to go?"

"Most emphatically. It is for me to order you, rather than for you to order me."

"Then here comes someone whose orders I think you will find it advisable to obey."

Up the steps came Mr Rodway—to the evident discomfiture of both Mr Ludlow and his companion. He was accompanied by Sidney Foster. Mr Rodway spoke first to Mr Ludlow's companion, with a degree of robust vigour which left no doubt whatever as to his meaning.

"Swire! You scoundrel! You have the impudence to show yourself here!" Some workmen had come with him. They remained at the foot of the steps. He called to them. "Take this fellow and march him through the lodge gates. If he offers the least resistance, hand him over to a policeman. Say that I give him into custody as being a notorious bad character—I'll show ample cause when he's brought before the magistrates in the morning."

Though visibly perturbed, Sam Swire tried to bluster.

"I ain't done nothing! Don't let anyone lay a hand on me."

"Lay a hand on you!"

The impetuous Mr Rodway laid two hands on him without an instant's hesitation, running him half way down the steps, and flinging him down the remainder of the distance in a style which must have been hurtful alike to his clothes, his dignity, and his person. As he showed an unwillingness to alter the horizontal posture to which he had been reduced, the workmen assisted him to regain his feet.

"Now, march him through the lodge gates," cried Mr Rodway.

They marched him; showing a willingness to observe Mr Rodway's directions, both in the letter and the spirit, against which Mr Swire evidently deemed it useless to protest. It is to be feared that he had been handled in a similar fashion more than once before. Rodway, returning to the hall, displayed a readiness to treat Mr Ludlow with equal lack of ceremony.

"Now, what are you doing here? Off you go, after your friend."

"Don't you try to bully me, Ben Rodway, nor allow yourself to imagine that I intend to let you drive me out of my sister's house."

"This is not your sister's house. It's my friend's. And I'm authorised by him to treat it as if it were my own till he returns—as you are perfectly well aware. Foster, this is the Theodore Ludlow of whose bad behaviour to his sister and mother you have already heard too much. You must forgive me if I treat him as he deserves."

"I'll take him in hand myself if you like."

Ludlow turned on the speaker, in the possible hope of succeeding better with him than with Mr Rodway.

"You'll take me in hand! I believe your name is Foster. Do you know the character of the man with whom you are associated—who calls this house his?"

"Very well indeed. I should advise you to be careful not to say anything against Mr Smithers in my hearing."

"Smithers! His name's no more Smithers than mine is. He's a criminal"

Mr Ludlow found himself standing at the foot of the steps almost before he knew it, having been assisted there by Sidney Foster, who, still with his hand upon his collar, was regarding him with sinister looks.

"Say another word against Mr Smithers and I'll knock you down."

"Duck him in the lake," exclaimed his sister from above. "It may cleanse his tongue, even if his heart be grimed beyond all hope."

Mr Ludlow made a gallant effort to retain some show of self-respect.

"You'll be sorry for treating me like this before long."

"I'll wait until that time comes."

"As for your sister—"

"I would recommend you not to allow any allusion to my sister to pass your lips."

Mr Ludlow looked at the speaker, and saw that he meant

what he said.

"Very good. Before many hours are past it will be my turn."

Mr Ludlow went after Mr Swire, holding himself with what, under the circumstances, was tolerable erectness. There remained Mr Chaffinch, to whom Mr Rodway addressed a question.

"Now, sir, may I ask who you are?"

Mr Chaffinch smiled, genially.

"Mr Foster knows me very well."

"I know you by sight."

"Rather more than by sight, I think, Mr Foster. And I fancy I may also call myself a friend of Mr Smithers."

"Scarcely a friend, Mr Chaffinch. I believe you spoke to him once in a train."

"Well, an acquaintance then, which I trust will soon ripen into friendship."

"I don't think it's very likely; and in any case, at present Mr Smithers isn't at home."

"I'll take the hint, Mr Foster—I'll take the hint."

He took it, smiling all the time.

When he was gone Miss Foster said to Mr Rodway:

"First blood's ours!"

"Yes," he replied. His tone was not so sprightly as hers had been. "But when it comes to business, it's last blood which counts. I shouldn't be surprised if that was theirs."

CHAPTER 31
HOME

"It's good to be in England again," Netta said to her husband, as they came off the boat on to the Admiralty Pier at Dover. Then she glanced up at him and laughed. "I suppose—at this moment it would be unpatriotic to say anything about the weather." They had had a cold crossing. The wind was a piercing north-easter. Yet, in spite of it, there had been more than the suspicion of a fog in the Channel. Now, as they landed amid the coldness and darkness of the late winter afternoon, it seemed as if they could scarcely have a more cheerless reception. Netta was glad to find herself in the compartment which had been reserved for them—in possession of a cup of tea.

"This is better—especially the tea. I am glad to be back again; but"—she looked at him with whimsical eyes—"I don't call Dover England. Do you? I shan't feel that I am back till I'm out of Dover."

When they were, and the train was speeding Londonwards, she sat very still, seeming to hug herself, as it were, in her corner. He observed her over the top of his evening paper.

"You're in a solemn mood."

"I am—tremendously solemn!" She was again silent for a second or two, then added, "This is a sort of between."

"Is it?—How?"

"One dream is ended; another's just going to begin."

"How can you tell?"

"Don't you know, when you're fast asleep and one dream's ended, how you do know that another is going to begin? The feeling you have that it's a sort of interregnum, during which you're passing from one strange happening to another? How you wait—and wonder—what the next is going to be?"

"Have you any notion?"

"I've a foreboding."

She said it with an odd little smile.

"A foreboding!—Is it so bad as that?"

"You see, I'm so happy, it makes me afraid. I never used to be afraid before I knew what happiness was; but now that I do know. I am. And the last dream was so beautiful! Oh, my dear, it has all been such rapture!—one can't expect the next to be like it."

"Monotony palls—sweetness cloys—a breath of a keener air is bracing."

"Yes—when you're in it and it's blowing all about you. But when you're petting yourself in your furs, and hear it whistling without, there's a moment when you hesitate to face it."

"As you stand in doubt on the edge of your bath?'"

"After the splash it's all right; but before—oh dear, you should see me shiver!"

"I do. But it's no good shivering. There's a huge house wait-ing for its mistress, and it insists on having her. When you find yourself sovereign lady of all you survey, you'll discover that the plunge was well worth making. As a country madam you'll be immense. When you see it growing, I don't believe you know wheat from barley."

"I don't."

"And you can't ride—or golf—or play tennis—or even ping-pong."

"I'll do all those things before long—and so well that no one will guess how late my education began. You wait till I get a chance! I'll show you that I'm a natural female athlete, and quite capable of doing anything that any woman ever did."

"I believe you are."

"You believe!—I'm sure! I've an instinct for all kinds of games—I am convinced of it—and I'll show the people about Dene Park that at that sort of thing I'm the lady champion of everything."

They dined in town; then a special train took them home. It was midnight when they arrived at Birchester. The weather had cleared. It was a cloudless, starlit night. Netta had the carriage windows down as they rolled through the lanes over the frosty roads. Suddenly a church clock struck the hour.

"Twelve o'clock—Christmas Day. A merry Christmas, Frank!—the first your wife has ever wished you."

She snuggled up close to him. He put his arm about her, and they kissed.

"The same to you, dear wife, and many of 'em,—I believe that's how it goes. You're a Christmas bride."

"How can that be? I suppose a Christmas bride is a person who's married at Christmas, and I've been married to you all these months. I believe you've already forgotten how long we have been married."

"I've no head for dates. I'm bringing you home at Christmas, so I say you're a Christmas bride; and if I say you're a Christmas bride you are—even if you aren't."

"How masterful you really are!"

"Before very long they'll be saying you're the feminine equivalent, so we'll be even.—Here is the entrance to your home, and Mrs Brazier and her son are up to do the honours."

The carriage stopped at the lodge gates. In the lodge itself a light was burning. As soon as the vehicle came to a standstill the old lady and her son were out of the house, throwing the gates open. Mr Smithers called to them.

"How are you, Mrs Brazier? Good-evening, Sam—I've brought your mistress home."

Netta put her head out of the window.

"And very glad," she cried, "I am to get here."

The old woman took the hand which the girl advanced, and held it as if it had been some fragile thing.

"Welcome, sir and madam. A merry Christmas to you both!"

Mrs Brazier remained to curtsey and her son to touch his hat as the carriage rolled on down the avenue.

"Those," said the husband to his wife, "are the first of the great host of your retainers."

"She seems a very nice old lady, and her son is not an ogre. I'm not afraid of them." The carriage swept round a corner, clear of the trees. "Frank!—is that the house?—our house? It looks like a palace."

"I told you it was."

"But you didn't tell me it was a fairy palace;—and standing up there, all lit up against the night, it looks like one. I believe that it's an enchanted castle!"

"Not a doubt of it—to which the queen of the enchantments is coming."

So soon as the coachman reined up his horses the vehicle was taken by storm. The door was thrown open; Netta was in her mother's arms; Margaret Foster had one of her hands; Mr Rodway had the other. Sidney Foster had both her husband's hands in his. The air was alive with their voices and cries of welcome.

"Netta, how late you are! I was beginning to be afraid that something must have happened."

This was her mother—who was disposed to tears.

"Well, young woman, so he has brought you back alive. We hardly expected it."

This was Margaret Foster. Mr Rodway was slightly inarticulate. Sidney was more audible—as he addressed the husband.

"I don't know if it's the light or what it is, but you seem to be as "brown as a berry."

"How did you expect I was going to be ?"

"Well, when a fellow returns from his honeymoon, one never knows how he's going to look."

Netta turned to him.

"Thank you, Mr Foster. I'll remember your words when you are starting on yours."

They went up the steps in a crowd laughing and talking all together.

"Didn't I tell you," exclaimed Netta, "that this was an enchanted castle? These are the sort of steps enchanted castles always have."

"Of course it's an enchanted castle," rejoined Miss Foster. "And within are divers strange enchantments—as you are soon to learn."

Indeed, it might have been an abode of faerie; for, to Netta, even when she was in the building, everything seemed wonderful—that she should be mistress in such a place, the greatest wonder of them all. Margaret Foster escorted her to her apartment. When they reached it Margaret commented, with characteristic freedom, on the alleged singularity of her appearance.

"How scared you look! Your eyes are notes of exclamation expressive of nothing but amazement. Don't you like the nest your lord's designed for you?"

"Nest, you call it? Palace, it seems to me and I'm supposed to be its mistress!"

"It's not a case of supposition—you are."

"I who used to be the maid-of-all-work in Dulverton

Road."

"I'd like to occupy a similar position in my establishment—I'd keep it more respectable."

"I never thought that a house could be so beautiful. But it's your home, not mine."

"There were some people named Foster who lived here once, so I'm rather glad you like the place. Judging from your looks, marriage seems to suit you.'

"Seems to suit me!"

Margaret was searching her friend with eyes which found out everything.

"Has he been beating you?"

"Beating me—Meg!"

"You convey to me the impression of being fairly happy—considering."

"I'm the happiest woman that ever lived."

"Dear me! Are you indeed? And pray how do you know how all the other women felt? But, anyhow, your words suggest that you've still some fragments of faith in the man that's got you—and after all, that's something."

"Faith! I know that the man who—as you put it—has got me, is incomparably greater, nobler, wiser, stronger, tenderer, truer, than I ever supposed he was. Faith has been exchanged for knowledge, my dear."

Mr Rodway had a few words alone with his partner before they went into supper. "Feeling fit?—you're looking it!"

"I am feeling all I look—and more."

"No clouds—even on the horizon?"

"My dear Ben, I've a physical peculiarity—I'm incapable of seeing a cloud, even when folks are saying that the sky is black with them."

"A convenient gift at times, but also, on occasion, a source of danger. It can't be nice to always go out without an umbrella when it's going to rain—hard."

"Ah!—but I'm impervious to rain."

"But those who are with you mayn't be."

"They'll have umbrellas—or, in the nick of time, I may be able to produce one from up my sleeve." The two men looked at each other. Mr Smithers laughed. But there was no sign of laughter on his companion's face—a fact on which he observed.

"Why, Ben, to look at you, one would think that you saw nothing else but clouds. That's a freak of vision peculiar to a large section of humanity—it's born of the liver, fry a pill."

"In my case you are mistaken. I assure you that I only see things which are in full sight. It seems to me that the man who doesn't see them is the one who's suffering from a freak of vision. Whether, for him, a pill would be a sufficient remedy I seriously doubt."

An odd thing happened while they were at supper—one of those odd things which seemed to dog Mr Smithers' footsteps. They were jesting, eating, drinking, speaking of a hundred things, for questions flowed, and answers came as readily. To all appearances their minds were entirely occupied with the pleasures of the moment; care was wholly absent from the board. Mr Smithers was telling a story of how, he declared, Netta had lost herself in Paris; and she was denying his assertions, when, just as he was in the middle of a sentence, he stopped as if to listen.

"What noise is that?"

The question was asked in a quick, sharp way, which was so foreign to his general manner, that coming, as it did, so unexpectedly, it was a little startling. They all listened. Sidney Foster spoke—as if the inquiry had been specially addressed to him.

"I hear nothing."

"Perhaps it was the wind."

He went on with his story. But it seemed that the salt had gone out of it. He brought it to a lame conclusion. Some desultory remarks were exchanged. Then again he startled them by whirling round in his seat and staring across the room.

"Don't you hear it?"

Once more they listened. This time it was Margaret who answered.

"I do hear something—it's out in the park—like someone

crying."

Netta looked at her in surprise.

"Meg!—Who can be crying, in the park, at this time of night? I hear nothing."

Mr Smithers raised his hand, as if commanding silence.

"Now can't you hear? It's coming closer."

"It's somebody serenading you."

This was Rodway. Netta half rose from her chair.

"It's not the whistler !"

"The whistler? No; this time it's not the whistler. It sounds to me as if it were some poor chap screeching."

The sound, whatever it was, grew obviously louder, as if it swelled in volume as it was borne towards them on the breeze. Suddenly Mr Smithers sprang to his feet. His words had an ominous significance—as if they burst from him in the shock of what was something more than surprise.

"It's the piper!"

Each second the sound grew greater as it seemed to come rushing across the park. Then, all at once, it went wailing past the window of the room which they were in; and then, at the very moment when it had reached its greatest height, all was still. The effect was peculiar—the approaching noise; the sudden wail; the instant silence. They looked at each other with startled faces.

"What was it?" demanded Netta.

Rodway answered. His glance was fixed upon his partner.

"It did sound like bagpipes; blown by a madman. It almost reminds one of the stories which are told of a great Scotch family, which is haunted by a ghost in the shape of a long dead-and-buried piper."

"Really?"

"Really. Haven't you ever heard of the Gairloch piper, who always warns members of the ancient house of Skye of approaching death?—You've heard the story, Smithers, I suppose?"

Mr Smithers had continued standing an instant after the sound had ceased. Then, without observing on it in any way, resuming his chair, he continued to eat what was on his plate. He answered Rodway's question without glancing up.

"Yes, I've heard of it." Laying down his knife and fork he looked at his watch. "It's tolerably late; Christmas is well in, Netta; you've been travelling—don't you think it's time?"

On the table in his dressing-room he found a blank envelope, which was sealed with what looked like a Masonic symbol. He summoned the servant.

"Did you put this on my dressing-table?"

The man looked askance at the envelope which he held up.

"No, sir."

"Who did ?"

"I don't know, sir. I was in here about five minutes ago, and it was not there then."

"Are you sure?"

"Quite, sir. I could not have failed to have noticed it."

Mr Smithers examined the man's face. He was a young fellow, with brown hair and a frank, open countenance.

"You can go." The man went. "If he didn't put it there, who did? Have I an enemy in my own household?"

He tore the envelope open. It contained a typewritten communication.

You will be required to give a final settlement on Jan. 1—the first day of the new year.

If you are a wise man, you will be at the Piccadilly corner of Waterloo Place at nine o'clock on the evening of that day. You will be accosted by a person who will have in his necktie, in the form of a scarf-pin, the seal of the Eight. He will conduct you to the place of settlement.

If you are not a wise man, you will not be at the rendez-vous at the appointed time.

In that case the settlement will take a more disagreeable form—you will have had due warning.

He pressed a spring in his dressing-case, and took out of the cavity which was disclosed two other sheets of paper, which he compared with the one which he had just received. In every respect they were identical.

"One at Florence; the next at Paris; the third one here. It looks as if they at last meant business. The first of January! Six clear days. It's a short time to have in which to put one's affairs in order."

Netta's voice called to him from the adjoining bedroom.

"I'm so sleepy! Shall you be long?"

CHAPTER 32
CALM BEFORE THE STORM

At Dene Park that Christmas Day was one to be remembered. There was dinner for the tenants and the workpeople; a huge Christmas-tree for the children; there were games and dances for their elders. It was honoured in the traditional fashion. The new master and mistress were everywhere, winning golden opinions—she for her youth, and looks and smiles, and pleasant, kindly ways; he for the indefinable, sympathetic something which won him friends wherever friends were to be won. And then he was so tall, and strong, and handsome—so fine a gentleman—one whom any property would be proud to own as master. His smile was like sunshine; his voice like an instrument of many strings, from which he could produce at will the sweetest and merriest notes; he was so obviously without a care in the world.

None saw an incident which took place in his dressing-room. Netta and he, that morning, were late risers. When he reached his dressing room, learning that the papers had already arrived, he ordered them to bring up the *Times*. When it came, he allowed it to remain untouched until the servant had left the room. So soon as the man had gone he opened it, asking of himself a curious question as he did so.

"What did Shon mean?"

He searched the columns of the paper as if for an answer—it seemed that he found one.

"What's that?—'Accident to the Scotch Express. Serious Loss of Life. List of the Killed and Wounded.'"

It appeared that on the previous day a grave disaster had happened to a fast train to the North of Scotland. It had collided with some heavily laden baggage-trucks which—as usual—were where they ought not to have been. The result was a catastrophe. For many—in that moment' the festive season' was turned to one of mourning. There were some among the passengers who had been killed upon the instant; others who had been better killed. Among the dead were the occupants of a specially reserved saloon which had been in the front of the train. They were four—three women and a child—the Marchioness of Skye; her infant son, Lord Alec Bruce of Gairloch; his nurse, and her maid. All four must have gone without a moment's warning straight to their account. Their bodies had been taken out of the ruins of the telescoped carriage, "presenting"—so the paper said—"a dreadful spectacle."

Mr Smithers read and re-read these words until they must have taken strange shapes before his eyes.

"That's what Shon meant!" It came from his lips like a wail.— "That's what he meant!"

The hand which held the paper dropped to his side. He stood in his shirt-sleeves, staring into vacancy, as if it contained a ghost, at which he was constrained to stare.

"Now, what shall I do?"

The question seemed to force itself between his lips. As if in despair of finding an answer, he dropped down on to a chair which was behind him—and stared.

Netta's voice was heard speaking to him from the next room—as it had done the night before.

"I'm going down to breakfast directly; are you nearly ready?"

"I shall be ready in five minutes."

And he was.

At the breakfast table there was an exchange of Christmas gifts; each had something for everyone else. The air was full of expressions of surprise and pleasure. Thanks and laughter were on all lips. The host's mood was in harmony with the rest. His wife's presents to her friends were the theme of admiration.

"I believe," declared Margaret, "that you'd like to pass your life giving people things, the most lovely things that you could find."

"I should. It wouldn't be bad fun. Do you think it would? You see, in my time I've had so little chance of giving anybody anything that I must make up for lost opportunities. But as for the lovely part, if there's anything specially charming, you may be quite sure that Frank chose that. When my taste wobbles, and I can't think what to get, he steps in and at once discovers something that's a perfect dream. At buying presents there never was his equal!"

Margaret laughed.

"Mr Smithers, I'm beginning to suspect that your wife is under the impression that you've some good qualities."

He looked up at her, for a moment, with twinkling eyes.

"Miss Foster, my wife—being the wisest woman in the world—is well aware that I'm compact of them."

They spoke of the accident to the Scotch Express; remarking on how frequently the Christmas season was heralded by some misfortune to ship or train, as if it were a law of nature that tragedy should be associated with comedy, laughter with tears. Mr Smithers joined in the conversation, pointing out the special dangers of that portion of the line on which the accident occurred, as if he had been over the ground and knew it well.

When the party had separated, and he and his partner were lighting their pipes, preparatory to sallying out into the open air, Mr Rodway commented on a point which had not been touched upon at table.

"Odd that the Marchioness of Skye and her son should have been on board!"

Mr Smithers' reply was brief: "Very."

"Especially after what took place last night."

"How do you mean ?"

"That wailing noise."

"What about it?"

Mr Rodway looked at his partner who was occupied in inducing his pipe to draw to his satisfaction—almost as if his temper was a little ruffled.

"You seemed interested enough in it at the time."

"In what?"

"Man, you're a masterpiece!"

Mr Rodway's tone was so explosive that the other stared at him in unmistakable surprise.

"Ben! what's wrong? I know I'm a masterpiece on general principles, but why on this particular occasion?"

"You don't know? Of course not!"

"Ben, you've been overworking—the Power's got too much upon your digestion. Take my very strong advice—do try a pill!"

By way of reply to this friendly suggestion Mr Rodney's manner was vitriolic.

"I suppose you never heard of the Gairloch piper, or how the death of a member of the reigning house of Skye is announced by the wail of his pipes—no hint of the story ever came your way?"

"You are mistaken. I'm probably as familiar with the legend as you are. But why, on that account, this fluster?"

"Do you mean to tell me that that wasn't the Gairloch piper we heard last night?"

"Heard last night! I say—Ben!" The ladies came downstairs. "Please, Netta, are you ever coming? Both Rodway and I are spoiling for a mouthful of fresh air. Miss Foster, this partner of mine has been overworking himself. If he doesn't look out I tell him he'll fall a victim to the fiend dyspepsia."

Mr Rodway said nothing—not even when Miss Foster murmured in his ear:

"Now, what silly thing have you been saying or doing? It's extraordinary what one has to endure from geese."

She sighed. He gasped and glared. Some moments afterwards he observed, apparently *apropos* of nothing in particular :

"The man's a masterpiece!"

The day's festivities went off without a hitch. Mr Glasspoole, who was understood to be responsible for all the details of the arrangements which had been made, was congratulated on his success. Indeed, the little man was in his element—here, there, and everywhere at once. So, also, were his wife and daughters. Late in the day Netta expressed to her husband her conviction that they were in no slight measure indebted for the day's success to the steward and his family.

"Frank, I like those Glasspooles. They're so natural, and simple, and willing to oblige; and somehow there's something about them—their looks, voices, manner, or something—which seems to say they've had a history. Have they?"

"You shrewd student of human nature, we all of us have had a history."

"All of *us?* I'm not so sure—not in the sense I mean. Have you?"

"My history is just beginning."

If such was the ease, it continued uneventfully for six clays, which were spent in making himself and his wife acquainted with their new possessions. Netta enjoyed the process of finding out the full extent of her domain with the outspoken frankness of a healthy, unspoilt child. To her it seemed so wonderful that it should all be hers. She never wearied of telling her husband that she found it impossible to realise that it really and truly was her own—that she was its mistress and its queen. And he, on his part, seemed to find it pleasant to listen to her enthusiastic outbursts—as a parent likes to witness a child's rapture on finding itself the recipient of the toy which its heart desires.

The holiday season passed in making holiday. On the eve of the new year they all went together to the village church, of whose living Mr Smithers was the patron. The vicar was easily induced to make what, for him, was a new departure, and to hold a 'watch-night' service. Husband and wife greeted the new year in God's house. As they walked home across the park, the joy-bells crashing through the midnight air, the young wife broke the silence which had momentarily prevailed between them by delivering herself of an observation which the whole world has uttered in its time.

"I wonder what the new year will bring to us."

She had not long to wait to see.

CHAPTER 33
MR LUDLOW SPEAKS OUT

On the morning of the first of January Mr Smithers went to London by the train which left Birchester at half-past eleven. He told his wife that he had business in town which would probably prevent his returning until the following day. She knew that during their absence abroad arrears of business had accumulated which required his attention. A man in his position cannot take a prolonged holiday with complete impunity. And although, for some cause, which she could not have adequately explained even to herself, reluctant enough to let him go, she acquiesced in his departure. She accompanied him in the dogcart to the station; saw the train start, with him in it; then turned to leave the platform. As she moved towards the entrance someone took off his hat to her—a very fat, barrel-shaped man, with a small bullet head and a hairless face, which, as he smiled, became a network of wrinkles.

"I beg your pardon. I believe I have the pleasure of speaking to Mrs Smithers. May I ask if Mr Smithers is at home?"

"My husband has just gone to town."

"To town? Is he likely to be at home this afternoon? My name is Chaffinch—I rather wished to see him."

"He will not return until tomorrow."

"Not until tomorrow?—Thank you very much."

He dismissed himself with a sweeping bow. She made for her dogcart, he for the telegraph office, from which he despatched the following telegram:

To Samuel Waterson, Hotel Cosmopolitan, London:
He comes on by this train; she will come on later.

As the groom drove her homeward, her mood was a little melancholy, as was but natural. It was the first time since their marriage that they had been parted. Had she known that in a drawer in her husband's dressing-table there was a sealed envelope, which was inscribed in his handwriting—"To be opened by my wife should nothing have been heard of me by noon on January the second.—Francis Smithers."—she might have had reason for something more than melancholy. But she did not know that it was there; nor did she dream that actual peril—in any shape or form—was close at hand. Her mood was sentimental—not for some months had she been alone; she was disposed to prolong her solitude rather than to bring it to an immediate close.

Alighting at the lodge gates, she bade the groom tell Miss Foster, or anyone else who might inquire for her, that she was walking home through the park. As the cart went on down the avenue she struck off among the trees. It was a clear, crisp morning, dry under foot; the copse, which stretched in front of her, invited one who was meditatively inclined. Not a creature was in sight, or apparently in hearing. This was the spot in which she could think out the thoughts which all at once were pressing on her.

Vague fancies they were rather than tangible reflections—the shadowy conceits which are apt at times to compass a woman round about, and to lift her, wide-awake, into something very like a world of dreams—especially if she is young, imaginative, and in a position to whose entire novelty she has not yet become accustomed. As, even in her most practical moments, she still seemed to herself to be an actor in a fairy tale, it was not strange if, when the fit was on her, it scarcely needed an act of conscious volition to transfer her to that land of romance in which young girls love to wander. Her story of the last few months transcended any romance of which she had ever heard; and in all its parts it had been, and was, so beautiful.

Like Cinderella, she had been transformed, as if by magic, from the hopeless household drudge into the Prince's well-loved wife. And what a Prince he was! His virtues,—how unique! his affection—how unbounded! The ideal man of whom countless women dream was actually hers! What had she done to deserve this great good fortune? What could she do? She might give him all she had; yet how little, after all, was that. How, by her future life, could be least shown her manifold unworthiness of him? Worthy she could never be—she was sure of that; never though she lived to untold years!

So strenuously was this borne into her that, as she walked, she clenched her fists, demanding of herself:

"Frank! Frank! What did you see in me? There's nothing to be seen—nothing—absolutely nothing. I wish I could do something—just some little thing!—in return for all you've done for me."

As she addressed to herself this profound aspiration something caught her ear: she saw, advancing towards her along the path which wound among the trees upon her right, a man. Her knowledge of the geography of her own estate was still more than a trifle vague, nor had she any certain knowledge of what were public footpaths and what were not. Still, she felt persuaded that where she was was private; and that this man, if he was a stranger, trespassed. That he was a stranger, as she looked at him, she had no doubt.

His appearance, as he approached, did not favourably impress her. He seemed to have been quite recently in the wars. His ill-fitting clothes were ill-kept, as if he had lately lain in the mud or been rolled in the dust. He slouched rather than walked, with a hangdog-air which was unpleasantly suggestive. He was coming towards her at right angles. Should she stop and inquire what he was doing there, or walk on and ignore his presence? The question was answered by the man himself. He called out to her.

"Excuse me, Miss, I want to speak to you."

She stood still, in sudden indignation. How dare he call her 'Miss' when she was a married woman—or address her at all?

He, such a disreputable creature; she, the lady of the manor. When he came close she hurled at him an inquiry:

"Do you know that you're trespassing?"

His answer was not what she had expected.

"Trespassing? Me trespassing? On my own ground, or on what ought to be my own ground? I like that!"

"If you don't take yourself off instantly I shall summon a keeper, and then you'll regret it."

"Summon a keeper! You will? For me? Who do you think you are, to talk to me like that?"

"I am Mrs Smithers, and the ground on which you are is my husband's property, as you will quickly learn."

"You're Mrs Smithers!" The man expectorated, as if the name tasted badly in his mouth. "You're no more Mrs Smithers than I am. 'Cause why? Because your husband's name—if he is your husband—is no more Smithers than mine is."

Netta went a little white.

"You have been drinking, my man. I will leave someone else to deal with you."

She made as if to pass on. He blocked the way.

"Oh no, I haven't been drinking; and I'm not going to deal with anyone else but you—at least, not yet awhile. My name's Swire—Sam Swire. Have you ever heard the bloke what calls himself your husband speak of me?"

"I have not. He is not likely to speak to me of such a person as you are, even if he's aware of your existence."

"I daresay not; he's that sort of cove. He never told you that he murdered me as near as a toucher for trying to get what was my own, and that I could send him to penal servitude for life for that alone?—Of course not! He wouldn't. He likes to keep that sort of thing private. It's his way."

"If you don't let me pass at once I shall call for help."

"You can call till you're hoarse for all I care; only, if you've a mite of sense, you won't do anything so foolish till you've listened to what I have to say. I don't mean you no harm, not a morsel. He's done you, like he has me, and everyone he's come across. Oh, he's a gem! I tell you, you're not Mrs Smithers, because, whatever his name is—and that's between him and his mother!—it isn't Smithers. He married you under a false name. When I was sent to Canterstone Jail to do three months, I found him there doing two years; and he was jailed as Bruce—Andrew Bruce. He took the name of Smithers when he came out of stir because, by taking it, he saw his way to the biggest robbery that ever yet was done."

"Will you let me pass?"

"No, I won't; not till you've heard me out. What do you know about him, except what he's told you? Nothing at all. I tell you that when he came out of prison I don't believe he had more than a sovereign he could rightly call his own, and every farthing he's got now he's got by blasted robbery."

"Do you suppose I am paying the slightest attention to your ridiculous drunken lies?"

But her cheeks were pale, her lips trembled, fear was in her eyes.

"I'm not drunk, and they're not lies, as I'll prove to you quickly enough. You're the best done young woman in England, and the chap what's done you is the biggest all-round scoundrel that's managed to cheat the gallows up to now. But he's bound to end on them, as sure as I'm alive."

"I'm afraid, Netta, that what Mr Swire says is only too true."

The words came from behind her, in a voice which she knew well. Turning, she found that her brother was within half-a-dozen feet of where she stood, dressed as for the City, in his frock-coat, silk hat, black kid gloves. He rested both hands on the top of an umbrella. His appearance so reminded her of a certain type of stage figure with which she had become familiar that, an irresistible appeal being made to her risible nerves, she burst into an hysterical fit of laughter.

"Do you think that costume's suited to the country, Theodore? You don't know how funny you look in it—like a man in a play!"

Theodore, unfortunately, was wholly devoid of a sense of humour. Neither her remarks nor her merriment seemed to please him. He bestowed on her the look before which, in the old days, his mother and sister had often cowered.

"Since you find entertainment in the idea of being a nameless creature and a scoundrel's plaything, I shall understand that, in dealing with you, it is not necessary to chop phrases. What Swire says is even less than the truth. The blackguard with many aliases who pretended to marry you is not only a jailbird and an impudent swindler, but a convicted murderer, who only escaped the hangman by the skin of his teeth."

"And what are you? Although I regret to say that you are my brother, are you not a blackmailer and a fraudulent clerk, who was glad to save yourself from the consequences of your own misdeeds by accepting a large sum of money from the man of whose absence from home you are taking advantage to vilify to me—his wife."

"You are not his wife. I suspected, from the first, that he was a rogue, as you are perfectly well aware, because I continually warned you against him; but at the time of which you speak I had no notion that he was such a rogue, or he would have had to walk over my body to have reached you. He was tried for murder— the murder of Colonel Raymond Verinder. Owing to a technical flaw, the capital charge was withdrawn, and he was found guilty of manslaughter, for which he was sentenced to two years' hard labour. He then called himself Andrew Bruce. He was a married man, and his wife still lives. You will perceive in what a position that one fact places you."

"It is false—every word of it."

But she had to press her fingertips into the palms of her hands and to bite her lips to keep herself from crying.

"Does not your commonsense tell you that I should not make such a positive assertion had I not taken the necessary steps to ascertain that it was correct? This man was in jail with him."

"That's true—true as gospel. He was Bruce then—that I'll swear."

"While in jail he appears to have planned what has turned out to be perhaps the most remarkable fraud that ever was per- petrated. When he emerged from prison he assumed the name of Smithers, for the purpose of getting hold of moneys which were the fruits of a series of rascalities which had been the work of a villain who had been almost a kindred spirit. To enable him to gain possession of the shameful hoard, with brazen assurance he committed a hundred offences against the law.

"With this money he financed Rodway's invention. As it was never his, nor the rogue's that hid it, all the profits of that invention are forfeit to the law, and, when the facts become known, will be claimed and seized. So you see that this man's a criminal monster—a thief, a forger, an impostor, a murderer, a bigamist— soon to be a beggar. You stand on the edge of an abyss of shame, too terrible to contemplate—as his latest plaything."

"It's not true; not—not a word of it. You would never dare to talk like this if he were here!"

"No, that he certainly would not."

The speaker was Miss Foster, who came quickly towards them through the trees. Netta ran to her with a cry.

"Oh Meg, I'm so glad you've come! They've been saying such wicked things of Frank!"

CHAPTER 34
NETTA LEARNS THE TRUTH

Margaret Foster, putting her arm round, Netta, drew her closely to her, contemplating the two men in front of her with looks which were not flattering.

"So it's you again, Mr Ludlow, and your prison friend. Netta the other day this animal"—the allusion was to Mr Swire, who seemed to resent it—"was assisted off the premises, and I regret to say that your brother had to be sent after him. I trust that you have not paid, them the compliment of listening to anything that either of them may have to say."

"They have made me listen; but I haven't believed a word— not a word."

"That's right. It's impossible to treat them with the contempt which they deserve, but it's as well to get as close to it as one conveniently can."

"Miss Foster, I have cause to believe that in this matter—for reasons—which I am at a loss to understand—you are not so innocent as you would desire to appear. Can you tell my most unfortunate sister that the man whom she supposes to be her husband is not a convicted criminal, and that he did not marry her under a name to which he has no title? Don't you know, of your own knowledge, that this is true?"

"Mr Ludlow, be so good as to let me pass."

"Not until you have answered my question."

"I ask you, for the second and last time, to let me pass."

"Netta, you are surrounded by a conspiracy of silence. Rodway knew the truth on the day that you were married. I believe this girl has gagged his lips,—why, since she pretends to be your friend, and is presumably a lady, is beyond my comprehension. Ask her, in my presence, if what I have told you is not true."

"I told you it was the last time!"

With the intention of compelling him to allow them a passage, Miss Foster flung herself at Ludlow almost as if she had been a man. But she had neither a man's strength, nor—in affairs of this sort—his adroitness. Mr Ludlow—not himself by any means a physical-force man—had no difficulty in gripping her wrists, and in continuing to hold them, despite her struggles.

"No you don't, Miss Foster! Your attendant bullies are not now at your beck and call to assist you in your nefarious scheme to cover up the truth from the light of day."

Netta, with a white face, went close up to him.

"Theodore, let Margaret go!"

"With the greatest possible pleasure. It is my wish to remember that she is a lady, so long as by her conduct she does not compel me to forget it. Question her now as to the truth of what I have told you."

As Mr Ludlow released her, the young lady, with crimsoned cheeks, seemed endeavouring her utmost to conceal her consciousness of her loss of dignity.

"Meg, of course I know that all he has said is false, but, for form's sake, tell me that you too know that it is lies."

"Oh, I've no doubt that he has told you lies." Your looks hardly suggest such knowledge, Miss Foster; nor does your manner of fencing with my sister's question.—I'm afraid, Netta, that you will have to make your inquiry clearer. Ask her if she is cognisant of the fact that your husband married you under a name which is not his."

"That, Meg, I am sure you will find it easy to deny."

"On such a point I should certainly not advise you to accept your brother's statement."

"You hear how she juggles with phrases! This young lady has a nimble tongue. Now, ask her if she is not perfectly well aware that the man whom you suppose to be your husband is a convicted felon."

"Netta, don't trouble yourself to obey this—gentleman. I decline to answer, here, any question which may be prompted by him or by his friend; for reasons which, later on, you will appreciate."

"But, Meg, surely you will not allow him to say such a thing—before me!—without telling, him, on the instant, that he lies?"

"That's the way in which to put it to her."

"Netta, there are two ways of telling a story—a wrong way and a right way. You may take, my word for it that your brother has told, his story the wrong way. Your husband returns tomorrow. I would recommend you to put your questions to him then, and he will give you all the information you require."

"In other words, she recommends you to afford him another opportunity to continue his campaign of lies; for to suppose that such a character as he is will admit his guilt—even when confronted by irrefutable proof—is an absurdity.—I regret, Miss Foster, that you drive me to the conclusion that you are willing to assist in duping, betraying, and ruining the credulous girl whom you pretend to call your friend."

"You dare say such a thing!—you!"

"I dare say more. This unfortunate child—she is little else—is my own flesh and blood. I am her brother. As such, until you give plain answers to the plain questions which she has put to you, I shall decline to allow her to return to the house of which this scoundrel has obtained possession by fraud and falsehood, and in which he wishes her to figure as his associate and mistress."

"Your language is quite in keeping with your well-known character, Mr Ludlow; but I don't fancy your permission will be asked. Here comes someone who will be better able to cope with you than two helpless women." She pointed to Mr Rodway, who was hurrying towards them along the woodland path. She called to him.—"Mr Rodway, you are not coming before you are wanted. Be quick, please!"

Ludlow moved towards him as, at the lady's bidding, he quickened his steps almost to a ran.

"Rodway, before you speak, listen to me!"

Miss Foster interrupted him.

"Don't do anything of the kind.—Have him thrown into the road instead!"

Rodway looked from one to the other in. evident perplexity.

"What has happened?"

Ludlow got his words out first.

"This has happened—that I want to know why you have concealed from my sister your knowledge of: the fact that the man. whom she supposes to be her husband is an impostor and a convicted felon?"

As Mr Rodway turned to look at. Netta, on his face there was a very curious expression—as of one who suddenly finds himself amid the throes of an earthquake, against whose manifold perils he has no means of defence, and of whose consequences he is fearful, rather for others than for himself. There are situations in which a, man becomes conscious that he may sacrifice even his life in vain. His actual utterance was bold enough.

"Margaret, take Netta home."

But Netta interposed, tremulous and pale.

"I am not to be taken home so easily—as a child by its nurse.—Ben, it appears that Meg refuses to give Theodore the lie, so I ask you to tell me if there is the slightest shadow of a shade of truth in what he says."

"Tell her. I have never known you to utter a falsehood yet."

"I am not going to utter a falsehood now—even for the sweet pleasure of baulking you."

"Then tell her if it's not true that he came straight from prison to be a lodger in my mother's house, and then and there commenced the career of fraud which he has continued to the present hour."

"I should like to kill you!"

"Ben, don't you understand that by your silence you are killing me? "

There was that in her voice which set the strong man trembling. It seemed that he could hardly stammer out a reply—which was no reply.

"Netta, go home."

"But if what Theodore says is true, I have no home, and no husband."

"You certainly have no husband."

Ludlow's tone was cold and measured. Rodway's was hot and eager:

"That's false!"

'Ludlow persisted.

"At the time of his conviction he was a married man, and his wife still lives."

"I don't believe it."

"It is none the less a fact."

"Theodore, if you're telling a lie I'll—I'll!"

Rodway was quivering with passion, which it was plain he found it hard to repress. The other regarded him with unflinching eyes.

"If it is a lie, you may use me as you will—but it is not a lie."

Netta plucked Rod way by the arm.

"Then I suppose—in any case—that the rest is true?"

"Margaret, take her home!"

"Thank you—I need no taking—I can take myself. Margaret may come with me if she likes."

Ludlow made as if to slop them. Rodway caught him by the arm.

"Don't move, or you'll be sorry."

Apparently he saw that in the speaker's face which induced him to esteem discretion the better part of valour. He let the women go. Rodway remained behind, to deal with the two men in his own fashion. Already Mr Swire was evincing a disposition to slink away in the rear.

The girls walked home in silence, each with her eyes fixed straight in front of her, and neither attempting to utter a word. When they reached the house Netta went straight up to her bedroom, and, although uninvited, as if in virtue of a tacit understanding which existed between them, Miss Foster went with her.

As soon as the door was closed, Netta turned to her companion with a face, the expression of which had become so singularly transformed, that her friend regarded her with a sudden consciousness of physical pain.

"Meg, what has happened to the world? Just now it seemed so beautiful, and now it's hideous."

"It's still a very good world to live in."

"How can you say that—when it's hideous? Meg, is it all true—what Theodore said?"

"Netta, have I ever struck you as being the sort of person who would be likely to tell you. falsehoods?"

"Never—till now,"

"The reservation's unkind. Now I'm going to tell you the simple, honest truth."

"Yes, do—tell me the truth—at least. It seems that I have been living in a world of lies."

"You have been doing nothing of the kind."

"But it seems that I have."

"I tell you that it's only seeming. Don't you know your husband well enough to know that?"

"Is he my husband?"

"Netta, I know nothing about the truth of what your brother

has just now told you.—I mean about his having had a wife when he married you."

"But you know about the rest!"

"I am coming to that. But I am convinced that he has never done you a conscious wrong. Don't you yourself know enough of him by now to be sure of that?"

"Not if he had a wife when he married me."

"I don't know what foundation of truth there is in your brother's story. Frankly, I have no great faith in your brother."

"I didn't use to have."

"I haven't now. I have an innate persuasion that, on examination, his story will not be found to bear the interpretation he wishes it to convey."

"But the rest of it is true. Meg, can it be possible that he came straight from prison to our house, and that—he committed murder'"

"I have not the faintest notion what he did; but I'm sure it was nothing of which he has cause to be ashamed, though, I'm afraid, it is true that he was in prison."

"You knew that all along?"

"I did not know it till after you were married."

"You are sure of that?"

"You remember the man who made the disturbance outside the church? That was Swire. He told your brother and Mr Rodway, there and then. After you had left for your honeymoon, Mr Rodway told me."

"Then he knew before I left?"

"Do you reproach me for not letting him tell you then?—after the time you've had abroad?—that dream of perfect happiness.'

"Yes, but if it was only a dream? One would rather be saved from dreams, however pleasant, if the awakening is likely to be disagreeable. For the awakening stays, while the dream goes."

"But this has not been a dream of yours, Netta; and there will be no awakening from it of the kind which you suggest. I know nothing of your husband's story, but I believe he has been greatly sinned against. I thought so from the first moment that I saw him. I am sure he is a true and honest gentleman. Do you think that I should be proud to call him my friend if I was not sure? I preferred to tell no tales of him; first, because I was conscious that I had but an imperfect knowledge of the facts; and second, because I trusted him, and felt that when he knew the proper time had come he would tell you everything, and lay his heart and life bare before you. I should have thought that, as you loved him, you would have felt that way too; realising that he would hold you dearer because, in such a matter, you left it all to him."

"I am only just beginning to understand in how many respects your point of view is different from mine. Yours appears to me to be—peculiar. For instance, you don't seem to perceive that while you have all been wise, I have been the only fool among you; and as I'm the person principally concerned, that cannot be nice for me."

"You've been no fool;—ask him if he thinks you have."

"Ask him? Who do you mean by 'him'? The person whose name I supposed was Smithers?"

"Netta!"

"Well? Why do you look at me like that? It was the merest supposition, wasn't it? It's easy for you to talk prettily, and to say smooth things; but you have a name—I haven't."

"Netta, I understand your frame of mind—how all the foundations of the world seem to have given way."

"It's very good of you."

"But it's not so bad as you imagine—indeed, it's not bad at all—it's only a cloud that has got for a moment before the sun. Wait till your husband returns tomorrow—you'll find that at his touch it will melt away."

"Wait?—I suppose I shall have to wait—even if in the interval I go mad. I don't know where he is or I'd telegraph to him to return—and perhaps he wouldn't come."

"You'd be very foolish if you did anything of the kind."

"I daresay. I have been foolish in my time. But moments seem precious when you're as I am." She bit her lip, and clenched her fists, and turned away. "If you don't mind very much, I'd rather you left me."

Without a word Margaret Foster went out of the room. Netta, waiting till she heard the door shut, turned as if to see if the girl had really gone. Then, crossing the room, she stood before a mirror, studying the reflection which appeared in it.

"That's not my face. I thought I shouldn't know it if I saw it again. I felt I changed with everything else. I seem to have died.—I wonder what it feels like to be dead. I wish I could die before he comes back. I'm afraid of his coming. I daren't think of the stranger I shall see. My husband and my lover went away this morning—forever. I didn't know he was going away forever I wish I had, it'd have been so different—and this man's coming in his place What shall I do?"

CHAPTER 35

COUSINS

About three o'clock on the afternoon of that day Mr Smithers was in Piccadilly. Just after he had passed Arlington Street someone spoke to him, who had approached him from behind.

"Drew!"

At the sound of the voice he gave a perceptible start. One might have suspected him of a desire to ignore the speaker and march straight on. But if such was his intention it was frustrated by the other's insistence.

"Drew, I say!"

The words were uttered with an emphasis which refused evasion. After what was plainly enough a further moment's hesitation, Mr Smithers turned, to find himself confronted by a man who had both a singular likeness and unlikeness to himself. This other man was shorter, smaller altogether. He was not so broad. He had not that air which compelled attention—at first sight, Mr Smithers' most striking characteristic. Yet, when you observed more closely, you perceived that even in his bearing and his figure he recalled the bigger man. There was about him an ease, a grace, one might add a touch of conscious, yet careless, superiority, which was as a reminiscence of the other's splendour.

One saw it clearly as they stood together. About his face were recollections. His hair and beard were thin and sandy, while the other's were luxuriant and golden; his countenance was thin and peaked, while the other's was radiant with health and vigour; yet in the features, their expression, above all in the large blue eyes, which smiled, and would smile though the heart was weeping, there was kinship. The newcomer was attired in apparel-each detail the production of a master hand—whose hue, from head to foot, was black.

He was gazing at Mr Smithers in unmistakable surprise.

"Man, is it a sea-king or a painter's model that you are? I'd not have known you in that beard. You're like a picture!"

Mr Smithers laughed—and when he spoke it was odd how like their voices were.

"Yes—my beard has grown."

"Grown—when I never saw you with a hair upon your face! It's just magnificent. I believe you meant to cut me."

"I had for the moment some intention of walking on."

"It's pretty of you to admit it. You're a pretty fellow altogether!"

"Yet, Alec, I'm glad to see you. I've ached for a sight of you."

"You've kept your aches out of your face."

"I've learnt to do it."

The other observed it shrewdly; then something came on to his face which made it beautiful—a look of understanding. But he only said :

"Come to the house with me." When the other seemed to hesitate, he continued, in gentle yet peremptory tones, "It's no good thinking whether you will or whether you won't, because if you won't I'll have you carried."

"I'd sooner walk."

"Then walk with me."

He passed his arm through the other's. As, arm in arm, they

crossed the road together, it was plain that they were kin. They strolled almost completely silent, finding sufficient content in each other's society in the Marquis of Skye's house, which is in Park Lane—as the world knows, one of the most famous of London's famous houses. There they entered a room which overlooked the garden. And being alone in it, the Marquis of Skye placed his kinsman before a window, and stood in front of him at a distance of about an arm's length.

"Let's stare at you," he said. And he stared; the other bearing his inspection with smiling equanimity. "Do you know you've used me very ill?"

"Such was not my intention."

"And what kind of an intention had you then?"

"To hide myself."

"And what kind of intention do you call that? When I've been picturing you in all sorts of piteous plights, with shoeless feet, contending with fearful creatures in fearful places, without a sup of whiskey with which to warm yourself, and here you are, a radiant vision, looking a credit to your family, and I'll be betting that you've money in your pocket."

"I have a pound or two."

"It's more than the rest of your family has got. Like everything else, money's scarce with us. Why didn't you come to me when you quitted that prison place? I didn't like to write. I know the black spirit that's in you, and I thought you mightn't fancy the address; and I'm told, besides, that they've a nasty little trick of editing your correspondence, and I never wrote a letter that didn't want it—but why didn't you come?"

"I couldn't."

"And why couldn't you?"

"I'd no money."

"And can you stand there and tell me that you didn't know I'd give you money if you wanted it?"

"I'm not so foolish. But I also suspected that you'd none to spare."

"Suspected!—The word is good. I've never had money to

spare, nor ever will have, but that's no reason why I shouldn't have got money for you if you had wanted it. You talk strangely."

"And do you think I could have come to you straight from the shadow of a prison?"

"Why not? Do you think that you're the first Bruce who's been jailed? You've scandalously neglected the study of your family history if you do. We've been a gallows crew since the day that we began—murdering and thieving down the ages—as people of family did. I doubt if there's a jail in Scotland that hasn't held us. And what jailed you? Doing what did you honour—killing a scoundrel—that was all. If you hadn't killed him, then I mightn't ever have spoken to you again. Our fathers would have run him through in the Park, or put a bullet in him, like gentlemen. Other times, other manners. You being in the movement—as a gentleman should be—killed him in the fashion of the hour."

"I never meant to kill him."

"No; of course not. When a gentleman drops another gentleman out of a fourth-floor window, he never imagines that anything will hurt him. It's against nature to suppose it."

"I was blind with fury."

"And, as things are, a very good thing it is to be blind in moments of that sort. To suppose that you did anything unbecoming a gentleman is absurd—you'd call the man to account who suggested it. You know—as well as I know—that there isn't a man in London—that is a man!—who wouldn't be proud to take you by the hand—or a woman either." Suddenly changing the subject, the Marquis waved his hand towards a water-colour drawing of a lady which hung over the mantelpiece. "You've heard?"

"I saw it in the paper—and I heard the pipes."

"I also.—Well, she was a good wife to me—in her way; and I wasn't a bad husband to her—as husbands go—which isn't saying much for either side. I'm endeavouring to reconcile myself to the inscrutable decree of an all-seeing Providence—and I hope she is. The boy wouldn't have lived in any case."

"Is that so?"

"You had only to look at him—Sarah knew it herself—the doctors were unanimous. He was a weak, puling brat, without a hearty yell in him.—So you're the heir."

"God forbid!"

"What might you be meaning? Aren't you the heir?"

"You'll marry again."

"Never. I'm doomed."

"Doomed?"

"You'll be Marquis of Skye within—let's take the extreme limit—let's say inside a week."

"What rubbish are you talking?"

"Shon piped to me last night."

"Alec!"

"He favoured Sarah the night before she started on her last journey. I only heard of it yesterday. It appears that in the middle of the night she rang for her maid and asked her who was piping. The girl told my man; yesterday I had the tale from him. On my return this morning Shon performed for my special benefit his own particular version of *Buaidh no Bas*."

"It was a hallucination. You were thinking of your man's story; you imagined that you heard."

"You know how a Bruce imagines *Buaidh no Bas*. Nor was I thinking of my man's story—I was thinking of my infernal luck—I had been playing Bridge in Fossdyke's room. I walked home. As I came into the gate I heard the piper—it was as though he was playing to himself just behind my back. I turned, fully expecting to see someone there. When I saw that I had the whole place to myself for a moment I was startled. Then I understood."

"It's the rankest superstition—one of which we Bruces ought to be thoroughly ashamed. I don't believe that there's a particle of truth in the whole mad legend."

The Marquis looked at him—queerly. His tone became suddenly sardonic.

"If I were you I shouldn't lie—on such a point. If you have

262

lies to spare, don't waste them. You know how it goes—for a cadet, twelve hours' notice; for the head of the family, twenty four Shon is good enough to assume that he may want a little longer to make ready. So it would seem that it's by the mercy of Providence I've run across you in the nick of time. It was this morning at a quarter past four that I heard him. So if you look round about noon tomorrow you'll find that Preston—you remember Preston? he's still head-jack-in-office—will greet the Marquis."

"Nonsense! I wish you wouldn't talk in that strain—you've always had that eerie streak in you."

"I daresay. Still—I should advise you to keep a carpet-bag packed ready. Have you seen that?" He took a photograph out of a heap of others and threw it across. She's Esme Papillon now—I suppose you've heard."

"Yes; I've heard."

"She's gone on to the stage—where they all go now. It's quite the fashion—so is she. A name like Esme Papillon looks well on the bills—she certainly looks nice on the boards. Made a huge success—draws all the town to the Pandora."

Although the Marquis paused, the other was silent—he was regarding the photograph he held in his hand as if it had been some sort of curio. His cousin went on observing him closely, as a surgeon might a subject on whom he was using his scalpel:

"She's married again—Bellamy the actor—Frederick Bellamy, you know. Plays fools—and plays them perfectly. I'm told that he's as proud of her as if she were something altogether too fine for human nature's daily food—and yet he must know everything. Man's queer!"

"I also am married again."

"What!"

The Marquis started, almost as if the other had struck him. Mr Smithers met the other's gaze and smiled.

"To the dearest girl in the world. The phrase is not original, but in this case it's an accurate description."

"Are you—joking?"

"I am not."

"Then, if you're in earnest, it's the best news that ever I heard—but as to that I needn't be telling you. Say there are at least two pair of twins—four bouncing, bonny boys, that can make themselves heard from here to the other side of the Park—there's nothing like good lungs. Knowing your record and mine, and that we're the last of the stock, each time I've looked at Sarah, and at the puling brat which was all that she could give me, it's been like a nightmare to me to think that the Bruces were done. But if you'll promise that you'll have at least a baker's dozen of lusty, long-legged, strong-lunged lads, built on their father's lines, it's with the greatest pleasure that I'll be joining Sarah."

"I've not been married six months."

"To be sure that's a wee small time. But say there are hopes?"

"I hear there are hopes."

"Then take me to your wife at once—or rather, bring her here. Don't let her keep out of the home of her unborn babe a moment longer than she can help.—By the way, who've you married?"

"The daughter of the landlady who kept the lodgings which I occupied when I first came out of prison."

"Say that again—it sounds like a little complication." Mr Smithers repeated his words. The Marquis was still for a moment. Then he said—in his tone a suggestion of doubt—"Have you taken the long price again? The last time you didn't land it."

"You wouldn't ask me such a question if you knew her."

"Has she money?"

"Not a penny, except what I give her."

"Then I'm thinking that that's not likely to be much. It'll be the first time I'll be hearing that your pocket's overweighted;—yet you seem to have a tailor who trusts you. How have you managed?"

"I've had adventures."

"I'll be bound! Adventures are to the adventurous, and there's no mistaking that you're that. Have your adventures taken the shape of a gold mine?"

"Something like it, only more so.—May I have a cigar?"

He turned to a silver cabinet which stood upon a side-board.

"If you try the left top drawer you'll find the thing you're wanting—and hand me one. They're fine and black and strong,—rightly suited to a man with an empty pocket who's beginning to talk of gold mines."

Mr Smithers did as he was requested, proceeding to light the one which he himself had chosen.

"Have you ever heard of Francis Smithers?"

"The Francis Smithers who everybody's heard off?—the million a minute man?"

"That's the man. I'm he."

"What's that?"

The marquis lowered his cigar in the middle of the operation of lighting it, regardless of the fact that the flame of the match approached his fingers.

"I say, I'm the man you refer to."

"But the man I refer to is Francis Smithers, the Rodway Power man, who, from the coin point of view, is leaving the American multi-millionaires at the post."

"I am that Francis Smithers. Rodway is my partner."

The marquis laid down his cigar, still unlighted, and dropped the match with a start.

"Is this one of those samples of American humour in which the point consists in telling the biggest lie that ever was told; because, if so, it isn't fair for you to start off without giving me warning?"

Mr Smithers handed the other a visiting-card.

"That is my name and my country address. At present we haven't a house in town."

"Oh, at present you haven't a house in town! Is that so?"

"When I came out of prison I assumed the name of Smithers."

"Wasn't the name of Bruce good enough for you?"

265

"I didn't wish to bring more shame on it than I had done already. That was one reason, and there were others. In the same house in which I lodged lived Benjamin Rodway, who was then a bank clerk. I became his partner—as Francis Smithers. When I became engaged I took out letters-patent, and became Francis Smithers legally."

"Then am I to understand that there is no Andrew Bruce?— that Francis Smithers is your legal name?"

"You are. My wife is Mrs Smithers."

"And when I join Sarah—what then?"

"My dear Alec, you must marry again."

"Between this and tomorrow."

"Get that bee out of your bonnet. In an insurable sense yours is a better life than mine."

"But suppose—what then?"

"Would you wish that a man with my record should become a Marquis of Skye?"

"I would—a thousand times over—if that man be you."

"Then I wouldn't."

"Fortunately the matter is not one for your decision. The law gives you no option. It will make you marquis whether you will or not. By means of no letters-patent will you be able to stultify your birthright. Shame on you if force be needed. Are you such a coward that you dare not face your peers—because a woman tricked you once, and you paid the man that aided her? I know you better than you know yourself. The Bruce blood runs hot in your veins. You'll not play the skulking loon, seeking refuge behind a hedge, when the piper calls you to take the place that's yours;—you'll not deny your sires, or their heritage; but you'll take it—and hold it—like a man!"

"If you are convinced that I will not bring shame upon our fathers, then I will;—that is, if I survive you."

"Shame upon our fathers? Why, if you'd cut the rascal's head off at the shoulders and stuck it on your doorpost, you'd only have done what they've done often. How many times, I'm wondering, has there been a row of heads drying on the Gairloch battlements? So far from bringing shame, if you are Francis Smithers you'll bring great glory; for money's the one thing the Bruce has found it hard to get and keep. At the notion of a Marquis of Skye with the money of Francis Smithers, there isn't one of your sires that won't rub his hands together and chuckle with glee; and when Shon calls you, his pipes will skirl with joy."

"Alec, there's a question I wish to ask you."

"Ask, and be answered.—It's good for you that I'm away tomorrow, or I'd be wanting cash from you the day after. It's nothing but debts that you'll be succeeding to. I give you my word that I'm hard put to it to find someone that'll let me make them bigger."

"Any sum that you require I shall be only too proud and happy to let you have at once; and if you will let my men of business communicate with yours, I will see that all encumbrances are cleared."

"Hark at him!—Did any Bruce ever hear the like!—And he's afraid that he'll bring shame upon his sires! If it's shameful to free your family of a load of debt which has been dragging it through the dirt this many a year, then your opportunities in dishonour it on those lines will be many—when I've joined Sarah."

"That's the point on which I want to ask a question. You say that you heard Shon this morning." The marquis nodded. "Don't you think the warning might have been meant for me?"

"Why?—Did you hear him?"

"I think it possible that what you heard was meant for me, since it's on the cards that this time tomorrow I may be—with Sarah."

"Why do you say it?—What's in the air"

"I have some business to transact tonight which may have that result. I merely speak of it because I wish to point out that it's extremely possible—from what you say—that I've been warned by deputy. So far as I was concerned, the warning was not required. I knew already."

"By this time tomorrow we'll both know."

"Probably.—Should the call be mine, you'll remember I've a wife."

"I will. She shall be bone of my bone—especially if it's a boy."

Mr Smithers expelled a cloud of smoke from between his lips.

"She's the dearest girl in the world—and I love her better than my life."

CHAPTER 36
BETWEEN THE STORMS

Again and again the same idea, in different settings, placed Netta upon a mental rack—which, by degrees, became a physical one as well.

"To think that I should have trusted him so implicitly, and that he should have been so hideously false—that his treachery should have been equal to my faith!"

The fashion of it continually changed, assailing her in a hundred different forms; but the thought, at bottom, remained identical—that he should have so imposed upon her credulity! Wherever she looked the reflection lashed her as with unescapable whips. She had esteemed him a god—and he was this thing of pestilent clay; she had believed him incapable of falsehood—and, from the first, in all that he had said and done, he had been a materialised lie; she had credited him with more than mortal virtue—and all the while he had been vice incarnate; she had imagined him upon a pedestal, at whose base all the world ought to fall down and worship—and he was this shameful thing, whom she would be fortunate if she would be able to hide in a ditch!

And she—she herself!—what a simpleton she had been—what a credulous fool! As she beat her fists against the arms of the chair on which she was sitting, she told herself that it really was incredible that she could have been such a monstrous idiot. How he must have been laughing at her—making a jest of her behind her back! From that first moment when, fresh from jail—oh ye powers, think of it! fresh from jail!—he had been her mother's lodger, he had been smiling at her in his sleeve. Piling lie upon lie, and tickled beyond measure at the gullibility with which she swallowed them; adding fraud to fraud, and splitting his sides with amusement at her persistence in regarding him as an honest man. When she recalled how she had boasted of him to Margaret Foster, among others, as being a stainless knight, without fear and without reproach, she writhed and bit her lips, and could have beaten her head against the wall in her abandonment of shame.

Hers was a nature which was peculiarly sensitive to ridicule. To know that she had become a common laughing-stock was in itself sufficient to cut her to the quick—especially as, in her sublime unconsciousness, in her inconceivable blindness, she had held her head so high. Even Theodore would have the laugh of her; he would never allow her to forget until one of them was dead. And Rodway—whom she had always regarded as a good-humoured bull; the reiteration of whose desire that she should marry him she had looked upon as a sort of standing joke she would suspect him of indulging in at least an inward smile whenever he looked her way.

As for Margaret Foster, that sly cat—so she called her—who, under the guise of friendship, had set herself deliberately to deceive her, and while pretending to envy her, had been enjoying her crass stupidity—she had never had a girl friend before—her first would be her last! She had heard of woman's treachery to woman, now she knew what it meant. And her mother, of whose simplicity she had made fun—what would her mother think and say when she saw her tumbled off the pinnacle on which she had supposed herself to be immutably fixed?

As tormenting demons chased each other through her fevered brain, rage seemed to contend with agony. If there only had been something in reach on which she could wreak her wrath; or if she had only been able, at that very moment, to erase herself from off the face of the earth, as if she had never been!

At the best, the position was too terrible to permit as yet of sane contemplation; and at the worst—what then? A sobbing fit shook her as with palsy. She dare not think of it. Suppose, when he returned—if he ever did return; she was not sure that she wished him to return—and she put to him those questions which she would have to put; and he, stripped of the subterfuges of which he had taken such diabolical advantage, constrained to the bare truth, was to admit that what was not the least of Theodore's accusations was true, and that he had already another wife—what would she do then? What could she do? Nothing. There was the lake. She might find refuge there!

While—to use the apostolic figure—she contended with the wild beasts which her brother had gone out of his way to let loose upon her, that model relative was himself by no means happy. One might have supposed that he would have been content with the fruit of his labours, but he was not. Nor was his associate, Mr Swire.

After the ladies had departed, and left him confronting Mr Rodway in the copse, there had been a painful scene. He certainly had found it painful. To be handled—by a muscular person in a very bad temper—as if one were something between a football and a lay figure, cannot be comforting to the feelings of any gentleman. Mr Swire, with a discretion which did more credit to his head than to his heart, made the best possible speed along what he believed to be the shortest cut to the high road. When Mr Ludlow rejoined him—which he did only after a considerable interval—that pillar of the commercial fabric looked as if he had been treated very badly,—and he had. Mr Swire greeted him with an unsympathetic grin.

"You look a pretty sight!"

Mr Ludlow did not look a pretty sight. He was hatless; his collar was missing; his shirt was torn open at the neck; his nice black clothes not only looked as if they had come off a ragman's barrow, but they seemed to be attached to him only by accident. His nose was bleeding. His face and hair were so plastered with mud that he was unrecognisable. Mr Swire's words were intended to be ironic—as Mr Ludlow was not slow to perceive.

"If there's a law in the land, that man Rodway shall smart for this.—Why didn't you stand by me?"

"I did stand by you till the fight began. Then, as it wasn't any business of mine, and I didn't want to be mixed up in a little family affair of that kind, of course I came away. There was one to one—you didn't want there to be two to one, did you? Did you kill him?"

"Kill him!"—Mr Ludlow ground his teeth—what was left of them.—"Before I've finished I'll make him wish I had killed him.—You've made a pretty mess of things!"

"Me! that's good. What price you? When I think of how you looked when you came away from town this morning, and how you're looking now, it seems to me that you haven't made a very good job of it up to this.—What I want to know is, what I'm going to get out of it."

Mr Ludlow glared at the speaker as well as the state of his optics permitted.

"May I ask what you expect to get out of it after the way in which you've behaved?"

"You said that this ought to be as good to me as ten thousand pound—what I want to know is, where's that ten thousand coming from?"

"You may well want! I supposed you were going to behave like a reasonable being. I never imagined you were going to blunder out everything in the way you did. Before I had a chance of speaking you had ruined all."

"How do you make that out? Now look here, I've seen your hanky games before today, so don't you try to play no more of them off on to me, or I'll start talking. I done just as you told me, and now I expect you to be as good as your word; and what I want and what I mean to know is, where's that ten thousand a-coming from?"

Mr Swire was regarding his companion in a manner which hardly suggested friendhip. Mr Ludlow, indeed, resented his hearing with as great a show of dignity as his unfortunate condition permitted.

271

"Be so good as to stand further off, and not to thrust your face at me like that. I shall also be obliged by your going your way and allowing me to go mine."

"With the greatest of pleasure. It ain't no catch to be seen with a scarecrow like you, what's treated your own sister worse than I'd treat a blooming copper. Only, before I do go, perhaps you'll hand over."

"Hand over what?"

"That ten thousand pound you said this lay was going to be worth to me."

"Don't be an idiot!"

"What you call me?"

"I ask you not, if possible, to behave as if you were an—"

Mr Ludlow did not finish his sentence. Before he could do so his companion took, or rather tried to take, him by the throat. The cashier, having had a recent object lesson in the inconveniences of that kind of thing, warded off the threatened attack by planting his fist in Mr Swire's right eye with such a sudden force and directness that Sam, as he staggered backwards, seemed to have some difficulty in keeping himself upon his feet. It was a second or two before he recovered from the pain and shock. When he did, he rushed at Theodore in the fashion of his class—with head down and arms whirling like the sails of a windmill. Then and there the whilom allies engaged in a rough-and-tumble bout of fisticuffs of a sort in which one hardly expects to find a gentleman of Mr Ludlow's type engaged.

Matters, however, had not proceeded far when law and order came upon the scene in the shape of Jaikes, the village constable. Mr Jaikes' methods proved rough and ready. He saw two men fighting; he did not stop in inquire into the why and wherefore—the sight of contention was enough for him.

"Now then! What's all this? We don't want none of this sort of thing here! Off you go—both the two of you!"

Swire, experienced in such matters, was not slow to take the hint. Disengaging himself from the fray, he slunk off with a degree of expedition which showed unequivocal readiness to obey the official mandate. But Mr Ludlow, unaccustomed to being addressed by a policeman in such a tone, evinced a disposition to remonstrate.

"I've been assaulted by two persons."

That he had been subjected to considerable violence was sufficiently plain. But Mr Jaikes did not wait for him to go into details. His manner was curt.

"I've heard! I know all about you! And serve you right! Your friend knows on which side his bread's buttered—if you take my advice you'll go after him."

"That fellow's no friend of mine. My name is—"

Mr Ludlow began fumbling for his card-case. The constable cut him short.

"I don't want to know what your name is, and I don't want to have anything to say to you. Are you going to take yourself off, or am I going to lock you up?"

Moving forward, the policeman showed an inclination to take him by the collar of his coat. As that would have been the third time, in the course of a single morning, of his being subjected to such an indignity, Mr Ludlow's soul rebelled. He took himself off; though painfully conscious—as the policeman's eyes followed his hatless figure—that it was an exceedingly undignified position for a man in his position to have to occupy.

With regret it has to be stated that while Mr Ludlow was falling out with his associate, a difference of opinion was also taking place between another pair of allies. When Miss Foster left Netta in her bedroom she marched straight in search of Mr Rodway. And she found him—at a moment when it would have been perhaps well if she had failed in finding him. He had recently concluded his interview with Mr Ludlow.

And though there was no evidence of his having suffered damage, his apparel was not in the best of order, and there were abundant signs that he was both hot and excited. As coolness and calmness were not at that instant the most prominent characteristics in the young lady's deportment, it did seem unfortunate that they could not have managed to miss each other.

She opened proceedings by looking him up and down with an air which in itself was provoking.

"So you've been fighting?"

His tone in reply was grim.

"If you like to call it so. I've treated Theodore Ludlow to the best thrashing he's ever had in his life—as yet!"

"I suppose it has made you happy. I believe that sort of thing does make some men happy—of a certain nature."

"On the contrary, I'm the most miserable brute in England; and I'm rendered so by the consciousness that this would not have happened if I had persisted, as I ought to have done, in disregarding your advice. If I had only acted honestly and straightforwardly, as I wanted to, it might all have been avoided."

"That's just the sort of remark I expected you would make—just the remark. Allow me to tell you that if you had been half the man I supposed you were, poor dear Netta would not have been in the condition she now is."

"What could I have done to save her, then?"

"You might have contradicted her brother's assertions, as she begged and implored you to."

"And told a lie?"

"Told a lie! You might have found means of silencing his wicked tongue without committing yourself to an actual falsehood. I tell you frankly, Mr Rodway, that I never imagined that you would have behaved as you have done." He gasped, as well he might. "There is that poor girl contemplating suicide."

"Contemplating suicide!"

"What else is there for her to contemplate, since she supposes herself to be falling through the bottomless abyss into which you have allowed her to be plunged?"

"I allowed her to be plunged!"

"If you had thrashed that man at the beginning instead of afterwards, you might have saved her from everything."

"But the mischief was done before I arrived on the scene."

Perhaps it was the consciousness that this was so which made her bite her lips and tipped her tongue with spite.

"We girls were alone. What could we do against two great men? But when you came, you might easily have made them eat their words, if you had not preferred to break poor Netta's heart instead."

He threw out his arms, as if appealing to the silent trees.

"I never heard anything more monstrous! Let me tell you—in face of your cruel accusations—I will speak out!—let me tell you that you are in no small degree responsible for the hideous position into which affairs have drifted."

"That's right! Lay the blame on me! I thought you would. Having thrashed Mr Ludlow—after carefully waiting till after he had broken his sister's heart—now thrash me."

"If you had suffered me to act honestly—"

"Are you suggesting that I advised dishonesty, by word, look, or action?"

"If you had let me tell her the truth about that black-guard—"

"Of whom are you speaking?"

"I am speaking of the scoundrel who is bringing shame upon us all."

"Are you referring to Mr Francis Smithers?"

"Francis Smithers!—bah! Don't let there be any of that hypocrisy between us two."

"And let there be still less of that kind of talk, if you please, Mr Rodway. It is because you are so utterly incapable of dividing the true from the false; of detecting the fundamental lie which is at the root of the pseudo truths, which come from the lips of such men as Theodore Ludlow, that I say that the responsibility is yours for the trouble which has come, and still is coming. I know, it you don't, that there is more manhood in the man you call a scoundrel, than could be obtained from a hundred such men as you and Ludlow and Swire, if you were boiled down into Liebig's extract—more of all the fine, the virile qualities.

"More truth, more honesty, more courage, more wisdom, more dependability—I'd rather trust him with my whole body than you with my little finger. And if you encourage Netta in supposing, for one single instant, that he's anything remotely like the creature that vile man's vile lips have suggested, then you deserve to be whipped at the tail of your own unresting machines as long as they keep running."

The young lady spoke with so much vigour that Mr Rodway—in open-mouthed astonishment—shrank from her, as if fearful of a personal assault.

And while she was emptying on him the vials of her scorn, Netta was suffering herself to stumble into the nets which had been spread to catch her.

CHAPTER 37

THE SETTING OF THE SNARE

It had ended in tears, the passion and the pain, the rage and the frenzy. The climax had come in the form of a paroxysm of weeping. Netta had thrown herself upon her bed to cry. And there she still lay when someone knocked at the door. The knocking came a second time before she heeded. Then she sat up in sudden fright.

"Who's there?" Someone tried the handle, to find the door was locked. "You can't come in. What do you want?"

"A lady wishes to see you, madam."

"A lady—what lady?"

"I understand that she declines to give her name, but that she is very desirous of seeing you. She says that her business is of the utmost importance."

The voice was her maid's. Apparently she had been deputed by one of the men-servants to bear a message.

"Where is my mother? or Miss Foster? I'm not well—tell one of them to see her—I can't."

The maid departed, shortly to return.

"I'm very sorry, madam, but Parker tells me that the lady declines to go without seeing you." Parker was the butler, a personage with imposing manners, of whom Netta herself stood somewhat in awe. "She has sent this note."

Netta descended from the bed, opened the door about three

inches, took the envelope which was passed through the inter-stice, and shut the door again in the woman's face. She had to wipe the tears out of her half-blinded eyes before she could see to read. Then she found that in the envelope was a sheet of paper on which was pencilled, in clear, bold writing, the following :

I am sorry to hear that you are ill, but I must see you at once on a matter which is literally one of life and death. I regret to appear insistent, but as no one will serve but you, I must request you not to keep me waiting.

The writing was strange, there was no signature—nothing to show from whom the communication had come. She had to read the words over two or three times before she was able to grasp their meaning. Then her face assumed a grimmer set-ting. Her blurred eyes became set and rigid. She asked herself a question:

"Now, what else is coming?" She called to the maid with-out—"What sort of looking person is this lady?"

"I haven't seen her, madam."

"Is she young?"

"Parker didn't mention, madam."

"And she won't give her name?"

"She absolutely declines to give her name. Parker says that she says she will give her name to you, but to no one else."

Netta repeated to herself, *sotto voce:* "She'll give her name to me, will she, and to no one else?" She reflected for a few mo-ments, then asked aloud, "Where is she?"

"She is in the oak room, madam."

"Tell her that I will be with her in five minutes."

The maid bore away the message. Netta reread the pencil-led note; stood for a second, as if considering; washed her face and sponged her eyes—the marks of the tears would not come out of them; retouched her hair before the mirror; then began to look for a particular bottle of smelling-salts. It was not upon her dressing-table, nor anywhere in sight. She went into her husband's dressing-room, thinking that it might be there;—he liked the pungent odour of the contents of that particular bottle, and had a trick of appropriating it for his especial use. As it was nowhere to be seen, she drew out his dressing-table drawers, one after the other, supposing that it might be in one of them. In one of the drawers she saw an envelope, but in none of them the bottle.

The envelope was that which was addressed—"To be opened by my wife should nothing have been heard of me by noon on January the second.—Francis Smithers." Had she observed it, it might have put her on the alert; and might even have saved her from the peril which was momentarily coming closer. But she did not observe it, and she went blindly to her fate. Since there were no signs of the bottle, she returned to her bedroom. As she did so the door—which she had not relocked opened. Supposing that it had been opened by her maid, she began to address her.

"Forbes, have you seen my blue smelling-bottle With the—?"

Something which she saw in the mirror in front of which she was standing caused her to slop and turn. Someone had entered the room who was not Forbes—a strange woman, who had closed the door after her as she came in, and who now stood in silence, observing Netta. She was about forty years of age; not bad-looking, in a hard, garish fashion; big, and squarely built; the unmistakable suggestion of muscular strength which was conveyed by her figure being in keeping with the squareness of her jaw and the spirit of domination which looked out of her eyes.

Expensively and even well dressed in tailor-made tweeds, there was that about her which forbade her being mistaken for a woman of gentle birth and breeding. Netta decided, on the instant, that she was a type of person whom, under any circumstances, she would dislike—even had she not presented herself in such a very unusual fashion. Her tone was as severe as she could make it.

"Who are you? And what do you mean by intruding yourself uninvited in my room?"

The woman showed no discomposure. She replied to Netta's inquiries with another—which she left unfinished.

"You are?"

"I am Mrs Smithers."

"Pardon me, I am Mrs Smithers—Mrs Francis Smithers."

Netta swayed a little backwards, so that she was glad to have her hand upon the dressing-table. It was what she had expected.

"I don't understand."

"Don't you really?" There was an insolent intonation in the voice which suggested something more than doubt.

"My husband's name is Smithers."

"Excuse me, your husband's name is not Smithers. That was my husband's name. I am his widow."

What did the woman mean?"

"My husband is dead."

This time Netta's feel refused altogether to support her, even with the aid of the corner of the dressing-table. Fortunately there was a chair al hand to save her from falling on to the floor. Apparently this woman was on a different errand from that which she had feared. Although she had not a notion what it was that had really brought her, her heart leapt within her bosom as if with relief. She said again—this time with truth—

"I don't understand."

"I will make it plain enough. Neither you nor I married a model man. We both married scoundrels. But you seem to have hit upon the greater scoundrel of the two."

"How dare you say it?"

"I dare to say it because it's true. Both our husbands were in jail together."

"I don't believe it."

Netta spoke as if she was choking. The other's voice was hard and clear—pitiless.

"You'll have to believe it. My husband died in jail. Yours sat by his deathbed. When he was dead he set himself to rob him, And in robbing him he robbed me. All that you have is mine—

even to the name by which you call yourself."

"Can you—can you prove that what you say is true? I have heard something of this a little time ago I only want to know."

Netta put her hand up to her forehead, as if it ached.

"Do you think that I would come to you with a tale like this if I couldn't prove that it was true? If I'm forced, I'll prove it in every court in England. The man who calls himself your husband is as little moved by appeals to his sense of mercy and of justice as if he were made of steel. If I must, I'll drag from him what is mine by the help of the law—I'll not get it in any other way. But you—you are young; too young to be wholly bad; you may be different. You may have a heart within your bosom which can be moved to pity. You may be willing to help me against this man—who has wronged you almost as much as he has wronged me!—to get back at least some of the things of which he's robbed me."

"If you are able to show that any of the things I have are yours, I'll not keep them from you for an instant."

"You mean it?"

"I do."

They looked at each other. The one so simple; so easy to deceive; so nearly broken-hearted. The other so unscrupulous; so versed in devious ways; so ready to snatch at an unfair advantage. The elder woman perceived that, because of the girl's piteous plight, she was likely to have an easier task than she had foreseen.

"You will let me prove to you that the man who calls himself your husband has done what I say he has?"

"If you can."

"If I can!—Come with me and I'll show you if I can."

"Come with you?—Where?"

There was a sudden eagerness in the woman's manner from which she instinctively shrank.

"Tonight he's to be called to an account."

"Called to account?—What do you mean?"

"I am not the only one he's robbed—he's robbed others.

When we've asked him to disgorge—to give us back what is our own—he's laughed in our faces. I tell you he's like steel for hardness. But he'll do no more laughing after tonight. He's going to meet those face to face who'll put a stop to that. We've borne enough—as he'll find out. If you mean a tithe of what you say, and are not a brazen-faced liar such as he is—and you don't look it; you look good!—you'll come with me and help us—persuade him to give us back our own."

"Where is he?"

"I'll take you to him."

"I ask you to tell me where he is."

"He's in London. Tonight he's going to a house which is one of his own particular haunts, and there he's going to meet his victims; the unfortunates whose property he has—and you have."

"Not I."

"Yes, you!—you! I see it all about you!—you even have my name! You'll see that he'll start laughing at us again—bid us whistle for the return of a pennyworth he's stolen. And if you're not there to help us, there'll be mischief done."

"Are you sure of what you say?"

"What I tell you is the truth, the whole truth, and nothing but the truth. Can't you see that I am speaking truly?"

"You seem to be—but I have been so much deceived."

"You have!—God knows you have! But if you do as I ask you, deceit will be at end. You'll at least have a quiet conscience, whatever happens; and that is something. If you like, I'll go down on my knees to implore you;—I'll sacrifice my heart's blood to touch yours."

"You need do nothing violent. If you are sure that tonight my husband will be at the house you speak of, under the circumstances you mention, no pressure will be needed to induce me—to be also there."

"I swear that I've told you nothing but the truth—he will be there.—What object could I have in telling you a falsehood?"

That was the inquiry which Netta was putting to herself. She saw no object—then. She arrived at a decision—which was to deliver her into hands which knew not what it was to show—mercy.

"I will come with you.—When shall we start?"

"Now!—At once!—Every moment's precious. The one thing to be feared is to be late. If you are too late, you may have cause to regret it to the last moment of your life."

If Netta could have only known it, the woman, was looking at her with eyes from which—at that very second—there gleamed murder. She was saying to herself that the moments of the pretty fool in front of her were numbered, and enjoying in anticipation the epicurean pleasure of assisting at her despatch. But the girl saw nothing—understood nothing—-guessed nothing. She was only filled with a divine desire at any cost to right the wrong. So she allowed herself to be trapped as easily as if she had been some woodland creature, ignorant of lures.

"If you will sit down, I will put on my hat and jacket and come with you directly." The woman, placing herself on the easiest chair which she could find, watched the girl making ready with a grin which she seemed to find it impossible to restrain. If Netta had noticed it, its peculiar quality might have hinted to her that it might be advisable at least to consult with someone else before she placed herself in this stranger's power. But she noticed nothing.

CHAPTER 38
THE CABMAN

As the voice of Big Ben came across the Park announcing that it was nine o'clock, Mr Smithers strolled up Waterloo Place. It was a fine evening, but very cold. A slight shower of sleet had fallen in London during the earlier part of the day; the roads and pavements were like glass. As he strolled up towards the Circus a hansom kept pace at his side, scenting a possible fare. Mr Smithers smoked as he went. As the hour struck, he removed the cigar from his mouth and stood for a moment to listen. The cabman stopped too; apparently under the impression that the tall figure on the pavement was hesitating whether to walk or ride. Ignoring the driver's hint, Mr Smithers continued his leisurely walk. As he approached the Circus he scanned the loiterers and passers-by.

At the corner he stopped. In the shadow, against the shuttered window of a shop, a man was standing. The two had that part of the pavement to themselves. Mr Smithers, crossing to where he stood, subjected him to a close examination—which the other showed no sign of resenting. He was an undersized fellow, with a thin, dark face—a Jew. In his scarlet necktie was a scarf-pin fashioned to represent the symbol with which Mr Smithers was so well acquainted. Mr Smithers, putting out his fingers, was about to withdraw the pin from its place when the wearer covered it with his hand. He remonstrated—with a strong cockney twang.

"What are you up to? No tricks!—I know you're good at them, but I don't want you to play none of them with me."

Mr Smithers laughed.

"I only wanted to look at it closer. I have wondered, more than once, what it's intended to represent. What's the notion ?"

"Never you mind what the notion is—you keep your hands off, that's all you've got to do.—So you've come, have you? About time too. You're late, you are. Lucky for you you ain't later."

"Why is it lucky?"

The man grinned—unpleasantly.

"As you ain't later, you needn't trouble yourself about the why. I tell you it is lucky.—Are you coming with me?"

"I'm here for that especial purpose."

"Then we shall have to have a cab."

Two hansoms were drawn up against the pavement.—the one which had followed Mr Smithers up Waterloo Place, and another, in front of it, which, it seemed, had been there before the other came. The stranger moved towards the first, Mr Smithers towards the second.

"Here," exclaimed the stranger, "this cab will do. Jump in."

"Thank you," returned Mr Smithers. "I think I prefer this

one. The horse is better."

"What are you giving us? There's nothing the matter with this horse. Come on in here—this one came first."

"All the same, I think I prefer this one. If you are going to oblige me with your company, I should recommend you to take a seat."

Without waiting for the other, Mr Smithers stepped into the cab by which he was standing and sat down. The Jew came and addressed him from the pavement:

"What do you think you're doing? The other cab's mine—I came in it; it's been waiting for me."

"I really think that I would rather ride in a cab which has not been waiting for you."

Mr Smithers' tone was so courteous and pleasant that the other scarcely seemed to know what to make of him.

"Are you coming out of that?"

"I am not. What is more, I am afraid—if you are not coming into this—that I shall have to go."

"Where do you think you're going?"

"My good fellow, what business is that of yours?"

The man returned the speaker's smile with a glance which was not friendly. His tone was sullen.

"Wait half a mo."

Mr Smithers waited. The Jew, going back to his own cab, commenced a colloquy with his driver. Presently a tall man came across the road and joined them. Then the Jew came and look his seat in the cab which Mr Smithers already occupied, seemingly not in the best of tempers. When the driver opened the trap in the roof he called to him through it.

"Hanover Gate, Regent's Park—and don't move as if that horse of yours had only got three legs to go on."

When they had gone some little distance Mr Smithers observed, in his most genial tones :

"I am afraid that my preference for a hansom which had not been waiting for you has caused something in the nature of a hitch in your arrangements."

His companion's tone, as he replied, was not by any means so pleasant as his own had been.

"Don't you put yourself out. There won't be no hitches in our arrangements by the time we're through with them."

"Our?—Your friends are in the plural number, I see. I presume that one of them is following us in that cab of yours."

"Look here! if you don't want to make things worse than what they are, you won't see nor hear nothing, and you won't presume nothing either. You just keep a still tongue in your head, and come along with me."

"Your advice sounds excellent. Will you try a cigar?"

"I don't mind if I do." The Jew selected one from the case which the oilier proffered. "I suppose there's no hanky about them? I understand that you're a bit too fly, my bloke; that's why I ask. I've heard of drugged cigars before today!"

"I'm beginning to fear that you're a bit of an ass."

"Now then! Don't you call me no names, or you'll be sorry."

"Since I imagine that I might have less difficulty in throwing you out of the cab than you would have in throwing me, I take it that the probabilities of sorrow are with you."

The Jew, who was biting off the end of his cigar, turned sharply on the seat.

"If you were to throw me out of this cab—and I'm not denying that, by the look of you, you could do it—you'd be about one of the sorriest men that ever lived."

"I've half a mind to throw you out, merely for the purpose of ascertaining on what grounds that assertion is based."

"I'd keep to the half mind if I was you.—Got a match?" Mr .Smithers handed him a gold match-box which had been a present from Netta—one of the many presents which she was so fond of presenting to him with his own money. The Jew admired it. "That's something like a match-box, that is; it would pawn for a tenner."

"Do you think so ?"

"Lay a dollar it would. I've done in a few things like that in my time. I ought to know." Apparently, having recovered from his bad temper, he was becoming talkative.—"This ain't a bad smoke. Daresay they stand you in a bob apiece. I know where you can get 'em for eightpence."

"You might give me the address."

"It wouldn't be no use—to you."

"Why not? One likes to buy in the cheapest market."

"I daresay."

About his curtness there was something which was almost ominous; as if it conveyed—and was intended to convey—a threat. It moved Mr Smithers' mirth. He laughed.

"You speak as if my buying days were over."

The other's reply was distinctly not an answer to his words.

"It's a fine night, ain't it?"

"But cold—a cold night on which to die."

For the second time the Jew turned sharply in his seat—regarding the other with his dark, inscrutable eyes.

"Do you think you'd find it so?"

"I haven't considered the matter from the personal point of view. I fancy one doesn't till one gets close to it."

"Then, if I were you, I should consider it."

"You think that I am close to death?"

"You may be."

"On the other hand, I mayn't. One should always weigh all the possibilities.—May I inquire your name?"

"Brown—Sam Brown. You've heard it before."

"I've seen it written—followed, I think, by a note of interrogation."

"I shouldn't be surprised. Some folks always do look like questioning me when I tell them that my name's Sam Brown—they seem to think it ought to be Moses." The cab drew up. "Here we are—Hanover Gate. This horse has got four legs. Out you skip."

"How much farther have we to go? I think I would rather ride all the way."

"Then you ain't going to. I ain't going to take no strange cab of which I don't know nothing up to my crib—not quite I ain't. As it is, we ain't got more than a hundred yards to go.—Are you going to get out?"

"Are you sure that we haven't more than a hundred yards to go?"

"I ain't measured it with a tape, and so I tell you straight.— Once more I ask you, are you getting out?"

Mr Smithers stepped on to the pavement.

"It's just possible that I may be able to walk that hundred yards of yours. I'll at least give it a trial. Your following friend doesn't appear to be in sight. Driver, what's become of that cab which I wouldn't take?"

"Followed us to the top of Baker Street, then turned off towards Dorset Square."

"Did it? Perhaps your friend has gone to prepare for us.— Thank you, driver; here's half-a-crown for you."

The cab remained stationary while the two men, crossing the road, passed into Grove Gardens. Then the cab moved after them. As it neared the corner a policeman approached. The driver, pulling up, descended from his box, addressing the constable in a peremptory fashion which seemed to startle him.

"Mind my horse!" He spoke a few words in an undertone, which seemed to startle the constable still more. Then added aloud, in the abrupt *staccato* tones of the man who commands, "Stay here till I come back."

Without further ceremony he also disappeared into Grove Gardens, leaving the policeman in charge of his horse and cab.

Well, well," exclaimed that officer to himself, evidently taken aback by the unexpectedness of his position, "this beats anything! I wonder what's up now?"

When this very original cabman entered the Gardens, the two men were still in plain sight. Mr Smithers was laughing. In the prevailing stillness the sound was distinctly audible to the man at the back, who indulged in a comment of his.

"He's got presence of mind and pluck. He'll want 'em both. Unless I'm mistaken, he's walking into a hotter place even than he fancies."

The two men turned one corner, then another, then a third, the cabman, still apparently unobserved, keeping judiciously in the rear. He refrained from following them round the last corner, but when he gained it, stopped to listen. He could hear the footsteps of the men in front. Then they ceased.

"I thought so. Mr Brown's looking to see if there's anyone behind."

It must have been a pure guess, but it was a correct one.

The road which the Jew had entered had trees on either side. Old-fashioned houses stood in grounds of their own. In most cases each was surrounded by its own high wall, so that, from the street, it was difficult to see what lay beyond. It seemed a very quiet neighbourhood. Lying, as it did, off the main road, traffic was practically non-existent. Not a creature seemed to be about. As Mr Brown, suddenly pausing, turned right-about-face, his companion remarked on the entire absence of any sort of going to-and-fro.

"There's quite an atmosphere of remoteness about this place, Mr Brown. To all intents and purposes, it's a thousand miles from the traffic of the city. May I inquire what you're looking for?"

"I'm looking to see if there are any friends of mine about."

"Indeed. Do you expect friends of yours to be about?—here, in the open street?" Mr Brown was whistling beneath his breath, very softly. Mr Smithers recognised the air. "So you're a whistler too? Wherever I go, that air seems destined to haunt me.—You must pardon my observing that that hundred yards has already stretched to half-a-mile. If it's likely to extend much farther, I'm afraid I shall have to ask you to excuse me."

"Excuse you "

The Jew looked at him with a grin. Mr Smithers met his glance with a smile.

"I said—I'm afraid I shall have to ask you to excuse me."

"Ah! Well, we won't talk about that; because, as it happens, we're there."

"There? Where's 'there'? And what's 'there'?"

"This is the place—over you come."

Mr Brown moved across the road. Mr Smithers remained where he was. Instantly the other, pausing, turned to look at him.

"Are you coming?"

"Is that the house inside that ten foot wall?"

"That's it."

"I suppose there is a house—nothing's visible from here—it's completely cut off from the world."

"There's a house right enough—as you'll see."

"It would be rather a joke if, after all the trouble you and your friends have taken, I changed my mind, and declined to come."

"You'd find it a joke—I wouldn't advise you to try it."

There was something in the Jew's tone which was very grim indeed. Mr Smithers laughed.

"I think that—once more—I'll take your advice, and won't."

"You hadn't better.—Come on."

The two men moved towards the ten-foot wall side by side.

"Do you know, Mr Brown, that you've a way of addressing one as if one were a dog?"

"It's manner."

"Rather an unpleasant manner. If you, in turn, will take advice, you'll change it."

A gate opened in the wall under whose shadow they were moving. As if in response to a preconcerted signal, two men came out. They placed themselves on either side of Mr Smithers. Pausing, he regarded them with his sunny smile—his hands in the pockets of his long overcoat.

"Friends of yours, Mr Brown?"

"Yes—friends of mine."

One of the men was tall and thin—with a thinness which suggested sinews. Mr Smithers recognised in him the individual who had crossed from Mr Brown's cab at Piccadilly Circus. The other was a negro. Without a word each took Mr Smithers by an arm—manipulating him with such dexterity that, almost before he knew it, he found himself standing with the three men inside the gate, which was shut behind him.

Two minutes afterwards the driver of the hansom came dashing into Park Road as if he were running for his life—to find the policeman still in charge of his horse and cab. Without seeming to pause in his flight, he sprang on to the box.

"Let go her head!" he gasped;—the pace at which he had come had left him almost speechless for want of breath.

The policeman stepped back. The driver snatched at the reins; turned the mare; and—without vouchsafing another syllable to the constable—sent her pelting along the road at a rate of speed which was considerably beyond the statutory limit.

The officer stared after him with feelings which were plainly mixed. "He'll soon get himself pulled up if he keeps on like that. I wonder what is up. I suppose it is all right, and I've not been hoaxed. It'll be a nice lookout for me if I have been."

Judging from the expression of his countenance, it would seem that he was in a state of almost painful uncertainty.

CHAPTER 39
AMONG THIEVES

Mr Smithers looked from one to the other of the two men who had been responsible for the rapidity of his passage through the gate.

"Gentlemen, wasn't that a little uncalled for? I have a constitutional disrelish for the touch of a stranger's hand."

The tall man answered—with a nasal twang—

"Perhaps it was a little unceremonious, but there are occasions on which ceremony has to take a back seat. I'll ask you to be so good as to step along."

They were standing in what was evidently a covered passageway leading from the outer gate to the house. The sides were apparently of brick, covered with painted plaster; the roof was of glass. A faint light glimmered in the hall beyond, but where they were it was all in shadow.

"You're an American, sir?"

"I am; so you'll understand that I come from a country where they don't like to be kept fooling around so perhaps you will step along."

"Then, since you are an American, you will probably understand what these are. I believe that in certain sections of your society they are common playthings."

He took a quick step to the rear, so that he had his back against the door. As he took his hands out of his overcoat pockets it was seen that he held a revolver in each, the muzzles of which were pointed in their direction. Without a moment's hesitation the negro, ducking, came straight at him; there was a report; he went over on to his back with a sound which was more like a bellow than a human cry. The others, who had shown a disposition to join him in his onward rush, were equally prompt to display a readiness to keep their distance—the gleaming muzzles were still trained on them.

"That's intended for a hint. He's got the bullet in the fleshy part of his thigh; I don't suppose it'll do much damage to a hide like his; he'll be able to pick it out at his leisure. You, as an American, ought to know better than to set black scum like that at a white man."

The American spoke to the writhing black, who still continued to give utterance to his feelings,

"Stop that noise; it isn't the first time you've had a piece of lead inside you." Then he put a question to Mr Smithers, which smacked of the ironical. "Is that how you're going to take it?"

"It is. I must request you, sir, not to let your hands go near your pockets; nor you, Mr Brown—or I shall have to ask you to hold them up."

Brown acted on the suggestion then and there.

"My goodness! I'll hold mine up with all the pleasure in life."

He held his hands up in front of him in a fashion which seemed to strike the American as funny. He laughed.

"I didn't know you were just that sort of man, or I wouldn't have come out without my guns. I haven't so much as a pea-shooter on me. If I'd brought a gun you wouldn't be standing there quite so cock-a-doodle; but I didn't understand that they were quite so spry with them over here."

"That's frank. I will be equally candid. I have come to meet you, gentlemen, at your particular request, but the meeting is to be on my own terms. By that I mean that I am prepared to behave myself so long as you do; but that if there's going to be trouble, the trouble is not going to be all on one side. And in that connection I would again observe that I've a constitutional disrelish to the touch of a stranger's hand. Now, if you'll lead the way into the house—and take your black friend with, you; by the wool, if that's easiest—I'll follow."

"You will?"

"I am in the habit of stating my meaning exactly. I tell you, if you will lead the way into the house, I will follow."

The American spoke to the negro. "You ain't dead, nor yet dying. Stand up."

With his assistance the black managed to stagger to his feet, clapping his hand to his thigh as he did so, and glancing at Mr Smithers in a manner which was an eloquent expression of his feelings. The trio moved on ahead, the black floundering along with the aid of the tall man's arm; emitting groans and imprecations, which were received by his supporter with a silence which was scarcely sympathetic. Mr Smithers strode after them, his arms dangling at his sides, the revolvers in his hands. It was a singular procession. The passage was a long one, the house evidently standing at some distance from the road. The three in front moved slowly, hampered by the stumbling black.

When the Jew quickened his pace, seemingly with the intention of announcing their arrival, Mr Smithers pulled him up.

"Gently, Mr Brown;—keep together, if you please. Your friends indoors must be quite aware of what has happened, and will have made all preparations for your arrival that you can possibly desire. They do not need you to recruit their forces."

Brown obeyed, keeping close to his associates with an apparently punctilious desire to avoid the resentment of the man with the revolvers, which, in its way, was amusing They approached the end of the passage. In front were stone steps, ascending, through an open doorway, to what looked like a dimly lighted hall.

"Stop!" cried Mr Smithers. They stopped, as at the word of command. "What's beyond that doorway?"

The American replied :

"A house. At least, there was a house when I came out to bid you how-d'ye-do. Perhaps surprise at your behaviour has caused it to take itself off the face of the earth."

"Let me again recommend you, and, through you, your friends, not—if they wish to avoid trouble—to cause it. They may think me simple to venture alone into a building in which they are; but let me assure them that I m capable of showing adequate resentment—even though alone—for liberties which they may be thinking of taking."

Mr Smithers' clear tones were probably distinctly audible to any unseen audience which might have been beyond that open door. The American, in reply, was jocular;

"Hear, hear! Now, if the address is finished, may we move on?"

"You may. Only, do let me urge you to remember."

"You can bet that we'll remember. Remembering is what we're best at."

The three men in front, mounting the steps, entered the house. Mr Smithers came closer. They moved across the shadowed hall. He went after them. So soon as he had crossed the threshold, and was about to look about him, in the dim light, to see what sort of place it was which he was entering, someone sprang at him from out of the shadows on either side. *Crack, crack*, went his revolvers. A cry of pain seemed to show that someone had been hit. But apparently it was neither of his immediate assailants. They clung to his wrists with a pertinacity which not only made it impossible for him to throw them off, but rendered it difficult for him to use his weapons with advantage.

Suddenly someone came at him from behind. The men in

front, relieved from their fear of being used as his targets, returned to join in the attack. The American's long fingers closed about his throat in a fashion which was not pleasant. Others came running down the stairs—he could hear them shouting words of encouragement to their friends as they descended. Against such odds resistance was vain. By sheer weight of numbers they bore him to the ground; and having got him down, they kept him there. The American proffered him a piece of advice.

"If you move, we'll have to break your head; and as that might hurt, I'll use your word and recommend you to keep still."

Another voice came from the background—which also had an American twang in it, and which, although soil and gentle, had in it a suggestion of menace and authority:

"Tie him up—tight."

When he heard this, Mr Smithers made another violent effort to throw off his antagonists. So soon as he recommenced his struggles, the same unimpassioned voice pronounced two words: "Bash him!"

By dint of exerting his utmost strength it almost seemed for a moment or two as if Mr Smithers might regain his liberty. Compelled to take advantage of such means of defence as were within his power, bringing his leg up suddenly, he dealt the American—who was kneeling upon his prostrate body—such a violent blow in the back, that he was forced momentarily to release his hold.

In the confusion which ensued, Mr Smithers all but regained his feet. Shaking off at least some of those who held him down, he raised himself clean off the ground.

But as he was scrambling on to his knees, something struck him a blow on the head which seemed to knock the life right out of him. Falling back with a thud upon the floor, he lay still. When they were sure that his silence was obligatory, and not designed, his assailants loosed him. As Mr Brown stood up he rubbed his arms and shoulders. "That done him, that did! He very nearly done me first, though."

The tall American, who seemed to be a little uncertain on his feet, was apparently endeavouring to ascertain the condition of his spinal column.

"If there'd have been a little more powder at the back of his knee, I'm thinking that I never should have sat or stood up straight again. There's steel springs in the muscles of his legs."

His compatriot remarked, in his curiously gentle voice:

"You'd better look spry and tie him up before he starts with his leg work again." A short stout man stood looking down at the recumbent figure, rubbing his hands together and smiling as he did so. It was Mr Chaffinch.

"I told you that we should have trouble with him. He is not an ordinary man—he has such high spirits—and he's so difficult to persuade—he won't hear reason."

"He's a devil, that's what he is! But we will show to him that there are other devils also."

The speaker was Gustav Kronberg—the gentleman in the yellow suit, who had visited Mr and Mrs Smithers in the hotel at Rome. His opinion was corroborated by Mr Bob Hammick's husky tones:

"He's a bitter bad bargain, that's what I call him. And as for owdacity, I never see his equal—strike me pink, I never have! He's a fair red-hot 'un—that's what he is!

Mr Hammick moved the motionless body, round which they all were grouped, with the toe of his boot. The smooth, authoritative tones made themselves heard again.

"Gentlemen, not so much talking, if you please. We're here for business; and, so far as I'm concerned, time's of value. I'm ready to credit our friend with all the qualities with which you endow him, and yet I'm betting that he's met his match at last. When he leaves this edifice he won't be the man he was when he came in—not by a deal. Tie him tight there—never mind about cutting into his arms.

"We don't want any more wrestling matches just yet awhile. If we've got him so that he can't move, wishing to heaven that he could, maybe we'll find him more handy for that means of persuasion we're going to employ."

Chapter 40
The Eight

When Mr Smithers returned to consciousness,, he first became aware of two things. One was, that he was sopping wet; the other, that, regarding him with a malignant grin, was the hideous and evil countenance of the negro he had wounded. The cause of his being wet was made immediately apparent by the fact that, so soon as his eyes were opened, a quantity of ice-cold water was dashed into his face. It was thrown with such force that it not only blinded him, but it also deprived him for a second of his just returning breath. So soon as he could, he turned his head to see who was the cause of the outrage. A man was standing a foot or two away from him, holding an empty zinc pail. He recognised him.

"I've seen you before. You're the man who spoke to me in Chancery Lane."

Mr Hammick grinned.

"And now you see me again—it's going to be quite a happy little meeting, as you'll find."

"You also see me again—leastways you will, when you've got rid of that."

Mr Smithers suddenly realised that by Hammick's side Mr Brown was standing, and that he also held a pail—a full one. While he still was speaking, he lifted his pail and flung its contents into Mr Smithers' face. The icy water entered both his eyes and mouth. He gasped and spluttered in his efforts to be rid of it, seeming to cause much amusement by the grimaces which these proceedings necessarily involved. Laughter seemed to resound on all sides of him.

When he had regained the use of his eyes, he perceived that in front of him was a plain wooden table, round which men were seated, regarding him with expressions on their features which suggested that they found the spectacle he presented most diverting. His head throbbed, his senses seemed dulled, he was conscious of such exquisite pain that he was prevented from taking advantage of the few wits which he seemed to have at his command. So stupid did he feel that a perceptible interval elapsed before he understood what it was that was paining him. Then the thing became plain enough—too plain.

He was secured to a chair—which, in its turn, seemed fastened to the floor—by slender cords which were wound round and round his legs and arms and body, with such remorseless tightness that they not only cut into his flesh like knives, but, by biting into the veins, and so preventing the proper circulation of the blood, tortured him as if they had been red-hot wires. He had to bite his lips to stifle the exclamation which, in the first stress of his agony, involuntarily rose to them.—for he realised that these were men who would find the most delicious entertainment in his confession that he smarted at their hands.

He was yet, however, so little master of himself, that some instants passed before he was able, not only to open his eyes, but to keep them open—wearing a smile which he made it his utmost endeavour should be as a mask to conceal the pains as of hell, which seemed every instant to increase in intensity. While he steeled himself to show an indifferent front to the men who, he was aware, looked eagerly for signs of the agonies which racked him, someone spoke to him from the other end of the table. It was the American, whose soft rounded tones seemed to suggest—to the quivering man in front of him—oil of vitriol, as if he meant his every word should burn.

"We are glad to welcome you among us, Mr Francis Smithers; and regret that the singularity of your behaviour should have constrained us to commence by handling you in a fashion which we had intended to postpone till later in your visit. You're sitting there as in a suit of fire, and it rests for you to say to what temperature it has still to be raised."

With an effort which was almost superhuman, Mr Smithers fixed his glance upon the speaker—and smiled. He was a man of between thirty and forty years of age;—a commonplace looking man; suggesting, in his appearance, nothing unusual, either physical or mental. He had light brown hair and a slight sandy moustache. His eyes, which were grey, were his most peculiar feature—the pupils had a trick of dilating, as it seemed at will, which reminded one of a cat, and which was both startling and disagreeable. He sat forward, with his arms upon the table, twisting a pen between his fingers. Mr Smithers put to him a question :

"May I venture to ask to whom it is that I have the pleasure of speaking?"

"You may that. I'm Waterson—Samuel Waterson, of Philadelphia, Penn.; and as this little association is one of my pet notions, and I've sunk a Satan of a pile in it, and taken any amount of trouble, you may reckon that I take a real interest in you."

"I fancy I have heard the name of Samuel Waterson before—in connection with the police?"

"It's in the betting."

"As a forger of banknotes?"

"I have seen myself described in cold type as—the Banknote King."

"Judging from your tone, you would appear to pride yourself upon the fact of your being a blackguard, a thief, and a coward, Mr Waterson. I have always understood that all thieves were cowards, but I have not realised how true that was till now."

"Clip him over the mouth, Linkman! He's too much tongue."

The black, who was seated on his left, stood up and struck him with his clenched fist upon the mouth. The blow was a sufficiently severe one to fuddle him for a moment. When he had regained enough self-possession he turned to the black with a smile :

"You coloured gentleman!"

The words, or the manner in which they were spoken, or both, roused the negro to fury. Gripping the helpless man's hair with the fingers of one hand, with the other he began to pommel him about the head and face, no one endeavouring to stay him with so much as a word. Indeed, when he had amused himself sufficiently, Waterson said, as Mr Smithers sat dazed and bleeding in front of him:

"You see, that's the sort we are. We like people to keep civil tongues in their heads. *And* if you don't do as we tell you, we'll do you."

Mr Chaffinch, who was on the speaker's right, added a kind of postscript—rubbing his fat hands together, and wrinkling his face with his smile :

"I advised you to behave judiciously; you took no notice, and you see what comes of it."

Mr Smithers' rejoinder was scarcely courteous :

"So, Mr Augustus Chaffinch, you are at last in your proper place among your brother blackguards!"

The fat man waved his hands.

"Now do you call that judicious? A person in your position should have more sense. If your conduct were only judicious, even yet things might be made so much more pleasant."

Mr Kronberg interposed;—he was on the other side of Waterson :

"For me, I do not think it matters what he says. We owe him so much already that a little more makes no difference."

Waterson tapped on the table with the end of his pen; his tone was blandly sardonic

"What our friend Kronberg says is true; we owe you so much already. We had arranged the biggest coup we had ever planned; bent all our energies to carry it into execution; spent ourselves in our determination that there should be no hitch; we actually saw our fortunes made, when you—a perfect stranger—come suddenly out of nowhere, and calmly appropriate—entirely to yourself—the priceless treasures which we had accumulated at the cost of so much time, pains, skill, and money, and which were the common property of us all; and you laugh! You will easily believe that the humour of the situation is hardly likely to strike us in quite the same way as it does you. You have enjoyed the jest for a really considerable space of time. You must admit that the moment has arrived for us to share in your enjoyment."

Mr Chaffinch held out his hands in front of him, with what he perhaps intended for a persuasive gesture:

"You must admit it—as a reasonable person, you must certainly admit it."

Mr Smithers was silent. The fact that the continually increasing pressure of the cords which bound him was bringing out drops of anguished sweat upon his forehead did not prevent his smiling. Waterson continued :

"To proceed to details. You have in your possession banknotes—or what resemble banknotes—of the face value of over a million sterling. You hear what I say?"

"I do."

"You also hold the finest set of plates for the production of banknotes which ever came out of an engraver's hand, and an absolutely invaluable stock of real banknote paper; what we went through, severally and collectively, to get that paper, you are possibly incapable of realising. You continue to follow me?"

"You have still left me my sense of hearing."

"Then continue to make the best use of it while it is still yours; it is possible that it will not be yours much longer. You are also the custodian—the involuntary and unintentional custodian, so far as we are concerned—of a practically unique collection of jewellery. It would not be placing an immodest valuation on it were we to state that it is really worth a million sterling. These things—the notes, the plates, the paper, the jewels—are ours."

"In what sense are they yours?"

"We printed the notes, engraved the plates, bought the paper; in our own fashion, annexed the jewels; in that sense they are ours."

"But if—as would appear to be your own rule possession is nine-tenths of the law?"

There is the crucial point! In that sense, at present they are ours which is the reason why you are here. We placed these things in charge of one of ourselves, on the understanding that, on a certain day, certain things should be done with them. Before that day arrived our friend met trouble. For a long term of years we had to eat our heart out in the consciousness that our fortune was where we couldn't get at it, for we had made the stupendous and stupid error of allowing it to be placed where it was only accessible to our unfortunate friend, who was himself secluded both from it and from us. But we bore up, I hope, like men; secure in the conviction that the time would come when we should enter into the enjoyment of our own. You perceive the situation?"

"I listen to your words."

"Then I cannot but think that they must move you near-ly to tears. Talk about patience on a monument! Think of the patience with which we eight men waited for an opportunity to get at that box which was being guarded—theoretically, for us—by that Safe Deposit Company. Then picture our feelings when our friend Hammick informed us that an individual— who might have dropped from the moon, for all we knew, and for all the warning we had had of his approach—had entered that company's premises—under his very eyes!—and used our box as if it were his own. Can't you imagine the sensations with which we heard that news?"

"Weren't you pleased?"

"Oh we were—down to the ground. When we learned what kind of an individual that individual was; how he laughed and laughed, and kept on laughing, when hints were given to him of the injury he was doing to eight hardworking and patient men, our pleasure grew greater; only there wasn't enough of it to go round. The earnest and heartfelt applications of separate indi-viduals of our little society have only amused you—so I under-stand. Contradict me if I'm wrong. Various honest and peaceful avocations have served to keep us scattered over the face of the earth—we're a globetrotting little crowd. This is the first oppor-tunity we have had of introducing ourselves to you collectively; and we therefore propose to take advantage of it to ask you one or two questions. Have I made myself clear to you so far?"

"Clearer than you imagine."

"You flatter me; because, in that case, so to speak, I shall have penetrated to the very marrow of your bones. Kindly pay careful attention to the questions which I am about to have the honour of putting to you, and weigh your words before you answer them. In the first place, will you be so good as to tell us where our property now is?"

"I decline to admit that it is your properly."

"We haven't time to argue that, though I'm free to allow that it may seem to you to be arguable; but age comes fast, and we're in a hurry. Will you be so good as to tell us where the property which you decline to admit is ours now is?"

"I will not."

"That's final?"

"It is."

"You're sure?"

"I am."

"You hear, my dear friends, that this gentleman declines to tell us where our fortune is located. Perhaps that's because it has vanished into air; let's hope it isn't because he's wasted it all on riotous living. In the second place, are you prepared to hand over to us the property in question, say, within twelve hours of this?"

"I am not."

"You are not ?"

"You heard what I said."

"Yes; but as this is a matter of some little importance, I am real anxious to be sure that I hear right; and to give you a chance of changing your mind before it's altogether too late. So perhaps you'll excuse me if I ask you just once more if you'll disgorge inside twelve hours?"

"You have had my answer."

"And I may again take that answer to be final?"

"You may."

"Since this fortune which you won't admit to be ours may be stowed away in quarters where it mayn't be just handy to get at, perhaps twelve hours is too short a period to want to tie you down to. So I will now ask you to be good enough to state to this assembled company when it will be convenient to hand it over."

"Never."

"That's a hard word, 'never.' Perhaps some of it is spent; other people's money is dreadful easy to burn. Would you like to take advantage of this occasion to mention when you'll let us have what's left?"

"You'll have nothing from me—ever."

"To hear you one would judge that your words were fast to the bed-rock. Shall we talk of shares? You can't want to keep it all; it's against nature. There's notes, plates, paper, jewels. Would you kindly like to mention what you'll let us have? You can't be such an all-fired monopolist as not to want to give us something?"

"The jewels, I believe, were stolen. The notes, plates, and paper represent a form of criminality against which society has to be continually on its guard. You seriously misjudge my character if you suppose that I am capable of placing in the hands of professional criminals, such as you confess yourselves to be, tools which you propose to use to work serious, and possibly irreparable, mischief to innocent men and women."

"You take a high and comical tone, considering your record. You might be a gospel-pitcher, instead of the worst egg in the basket."

"I fancy that your knowledge of me is merely superficial. With men of your type I have not only no sympathy, but very much the contrary."

Men of my type! You have a face. I'd been told of it before, but I didn't understand what a face till I'd had the pleasure of meeting you. And what do you call men of your type?"

"Have you brought me here for the purpose of furnishing you with what I conceive lo be a correct analysis of my own character?"

"We have not, and that's a fact. I'm obliged to you for the reminder—Well, we've put our questions and we've had your answers; and I daresay you understand that we rather expected what kind of answers they would be. We've kind of hung out

303

the olive branch before; you didn't snatch at it, and we didn't suppose you'd do much in the way of snatching now. We are sorry; we would have liked you to have behaved as if you were a white man.

"It'd have revived our belief in human nature if you'd have handed over, cheerful and without a murmur, the fruits of our earnest and very real labours. But since you're not built that way—and begging your pardon for this little speech—we're going to use persuasion, and so endeavour to supply deficiencies in your architecture. Now how much persuasion do you think you'll want before you're brought to see that it might be worth your while to hand over to us what's our own?"

"Nothing you can do will induce me to change my mind."

"Nothing? That's a vague expression—covers a deal of ground. You're sure that's the word you want to use?"

"I am."

"Ever heard of the tortures of the Spanish Inquisition? Suppose we try some of those?"

"You can try what you please. I've no doubt you're scoundrels and cowards enough for anything."

"Suppose we drop you into boiling oil?" Mr Smithers laughed outright. "Funny idea, isn't it? I notice you're easily amused; it's one of your strongest points. We'll fill you right up with amusement before we've done. You know we mean to get back what's our own if we have to tear the soul right out of you to do it."

"My soul is beyond your purview."

"You think so? Your body isn't—that's a dead sure thing. What's to hinder us from tearing the flesh from off you with a pair of red-hot pincers?"

"The law of England will have its pound of flesh from you in exchange for all that you may take from me."

"That's your conviction—and a very comfortable one it must be to have. When we're stripping the flesh off your bones it must be so soothing for you to be able to, reflect that someone will serve us just the same in the good time that's coming. Now you might hardly believe it, but I believe we've hit upon a means of persuasion which will so appeal to both your soul and body as to induce you to return that lot of goods to their rightful owners inside of half-an-hour."

"I do not believe it."

"Are you a sporting man?"

"Not where vermin are concerned."

"Meaning me. Thank you very much. If you were a sporting man—where vermin are concerned—I'd be willing to have a nice little bet that when this means of persuasion is brought to bear on you, you'll come round to our way of thinking well inside the thirty minutes."

"You'd lose your money."

"Not much I shouldn't. Do you know what the means of persuasion is?"

"I neither know nor care."

"Can you guess? I can see you can't, by the face of you, or you wouldn't be sitting there so nice and pleasant—though, as it is, you look as if your beauty was spoiled for good, and half the senses beat out of you; and there's great drops of wet trickling down your forehead and your cheeks that's being wrung out of you by the whipcord that's burning into your head's marrow—and may it burn! But all that's nothing to what you'll look like, and feel like, thirty seconds after I've rung this hell."

He struck the gong of a hand-bell which was before him on the table three times Almost before the last stroke had ceased vibrating, a door opened at the end of the room. A woman, coming in, continued to hold it open, as if to enable someone else to pass.

And Netta entered.

Chapter 41
The Means of Persuasion

What Mr Smithers had been expecting to see he could not himself have said—possibly some grotesque implement of hideous torture, but not this.

Indeed, so wholly taken was he by surprise, so far from anticipating any visitation of the kind, that he at first supposed that the agony which his bonds were causing him had mounted to his brain, and that what he seemed to see in front of him was an optical delusion. So it happened that for some seconds he continued to stare in silence at Netta, and she at him, both appearing unable to credit the evidence of their own senses.

Her veil, which was drawn aside, drooped over the brim of her hat. Her cheeks were colourless; then, on a sudden, they went fiery red, and paled again. Her eyes showed signs of weeping; even now, in the corner of each a tear was standing. Her lips were tremulous. She drew quick breaths, as if her heart beat fast. She stood very straight, her head a little back, her hands held a little in front of her—as if expectant of a blow. But it was plain that the blow which she actually received was altogether beyond anything which her imagination had foreshadowed.

She stared at the man tied in the chair, with yards and yards of thin cord lacing him about, confining him as if in a vice, with the torn, disordered, dusty clothing, with the rumpled hair, and bruised and bleeding face, as if incredulous of the idea that this could be her husband. But when she began to realise that this indeed was he, this creature in such a sorry plight, she gave back a little, breathing faster and faster, the colour corning and going in her checks.

At the same time it dawned on Mr Smithers that this woman, this girl, appearing so miraculously in this haunt of villains, was his wife, his bride of a few months' standing, whose innocence of evil still was virginal. And when he saw her moving back, and her agitation at the sight which he presented, he forgot his own condition, and made as if to rise and go to her. But so soon as he moved, his bonds bit him tighter, so that, before he knew it, a groan of agony had escaped from his lips. As she heard it Netta gave an answering cry, moving towards him as if to offer aid and comfort. But before she had taken a second step the woman who had brought her there held her by her right arm, and Bob Hammick had planted himself directly in her path.

"None of that," said Mr Hammick. "You stop where you are.

Hands off—no touching's allowed."

"But," returned Netta, looking at him as if she supposed him to be ignorant of the relation in which she stood to the man in the chair, "he's my husband."

"Never you mind what he is. You stop where you are, or you'll be made to."

The intentional brutality of the speaker's tone seemed to add to her already sufficiently obvious bewilderment, as if she could not but fancy that he had made some strange mistake in addressing her so. Waterson, since her entrance, had been observing her with an air of amusement; now, waving his hand towards her, he spoke to Mr Smithers.

"This is the means of persuasion we propose to use. Hadn't you better own at sight that you are beaten?"

Mr Smithers, ignoring him, addressed his wife. His voice was a little hoarse, his face a ghastly white.

"Netta, how is it that you are here?"

She replied, in tones which trembled :

"I came with this lady. I understood from—"

Waterson cut her short.

"Excuse me, Miss—sorry to interrupt a lady, especially when she's young and pretty—but you've been brought here to speak when you're spoken to by me, and by me only. If you're as smart as you look, you'll he careful not to pay attention to any other creature in this room." He turned to her husband. "As for you, the next time you speak to her without my leave I'll have her tied up. I mean what I say, so if you care a tin cent for the young lady's comfort, you'll just watch out."

"You hound!"

"Now, look here, that's not talk for one gentleman to use to another; you know it isn't, and if you don't I'll have to learn you manners. It doesn't seem to be much use to knock chips off you, so the next time you pitch any of that sort of talk this way I'll knock chips off her and you shall see me do it. I'll use her as a whipping-boy, to keep you in good order—so long as you behave, all right; when you misbehave, she'll smart."

If looks could kill, the speaker would have fallen dead in his chair. Mr Smithers' face became transformed. All thought of his own sufferings seemed swept away by the flood of rage which came rushing over him. He seemed to swell in his chair. Waterson commented on the change in his humour.

"So your dander's rising?—I thought it would. Up to now you've been too dead calm for me, my sonny. There are times when I like to deal with a man who's got hell inside him, and this is one of them. Once more—you see what are the means of persuasion we propose to use. I understand that this isn't the first time you've met the lady. You're thinking that a man who would mishandle a woman isn't a man, and there I'm with you. If she is mishandled, it's you that'll do it. You've got the whip-hand of us; and if to keep it you choose to sacrifice the woman who loves you, the responsibility's yours—don't you throw dust in your own eyes—it's yours.

"You've made free with our property, and you've used it to live on the fat of the land and to buy yourself a wife—and here she is. If you've a spark of manhood in you, which you pretend is wanting in us, you won't try to hang on to what isn't yours at the cost of the woman who's trusted you; for she'll have to pay—dearly—for what you keep. If you choose to keep your pockets filled at such a price, then you're the kind of skunk for whom there isn't any use; and we're going to prove it before we've done with you.—You hear what I say?"

"I hear language which, coming from such a quarter, is the highest compliment you can pay me."

"Oh, you may sneer—just for a little while; then every sneer of yours she'll pay for. You want breaking in, and by ——! you shall be broken. I've seen your sort tamed before today. It isn't a pretty business, but it's wonderful how they come to heel when it's through.—Now, for the last time, are you going to give us back our own, or shall we have to use this means of persuasion to make you?"

"Each time you insult or hurt that lady you shall pay for it a thousand times."

"That's not an answer to my question. Are you going to hand over? If you aren't, we'll take the risk of all you promise us, and you shall see her whipped to ribbons before your eyes."

"You unspeakable thing!"

"Didn't I tell you what would happen next time you pitched that sort of talk this way?"

He picked up a lady's riding whip which lay before him on the table and struck Netta with it smartly over the knuckles of her ungloved hand. Taken unawares by the unprovoked assault, she started back with a cry of mingled pain and fear. Before she could make a further movement, the woman who had served as a lure held her on one side and Hammick on the other.

"You coward" she exclaimed.

In an instant the blow was repeated.

"Weren't you warned not to speak unless I told you? You'll find—and he'll find—that my word goes here; so don't either of you make any mistake about it." He looked at the helpless man in front of him. "Well? Wouldn't you like to relieve yourself of some of those big words that are trembling on your tongue— and get her another cut or two?"

Mr Smithers replied with a show of self possession which, under the circumstances, seemed unnatural.

"I should be reluctant, Mr Waterson, to do anything which would be likely to incur your further displeasure."

"What do you mean by that? Sneering on a fresh tack—is that it? You're a nut that takes some cracking; but we'll crack you—never fear."

He turned to Netta, pointing at her the riding whip which he still held in his hand :

"Listen to me. Eyes front, if you please—and a pair of sparklers they are—real stones. I don't wonder that there's a glint in them as you look at me, and I don't suppose that just now you're feeling that I'm quite the sort of man whom you would like to fall in love with. For that I'm sorry; because I assure you that I'm just as unwilling as any other man to lay a hand upon a woman save in the way of kindness. But this is a case of stern necessity—

as you'll yourself allow when I've explained. You see the man who calls himself your husband—he doesn't look pretty just now, does he?

"And I believe that he's no more your husband than I am. He's robbed us—all the eight gentlemen you see here—of what cost us years of thought, and anxiety, and labour, besides a heap of money. And all we want him to do is to give it to us back again—just that, and nothing more. I'm sure you'll perceive how extremely reasonable that is of us. And therefore it is with the utmost confidence that I appeal to you to ask him to play the honest man. You have my permission to speak."

He gave his whip a little flourish. Netta seemed to be at a loss as to what was required of her.

"What do you want me to say?"

"I wish you to give free rein to the noble impulses of your beautiful feminine nature, and to ask this gentleman, with all the eloquence at your command, to give us what we're wanting."

"I am to speak to him?"

"That's what I'm requesting."

"And I shall not be struck if I do?"

"You will not. It's with extreme regret that I have to say it, but it's just possible that you'll be struck if you don't."

"Thank you." She looked towards her husband, and she smiled. In her voice there was actually a jubilant ring. "Frank, all sorts of stories have been told me about you today, and it is because of them that I am here. But I am not sorry that I came, since my coming has relieved my heart of such a weight of foolish doubt and trouble. For no one can be in this room and look at these men, and fail to understand that in any difference that may be between you and them you are sure to be in the right, and they in the wrong. Their mere appearance is sufficient to render me assured that all the evil things which have been told of you are false.

"As I have trusted you always, I trust you now. Do what you think is right. Have no fear for me. I have none for myself. If they do me wrong, who have done no wrong to them, it is they who will suffer, not I. Act, dear, as you would if I were not here."

"You are not afraid?"

"Indeed, no—not a little bit."

"Then neither am I. You know, Netta, that I love you?"

"Of course. It is worthwhile having come to be able to say again—of course." She turned to Waterson, still smiling. "Is there anything more that you would wish me to say?"

"I hardly think that there is."

The words were uttered with a dryness which—despite the menace which was at the back of them—moved Netta to laughter.

She had been listened to in silence, though her observations had been couched in such a different strain to that which her auditors desired. During the brief colloquy between husband and wife the faces about the table had assumed a more truculent expression, but none had interrupted. Now, as if by general consent, they waited for Waterson to play the part of spokesman. He sat twiddling the riding whip between his fingers, as if he were considering what shape to give his words. When he spoke his voice was as bland as it had been throughout, but the pupils of his eyes had become distended to twice their normal proportions.

"Those were very high-toned remarks of yours, though they weren't exactly what we wanted. What puzzles me is, if you quite understand what kind of man it is to whom you have been talking. You seem to think that he's a painted saint, but he isn't. He's done you quite as brown as he has us, and that's very brown indeed. Let me give you some pointers as to where he's done you. To begin at the beginning—his name isn't Smithers."

"Pardon me, Mr Waterson; you possibly make that assertion in good faith, but you are in error none the less. I was careful to make that my name before I married this lady."

"Well, we'll let it go at that. We'll allow that he made his name Smithers to marry you, though it wasn't Smithers up to then. Do you know that he's a jail bird? That he came straight out of jail to sneak our pile, and make up to you?"

"It may be news to you, Mr Waterson, to learn that I was sentenced to a term of imprisonment for doing that of which no man would have cause to be ashamed."

Netta looked at him and smiled, but she did not speak—being mindful, perhaps, of Waterson's whip.

Mr Chaffinch intervened:

"My dear friend, you must forgive my pointing out that reason and argument have been tried before. Every effort has been made to induce this person to behave in a right-minded manner. In vain;—to all appeals he has turned a deaf ear. This young woman appears to be a bird of his own feather. It is no use wasting valuable moments in talk. The time has come to proceed to deeds."

"Hear, hear! Them's my sentiments. Tie her up and whip her—that's the only kind of talk you'll find he'll listen to; and if you'll let me get my fingers round that whip, he'll soon start talking."

This was the Jew, who called himself Sam Brown. His eyes were fixed on Netta as if already, in anticipation, he revelled in the part he pictured himself as playing. The tall American, who had met Mr Smithers at the gate, joined for the first time in the conversation. He was a peculiar-looking man, with black hair parted in the centre, which was so long that it hung down the nape of his neck. He spoke with a pronounced drawl.

"I'm a man of principle, and it's against my principles to hurt a woman; but if the only way of hurting that man is by hurting this woman, and that seems to be about the size of it, then this is a case in which principles must go by the board, and I say hurt her till he feels that he has had about enough of it. Only do let's hustle. The sooner we start, the sooner we'll be through."

Kronberg spoke next—his voice hard, metallic, domineering.

"Why do we wait? I thought we were here for business, not for talk. There has been too much talk already. Does he talk before he does? He is not that kind of man—have I not had the proof of it on my own body? Then why do we talk so much? If he does as we want, good; then we will talk. But if not, string her up—at once, this instant. My time here is short; I myself must go and cut pieces out of her with a whip, or with what you will, until he does."

Waterson sat drawing the thong of the whip through his lingers, as if amused at the vehemence of some of his colleagues. As he looked at Mr Smithers, the pupils of his eyes seemed to have grown still larger.

"You perceive that my friends are of one mind, and that mind is mine. We've talked enough. We'll now do.—Hammick, show him what we've got behind there."

The wall on one side of the room was shrouded by green baize curtains. Mr Hammick, drawing one of these aside, disclosed a triangle, fashioned somewhat on the lines of the frame which is used in jails for flogging refractory prisoners. There were straps at the top to secure the victim's wrists, and others at the bottom to secure the ankles. Netta looked at the thing, with evident lack of comprehension of the purpose to which it was applied. Waterson, calling her attention to himself by flicking her lightly with the end of his whip, proceeded to explain.

"You see this is a sort of scaffold on which we are going to whip you. We take off your pretty bodice, and bare your pretty back, and fasten your pretty wrists there, and your pretty ankles here; then, when you're trussed up so that you can't do anything else but squeal, we—" he drew the whip through his fingers with a gesture and a look which were not pleasant—"we cut into your pretty back with this whip.—How long do you think it'll be before you squeal?"

The negro, leaning over the board, proffered a petition:

"Let me cut into her. I will show you how to use a whip like that. I will cut you out a fine pattern on her back; at every cut I will take off a strip of flesh like that." He drew his fingers apart to illustrate his meaning. "I will pay him for his bullet."

"But, my dear Linkman, won't that prevent your standing?"

The negro grinned horribly.

"Not for a job like that."

The tall American interposed.

"It seems against nature to let a black man cut into a white woman."

Kronberg spoke, bringing his fist down with a bang upon the table.

"All the better so. The more it is against nature, the less will he like it—and that is the point."

Waterson followed; his bland tones in such odd contradiction to the menace which was in his dreadful eyes.

"I am inclined to agree with you, my dear Kronberg; the more drastic the remedy, the more rapid the cure." He pointed his whip at Mr Smithers. "Now, for the very last time, I'm going to repeat the question that I've put to you already; and as the responsibility for all that follows will be yours, I earnestly advise you to weigh your words before you answer. Are you going to sit there and enjoy your best girl's squeals, while our coloured friend cuts into her, to save your pockets; or, to save her, are you going to give us what's our own?"

"You will not dare to touch my wife."

"Not dare? Really, I didn't know you were so simple. Is that your answer to my question?"

"Except to warn you against the consequences of any act of ultra-blackguardism of which you may be guilty."

"Gentlemen, you hear him! You all must feel that nothing could exceed the patience with which we have treated him, except the colossal insolence with which he persists in treating us. Do I voice the sense of the meeting in expressing the fear that there is nothing left for us except to proceed to extremities?"

Various speakers gave simultaneous expression to their feelings.

"Tie her up!"

"Tear the clothes all off her!"

"Cut her into ribbons!"

"Seeing the blood streaming down her back and hearing her squealing like a stuck pig will bring him to his senses."

"Frankly, gentlemen, I am afraid that nothing else will. Hammick, is that triangle ready? Remember that it's a lady we have to deal with; let everything be in order. The feminine soul loves order!"

While Mr Hammick was busying himself with the straps on the triangle, Netta was left with, as sole custodian, the female who had enticed her from her home, and who up to then had not uttered a single syllable. The outward composure of the girl's bearing had possibly conveyed a wrong impression of her character, so that it was taken for granted that, for very lack of spirit, she acquiesced in the frightful role which she was destined to fill. The woman, more engaged in observing Hammick than in considering her charge, held her loosely with a single hand. In an instant she had wrenched herself free, had snatched up a bowie knife and a revolver which lay on the table in front of Waterson, and, with them in her hands, was rushing to her husband at the other end. It was all done so suddenly that she had reached his chair before anyone could stop her, and, with eager hands was cutting at the cords which held him.

"An arm first," he said;" then give me that revolver."

She did her best to do his bidding; but, though slender, the cords were many. Before she was halfway through them the room was in an uproar. The black at her side reached out at her. Unhesitatingly she discharged at him the revolver which she held, taking aim as best she could. From the roar of rage and pain which came from him it was plain that the bullet had struck him somewhere, but it was equally plain that it had not disabled him. Gripping her about the waist, he tore her from her husband's side, whirled her over his head and flung her from him—her revolver discharging harmlessly while she was in midair. She descended on to the floor with a crash which shook the room. In a second they were on her, tearing from her the revolver and the knife.

"Linkman," cried Waterson, "it's a dead sure thing that now you have earned the right of cutting into her, so cut into her you shall. Tie her up right straight away." The woman who had served as lure delivered herself of her first remark: "If you're going to bare her back you'll have to do it before you tie her up."

"Is that so? Then bare her back, right now—then, gentlemen, we'll see what sort of shoulders the lady has."

"What's that?"

The inquiry came from Mr Chaffinch. Like the rest he had risen from his chair, but unlike them his attention was not wholly absorbed by what was taking place inside the room. He spoke sharply, as if resenting the noise which his friends were making. "Can't you be still for a second?—What's going on downstairs?—Listen!" They acted on his hint and listened, momentarily quiet. A sound proceeded from below as if someone was raining blows—heavy blows—upon a door.

CHAPTER 42
MR CARPENTER

The Marquis of Skye was a man of many acquaintances. Being in the mood, he dined that night at a certain restaurant which was much frequented by the people. The diners there were, for the most part, comparatively early folk, going on to some theatrical entertainment, and desirous of reaching it before the curtain rose. When the marquis entered, the greater part of them were already gone. Only a few of the tables continued to be occupied. At one of them sat a man alone. He saw the marquis as soon as he entered, and nodded. The marquis crossed towards him with a smile of pleasure.

"Have you room at your table for me?"

"I have."

"Then we'll dine together."

"But I'm halfway through my dinner."

"That doesn't matter; I'll catch you up. I eat at a gallop. I'll undertake to give any man a start and a healing."

"You shouldn't, you should eat slowly; give so many bites to each mouthful before you swallow it. It preserves your digestion."

'Thank you; but I've no taste for preserves—even for a preserved digestion. Waiter, what can you give me to eat?"

The other watched him as he chose his dishes. He was a young man of about thirty. His black hair was cut very close; his moustache waxed at the ends. He had lean cheeks; a short, straight nose; and keen dark eyes. He showed his teeth when he smiled. There was about him an air of alertness which suggested that his vitality was strong, and that he enjoyed his life. His name was Frederic Carpenter. Even by casual acquaintances he was known as Fred; being a man with whom almost anyone could take liberties up to a certain point, but not too far. He was a Civil Servant; having some sort of a position—nobody outside the office seemed to know quite what—in the Criminal Investigation Department at Scotland Yard.

The marquis, attacking his soup, commented on an unusual something which he seemed to notice in his companion's demeanour.

"From what quarter is the wind blowing? You look as if you were scudding along in front of it, with all sails set."

"I'm going to have a lark tonight."

"No?—A real lark ?"

"A very real lark."

"You've let me share the table—can't we share the lark ?"

"I'm afraid not. I'm not sure that I oughtn't to keep outside of it."

"What's that matter—if it's a real good thing? Never did a thing that I ought in my life. Is it a secret ?"

"It is up to the present moment; but as probably all the world will be talking about it tomorrow morning, I don't mind giving you a little early information—especially as I take it that you won't pass it on."

"Mum's the word—though I'm not quite sure that I know what mum means; but that's by the way. Let her go."

"You've heard of a man named Bruce—Andrew Bruce?"

Suddenly Mr Carpenter, laying down his knife and fork, sat up straight in his chair, with an air of extreme confusion. "Why—what an ass I am —I believe he's a relation of yours?"

"He's the only relation I have in the world—my cousin; and my heir—thank God!"

"I'd forgotten all about it—I deserve well kicking."

"Why? Because he's my cousin? What were you going to tell me about Andrew? Nothing to his discredit?"

"Very much the other way."

"Then let her go."

"Well—really I never felt such a fool in my life!"

"You're over young. You'll have felt all kinds of a fool by the time you've reached my years. You're slow at starting."

"Of course you know that he got into a little trouble."

"I know that he threw Raymond Verinder out of the window if that's what you call trouble?"

"Just so—and, of course, we all know that it served the brute well right; only when one man helps another to smash his head on the pavement, the law has a way of its own of looking at it."

"That's the cold truth. And especially the fellows inside your office. It's their trade."

"Have you seen him lately?"

"No later than this afternoon."

"Then perhaps he told you about what's going to happen tonight."

"Not a word. Though I surmised from his manner that for some reason or other tonight was going to be big with the fate of Rome."

"I shouldn't be surprised if it was—for him. I'll tell you all about it"

"You've been telling me some minutes, but up to this it seems all preface."

"Some time ago he came to see the chief. I happened to be in the room at the time, and was present at the interview. He told us a most extraordinary story. It seems that he met a man when he was—you know where."

"In jail—I know."

"A man named Edney—one of the kind who ought to have been drowned at birth. He nursed this man while he was on his deathbed. The fellow actually made him his heir—of course in informal fashion, but the intention was real enough. He told him that he would find certain property in a certain place, and that he might have it. Edney was one of nature's liars, and your cousin didn't believe a word he said; still he thought it might be worthwhile to examine the spot which he'd described with very curious minuteness—and there, to his surprise, were the things he'd spoken of. What do you think formed part of them?"

"Haven't an idea in my head—never had."

"Most of the jewels which had figured in some of the biggest jewel robberies which had been brought off in all parts of the world during the last twenty years or so."

"They ought to have been worth something."

"They were—untold gold."

"It's like my luck. I wish I'd been sent to jail instead of him; then they might have been left to me. Why wasn't it I who helped Verinder out of the room?"

"They were in the family !"

"It's little you know about relations if you think that that would be likely to benefit me."

"Another part of that legacy consisted of the finest stock of forged banknotes of all nations, and the finest plant for manufacturing them, that ever was. If those notes had been put into circulation they'd have disturbed the banknote currency of the world, because no one would have been able to tell the real article from the imitation. Bruce had all the things with him in a tin box—the actual tin box in which they had been stored. When he turned them out in front of us upon the table, the sight of those jewels would have made your mouth water."

"It waters at the thought of 'em!"

"In that box had been a notebook filled with secret writing. He'd puzzled out the key to it—he's got brains."

He has—mine! That's how it is I haven't any."

"He'd made out what the book was all about. It contained a detailed account of the dates on which the jewels had been stolen, from whom they had been stolen, by whom—and in short all about them; the very things we at the office wanted to know. He'd a great idea—he's a wonderful chap!"

"We're a wonderful family—on his side of the house."

"The fellows to whom the things belonged had found out that he had them, and had tried all sorts of dodges to induce him to fork up."

"He must have had an enjoyable time!"

"He felt sure—for reasons—that before very long they'd *try* to bring him to book before the entire crowd. His idea was to say nothing about what he'd done with the things, but to let them think that he still had them; and then, when the time came, give us the office, and let us collar the whole jolly lot. They seem to have got tired of trying to get at him singly. The other day they gave him notice that, as he'd expected, they meant to make him render an account to the whole blessed gang. He communicated at once with us, we made our preparations, and the thing is coming off tonight."

"Tonight?"

"Tonight. That's the lark I was telling you about. It's going to be a great game. Bruce is going to meet one of their chaps at Piccadilly Circus at nine o'clock."

"Nine o'clock! It's past nine now."

"I know it is; there's a clock behind you, and I've got my eye on it all the time. I'm expecting news every minute. He's going to get with this chap into a cab driven by one of our fellows—because he hasn't a notion where the real place of meeting is going to be, any more than we have. So soon as the cab puts them down, our fellow is to lick back to us as hard as he can tear. Directly he returns a body of picked men will start for that crib of theirs, and before they guess that we're on their tracks we shall have nabbed the crowd."

"It's a very pretty scheme of yours, but my cousin plays a leading part in it which I don't altogether relish."

"He's a good plucked one—there's not a doubt of it."

"Pluck be hanged! He's all the family I have. Suppose harm touches him, what will become of the marquisate? Now I understand what he was talking about this afternoon; if I'd understood then, I'd have spoilt your scheme—my word for it! To commence, suppose the chap he's gone to meet won't get into that cab of yours?"

"He'll manage that; he's a way about him there's no resisting."

"You're surer than I am. Anyhow, maybe the place you call their ' crib' is the other side of London. Between the time your fellow returns to you and you get back to Andrew, what's to prevent their cutting his throat, or getting rid of him in any other way they fancy; and if they're the sort you say they are, they'll not stick at a trifle—and then what's to become of the marquisate?"

"We pointed out to him the risk which he was running, but he insisted that he would be able to protect himself till we came to his assistance."

"Protect himself!—against a murdering crew like that! It's nearly a quarter to ten, and you hearing nothing! They'll have cut him into pieces while I've been eating my dinner."

"We'll hope not."

"What's the good of hoping?"

"There's our fellow!"

A man appeared at the door, who signalled to Mr Carpenter. In a second that gentleman was on his feet. The marquis also rose, declaring:

"With or without your leave, I'll share this lark with you—and a pretty lark it's like to be, I'm thinking!—just as I've shared your table.—Waiter, take the bill out of that."

Tossing some money on to the table, he followed close on Mr Carpenter's heels the door.

CHAPTER 43
WITHOUT

The person who had signalled to Mr Carpenter seemed to be in so great a hurry that he was unable to even wait for that gentleman's approach. By the time he had gained the hall of the restaurant the stranger was in the street. When Mr Carpenter joined him on the pavement he was standing beside a hansom cab, which he straightway invited the other to enter.

"Jump in!—time's precious."

Mr Carpenter hesitated—to ask a question :

"Well, Daniells, what's the news?"

Mr Daniells' manner was curt.

"I'll tell you as we go along—jump in!"

The marquis interposed:

"You'll have to take me with you."

Mr Daniells turned sharply round.

"Take you? Who are you?" Then, in sudden recognition, he raised his hat. "I beg your pardon, my lord. I didn't see it was you."

Mr Carpenter nodded.

"You know the Marquis of Skye?"

"By sight, of course."

"Mr Bruce is his cousin. He wants to come with us."

"He means to come with you."

The correction was his lordship's. Daniells looked at him inquiringly, then addressed Mr Carpenter:

"You've told him what's up?"

"I have. As it's his cousin to whose assistance we are going, he naturally feels interested."

"He being all the family I have, I've a fancy for being present at his last moments."

"It's likely to be a case of his last moments if we're not soon moving. Jump in both of you if you're going. For every moment we waste now, there may be the deuce to pay later on."

The marquis and Mr Carpenter got in first; Mr Daniells packed himself in after them. All three were thin. The cab was off. Mr Carpenter began a catechism.

"Well, Daniells, now what's the news ?"

"The news is that I'm out of condition." He had his hat off and was wiping his brow, although the temperature was considerably below freezing-point. "A man in my walk of life ought always to be just fit. I shall have to leave off milk in my tea."

"According to the tale I'm told about the way in which you diet yourself, I should think that that's about all you have to leave off."

"I haven't much—unless I starve. There are few men who stoke their bodies with less fuel than I do. But milk will have to go—it's heating."

"How did you manage with that cab of yours?"

"Followed him up Waterloo Place. Picked him up at the Circus. The chap who met him was tried at Clerkenwell Sessions twelve years ago for burglary and the murder of a policeman. He was acquitted on the charge of murder. According to the way in which the tale got itself told, it was his pal who did for the peeler, while he was taking himself off with the spoil. For that he had seven years."

"A nice sort of character to meet!"

"That chap's been lucky. He's one of the worst regular hands we have in town. We've only been able to bring it home to him three times, but we've nearly done it again and again. However it might have been about that other job, there isn't a morsel of doubt that he's earned the gallows since then."

"Did he come with you in your cab?"

"Mr Bruce managed that beautifully. He'd a cab driven by a pal of his own, and he was very strong on having that. But Mr Bruce wasn't taking any—he had to come with me. I listened to what they were talking about as they went along—he as good as told Mr Bruce that they meant to do for him."

The marquis groaned.

"That's pleasant hearing, since he's all my family!"

"He wouldn't ride any further than Hanover Gate—for all Mr Bruce's trying to get him to let me drive them to the door. So I followed them on foot."

"See where they went?"

"I did. Then made for the nearest station, and telephoned to them at Bow Street to send our chaps right on. Then came round for you—and that's what's wasted precious time, because our chaps ought to be pretty nearly their by now."

"And my cousin dead!"

"You seem to have made up your mind upon that point," observed Mr Carpenter. "But I both hope and believe that you'll find that you're wrong."

"It's easy talking! What's your notion, Mr Daniells? What do you think that lucky chap, of whom you've been telling us, and his lucky friends, are likely to do to my cousin when they've got him all to themselves?"

"That's more than I care to think. I wouldn't like to be in his shoes, I do know that; and no one's ever called me a cur. Considering how he's had them all on toast, they'll have their backs up, and they'll stick at nothing—they're that sort. Anyhow, he's in for the very worst hour he's ever had in all his life; that I'll swear to. When I remember what a gentleman he is—an all-round, true English gentleman."

"He's Scotch."

" He's as good as if he were English—I don't like to think of it. Him at the mercy of that scum!"

Thrusting up the trap door he spoke to the driver. "Push along! unless you want to be hung for murder."

There was an interval of silence, broken by the marquis.

"If they harm him they shall pay!"

"Oh, they'll be made to pay right enough. I shouldn't be surprised if we snapped the lot; then this'll be the last flutter they'll have for a good many years to come. More than one of them will go for life. But whether he won't have to pay too dearly for helping us to get them is another question altogether."

Conversation languished. Each was engaged with his own thoughts. Mr Daniells was plainly fidgeting; he kept urging the driver to further haste. At last that individual expostulated :

"What's the good of your keeping on at me? You, as a policeman, ought to know. My mare's doing her best. If I start galloping her, I shall have some blessed copper pulling me up sharp; then where'll you be?"

Suddenly they turned into a road in which it was obvious

that something unusual was happening. A number of men were descending from what looked like a private omnibus, which had been crowded to its utmost capacity, both inside and out. Behind was an ominous looking vehicle—'Black Maria'—the official van used for conveying prisoners from court to jail. From it also men were emerging. The whole cortege was drawn up before a high dead wall. In that quiet street, at that hour, the proceedings seemed uncanny. Mr Daniells pulled the cabman up.

"Just in time!" he exclaimed. "Our chaps have just come."

The trio descended on to the pavement—to find themselves in the midst of a crowd of men, dressed in civilian clothes, all of whom seemed curiously in earnest. What little talking there was took place in undertones. Mr Daniells was the only person who spoke above a whisper.

"Where's Inspector Barnes?" he inquired. A tall man stepped forward. He had a short black beard, and was apparently the only person present in official costume. Oh, there you are, Barnes. Everything all right?"

"Can't say—only just come. I suppose this is the place. We can't see much from outside here; and from what we can see, it looks as if it were empty. From the top of the 'bus the house seems to be all in darkness."

"I daresay; shutters up all round. But this is the place safe enough, and I rather fancy that you'll find plenty inside ready to receive you warmly.—How many men have you got?"

"Forty altogether, barring the driver."

"Got the ladders?"

"In the van; they're fetching them out."

As a matter of fact, while the inspector was speaking, two short ladders were being produced out of the recesses of Black Maria and brought forward on to the pavement. Mr Daniells issued his instructions.

"Stand one of those ladders against the wall, then lower the other over the other side.—Barnes, leave a dozen of your men here—tell them to keep a special eye upon that door—and send the rest over the wall to surround the house. You and I'll go with them. I think we shall be able to get into the house with less fuss from the garden than from the street."

The inspector, picking out eleven men, placed them under a sergeant, with instructions to detain anyone who attempted to emerge from the premises. The others, following each other over the ladder, vanished over the wall. Mr Daniells addressed Mr Carpenter.

"Are you coming with us?"

"I am."

The marquis, unasked, announced his intention.

"Count me in. Where you lead I will follow. All I want is to get to my family by the shortest road."

Daniells shook his head.

"You quite understand, my lord, that we can assume no responsibility for whatever happens. I oughtn't to have let you come—it's irregular."

"My life has been irregular up to now; it's only fit and proper that the end should be in keeping."

"The end? What do you mean?"

He looked at the other sharply, with keen, inquiring eyes. The marquis laughed.

"I mean that I'll be obliged by your requesting your friends not to monopolise that ladder unduly long."

The ladder was scarcely high enough; reaching the top, one had to lever oneself on to the wall. Daniells balanced himself momentarily on the summit.

"What's down there ?"

"Seems like some sort of shrubbery. 'Ware how you come; without a light it isn't easy to see where you're going."

Presently all were over. As the speaker had said, the whole garden seemed to take the form of a large shrubbery, that is, so far as they were able to ascertain. In the prevailing darkness it was difficult to make out their surroundings. They stumbled over unseen obstacles; against branches which only became visible too late. They seemed to have suddenly entered a place of mystery. Sounds were audible for which there were no ostensible causes. All at once, from someone there came an exclamation which was louder than the other. The inspector's voice inquired into the reason.

"Who's that? What's the matter there?"

"It's me, sir," replied an unseen person. "I've tripped over a root or something—afraid I've twisted my ankle."

The inspector was unsympathetic.

"Not you. You'll be all right if you stand up and pull yourself together. What's this? A path?"

It appeared that it was; also that it ran round the house.

"Shine a light here, someone, and let's see what this is."

The shutter of a lantern was opened; a bright ray ran up and down, to and fro—sufficient to show that the path on which they were was a narrow and a winding one. Reclosing the lantern, they followed it as best they could towards the left.

"Place is like a maze," grumbled the inspector. "In this light a man might keep on walking round and round, and come to nowhere after all"

"In the meantime," murmured the marquis," my family is being slain."

"Here's another path," observed someone in front. "Why, there's two; they branch off to the right and left; this one goes straight on."

"That's all right. You pay your money and take your choice— to find that they all lead nowhere."

"The one to the left ought to lead to the house. Hullo! we're right up to it; this feels like a wall. Let's have another glimpse of light there, and let's see where we are—the place is as black as Hades."

Again a shutter was turned. A gleam of light ran up and down a building which was right in front of them, so close that if they had taken another step the leaders would have struck their heads against it. As revealed by the lamplight, a door stared them in the face.

"I see how it is," exclaimed Mr Daniells. "We've struck the covered passage which leads into the house, and this is the door which opens out of the passage into the garden. What we have to do is to get through it. I expect that path we've just left goes right round the house. Barnes, you take some of your men along it and station them within easy hail of each other. Mind, you chaps, you're down on anyone who tries to pass. Leave me ten. I'll wait here till you come back. Be as quick as you can."

Doubtless the inspector obeyed orders to the best of his ability, but, under the circumstances, rapidity of motion was difficult. He and his men moved off; they heard them tramping as they went—their occasional stumbles.

"It strikes me," remarked Mr Carpenter, "that either this house is empty, or else its inmates are intent on some very engrossing business. If they were merely fast asleep, they'd have shown signs before this of being roused by the row we're managing to make."

"They're too much engaged, that's what it is; and probably the last thing they're expecting is a visit from us. Mr Bruce never let them have the least idea that he was communicating with us. They think they've got him all to themselves by himself; when they see us they'll look funny—and act funny too, unless I'm wrong. Barnes is taking his time."

"It isn't easy to make out the geography of an unknown garden on a night like this. You don't want him to leave them a chance of getting off—he has to post his men."

Some minutes passed. They could hear the diminishing tramp of the police officers as they passed farther round the house. Then there was silence—almost ominous silence. Then footsteps were heard returning towards them along the unseen winding path.

"Here's Barnes!"

"And time it was Barnes. Hullo! what's that?"

There was a sound within the house—a sound which startled those who were without.

"It's a pistol shot!"

"By George, it was a pistol shot! That sounds as if someone was inside, and as if business was being done."

"Break the door down! Don't wait for Barnes! While we're waiting, murder's being done."

This was the marquis—his tones betrayed excitement. In comparison, Daniells' voice, though eager, was businesslike and cold.

"If we give the alarm before his men are ready, the whole lot of these chaps may get away scot-free.—Who has the cold chisels and hammers?"

"Here you are, sir."

"Is that you, Barnes? Placed your men all right?"

"So far as I can see in this darkness."

The sound within the house was repeated—a second shot was heard. The marquis's excitement grew apace.

"Confound you, Mr Daniells! what are you keeping us hanging about like this for? It's sheer murder!"

"Keep calm, my lord.—Now, you men there, open this door!"

In a surprisingly short space of time the door was opened. They streamed through it—to find themselves in pitch blackness.

"Let's have some lights."

Lanterns gleamed—to disclose that they were in the covered passage which led from the street to the house, and that the hall door was closed in front of them. Mr Daniells' instructions were short and pithy.

"Break open that door!"

Instantly chisels and hammers were carrying out his orders. Under their persuasive influence the door was being wrenched from its hinges.

CHAPTER 44
WITHIN

It was the sound of that hammering which Mr Chaffinch heard in that upstairs room—which shortly penetrated to the consciousness of his companions. Each man seemed to hold his breath to listen. The fashion of their faces changed. Rage and lust of cruelty, fading for a moment into the background, gave place lo something which was almost fear. With odd unanimity, all eyes turned towards the door. Mr Waterson voiced the common doubt:

"What's up now?"

The woman who had lured Netta answered :

"I'll go and see."

"Do! Someone catch hold of that girl while you're gone—she's marked dangerous."

The woman hurried out There was no necessity for anyone to take her place in guarding Netta, who was already held by three or four. The noise below seemed growing louder. The threat which it conveyed was unmistakable. Men were producing revolvers which had hitherto been hidden. Mr Chaffinch, whose huge countenance had assumed a pasty look, deprecated their appearance.

"Put those away. Remember, gentlemen, that you're in England, and that here that sort of thing won't do.'

The tall, thin American was the only one who commented on the hint:

"I reckon lead's lead even in this darn country—it's a stopper!"

Waterson asked a question of Mr Chaffinch:

"Is there any way out—for us?"

"There's only the one entrance."

"Then if it's the cops, they've got us like rats in a trap."

"But how can it be? They've no reason to suppose that we are here?"

The Jew, Sam Brown, interposed, with a jerk of his elbow towards Mr Smithers.

"Haven't they? What price him?"

"He'd no notion where he was coming to."

"Perhaps; but he's fly enough for anything, he is. If it is them, I know how they got on to us—through that blamed cabman."

"You think," added the tall American, "that that cabman he was so anxious to patronise at the Circus was a friend of his?"

"That's about the size of it. I wish I'd seen him hung before I got inside his blamed cab."

"What's that your talking about?" asked Waterson.

Before any could answer the woman came hurrying in, in evident perturbation.

"There's a crowd of men at the door, and there's more in the garden; but it's so dark I can't see properly."

"It's the tecs, sure enough!" cried Brown. "He's given us away! Damned if I don't believe it's been a plant of his from the beginning!"

The tall American pointed his revolver at Mr Smithers.

"It's the last time he shall give me away."

He fired, but Mr Chaffinch, rushing forward, struck up his arm. The bullet lodged in the wall.

"What did you do that for?" he demanded angrily.

"Don't make things worse than they are already, you fool," retorted Chaffinch. If the tecs are on to us, I don't mean to stand my trial for murder if you do."

"Gentlemen," exclaimed Waterson," it's been suggested to me that we put out the lamps, then scatter over the house, each man for himself. It seems to me that that'll be our best chance."

Scarcely were the words out of his mouth than Kronberg, without waiting to hear what was the opinion of the company, springing on to the table, blew out the lamp which was suspended in the centre of the room. Another lamp, a common glass one, stood lighted on the mantelshelf.

"Steady there!" cried a voice. "Let's have the door open before you leave us all in darkness!"

"And let me make my mark upon that beauty!"

Again the American fired at Mr Smithers; again Mr Chaffinch thrust aside his pistol arm; and again the disappointed marksman turned on his associate in anger.

"See here, my fat friend, do you want some lead in you?"

There was a crash below, which seemed to set the whole house in a tremor.

"They've got the door down!—Put out that light!"

Someone dashed the glass lamp off the mantel on to the floor. Fortunately it became extinguished as it fell; it was obvious from the sound that it had been shattered into fragments. In the darkness which ensued there arose a singular hubbub of voices; of men making the best of their way past unseen obstacles towards the door. Out of the confusion came the sound of a woman's voice. It was Netta screaming.

"Frank!—save me!—the black!—the black!"

Something was happening to her, but in the darkness it was impossible to see what. There was the sound of a thud, thud, as of blows being struck by some heavy weapon; then a sort of whimpering noise, as of broken hysterical sobs; then only the previous confusion. Mr Smithers was heard above the din.

"Netta!" he shouted. "Netta!"

But none answered. Only a voice addressed him, belonging to someone who was standing; close at his side.

"Now, my friend, don't you disturb yourself about Netta. Our coloured friend will look after her—he's dead on to a white girl is the Linkman. You talk to me. It's my turn to have a gun and a tickler. Perhaps the tickler'll make less noise."

The prick of a sharp point in his arm made it plain to Mr Smithers what the speaker meant by a 'tickler.' It was evidently some sort of a knife, as indeed his further words explained.

"If I cut your head clean off your shoulders, your friends coming up the stairs may have what's left of you, with my best compliments."

If the speaker proposed to put his bloodthirsty suggestion into actual execution he reckoned without his host. Although Netta, in her desperate dash to effect her husband's freedom, had only sundered a few of the cords which bound him, she had yet done more than at first appeared to bring about the end she had in view; for, by judicious movements of his muscles, he had taken advantage of the cords which she had cut to loosen the others. When the knocking had been first heard without, he alone had kept his head, for he alone had been prepared for it. In the confusion which followed he had busied himself by straining every nerve to improve on what he had already done, to such good purpose that, when he felt that point entering his flesh, he had succeeded in almost entirely freeing his right arm. It needed but that prick to supply a final impetus. With sudden rage he put forth his entire strength—his arm was free. He gripped the other by the wrist, and, taking him wholly unawares, twisted the knife out of his hand.

"You beauty!" exclaimed a voice. "Then it'll have to be lead!"

Mr Smithers felt something cold touch his forehead—it was the muzzle of a revolver. He wrenched his head aside, striking out blindly with the knife of which he had gained possession.

It came into contact with something. There was an exclamation of pain and fury. Coincidently the weapon was discharged. The flame scorched his skin, but the bullet missed him. That something serious had happened to his assailant was shown by the fact that the weapon went clattering to the floor, while his voice was heard declaring:

"I do believe the beauty's hacked my hand off at the wrist!"

Mr Smithers, finding himself the recipient of no further immediate attentions, began to make eager use of his knife to sunder his remaining bonds.

The encounter, such as it was, had occupied but a moment. Chaos still reigned in the room. The extinguishing of the lights had apparently caused its occupants to forget their bearings. Judging from the sounds, they experienced a difficulty in finding the door. Suddenly a voice exclaimed :

"Look out!—They're coming up the stairs!"

Confusion became confounded. Men seemingly came into collision with each other, some pressing forward while others pressed back. Oaths and. execrations filled the air. All at once authoritative tones were heard without.

"Show a light there!—quick! They're in this room!"

Bull's eye lanterns gleamed through the doorway. Men endeavoured to escape the channels of light which they opened out in front of them. Mr. Daniells thundered an inquiry:

"Mr Smithers!—Are you in there?"

"I'm here all right, but they've got my wife!"

"Andrew!" came a shout, which Mr Smithers recognised.

"Alec!" he replied.

The marquis came rushing down one of the channels of light; it threw his figure into vivid relief. He had his hat off—was apparently waving it in exultant salutation to his cousin. There was a shot. He threw out his arms on either side of him, as if to prevent himself from falling:—and fell, crying, as he went tumbling backwards:

"That's got me! Where's Shon?"

In the confusion and uncertain light, it was impossible to see who had fired. Only Mr Chaffinch was heard protesting :

"Gentlemen, gentlemen, none of that, I beg of you. Officers, I call you to witness that we are not responsible for that shot. We surrender."

A lantern was turned full on to him. Mr Daniells was seen standing in the door.

"I know you—you're Augustus Chaffinch; and you know me—I'm George Daniells. There are forty constables in the house and grounds. You chaps have done enough mischief already; if you're wise, you'll act on Mr Chaffinch's suggestion and do no more."

Someone struck a match. It was seen to be Kronberg. Climbing on to the table, he lighted the centre lamp, which he had himself put out. "Let us see what we are doing," he remarked. There was another shot—someone else dropped on to the floor.

"Who's that?" demanded Mr Daniells. The tall American was seen to be lying in a heap. Chaffinch explained :

"It's Philip Fenturn. It was he who fired the other shot."

Such was the presumption, though it was never actually proved. He had blown his own brains out, preferring self-destruction to the fate which he knew was certainly in store for him. The officers, entering, began to take possession of their prisoners, no one offering the slightest resistance. Messrs Carpenter and Daniells between them freed Mr Smithers from the remainder of his bonds.

"Are you hurt?"

"Not seriously; but" He had raised himself to his feet. The agony caused by the restored circulation was too much for him. He sank back with a groan. A woman's shriek rang through the house. He made a further effort to regain the use of his limbs—in vain. "That's my wife!—Save her!—I can't!—I'm done!" His head drooped over the arm of the chair. He had swooned. The woman's shriek rang out again, coming from an upper floor.

"There's some devilry taking place upstairs. If some of you chaps will come with me we'll stop it."

Guided by the continued cries, which were growing fainter and fainter, they discovered a room above, with the door locked. They burst it open, to find the black inside with Netta. They had arrived just in time.

The negro's strength must have been herculean. Although he had still a bullet in his thigh, in his frenzy at being baulked of his prey, he fought his would-be captors like a madman, succeeding in inflicting serious injuries on more than one of them before they had him fast. When he was finally secured, the two leaders of the expedition exchanged notes.

"How many have you got?" asked Mr Daniells.

"Counting the one who shot himself, this one"—meaning the black—"makes eight. Then there's a woman besides, who says that she doesn't know what we want to arrest her for, because she's done nothing."

"Hasn't she? We shall see about that later."

And they saw.

CHAPTER 45
THE MARQUIS AND MARCHIONESS

"You see it was the chief whom Shon was calling,"

They had removed the Marquis of Skye to the great house in Hark Lane. He had insisted; and as, in any case, it was only a question, of hours, it had seemed to the doctors that it did not matter. The bullet had not killed on the spot, but it had produced internal haemorrhage, which was beyond the reach of medicine. The marquis was bleeding, to death.

It was between two and three o'clock in the morning. Beside the bed were his cousin, whom we have known, through the greater part of this story as Francis Smithers, and his wife, Netta. Both looked as if they had been in the wars. Netta, in particular, was disposed towards silence. During the last few hours events had come marching upon her with such breathless rapidity that it was not strange that she felt bewildered. And now, scarcely had she escaped what was worse than death, than she found herself in this great house, in the presence of this dying man, confronted by the fact that she was within measurable distance of becoming the wife of one of the greatest of England's peers No wonder that she asked herself if these things could be happening in a world of dream.

The marquis was conscious of no pain. On the contrary, he was completely at his ease—-more so than were the watchers at his side. Only his voice grew ever fainter. He spoke to Netta, who regarded him with the strangest mixture of awe and pity. He was a little beyond her understanding.

"I am sorry, cousin, that our acquaintance has been so brief an one, but I comfort myself with the reflection that knowing you has enabled me to die in peace. I am persuaded that I am leaving the Bruces in safe hands."

He watched her in silence for some seconds, seeming surprised at the tears which were rolling down her cheeks. He put out his hand and touched one with his fingers.

"Why, it's a tear! You shouldn't cry—it isn't worth it. Between ourselves, it'll be best thing for me—to be dead. Everything I've cared for has been dead some time. And I'm tired—you don't know how tired one gets. Besides, I'm leaving behind me so excellent a representative—one who'll be in every respect a better chief than ever I have been."

"That is not so."

Andrew was standing by his wife's side, as she kneeled upon

the floor. It was from him that the point-blank contradiction came.

"It is so; your little finger would make a better chief than my whole body." Then, to Netta, "You don't know my cousin, although you've married him. He's the dearest fellow, but he's had a deal of trouble. One woman destroyed him; it's only fair that another should build him up again. You'll not bring him any hurt or harm?"

"I'll try not—I'll try hard."

"You'll not need much trying. I thank you for having married him—it's a compliment to the family."

That was the last set speech he made, and it was uttered with a smile. There came from him at intervals a few disconnected remarks, but they became rarer and fainter. At last he said something in so low a tone of voice that she had to bend over to catch what he said.

"Kiss" he whispered, and then stopped, as if his strength was spent, and he could say no more.

But she understood, and kissed him. And her husband kissed him too.

Almost immediately afterwards the wailing sound of bagpipes seemed to be borne on the wind past the window.

"What is that?" she asked; for up to that moment everything had been very quiet.

"It's Shon." Her husband lifted her up from her knees and took her in his arms. "Alec is dead."

Later in the day the husband and the wife talked together. Youth is elastic. Its moods soon change. Netta had had a refreshing and a dreamless sleep. When she awoke the world looked brighter. After all, this man had been nothing to her—the acquaintance of an hour. And he was dead. There was an end.

It was the singularity of the position which made its strongest appeal to her. She said to her husband:

"Are you really the Marquis of Skye?"

"I am afraid I am—unfortunately."

"And am I the Marchioness ?

"You are; that burden is laid upon you."

But this time he smiled, for he perceived from something which was on her face that she might not regard it as such a burden after all. She drew a long breath, as if to assure herself that she was awake.

"And the other day I was cleaning the lodger's boots—and you were the lodger."

He drew her towards him with a laugh.

"You will admit that I always protested."

"But I did them all the same. And now I'm a marchioness. Oh dear! I never thought that it would come to this." A sudden thought occurred to her. "Frank—whatever grand names you have, I shall always call you Frank."

"I hope you always will."

"Frank—is it true that you've been married before?"

She drew a little away from him, regarding him with anxious eyes.

"Perfectly. I divorced my first wife, for sufficient reasons. She has become an actress. You have seen her at the Pandora Theatre. She calls herself Esme Papillon, and is married again—to Mr Frederic Bellamy, whom you saw acting with her in the piece in which she played the heroine."

"Frank! Was Esme Papillon your wife?"

"She was, once—to my cost. She ruined me by her extravagance—lock, stock, and barrel. I never was a rich man. When I tried to check her, she grew to hate me. And there were other things. I'll do her the justice to admit that I don't believe that she meant much harm. That was the worst of it—she was incapable of meaning anything. She was that sort of woman—irresponsible. She had acquaintance who helped to ruin her—and me. One was a man who called himself my friend—Raymond Verinder. One night I found her in a room with him. I was very angry. We fought. I threw him out of the window. He was killed."

"Killed!"

Netta's face had grown whiter.

"They charged me with murder. It was not murder. I had not

338

meant to kill him. They perceived that themselves. They altered the charge to manslaughter. Of that they found me guilty, and sentenced me to two years' hard labour."

"Frank!"

She put her hand upon his shoulder and snuggled closer to him.

"You will understand that that was not nice for me. I resolved to put the past—the world in which I had lived—behind me; to submerge my own identity; to begin life again at some fresh starting-point. So I came to Putney—and fell in love with you—which I ought not to have done."

"Why oughtn't you to have fallen in love with me? You were divorced before you came."

"Oh yes; I was divorced before I came."

"Then why oughtn't you to have fallen in love with me?— Because I wasn't good enough?"

"The idea! Because of my record. A man with such a record as mine ought not to have allowed himself to fall in love with such a woman as you—for her sake, not his."

"Indeed! And pray what's the matter with your record? If I found out that a woman was trying—even trying, mind!—to steal your love from me, do you suppose that I shouldn't feel like killing her? And I shouldn't be surprised if I did it too."

"You need never have any fear of anyone alienating my love from you. I owe you too much."

"You owe me too much! What do you owe me?"

"I owe you happiness."

"And don't I owe you happiness?"

"I hope to succeed in making you happy before I've done."

"Before you've done? What do *you* think you've been doing up to now?—Frank, you're a wise person, but I'm beginning to wonder if, after all, on some points you're not a little dull. Aren't you perfectly aware that long ago you made me the happiest woman that ever lived?"

"But happiness in your mouth means one thing, and in mine another."

"Does it?—How pleasant!—I am learning!

"By consenting to become my wife you restored me to my self-respect—you raised me out of the ditch into which I'd fallen. The consciousness that a good woman had consented to entrust her life to me made a better man of me than I ever thought I should have become again. It is in that sense that I mean that I owe you happiness."

"Is it?—Very pretty, and excellently expressed!—Now perhaps you will allow me to ask you just one question—what would have become of me if it hadn't been for you?"

"That is a question which neither I nor any other man can answer."

"Is it? Then I can at least supply you with the probabilities.— At best, I should have been still the household drudge I was when first you saw me. But the probabilities are that I should have been on the streets—a pauper, hopeless and downtrodden, begging my bread. Instead of which, you have not only made me your wife—than which no greater honour could have befallen a woman—but you have also made of me a marchioness.—No, sir—or, dear my lord, as I suppose it'll have to be—don't you ever attempt to drop even the very faintest hint that you owe me more than I owe you; because the thing is, on the face of it, so utterly preposterous, that if you will descend to such absurdities, you'll put me in such a temper that I'm nearly sure we'll quarrel."

CHAPTER 46

SUMMING UP

Mr Chaffinch and his friends met with their deserts, or, at least, with a considerable part of them. For it may be taken for granted that gentlemen of their kidney never do receive quite all that they deserve from the hands of the law. That little book, filled with the secret writing, which Mr Edney's heir found in safe No. 226, contained matter which proved to be their complete undoing. When Mr Smithers, having puzzled out the key, went with it and the rest of his find to the authorities, he was able to lay before them a history of certain criminal transactions in which the association had been engaged which was in its way unique. The late George Edney, besides being a player of many parts, must have been a man of subtle humour. He had recorded with circumstantial details, the particulars of all the crimes in which he and his associates had been concerned.

It is within the range of possibility that, in bequeathing his ill-gotten booty to his fellow-prisoner, he foresaw the use which might be made of this interesting volume, and chuckled at the prospect. For it is hardly likely that so astute a person could have so misread the character of Andrew Bruce as to suppose that he would be willing to continue as his posthumous partner in his innumerable rascalities. However that may have been, the entries which he had made with his own hands did settle the fate of his friends, more than one of whom was sentenced to penal servitude for life.

Mr Theodore Ludlow failed one day to put in an appearance at the office of the bank which he honoured with his services. On inquiries being made into the condition of his accounts, a sufficient reason for his absence was discovered. He had apparently taken a little trip abroad; and, so far as is known, has not since revisited his native land. Of Mr Sam Swire, his whilom associate, nothing has been seen or heard.

Shortly after succeeding to the marquisate, Mr Francis Smithers that was presented the Dene Park estate to Mr Sidney Foster. When the young gentleman naturally hesitated to accept—so munificent a gift, the marquis told him the whole story of George Edney's legacy, explaining that his chief reason for appropriating it was to enable him to make restitution to the testator's victims.

One day Mr Benjamin Rodway, now a multimillionaire, asked Miss Margaret Foster to be his wife; and strange to say—for they hardly ever said a civil thing to one another—the young lady consented.

"I don't mind," she observed. "I'll marry you. I've done you so much good already that I may as well place myself in a position which will enable me to do you more."

He pulled a face—for his manners were still uncouth.

"I don't see what good you've done me up to now?"

"That's merely an illustration of your phenomenal opacity. To begin with, I saved you from making a fantastic spectacle of yourself on at least one historical occasion—and even then you went as far in that direction as you possibly could. I suppose that now you will admit that I was right in all that I said of Netta's husband—that he is the truest, bravest, noblest gentleman."

Mr Rodway ran his fingers through his hair—he has the trick of it unto this hour.

"I tell you what he is—he's the luckiest man in the world."

"My dear Benjamin—I shall always call you Benjamin in full; you look a Benjamin, with your hair standing up so beautifully on end; you're a tidy man—my dear Benjamin, in a sense we may be fortune's fools and playthings, but after all there's a certain kind of luck which only goes with character."

Not long ago Mr and Mrs Benjamin Rodway entered on the responsible position of godparents to the infant son and heir of the Marquis and Marchioness of Skye. Both the mother and the godmother perceived, the moment that each of them set eyes upon him, what a striking resemblance the boy bore to his father. It's extraordinary what insight, in such matters, women have! Compared to them, men are as nothing.

The Chase of the Ruby

CHAPTER 1
GHOSTS IN AFRICA

'Upon my word, this is—' He hesitated, then chose another form of words with which to conclude his sentence. 'This is extraordinary.'

He allowed the paper to flutter from between his fingers, stood staring at nothing, then, stooping, picked up the sheet of blue post from where it had fallen at his feet

'Extraordinary!' he repeated.

He regarded it and handled it as if it had been some uncanny thing—though, on the face of it, it was nothing of the kind. It was a formal letter addressed to 'Guy Holland, Esq., 37A Craven Street, W.C It began 'Dear Sir,' and ended 'Yr. obedt. servant, Saml. Collyer.' Between the beginning and the end it informed him that his uncle, George Burton, had died at Nice on February 23, and that the writer would feel obliged if he would call upon him at his earliest possible convenience.

'I wonder if I saw him die?' Mr Holland knit his brows as he asked himself the question. 'How could I, when I was in Mashonaland and he was in Nice? Absurd!'

He laughed, as it has been written, 'hollowly'; the laugh of uneasiness rather than mirth.

Then he went and saw the lady.

She was waiting on a seat by a certain piece of water in Regent's Park. She must have had eyes behind, because, although she was sitting with her back to him, directly he stepped upon the grass she sprang up, and, as if she had been observing him all the time, went to him at something very like a run. He advanced at quick step. They met in the middle of the grass plot, contrary to regulations, which forbid people to walk upon the grass. They each gave two hands, and that with an air which suggested that if that had not been a public place they would have given each other something else as well.

'Guy! she exclaimed. 'I thought you were the other side of the world. What a time you've been!'

'Coming from the other side of the world? or from Craven Street? It is some distance from Craven Street to Regent's Park.'

'You are in Craven Street, are you? What's it mean? You're looking well—sort of coppery colour; it suits you.'

'That's the air of the *veldt*; it burnishes a man's skin. You're looking sweet. I say, it's awfully hard lines that I can't kiss you. Mayn't I—just a little one?'

'In broad daylight, in Regent's Park, with a hundred pairs of eyes observing us from Hamilton Terrace? Thank you; some other day. When I had your note—what a note! "Meet me at the old place at noon"—I wondered who I was to meet, you or your ghost. As a matter of fact, I had a most important engagement— just at noon; but I put it off on purpose to come and see.'

'That was very dear of you. I'm not my ghost, I'm me.'

'But—Guy, have you made your fortune? You didn't seem as if you were going to make it at quite such a rate when you wrote last'

He shook his head.

'Came back with less in my pockets than when I left'

'Then—what does it mean?'

'My uncle's dead.'

'Mr Burton?'

He nodded.

'Has he left you his money? Oh, Guy!'

'As to that, I can't say. At present I know nothing. The fact is, Letty, it's—it's a queer business. You won't laugh?'

'What at?'

'Well'—he held out an envelope—'if I hadn't found this letter awaiting me telling me of the old man's death, I should have accused myself of softening of the brain, or something of the kind. As it is, I believe I've had a vision.'

'A vision! You? Guy, fancy your discovering that there are visions about.'

'You're laughing at me now.'

'I'm doing nothing of the kind. How can you say such a thing? I'm the soul of gravity. Do I ever laugh?'

As a matter of fact, there was a twinkle in her eyes even as she spoke, which he perceived.

'All right; laugh it out I don't mind. All I can say is that it's gospel truth, and seems queer enough to me, though I daresay it's extremely comic to anybody else.'

'What seems comic? You haven't said a word.'

'Let's find a seat, and I'll say a good many.'

They found a seat—not the one she had been sitting on, but one which was sheltered by a tree. It was, perhaps, because it was in the shade that they temporarily ignored the fact that they were yet in Regent's Park. They were still pretty close together when he began to tell his tale.

'On the 23rd of February I had had a long day in the open. It was broiling hot, and in the evening I was glad to get back under cover. As I sat at my tent door, too tired even to smoke, I saw, right in front of me, my uncle.'

'Your uncle? Mr Burton? Where was this?'

'Perhaps three hundred miles north of Buluwayo.'

'But—what was your uncle doing there?'

'I told you it was a queer business, and so it was. Let me try to explain. Straight in front of where I was sitting the plain stretched for heaven knows how many miles right away to the horizon. There were no buildings; scarcely a bush or a tree was to be seen; just the monotonous level ground. All at once I perceived, certainly within a hundred feet of where I was, a flight of steps.'

'A flight of steps?'

'Well, I had a sort of general idea that there was a building in connection, but my eyes were fixed upon the steps. I seemed to know them. There was a wide open door at top. I felt that I was well acquainted with what was on the other side of that door. On the steps my uncle was standing. Mind, I saw him as well as I see you, and, thank goodness, I can see you pretty well. I can't tell you what he wore, because I'm no hand at describing clothes; but I've an impression that he had on a suit of tweeds and a bowler hat. He was apparently lounging on the steps, watching the passers-by. He did not see me—of that I was sure. On a sudden someone else came towards him up the steps. He was a stranger to me, though I think I should know him if I saw him again. He was taller than my uncle, and, I imagine, younger.

'Anyhow, he was altogether a bigger and a stronger man. He had a walking stick in his hand, with a horn handle. Directly he got within reach, without, so far as I could judge, uttering a word of warning, with this stick he struck my uncle with all his force across the face. I suspect that my uncle had seen him coming before I did, and, for reasons of his own, had stuck to what he deemed his post of vantage on the steps, being unwilling to go and meet him, and ashamed to run away. That he was not so taken aback by the suddenness of the attack as I was I felt persuaded. He put out his hand to guard himself, and, I fancy, at the last moment was disposed to turn tail and flee.

'But it was too late. The blow got home. He staggered back and would have fallen had not the stranger gripped him with his left hand, and commenced to belabour him with the stick which he held with his right People came streaming out of the open door above and up the steps from the street. My uncle made not the faintest attempt at resistance. When the people came close enough to hamper the free action of his arm, the stranger, giving his victim a push, sent him head foremost down the steps. In an instant the whole thing vanished.'

Mr Holland ceased. The lady had been regarding him with wide-open grey eyes.

'Guy!' she said.

'Wasn't it odd?'

'Odd? You must have been dreaming.'

'I was as wide awake as you are. It was a mirage, or vision, or something of the kind. The queerest part of it was that it was so amazingly real, and so near. When the thing had gone I kept asking myself why I hadn't jumped up and interfered. I could have got there in a dozen strides.'

'Then what happened?'

'I sat for a long time half dazed, half expecting the thing to come again, or to continue from the point at which it had left off. Then I went and told a man with whom I was chumming what I'd seen. He said the sun had got into my eyes, advised me to have a drink—made fun of it altogether. But I knew better; and, as it turned out, I was haunted by my uncle all through the night.'

'Awake or sleeping?'

'Awake. I couldn't sleep. I was haunted by a feeling that he was dying. The stranger had not killed him; but in consequence of the thrashing he had received he was struggling with death, and kept calling out to me to come to him; and I couldn't'

'Poor Guy!'

The lady softly stroked the hand of his which she held between her two.

'I wondered if I was on the verge of an attack of illness or going mad, or what, though personally I felt as fit as a fiddle all the time, with my senses as much about me as they are now. I kept hearing him call out, over and over again, "Guy, Guy!" in the voice I knew so well and wasn't particularly fond of. There was something else which he kept repeating.'

'What was that?'

'"The ruby."'

'The ruby?'

'I haven't a notion of what he meant or what the whole thing meant, but at least a dozen times that night I heard him referring to a ruby,—the ruby, he called it. Long and seemingly involved sentences I heard him utter, but the only two words I could distinguish were those two—"the ruby"; and, as I have said, those two I heard him pronounce certainly a dozen times. And in the morning I was conscious of an absolute conviction that he was dead.'

'How very strange.'

'I'm not one of your clever chaps, so I don't pretend to be able to suggest a sufficient explanation, but the entire business reminds me of what I've heard about second sight. Although in the body I was out there on the *veldt* I seemed to know and see what was taking place heaven knows how many thousand miles away. In spite of the persuasion which was borne in upon me that he was dead, every day, and sometimes all day, I heard him calling out to me, "Guy, Guy!" and every now and then, " The ruby!" It was as if he were imploring me to come to him.'

'So you came.'

'So I came. The truth is I couldn't stand it any longer. I should have gone off my head if I had had much more of it. I was good for nothing, my nerves were all anyhow, everyone was laughing at me. So I slipped off by myself without a word to a creature; got down to Cape Town, found a boat just starting, and was off on it at once. Directly the boat was away the haunting stopped. My nerves were all right in an instant I told myself I was an ass; that I ought to have wired or written, or done something sensible. Since, however, it was too late I tried to make the best of things. I ran up to London so soon as we reached port, meaning, if it turned out that my imagination had made a fool of me, to go straight back without breathing a word to anyone of my ever having come.'

'Not even to me?'

'Not even to you. You wouldn't have liked me to turn up with nothing but a bee in my bonnet.'

'So long as you turned up, I shouldn't have cared for forty thousand bees. The idea!'

'That's very sweet of you. As it happened, no sooner did I appear at my old quarters than Mrs Flickers produced a letter which had arrived for me—she did not know how long ago, and which she had not known what to do with. It turned out to be an intimation from Collyer that that my uncle had died on the 23rd of February, the very day on which, out on the *veldt*, I had seen him assaulted by that unknown individual upon that flight of steps.'

'Guy, is this a ghost story you have been telling me? I don't want to be absurd, but it really does look as if it were a case of the hand of destiny.'

'I don't know about the hand of destiny, but it does look as if it were a case of something.'

'I shouldn't be surprised if, after all, the old reprobate has left you some of his money.'

'Nor I. Oh, Letty, if he has! We'll be married on Monday.'

'As this is Friday, couldn't you make it Sunday? Monday seems such a long way off. My dear Guy, first of all interview Mr Samuel Collyer. Then you'll learn the worst.'

'I am going to. Of course I had to see you first—'

'Of course.'

'But I wired to him that I'd call this afternoon.'

'Then call.'

And Mr Holland called.

CHAPTER 2
THE QUEST ORDAINED

Mr Collyer's offices were in Pump Court, first floor front Mr Samuel Collyer was a somewhat short and pursy gentleman of about fifty years of age, with a clean-shaven face, and a manner which gave such a varying complexion to the words he used as to cause it sometimes to be very difficult to make out exactly what it was he meant; an extremely useful manner for a solicitor to have. As with alert, swinging stride Mr Holland entered, Mr Collyer rose, greeting him with his usual stolid air, as if he had just looked in from across the road, instead of from the wilds of Africa.

'Good morning, Mr Guy. You're looking very brown.'

'Yes, I—I'm feeling very brown.'

The words seemed to come from him almost before he knew it, on the spur of the moment, as if the presence of a third person lent them a special significance. Reclining in the only armchair the room contained was a young gentleman of about Mr Holland's own age. He was well dressed, good looking, very much at his ease, and he regarded Mr Holland with a suggestion of amusement which seemed somehow to be very much in character.

'In questions of feeling is brown the equivalent of blue?'

Mr Holland's bearing was not so genial as the other's.

'I did not expect to see you here.'

'Nor, my dear Guy, did I expect to see you. I did not even wish to.'

'That I can easily believe.'

'It is Mr Collyer's fault that I am here, not mine. I should have been content never to set eyes on you again; and as for being in the same room with you—'

He left his sentence unfinished, with a little airy movement of his hand, which seemed to round it off with a sting. He continued to smile, although Mr Holland regarded him for a moment with eyes which were very far from smiling. The newcomer turned to the solicitor.

'I have your letter.'

'I presume, Mr Guy, that you had my letter nearly three months ago.'

'I had it this morning. I only came back from Africa last night'

'From Africa? I was not aware you had gone so far.'

'Dear Guy is such a gadabout'

The interpolation came from the young gentleman in the armchair. The solicitor went on.

'The only address I had was the one in Craven Street. As my letter did not come back I supposed it had reached you safely; but that, for reasons of your own, you chose to take no notice of it. You know, Mr Guy, that in such matters you are a little erratic'

'I know. You needn't remind me. So my uncle is dead. Of what did he die?'

'The immediate cause was apoplexy, brought on, it is to be feared, by something which happened on the afternoon of his decease.'

The young gentleman in the arm-chair struck in.

'He was thrashed within an inch of his life, and very properly he was served.'

'Thrashed! Where? On a flight of steps?'

'On the steps of the Hôtel des Anglais at Nice.'

'Good God! I thought I knew the place; of course it was the Hôtel des Anglais; it's—it's past believing.'

The solicitor misapprehended the cause of Mr Holland's excitement.

'It does seem almost incredible; none the less it is a lamentable fact'

The young gentleman put in his word.

'How incredible? The dear man misbehaved himself with another man's wife, as was his invariable custom when he had a chance. The other man thrashed him for it. What could be more natural? or simpler?'

Mr Holland ignored the inquiry.

'What is it, Mr Collyer, which you wish to say to me?'

'It is not so much that I have anything to say to you as that I have a duty to perform. I have to read to you your uncle's will. His instructions were that it was to be read only in the presence of both his nephews, his sole remaining relatives.'

'He has probably left all his money to found a hospital for cats, and wished us both to be present, my dear Guy, so that we might enjoy each other's discomfiture.'

Mr Holland said nothing. Mr Collyer was taking some papers out of a metal box which stood against the wall, and on the front of which was painted in white letters the name, 'George Burton.' Reseating himself behind his table he held up a large white linen envelope, such as is used in England for registered letters.

'I will read you the endorsement which is on it "This envelope, which he told me contained his will, was delivered to me by Mr George Burton, on the 22nd of June 1899, and was then and there sealed by me in the presence of my two clerks whose names are undersigned." Then follow my own signature, and the signatures of the clerks in question, both of whom are still in my employ, Ferdinand Murpeatt and Benjamin Davis. Would either of you gentlemen like to see them?'

'My good Mr Collyer, we don't want to see your clerks. Your clerks be sanctified. Why all this form and fuss? Make an end of it Let's know if it's cats or dogs Uncle Burton's favoured.'

'And you, Mr Guy, are you content that I should proceed at once to the contents of this envelope?'

Mr Holland said nothing; he simply nodded. The solicitor, taking a penknife, began to cut open the top of the envelope with a degree of care which perhaps erred on the side of over-caution. He addressed them as he did so.

'I may say that, beyond Mr Burton's own statement that it holds his will, I have no notion what this envelope contains. I have no knowledge of the purport of the will; Mr Burton never gave me the faintest hint as to what were his testamentary intentions. You are aware that your uncle was a man who did what he liked, in his own way; and I say this, therefore, in order to give you to understand that whatever form the will may take, I am not to be held responsible.'

The young gentleman in the armchair laughed.

'My dear Collyer, do cut the cackle, and do let's come to the 'osses.'

Mr Collyer took out from the envelope a single sheet of paper. Without further preamble he commenced to read what was written on it, in a slow, monotonous, sing-song voice, as if it were something sacred which he almost felt it his duty to intone.

I, George Burton, of Hyde Park Terrace, London, W., do hereby announce that this is my last Will and Testament, as written with my own hand on June 17, 1899.

'" I have only two relatives living, *viz.*, my two nephews, Horace Burton, my brother's son, and Guy Holland, the son of my sister; and, since I love them equally well, I desire to do them equal justice.

The reading was interrupted by prolonged laughter from the young gentleman in the armchair.

'The dear man!' he cried.

Mr Collyer continued.

I therefore give and bequeath all that I die possessed of, in real and personal estate, to my nephew, Guy Holland—

'Good Lord!' exclaimed the young gentleman in the armchair.

Mr Holland's lips might have been closed a little tighter. The lawyer went on unmoved.

Absolutely, to do with as he pleases, on condition that he recover from May Bewicke, the actress, whom he knows, my ruby signet ring, which she obtained from me by means of a trick on the 27th of this last May. The ring is well known to him, and to Horace, and to my lawyer, Samuel Collyer. The ring is to be delivered to Samuel Collyer, whom I hereby appoint my sole executor, by my nephew, Guy, within three months of the day of my death. Should he do so within the period mentioned, then I do hereby name him as my sole heir and residuary legatee. In default, however, of such delivery within the time stated, for any cause whatever, then my whole estate, without any deduction whatever, is to become the absolute property of my other nephew, Horace Burton.

Since the chances that Guy will obtain the ring from Miss Bewicke are not very large, that young woman preferring to keep tight hold of anything she has once laid her hands on, in making this will I am doing Horace even more than justice.

In the improbable case of the delivery of my ruby signet

ring by Guy to Samuel Collyer, within the aforementioned three months of my decease, it is to be held by the said Samuel Collyer, and not to pass out of his possession until his death, when it is to be sold, and the proceeds devoted to form a Society for the Reformation of Actresses.

As witness my hand and signature this seventeenth day of June, Eighteen hundred and ninety-nine.

George Burton.

Witnesses—

John Claney, 13 Porchester Terrace, W.
Augustus Evans, 83 Belgrave Row, S. W.'"

The reading was followed by silence, broken by a question from Mr Holland.

'And pray what is the plain English of it all?'

'The will is plain English. You are to obtain a certain ring from a certain lady and deliver it to me within a certain time. If you do so you are your uncle's heir; if you do not, Mr Horace is.'

'Within three months of his death. He died on the 23rd of February. This is the 19th of May. I have four days in which to get the ring.'

'Apparently that is the case.'

'Supposing this lady refuses to give me the ring when I ask for it, as, so far as I can perceive, she will be perfectly justified in doing.'

'Perfectly!'

The murmur came from Horace.

'How am I to get it from her within four days? Where is Miss Bewicke now?'

'In London. She is acting at the Modern Theatre. I am afraid I am unable to assist you with any advice as to how you are to procure the ring should she refuse to hand it over.'

Mr Holland stood up.

'Is that will a good one?'

'You mean in a legal sense. I should say so, perfectly. It is just the sort of will I should have expected your uncle to make. It is distinctly characteristic of the man.'

'My uncle was a most delightful person. Then, if I do not succeed in jockeying this lady out of her property inside four days I'm a pauper.'

'At least you will not inherit under your uncle's will.'

As Mr Holland stood with knitted brows his cousin gave him a friendly pat upon the back. Mr Holland whirled round to him in a manner which was distinctly not friendly.

'How dare you touch me, sir!'

'My dear Guy! May not a cousin give a cousinly salutation to a cousin? My congratulations, my dear boy. You're sure to be the heir. You always were so clever at diddling a woman.'

The blood showed even through Mr Holland's bronzed cheeks; his clenched fists twitched. The other, however, paid no heed to these signs and portents.

'I believe you managed to diddle Miss Bewicke once before, eh, Guy?' He turned upon his heels, with a little movement of his shoulders. 'Let's hope you'll succeed the second time as well as I've been given to understand you did the first. Goodbye. Good luck, dear boy. Collyer, I'll look in on you again.'

Mr Horace Burton strolled from the room. Presently Mr Holland followed him.

'I, also, Mr Collyer, will talk things over when I look in again. I don't feel equal to the task just now.' He said to himself as he was going down the stairs, 'Nice to have to rob your old sweetheart to keep yourself out of the gutter. He knew very well there had been passages between us; so he set me the dirtiest job to do which he could think of. The brute! I'd better have stayed in Africa than have come back to this. I wonder what Letty'll say.'

The solicitor, left alone, leaning back in his chair, stroked his chin with his hand as if to discover whether it wanted shaving.

'They don't know that Miss May Bewicke is Mr Samuel Collyer's niece. I fancy that there are only one or two persons who are aware that he has a niece upon the stage. George Burton certainly was not'

He smiled as if his own thoughts tickled him.

CHAPTER 3
MISS BROAD COMMANDS

They were in Regent's Park again; at the same place; on the same seat. She said to him as he came up,—

'I told papa that you were here. I'm of age, and I suppose I'm entitled to do as I please; but I made up my mind that I'd have no secrecy. It's degrading.'

'Well, degrading's strong. And what did papa say?'

'I mentioned, at the same time, that your uncle was dead, and under the circumstances he perhaps thought it advisable not to say much. At any rate he didn't.'

'He might have done; and he will do soon.'

Something in his tone caught her ear.

'Guy! What's the matter? You don't mean—?'

'Not exactly, though I'm not sure it isn't worse.'

She half rose from the seat

'Has he left you nothing?'

He told her the purport of his uncle's will; she listening eager-eyed and open-mouthed.

'Do you mean to say that you're to get this ridiculous ring out of Miss Bewicke's possession in four days, by fair means or foul?'

He nodded.

'But it's monstrous.'

'It is a pretty tall order?'

'What do you propose to do?'

'I propose to call upon Miss Bewicke.'

In a moment, without any warning, she was standing up beside him stiff and straight

'I see. Now I understand. That's the idea. I've no doubt that Miss Bewicke will find you a most persuasive person.'

'My dear Letty!'

'Weren't you and Miss Bewicke once engaged to be married? Pray don't trouble yourself to explain. I know all about it.

You need have no fear of losing your uncle's inheritance. You are quite sure to understand each other. She'll be delighted to give you the ring in exchange for another. Would you like to give her mine?'

She actually began to unbutton her glove. He groaned.

'It's worthwhile seeing ghosts in Africa for this!'

'And what do you propose to say to Miss Bewicke when you call upon her?'

'That's what I want you to tell me.'

'I tell you! As if you didn't know! After the stories I have heard of her I had hoped that you would have had no more to do with Miss Bewicke. But, of course, my wishes do not count.'

'If the stories you have heard are to Miss Bewicke's discredit, you may take my word for it that they are libels.'

'You are sure to know. I am glad you have such a high opinion of her. When you have seen her you might let me know what she says. That is, if she should say anything which was not spoken in the strictest confidence.'

She actually walked away. He went after her.

'My dear Letty, don't you want me to try to get the ring?'

'By all means act in accordance with the dictates of your better judgement You are so much wiser than I.'

'But, Letty, if I don't get the ring, I—I won't say I lose you, because God knows I hope I never shall do that; but it means that I shall have to wait for you, the Powers above alone can tell how long. While getting it means getting you at once.'

'Guy, weren't you once engaged to be married to Miss Bewicke?'

'Yes, I was.'

'And I suppose you loved each other?'

'Letty, it's not like you to rub it in like this.'

'My dear Guy, let us look the situation fairly in the face. This person, from whom you are going to ask this weighty favour— in effect you are going to ask her to bestow on you a fortune— is the woman whom once you loved, and who was once your promised wife. I don't like it; it's no use pretending to you that

I do.'

'My dear Letty, do you think I like it? If it weren't for circumstances I'd let the ruby and the fortune go together. Listen, the decision shall be in your hands. Shall I try to fulfil the old man's preposterous and malignant condition? or shall I throw the whole thing up at once, let the money go to Horace Burton, return to Africa, and keep on pounding away in the hope of making enough to win you in the end? Now, which is it to be? You shall say.'

'It's not fair to place the entire responsibility upon my shoulders.'

'Since this is a matter in which you are primarily interested, my one desire is that your views should be treated with the utmost possible deference.'

'Then get the ruby.'

'But how?'

'Tear it from her if you like; knock her down and steal it; I don't care. Only don't make love to her under the pretence of doing me a service. Guy, if you're even civil to her—'

She left the sentence unfinished; the air with which she spoke was eloquent enough.

'My dear Letty, as if I should! Then do you suggest that I should go and see her?'

'Of course. Tonight.'

'Tonight?'

'At once. And get the ruby from her somehow; I don't care how, but get it. And meet me here in the morning with it in your hand.'

'But, dearest, Miss Bewicke goes to the theatre.'

'I don't care where she goes.'

'Exactly, but I can hardly interview her in the theatre; and, in any case, she would scarcely have the ruby with her there.'

'Then see her after.'

'After the theatre?'

'Oh, Guy, don't keep asking me questions! If you only knew how I hate the notion of your seeing her at all, especially to solicit a favour at her hands. But since I suppose you must, you must get it over. Only I know what took place between you before; papa knows and everybody knows—heaps of people have told me.' A curious something came into her voice, a sort of choking sound. It frightened Mr Holland. 'Guy, you must see her tonight—tonight—and never again. Get the ruby from her if you have to fight her for it, and meet me here tomorrow morning with it in your hand.'

Without a word of warning she scurried from him down the path. He called after her.

'Letty!'

'Don't try to stop me. I don't want to speak to you when you're going to see that woman.'

There was that in her voice which caused him to deem it advisable to take her at her word. He let her go. He remained behind to objurgate fickle fortune and other things. He told himself, not for the first time,—

'It really was not worthwhile to see ghosts in Africa for this. If spectral visitations all tend this way I bar them. The next ghost I see I'll decline to notice it. It shall lead somebody else into a mess, not me.' He began to stroll towards the gate, kicking every now and then at the pebbles on the path. 'Never thought Letty was such a little spitfire. Bless her heart! I love her for it all the more. Who can have told her about the mess I made of things with May? I'll swear I didn't. These things will out.' He groaned. 'It's past seven. I'll go and get something to eat. Then if food screws my courage to the sticking point I'll go and interview Miss Bewicke a little later. But as for taking that ruby from her *vi et armis*—oh, lord! If ever there was a forlorn hope, I'm down for one tonight.'

Miss Bewicke had a flat in Victoria Street. A little after half-past eleven Mr Holland addressed himself to the hall porter with an inquiry if she was in. There was that in his bearing which suggested that the food which he had consumed had not exhilarated him to any appreciable extent. In fact, so melancholy was his air that one would not have been surprised to learn that it had injuriously affected his digestion. The porter regarded him askance.

'Do you know Miss Bewicke?'

'I have that honour.'

'Sure?'

'Tolerably sure.'

'You'll excuse my asking you, but such a lot of people, perfect strangers, come hanging about and annoying her that my orders are not to let anybody go up if I can help it who isn't a friend of hers. I understand you to say that you are a friend.'

'A friend of some years' standing.'

Mr Holland sighed. The porter observed him with dubious glances, being possibly doubtful as to the meaning of the sigh.

'I suppose it's all right if you're a friend of hers; you ought to know best if you are. I can only say that you'll do no good if you're trying it on. I don't know if Miss Bewicke is in; I don't think she's returned from the theatre But you can go up and see. I'll take you up in the lift if you like.'

The porter took him up in the lift. On the way Mr Holland asked a question.

'Do Miss Bewicke's unknown admirers allow their admiration to carry them as far as her private residence?'

'I don't know about admiration. Idiots I call them; and sometimes worse. People hang about here all day, and sometimes half the night, trying to introduce themselves to her, and I don't know what rubbish. Why, I've known half-a-dozen cabs follow her from the theatre to the very door.'

'Empty cabs?'

'Not much; a fool, and sometimes two fools, in each.'

'Ah!' Mr Holland reflected. 'If Miss Bewicke had been destined to be my wife I wonder how I should have enjoyed her being the object of such ardent admiration. Under such circumstances a husband's feelings must be worth dissection.'

In reply to Mr Holland's modest knock, the door of Miss Bewicke's apartments was opened by a young gentleman well ever six feet high, who appeared to be in rather a curious frame of mind.

'What the deuce do you want?' was his courteous salutation.

'I want Miss Bewicke.'

'Oh, you do, do you? then just you come inside.'

He took Mr Holland by the shoulder, and that individual, although a little surprised at the young gentleman's notion of the sort of reception which it was advisable to accord a friendly visitor, suffered him to lead him to an apartment which was beyond. This was apparently a sitting-room, prettily furnished, particularly with photographs, as is the manner of ladies who are connected with the theatre, and contained a table which was laid for two. The young gentleman still did not release Mr Holland's shoulder. He glared at him instead, and put to him this flattering question,—

'Are you the blackguard who has been making himself a nuisance about the place this last week and more?'

Mr Holland's reply was mild in the extreme.

'I hope not'

'You hope not? What do you mean by that? Don't you know you are?'

'I do not I think the mistake, sir, is yours. May I ask who you are? You have your own ideas of how to greet the coming guest Does Miss Bewicke keep you on the premises in order that you may mete out this kind of treatment to all her friends? You should be popular.'

'You're no friend of Miss Bewicke's. Don't try to bounce me, sir. I'll tell you in two words who I am. My name's Dumville— Bryan Dumville. Miss Bewicke is shortly to be my wife. As her affianced husband I consider myself entitled to protect her from the impertinent attentions of any twopenny-ha'penny bounder who chooses to think that because she condescends to appear upon the stage of a theatre he is at liberty to persecute her when and how he pleases.'

'Your sentiments do you credit, Mr Dumville.'

'Don't try to soft-soap me, sir. You can speak smoothly enough to me; but I will give you ten seconds, before I throw you down the stairs, to explain the meaning of your presence here.'

'I think, Mr Dumville, that, if I were you, I should make it a little more than ten seconds before, as you put it, you throw me down the stairs. I have come to see Miss Bewicke. I am afraid I can only explain myself to her.'

'No, you don't. That trick's been played before! It's stale; out you go!'

'Don't be an ass, sir!'

'Ass!'

The epithet seemed to add fuel to the excitable Mr Dumville's flame. Throwing both arms round Mr Holland, trying to lift him off the ground, he proceeded to hustle him towards the door. Mr Holland, unwilling to be treated in quite such unceremonious fashion, displayed a capacity for resistance for which, possibly, the other was unprepared. There was every prospect of a delightful little bout of rough and tumble, when an interruption came.

'Bryan! what are you doing?'

The interruption came from a young lady who was standing at the open door.

CHAPTER 4
MR HOLLAND FAILS

A small young lady, daintily fashioned, with a child-like face. She was charmingly dressed; a big feather boa was round her neck. As she stood there, in spite of the perfection of her attire, she looked more like a child than a woman. The men released each other. Mr Dumville explained.

'I was only going to throw the fellow down the stairs.'

'Is that all? And what has'—there was a little hesitation; then the word was softened by a smile—'the fellow done? And who may the fellow be?'

'I don't know. Some bounder, I suppose.'

Mr Dumville seemed slightly disconcerted, as if the situation had not quite shaped as he had expected. Mr Holland's hat and stick had fallen to the floor. He stooped to pick them up. When he turned there came an exclamation from the little lady at the door.

'Guy!'

'Miss Bewicke.'

'Whoever would have thought of seeing you? Why, this is Mr Holland, a friend of my childish days.'

She advanced with a tiny gloved hand held out to him. Mr Dumville, whose hands were in his trouser pockets, seemed disposed to be grumpy.

'It wasn't my fault; he should have told me.'

'You hardly gave me an opportunity.'

'My dear Bryan, I believe you're a little mad; that is, I believe you're a little madder even than I thought you were. Guy, this is Bryan Dumville, a gentleman who thinks that he has claims on me. Bryan, this is Guy Holland, who was a friend of mine when I was quite a little child; and that—how long ago that is!'

'I don't see how I'm to blame. The porter was talking about the fellow who has been such a nuisance, saying that he has been making himself particularly objectionable today, trying to force his way upstairs, and I don't know what; and he added that he was hanging about at that very moment, and if he turned his back he shouldn't be surprised if the blackguard made another try to get at you. I made up my mind that if he did I would give him what for. So, when someone knocked at the door, and I found it was a man, I went for him.'

'Nothing could be more natural.'

If Mr Holland's tone was a little dry Mr Dumville did not seem to notice it; but the lady regarded the speaker with laughter lighting all her pretty face.

'Guy, you must sup with us.'

'Thank you, I have not long dined.'

'That doesn't matter; you must eat with us again.' She rang the bell. A maid appeared. 'Bring another plate; Mr Holland will join us at supper.' Miss Bewicke proceeded to remove her outdoor things, handing them to Mr Dumville one by one, talking as she did so. 'Someone told me that you were at the other side of the world—at the North Pole, I think.'

'Not the North Pole; but I have been to Africa. I only re-turned last night'

'And you came today to see me? How perfectly delightful of you.'

Mr Holland winced. He was conscious that the lady might misapprehend the situation.

'The fact is, I have something rather important which I wish to say to you.'

'Indeed? How interesting! I like people to say important things to me. Say it while we're at supper. That is, if it's some-thing Bryan may be allowed to listen to.'

'If I'm in the way I'll go.'

Mr Holland was silent He felt that Mr Dumville was in the way, but that he himself was hardly in a position to say so. Miss Bewicke spoke for him.

'My dear Bryan, when you're in the way we'll let you know. Now, people, will you please sit down?' They seated themselves at table. 'What is this very important thing?—must it out?—or will it keep?'

Mr Holland reflected. He thought of Letty, and other things. Miss Bewicke seemed disposed to be friendly. Perhaps it was as well there was a third person present. He decided to make the running.

'It's this way. My uncle's dead.'

'Your uncle? Mr George Burton? I hope you won't think me dreadful, but I cannot say I'm sorry. He was not a person for whom I entertained feelings of profound respect.'

'He—he's left rather a peculiar will.'

'I'm not surprised. I should be surprised at nothing he did which was peculiar. I never knew him do anything which wasn't. Or worse.'

Mr Holland resolved to plunge.

'He says you have a ruby ring of his.'

'He says ?—who says?'

'My uncle—in his will.'

364

Miss Bewicke laid down her knife and fork.

'Mr Holland, do I understand that you intend to suggest that I have in my possession another person's property?'

'It's like this. He had a ruby ring, I know it very well. In his will he says you have it. He may have given it to you for all I know; he did queer things—'

'Thank you.'

'I don't mean that'

'It doesn't matter. Go on.'

'Anyhow, it's a condition of his will that I'm to get it back from you, and if I don't get it back within three months of his death I'm to lose his money.'

'I don't in the least understand you. Will you please be so good as to make yourself quite clear.'

He made himself as clear as he could, though he did not find it easy. Nor was his explanation well received.

'Then am I to gather that you have come to me at midnight, hot-foot from Africa, in order to get from me—a ring; a ruby ring?'

'It doesn't sound very nice, but that's the plain truth of it.'

'It's very flattering.'

'Very!'

The chorus came from Mr Dumville, and was accompanied by a glare.

'I can only throw myself upon your mercy, Miss Bewicke, and implore you to let me have this ring to save my inheritance.'

Miss Bewicke resumed her knife and fork, which had all this time been lying idle. There was a change in her manner, which, though subtle, was well denned to Mr Holland's consciousness.

'By the way, Mr Holland, the other day I heard your name associated with a person called, I think, Broad. Was it merely idle gossip, or do you know anything of a person with a name like that?'

'I do. I know Miss Broad, and very well. I hope she will be my wife. She has promised that she will.'

'Ah, you and I know what is the value of such promises, don't we, Mr Holland? Is she any relation to Broad, the teaman, in Mincing Lane?'

'She is his daughter; his only child.'

'Indeed! His only child? How delightful! Old Broad has bushels of money. How nice for you, of all men, to be received in such a family.'

The airy insolence of the tone was meant to sting, and did, though he endeavoured to conceal the fact.

'You haven't answered my question.'

'Haven't I? What was your question?'

'Will you let me have the ring, to save my inheritance?'

'It's such an odd question—isn't it, Bryan? So mysterious. Melodrama's not at all my line. They say I'm too small. Do you think that I'm too small?'

'I should imagine that you were better fitted to shine in domestic comedy.'

His words conveyed a meaning which this time stung her, although she laughed.

'But, my dear Mr Holland, what do you want with an inheritance when you are going to marry a rich wife—the only child of her father, and he a widower. I'm told that old Broad's a millionaire.'

'I'm not marrying her for her father's money; nor for her own. Nor do I intend to go to her empty-handed.'

'How chivalrous you are! So changed!'

'Am I to have the ring? '

'Really, Mr Holland, you speak to me as if it were a case of stand and deliver. You can hardly know how your uncle behaved or I do not think you would broach the subject to me at all. In any case it is not one which I can discuss with you. Talk it over with Mr Dumville. Whatever he wishes I will do. I always act on his advice; he is so very wise. Goodnight, Mr Holland. So glad to have seen you. Come soon again. Goodnight, Bryan, dear.'

'But you haven't had any supper.'

'Mr Holland has taken my appetite away; he has caused my mind to travel back to events which I am always endeavouring to forget But it doesn't matter. Hear what he has to say, and decide for me. King will let you both out when your discussion's finished.'

Mr Holland stood up.

'Miss Bewicke, I am very sorry if I have said anything which has given you pain or offence. Nothing could have been further from my intention.'

'Thank you.'

'But this matter which you treat so lightly—'

'Lightly!'

'Is to me almost one of life and death. I believe that my uncle has left something like a quarter of a million.'

'What a sum, Bryan! Doesn't it sound nice?'

'If I can hand this ring to Mr Collyer—'

'To whom?'

'To Mr Collyer, my uncle's solicitor, the money is mine. I have only four days left to do it in.'

'Four days! Just now you said three months.'

'The time appointed is three months after my uncle's death. He died on the 23rd of February. I have only just become acquainted with the terms of his will. So in four days it will be decided if I am to be a rich man or a pauper. You see, Miss Bewicke, that my fate is in your hands.'

'I really cannot discuss the matter with you now. It would make me ill. The strain would be too much for me. I refer you to Mr Dumville. Bryan, dear, I leave the matter entirely in your hands.'

'Miss Bewicke—'

Mr Dumville rose.

'Mr Holland, you have heard what Miss Bewicke has said. So far as she is concerned the discussion is closed. My dear, let me open the door for you.'

He opened the door for her. She passed out, with her handkerchief to her eyes. A fact on which Mr Dumville commented.

'You see what you have done, sir—affected her to tears.'

'To what?'

'To tears!'

'Oh!'

'Well, sir, what have you to say to me?'

'To you?'

'Yes, sir, to me. You have said more than enough to Miss Bewicke. Now, perhaps there is something which you would like to say to me, as her affianced husband.'

'There are one or two things which I should like to say to you, but I am inclined to think that I had better not say them to you here. Nor do I quite see my way to ask you to come outside, though I should like to.'

Mr Holland was savage, and unwise enough to show it. Mr Dumville, having polished his eyeglass, replaced it in his eye so that he might scan the speaker with a greater show of dignity.

'What on earth do you mean by talking to me like that? If that's the kind of remark you wish to make the sooner you get away the better.'

'I am quite of your opinion, Mr Dumville. I shall always remember with pleasure that I was able to get away from you.'

Mr Dumville strode forward.

'You be hanged, sir!'

'After you, Mr Dumville, after you.'

'You had better be careful; although I don't want to have a vulgar row with you here.'

'Would you mind mentioning a place at which you would? I will try to make it convenient to be there.'

Mr Dumville turned and rang the bell.

'What's that for?'

'For the servant to show you out.'

Mr Holland laughed, showing himself out without another word. He was conscious of two things—that he had not been particularly discreet, and that he would like to make his indiscretion greater by 'taking it out' of somebody. It was not often his temper gained the upper hand ;-when it did he was apt to be dangerous both to himself and others.

Nor was his mood chastened by a little incident which took place as he was about to descend the staircase. From a door which opened behind him Miss Bewicke addressed him in mellifluous accents.

'Oh, Mr Holland, will you give my fondest love to dear Miss Broad? It's true that I don't know her, but if you tell her what good friends you and I used to be I'm sure that she won't mind. I hope to make her acquaintance one of these days, and then I'll tell her how fond you and I were of one another. Goodnight'

Before he had a chance to answer the door was closed. He went down the stairs in a rage.

'The little cat!' he muttered. 'The little cat! who would have thought she had such claws?'

As he was going out into the street a woman, running against him, almost knocked him over. She was entering the house, apparently in hot, unseeing haste; putting up her hand as if to prevent his observation of her features; flying up the stairs as if danger was hard upon her heels.

Mr Holland adjusted his hat, which she had knocked almost off without offering the least apology.

'I wonder what mischief you have been up to? Women are beauties, real beauties!'

Having indulged himself in this very cheap piece of cynicism, he, metaphorically, shook the dust of the house from off his feet, but had not gone a dozen paces when he found himself face to face with his cousin, Horace Burton.

CHAPTER 5
A WOMAN SCORNED

Mr Burton might have been awaiting Mr Holland. He did not seem at all surprised to see him there, even at that hour of the night, or, rather, morning, for midnight had long since chimed.

'How do, dear boy? So you haven't been letting the grass grow under your feet. That's where you beat me; you are so energetic'

And Mr Burton smiled. That smile was his most prominent feature. It was always there. Not that it necessarily denoted mirth. Not at all. It might mean anything, or nothing. When he was in a rage he smiled, and when he was in the best of tempers; when he wished to be agreeable, and when he wished to be nasty— and he could be nasty. He was not a bad-looking man, in his way, though there was something about him a little suggesting the worst side of the Semite, which rather detracted from the general effect It was difficult to say exactly what it was.

Whether it was that his nostrils were unduly thick, or that so much of his mouth as his heavy moustache suffered to be visible was animal, or that his eyes, which were fine of their kind, had an odd trick of intently observing you when you were not looking at him, and of wandering away into space when you were, it would have needed an acute physiognomist to determine, and then that physiognomist might have been in error.

Certainly there was something about Mr Horace Burton which nearly always caused an experienced man of the world, on first making his acquaintance, to glance at him a first, a second, and again a third time, and then start thinking. Perhaps it was that, in spite of his moustache, his chronic smile displayed his teeth, which were not nice ones; or because of his soft, purring voice, which, when he became excited, had a squeak in it; or because of his feline trick of touching a person, with whom he might be conversing, with his fingertips, and stroking him, when he got near enough to do it.

Mr Holland regarded his cousin in silence. The encounter did not appear to astonish him, nor to add to his pleasure either. Mr Burton continued.

'Well—have you got it?'

'Have I got what?'

'Ah—you've answered. You haven't. I see. Thanks. It was rather sharp work to raid the girl at this hour of the night, don't you think? But you always were so keen. Was she nice to you? She used to be, didn't she? You've been a lucky chap. I never could make out what women saw in you to like. A lot of them have seen something. There's Miss Broad, for instance—'

'Don't mention that lady's name.'

'Not mention her name? My dear chap!' Mr Burton placed the fingertips of his right hand against Mr Holland's chest, to have them brushed aside as if they were some noxious insect He went on unmoved. 'She's to be my cousin; so I'm told. Unless you've jerked her up. I hear her father kicked you out of the house; perhaps you anticipate more kicking; in a case like that you can't kick back again. So perhaps you're wise to chuck the girl. I tell you what, dear boy.' The fingertips returned, again to be displaced. 'Marry the Bewicke girl. Get a special license to marry the girl out of hand. Then you'll get the ruby and the money too. It's the only way you will Hearken to the words of a wise man.'

'Mr Burton, although I am so unfortunate as to be a relative of yours, I have on a previous occasion been compelled to inform you that I decline to hold communication with, or afford you recognition of any sort or kind. I repeat that intimation now. With my reasons you are well acquainted; their name is Legion. Have the goodness, therefore, to let me pass.'

'But, my dear Guy, how about our uncle's money?'

'What about my uncle's money?'

'Our uncle's; forgive the plural, Guy. Hadn't we better come to some friendly arrangement while there still is time. You'll never get the ruby out of the Bewicke woman; I know her; she's a daughter of the horse-leech; she'll see you damned first. Relinquish the chase at once—you'll have to in a few hours, anyhow—and throw yourself on my magnanimity. There's a suggestion, Guy! Give it up; withdraw at once from what you know is a lost game, and I'll present you with a thousand pounds. Push the thing through to the bitter end, and you'll get nothing.'

'A thousand?—out of a quarter of a million?'

'It would be a gift, Guy—a free gift. It isn't every man who'd present a cousin who'd used him as you've used me with a free gift of a thousand pounds.'

'Mr Burton, if the money is to be yours, I'll have none of it.

371

I'm not disposed to be beholden to your charity, nor to you in any way, as you are aware. If it is to be mine, you'll have none of it; I know your tastes, and will not pander to their gratification. Let me pass.'

'See how different we are. If the money is to be mine—and it will be; it's as good as mine already—I'll give you a few coppers every time we meet; I'll even send you some occasionally through the post. Goodnight! My love to both the ladies!'

Mr Burton hailed a passing hansom and was driven off. Mr Holland continued his promenade, but had not gone far before he was accosted from behind.

'Mr Holland! Mr Holland!' exclaimed a female voice, as if the speaker were in distress for want of breath.

'Who's that?' He turned to see. A feminine figure was hastening towards him. 'This promises to be a night of adventure. Has that little hussy become humanised and changed her mind?'

The caller approached, holding her hand to her side.

'I wish to speak to you. You know me?'

They stood close to a lamp. Mr Holland looked her up and down.

'I seem to have seen you before. You are the person who rushed into the house as I came out.'

'That is it; I rushed—from him!'

She threw out her hand with a dramatic gesture, pointing down the street.

'From whom?'

'From your cousin—from Mr Horace Burton. Oh, he is a nice fellow! If I had stayed with him much longer I should have killed him; so to save myself from killing him I rushed away."

'My cousin's concerns are not mine. I cannot assume responsibility for anything he may do or have done. You are mistaken if you suppose I can.'

'I am not mistaken; I know all that. You men are all the same; you hang together. If your own brother drives a woman into the gutter, you say it is no affair of yours; you pass on, you leave her there. Before you open your mouth I know you cannot be responsible for what he has done. But you can make me to be revenged on him.'

'Even that I cannot do.'

'You can! I say you can!'

The woman spoke, not loudly, but with such passion and intensity of meaning that Mr Holland was conscious of a curious sensation as he heard her. She was tall and thin, about thirty, not bad looking, but precisely the type of woman the ordinary rake, seeking for a victim, would, if he had his senses about him, have left severely alone. She was distinctly not a person to be trifled with. Apparently a foreigner, because, although she spoke fluent English, there was now and then a slight accent and a curious idiom which betrayed her. Written large all over her was what, to a practised eye, was unmistakable evidence that she was of the number of those who take all things seriously, even rakes.

One could easily believe that to her a promise was a promise, though it came from the mouth of a man; and since there are men who regard promises made to women as a sort of persiflage, one would have thought that gentlemen who take that standpoint would carefully avoid an individual who eyed matters of the kind from such an inconveniently different point of view. Mr Horace Burton, however, was in some respects an unusual specimen even of his class. Possibly the consciousness that he ran the risk of burning his own fingers by playing tricks with this particular fire was the lure which drew him on. Anyhow, Mr Holland told himself that this time his cousin had caught a Tartar, and became more and more convinced of it as the woman went on.

'My name is Louise Casata; I am Corsican, as he will find, your cousin. I am the companion of Miss May Bewicke.' Mr Holland pricked up his ears at this, which the woman, with her keen instinct, perceived. 'Now do you not remember me? I was with her when you used to make love to her. I used to think you did it very well. But in those days you were fond of her. Now it is of another woman you are fond. Although you may have forgotten, do not believe she has.'

This time Mr Holland winced.

'I think that now I do remember you. You used to write letters for her and that kind of thing.'

'All sorts of kinds of things. I do everything she tells me to; I am a Jack-of-all-trades. I would act for her one day; I can act, but I am too large a size. But that does not matter; nor does it matter what your cousin has done to me, though you can guess. But you cannot guess how he has lied and juggled.'

'I think I can.'

'Then you must know him very well. In which case you have my sympathy. What does matter is what you are going to do to him.'

'I am going to do nothing to him.'

'We will see; you will see; they all will see. Be still! Let me speak. He has told me about your uncle's will—about the ruby which Miss Bewicke has. How, if you get it from her, you are to have all the money; how, if you don't, he is to have it all. I know! Very well; you will get the ruby. That's what you will do to him. He will be ruined, body and soul; though, for his soul, that was lost long ago. If he wishes to keep his body out of prison he will have to be quick out of England. He will not find it easy. There are those who are watching for him too well.'

'Are you sure of what you say?'

'Am I sure! Do I not know? It is only because they think he will get his uncle's money that he has not been in prison before. I tell you there is a convict's uniform waiting for him in more than one place. You will fit it on his back. I shall be revenged. I will go and see him when he is in gaol. Every three months he will be allowed to receive a visit I will be his visitor. To see me will give him pleasure. I shall have such nice things to say. Oh, yes!'

Mr Holland shivered. There was that about this woman which filled him with a sense of vague discomfort.

'I don't like your way of putting things at all!'

'What does it matter what you like? To get the ruby—that is your affair.'

'How do you suggest that I am, as you phrase it, "to get the ruby"?'

'You will have to take it.'

'Take it?'

'She will never give it to you—never. She hates you. She also has been looking for revenge. Now she has her chance. You behaved badly to her. Now she will behave badly to you.'

'I deny that I behaved badly to her. If you were acquainted with all the facts you would not judge me with such hard judgement'

'She thinks that you behaved badly to her, and, for a woman, that is enough.'

'Then am I to take it that you only think that Horace Burton has behaved badly to you?'

The woman favoured him with a look which made him realise more clearly than anything which had gone before what a Tartar his cousin had encountered. She was silent for a moment or two. When she did speak, she spoke quietly; but it was a quietude in which there was a quality which was not peace.

'You think to get me in a rage I am not such a fool. When I am in earnest I am not so easily angered. It is no affair of yours if it is only that I think he has treated me badly. It is your affair to get the ruby; and I tell you that to get it you must take it.'

'I am so dull as not to understand what you mean when you say that I must take it'

'I will make it clear. You have four days— four only. Good! At one o'clock tomorrow night you will come to Miss Bewicke's rooms. She will be out. It is Saturday. She goes by the midnight train to Brighton until Monday. All will be dark. The front door you will find open. You will have but to push it to enter. You will go to her bedroom; it is in front of you, the second door on the right as you go in. That door, also, will be open. The dressing-table is before the window on the left. It has many little drawers. In them are a great number of her jewels. In the bottom little drawer on the right-hand side facing the glass there is one thing only; it is your uncle's ruby signet ring. I know. I have seen it very often. She is not proud of the way in which she got it; she calls it "old Burton's scalp." It is to her a trophy which she won in battle, so she keeps it all by itself in that little bottom drawer. You have but to put your hand in; it is yours. You go away; you close the doors behind you; for you the game is won.'

Mr Holland stared. The matter-of-fact air with which the proposal was made almost took his breath away.

'You are suggesting that I should commit burglary.'

She made a contemptuous movement with her head and hands.

'It is but a word; what does it matter—a word? It is a burglary of which you will hear nothing more. I promise you that Miss Bewicke will do nothing.'

'And the morality of the proceeding, what of that?'

'Morality!' She laughed. 'The morality! Do not talk to me such nonsense! Bah! As if anyone cared for morality except for the sake of a—. But I shall not contend with you; you but amuse yourself. You understand what I have said?'

'Perfectly. Too well.'

'Very good. Then I shall see you tomorrow night at one o'clock.'

'You will do nothing of the kind.'

'No, I shall not see you, because it will be dark; but you will be there. You will find the doors open, and everything as I have said. It is already late; I must go. Goodbye.'

She went, fluttering from him up the street at a gait which was half walk, half run. He stood looking after her, a little taken aback by the abruptness of her departure.

'That woman appears to have formed a high opinion of my character. She flatters me.'

CHAPTER 6
Miss Broad Commands a Second Time

The next morning, although he was early at the rendezvous, Miss Broad was there before him. He saw her before she saw him—or thought he did—and, unperceived, as he fancied, stood and watched her. She was reading a book, sitting a little sideways, so that he saw her profile clearly. It was a brilliant morning, and she was attired for the sun. She had on a light grey silky dress, which was covered with flowers, and a huge hat, about a yard round, which matched the dress. He thought how nice she looked. Of a charm so delicate. Instinct with the essence of all things spiritual. He had been depressed as he had come through the park. The mere sight of her dispelled the clouds. The blood moved brisker through his veins. Seeing how engrossed she was by what she read, thinking to take her by surprise, he began to steal towards her across the grass—which he ought not to have done. Hardly had he stepped over the little iron fence than a stentorian voice bawled,—

'Come out of that!'

The invitation was addressed to him, as others, including Miss Broad, perceived as well as he did. It was a keeper's civil method of suggesting that he should keep off the grass, which, just there, was fenced about. He bowed to Miss Broad with a feeble smile, she merely nodding in return, without rising from her seat As he advanced towards her along the proper gravel path, he was a little conscious that his approach had been robbed of dignity. She received him with an air which was a little frigid—still without rising—and beginning at once on a subject which he would have liked postponed.

'Well? Have you got it?'

'Have I got what?'

'You know very well what I mean. Have you got the ruby?—as you promised.'

'As I promised? My dear Letty, I think that statement is—is a little unauthorised.'

'Does that mean that you haven't got it?'

'I'm afraid it does—as yet'

'Did you try to get it?'

'I did.'

'Did you go and see that woman?'

'I called upon Miss Bewicke.'

'And do you mean to say that she refused to let you have it?'

'If you'll allow me, I'll tell you what took place.'

He told her—a trifle lamely, but still he presented her with a sufficiently clear picture of what actually occurred—sufficiently clear, that is, to inflame her with indignation. She listened with eyes which grew brighter and brighter, and lips which closed tighter and tighter. The spiritual side of her became less obvious.

'And do you mean to say that you allowed the creature to trample on you without a word of protest?'

'I am not aware that she did trample on me.'

'Not when, according to your own account, she treated you as if you were a dog? I wonder you didn't take her into your hands and strangle her.'

'My dear Letty!'

'Of course I don't mean that; but you know what I do mean. As for that man—that Mr What's-his-name—why didn't you knock him down?'

'In a lady's room? I did suggest that if he liked to step outside I should be happy to do him any little service which was in my power.'

'And what did he do?'

'Rang the bell and requested the servant to show me out.'

'And you went? You actually allowed this man to kick you out—for that was what it came to—without a word.'

'Well, my dear, Miss Bewicke called out to me as I was going down the stairs to say that she sent her love to you.'

'Guy! you dare to tell me such a thing? You allow that creature to insult me by sending such a message, or pretending to; and then you repeat her insolence to me. The little wretch! So you are ruined.'

'Not yet. There are still about four days between me and the worst.'

'Then do you propose to allow her to have you kicked out of her apartments on each of those four days? Besides insulting me? I had hardly imagined that you were that kind of person.

But one learns. Well, I suppose if you don't mind, I needn't. Though I really think you might be better off if you returned to Africa before instead of afterwards.'

'That is something like the advice which Horace offered.'

She sat up straighter.

'Did you also see Mr Burton last night?'

'He was waiting in the street when I came out of Miss Bewicke's. He congratulated me on the result of my visit'

'Really, you appear to have had a thoroughly enjoyable time. Everybody seems to have had a kick at you. For my part, Guy, rather than allow people to ride over me rough-shod, as you appear disposed to do, I'd—I'd—steal the ruby.'

'You are in accordance with still another piece of advice which I received.'

'Guy! what do you mean?' He told her of his interview with Miss Casata. When he had finished she drew a long breath. 'Guy, I should do as she says.'

'Letty!'

'I should, I really should. So long as you get the ruby, no matter what happens, you can't be worse off that you will be if you don't get it If you don't get it, you are ruined. You will have to go back to Africa and stay there for the rest of your life, or, at any rate, till both of us are old; because you know you've no more chance of getting money there than you have here, and that's none at all. And you know you promised papa, and I promised papa, that you wouldn't marry till you had money of your own. And that doesn't mean a pound or two; it means a lot He doesn't like to think you're marrying me for his money.'

'Letty!'

'Well, he doesn't; you know he doesn't. Of course I know you're not, or should I be sitting here talking to you now? But papa's different. And, anyhow, we promised. If there was nothing else to be gained, I'd like you to take it if only for the sake of spiting that actress creature. I'll teach her to send me messages.'

'But, my dear Letty, I fancy you don't quite realise that you are suggesting that I should commit a felony.'

'Felony! Don't talk such stuff and nonsense.' Her words reminded him of some of Miss Casata's of the night before. For some cause he shivered. 'Doesn't your uncle as good as say she stole it from him? And didn't that woman tell you that she's ashamed of it herself, and that therefore she hides it away all alone in a drawer? That shows that she's perfectly conscious that it's as much your property as hers. Indeed, it's much more your property. Your uncle left it to you, and she's no right to keep you out of it a single moment And she wouldn't, you know very well that she wouldn't, if it wasn't for me. You threw her over—'

'Pardon me, I did not.'

'Then did she throw you over?'

'That's nearer the mark.'

'Really, Guy, you have an agreeable way of commending yourself to me. Then am I to understand that she regards you as her cast-off rubbish?'

'We agreed that we had made a mistake. That is the truth of the matter. There was no throwing over on either side.'

'Now, Guy, I know more than you suppose. Do you mean to deny that she resents the idea of your being about to marry me?'

'She congratulated me on the fact last night.'

'Did she, indeed? How very good of her. And pray how did she congratulate you? As if she meant it?'

'I suppose she meant it.'

'You suppose! Do you dare to tell me that you don't know quite well that her congratulations were ironical?'

'Well, I confess I had my "doots."'

'There! Didn't I say so all along? Oh, Guy, how difficult it is to get things out of you. Now, try to be equally truthful again, and tell me, on your word of honour, if you don't know that she would give you the ruby without a moment's hesitation if it wasn't for me; that is, if the fact of our being engaged to each other didn't prevent you paying attention to her?'

'I shouldn't like to put it in that way; but I think it possible that Miss Bewicke might prove more malleable if the circumstances were other than they are.'

'Precisely. That is what I mean. So promise me that tonight you will take your own.'

'My own! Letty!'

'Promise me!'

'But, my dear Letty—'

'Of course there is an alternative. You can throw me over. We, in our turn, can agree that we have made a mistake. Then you will be able to make yourself agreeable to her; and you will be able to get the ruby that way.'

'But, my dear Letty, if you will only be reasonable—'

'It is you who are unreasonable. You allow an idea to mar our lifelong happiness. Before you realise how hollow it is it will be too late. There will be nothing in front of us but dreary years of waiting. You let the cup of happiness be dashed from your hand even when it is already at your lips. I release you, Guy. I will not be a clog on you, perhaps through all eternity.'

Her tone was sombre, funereal Mr Holland groaned.

'Oh, Lord! Your logic is as beautiful as you are. It really was worthwhile seeing ghosts in Africa for this!' She stood up.

'Then go back to Africa and see some more. You shall not stay here to laugh at me. Goodbye.'

He caught her by the hand. 'Letty! How can you be so cruel.'

'Then you should do as I ask you. As you would do, without hesitation, if you really had a spark of the love you pretend to have for me.'

'I will; I'll do whatever you ask, though I'm ashamed of myself when I say so.'

'Promise that tonight you'll take your own?'

'I promise.'

She sat down again, and was as nice as she could be; he only knew how nice that was. He would have been as happy as is possible if it had not been for the thoughts which were at the back of his head, and the prospect which lay in front of him.

Unfortunately, nearly all the time Miss Broad was causing

him to realise his good fortune in winning the love of such a girl as she was he was picturing himself stealing up a flight of darkened stairs, like a thief.

CHAPTER 7

THE BOTTOM DRAWER

That night he realised his own picture.

One o'clock was the hour suggested by Miss Casata. Twenty times before that hour arrived he told himself that he had better return to Africa—ghosts or no ghosts—than do this thing. It seemed to him that dishonour hedged him round about; that whichever way he went he would find himself among the thorns. If he did this thing he would break his plighted word; quite possibly lose his love and his fortune too. If he did the other he might quite possibly find himself up to the neck in a slough of misunderstandings—to speak of nothing worse—from which he could never emerge as clean as he went in. The choice was a pleasant one. Yet he never hesitated as to which horn of the dilemma he would thrust himself on. Although very much against his will, he was set on burglary. And, being once resolved, set about the business, to all outward appearances, as calmly as if such incidents were the mere trivialities of his nightly life.

At a quarter after midnight he started to stroll from Charing Cross. At the half hour he was sauntering in the Westminster Abbey Gardens. He glanced along Victoria Street as far as he could see. An occasional omnibus came rumbling along. Cabs flitted to and fro; sometimes carriages. But foot passengers were few and far between. And, so far as could be seen from the street, the buildings on either side of the way were in darkness.

He strolled gently on, swinging his stick, smoking a cigar, as any other gentleman might have done who enjoyed the cool night air. Under a lamp-post stood a policeman. Mr Holland smiled.

'Goodnight, officer!'

He bestowed on him a genial salutation, which the other returned in kind.

'Goodnight, sir.'

He seemed rather a youngish man, well set up, with broad shoulders and a shrewd face. Mr Holland wondered if he should have any professional intercourse with him before the night was over. He laughed to himself as he thought of it. When he had gone some distance further he stopped and turned. The constable had vanished. Presumably his duty had led him down one of the side streets. An omnibus was coming in one direction, a couple of cabs in the other. Miss Bewicke's rooms were close at hand. Should he let the vehicles pass before he came to business? It was not yet one. He hesitated, then walked slowly past the house, noticing as he went that the front door was closed. What did it mean? Was he supposed to knock, calling upon the porter to let him in? The notion was absurd. Perhaps Miss Casata had only been playing with him after all.

At the idea he laughed again. What would Miss Broad say—and think—if the woman had promised more than she could perform? He went nearly as far as Victoria, then retraced his steps. As he approached the house again Big Ben struck one; He stopped, threw away the butt of his cigar, moved to the door. There was a handle. He turned it, it yielded, the door was open.

So it seemed that there was some sort of method in Miss Casata's madness.

The question was, where was the porter? Was he within? Upstairs or down? He peeped inside the door, or tried to. The street lamps did not penetrate; it was pitch dark. He entered, closing the door behind him. All was still. As he listened, seeking to peer this way and that, it seemed to him that the darkness was like a wall on every side.

'What am I to do? I shall tumble over something if I don't look out; I don't even know where the staircase is; Dare I strike a match? I wonder what professionals do under circumstances such as these. I've heard of their carrying dark lanterns, and such-like mysterious things. Unfortunately, I haven't got so far as that, though there's no knowing how far I shall get before I've done.'

He moved forward, and kicked against something which made a noise.

'This will never do. I shall come to grief if I don't look out. It'll have to be a match.'

He struck one; it ignited with a spluttering noise which seemed to him to resemble the explosion of a dynamite cartridge, fizzled, then went out.

'This is pretty. But I caught a glimpse of the staircase. I suppose I'll have to be content with seeing so much.'

He felt his way to the stairs, presently had his hand upon the rail, then commenced to ascend. All at once he stopped.

'Hanged if I haven't forgotten on which floor her rooms are! That's a comfortable state of affairs. I can't go prowling all over the place playing a game of hide-and-seek with Miss Bewicke's rooms. There'd be trouble. Now, what am I to do?'

The question was answered in rather a curious way. Looking up he gradually became conscious of what looked like a gleam of light somewhere overhead.

'I wonder if that's a hint to me, or if it's the porter. I'm off to inquire. If it's the porter I'll have to explain.'

He chuckled to himself at the reflection of the sort of explanation he would have to offer. He continued to ascend.

'I hope it's all right, but it seems a good way up. I didn't think she occupied quite such an elevated position as this.'

He reached the floor on which was the light, perceiving now that it proceeded from a door upon the right which was open but the merest fraction of an inch.

'Is that where she resides? I wonder. At least I'll make inquiries. I'll knock, as an honest man should do, and see who answers.'

He tapped at the panel softly with his knuckles, so softly that one might have been excused for supposing he had no desire that his tapping should be heard. There was no response. He tapped again; still none. He pushed the door wider open, finding himself in what appeared, in the dim light, to be a little hall.

Another open door was on his right. It was on the other side of this that the light was burning. He remembered what Miss Casata had said about Miss Bewicke's bedroom; that it was the second door on his right as he entered. Apparently she had been as good as her word; better, indeed, for she had placed a light to guide him. He advanced to find himself in what was evidently a lady's bedroom.

A night light flickered on a table in the centre; it was that which had lightened his darkness. He glanced around. Everywhere were traces of feminine occupation; knick-knacks which no man would willingly suffer in the chamber in which he slept; numerous examples of the inevitable photograph. Against a wall hung a crayon portrait. He recognised the original—the owner of the room. The pictured face seemed to return him look for look, reproaches in its glances. He removed his eyes, abashed.

On one side was the dressing-table of which Miss Casata had spoken. A gorgeous piece of furniture, of some delicate light wood, with gilt and ivory insets. Columns of drawers were on either side; a full-length cheval glass swung between them. As he stood in front of it he was startled by the reflection of his own image; he felt that there was something sinister in the bearing of the man who spied on him. The little drawers were those of which he had been told. They contained many of Miss Bewicke's jewels. What he sought was in the bottom drawer upon his right Somehow, since he had entered the house, everything seemed on his right He stooped to open it The drawer was locked.

The discovery staggered him more than anything which had gone before—that the drawer was locked. At last he was confronted with the real nature of the errand he had come upon. Hitherto he had been able to salve his conscience with the fact that he had simply passed through open doors. Now, if he wished to effect an entrance he would have to force one, like any other thief. He gave another try at the handle. The drawer refused to budge. It certainly was locked. His eye was caught by something which was lying upon the floor, within a foot of him. It was a screwdriver. The juxtaposition was suggestive; the screwdriver, and the locked drawer. Miss Casata was no half-hearted ally; she was thorough. She was aware that, as an amateur, he might forget to bring the proper tools; so, with praiseworthy thoughtfulness, she had supplied, in advance, his possible omissions.

He was not so grateful as he might have been. He used strong language.

'Curse that woman! It is such as she who drive men along the road to hell.'

None the less he took the screwdriver in his hand. He felt its edge. It seemed sharp.

'I suppose, since I've gone so far, I may as well see the thing right through. It's no good shying at a gnat after tackling a whale. Here goes!'

Thrusting the chisel between the woodwork and the drawer, he proceeded to prise it open. The lock was but a slight one. It quickly yielded. The drawer shot out He peered within. It contained a small white box, apparently of deal. He took it out. Inside was a ruby signet ring. He rose with the ring between his fingers.

As he stood up, someone came into the room. Turning, he found himself staring at Miss Bewicke.

Chapter 8
The Lady—and the Gentleman

Apparently each of the pair was equally surprised. Each stared at the other as if tongue-tied; Mr Holland motionless, holding the ring a little in front of him, as if suffering from at least temporary paralysis; Miss Bewicke, equally rigid, with her fingers up to her throat, just as she had raised them intending to remove the boa which was about her neck. It was she who first regained the faculty of speech.

'Guy!' The word came with a little gasp, as if she uttered it unwittingly. He was still; staring at her as if he were powerless to remove his eyes from off her face. 'What are you doing?'

Still silence from the man. His incapacity seemed to inspire her with confidence. She removed her boa, smiling as she did so. She sauntered here and there, eyeing things. She walked right round him, peering at him as she went. He might have been some mechanical figure, he endured so stolidly her ostentatious curiosity. Only he followed her with his glance as she passed round.

She did not speak when she had finished her inspection; with apparent indifference to his presence she took off her hat and coat. Unable, perhaps, to endure the situation any longer he struggled to obtain possession of his voice. It sounded harsh and husky.

'I thought you had gone to Brighton?'

'So you keep an observation on my movements, I see?' The words were accompanied by a smile which made him clench his fists so tightly that he drove the nails into the palms. She was folding up a veil, with a dainty show of peculiar care. 'I ought to be at Brighton; but I'm not. I meant to go; but I didn't. It was so late that I put off my journey till tomorrow; so I went to see some people instead. It was painfully slow; this promises to be better.'

Her airy manner, which seemed to him to be so pregnant with contempt, tried him more than reproaches might have done, or rage. He was so conscious of his position that indifference stung more than lashes. A policeman he could have faced, but not this smiling girl. All his self-respect had gone clean out of him; he felt she knew, and floundered in his efforts to regain some part of it.

'Miss Bewicke, you know why I am here.'

'To see me, I suppose. So good of you, Guy. Especially as I take it that you intended to wait for me till I returned from Brighton.'

'I came to take my own.'

'Your own?'

'This.'

He held out the ring between his finger and thumb. She came nearer, so that she might see what it was he held, smiling all the time.

'That—that's mine!'

'It was bequeathed me by my uncle.'

'Your uncle? Impossible; it wasn't his to bequeath."

'You know the conditions which were attached to its possession. Since you declined to give it me—'

'I did not decline.'

'I don't know what other construction you put upon your conduct of last night I gathered that you declined. Therefore, since its immediate possession was of capital importance, I came and took it'

'How nice of you. And you waited till you thought I was at Brighton to show your mettle? How discreet! Guy, weren't you once to have been my husband?'

Nothing was further from his desire than to become involved in a tangle of reminiscences, so he became a little brutal.

'I have the ruby; that is the main point.'

'Are you proud of having robbed me—the girl who was to have been your wife?'

'You would have robbed me.'

'Even supposing that to be true, does that entitle you to throw aside all those canons of honour to which you have always given me to understand you were such a stickler, and become —a thief? Oh, Guy!'

'I do not propose to bandy words with you. I know of old your capacity to make black seem white—you were ever an actress, May. How the ruby originally came into your possession I cannot say.'

'It's not a pretty story, Guy; scarcely to your uncle's credit.'

'But you were perfectly well aware that morally it was mine. It was nothing to you; it was all the world to me. I believe that you refused to let me have it precisely because you knew that your refusal might entail my ruin; and so your cup of revenge might be filled to the full. Under those circumstances I hold that I was justified in using any and every means to save myself from being utterly undone by the whim of a revengeful woman.'

'I meant to let you have it.'

'That was not the impression you left upon my mind last night.'

'You took me unawares—I had to think things over.'

'Then if it was your intention that I should have it you cannot but be pleased to find that my action has kept abreast of your intention.'

Miss Bewicke was silent. She was drawing imaginary pictures with her finger-tip on the table by which she was standing, looking down as she did so. His desire was to get away; it was not an interview which he wished to have prolonged. But his departure was postponed.

'Why do you say I am revengeful?'

'You know better than I.'

'Do you think I wish to be revenged on you because once you pretended to love me, and now you keep up that pretence no longer?'

'It was no pretence.'

'I am glad to hear that, because, Guy, I love you still.'

She looked up at him in such a way that she seemed to compel him to meet her eyes. He shivered.

'I wish you wouldn't say such things.'

'Why? Because they're true? I like to tell the truth. I have always loved you, and I always shall, though I shall never be your wife.'

'I thought you said you were engaged to Dumville.'

'So I am. And I daresay that perhaps one day I shall marry him. I don't know quite why. But it certainly isn't because I love him. I have never pretended to. Ask him; he's frankness itself; he'll confess. Although, as you have only told me, I am a woman with ill-regulated passions and irresponsible tendencies, I'm a woman with only one love in her life, and you are he. Goodnight, and goodbye.'

Now that she had formally dismissed him he felt that it was difficult to go. He fidgeted instead.

'I know you think that I have behaved meanly.'

'Not at all. I suppose you have acted according to your

lights.'

'I'm not so sure of that. But, the truth is, I was desperate.'

'Indeed? Is that so? Like the man with the twelve starving children, who steals the bottle of whisky. I know. If I were you I wouldn't trouble to explain. This sort of situation is not improved by explanation. I think you had better pocket your booty and go.'

'As for the ruby'—he was holding it out on the palm of his open hand—'I will give you another for it a dozen times as good as this.'

For the first time she fired up.

'You dare to do anything of the kind—you dare! Do you think I am to be bought and sold?'

'I simply don't wish you to suffer from my action.'

'Do you think that your giving me one piece of stone in exchange for another piece of stone will prevent my suffering? Guy, please, go.'

He placed the ring before her on the table.

'There is the ruby.'

'Take it'

'Do you mean that?'

'I do. If it is of the slightest use to you, by all means take it'

'You give it to me—freely?'

'Oh, yes, so freely! Only—I wish you'd go.'

Thrusting the ruby into his waistcoat pocket, he went, without another word. Without it seemed darker even than before. He stumbled, blindly, down the stairs. Presently the darkness lightened; a gleam descended from above.

Glancing up he perceived that Miss Bewicke was leaning over the railing with a lighted candle in her hand. He said nothing; attempted no word of thanks. So far as he knew she, too, was still; but as he descended, assisted by the light she held, he felt as he was convinced the whipped cur must feel, which sneaks off with its tail between its legs. The candle was still showing a faint glimmer of light as he passed into the street. He applied a dozen injurious epithets to himself as he thought that he had not even acknowledged the courtesy he had received. But for the life of him he could not, at that moment, have uttered a word of thanks.

Now that he was out in the street he raged. In his first mad impulse he would have taken what Miss Bewicke had called his 'booty' from his pocket and hurled it from him through the night Prudence, however, prevailed. He told himself, again and again, that he was an ineffable thing to allow it to remain a second longer in his possession. It stayed there all the same. He was conscious that nothing could be less romantic than the whole adventure; nothing more undignified than the part which he had played in it. He had been throughout a mere figurehead—a counter manipulated by three women—he who thought that if he had anything on which to pride himself it was his manhood. His rage waxed hotter as he strode along; he was angry even with Miss Broad.

'If it hadn't been for her—' he began. Then stopped, stood still, struck with his fist at the air—his stick, it seemed, he had left behind him. 'What a cur I am! I try to put the blame, like some snivelling sneak of a schoolboy, upon everyone except myself, as though the fault was not mine, and mine alone. Am I some weak idiot that I am not responsible for my own actions? that I do a dirty thing, and then exclaim that someone made me? Well, it's done, and can't be undone, and I stand, self-confessed, a hound; but, as I live, I'll return at once and make her take the ruby back again. Then off once more for Africa. Better to be haunted by my uncle's ghost than by my own conscience.'

He turned, prepared to put his new-born resolution immediately into effect, and found himself confronted by an individual by whom his steps had been dogged ever since he left Miss Bewicke's. Had he had his wits about him he could hardly have helped noticing the fact, the proceedings of the person who took such a warm interest in his movements had been so singular. To begin with, he had been on the other side of the road. When Mr Holland first appeared he had slunk back into a doorway, from which he presently issued in pursuit, keeping as much as possible in the shadow. When, however, he perceived himself unnoticed he became bolder. Until, at last, making a sudden dash across the street, he began to follow within a few feet of the unconscious pedestrian. He carried something, which every now and then he gripped with both hands, as if about to strike.

The mathematical moment came when Mr Holland turned. Without giving him a chance to speak the man swung the something which he carried through the air, bringing it down heavily, with a thud, upon his head. Mr Holland dropped on to the pavement. And there he lay.

CHAPTER 9
THE FLYMAN

The assailant remained, for a second or two, looking down on his recumbent victim. He retained his grip upon his weapon, as if anticipating the possibility of having to strike with it another blow. But, no, the first had done its work. Mr Holland lay quite still, in an ugly heap, as men only lie who have been stricken hard. His assailant touched him with his foot, as if to make quite sure. Mr Holland did not resent the intrusion of the other's boot; he evinced no interest in it at all. The man was satisfied.

'That done him.'

It had, for sure. The fellow glanced up and down the street No one was in sight That was a state of things which could hardly be expected to continue. Time was precious; at any moment a policeman might appear. Under certain circumstances a policeman is inquisitive.

The man, dropping on one knee, began to handle Mr Holland as if he had been so much dead meat; indeed, a butcher might have been expected to finger the carcase of what he had just now killed with greater ceremony.

'I wonder where he put it'

He appeared to be searching for something, which, at first, he could not find. He went quickly through the stricken man's pockets, emptying each in turn of its contents. He made no bones about putting back what he took out, but threw everything into an inner pocket in his own jacket Watch, money, cigar-case, keys, various odds and ends all went into the same receptacle. Still he did not appear to light on what he sought

'Suppose he never got it? That would be a pretty little game. My crikey!'

He went through the pockets a second time more methodically; coat, waistcoat, trousers, nothing was omitted. The result was disappointing; they all were empty.

'Has he got it in a secret pocket?' Tearing open the waistcoat, he ran his fingers up and down the lining. 'I can't undress the bloke out here.' He went carefully over the lining, fingered the trousers. 'I don't believe he's got it If he hasn't, then I'm done. It wasn't worth bashing him for this little lot' The reference was, possibly, to what he had transferred to his own jacket 'If he hasn't got it, there'll be trouble. Strikes me I'd better take a little trip into the country. He might think I'd got it and done a bunk. I might get a bit out of him like that. If he's anything to get. I wish I'd never gone in for the job. What's that?"

All the while he had never ceased to finger the silent man, submitting his garments to the minutest possible examination which the position permitted. Constantly he glanced behind and in front, well knowing that the risk of intrusion grew greater with every moment. With what looked very like impertinence, he turned the object of his curiosity over on to his face. As he did so his eye was caught by something which was lying on the pavement, and which apparently had hitherto been covered by the body of the silent man. It was a ring. He snatched at it

'Got it, by the living jingo! The whole time the fool was right on top of it If I hadn't overed him I might have gone away and thought he'd never had it after all. That'd been a pretty how-d'ye-do. I suppose he dropped it when I downed him, and covered it when he fell. He might have done it on purpose, just to spite me.'

He was standing up, turning the ring over and over between his fingers. 'It's all right, there's no mistake about that much. This is fair jam, this is. A thousand quids into my pocket' Something attracted his attention. 'Hollo!—sounded like a footstep—a copper's, unless I'm wrong!'

Without pausing to look behind he crossed the street, keeping well within the shadow of the houses, and walking fast, yet not too quickly, in the direction of Victoria. As he went he disposed of what had proved so efficient a weapon. It was a narrow bag, about a couple of inches in diameter, and a little over a foot in length. It was stuffed with sand. Untying one end, he allowed the contents to dribble out into the areas of the houses as he passed. Nothing remained but a strip of canvas. He was cramming this into his pocket as he reached the corner of a street into which he turned. A constable was standing on the kerb as if waiting for him to come. His wholly unexpected appearance might have startled a less skilful practitioner into doing something rash. But this gentleman had had too many curious experiences to permit himself to readily lose his wits.

'Goodnight, p'liceman. Fine night!' he sang out, moving quickly on, as if he were hastening on.

'Goodnight,' returned the policeman.

He eyed the other as he passed, as if he wondered who he was, yet was conscious of no legitimate reason why he should stop him to inquire.

The man drew in the morning air between his teeth, as if he desired to inflate his lungs to the full.

'That was a squeak. It wasn't him I nosed. Who'd have thought that he was there. If he'd come round the corner a minute or two ago there'd have probably been fun. Lucky I emptied the bag before I came on him. Hollo! He's going into Victoria Street. If he uses his eyes he'll spot my bloke in half a minute from now. I'd better put the steam on.'

He quickened his pace, not breaking into a run, for he was aware that nothing arouses attention more than the sight of a man running at that hour in a London street. But for the next ten minutes he moved at a good five miles an hour, going fair toe-and-heel. Then he slackened, judging that for the present he was safe; and, moreover, he was blown.

By what at least seemed devious ways he steered for Chelsea, to find himself, at last, in the King's Road. Thence he made for the river side, pausing before a house which faced the Thames. The house was an old one. In front was a piece of ground which was half yard, half garden. The approach to this was guarded by an iron railing and a gate. The gate was locked. By it was a rusty bell handle. At this he tugged. Almost immediately a window on the first floor was opened about three inches. A voice was heard.

'Who's there?'

'It's me, the Flyman.'

'You've been a devil of a time.'

'Couldn't be no quicker.'

The window was shut again. Presently the front door was opened instead. A man came out It was Horace Burton. He sauntered to the gate.

'Have you got it?'

'You let me in and then I'll tell you.'

'Don't be an idiot! Tell me, have you got it?'

'I sha'n't tell you nothing till I'm inside.'

'You're an ass! Do you think I want to keep you out?' He fumbled with the lock. 'Confound this key; it's rusty.'

'Your hand ain't steady; that's what's wrong with it.'

'Hang the thing!'

The key dropped with a clatter to the ground.

'You let me have a try at it; perhaps my hand ain't so shaky as yours.'

The man outside picked up the fallen key, thrusting his hand through the railings to enable him to do so. Soon the gate was open. When he had entered he locked it again behind him. The two men went into the house. When they were in the hall Mr Burton repeated his assertion.

'You've been a devil of a time. Do you think I want to stop up all night waiting for you?'

'That's all right I'll tell you all about it when we get upstairs. Who's there?'

'Old Cox is there, that's who's there; and he looks to me as if he were going to stop there the rest of his life—hanged if he doesn't'

Possibly Mr Burton had been quenching his thirst too frequently with the idea of speeding the heavy hours of his vigil. The result was obvious in his speech and his appearance. At the foot of the staircase he stumbled against the bottom stair. The newcomer proffered his assistance.

'Steady, governor. Let me lend you a hand.'

Mr Burton was at once upon his dignity.

'Don't you touch me. I don't want your hand. Do you think I don't know my way up my own staircase?'

He ascended it as if in doubt The Flyman kept close behind in case of accident. Which fact Mr Burton, when he was half way up, discovered. Steadying himself against the banister he addressed his too-assiduous attendant.

'Might I ask you not to tread upon my heels? Might I also ask you to go down to the bottom of the stairs and wait there till I'm at the top? There's too much of it'

'All right, governor. Only don't keep me here too long, that's all.'

'You haven't kept me long? Oh, no! Not more than thirteen hours.'

When he had reached the top Mr Burton threw open the door of a room in which the gas was lighted. In an armchair a gentleman was smoking a cigar.

'This confounded Flyman thinks that he's the devil knows who. Seems to think he owns the place. I think I'll have a drink.'

The gentleman in the armchair ventured on remonstrance.

'I wouldn't if I were you; at least, not till we've got this business over.'

'Wouldn't you? Then I would. There's something the matter with this beastly siphon.'

The matter was that while he directed the nozzle of the siphon in one direction he held his glass in another. The result was that the liquor did not go where he intended. So he drank his whisky neat.

While Mr Burton was having his little discussion with the siphon, the man who had described himself as 'the Flyman' came into the room. He was rather over the average height, slightly built, with fair hair and moustache and very pale blue eyes. The *eyes* were his most peculiar feature. He was not bad looking, with an agreeable personality; at first sight, a likeable man, until you caught his eyes, then you wondered. They were set oddly in his head, so that they seldom seemed to move. He had a trick of regarding you with a curiously immobile stare, which, even when he smiled— which was but rarely—seemed to convey a latent threat. He was dressed like a respectable artisan, and had such a low-pitched, clear, musical voice that it was with surprise one observed how peculiar were his notions of his mother tongue.

As soon as he was inside the room Mr Burton repeated his former inquiry.

'Now, then, have you got it?'

'I have.'

'Then hand it over.'

Mr Burton held out a tremulous hand.

'Half a mo. I've got a word or two to say before we come to that. I should like you to understand how I did get it. It wasn't for the asking, I'd have you know.'

The gentleman in the armchair interposed. He waved his cigar.

'One moment.'

'Two, if you like, Mr Cox.'

He was a little, paunchy man, with 'Jew' written so large all over him that one asked oneself why he had been so ungrateful to his forefathers as to associate himself with such a name as Cox— Thomas Cox. He got out of his chair, which was much too large for him, so that he could see the Flyman, who still kept himself modestly in the background. He punctuated his words by making little dabs in the air with his cigar.

'What we want is the ruby; that's all we want We don't want the schedule of your adventures. We're not interested. You understand?'

'Yes, I understand you, Mr Cox, but it don't go.'

'What do you mean, "it don't go"?'

'I'm not all alone in this. There's three of us in this game.'

'Listen to me. You say you've got the ruby. Very well, hand it over. I will see you have what Mr Burton promised you. We'll say no more about it, and there'll be an end of the matter.'

The Flyman's manner became a trifle dogged.

'I don't hand over nothing till you've heard what I've got to say.'

Something in the speaker's manner struck the observant Mr Cox. He showed signs of perturbation.

'Flyman, you haven't killed him?'

'I don't know whether I have or haven't I hit, perhaps, a bit harder than I meant. He was as good as dead when I saw him last; anyhow, he'll be silly for the rest of his days, or else I'm wrong. I know what a good downer with a sand bag means. I'm a bit afraid I gave him an extra good one. I didn't like the looks of him at all.'

'You're a fool! Why did you do it?'

'Because you told me?'

'I told you! What the devil do you mean?'

'You set me on the job—you and Mr Burton together. You said to me there's a bloke coming out of a certain house at a certain time. He's got something on him which you're to get You knew very well I wasn't going to get it out of him by asking.'

'Did anyone see you?'

'Not while I was at it, so far as I know. But a copper did directly afterwards. For all I can tell, he's seen me before, and'll know me again.'

Mr Cox's perturbation visibly increased.

'Did he—did he try to arrest you?'

'He didn't know what had happened then; but he was going straight to where I'd left the bloke lying. Then, of course, he'd put two and two together, and think of me.'

'Flyman, you're a fool! Did anybody see you come in here?'

'That's more than I can say. But somebody'll soon know I did come in here if anything happens to me. I'm not going to be on this lay all on my own.'

Mr Cox threw his unfinished cigar into the fireplace. It had gone out His attention was occupied by matters which rendered smoking difficult. He stood knawing the fingernails of his left hand. The Flyman watched him. Mr Burton seemed to be endeavouring to obtain sufficient control of his faculties to understand what the conversation was about. Presently Mr Cox delivered himself of the result of his cogitation.

'I tell you what, I shouldn't be surprised if a little trip abroad would do you good.'

'I'm willing.'

'Then I'll see that you have a berth on board a boat I know of, which leaves the London docks tomorrow for America.'

'I'm game.'

'Now, let's have the ruby.'

'Against the quids?'

'Against the quids. You don't suppose that Mr Burton and I carry a thousand pounds about with us loose in our pockets?'

'No quids, no ruby.'

'The money shall be handed to you when you're on board the ship.'

'I'll see that the ruby isn't handed to you till it is.'

'Do you think I want to do you?'

'I'm dead sure you do, if you only get a chance. I've done a little business with you before today, Mr Cox. You must think I'm soft. Why, nothing would suit your book better than to do me out of the pieces and get me lagged. But if you try that game, I'll see you get a bit of it Thank you; I don't trust you, not as far as I can see you, Mr Cox.'

The gentleman thus flatteringly alluded to laughed, a little mechanically.

'I'm sorry to hear you talk like that, Flyman. There's no time now to try to induce you to form a better opinion of me; but you'll discover that you have done me an injustice before very long. Anyhow, let's see that you have the ruby.'

Mr Burton chose this moment to awake to the fact that he had a very definite interest in the discussion which was being carried on. He banged his glass against the table.

'I'm going to have that ruby! I'm going to have it now!'

'So you shall, when you've given me the thousand pounds.'

'I don't care about the thousand pounds; I'm going to have the ruby!'

'Then, I'm damned if you are!'

'I say I am. Now, then! So you'd better give it to me—before I take it.'

The speaker staggered towards the Flyman.

'Don't you be silly, Mr Burton, or you might find me nasty; and I don't want to have to be nasty to you.'

'Give me the ruby; it's mine.'

'That's where you're wrong. Just now it happens to be mine.'

Mr Cox placed himself between the pair.

'Pretend to be sober, Burton, even if you're drunk.'

'I am sober. I don't care that for him.' He tried to snap his fingers, but the attempt was a disastrous failure. 'I say, I'm going to have the ruby now, and so I am.'

'Shut it!'

Mr Cox's treatment of the intoxicated gentleman was vigorous and to the point He gave him a push which propelled him backwards with such unexpected force that, before he was able to recover himself, he was lying on the ground.

There for a time he stayed. The others paid no attention to him whatever. Mr Cox continued the discussion on his own account

'Let me see the ruby.'

'Let me see the quids.'

'Look here, Flyman; you say you know me. Well, I know you; I know you for a windbag and a liar. It's quite likely that all you've been telling us is humbug, and that you've not been within miles of what we want. If you've got the ruby, you let me look at it; there'll be no harm done. I'm not going to buy a pig in a poke, and I'm not going to steal it'

'I lay you are not going to steal it; I lay that. There it is. Now, you can take and look at it'

Taking a ring from his waistcoat pocket, slipping it on to his little finger, he held it out for the other's inspection, eyeing Mr Cox in a very singular manner as that gentleman bent over to examine it 'Did you get that from—the person we've been talking about?'

'I did.'

'Tonight?'

'Tonight. Not an hour ago—as he came out of the house.'

Mr Cox turned to Mr Burton, who was sitting upon the floor.

'Get up, you jackass! Come here and see if this is what we're after.'

Mr Burton's answer was not exactly a response to this peremptory invitation.

'I'm not feeling—as I ought to feel.'

'So I should think. You'll soon be feeling still less as you ought to feel, if you don't look out.' He assisted the gentleman on to his feet 'Now, then, pull yourself together. Come and see if what the Flyman's got is your uncle's ring.'

As Mr Burton advanced, the Flyman dropped the hand with the ringed finger.

'Don't you let him snatch at it, or I'll down him.'

'He won't snatch at it. You needn't be afraid of him.'

'I'm not afraid of him—hardly; only I thought I'd just give you a little warning, that's all. There you are, Mr Burton; there's what's worth more to you than you're likely to tell me.'

Mr Burton only bestowed upon the outstretched hand a momentary glance; he drew back as if what he saw had stung him.

'It's not!'

'What d'ye mean?'

'It's not my uncle's ring.' The fall, or something, had sobered him. He had become disagreeable instead. He snarled, showing his teeth to the gums, as if he would have liked to assail the man in front of him with tooth and nail. 'Curse you, Flyman! what's the game you're playing?'

'What's the game you think you're playing, that's what I want to know?'

'That's not my uncle's ring, and you know it's not. Come, out with it! no tricks here!'

'This is your uncle's ring, and you're trying to kid me that it isn't, thinking to do me out of what you promised. Don't you try that on, Mr Burton, or you'll be sorry.'

The two men glared at each other with their faces close together, Mr Burton meeting the Flyman's threatening glances without flinching. He turned to Mr Cox.

'Cox, what he's got on his finger is no more my uncle's ring than I am.'

'You're sure of that?'

'Dead certain. The stone in my uncle's ring was much larger, better colour, finer altogether. It bore his crest—on that thing there seems to be a monogram—and inside the gold mount, at the back, his name was engraved—"George Burton."'

'We can soon settle that part of the question. Flyman, is there a name inside that ring?'

The Flyman was already looking for himself.

'There's not; there's no name. Is this a plant between you two to do me out of my fair due?'

'Don't you make any mistake about that, my man. If that's the ring we want you shall have your thousand right enough. It's worth all that to us. If it's not, then it's worth nothing, and less than nothing. Don't let's have any error about this, Burton. You're quite sure that you recollect what your uncle's ring was like?'

'I'd pick it out among ten thousand. I've seen it hundreds—I should think, thousands—of times. I wore it myself for a year. It used to amuse the old man to fool about with it, lending it to all sorts of people. He lent it to me, and he lent it to Guy. I believe he lent it to Miss Bewicke; and it was because, when he asked her, she wouldn't give it him back again that he got his back up.'

'I suppose, Flyman, it was Mr Holland you tackled?'

'It was the bloke you pointed out to me this afternoon—that I do know. Here, I borrowed these things from off him—took them out of his pockets.' He produced a miscellaneous collection. Here's a cigar-case with initials on it, " G. H.," and cards inside with a name on them, "Mr Guy Holland." I should think that that ought to be about good enough.'

'You're sure that that was the only ring he had about him?'

'I'll swear to it. I ran the rule over him quite half a dozen times. He only had one ring—there wasn't one upon his hands—and that's it'

'And you, Burton, are certain it's not your uncle's?'

'As sure as that I'm alive.'

'Then, in that case, we're done.'

The trio looked as if they were.

CHAPTER 10

SHE WISHES THAT SHE HADN'T

Miss Broad had a very bad night That was because of her conscience, which pricked her. Almost as soon as Mr Holland had left her she regretted the advice she had given him—advice, she had the candour to admit, as applied to this case, being but a feeble word. She had bullied him into committing burglary! It was awful to think of, or, at least, it became awful by degrees. A sort of panorama of dreadful imaginings began to unfold itself in front of her. She even pictured him as being caught in the act, arrested, thrown into gaol, tried, sentenced to penal servitude, working in the quarries—she had heard of 'the quarries'—because of her. She did not pause to consider that, after all, he was responsible for his own actions. He loved her; by obedience he proved it, even to the extent of committing burglary. Therefore, the blame of what she did was on her shoulders. So she upbraided herself, regretting too late, as ladies sometimes do, the line of action she had taken up with so much vigour.

'I wish I'd bitten my tongue off before I'd been so wicked. The truth is, I really believe I'd like to kill that woman. Ellen, you needn't pull my hair right out.'

The first two remarks were addressed to herself, the last, aloud, to her maid. That young person, who was dressing Miss Broad for dinner, found her mistress in rather a trying mood.

'If he was detected in the act, he would be at that woman's mercy. She might compel him to do anything in order to avoid open humiliation and disgrace and ruin.'

At the thought of what he might be compelled to do, she was divided between terror, tears and rage. Since the woman had once pretended to love him, and, no doubt, was still burn-ing with a desire to be his wife, she might even force him—oh, horrible!

'Ellen, you're pulling my hair again.'

Which was not to be wondered at, considering how unex-pectedly the young lady jerked her head.

She ate no dinner, excused herself from two engagements, made herself generally so agreeable that she drove her father to remark that her temper was not improving, and he pitied the man who had anything to do with her. Which observation added to her misery, for she knew quite well that her temper was her weakest point She was a wretch, and she had ruined him!

Throughout the night she scarcely slept. She was continually getting off the bed to pace the room, exclaiming,—

'I wonder if he's doing it now?' She must have wondered if he was doing it 'now' nearly a hundred times, apparently under the impression that 'it' was an operation which took time.

The result was that, when the morning came, she did not feel rested, and looked what she felt, causing her father—an uncom-fortably observant gentleman, who prided himself, with justice, on being able to say as many disagreeable things as any man—to remark that she looked 'vinegary,' which soured Miss Broad still more.

She had an appointment with Mr Holland, at the usual place in Regent's Park, for ten. They were to have a little conversation; then, together, they were to go to church. She was at the rendez-vous at nine, though how she managed to do it was a mystery even to herself. At ten minutes past she began to fidget, at the half-hour she was in a fever, and when ten o'clock struck, and there was no Mr Holland, she was as nearly beside herself as she could conveniently be.

'He's never been late before—never, never! Oh, what has happened?'

She went a little way along a path by which she thought that he might come; then, fearful that after all he might come another way, tremulously retracing her steps, she returned to the seat. But she could not sit still, nor stand still either. She was up and down, sitting and standing, fidgeting here and there, glanc-ing in every direction, like the frightened creature she was rap-idly becoming. Every nerve in her body was on edge. When the quarter struck, and there were no signs of Mr Holland, she could restrain herself no longer. Tears blinded her eyes; she had to use her handkerchief before she could see. It would have needed very little for her to become hysterical.

She knew her man—his almost uncanny habit of punctuality. She was certain that, if nothing serious had happened to prevent him, he would have been in time to a moment She was sure, therefore, that something had happened. But what?

As she vainly asked herself this question, a boy came along one of the paths. He was a small child, about nine years of age, evidently attired in his Sunday best. He carried something in his hand. Coming up to her, he said,—

'Are you Miss Broad?' She nodded; she could not speak. 'I was told to give you this.'

He handed her the envelope. She jumped to the conclusion that it came from him. Her delight at receiving even a message from him about scattered her few remaining senses.

'I'll give you sixpence.' She spoke with a stammer, fumbling with her purse. 'I haven't one; I'll give you half-a-crown instead.'

The boy went off mumbling what might have been meant for thanks, probably too surprised at the magnitude of the gift to be able to make his meaning clear. She tore the envelope open. It contained half a sheet of paper, on which were the words,—

If you want Mr Guy Holland, inquire of Miss May Bewicke.

Chapter 11
The Pursuit of the Gentleman

That was all.

Miss Broad's first blundering impression was that somebody was having a joke with her—that she was mistaken, had read the words askew. She looked again.

No; the error, if error there were, was, to that extent, certainly not hers; the words were there as plain as plain could be, and they only.

'If you want Mr Guy Holland, inquire of Miss May Bewicke.'

They were typewritten, occupying a couple of lines. The rest of the sheet was blank—no address, no date, no signature; not a hint to show from whom the message could have come. She looked at the envelope. The face of it was blank; there was nothing on it, inside or out Where was the boy who had brought it? She turned to see. He had gone, was out of sight So far as she could perceive, she had the immediate neighbourhood entirely to herself. What did it mean?

The disappointment was so acute that, as she sank back upon the seat, the earth seemed to be whirling round in front of her. She never quite knew whether for a second or two she did not lose her senses altogether. When next she began to notice things, she perceived that the envelope had fallen to the ground, and that the half sheet of paper would probably have followed it had it not been detained by a fold in her dress. She examined them both again, this time more closely, without, however, any satisfactory result

Of the typewritten words she could make neither head nor tail. Were they meant as a hint—a warning—what? Anyhow, from whom could they have come—to her, there, in the Park? Why had she not asked the boy who had instructed him to give the envelope to her? What a simpleton she had been!

'"Inquire of Miss May Bewicke."What can it mean? "Inquire of Miss May Bewicke." Unless—'

Unless it meant something she did not care to think of. She left the sentence unfinished, even in her own mind.

She arrived at a sudden resolution. It was too late for church, or she told herself it was, supposing her to have been in a church-going mood, which she most emphatically was not. Instead of church she would go to Mr Holland's rooms in Craven Street, and inquire for him there. Under the circumstances, anything, including loss of dignity—and she flattered herself that dignity, as a rule, was her strong point—was better than suspense.

She had some difficulty in finding a cab. In that district of town, cabs do not ply in numbers on Sunday morning. By the time she discovered one she was hot, dusty and, she feared, di-shevelled. As the vehicle bore her towards the Strand, her sense of comfort did not increase. If he was not in Craven Street, what should she do? Ye saints and sinners! if he were in gaol!

He was not in Craven Street

A matronly, pleasant-faced woman opened the door to her.

'Is Mr Holland in?'

'No, miss, he's not.'

'Has he been long gone out?'

'Well, miss, he hasn't been in all night'

The young lady shivered. The landlady eyed her with shrewd, yet not unfriendly, eyes. She hazarded a question,—

'Excuse me, miss, but are you Miss Broad?'

'That is my name.'

'Would you mind just stepping inside?'

The landlady led the way into a front room. The first thing the young lady saw on entering was her photograph staring at her from the centre of the mantelshelf. A little extra colour tinged her cheeks. The landlady glanced from the original to the likeness, and back again.

'It's very like you, miss, if you'll excuse my saying so. You see, Mr Holland has told me all about it. You have my congratulations, if I might make so bold, for a nicer gentleman I never want to see. I was that pleased when I saw him come walking in the other day. Did you expect to see him, miss?'

'I had an appointment with him. He never kept it. As he has never done such a thing before, I scarcely knew what to think.'

'Well, miss, the truth is, I hardly know what I ought to say.'

'Say everything, please.'

'It was only his nonsense, no doubt, but when he was going out last night I asked him if he should be late. "Well, Mrs Pettifer," he said, "if I am late, you'd better make inquiries for me at Westminster Police Station, for that's where I shall be; they'll have locked me up." When Matilda told me this morning that he hadn't been in all night, I thought of his words directly, because he'd ordered his breakfast for eight o'clock this morning, and, as you say, he's always so dependable—Why, miss, whatever is the matter?'

Miss Broad, who had found refuge in an armchair, was looking very queer indeed.

'Don't you take on, miss. It was only his fun. Mr Holland's full of his jokes. Heaps of gentlemen stay out all night; nothing's happened.'

But the young lady was not to be comforted. She had her own reasons for being of a different opinion. That allusion to Westminster Police Station did not sound like a joke to her. When she quitted Craven Street, she directed the cabman to drive her to a certain number in Victoria Street She was staring as she went at the two typewritten lines which the mysterious boy had brought in the mysterious envelope.

'I will inquire of Miss Bewicke. It will be better to begin there than—at the other place. There will be time enough for that afterwards. If—if she should have locked him up!'

The potentiality was too horrible. She could not bear to contemplate it. Yet, willy-nilly, it intruded on her fears.

She ascended in the lift to Miss Bewicke's apartments. She knocked with a trembling hand at Miss Bewicke's door. She had to knock a second time before an answer came. Then the door was opened by a tall, thin, saturnine-looking woman, to whom the visitor took a dislike upon the spot

'Is Miss Bewicke at home?'

'Will you walk in?' It was only when Miss Broad had walked in that she learned that her quest was vain. 'Miss Bewicke is not at home. She went to Brighton this morning.'

'This morning? I thought she was going last night.'

'Who told you that?'

There was something in the speaker's voice which brought the blood to Miss Broad's cheeks with a rush. She stammered.

'I—I heard it somewhere.'

'Your information was learned on good authority; very good. Oh, yes, she meant to go last night, but she was prevented.'

'Prevented—by what? '

'I am not at liberty to say. Are you a friend of Miss Bewicke's?'

There was something in the woman's manner which Miss Broad suspected of being intentionally offensive. She stared at her with bold, insolent eyes, with, in them, what the young lady felt was the suggestion of an insolent grin. That she knew her, Miss Broad was persuaded; she was sure, too, that she was completely cognisant of the fact that she was not Miss Bewicke's friend.

'I am sorry to say that I am not so fortunate as to be able to number myself among Miss Bewicke's friends. I have not even the pleasure of her acquaintance.'

'That is unfortunate, as you say. About her friends Miss Bewicke is particular.'

The suggestion was so gratuitous that Miss Broad was startled.

'Are you a friend of hers?'

'I am her companion; but not for long. You know what it is

for one woman to be a companion to another woman. It is not to be her friend. Oh, no. I have been a companion to Miss Bewicke for many years; but soon I go. I have had enough.'

The woman's manner was so odd that Miss Broad wondered if she was a little touched in the head, or if she had been drinking . She looked round the room, at a loss what to say. Her glance lighted on a large panel photograph which occupied the place of honour on the mantelpiece. It was Mr Holland. She recognised it with a start It was the best likeness of him she had seen. He had not given her a copy, nor any portrait of himself, which was half as good.

Miss Bewicke's companion was watching her.

'You are looking at the photograph? It is Mr Holland, a friend of Miss Bewicke's, the dearest friend she has in the world.'

'You mean he was her friend?'

'He was? He is—none better. Miss Bewicke has many friends—oh, yes, a great many; she is so beautiful—is she not beautiful?—but there are none of them to her like Guy.'

The woman's familiar use of Mr Holland's Christian name stung Miss Broad into silence. That she lied she knew; to say that, today, Mr Holland was still Miss Bewicke's dearest friend was to attain the height of the ridiculous. That the young lady knew quite well. She was also aware that, for some reason which, as yet, she did not fathom, this foreign creature was making herself intentionally offensive. None the less, she did not like to hear her lover spoken of in such fashion by such lips. Still less did she like to see his portrait where it was. Had she acted on the impulse of the moment, she would have torn it into shreds. And perhaps she might have gone even as far as that had she not perceived something else, which she liked, if possible, still less than the position occupied by the gentleman's photograph.

On a table lay a walking-stick. A second's glance was sufficient to convince her of the ownership. It was his—a present from herself. She had had it fitted with a gold band; his initials, which she had had cut on it, stared her in the face. What was his walking-stick—her gift—doing there?

The woman's lynx-like eyes were following hers.

'You are looking at the walking-stick? It, also, is Mr Holland's.'

'What is it doing here?'

The woman shrugged her shoulders.

'He left it behind him, I suppose. Perhaps he was in too great a hurry, or Miss Bewicke. Sometimes, when one is in a great hurry to get away, one forgets little things which are of no importance.'

She called his walking-stick—her gift to him—a thing of no importance! What was the creature hinting at? Miss Broad would not condescend to ask, although she longed to know.

'As I tell you, Miss Bewicke is not at home. She is at the Hotel Metropole at Brighton. Would you like to take Mr Holland's walking-stick to—her?' There was an accent on the pronoun which the visitor did not fail to notice. 'What name shall I give to Miss Bewicke?'

'I am Miss Broad.'

'Miss Broad—Letty Broad? Oh, yes, I remember. They were talking and laughing about you—Mr Holland and she. Perhaps, after all, you had better not go down to Brighton.'

When the young lady was back in the street, her brain was a tumult of contradictions. That the woman who called herself Miss Bewicke's companion had, for reasons of her own, been trying to amuse herself at her expense she had not the slightest doubt. That Mr Holland's relations with Miss Bewicke were not what were suggested she was equally certain. None the less she wondered, and she doubted. What was his portrait doing there? Still more, what was his walking-stick? He was carrying it when they last met Under what circumstances, between this and then, had it found its way to where it was? Where was Mr Holland? That there was a mystery she was convinced. She was almost convinced that Miss Bewicke held the key to it.

Should she run down to Brighton and find out? She would never rest until she knew. She had gone so far; she might as well go farther. She would be there and back in no time. The cabman was told to drive to Victoria. At Victoria a train-was just on the point of starting. Miss Broad was travelling Brightonwards before she had quite made up her mind as to whether she really meant to go. When the train stopped at Clapham Junction, she half rose from her seat and all but left the carriage. She might still be able to return home in time for luncheon. But while she dilly-dallied, the train was off. The next stoppage was at Croydon. There would be nothing gained by her alighting there; so she reached Brighton, as she assured herself, without ever having had the slightest intention of doing it. Therefore, and as a matter of course, when the train rattled into the terminus she was not in the best of tempers. She addressed sundry inquiries to herself as she descended to the platform.

'Now what am I to do? I may as well go to the Metropole as I am here. I am not bound to see the woman even if I go. And as for speaking to her'—she curled her lip in a way which was intended to convey a volume of meaning—'I suppose it is possible to avoid the woman, even if I have the misfortune to be under the same roof with her. The hotel's a tolerable size; at any rate, we'll see.'

She did see, and that quickly. As she entered the building, the first person she beheld coming towards her across the hall was Miss May Bewicke.

Which proves, if proof be necessary, that a building may be large, and yet too small.

CHAPTER 12
THE TENDER MERCIES OF TWO LADIES

By way of a commencement, Miss Broad was conscious of two things—that Miss Bewicke was looking her best; that she herself was looking her worst; at least, she was nearly certain she was looking her worst, she felt so hideous.

Miss Bewicke had a knack of walking—it came by nature, though there were those who called it a trick—which gave her a curious, and, indeed, humorous, air of importance altogether beyond anything her stature seemed to warrant This enabled her to overwhelm men, and even women who were much taller than herself, with a grace which was positively charming. She moved across that spacious hall, looking straight at Miss Broad, as if there was nothing there; and was walking past with an apparent unconsciousness of there being anyone within a mile, though she brushed against the other's skirts as she passed, which was a little more than Miss Broad could endure. She was not going all the way to Brighton to be treated by that woman as if she were a nonentity.

'Miss Bewicke!'

The lady, who had passed, turned.

'I beg your pardon?'

'Can I speak to you?'

'Speak to me?' She regarded the other with a smile which, if pretty, was impertinent. 'I'm afraid I haven't the pleasure.'

'I am Miss Broad.'

'Broad ?—Broad? I don't seem to remember.'

'Perhaps you remember Mr Holland.'

'Mr Holland?—Guy Holland? Oh, yes, I have good cause for remembering him.'

'Mr Holland has spoken of me to you?'

'Oh! You are that Miss Broad! I have pleasure in wishing you good morning.'

Miss Bewicke walked off as if, so far as she was concerned, the matter was at an end; but so abrupt a termination to the interview the other would not permit

'I am sorry to detain you, Miss Bewicke, but, as I have said, I wish to speak to you.'

'Yes. What do you wish to say? '

'Can I not speak to you in private?'

'By all means.' Miss Bewicke led the way into a sitting-room. As soon as they were in, and the door closed, before the other had a chance to open her lips, she herself began the ball. 'Miss Broad, before you speak, there is something which I wish to say to you. You incited Mr Guy Holland to commit, last night, a burglary upon my premises.'

If she expected the other to show signs of confusion, or to attempt denial, she was mistaken. Miss Broad did not flinch.

'I did'

'You admit it?'

'I do.'

'Are you aware that in so doing you were guilty of a criminal action?'

'As to that I know nothing, and care less.'

'I have only to send for a policeman to have you sentenced to a term of imprisonment'

'I understand how it is you have been so successful on the stage. You really are an excellent actress. You bear yourself as if you were the injured party, while all the time you know very well that it was precisely because you had robbed him that I advised him to despoil you of your booty.'

'You are perfectly aware that that is false.'

'On the contrary, I am perfectly aware that it is true. Where is Mr Holland? Is he here with you?'

'Miss Broad!'

'Or did you dare to make his doing, what you know he was perfectly justified in doing, an affair of the police?'

'I came upon Guy Holland, at dead of night, engaged in robbing me, and I sent him from me with my blessing.'

'Then where is he?'

'I know no more than this chair.'

'Miss Bewicke, I called at your rooms this morning. I saw his walking-stick upon your table. When I asked how it came there, the woman who had opened the door said, in effect, that he had left it behind in his hurry to go away with you.'

'The woman! What woman?'

'She said she was your companion.'

'Casata? Louise Casata never said anything so monstrous.'

'Not in so many words; but that was what she intended me to understand.'

'You believed it? What a high opinion you appear to have of us! Guy must be worse even than I imagined, or you, his promised wife, would not judge him with such hard judgement'

'I did not believe it; but I did believe that you called in the police last night.'

'I didn't; I called in no one. I simply told him to go, and he went'

'You are laughing. You know where he is. I can see it in your face.'

'Then you are indeed a seer.'

'This morning, when he did not come, as he promised he would, and always has done, someone gave me this. What am I to think?'

Miss Broad handed Miss Bewicke the two typewritten lines, which that lady carefully regarded.

'Someone? Who was someone?'

'A little boy. I thought it was a message from Guy. By the time I found it wasn't, he was gone. I don't know who he was, nor from whom he came, if it wasn't from you.'

It certainly did not come from me. Miss Broad, I begin to find you amusing. I also begin to understand what it is Guy Holland perceives in you to like. You are more of a woman than I am; that is, there is in you more of the natural savage, which, to a man of his temperament, goes to make a woman.'

'I want none of your praises.'

'I'm not going to give you any, or compliments either. I doubt if you're in a frame of mind to properly appreciate any sort of sleight-of-hand. Let me finish. I had an engagement for luncheon; as you have made me late for it, perhaps you will do me the honour of lunching with me here.'

'No, thank you.'

'Pardon me, you will.'

'Excuse me, I won't'

'We shall see.'

Miss Bewicke touched the bell button. Miss Broad eyed her with flaming cheeks.

'It's no use your ordering anything to eat for me, because I sha'n't touch it. You treat me as if I were a child. I'm not a child.'

'My dear Miss Broad, we are both of us women—both of us; and there are senses in which women and children are synonyms. Mr Holland was once in love with me—he was, I assure you. He is now in love with you, which fact creates between us a bond of sympathy.'

'I don't see it.'

'No? I do. You will. He appears to have got himself into, we will put it, a rather equivocal position. It is our bounden duty, as joint sympathisers, to get him out of it. We will discuss our bounden duty; but I never can discuss anything when I'm starving, which I am.'

To the waiter who appeared Miss Bewicke gave orders for an immediate lunch for two. Miss Broad kept silence. The truth was, she was not finding Miss Bewicke altogether the sort of person she expected. That little lady went on,—

'I'm free to confess, my dear Miss Broad; by the way, may I call you Letty?'

'No; you may not'

'Thank you; you are so sweet. As I was about to remark, my dear—Letty'—the other winced, but was still—'I'm free to confess that I think it not improbable that something has happened to Mr Holland.'

'You know that something has happened?'

'I don't know—I surmise. I put two and two together, thus:—To begin with, I don't think that you were the only person who egged him on to felony.'

Miss Broad again was speechless. She remembered Mr Holland's tale of his encounter with Miss Casata.

'There was a preciseness about his proceedings which set me thinking at the time, and has kept me thinking ever since. I'm pretty shrewd, you know. Now, I happen to be aware that a certain person of my acquaintance has been on too good terms with Mr Horace Burton. You have heard of Mr Horace Burton? I thought so. Such a nice young man! Now, however, this certain person is on the worst terms with Mr Horace Burton. For sufficient reasons, I assure you. She has been evolving fantastic schemes of vengeance on the deceitful wretch; she's just a little cracked, you know. To ruin Mr Horace Burton by assisting Guy Holland to deprive him of his fortune would be just the kind of notion which would commend itself to her. I fancy that that's exactly what she did do. Didn't she, my dear?'

Miss Broad was breathing a little hard. The other's keen intuition startled her.

'It was I who told him to take what was his own.'

'Yes, I know; but the first suggestion did not come from you. However, so long as we understand each other, that's the point. To proceed—Mr Horace Burton would be cautious that this certain person's sweetness had turned to gall, and also that she was wishful to pay him out in his own coin. He might even have a notion of the form that payment was to take, having learned it from the certain person's own lips. If so, you may be quite sure that he or his friends saw Guy Holland enter my premises, if nobody else did. They saw him come out. They were to the full as anxious to obtain possession of that ruby as ever he could be. So they took it from him.'

'Took it from him—with violence?'

'Do you think they could take it from him without violence—that he would hand it over practically upon request? That's not like Guy; not the Guy I knew. He'd fight for it tooth and nail himself against a regiment'

'Do you think then they hurt him?'

'It looks as if they did something to him. He never went home. There must have been some reason why he didn't There is at least a possibility that it was because he couldn't'

'Do you think they—killed him?'

'Ah, now you ask too much. I should say certainly not It would be unintentionally if they did. That would be too big a price even for Mr Horace Burton to pay. If they attacked him in fair fight, I should say that he killed someone before they did him; and that when they did it was because they had to. But the possibility is that they never let him have a chance; that they stole on him unawares, and had him at their mercy before he knew that danger threatened.'

'Miss Bewicke, you are so clever—so much cleverer than I—'

'My dear!'

'Come up to town with me and help me look for him, and go with me to the police, and—'

'Set all London by the ears? I know. We'll do it; but here comes lunch. You sit down to lunch with me, and we'll talk things over while we lunch. You see how far talking things over has already brought us; and after lunch we'll go to town, as you suggest, and find out what's happened to Guy Holland, and where he is, or we'll know the reason why. But if you won't lunch with me, then nothing remains but to wish you good day, and, so far as I'm concerned, there'll be an end of the matter. I'll have nothing to do with a person who won't eat my bread and salt'

So the ladies lunched together. Although Miss Broad declared that she could not swallow a morsel, Miss Bewicke induced her to dispose of several. Indeed, she handled her with so much skill that by the time the meal was through—it was not a long one—one would have thought that they really were on decent terms with one another, though Miss Broad was still a trifle scratchy. But then her nerves were out of order, and when a lady's nerves are out of order, she is apt, occasionally, to stray from those well-defined paths which etiquette and good breeding require her to tread; in short, she does not know what she is doing, or what anybody else is doing either, which Miss Bewicke quite understood, so that her guest's eccentricities, apparently, simply amused her.

And the two young ladies went up together in the same compartment to London to look for Mr Holland, and to call down, if necessary, vengeance on his enemies and those who had despitefully used him.

Chapter 13
Visitors For Miss Casata

Miss Casata had a razor in her hand—an open razor. She examined its edge.

'It is very sharp. Oh, yes, how sharp! One cut; it will all be over. Will it be over with one cut—that is it—or shall I have to hack, and hack, and hack? That would not be agreeable.'

She stood in front of a looking-glass, regarding her own reflection.

'I am not bad looking; no, I am not I have a certain attractiveness, which is my own. To use the razor would be to make a mess. I should be a horrible sight. Would he care? He would not see me. If he did, he would laugh, I know. He has what he calls a taste for the horrible. It would amuse him to behold me all covered with blood.'

She turned her attention to some articles which were on a table.

'Here is a revolver. The six barrels are all loaded. It would not need them all to blow out my brains—that is, if I have any to blow. Here is a bottle of hydrocyanic acid. What lies I had to tell to get it; what tricks I had to play! There is enough in this little bottle to kill the whole street I have, therefore, the keys of death close to my hand—painless, instant death. Three roads to eternal sleep, and I stand so much in need of rest. Yet I hesitate to use them. It is very funny. Is it because I am going mad—I did not use to be infirm of purpose—I wonder?'

She handled, one after another, the three objects—the razor, the revolver, the little bottle—as if endeavouring to make a selection.

'I am too optimistic. There is my fault—I always hope. It is an error. I have always had in my life such evil fortune that, when happiness came, I should have known it would not endure—that the night would be blacker because the sun once shone; that for me, henceforward, it would be always night. I was a fool; so happy I forgot, so I pay for it Well, I will take my fate into my own hands and make an ending when I choose. I should have liked to see the little one—my little one.' A softness came into the voice of which one might hardly have thought it capable. 'To have held it in my arms; to press it to my breast; to touch its lips with mine. I should, indeed, have liked to be a mother.

Yet better not; it might have been like its father. That would have been the worst of all. Which is it to be—steel? lead? a little drink? Why is it I cannot decide? What's that?'

She had Miss Bewicke's dainty drawing-room to herself. An incongruous object she seemed in it, she and her gruesome playthings. A sound appeared to have caught her ear. She put her right hand behind her back; in it, the three assistants of death. Moving to a door which was on the opposite side of the room, turning the handle softly, she passed half-way through it, then stood and listened.

'Quite still, yet. The noise did not come from there. There was a noise. Ah!'

The interjection was in response to a rat-tat-tat on the knocker. The room was illuminated by a dozen electric lights. Disconnecting one after the other, she allowed but a single one to remain alight. Comparatively, the apartment was in darkness.

'That's not Ellen's knock, nor Jane's; she is not already back again. Besides, she also does not knock like that. Who is it?'

The knocking came again—slightly, more insistently than before.

'If it is some bothering visitors, they will have a short answer, I promise them. When I do not open, why do they not take a hint and go? I am not to be disturbed when I am making my arrangements to remain undisturbed forever.'

The knocking was repeated for a third time.

'So, they persist! Well, I will show them. They shall see.'

Cramming her trio of treasures into the pocket of her dress, where one would have supposed them to be in uncomfortable, not to say dangerous, juxtaposition, she strode to the door, intent on scarifying the presumptuous caller. When, however, she perceived who stood without, surprise for the moment made her irresolute.

The visitor was Mr Horace Burton, at whom Miss Casata stared, as if he were the very last person she had expected to see—which, probably, as a matter of fact, he was. Mr Burton, on the other hand, bestowed on her his blandest smile. He sauntered past her as if he had not the slightest doubt in the world that he would be regarded as a welcome guest.

'Hollo, Lou! come to pay you a visit.'

His tone was light and airy, in striking contrast to her demeanour, which was about as tragic as it could be.

'Go! Do you hear me, go, before you are sorry, and I am sorry, too!'

Her manner seemed to leave him quite unmoved.

'Now, my dear girl, don't look at me like that; it isn't nice of you. I'm here as a friend—a friend, you understand—and something more than a friend.'

'You are no friend of mine; no, you never can be. I tell you again to go at once, or you will be sorry. I have warned you.'

'That's all right; you'll change your tone when you hear what I have to say. I've come here to bring sunshine into your life, to ask for your forgiveness, to undo the past. Be sensible; there's a good girl.'

'Sensible? Oh, yes, I will be sensible. There's someone else here.'

'Yes, that's Cox; he's a friend of mine. He's come here to see fair play and witness my repentance. Come in, Cox.' Mr Thomas Cox entered, looking, if the thing were possible, less like a Thomas Cox than ever. 'Cox, let me present you to Miss Casata, the only woman I ever loved. There have been times when I have been forced to dissemble my love. Hang it, Cox! you know how I've been pressed. When a man's in such a hole as I've been in, he crushes down the love which he feels for a woman; he has to, if there's any manhood in him. He doesn't want to drag her down into the ditch in which he lies. But, Cox, you know how I have loved her all the time.'

Mr Burton turned away his head—whether to hide a tear or a smile was uncertain. He spoke with a degree of volubility which, under the circumstances, was remarkable. As Miss Casata appeared to think, her tone remained inflexible.

'There still is someone else.'

'Ah, that's the Flyman; he's nothing and nobody; he doesn't

count. Let him have a chair, and he can wait in the hall, Lou, till you and I come to an understanding.'

Mr Burton's suggestion was carried out A chair was taken into the little hall, on which the Flyman placed himself. How long he remained on it, when their backs were turned, was another matter. The outer door was closed, as also, Miss Casata having entered, was the door into the drawing-room. But that was of no consequence; the Flyman's ears were keen.

There was a curious glitter in the lady's eyes when she confronted her quondam lover. Now and then she touched her lips with the tip of her tongue, as if they were dry. Her hands continually opened and shut, apparently of their own volition. Occasionally one of them found its way into her pocket, feeling if her treasures still were there. She spoke as if her throat were sore.

'Well, what is it that you want? what new lie have you to tell?'

'I want to marry you; and, Lou, that's no lie'

She was silent. One could see her bosom moving up and down. Then, becoming conscious of the two men's scrutiny, she drew herself up straighter, as if resolute to keep herself in hand.

'You insolent!'

'Insolent! Now, Lou, that's not nice of you. A man's not insolent who wants to marry the woman whom he loves, and who loves him.'

'I love you? I?' She tapped her chest with her forefinger. 'I love you so much that I would like to tear you to pieces! That is the sort of love I have for you. You—thing!'

'Lou, you're letting your temper get the better of you. I know I treated you badly.'

'Badly!'

She laughed—a mirthless little laugh.

'I know you've a right to feel annoyed with me—'

'Annoyed with you? Oh, no, not that!'

'But I was forced to do what I did; I couldn't help myself.'

'No doubt!'

'But now it's different altogether. I see things in a new light I know what a mistake I've made. I've found out that I love you even more than I thought I did, and I've come to ask you to give me another chance—to forgive me. You're a woman, Lou, the best of women, and you've a forgiving heart; I know you have. Let me be your husband. I'll treat you better in the future; really, now!'

'What does all this mean?'

'It means what I say. Doesn't your own heart tell you so?'

'Oh, yes, it tells me. It tells me all sorts of things. It is a fool and a liar. It is of you I ask what does it all mean? It is you I want to tell me. Never mind what my heart says; we will leave my heart alone I think we'd better.'

'Well, look here, I'll be candid. You're clear-sighted, whatever else you are, and level-headed; a cleverer woman I never met. I've told you so scores of times. With a woman of your type, candour's the best policy, as you say. So here's the matter in a nutshell. I'm in a hole; you're in a hole. You help me out of the hole I'm in; I'll help you out of the hole you're in. That's what I've come to say to you tonight. You appreciate frankness; there you have it.'

'What is the hole you are in?'

'My dear Lou, you know quite well. I've never kept it secret from you; I've always made you my confidant. What I want is my uncle's ruby. You tell me where it is, and help me to lay my hand upon it, and I'll marry you in the morning. And there's the proof that I mean what I say.'

He handed her an official-looking document, which purported to be an announcement of the fact that notice had been given to a certain registrar requiring him to perform the ceremony of marriage, by special licence, between Horace Burton and Louise Casata. The lady, however, scarcely glanced at it. She kept her eyes fixed on the gentleman.

'Your uncle's ruby!'

'That's it. As you know, if I can get it in my possession, it means fortune; if I can't, it may mean misfortune of a bad type.

As I'm not taking any chances, if you'll help me to lay my hand on it, I'll marry you in the morning.'

'What a liar you are!'

'My dear Lou, all men are liars; somebody else said it before you. But where's the lie in this particular case? You've the proof in your hand that I mean business. Cox shall come with us and see it done. Won't you, Cox?'

Mr Thomas Cox bowed.

'Pleased to do anything to oblige a lady.'

'There you are! If you like, you needn't lose sight of me until we're married.'

'You say you want your uncle's ruby?'

'Of course, you know I do.'

'I know that you have it already.'

'I wish I knew as much. If I had it, I shouldn't be here to-night. There's another piece of candour.'

'I saw him take it'

'Him? Who?'

'The man outside whom you call the Flyman. I saw him from a window take it last night from Mr Holland.'

Mr Burton turned to Mr Cox.

'There you are! There's one witness. How many more might there have been? The Flyman's a fool to transact a delicate piece of business of that description in a public thoroughfare!' He returned to Miss Casata. 'My dear Lou, you saw him try to take it, unfortunately without success.'

'He took everything Mr Holland had.'

'You appear to be well-informed upon the subject, though I don't know from what quarter your information comes. Still, what you say is pretty accurate. He did take all he could. He even took a ruby. Here it is for you to look at. Unluckily, it's not my uncle's. Hence these tears.'

He handed her the ruby signet ring which the Flyman, when he turned Mr Holland face downwards on the pavement, found that gentleman had been lying on.

CHAPTER 14
WHO KNOCKS?

Miss Casata examined the ring with every show of interest
'This is the ruby he took from Mr Holland.'

'It is.'

'It is the only one which Mr Holland had.'

'So the Flyman said. He ought to know. I believe, on this occasion, he's no liar.'

'And it's not your uncle's?'

'It is not'

'You are sure?'

'Dead.'

'Then, now I understand.'

'I wish I did share your understanding.'

'I understand why she laughed when he had gone, and why she said, "Poor Guy, how disappointed he will be!"'

'What is it you're talking about? Would you condescend to explain?'

'Yet—I do not understand. It was the box. Wait; in a second I will be back.'

She was back in less than a minute, bearing in her hand a small leather-covered box. On the lid was gummed a narrow strip of paper, on which was written, in delicate characters, 'The Burton Ruby.' Mr Burton received it with a cry of recognition.

'It's it; but the writing's strange.'

'It is her writing.'

'It's uncle's box—the one in which he always kept the blessed thing. There's his crest; there's where I dropped it in the ink.' He raised the lid. 'It's empty!'

'Last night Mr Holland took from it the ring which was inside. I always imagined that in it she kept your uncle's ruby, which was what I said to Mr Holland, as I told you I would do.'

'You're a nice girl, Lou!'

'And you're a nice man! Are you not a nice man?'

Mr Cox interposed.

'Now, don't let's have any quarrelling. Stick to business. Time's precious. Go on with your story.'

The lady turned and rent him.

'I will not go on with my story for you. What business of yours is my story, you dirty Jew?'

Mr Burton smiled benignly.

'Personalities! personalities! Don't call the man a Jew, my dear. Cox is no Jew; he's an anti-Semite. Continue your story for me, my love.'

Miss Casata complied with his request, although not in the most gracious manner.

'Do not call me your love, or you will be sorry. As Mr Holland was taking the ring out of the box, she came in—'

'And caught him at it? It must have been exciting. Wicked Guy!'

'He wished to give it to her back again, but she said, "Go, and take it with you." He took it, and went. Then, when he had gone, she began to laugh. She kept on laughing—it was true laughter, not false—as if it was the best joke in the world, and she said, "Poor Guy, how disappointed he will be!"'

'You notice things.'

'I am not a fool.'

'Is it possible that anyone ever mistook you for one?'

Mr Cox dug him with his elbow in the ribs, by way of a hint to him to hold his tongue. Miss Casata went contemptuously on,—

'I perceive now that she laughed because she knew that he had not taken with him what he supposed; but what I do not understand is, where, then, is the ring? I know she kept it in this box.'

She examined minutely the one she held. Mr Cox put a question to Mr Burton.

'For the last time, Burton, I suppose you're quite sure that it's not your uncle's ring? Nice we should look if it was afterwards discovered that you had made a mistake.'

'Don't be a silly ass! How many more times do you want to

hear me swear? I say, Cox, have you two legs, or four, and which end of you are they? I might just as reasonably put such questions to you. I tell you, I know.'

Miss Casata was still continuing her scrutiny.

'It is not the ring; you are right. It is not the ring which she used to keep in the box. The stone in that, I think, was larger. It had a crest on it, I remember. And inside there was a name engraved, "George Burton." She showed it me one day, and she said, "I shall have to have this stone remounted. I cannot wear a man's name upon my finger, especially that man's name." I remember very well. Oh, no, this is not the ring at all.'

Mr Burton turned in triumph to Mr Cox.

'You hear? Now, who's right?'

'You have seen the ring which you describe?'

'It is certain; more than once. When was the last time? Not many days ago. It was in this box. She took it out of this box, she put it back into the box, and the box she put into the little bottom drawer. I remember it very well. When I heard of Mr Burton's will, I thought of it at once.'

'Then where is it now?'

'She must have taken it out of the box and put it somewhere else.'

'But where? Think!'

'How do I know? how can I think? She must have put it with some of her other jewels. They are everywhere—all over the place.'

Mr Cox and Mr Burton exchanged glances. The young gentleman took up the running.

'In that case, we'll look for it all over the place.'

'What do you mean?'

'My dear Lou, I'm going to have that ruby, and before I leave these premises. So, now, you've got it.'

'You will not touch her things?'

'I've no desire to do anything so indelicate. You tell us where it is, or give us a hint.'

'I have not the slightest notion.'

427

'Then we'll investigate for ourselves.'

'You shall not touch her things!'

'Lou, you gave Guy Holland the tip. You helped him to commit a burglary. Why should you be squeamish now?'

'That was different'

'Of course it was. He's not attached to you like I am; he doesn't worship the ground you stand upon. It isn't as though you were smitten with Miss Bewicke, because you're not; you've told me so a hundred times. She's going to play some pretty trick on her own account; that's the meaning of her taking out the ruby, which she knew you knew was in that box. And it's a thousand to nothing that she means to play it at my expense. If I can help it, I don't mean to let her have the chance. Your fortune's bound with mine; we sink or swim together.

'If I don't get that ruby, and tonight, it'll probably mean that I go under, and, if I go, you'll go too. My dear girl, you know you will. Come, be sensible; be something like your dear own self. Do only half for me what you did for Guy. Let me just have a look round for that wretched ruby. By your own account, it must be somewhere close at hand. I'm sure to get it, and, when I do get it, I'll not forget the part you played. It'll not be my fault if I don't still make you the best husband a woman ever had.'

'I was not here when Mr Holland came. I did not see what he did. I knew nothing.'

'You need not see what we do. We have a little something somewhere which will make you as unconscious of anything that may take place as you can possibly desire Then, if there is a bother, you will be able to assume, with perfect propriety, the *rôle* of injured victim. But I don't see that there need be trouble, if you keep still. I've as much right to that ruby as anybody else. I'm going to assert that right, that's all. Now, be a good, kind girl. Go into another room and have a nice little read. We're going to have a ruby hunt. Flyman!'

The Flyman appeared at the open door. At sight of him, Miss Casata broke into a storm of exclamations.

'Not him! He shall not come in here. He killed Mr Holland!

I saw him! Mr Holland's blood is on his hands! I will not have that he come in here!'

'My dearest girl, but that's absurd. He's the only one of the three who understands locks. You don't want us to irretrievably ruin Miss Bewicke's property owing to our sheer want of skill? And for a nose for such a trifle as that ruby we are hunting for he has not his equal. Now, you go and have a nice little read.'

He moved forward with the possible intention of taking her by the arm and leading her from the room. If such was his design, it failed. As he advanced, she slipped past him. Rushing to the door which led into Miss Bewicke's bedroom, she placed herself in front of it. She took out one of the three treasures which were in her pocket—the revolver. Before the three men had even dreamed that she might be in possession of such a weapon, it was pointed at their heads. Her tone when she spoke was as significant as her attitude.

'If one of you tries to come through this door, I will shoot him dead. Do not think this revolver is not loaded. I will show you.'

She fired, the bullet penetrating the opposite wall. Mr Thomas Cox ducked as it passed. His companions instinctively shrank back. Her lips parted in a grim smile. Apparently this was her idea of humour.

'You see I am not so helpless as you perhaps supposed. I am not nervous, not at all. I am used to handle a revolver. I have won prizes for pistol shooting, oh, several times. There are five more barrels which are loaded. If I aim at you, I promise that I will not miss. You shall see.'

The bearing of the trio, in its way, was comical, they were evidently so completely taken by surprise. Mr Thomas Cox, in particular, looked as if this were an expedition in which, under the circumstances, he wished he had not taken part He said as much.

'Look here, Burton, this is more than I bargained for. Before we came I told you that I was not going to be mixed up with anything equivocal I have my character to consider. You said your lady friend would listen to reason; if your lady friend won't listen to reason, then I'm sorry, but I'm off.'

'Then you'll lose your money.'

'In that case you'll have to smart for it'

'That won't give you your money. It's a nice little lot.'

'I know it's a nice little lot, and I can't afford to lose it; you know I can't afford to lose it. But there's something I can afford to lose still less, and that—that's my character.'

'Your character! Why, if you only could manage to get rid of your character—I don't believe you yourself realise what an awful one it is—it'd be the best stroke of business you've done for many a day, my dear Cox!'

Mr Burton advanced, as if to tap his friend, in an affable manner, on the shoulder. This brought him within a few feet of where Miss Casata was standing. Laying his left hand on Mr Cox's shoulder, with his right he snatched away that gentleman's walking-stick, swung round and struck Miss Casata's outstretched wrist with such violence that the revolver was driven from her grasp and sent flying across the room. She gave a cry of pain. Her arm fell limp at her side. The blow had been delivered with so much force that it was quite possible her wrist was broken.

'You devil!'

'You wild cat!' returned the gentleman. 'Now, Flyman, on to her!'

The Flyman obeyed. The two gentlemen attacked the lady. Although she fought gamely, especially considering her injured wrist, she was no match for the pair. They got her down upon the floor, still struggling for all that she was worth.

'Now, Flyman, where's that stuff of yours?'

'I'm getting it. She's a oner. She's bit me to the bone.'

With difficulty—he only had one hand disengaged—he evolved a tin canister from his jacket pocket.

'Bite her to the bone! Let her have the lot!'

From the canister the Flyman managed to take a cloth—a cloth which was soaked with some peculiar-smelling fluid. This he jammed against the lady's face, even cramming it between her lips. She writhed and twisted, then lay still.

As the Flyman got up, he examined the hand which she had marked with her teeth.

'She takes a bit of doing. I shouldn't like to have to tackle her single-handed.'

Mr Burton smiled. His clothes were a little rumpled. As he rose he arranged his tie.

'Nice wife she'd make! What do you think?'

Mr Cox had occupied his time in picking up the revolver of which the lady had been relieved. He seemed genuinely concerned.

'You know, Burton, I tell you again I didn't come here for this sort of thing. I wouldn't have had this happen not—not for a good deal. I shouldn't be surprised if we get into trouble for this.'

'My dear Cox, we should have got into trouble anyhow. We may as well be hung for a sheep as a lamb. I'm going for the gloves.'

'Hung! Don't talk about hanging. You make a cold shiver go down my back. You haven't—killed her?'

'Killed her? You innocent! She's the sort who take a deal of killing. My good chap, when she comes to, she'll curse a little and go on generally; but she'll forgive me in the end. I know her; she's a dear!'

While the three men stood looking down at the unconscious woman, there came a knocking at the outer door.

CHAPTER 15
AN HONOURABLE RETREAT

It was not what they expected. Their faces showed it; they were so unmistakably startled. They looked at each other, then at the unconscious woman, then back again at one another. Mr Burton bit his lip.

'Who the deuce is that?'

'Servants, perhaps.'

'The suggestion was the Flyman's.'

'Then confound the servants! Why can't they take a little extra time tonight? They know their mistress is away.'

The knocking came again—a regular *rat-tat-tat*

'That's no servants. They wouldn't make that row.'

'You can never tell. Nowadays they make what row they please; they fancy themselves. Brutes!'

'Visitors, perhaps.'

'Confound them, whoever it is!'

They spoke in whispers, an appreciable pause between each man's speaking, as if each in turn waited for something to happen. Mr Burton was outwardly the most self-possessed, being the kind of man who would probably smile as he mounted the gallows. The Flyman had his eyes nearly shut, his fists clenched, his shoulders a little hunched, as if gathering himself together to resist a coming attack. Mr Thomas Cox was visibly tremulous; his great head twitched upon his shoulders; he was apparently in danger of physical collapse. It was curious to observe the contrasting attitudes of the three men as they stood about the recumbent woman.

The knocking was repeated, still more loudly, as if the knocker waxed impatient.

'We shall have to let 'em in. Anyhow, we shall have to see who's there. They'll knock the door down.'

This was the Flyman. Mr Cox suggested an alternative.

'Can't we—can't we get away? Isn't there another way out?'

Mr Burton enlightened him.

'My dear Cox, there's only one way into a flat, and there's only one way out, unless you try the window, which means a drop of perhaps a hundred feet. I'm not dropping. The Flyman's right; we shall have to see who's there. There needn't be trouble, unless you give yourself away. It depends who it is. I'll lay this dear little girl of mine upon her bed; she'll be more comfortable there, and not so conspicuous. I know which is her room. Then we'll see who's come to call on you.'

Displaying a degree of strength with which one would hardly have credited his slight figure, lifting Miss Casata off the floor, he bore her from the room. During his absence there came the knocking for the fourth time, this time furiously. When he returned, a marked change had taken place in his appearance. There were signs of strange disorder on his countenance, as if during his brief withdrawal he had been unstrung by some overwhelming shock. The Flyman at once observed his altered looks.

'What's happened? What's the matter?'

'Curse you, Flyman!'

'What have I done now?'

'I say, curse you!'

'Is she—dead?'

'No, she's not. I'm going to open the door. If it's the servants, I'll send them away, pretending to give them a message from her; if it's callers, I'll tell them a lie; if it's anybody who wants to make himself unpleasant, you two lookout I'm not going to be bluffed out of this before I've got that ruby.'

'Burton, be careful what you do, for all our sakes.'

This was Mr Cox. The retort was hardly courteous.

'You be hanged!'

Mr Burton reached the front door as the knocking was re-commencing. From where they were they could not see what he did, but they could hear. They heard him open; a feminine voice inquire, in tones of indignation,—

'What's the meaning of this? Why am I kept waiting?'

Then the front door slammed, the drawing-room door was thrown violently open, and two young ladies came through it, one after the other, with such extremely indecorous rapidity as to suggest that they could scarcely be entirely responsible for their own proceedings, as, indeed, they were not Mr Horace Burton had propelled them forward with his own right arm before they themselves had the least idea what was about to happen. And, following right upon their heels, he closed the drawing-room door, turned the key and stood with his back against it, surveying them with his habitual, benignant smile.

It was what they call upon the stage a tableau. The smiling gentleman, the two bewildered ladies, the two other almost equally bewildered men, for it was an open question which were the more surprised by the singularity of Mr Burton's behaviour—Miss Bewicke and Miss Broad or Mr Thomas Cox and the Flyman.

The peculiar nature of her reception seemed to have driven Miss Broad's wits completely from her. She gazed around like a woman startled out of sleep, who has no notion of what has roused her. Miss Bewicke had apparently retained some fragments of hers. She looked at Mr Burton, then at Mr Cox and the Flyman, then back at the gentleman who stood before the door. She eyed him up and down with a mixture, as it seemed, of amusement, anger and contempt Could a voice have stung, hers would have stung him then. But this gentleman was pachydermatous.

'So it's you?'

'I guess it is.'

'How dare you come here?'

'That's the problem.'

'It's one which will soon be solved.'

She moved across the room. He checked her.

'It's no good your ringing the bell. There's no one to answer.'

As she turned to face him, Miss Broad spoke, with an apparent partial return to consciousness.

'Who is this person?'

'This person is Horace Burton, of whom you may have heard. I cannot tell you who the other persons are. They look as if they were friends of his.'

'So this is Horace Burton?'

Miss Broad regarded the gentleman in question as if he were some unclean thing, which, possibly, she considered him to be. He, on the other hand, continued genial as ever.

'And you're Miss Broad—Letty, I believe? I'm pleased to meet you, cousin that is to be.'

434

'Cousin—your cousin? I shall never be a cousin of yours.'

'No? That's hard on Guy. He's counting on the money.'

'You despicable creature!' She turned away, presenting him with a good view of her back, and put a question to Miss Bewicke. 'What is he doing here? Surely you don't allow him in your rooms?'

Mr Burton took upon himself to answer for the lady.

'I'll tell you what I'm doing here; she can't. I'm now for the first time going to tell her also. It'll be giving her a little piece of information which I know she'll value. Miss Bewicke, I've come here in search of a quarter of million of money.'

'Is that so? You really are too modest! It was surely scarcely worth your while to come for such a trifle! I need hardly say that you will find several little sums of that amount lying loose about the premises!'

'Indeed? Well, I want one; that's all.'

'Mr Burton, will you be so good as to leave my rooms?'

'I'll leave them on the wings of the wind, whatever that may be, when I have my uncle's ruby.'

'When you have what?'

'My uncle's ruby. My dear cousin Guy committed burglary here last night in quest of it, so I'm sure you won't mind my paying you a little call this evening as a sort of sequel.'

'I suppose Louise Casata told you about Mr Holland?'

'There's no charge for supposing.'

'Probably the same person also informed you that he went away with what he sought?'

'Did he, Miss Bewicke?'

'You had better refer to your informant'

'I'm referring to you. I'm asking you if Guy Holland left these rooms last night in possession of my uncle's ruby?'

'Ask Miss Casata; ask your cousin even, but don't ask me.'

'I am asking you. You've been playing some confounded trick.'

'Mr Burton!'

'I don't wish to hurt your feelings, Miss Bewicke, so I'll say you've been amusing yourself with some dainty, delicate device, and I shouldn't be surprised to learn that you have that ruby on your person at this moment'

Miss Bewicke, walking to the bell, pressed her finger against the button, so that it kept up a continuous ringing. Mr Burton watched her with a smile.

'You see, there's no one there. You might have taken my word.'

'Where is Miss Casata?'

'Where is she? That's the question. Where's everyone?'

'If I am unable to attract the attention of my own servants, thanks to you, my friends in the next flat will hear the unceasing tinkling of the bell, and guess that there is something wrong.'

'I should be sorry, Miss Bewicke, to have to seem rude to a lady—'

'On the contrary, I should imagine that few things would give you greater pleasure; you are that kind of person.'

'At the same time, I must request you to leave that bell alone.'

He went closer to her. His moving away from it left the door unguarded. Over her shoulder she shot a glance at Miss Broad. That young lady, catching it, perceived the little ruse she had been playing. Hurrying to the door, she began to turn the key, and had already unlocked it when Mr Burton came rushing back to the post which he had been beguiled into deserting.

'You darling!' he cried.

Seizing Miss Broad by the waist he dragged her from the door. As he whirled her round, she struck him with her clenched fist on his right ear, the blow being delivered with such good judgment, force and fortune that it carried the young gentleman clean off his feet and right over on to his back.

'Bravo!' exclaimed Miss Bewicke. 'Now, Letty, open the door!'

But Miss Bewicke was a little hasty in supposing that the road was free. As Mr Burton fell, he prevented Miss Broad from moving by clutching at her skirts. She struggled to release her-

436

self in vain; he gripped too tight. And the Flyman, hastening to occupy the fallen hero's place, confronted Miss Bewicke as she advanced.

'It's no good,' he observed. 'There's no road this way.'

She was not to be baffled without an effort 'If you'll let me pass, I'll give you—'

'You won't give me anything, because you won't pass. Now, don't you be silly, or you'll be sorry. You won't bowl me over with a clip on the ear from your little fist.'

This was said because, encouraged, perhaps, by Miss Broad's success, Miss Bewicke showed signs of actual violence. The apparent recognition, however, of some peculiar quality on the face of the man in front of her caused her to relinquish her purpose, if it was ever formed. Instead, turning to Miss Broad, she took her by the hand.

'Come, quick!' she cried. Mr Burton, reassured by the Flyman's arrival, loosed the lady's skirt as he ascended to his feet. The quick-witted proprietress of the rooms, taking instant advantage of Miss Broad's freedom, rushed her towards the door through which, not long since, he had carried Miss Casata. Divining their purpose, he tore after them as soon as he had regained his perpendicular.

'Stop them, you fools! Move yourself, Cox!' But Mr Cox did not move himself. He remained motionless where he was standing, and Mr Burton, in spite of his impetuosity, was too late. They were not only through before he reached the door, but had banged it in his face, and turned the key on the other side. He shook the handle in vain.

'Open, you cats!'

They were not likely to comply with his civil invitation. He addressed himself to Mr Cox, on his face, all at once, a very peculiar look of pallor.

'I shouldn't be surprised if you swing for this.'

'Swing? For letting them through that door? Who do you think you're talking to?'

'I'm talking to you, my friend. What's the betting that your letting them through that door doesn't turn out a hanging matter for you? I'll take short odds.' He turned to the Flyman. 'Let me through there. There's another way into where they are; I'll see if I can get at them. You stay here, in case they try to double. Cox is no good. I'll be even with him for this.'

Mr Burton crossed to a door, which was on the other side of the little hall. Unlocked, it admitted him to the kitchen. From the kitchen he passed to another room, apparently where the servants slept. On the opposite side of this was still another door. He eyed it.

'If I remember rightly, that leads into her room.'

The door was locked; the key was in the lock upon the other side. He stooped to see; it was in a position which prevented anything being visible. He rattled the handle; rapped with his knuckles at the panel, without result. All was silent

'It is her room. I wonder what they're up to? They're very still. They can't—'

He stopped, probably because the stillness of which he spoke was broken by a woman's cry—a mingling of surprise, anguish, fear. He retraced his steps towards the kitchen, whispering to himself two words,—

'They have!'

Taking the key from one side of the lock, replacing it in the other, he locked the door of the servants' room behind him. The key itself he pocketed.

'Except through the drawing-room, there's only this way out, so we've trapped you anyhow.'

As if to make assurance doubly sure, he locked the door of the kitchen also. Again he pocketed the key.

Chapter 16
The Finding of the Ruby and the Locking of the Door

When Mr Burton returned to the drawing-room, he found that Mr Thomas Cox had been having a few words with the Flyman. That worthy jerked his thumb in the other's direction.

'Wants to sling his hook. Says he's had about enough of it'

'Oh, he has, has he? Now, Cox, listen to me. It's through you we're here—'

Interrupting, Mr Cox raised his hat and stick in a hasty disclaimer.

'Was there ever anything like that? It was your suggestion entirely. You said you could twist your lady friend round your finger—'

'Let's go a little further back, my Cox. You've told me—how many times?—that if I lose my uncle's money you'll send me to gaol. Not being anxious to go to gaol, I'm doing my best to get my uncle's money. So if it's not through you I'm here, I should like to know through whom it is.'

'That's different; you're entering on other matters altogether. You've committed—you know what you've committed; but it doesn't follow, because you've brought yourself within the reach of the criminal law, that I want to bring myself too.'

'You hand over those pieces of paper which you're always flicking in my face, and you're at liberty to go through that door, and down the stairs, and neither the Flyman nor I will ever breathe a word about your having been connected with the evening's entertainment.'

'Do you take me for a fool? You've robbed me on your own account already, and now you want to jockey me into robbing myself. Don't talk to me like that!'

'No, I won't talk to you like that; I'll talk to you like this. What there'll be to pay for this evening's proceedings I don't know; but you'll pay your share, whatever it is. This is a game of share and share alike, and of in for a penny in for a pound. The Flyman and I are going to see this through. I'm going to have the ruby before I leave, I tell you that; and you're going to be in with us right along.'

'Burton, you're a villain!'

'Cox, you're a scoundrel! Any use our saying pretty things to each other, you renegade Jew?'

Mr Cox was wiping his forehead with his pocket-handkerchief, as if he felt the heat

'I will not be spoken to like that, as if I were—as if I were a man of your own type. Where—where have those women gone?'

'The room on the other side that door is the dining-room; beyond is Casata's room. That's where they've gone.'

'Then—then they've found her?'

'Oh, yes, they've found her; not a doubt of it They've found a good many other things as well.'

His tone evidently struck Mr Cox as being disagreeably significant.

'For goodness' sake, Burton, let's go. You are so rash, don't let's make bad worse. Let's go while we have a chance, and before anything very serious has happened.'

'Something serious has happened.'

'What do you mean?'

'What I say.'

'You don't mean—'

'Oh, cut it! Flyman, Cox is too fond of cackle. We're losing valuable time, my child. You stay where you are, and keep an eye on things, while Cox and I find my uncle's ruby.'

The Flyman proposed an amendment.

'Excuse me, Mr Burton, but, if you don't mind, we'll have it the other way about You stay here, and Mr Cox and I will find the ruby.'

Mr Burton laughed.

'Flyman, Doubt was your sire, out of Suspicion. Still think I want to do you?'

'Sure.' The Flyman drew his finger across his lips. 'Mr Burton, you're cleverer than most, and a lot cleverer than me. If you once got that there stone between your fingers, I might whistle for my thousand, and keep on whistling. Besides, I am handier than you at looking for a thing like that'

'Then show your handiness; only look alive about it. We can't expect to continue in the enjoyment of these charming rooms forever.'

'Where shall I start looking?'

'There you are, displaying your handiness from the very beginning. How am I to know? I'm not informed as to where
she keeps her gewgaws. I believe that the pretty lady's sleeping-
chamber is on the other side of that door; look, there.' The Flyman looked in the direction referred to. 'Hold hard; take Cox
with you.'

The Flyman gripped Mr Thomas Cox by the arm.

'You come with me.'

Mr Cox objected,

'None of your handling.'

'Who wants to handle you? You come with me, that's all.'

'Yes, Cox, that's all. You go and assist our friend in prising
open the pretty lady's jewel-boxes and dressing-cases, and so on.
You know quite well that it isn't the first time you've been at
the game, dear boy.'

'I'll have no finger in anything of the kind; and as for your
imputations, I'll make you regret them, Mr Burton.'

'You will, will you? Take care, Cox; I'm in a nasty mood. If
you won't take a hand in this game, we'll play it in spite of you.
We'll count you out Not a farthing shall you have of my money,
and I defy you to put the law into execution against me. You
know you daren't—now. The moment you move, I'll give the
police the office to keep an eye on Thomas Cox. You've more to
lose than we have.'

'You—you brutes! Don't try to bully me.'

'Bully? I don't bully, Cox. Here, I'll open that door, and you
shall go through it at once, if you please. Only I'll go with you,
and at the foot of the stairs I'll denounce you for murder. If the
game is lost, as it will be if you won't play it out, I don't care if I
do hang, so long as you hang with me.'

'What—what the devil do you mean by keeping on dropping hints about—about murder?'

'You shall know, if you like, when you reach the foot of the
stairs. Take my earnest and well-meant advice, keep in with us,
and take my word for it that each moment you waste brings the
shadow of the gallows just a little nearer. I'll give you all the ex-

441

planations you want afterwards, if there ever is an afterwards.'

Mr Cox hesitated. He glanced from one of his companions to the other. What he saw on their faces seemed to have on him an odd effect. He went with the Flyman into Miss Bewicke's bedroom, looking as if he had all at once grown older. Mr Burton followed them with his eyes, the peculiar expression of his countenance seeming to endow his stereotyped smile with an unusual prominence. He looked, as he had said of himself, in a nasty mood.

'Leave the door open, Flyman. I also am interested in the proceedings, and should like to be instantly informed when you do light upon my uncle's precious jewel.'

He watched for a moment or two the Flyman pulling open such drawers as were unlocked and turning over their contents.

'Don't trouble yourself to look at the frills and laces. Women don't keep jewels among their underwear. Turn your attention to the dressing-table, man.'

The Flyman resented the comment on his mode of procedure.

'You never know where a woman does keep her things, especially the thing you're after, as you'd know if you'd as much experience as I have.'

Mr Burton, laughing, lit a cigarette.

'All right, man of many felonies. You're quite justified in resenting the criticism of the amateur. I was only telling you what was my own idea. Only do be quick and illustrate the handiness of which you bragged.'

He strolled towards the door which was on the opposite side of the room, the one through which the ladies had vanished. He softly tried the handle; it still was locked. Taking the cigarette from between his lips, he inclined his ear towards the panel and listened.

'They're quiet I suppose they're in her room. I wonder what they're doing? Problem for the papers which give prizes for puzzles. Under the circumstances, what might they be expected to be doing? Odds on that they're doing something else. One might easily see. It wouldn't take long to cut a piece out of this panel, or, for the matter of that, to take the lock itself clean off. But would it be worth one's while? They've seen enough. Ye whales and little fishes, they've seen too much! Better carry the thing to a conclusion without unnecessary witnesses. If they're content, we are. What's up now?'

The question was prompted by an exclamation which came from Miss Bewicke's bedroom. Mr Cox appeared at the entrance.

'Burton, you said that all we wanted was the ruby; that the rest of her things should go untouched.'

'Well?'

'The Flyman's pocketing her jewels.'

Mr Burton crossed the floor.

'That won't do, Flyman. We're here on an expedition of right We're not thieves.'

'You said yourself we might as well be hung for a sheep as a lamb.'

'I did; and you are aware that that is not the kind of sheep I meant. On this occasion I really must ask you to be honest.'

'But I never saw such shiners. Who could resist them, guv'nor? She's got enough to stock a shop. Why, if we take 'em away with us, we sha'n't be far out, even if we don't get that blessed ruby.'

'It's the ruby or nothing; also, and nothing. Put those things back.'

'I've only nobbled one or two. I've got to look after myself.'

'I, too, have to look after you. You know what was agreed; keep to the terms of the agreement, or, though you "nobble" every "shiner" the lady owns, you'll be a loser. Put those things back.'

There was something about Mr Burton just then which compelled respect, of a kind, which fact the Flyman recognised. His face darkened and, in audible tones, he grumbled. But he produced the trinkets, as requested, and replaced them, one by one, on their velvet beds.

'Is that all?'

'Every blooming one.'

'Cox, is that all?'

'Yes, I believe it is.' He glanced at the open jewel-case. 'No, there's a ring still missing.'

The Flyman cursed. 'Can't a bloke have one?'

'Not unless he wishes to pay for it more than it's worth. Come, man, look pleasant'

The Flyman did not 'look pleasant;' but he restored the ring. Mr Burton expressed approval.

'That's better. Now, show yourself as keen in the right direction. Give us a proof of the "handiness" you talked about, and find that ruby. It'll be worth to you more than all those other things.'

On this point the Flyman, from his manner, seemed to have his doubts; but he continued his researches. Mr Cox observed that they were strictly confined to what Mr Burton had called the 'right direction.' Mr Burton, returning to the locked door, pursued his meditations as he listened at the panel.

'It's odd that they're so quiet, and suggests mischief. In such a case, surely women are not quiet. Unless—unless what? That's what I should like to know.'

'Burton, is this the ruby?'

The words came sharply from Mr Cox, with a sudden interposition from the Flyman.

'You give me that! Don't you lay your fingers on the thing!'

'I'm only looking at it.'

'You give it me, I say.'

'Burton!'

The cry was almost an appeal for help. Mr Burton arrived to find something very like a tussle taking place. The Flyman was endeavouring to obtain possession of something which Mr Cox was holding, and which that gentleman was doing his best to keep.

'I found it!' he cried. 'Hand it over!'

'Burton! Quick! Catch!'

Mr Cox tossed something through the air which Mr Burton caught He had just time to see that it was a ring, set with a gleaming red stone, when the Flyman was upon him with an emphatic repetition of the demand he had made on Mr Cox.

'You hand it over before I down you.'

Mr Cox explained.

'I found it; he didn't I opened the box, and it was the first thing I saw. It had nothing to do with him.'

The Flyman paid no attention to the statement He merely reiterated his request.

'Now, Mr Burton, I don't want no patter.You fork up before there's trouble.'

The young gentleman, holding his hand behind his back, was smiling in the other's face.

'Gently, Flyman. Let's know exactly where we are before we come to business.'The Flyman flung himself upon him without another word. Mr Burton never for a moment seemed to lose his self-possession. 'You ass! what do you suppose you're going to gain by this?'

While they struggled, the bedroom door was suddenly slammed to. There was a clicking sound. The continuation of the argument was instantly deferred. Mr Burton hurried to the door.

'They've caught us napping; it's locked.Well, Flyman, I hope you're satisfied. Owing to your "handiness," of which we have heard so much, in our turn we are trapped.'

CHAPTER 17

THE FIGURES ON THE BED

'At any rate,' remarked Miss Bewicke, as, turning the key in the lock, she shut herself and Miss Broad inside the dining-room, 'you can't get at us for a time.'

The two girls stood and listened.They heard the handle tried; the rapping at the panel.

'You may knock, and knock, but it won't be opened. He's gone.That was Horace, dear. How beautifully you knocked him down!'

'What does he want?'

'It's pretty plain. Uncle George's ruby has the attractiveness of the Holy Grail. This is another quest for it'

'But they'll find it if we stop here.'

'And if we don't stop here, what do you propose to do? Fight them to the death? Nothing else will be efficacious. They're not the persons, and they're not in the mood, to stick at trifles.'

'What a wretch he is! I've heard Guy speak of him, but I'd no idea he was as bad as this.'

'My dear Letty, when a bad man is in a bad hole, you've no notion how bad that man can be. The question now is, Can we get out through the kitchen door, or can they get through the kitchen door to us?'

'Where does that door lead to?'

'Into Louise Casata's bedroom. The beauty of the average flat is that you can always pass from any one room into any other, which, sometimes, is convenient and sometimes isn't. I'm wondering whether Louise is responsible for Horace Burton's presence here, and also where she is. I've reasons for believing that it was not her intention to go out tonight'

'I shouldn't keep such a woman about my place, if I were you.'

'I don't intend to any longer. All the same, you've no idea how useful she has been. There have been times when I don't know what I should have done without her. Still, I fancy that henceforth she and I part company.' She opened the door which led into Miss Casata's room, then gave utterance to a startled exclamation. 'Why! what is the matter? Letty, keep back!'

Returning to the dining-room, she leaned against the door, which she had pulled to after her, as if she needed its support. For one who was, as a rule, so completely mistress of herself, she showed strange emotion. Miss Broad stared at her askance-.

'What has happened now? What's in there?'

'I don't know. Don't ask me. Let me get my breath and think, and I'll tell you all about it.'

She pressed her hand against her side, as if to still the beating of her heart. She seemed unhinged, thrown, in a second, completely off her balance. Her agitation was infectious. Probably, without her knowing it, Miss Broad's voice trembled and sank.

'Tell me—what it is.'

'Wait a minute, and I'll tell you—all.'

She made an evident effort to get the better of her infirmity. Bracing herself up against the door, the little woman looked Miss Broad straight in the face.

'Letty, something horrible has happened.'

'What is it?'

'I don't quite know myself; I didn't stop to look.'

'Let me go and see.'

'It's Miss Casata and—a man.'

'A man? What man?'

'I can't say; I only saw it was a man. They're lying on the bed—so still. Oh, Letty!'

'May!'

Miss Broad was probably wholly unaware that she had called her companion by her Christian name. The unknown horror in the other room had laid its grip on her. She was overcome by frightful imaginings, not knowing why. She gasped out an unfinished question.

'You don't mean—'

'I don't know what I mean. I only know that there's something there.'

The two girls had been speaking in whispers, as if they stood in a presence which compelled hushed voices. Now, suddenly, Miss Bewicke raised her tones, extending her small palm towards the door through which they had entered.

'Oh! you wretches! wretches!'

She broke into a passion of tears.

'May, for goodness' sake, don't cry!'

'I'm not going to. I don't know why I am so silly, but, for the moment, I couldn't help it.' Her sobs ceased almost as rapidly as they came. She dried her eyes. 'Letty, let's go and see what's happened. I'm afraid Miss Casata's—dead.'

'Dead?'

'Yes; and—the man.'

'The man?'

'They're so still. Let's go and see. Give me your hand.'

Miss Broad yielded her hand. Miss Bewicke opened the door. The two peeped through.

The room was not a large one. On one side was an ordinary French bedstead. A brass railing was on the head and foot On this railing were hung feminine odds and ends. These made it difficult for anyone standing at the door to see clearly what was on the bed. Miss Broad perceived that on the outer edge there lay a woman.

'Who's that?'

'That's Louise Casata.'

'Perhaps she's sleeping.'

'She wouldn't sleep through all the noise.'

'She may be ill; I'll go and look at her.'

'Don't you see—that there's a man?'

Miss Broad moved further into the room. She saw what the other alluded to. As she did so, she gave utterance to that cry which Mr Horace Burton heard, listening in the servants' room beyond—the cry in which there was such a mingling of emotions as they welled up to the lips from the woman's heart

Miss Casata lay almost on the extreme edge of the bed fully clothed. She was on her back. One arm dangled over the side; her head was a little aslant upon the pillow, so that from a little distance it looked as if her neck was broker.

The whole pose was almost as uncomfortable a one as a human being could choose; indeed, the conviction was irresistibly borne in on the beholders that it was not self-chosen, unless she had sunk on to the bed in a drunken stupor; but Miss Bewicke knew that she was no drinker.

However, it was not Miss Casata's plight which had drawn from Miss Broad that involuntary cry. Beside her, outlined beneath the bedclothes, was a figure, stiff and rigid. With the exception of one place, it was completely covered. Someone, curious, perhaps, to learn what the thing might mean, had drawn aside sufficient of the bedclothes to disclose a portion of the head and face. As a matter of fact, the curious person was Mr Horace Burton. When relieving himself of the burden of the lady who was once the object of his heart's affection, he had been struck by the outlined form which lay so curiously still, and had wondered what it was, and had seen; and because of what he had seen, had gone back to his companions with the fashion of his countenance so changed.

Now Miss Broad saw. The man beside Miss Casata on the bed was Mr Holland—Guy Holland—her Guy. It was when she perceived that it was he that her heart cried out. Miss Bewicke, who had only realised that it was a man, without recognising what man it was, came to her side trembling, wondering. When she also knew, she also cried aloud; but there was a material difference between the quality of her exclamation and Miss Broad's. Hers signified horror and amazement—perhaps something of concern; Miss Broad's betokened so many other things besides.

The two women went running to the bed; but when Miss Broad showed an inclination to lean over and to touch the silent man, the other, as if fearful of what actual contact might involve, caught her by the dress.

'No, no; take care!'

Even Miss Broad shrank a little back; for Miss Casata lay between.

'Move the bed!'

The suggestion was Miss Bewicke's. In a moment it had been put into force. The bed was wheeled more into the centre of the room, so as to permit of passage between it and the wall, and presently the girl was at her lover's side. She knelt and looked, but still she did not touch him. No tears were in her eyes; she seemed very calm; but her face was white, and she was speechless. On her face there was a look which was past wonder, past pain, past fear, as if she did not understand what it was which was in front of her. Miss Bewicke stood at her side, also looking; her dominant expression seemed sheer bewilderment

He also lay on his back. The bedclothes were withdrawn, so that his face was seen down to the chin. No marks of violence were visible. His expression was one of complete quiescence. His eyes were closed, as if he slept; but if he did, it was very soundly, for there was nothing to show that he breathed.

Suddenly Miss Broad found her voice, or the ghost of it. Her lips did not move, and the words came thinly from her throat.

'Is he dead?'

The other did not answer; but, leaning over, she drew the bedclothes more from off him, and she whispered,—

'Guy!' They waited, but he did not answer. She called again, 'Guy!'

Yet no response. In that land of sleep in which he was, it was plain that he heard no voices.

The further withdrawal of the bedclothes had revealed the fact that he was fully dressed for dinner, as he was when Miss Bewicke had seen him last, the night before. His black bow had come untied; the ends strayed over his shirt-front, which was soiled and crumpled His whole attire was in disarray. There were stains of dirt upon his coat Now that they were so close, they perceived that traces of dry mud were on his face, as if it had been in close contact with the ground. About his whole appearance there was much which was ominous.

The fact that this was so seemed to make a fresh appeal to Miss Broad's understanding; probably to something else in her as well.

'Guy!' she cried.

Her tone was penetrating, poignant. If it did not reach the consciousness of him to whom she called, in another direction it had a curious and unlooked-for effect. As if in response to an appeal which had been made directly to herself, Miss Casata, on the opposite side of the bed, sat up. The girls clung to each other in startled terror. To them, for the moment, it was as if she had risen from the dead.

Although she had sat up, Miss Casata herself did not seem to know exactly why. She seemed not only stupid, but a little stu-

pefied, and gasped for breath, her respirations resembling con-
vulsions as she struggled with the after-effects of the narcotic.
The two girls observed her with amazement, she, on her part,
evidently not realising their presence in the least.

It was Miss Bewicke who first attained to some dim comprehension of the meaning of the lady's antics.

'She's been drugged; that's what it is. Louise!"

Miss Casata heard, although she did not turn her head, but
continued to open and shut her mouth in very ugly fashion as
she fought for breath.

'Yes; I'm coming. Who's calling?'

'I! Look at me! Do you hear? Louise!'

This time, if she heard, Miss Casata gave no sign, but, sinking
back on the bed, clutched at the counterpane, making a noise, as
she gasped for breath, as if the walls of her chest would burst.

'Letty, let me go! I must do something. She'll relapse, or worse,
if we don't take care.'

Miss Bewicke hastened to the wash-handstand. Emptying a
jug of water into a basin, she took the basin in her hands and
dashed the contents, with what force she could, into the lady's
face.

The salutation was effectual. Miss Casata floundered, spluttering, on to the floor, more like herself.

Miss Bewicke confronted her, the basin still in her hands.

'Who did that?'

'I did. Louise, wake up!'

Miss Casata seemed to be endeavouring her utmost to obey
the other's command.

'What's the matter?'

'That's what I want to know. In particular, I want to know
what is the meaning of Mr Guy Holland's presence in your
room?'

'Holland?' She put her hand up to her head in an effort to
collect her thoughts. She spoke as if with an imperfect appre-
hension of what it was she was saying. 'He was in the street—
lying—on his face—so I brought him here—before the police-

man came.'

'Before the policeman came? What do you mean? How did you know that he was lying in the street?'

'I saw—the Flyman—from the window—knock him down—he took the ruby.'

'The Flyman? Who is he?'

'A man—Horace knows—I knew—Horace had set him on. I didn't want him to get into trouble, so I brought him here. It was all I could do to carry him up the stairs—he was so heavy.'

'And do you mean to say you've had Mr Holland hidden in your room all day and night?'

'All day—and night He's dead. The Flyman killed him. Horace will get into trouble—when it's known.'

Miss Casata, in her condition of semi-consciousness, said more than she had warrant for. Mr Holland was not dead. Even as she asserted that he was, he showed that her assertion was an error. While the still partly-stupefied woman struggled to get out of the darkness into the light, there came a cry from the white-faced girl on the other side of the bed.

'May, he moves!'

Startled into forgetfulness of what it was she held, Miss Bewicke dropped the slippery basin from her hands. It broke into fragments with a clatter. The noise of the shattered ware seemed actually to penetrate to Mr Holland's consciousness. Miss Bewicke would always have it that it was her breaking the basin which really brought him back to life. In an instant Miss Broad was half beside herself in a frenzy of excitement

'May! May! he lives! Guy! Guy!'

Miss Bewicke, turning, saw that he was alive, but that, apparently, when that was said, one had said all.

Chapter 18
Reinforced

Mr Holland had opened his eyes; he had done nothing more. The movement might have been owing to an involuntary contraction of the muscles, so rigid did his attitude continue to be, so apparently unseeing were the staring pupils. But, for the instant, it was sufficient for Miss Broad that he had shown signs of volition even to so small an extent She bent over the bed, addressing him by a dozen endearing epithets.

'Guy! My darling! my love! my dear! Don't you know me? It's Letty—your own Letty! Speak to me! Guy! Guy!'

But he did not speak. Nor was it possible, to judge from any responsive action on his part that he even heard. His continual unnatural rigidity cooled the first ardour of the lady's joy. She addressed Miss Bewicke. And now the tears were streaming down her cheeks.

'May, come here! Look at Guy! Get him to speak to me!'

To enforce compliance with her wish was not so easy, as Miss Bewicke saw, if the other did not. There was an uncanny look about Mr Holland's whole appearance which was not reassuring. He looked far indeed from the capacity for reasonable speech.

'He wants help. We ought to have a doctor at once.'

'Then fetch one—fetch one!'

That there was anything about the request which was at all unreasonable, seemingly Miss Broad did not pause to consider; she was too preoccupied with her own troubles and his. But to Miss Bewicke the difficulty of the errand forcibly occurred.

'You forget—' she began. Then stopped, for she remembered how easy it was, in the other's situation, to forget all things save one She knit her brows and thought, the result of her cogitations being a series of disjointed sentences.

'They can hardly be such brutes, when they know. And yet it was they who put him there. I wonder! Do I dare?'

It seemed that she essayed her courage. She went to the door, and, for a moment, listened. Then turned the key, opened it an inch or two. What she saw and heard increased her valour, especially what she heard. The drawing-room was empty. Loud voices came through the open door of the bedroom—her own bedroom on the opposite side—sounds which did not speak of peace.

'I do believe they're fighting.'

She stole on tiptoe a foot or two into the empty room, then stopped in a flutter as of doubt—what might not happen if they caught her?—then tiptoed further, till she had reached the centre of the room. Again she paused. If she was seen, it was a long way back to the haven of comparative safety she had quitted. But the noise, if anything, grew louder. From some of the words which reached her, she judged it possible that they were too much occupied with their own proceedings to pay heed to anything else. She perceived that, by some stroke of good fortune, the key was outside the door. She screwed her courage to the sticking-point, forming a sudden resolution. Darting forward, thrusting the door to quickly, she turned the key, then, when the key was turned, the deed done, the three gentlemen trapped, she leaned against the wall, went white, seemed on the verge of fainting.

She went still whiter when the handle was turned within, and Mr Horace Burton's voice was heard demanding that the door be undone.

'If they should get out!'

The possibility of the thing, and the fear thereof, acted on her as a spur. She tore to the door which led out of the flat, and, throwing it open, almost fell into the arms of the cook and housemaid who were returning from their Sunday evening out. Seldom have domestic servants been more heartily welcomed. She addressed them by their names.

'Wilson! Stevens! go at once for the police!'

Instead of promptly obeying, they stared at her in astonishment. Her hat, which she had not removed during the lively incidents which had marked the passage of the time since her arrival home, was on one side, at that unbecoming angle which is a woman's nightmare; and there were other traces of disarray which were not in keeping with her best-known characteristics, for, with her, a pin misplaced was the thing unspeakable. While the cook and housemaid stared, hesitating to start, as they were bidden, in search of the representatives of law and order, the lift stopped at the landing, and from it, of all persons in the world, Mr. Bryan Dumville emerged.

She flew into his arms, as, it may be safely said, she had never flown before.

'Oh, Bryan!Bryan! I'm so glad you've come!'

As the flattered gentleman was, no doubt, about to express his appreciation of the warmth of his reception, the lift commenced to descend. Something else occurred to her.

'Stop! stop!' she cried. The lift returned. The porter looked out inquiringly. 'Peters, there are thieves in my rooms! You had better come with us at once.'

'Thieves, miss? Hadn't I better—'

She cut the porter's sentence short, relentlessly.

'No, you hadn't. You must come with us at once. Don't you hear me say so?'

He went. They all went—the cook and the housemaid, the porter, Mr Bryan Dumville, and Miss May Bewicke. She went last As she went, she shut the front and drawing-room doors behind her. She pointed towards her bedroom.

'They're in there at this moment—three of them.'

The porter seemed to have his doubts.

'Three of them? You're sure they are thieves, miss?'

'Am I sure? Why do you ask me such a question? Do you think I'm likely to make a mistake in a matter like that? Pray, don't be absurd.'

'In that case, if they are thieves, don't you think I'd better fetch the police?'

Miss Bewicke's wits worked quickly. Even when circumstances seemed against their working at all—since instructing the cook and housemaid to do as the porter was now suggesting that he should do—she had already been turning things over in her mind, with the result that she was not sure that she desired official assistance after all. If the police came, arrests would be made; she would have to see the thing through to the bitter end. In view of such a possible consummation, there were many points to be considered. Had she been an actress, with a keen eye for an advertisement—a type which, it is understood, does exist—-the idea of figuring as the heroine of what the slang of

455

the hour calls a '*cause célèbre*' might have commended itself to her intelligence; but, as it happened, she was not that kind.

If these gentlemen did come into the hands of the police—at any rate, on this particular charge—it was possible that things might transpire which she, and possibly others, would not wish to have mentioned in court and in the papers. That the miscreants deserved all the punishment which the law might award them, she had no doubt whatever. At the same time, she was equally clear that they would duly, and shortly, receive their reward, if not at her instance, then at that of others. So, on the whole, she decided, in a twinkling, that she would take no final step till she saw which way the cat might jump.

'When I want you to fetch the police, I will tell you.' She turned to the housemaid. 'But there's one thing, Stevens, you might fetch, and must, and that's a doctor. Go to the nearest, and bring him at once.'

Even as she spoke, through the dining-room door there came three persons—Miss Broad, with Mr Guy Holland on her arm, looking the most woebegone figure imaginable, but still alive, and plainly walking; behind them Miss Casata. For the second time Miss Bewicke countermanded her instructions.

'Stay, Stevens! Perhaps the doctor won't be wanted.'

CHAPTER 19
STILL WITH A SMILE

The five stared at the three, then, after momentary inspection, as if for the purpose of satisfying herself on certain points by visual inspection, Miss Bewicke moved towards Mr Holland.

'Oh, Guy, I am so glad to see you better! I do hope that you're all right'

The words were, perhaps, a trifle banal, possibly because, for once, the nimble-witted lady was doubtful as to what was exactly the proper thing to say. Apparently, however, it was of little consequence what she said. The gentleman was still incapable of appreciating at their just value either words or phrases. That he knew she spoke to him was probable, for he turned and regarded her with vacant looks and glassy eyes; but that he realised who she was, or what she meant, was more than doubtful. Mumbled words proceeded from his stammering lips.

'All right—yes—quite all right—nothing wrong.'

Miss Broad looked at Miss Bewicke with eyes in which the tears still trembled. She appealed to her in a whisper, in tones which quivered.

'Won't you let them fetch a doctor?'

'Let them! Stevens, fetch the man at once.'

This time Stevens went in search of medical aid.

Mr Dumville had been observing Mr Holland with undisguised amazement Now he clothed his thoughts with speech.

'Holland, what on earth's the matter with you? May, what does all this mean?'

Miss Bewicke explained; that is, she told as much as she thought it necessary and advisable that Mr Dumville should know in the fewest words at her command. Mr Dumville professed himself to be, what he plainly was, amazed. The tale was very far from being complete in all its details, or he would probably have been yet more surprised, in a direction, as things were, which he little suspected.

'And do you mean that that man Burton is still upon these premises?'

'He was in my bedroom, when I turned the key, with his two friends.' Mr Dumville strode forward. She caught him by the arm. 'What are you going to do?'

'Slaughter him!'

'I would rather you did not do that. It would make such a mess upon the floor.'

'Do you think that scoundrel's behaviour is a thing to laugh at? I'll show you and him, too, where the laughter comes in.'

'My dear Bryan, I know very well that there's nothing laughable about Mr Horace. Burton or his proceedings. He is—oh, he's all sorts of things. I'd rather not tell you all the things I think he is.'

'I know.'

'Of course, you know. But, at the same time, when you have made sure that neither he nor either of his friends is taking away any of my property upon his person, I should be obliged if you would let them go.'

'Let them go! May, you're mad!'

'Believe me, Bryan, I am comparatively sane. I will tell you all my reasons later on. At present the thing is to get them gone. You may take my word for it that for Mr Horace Burton the day of reckoning is close at hand, and that it will be as terrible an one as even you can desire.'

'That won't be the same as if I'd killed him.'

'No, it won't be the same; it will be better. Could I creep between your arms if I knew that your hands were red with that man's blood? If you don't mind, as I locked the door, I'll open it. Please keep your hands off him as he comes out—for my sake, dear.'

She gave him a glance which possibly constrained him to obedience. She was famous in the theatre for the skill with which she used her eyes. Turning the key, throwing the bedroom door wide open, she stood before it with a little gesture of invitation.

'Pray, gentlemen, come out'

And they came out, the hang-dog three, for, though each endeavoured to bear himself with an air of unconcern, in no case did the endeavour quite succeed. As regards Mr Thomas Cox, the failure was complete. He looked like nothing so much as the well-whipped cur which only asks to be allowed to take itself away with its tail between its legs. The Flyman, who was probably more habituated to positions of the kind, succeeded a trifle better. He looked defiance, as if he were prepared to match himself, at less than a moment's notice, against whoever came. Mr Horace Burton it was, however, who might claim to face the situation with the most imperturbable front He looked about him, not jauntily so much as calmly, with his unceasing smile.

'More visitors, Miss Bewicke, I perceive. Ah! Guy, how are you? You're looking dicky. Louise, my dearest girl!'

Of its kind, his impudence was glorious. Mr Dumville strode up to him, as if forgetful of the lady's prohibition.

'By gad! I'd like to kill you!'

Mr Burton, glancing up at the speaker, did not turn a hair.

'I'm afraid I haven't the honour. Miss Bewicke, may I ask you to introduce me to the gentleman?'

'With pleasure. Mr Horace Burton, this is Mr Dumville. It is only at my urgent request that he refrains from breaking every bone in your body, as he easily could. But you know, and I know, that for you there's such a very bad time coming that I feel it's quite safe to leave you to the tender mercies of those to whom mercy is unknown. Turn out your pockets I'

'Charmed! I quite appreciate the motive which actuates your request, Miss Bewicke. Nothing could be more natural. But I give you my word of honour that neither of us has anything which belongs to you.'

Notwithstanding, Mr Burton turned his pockets inside out, smiling all the time. His companions followed suit, though scarcely with so much grace. So far as could be seen, neither of them was in possession of anything to which Miss Bewicke could lay claim, as she herself admitted.

'I really do believe you, Mr Burton, when you say that you— none of you—have property of mine. It sounds odd, and you may wonder why, but I do. Goodnight'

'Goodnight I am indebted to you, Miss Bewicke, for a pleasant evening's entertainment'

'Don't mention it When the time comes to balance your accounts, you'll find the sum-total of your indebtedness altogether beyond your capacity to meet. Go.'

And they went At least Mr Thomas Cox and the Flyman went—the first-named gentleman with an undignified rush, the second not very far from his heels; but Mr Burton lingered on the threshold to waft a kiss on his fingertips to Miss Casata.

'Best love, Louise.'

The lady made a dash at him, inarticulate with rage.

'You—you!'

Miss Bewicke stayed her progress.

'Louise!'

Mr Burton laughed

'My dearest girl, you can't expect to embrace me before all these people! Propriety forbids.'

When he had disappeared, Mr Dumville gave voice to his sentiments.

'I wish you'd let me kill him!'

Miss Bewicke nodded her head, with an air of the profoundest wisdom, as she laid her little hands on his two arms.

'My dear Bryan, before very long he'll be wanting to kill himself; that'll be so much nicer for us and so much worse for him.'

CHAPTER 20
HOW THE CHASE WAS ENDED

Mr Samuel Collyer was seated in his office. Spread open on the table in front of him was Mr George Burton's will, which apparently he had just been studying. The study seemed to have afforded him amusement Leaning back in his chair, he smiled. He referred to his watch.

'Twenty minutes past; they will soon be here. On these occasions, punctuality ought to be the rule, and generally is. George Burton was a curious man, and left a curious will. And yet I don't know. Why should I, or anyone, call it curious? By what right? When a man has neither wife nor children, and his only kindred are a couple of nephews to whom he is not particularly attached, surely he has a right to do as he likes with his own. It is his own—as yet And if he chooses to attach to the succession certain conditions which appeal, we'll say, to his sense of humour, what title has anyone, lawyer or layman, to comment adversely on the expression of his wishes?

'So long as they are not in opposition to the general welfare of the body politic, it seems to me none. In a sense, most wills are curious, when you get right into them and understand their ins and outs. I daresay mine will be. I'm a bachelor. Upon my word, I don't know who has the best claim to the few pence I shall leave. Why shouldn't I ornament my testamentary dispositions with a few characteristic touches? Why not?'

While the lawyer propounded to himself this knotty problem, two visitors were shown in—Mr Holland, again upon Miss Broad's arm. He still was not himself. The effects of the sand-bag, which the Flyman had used with more enthusiasm than he had perhaps intended, had not yet all vanished. He seemed uncertain about his capacity to steer himself. He did not carry himself so upright as was his wont. There was a look upon his face which it had not previously worn—of indecision, irresolution, as if he was not quite master of his mental faculties. That sandbag had landed on the brain. Miss Broad seemed to regard him as if he were a child; she watched over him as if he were one, and it must be allowed that he appeared to appreciate to the full her tender care.

The diplomatic lawyer chose not to see the things which were patent His greeting was,—

'I am glad to see you, Mr Holland, looking so much yourself. I was grieved to hear that you had had an accident'

'Accident!' The reiteration was Miss Broad's. 'You call it accident!'

'My dear young lady, the words which lawyers use are not always intended to bear their strict dictionary significance.'

Another visitor was announced—Mr Horace Burton, as much at his ease as ever. Miss Broad blazed up at sight of him.

'You dare to come here!'

'Dare! Collyer, who's this young lady? Oh, it's Miss Broad, my future cousin. May I ask, Letty—you'll let me call you Letty?—why you should speak of my "daring" to come to my own lawyer's office? Hallo, Guy, you look squiffy! Buck up, my boy!'

He would have saluted his cousin with his open palm upon the back had not Miss Broad caught his arm as it was descending and flung it away. He gazed at her with what was meant for admiration.

'You are a warm one, Letty, really now! If you propose to

slang Guy, as you seem fond of slanging me, you ought to have a pot of money to make it worth his while. He's likely to find marriage with you an expensive luxury, my dear.'

Mr Holland half rose from the chair on which Miss Broad had placed him. He spoke with hesitating tongue.

'You had better be careful—what you say.'

His relative laughed.

'You'd better be careful what you say, or you'll tumble down.'

Miss Broad laid her hand on Mr Holland's shoulder.

'Never mind what he says. I don't. He's not worth noticing.'

'Do you hear that, Collyer? Isn't she severe? But let's to business. I'm not come to engage in a tongue-match with a lady. The three months are up. Where's the ruby?'

Mr Collyer spoke.

'May I ask, Mr Holland, if you're in possession of the ring in question?'

It was Miss Broad who answered.

'No, he is not. Miss Bewicke calls herself his friend, and she even pretends to be mine, but her friendship does not go far enough to induce her to hand over property to its rightful owner which was never hers.'

Comment from Mr Burton,—

'How sad! That's very wrong of her. Shows such deplorable moral blindness, doesn't it? She is a wicked woman, is May Bewicke—heartless, hypocritical, selfish to the core. Well, Collyer, anyhow that settles it The money's mine, and I give you my personal assurance I can do with it.'

'I have not the slightest doubt of that, Mr Burton; but, before we conclude, there is something which I have been instructed to hand to Mr Holland. It was for that purpose I requested your presence here. Permit me, Mr Holland, to hand you this.'

From a drawer in his writing-table the lawyer produced a small parcel When Mr Holland had undone, with somewhat shaky fingers, the outer covering, it was seen that within was a leather-covered case. Inside was a note, which he unfolded.

Dear Guy, this is a wedding present from yours,

May Bewicke.

'This' was a ring—the ring—the famous ruby.

While they gathered round it, with a babble of voices, and Mr Burton showed himself disposed to bluster, Miss Bewicke herself appeared at the door with Mr Bryan Dumville. She advanced to Mr Holland and Miss Broad.

'My dear children, how are you both? So you have the ring? That's all right. Directly I heard of the will, I sent it to Mr Collyer—he's my uncle, don't you know? I thought it would be safer with him than it would be with me. A lone, lorn woman's rooms are always open to the machinations of the most dreadful characters, and you never know what may happen—burglaries and all sorts of things. And you see I do call myself Guy's friend, and I even pretend, Letty, to be yours. Don't I, Bryan, dear?'

Some of the latter words suggested that the little lady had been listening outside the door. Mr Dumville confined his attention to Mr Horace Burton.

'So it's you again? I shall have to kill you after all.'

Actually Mr Burton did not seem altogether at his ease.

'I suppose, Guy, you couldn't let me have a thousand pounds to get away with?' He laughed. 'No; it's no good. You'd better let me have it when I come out. They're waiting for me outside. A thousand would only be a drop in the sea. They wouldn't let me make a bolt of it for that.'

As he said, certain persons were waiting for him in the street When he appeared, and it was discovered that he was not to have his uncle's money, within an hour he was arrested on a charge of forgery. It was a remarkable case, and not a savoury one. Neither prosecutors nor prisoner showed to advantage; but as it was clearly proved that Mr Horace Burton had forged, and put into circulation, a large number of acceptances and other legal documents, the jury had no option but to find him guilty. A hard-headed judge sent him to penal servitude for fourteen years.

The Flyman soon followed him, it was understood, to the

same prison. His was a charge of robbery with violence in the City Road. The sand-bag again. As there were previous convictions against him, he suffered badly.

Mr Thomas Cox is still at large. He was seen lately on the cliff at Margate, with his wife and daughter, lounging on a chair listening to the band. He looked well and flourishing—an illustration of a sound mind in a sound body. But one never knows.

Mr Guy Holland and Mr Bryan Dumville were married at the same church, at the same time, on the same day. They are the best of friends. Their wives swear by one another. Mrs Guy Holland is convinced that Mrs Bryan Dumville is the most charming woman on the English stage, just as Mrs Bryan Dumville is certain that Mrs Guy Holland is the altogether most delightful person off it.

The Tipster

An Impossible Story
(A tale from *The Seen and the Unseen*)

1

"I've done it again! This is really rum!"

Mr. Gill tilted his hat towards the back of his head. Philip Major had come upon him in the Strand, standing in the middle of the pavement, staring at the fifth edition of the *Evening Glimmer*.

"That's what it is—rum! I can't help thinking, you know, that there must be something wrong."

"What's the matter?"

"Well," Mr. Gill put his hand up to his mouth: he coughed. "I've placed the first three horses for the Chichester Handicap. Here they are, large as life." Mr. Gill pointed to a paragraph in the paper. "Mary Anne, 1; The Duke, 2; and Coriolanus, 3; just as I sent 'em to my clients!"

Mr. Major laughed.

"That's all right I thought that you professed to send three winners, for seven-and-sixpence, isn't it?"

"But you don't understand. Yesterday I done the same. I placed the first three in the Billingsgate Stakes; sent 'em to every one of my correspondents, I did, upon my Dick! Why, Mr. Major, I've been a tipster—ah, I don't know how many years—and as for placing the first three, even at a donkey race, why, I haven't come within a million mile of 'em." Mr. Gill glanced round There was something curious in his glance. "But it isn't only horses. There's something up with me all round Why—"

He caught Mr. Major by the arm. They were by the pit entrance to the Lyceum Theatre. A hansom went rushing by.

"There's an old gentleman with a white hat crossing Wellington Street—that cab will knock him down!"

The cab whirled round the comer. An instant after there was a sudden tumult—someone had been run over. Mr. Major stared at Mr. Gill.

"I say, Gill!"

"I've been like that for the last day or two, but this afternoon I'm worse than ever. I keep seeing things."

"Excuse me, sir." Mr. Gill stopped and addressed a passer-by. "Your wife's just going to slip down the steps which lead to the nursery landing; and as she's in a delicate situation, if I was you I'd hurry home."

The passenger, a dignified-looking gentleman about forty years of age, appeared to be, not unnaturally, surprised at being addressed in such a manner by a perfect stranger.

"Who are you?"

"My name's Gill, sir—Thompson Gill. As your wife's going to be prematurely overtaken, all owing to a piece of soap which that there careless gal of yours has left upon the stairs, I thought you'd like me to mention it"

"Gill," observed Mr. Major, as they crossed the road towards Waterloo Bridge, "you're drunk."

"Not me. I haven't had so much as a drop this day. It's something wrong with the works, that's what it is. I keep seeing visions, or something. If I'd been a drinker I should say I'd got 'em. But it isn't that, I know."

"Perhaps you're going to be a prophet after all—not three winners for seven-and-six, but the *bona fide* article."

"That's what I'm afraid of," sighed Mr. Gill.

When they reached the centre of the bridge Mr. Major drew Mr. Gill aside into one of the embrasures.

"Come, Gill, I'll give you a chance to exercise your prophetic gifts. Am I going to sell that picture of mine which the President and Fellows have done me the honour to sky in their exhibition at Burlington House?"

Mr. Major asked the question lightly—but there was a suspicion of earnestness beneath the lightness. Mr. Gill paused before replying. His eyes looked out over the stream.

"Yes, you are."

"Oh, I am, am I? When?"

"Next week."

"So soon as that, my Gill! Come, we're getting on. And who will be the purchaser?"

"A gal."

"A gal!" Mr. Major started. "I presume by that you mean a young lady?"

"A dark gal, with big black eyes, and black hair curling all over her head. She'll go up to the picture and she'll say, 'So this is it, is it? They've hung it as well as it deserves. So this is the man who presumes to teach me painting? He can draw, but he will never paint—never.' Then she will look at the picture again, and she'll say, 'What a fool I am!' Then she'll go to a table, and she'll ask how much the picture is. And the man will say, 'Fifty pounds!' And she'll say to herself, 'That's more than the frame is worth.' Then she'll take out a sort of pocket-book, and she'll hand over five ten-pound notes. And the man'll say, 'What name?' And she'll say 'Briggs.'"

At this point Mr. Major started again—this time most perceptibly.

"What name?"

"She'll say 'Briggs.'"

"It's a lie!"

"It's not a lie. She'll say 'Briggs.' And to herself she'll say, 'I'm not going to flatter him by letting him know I've bought it. He's fool enough already.'"

Mr. Gill paused. Mr. Major stared at him. The little man had spoken with a quiet intensity which, in its way, was most effective. All the time he had kept his eyes fixed upon the stream,

"Anything more, Mr. Gill?"

"About the picture?"

"About the picture. Can you tell me, for instance, whether the name of the lady who is destined to become, in so flattering a way, my patron, really is Briggs?"

"Wait a moment When she goes away she'll tell the cab-driver to drive to Campden Hill Gardens." Again Mr. Major started "When she gets home she'll have a letter addressed to"—Mr. Gill hesitated—"to Miss Davidson."

"Oh! To Miss Davidson."

Mr. Major's voice was a trifle husky,

"The handwriting on the envelope will be very fine and small. The postmark will be Oban."

Mr. Major caught Mr. Gill by the shoulder.

"Gill!—stop! That will do! Come, let's get home. Gill, I should say that you were going off your nut"

"I don't know about going off my nut exactly, but there's something wrong with the works, I do believe."

"You don't suppose that I believe a syllable of all that nonsense you've been talking?"

"It's gospel truth, every word of it"

When they had gone a few steps further Mr. Gill stopped short

"Mr. Major, there's a man coming along the road, in a brown check coat, who's going to pay you half a sovereign which he owes you."

As a matter of fact, when they had proceeded about a hundred yards along the Waterloo Road they were approached by a man in a brown check coat, which was decidedly the worse for wear, who, at sight of them, pulled up.

"Hollo, Major! The very man I wanted to see. I think that makes us straight"

He thrust his hand into his waistcoat pocket In the outstretched palm which he held out to Mr. Major was—half a sovereign! That gentleman stared at the man, and at the coin, in undisguised amazement

"Hollo, Aldridge!"

"Rather unexpected, isn't it? I thought it would be—borrowed money back from me! Don't apologise, old chap! I've had a stroke of luck—so there you are!"

Mr. Major continued to stare at the coin after the man had gone.

"I say, Gill, this is very queer."

"That's what bothers me. It is uncommon queer."

2

It was the Tuesday morning afterwards. Mr. Major was at the house in Campden Hill Gardens in the capacity of painting-master. Towards the close of the lesson he asked his pupil a question. "Have you been to the academy yet?" Miss Davidson was in the enjoyment of her own fortune. It may therefore be taken for granted that she was of age. But she was more than that; she was in touch with those teachings of the age which tells us that a young woman can do without a chaperon. Her painting lessons were, as a rule, sacred to herself and her master—which, perhaps, enabled her to better concentrate her mind upon her searchings after art.

"Not yet I suppose I ought to have gone, but I really seem to have so much else to do."

Mr. Major said nothing. Perhaps he felt that even the most earnest searcher after art might be excused from attending that academy. Anyhow, that afternoon he himself was there. It was not his first visit by any means. He could have pointed out blindfold where all the most notorious pictures were. The position of one especial canvas he knew particularly well. It was in a far corner of the room, in a bad light, just above the line—exactly the position in which an indifferent work by an unknown man would be most likely to escape the casual visitor's eye. Mr. Major felt this very strongly as he approached that corner.

The rooms were crowded—though not, on that occasion, overcrowded—but just there there was not a soul. Apparently his picture was not attracting the least attention—nothing is more unsatisfactory to a struggling artist than to be aware of that. He advanced towards the slighted work of art with an uncomfortable feeling about the pit of his stomach. Suddenly he started. He hurried forward. The frame was starred!

"By Jove!" he exclaimed out loud. "Gill was right; it's sold."

In his surprise he was unconscious of the fact that he was staring at the frame as though he were paralysed by the merits of the painting. But others saw him. More people came to stare. Then he enjoyed that rarest of all rare pleasures—the pleasure which the gentleman enjoyed in Lord Lytton's novel, *The Disowned*—the pleasure of hearing his work criticised with perfect frankness.

A gentleman made an observation to a lady who was evidently his wife. " Don't care for that kind of thing," he said.

"I think it's silly," she replied.

They moved on. A gentleman—obviously a country gentleman—stared at the picture for, perhaps, two seconds.

"What's it all about?" he inquired of a friend.

"Don't ask me. Some stuff or other."

And they moved on. Then two parsons commented, as they went by. One of them was a dictatorial sort of person. He pointed out the picture with his umbrella.

"If I wanted an example to point the remark that I was just making, there is one. I say that art in England must be at a low ebb indeed when they're obliged to admit that sort of thing."

"The colouring's not bad," ventured his companion, who did not appear to be quite so critical

"Colouring! Pooh! Properly speaking, there is no colouring—that is, if you mean colour."

"Shows some idea of drawing."

"Drawing! After that, my good fellow, we'd better go and look at something else—say a Punch and Judy."

"Mr. Major."

As the two parsons were moving off—possibly in search of that Punch and Judy—the lucky artist, who seemed to have so hit the popular fancy, heard himself addressed by name. Turning, there was Miss Davidson, Mr. Major was momentarily confounded

"Where is your picture, Mr. Major?"

"Here is my daub."

"Daub?" The pupil seemed surprised. The master's manner was certainly ferocious. "Why do you call it a daub?"

"I only call it what other people call it, and some fool or other has bought it!"

"Mr. Major!" Miss Davidson drew herself back with distinct frigidity. Her naturally pale face, if possible, grew paler. Mr. Major immediately perceived how grossly he had blundered

"Forgive me, Miss Davidson. I mean that some good friend, with whom charity is esteemed a virtue, has been generous to me."

"But why should you suppose anything of the kind? Why should you suppose that a person would buy a picture he did not like, and for more than it is worth?"

"Why, Miss Davidson, ah, why?" He stood leaning on the hand-rail, his eyes on her. Her eyes she kept upon the catalogue. "It sounds ridiculous; but do you know that I am acquainted with a person who thinks himself a prophet, and he told me that this week someone would buy my picture."

"He need not be a prophet to have told you that" Lifting her eyes she looked him full in the face. "Hadn't we better be moving? Someone else may wish to look at the picture as well as we." She smiled as she said this. He flushed. "But what made you say so bitterly just now that your picture was a daub?"

"I had been the unintentional listener of the public verdict Besides"—he flung back his head with a petulant gesture—"do I not know myself that it is a daub! Do I not know what I meant it to be, and what it is! Do I not know how far it falls short of what I dreamed!"

She was silent for a moment Then she asked a question.

"I have more than once wanted to ask you, 'Do you think there is nothing worth living for but art?'"

"Indeed, I don't"

"I thought you didn't"

There was a dryness in her tone which stung him, especially

471

after the glance with which his words had been pointed He spoke coldly.

"There is only one thing better."

"Frankly, I am not quite sure what is my own mind upon the matter. There is so much talked about that sort of thing. But really I doubt if there is anything better worth living for than art"

"For a man there is a woman."

"You mean, I suppose, that for a man there are women."

"Miss Davidson! Don't say that" He put his hand upon her arm. His face was eager and flushed. "That, if you like, is the cant of the day. There is only one woman for a man."

She laughed.

"Suppose I put the converse, and say that for a woman there are men."

"Miss Davidson! That is not true!"

She laughed again, this time a little nervously.

"Don't let us stand in the middle of the room. Pray let us keep moving on."

Just then some acquaintances came up—acquaintances of hers, but not of his. He left her with them.

He wandered off into the sculpture gallery, which, so far as the general and appreciative public were concerned, he found, as usual, a howling wilderness.

"I wonder what I could do to win her love?"

This was the question which that young man addressed to himself among those lonely statues.

"I wonder if it could be won? By me? If it is won already?"

As this last thought occurred to him he actually trembled, which showed that, as a young man, he was something out of the common.

"One thing is necessary, that I should not come to her a pauper. I don't want the tale of the Lord of Burleigh told in just one more new edition. I wonder if I could do something to make money?"

Mr. Philip Major had the first-floor apartments in a house

in Stamford Street Mr. Thompson Gill had the ground-floor rooms. Thus chance, or necessity, had made the tipster and the artist acquainted. That night Mr. Major entered Mr. Gill's sitting-room, an uninvited guest

"Well, Gill, old man, been doing anything more in the prophetic line?"

Mr. Gill, his hands in his trouser-pockets, was seated, staring into vacancy.

"Mr. Major"—he got up; with a mysterious air he approached his visitor—"I do believe there's something wrong."

"How wrong? Has the prophetic tap run dry?"

"I tell you straight, I wish it had run dry. It's quite upsetting me, that's what it's doing. What do you think of the Exmouth Stakes?"

"What about the Exmouth Stakes?"

"I placed the first three horses; that's what's about it, and I sent 'em to all my correspondents—I'm making all their fortunes. I am, straight Why, you know, I'm a tipster; that's what I am, and I ain't ashamed to own it. But though I've been a tipster, I don't know how many years, I mention it to you in confidence that I don't know no more about horses than you do—perhaps not so much. The way I do in general's this. I take the list of probable starters, and I send one horse to one cove, and the second horse to another cove, and so on right through the whole boiling. So somehow, you see, I'm bound to strike the winner, and I don't forget to mention it! But of late I've been upsetting all my regular arrangements. Only the other day I sat down to sort out the bag of tricks as usual, but, if you'll believe me, I couldn't do it Do you thinly I could send every man a different animal? Not me! I sent the same animal to all the lot of 'em; and the queerest part of it is, the beggar won!

"When I see that in the evening paper, I tell you I did feel funny. When, the next day, I began dealing them round again, I couldn't do it no more than before. I sent the first three horses to every half-a-crown subscriber, and they romped in just exactly as I'd placed 'em. That was on Friday, in the Billingsgate

Stakes; on Saturday, when I saw you in the Strand, I'd just done the same in the Chichester Handicap. Yesterday was Monday, and there wasn't no racing; but today in the Exmouth Stakes I've placed the first three horses in the exact order that they came past the post. What do you think of that for a record? Wouldn't you say that there was something wrong with the works?"

"It does you great credit, Gill."

"It isn't so much the horses, I shouldn't mind if it was only them, but it's everything. I can't think of what has happened, but everything that's going to happen I can see quite well."

"Are you in earnest?"

"Try me and see! If there's anything you want to know about what's going to happen in the middle of next week, apply here for information. It's awful—I'm getting a regular freak of nature."

"Do you know, if what you say is correct, you could easily make your fortune—and mine?"

"I suppose I could."

"If, for instance, you were to act on your own tips."

"Just so."

"Then why don't you?"

"I'll tell you one reason why I don't—because I can see what's coming."

"But if you can, that's exactly the reason why you should."

"There's one thing coming tomorrow, and that's an end of me."

"What do you mean?"

"By this time tomorrow I'll be dead."

"You're carrying it too far, my friend."

"I am carrying it too far—I feel I am! I know I am! That's where it is! I don't only see the things I want to see, but I see the things I don't want to see; and I see that by this time tomorrow I'll be dead—ah, dead, sitting in that chair."

Mr. Gill pointed to the chair from which he had lately risen. Mr. Major eyed him. There certainly was something curious about the little man, although he spoke with a matter-of-fact straightforwardness which deprived his words of half their singularity.

"Don't be an ass, Gill! Perhaps you can tell me what, by this time tomorrow night, will have happened to me?"

"You! You'll have made your fortune."

Mr. Major laughed at this.

"Thanks awfully. Perhaps you can assist me with a tip or two?"

"That's just what I'm going to do. I'm going to give you all tomorrow's winners. You'll go down. You'll take every farthing you can beg, borrow, or steal You'll put the whole pile on the first race at starting prices. You'll put the whole pile on again, with all your winnings, on the second race; and you'll do the same on every race; and at the end of the day you'll have won— ah, what a pot!"

"Yes, what a pot! But suppose, in this going the whole hog system of yours, once, only once, I should happen to lose? Where shall I be then?"

"You won't lose; you will win. Take a piece of paper and write down the names of the winners."

Smilingly, perching himself on the edge of the table, Mr. Major took an envelope out of his pocket He prepared to write upon the back of it "Now then, my Gill."

Mr. Gill took a newspaper from the table. For a moment he studied it attentively.

"It's a long programme tomorrow. There are seven events upon the card The first is at half-past one; mind you're there. The Blenheim Plate—Ladybird will win that; write it down." Mr. Major wrote it down, still smiling. "The Windsor Stakes— King Bruce. The Maiden Plate—Sweet Violet The Churchill Handicap—Devil's Own. The Visitors' Plate—Estrella. The Hunt Cup—Ballet Girl." Mr. Gill folded up the newspaper. "Got 'em all down? No mistakes, you know. That's six races—that'll be enough for you; you'll have made your pot by then—and what a pot it will be!" Mr. Major, as he echoed the other's words, still smiled "Yes, what a pot it will be!"

3

"Yes, what a pot it will be!"

The words were still ringing in Mr. Major's ears when, on the morrow, he went down by train to that suburban racecourse. He had not carried out Mr. Gill's advice to the bitter end; he had not stolen, but he had begged and borrowed He had applied for help in as many quarters as he could manage in the limited time at his disposal. He had told some tall tales to get it too. He had pledged his credit to the straining-point He had in his pockets a sum of money which for him was fabulous. If he lost it he would be without a farthing in the world, almost without the hope of one.

He was quite aware that he was mad, that was the joke of it No one knew better than he that for a man who knew nothing of horses to go punting on the turf was an act of simple insanity. Nor did he suppose that the position was improved by the fact that he was about to back the fancies of an avowed humbug who, he himself believed, was at least half imbecile. Yet he never hesitated for a moment to carry out what he knew to be the folly in his brain.

The train was crowded—by that fragrant crowd which travels to a London racecourse, even in the specials. The conversation was horsey. Tips were freely offered. Mr. Major heard the chances of the animals whose names he had written on the back of an old envelope canvassed by persons who were without doubt much better judges of a horse than he. He paid not the slightest heed. All through the din of conversation Mr. Gill's words were ringing in his ears—"What a pot it will be!"

And wherever he looked he saw, as in a waking dream, a woman's face. This young man was simply mad. The most amazing nonsense was whirling in his head. Win a fortune—he'd win her. The two ideas were surging though his head in a sort of chime. He loved the woman—with a sort of honest pride he told himself how earnestly he loved her. He'd make his pile, and tell of his love. And to make his pile he had begged, and borrowed—and lied—all on the strength of an old fool's yarning.

"Would you like a tip, sir?—for the first race, sir? I'll give you a certainty, sir, for a shilling. I'd put it on myself if I had it, sir—so help me, I would."

This was the greeting which he received as he alighted from the train from an individual who evidently thought that he was green.

When he reached the course he made straight for the ring, and for a "leviathan penciller," whom, strangely enough, he knew by sight as well as by name. No welsher for him.

"What price Ladybird for the Blenheim Plate?"

He had never made a bet in his life before, but he had a sort of dim idea that when you did bet that was the way to set about it

"Lay you three to one."

"Put me on four hundred pounds."

Over a hundred pounds of that four hundred were his own savings, for he was beginning to keep his head above water in the artistic world; but how he got the rest of it—it was a sorry tale.

"Lay you seven to two, sir," interposed a lay-you-the-odds gentleman close by.

"I'll lay you seven to two," observed the leviathan calmly. "What name, sir? Mr. Blades, give the gentleman his ticket"

The four hundred pounds were handed over. Mr. Major received in exchange a slip of pasteboard. Someone spoke to him as he turned away, this time not a betting man; someone who had apparently been looking on.

"Jacobs has done you over that bet of yours. He has given you nothing like the proper odds. Anyone, including himself, would have given you five to one."

Mr. Major said nothing, not even to thank the speaker for the information. He took up a position to view the race. It was a fine day. Although it was probable that a crowd would come, it had not come yet. He had no difficulty in finding a favourable point of vantage from which to view the race on which he had staked more than all the money he had in the world. To show what sort of sportsman this young man was one need only mention that he had not even purchased a card. He did not know which was Ladybird, he was not acquainted with the colours she carried, he did not know who her owner was, nor her jockey—as a plain statement of fact he did not know if she was running in the race at all. He saw the start, he saw the animals rush by, he did not see but he knew that the race was over. He heard the roar of voices. He turned to a man beside him—"What's won?"

"Some"—flowery—"outsider." He turned to a friend:"What is it, Jim?"

"I don't know." There was a short pause. "There's the number. Ladybird! Who the somethinged something's Ladybird?"

Mr. Major went down to Mr. Jacobs in the ring. That dignitary greeted him with a nod.

"You were in the know, Mr. Major. Mr. Blades, give Mr. Major eighteen hundred pounds. Would you like to do anything on the next race, Mr. Major?"

Mr. Major counted over his eighteen hundred pounds. Taking out an old envelope from the inner pocket of his coat, he quietly referred to something which was written on the back of it

"Gent's got it all written down, Jake," observed a ribald—and a rival—penciller.

Mr. Jacobs paid no heed to him.

"What price King Bruce for the Windsor Stakes?" inquired Mr. Major.

"Lay you ten to three, mister," yelled one gentleman.

"Lay you eleven to three," bawled another.

Indeed, there was quite a chorus of offers. Mr. Major was indifferent to all of them.

"What price will you give me, Jacobs?"

"King Bruce?" The leviathan regarded Mr. Major with a curious glance. "Well, Mr. Major, I'll give you eleven to three."

"Put me on eighteen hundred pounds."

There was a slight pause of astonishment

"Who is he?" Mr. Major heard someone behind him ask.

"Another Juggins!"

The response was at least as audible as the inquiry had been. There was a laugh. Even Mr. Jacobs seemed amused.

"Eighteen hundred pounds, eleven to three, King Bruce, Mr. Major. Give Mr. Major his ticket, Mr. Blades."

"Look out, Jacobs," shouted a voice, "the young gent means having you."

There was another laugh at this. Mr. Major, serenely indifferent, walked away with Mr. Jacobs' ticket in his pocket

"Kyard, sir! Krect kyard, sir."

Someone thrust something beneath his nose. Then, for the first time, Mr. Major became conscious that he was without that convenience—especially for a novice—a programme of the day. He purchased a card. He found that for the Windsor Stakes there were five runners. King Bruce's colours were light blue. He picked them out when the horses were making ready for starting. As the animals tore past it seemed to him that the one with the light blue jockey on his back was bringing up the rear. It continued in the rear during the few moments in which the proceedings were in sight Suddenly there arose a tumult of many voices.

"By ——! He's won!"

The race was over. A man at his side, who had been following it through a pair of glasses, lowered them with a full-mouthed execration.

"Who's won?"

"King Bruce!"

Mr. Major was conscious of a little fluttering in the region of his chest, as though a pulse had all at once been set vibrating. The people were rushing off in all directions. For a moment he stood still. He studied an old envelope which he took from his pocket Then he started for the ring. Mr. Jacobs received him effusively.

"You are in luck, Mr. Major. You must have had some private information. I shall hardly like to bet with you. How much is it, Mr. Major? Mind you let me down easy." The artist handed in his "brief." "What do you make it, Mr. Blades? Eight thousand four hundred. Is that it, Mr. Major? Why, I shouldn't have so much money in the world if it hadn't been that some other gentlemen have been paying me. I tell you something in confidence. You're the only gentleman I know who was on King Bruce. What are you going to do on the next race, Mr. Major? Back another winner?"

"What price Sweet Violet for the Maiden Plate?"

Mr. Jacobs paused. He sucked the point of his pencil. The usual chorus broke out on either side of him: "I'll lay you two to one, sir."

Mr. Jacobs spoke. "Well, Mr. Major, it's my business to lay against horses at the market odds, I'll give you seven to three, though I'm not quite sure that I am doing the proper thing, you know. How much? The lot?"

Mr. Major held out to him the handful of banknotes which he had just received.

"I don't know, Mr. Major, if you think I've brought the Bank of England out with me, because I haven't; so if I run a little short—and you do seem as though you were going to bleed me—perhaps you wouldn't mind taking my cheque; you'll find it good enough."

"I shall be delighted."

The bet was made. Sweet Violet won easily was the general verdict; though as to that Mr. Major knew nothing. He saw the number go up upon the telegraph, and that was all he knew about it. He received back his eight thousand four hundred pounds, and an open cheque to boot The figures upon that cheque seemed to dance before his eyes. But as he handed over that cheque Mr. Jacob's mood seemed to be by no means effusive.

"That's enough for me, Mr. Major, for today. I'm going to take to backing horses for a change."

Whether Mr. Jacobs meant what he said or not, at any rate, he declined to have anything more to do with Mr. Major.

"You're too clever for me!" he declared.

The artist had to seek a market elsewhere. Not that it took him long to find one—offers to deal rained on him from every side.

"Deal with me—I'm George Foote, Mr. Major."

Mr. Major knew the name—through the sporting prints— "I'll cash Mr. Jacobs' cheque; though, mind you, I shouldn't be surprised if it was a stumer! This is the shop for cheques. What's your fancy, Mr. Major?"

"What price Devil's Own for the Churchill Handicap?"

"I'll give you seven to four, and I'll go you for Mr. Jacobs' cheque."

"Why," shouted a voice in the crowd, "just now you were giving six to one."

"Very well, Mr. Major, you deal with that gentleman over there. He'll lay you six to one—in pennies. Seven to four's my price."

"I want to go for more than the cheque."

"The cheque's big enough for me. What's the size of it? Nineteen thousand six hundred—yes, that's quite big enough for me."

Another penciller addressed himself to Mr. Major.

"How much more do you want to do?"

"Eight thousand five hundred."

"I'll do it at George Foote's price. You know me, I daresay, Tom Grainger, of Nottingham—Grainger with an 'i.'"

Directly the artist had made his bet Devil's Own seemed to be in general demand.

"Mr. Major! You here!"

As Mr. Major was thrusting Mr. Grainger's ticket into his pocket someone addressed him from behind. Turning, there was Miss Davidson. His heart seemed suddenly to cease to beat

"You!" was all that he could gasp.

She laughed.

"I did not know that you were a racing man. Allow me to introduce you to Sir Gerald Mason." Mr. Major was conscious that a resplendent middle-aged gentleman was acting as the lady's escort

"Are you alone?"

Mr. Major explained, stammeringly, that he was. Half unconsciously, he fell in by the lady's side. The three threaded their way among the crowd. They reached a drag.

"I daresay we can find a place for you, if it's only standing room."

Presently Mr. Major found himself, with other ladies and gentlemen, on top of a four-in-hand.

"Well, have you won?" inquired Miss Davidson, who seemed to have taken him under her wing.

"Yes." There was a choking m the artist's throat "Nearly thirty thousand pounds."

"What!"

The artist found himself greeted with a general stare.

"Nearly thirty thousand pounds."

"Today?"

"Yes, all of it today."

Sir Gerald Mason seemed to be particularly struck.

"That's a tidy little trifle," he observed.

Another gentleman came clambering on to the roof.

"I can't make it out There's something up. Just now they were laying anything against Devil's Own. Now they want three to one on."

"I expect," said Mr. Major, "it's because of me."

"Because of you?" The newcomer stared.

"Oh!"

"I've just been backing him for nearly thirty thousand pounds!"

"The deuce you have!"

"He's sure to win."

"Is he, indeed? May I ask how you know it?"

"A person with whom I am acquainted gave me yesterday the names of all today's winners. Devil's Own is one of them. I have them here." Mr. Major took out an old, soiled envelope. There was something written in pencil on the back of it He held it out in front of him. There was a universal smile. The artist was aware of it "I came out this morning with four hundred pounds. I have backed three of the horses whose names are on this envelope. I have already won nearly thirty thousand pounds. I have placed it all upon Devil's Own. Devil's Own will win. All the horses whose names are on this envelope will win. I am sure of it"

In his voice there was a ring of enthusiastic conviction. His eyes met Miss Davidson's. She smiled at him. "I hope they will, for your sake."

"Thank you. I knew you would."

He held out his hand to her. She gave him hers, blushing as she did so. The other people on the drag glanced at one another. When Miss Davidson withdrew her hand she turned to the course.

"We shall soon know if your prediction is true; they are starting."

They were starting, though they did not start just then. Racehorses are not to be induced to start by clockwork. But, at last, the flag was dropped. The runners came flying down the course.

"George!" exclaimed Sir Gerald Mason. "It's a procession!"

A horse had run off with the lead. He not only kept it, but increased it as he went The race was finished.

"A walk over for Devil's Own," remarked the gentleman who last had clambered on to the coach. He turned to Mr. Major, "I should like, sir, to know your friend."

"How much have you won, Mr. Major?"

The inquiry came from Miss Davidson. Mr. Major glanced at his couple of pasteboards.

"I have eight thousand four hundred on with one man, and nineteen thousand six hundred with another; that's twenty-eight thousand pounds, at seven to four that's forty-nine thousand pounds."

Someone so far forgot good manners as to whistle; it was the gentleman who had clambered on to the coach. Mr. Major's glance sought Miss Davidson's. Her eyes were gleaming.

"All won? I congratulate you."

"Really?"

"With all my heart"

His cheeks were flushed. His eyes were gleaming too. Words seemed trembling on his tongue. Before he could utter them he was assailed with a question.

"What's going to win the next?"

It came in half a dozen voices. He glanced at the back of the envelope.

"Estrella will win the Visitors' Plate."

"Estrella! She'll never stay the course; and she's nowhere in the betting."

"As for being nowhere in the betting, all the better for small punters like myself," remarked the elderly Sir Gerald.

He descended to the ground; the others seemed to be all talking together. Mr. Major and Miss Davidson for the moment were unnoticed.

"What are you going to do? You're not going to do any more betting?"

"I am. I am going to put every penny upon Estrella."

"Oh, Mr. Major!"

"Miss Davidson, I know that I shall win."

"You seem very confident But you know you cannot always have good fortune. And you are playing for high stakes, you must remember."

"I am, for the highest possible. I am playing for the greatest prize in the world."

His earnestness seemed to abash her.

"Whatever it is I hope you will win it"

"You mean it?"

She turned away.

"Of course I do."

He hesitated. He seemed about to speak. Then, with a sudden impulse, he too descended to the ground.

"Put on five pounds for me," she said to him as he went down. "I'll back your luck."

He looked up at her, his face peony red. But he was speechless. His entry into the ring was greeted with something like applause: already he was famous. In his mastering excitement he did not notice it

"Hollo! Mr. Major," cried Mr. Grainger of Nottingham, "don't you think you're knocking 'em? Are you going for the gloves? Do you want to break the lot of us? We've all got wives and children, and we don't want to see 'em in the workhouse. What' s the next article, Mr. Major?"

"What price Estrella for the Visitors' Plate?"

For a moment it seemed that there was no price. Then Mr. Grainger made a bid.

"I'll do you at evens, but not for a million, you know."

"I won't do you at any price," said Mr. Foote, who seemed unhappy. "I say with Mr. Jacobs—Mr. Major's too clever for me."

Sir Gerald Mason was standing by the artist's side.

"Evens!" he exclaimed. "Why, Estrella's quoted at forty to one."

"Oh, that was before Mr. Major was on. Mr. Major's hand-in-glove with the Old Gentleman—he's got the key of the stable."

Mr. Jacobs interposed.

"Look here, mister, I don't know who you are, but you've got twenty-eight thousand pounds of my money. Go you double or quits; evens against Estrella."

"I'll come in with you, Jacobs," cried an enterprising gentleman, whose name was Johnson—that well-known patron of "the fancy." "I'll do you the same price in any sum you choose, Mr. Major—a million if you like—I think I'm good for it!"

Mr. Major had to be content with the terms.

"I haven't done very well for you, Miss Davidson," he explained when he returned to the drag. "I've only got evens."

"It's a robbery," declared the elderly Sir Gerald; "rank robbery!"

"Rather too barefaced robbery for me." Thus Mr. Wilmot, which was the name of the gentleman who had clambered last on to the drag. "I don't think this time your friend has done you a good turn, Mr. Major. From her form Estrella hasn't the ghost of a chance. Personally, I should say the odds against her were more than forty to one."

"By Jove!" exclaimed a ruddy-faced young gentleman, with a "pane of glass" in his eye, "I hope she will win! I've a monkey on her!"

"Not to mention my five pounds," laughed Miss Davidson.

"Your money is quite safe. Estrella will win—I know it"

"Excuse me, Mr. Major," said Mr. Wilmot, "but your tone would almost suggest that you had been getting at somebody or something on a very extensive scale. You seem cock-sure."

"I am cock-sure."

"They're off!"

They were. Mr. Wilmot' s glasses followed the race.

"A capital start Bedgown's leading—Canute second. Hollo! The Squire's coming. Estrella's nowhere. The Squire's in front! What's that slipped through—Patience? Patience is coming! Come on. Patience; The Squire is racing her! Where's your Estrella, Mr. Major? She don't seem to be in this race. Patience is ahead! Bravo, Patience! By George, Canute's coming! He's in front! He's running away from 'em! Just look how he's going! It's all over—Canute for a million! Hollo! how about your Estrella, Mr. Major? What's that—what's that in blue and pink? It's—it's Estrella! Dashed if she isn't coming on; hang me if she isn't! My eyes, how she's travelling! If there's time, she'll overhaul the leader! She has! She's collared him! She's racing him! She's passed him! Gosh! she's won!"

"I've won over a hundred and fifty thousand pounds." With one accord they turned to Mr. Major, He seemed in a sort of ecstasy. He repeated the words, "I've won over a hundred and fifty thousand pounds. I knew Estrella'd win."

Mr. Wilmot looked a little white.

"It's uncommonly queer," he said.

"It is queer; I know it's queer. But I knew she'd win."

Miss Davidson spoke.

"I congratulate you, Mr. Major, with all my heart I never knew anyone who won a hundred and fifty thousand pounds before—and in a single day!"

"I shall win more before I've finished."

"You are surely not going to tempt Fortune again?"

"No—not fortune! The man who gave me the names of the horses which I have here was inspired. It was given to him to see behind the veil. I half suspected it at the time. I see it clearly now. It is not Fortune I am tempting; I am betting upon certainties. I know that every horse he gave me is sure to win!"

The people looked at one another. They were apparently in doubt as to whether this young gentleman was altogether sane. "What has this very remarkable friend of yours given you for the Cup?"

"Ballet Girl."

"That sounds more promising. Ballet Girl's my own fancy, and the favourite. But, if you take my advice, Mr. Major, you'll keep out of the ring. Let me deal for you. If they know you're dealing it'll knock the market all to pieces; you'll get no price at all"

"What does it matter what price I get? What does it matter if I have to give ten to one if I know the horse will win?"

Mr. Wilmot shrugged his shoulders.

"Of course, if you know, there's nothing further to be said."

Mr. Major found the ring in a panic. His entry was greeted with a roar of voices.

"Mr. Major, you've about broke me," yelled Mr. Jacobs. Then came a volley of adjectives. "I can't make things out at all. Upon my soul, I don't know that I didn't ought to appeal to the stewards."

Someone shouted in the crowd—

"Pay up, Jake, and look pleasant!"

"I'll pay up," said Mr. Jacobs; "but as for looking pleasant—"
There came more adjectives.

"What are you going to do in the Hunt Cup, Mr. Major?"
The inquiry came from neither Mr. Jacobs nor Mr.

Grainger.

"What price Ballet Girl?"

It was odd, after the previous tumult, to notice the silence with which Mr. Major's words were greeted—the completer silence still which followed them. No one made a price.

"You're surely not afraid of one man? What, all the lot of you?"

"Dash me!" roared Mr. Jacobs. "No man shall say that I'm afraid of him—not if I have to go into the workhouse tomorrow. I'll tell you what I'll do, Mr. Major. I'll give you the chance to make the biggest bet that was ever made in England. You've got over a hundred and fifty thousand pounds there, and by ——! most of it's mine. If you like to put the lot of it on Ballet Girl, at five to one on, I'll take you."

"Five to one on?" shouted the crowd.

"Five to one on!" vociferated Mr. Jacobs. "And that's an offer which I doubt if any other man upon this course will make you."

It was not a tempting offer, but Mr. Major took it

"You're a very foolish man, sir," said Mr. Wilmot, who was standing at his elbow.

"Why? I know the horse will win."

"You may know, but I don't, and you've spoilt the market for other men."

The start was a long time coming. While they waited for it there was considerable excitement on the top of the drag.

"Mr. Major," said Miss Davidson, "I do hope that mysterious friend of yours is right again. It will be a dreadful thing if Ballet Girl should fail us. We are all of us on her to a man."

"And at such a price!" growled Mr. Wilmot "Upon my word, I am ashamed of myself when I think that I ever allowed myself to be induced to back any horse at such a figure."

Mr. Major was standing by Miss Davidson. His eyes, which rested on her, were eloquent with many things. Always good-looking, just then he was even curiously handsome.

"Ballet Girl will win; I am sure of it. Then—then I shall never bet again."

"Never?"

"Never. I don't think I ever bet before. I never shall again."

"Your luck has been fabulous—really quite incredible. If I had been you I should have been content with what I'd won. To risk it all seems—seems dreadful."

"Why? You would be prepared to bet that two and two make four a thousand times in succession."

"But that is different."

"Not at all. Just as certainly as you know that two and two make four, I know that Ballet Girl will win. I shall have made my fortune. I shall have only one thing left to win. Only one!"

Someone said they were getting ready to start All eyes were turned towards the course. Mr. Wilmot's glasses again came into play.

"Isn't that Tragedy Queen who won't stand still? Up go her heels! Now there's Chappie joining her!"

Mr. Major, under cover of the gathering excitement, half whispered to Miss Davidson—

"I shall have only one thing left to win."

"I hope you will win it, whatever it is." She faced him. "Mr. Major, I do hope Ballet Girl will win."

"I know she will."

"They're off!"

They were. Mr. Wilmot favoured them with a running commentary.

"A good start! What's that in the black and white hoops in front? Hollo! Chappie's making the pace. Tragedy Queen seems to be funking it, or is young Blades holding her in? Ballet Girl seems to be running third. White will get himself shut in if he doesn't look out Hollo! Chappie's ahead! Mark Antony's challenging him! They're making a ding-dong thing of it, by George! Ballet Girl's creeping up; so's Tragedy Queen. What is that in the black and white hoops? Isn't it Bar One? It is Bar One! Ballet Girl is coming on. By gad, she is! Hark at the people shouting. Our five to one chance looks rosy, Mr. Major. She's collared

Chappie! Tragedy Queen is sticking to her. It strikes me it's going to be a race between the pair of them. Bar One's third. Isn't Ballet Girl just flying? Bravo! Why, there must be two lengths between her and Tragedy Queen! Hark at the people! I say, Mr. Major, the devil must be in that friend of yours; Ballet Girl's half a dozen lengths in front! She's having a lark with them! She's—why!—what is that? She's down! down! My God! Why don't White pick her up? There's something wrong! Tragedy Queen's passed her! So's Bar One! Bar One's gaining! Bar One's in front!—!—!" Mr. Wilmot must have forgotten the presence of ladies. And in that hot moment it is not impossible that his forgetfulness was overlooked "Bar One's won!" He turned on Mr. Major. "Bar One has won!"

There was a hubbub of many voices, a wild rush of people on to the course, where Ballet Girl lay motionless. Her last race was run. The flush had faded from Mr. Major's cheeks, the light from his eyes.

"I have lost!—lost !—lost it all!" He turned to Miss Davidson. You—you won't let it make any difference?"

"Make any difference?"

"I did it all for you. I—I did not like to come to you with empty hands."

"Mr. Major! What do you mean?"

"Although I loved you so, I did not like to think that you were rich and I was poor. If I had won I should have given it all to you—it would have been for you that it was won."

The lady turned away. It almost seemed that this remarkable young gentleman was making a declaration of affection, in public, on the roof of a drag, right before the eyes—the ears!—of a number of amazed and bewildered strangers.

"You—you won't let it make any difference because—because I have lost"

The lady favoured him with a front view. Her cheeks were a flaming red; but, in spite of it, she was the more self-possessed of the two.

"I think, Mr. Major, that excitement has turned your brain. It is rather a singular place in which to volunteer such a statement, but I don't know if you are aware that I am engaged to be married to Mr. Philip Cumberland?"

"Engaged? To Mr. Cumberland?" It was piteous to see the young man's face. "But he's in Oban."

"I don't know how you know he is in Oban. Nor do I see why his being in Oban should make any difference to the fact of our engagement"

"But—why did you buy my picture?"

"My good sir, I have never bought any picture of yours."

"Gill said it was you."

"You seem to be favoured with some curious friends. I have not the honour of Mr. Gill's acquaintance. Had I purchased your picture, I do not see how the purchase would have warranted your peculiar behaviour. As a matter of fact, I have done nothing of the kind."

Mr. Wilmot slipped his arm through Mr. Major's.

"Come, my friend, I think you and I had better take a stroll together. You seem to have let us in for a very nice thing!"

4

"Gill!" Mr. Major knocked at the door again. "Gill!" There was still no answer. He turned the handle. The door was open. Mr. Major entered. The lamp was still unlighted, but he could see that Mr. Gill was seated at the table. "Gill!" Mr. Gill continued silent Mr. Major went and touched him on the shoulder. "Gill!"

He started back. Mr. Gill was dead!

"Starvation—that's what it is."

Thus spoke the landlady, hastily summoned to the presence of the newly dead.

"Starvation!"

The young man turned his ghastly face to the woman's.

"Starvation. He's been slowly starving this ever so long. I don't believe he's tasted a morsel of meat these last two weeks. He owed me seven weeks' rent. But he was such an old lodger I didn't like to be hard on him. Now, I suppose, I shall lose it all"

"But I thought he had so many clients?"

"Not one. He used to have when first I knew him, but they turned him up—long ago! I don't believe he ever named a winner in his life. I know more than once he put me on a wrong one. Of late things have been preying on his mind. It's my belief that for nearly a week now he's been quite cracked."

Mr. Major wondered.

A Knight of the Road
(A tale from *Both Sides of the Veil*)

1

It was in a house that stood close by the Cocoa Tree. They had been playing high. Nor had they spared the wine. Still there was not one there whose hand was not steady enough to rattle the box; and that however much his brains might reel. And as if to show that there is not of necessity virtue in the teaching which bids a punter keep his head both cool and clear, the heaviest loser was the soberest man. And yet, again, how much of temperament there is in this! Be it the stomach, be it the head, one man can drain the sea where another cannot drain his glass. Right from the first Mr. Lovell had drunk deep, deeper than them all, and yet, while it would have needed but the gentlest persuasion to have induced more than one to have taken up for the night his lodging on the floor, he was as much himself as ever he was. By all the rules of play this man had won. But, the plain fact was, he had lost. In that one sitting lost all he had.

Sir Will Pettifer challenged him, with a hiccoughing tongue and a murky eye.

"O-one m-more c-c-cast!"

"I thank you, Will,—not one."

He brushed a grain of snuff lightly, with his frilled handkerchief, from the collar of his coat. Then he addressed to the assembled company this little speech—

"Gentlemen, I am drained—dry. I go from here—a beggar. This morning I drew from my man of business the remain-

493

der of my fortune. Tonight I have divided it among this gallant company. 'Twas seventeen thousand pounds. One may divide seventeen thousand pounds in a many parts, yet have I divided it almost in two. You have near nine thousand, Will. Mr. Pacy, you have six. To the rest of the company I desire my apologies if the division seems unsociable."

Mr. Pacy was a big man with a red face—a countryman. By him was a great heap of notes and gold. This he crammed into his pockets.

"Six thousand pounds! I'll with it to Hammersmith! I'll share it with Mistress Meg!"

When he heard these words Sir Will sprang to his feet and struck the table with his hand.

"Tha-at I've a m-mind to do!"

Mr. Pacy looked him straightly in the face. He bore his liquor with less ostentation than Sir Will.

"Then luck befriend the first!" he cried. And rose to go.

As he was going Mr. Lovell took him by the arm.

"To Hammersmith? That's a lonely road! With six thousand pounds! At this hour of the night! Have you a mind to carry the division further? To extend your charity to the gentlemen that ride the road?"

"Were there a thousand thieves that barred the road I'd ride to Hammersmith tonight! I have a mind to share my gains with Mistress Meg."

He was an obstinate man when the drink was out. When the drink was in an exposition of clear logic carried more meaning to a pig than it did to him. And where he was one fool, Sir Will, for very emulation's sake, made two. Besides, these were ancient rivals for the heart of Mistress Margaret Mathers. Mistress Mathers called herself a widow. God wot of whom! For they were many. So they rode off to Hammersmith. Mr. Pacy first, for his horse stood outside the door a-catching cold. Sir Will had none of his own. So he had to hunt for a steed to bear him to the fair. And since, in the middle of the night, horses are not to be had for whistling, it was a hunt which took some time.

Mr. Pacy went plodding steadily on. He rode fifteen stone, and perhaps a little more, so that it was not every beast that, with him on its back, went like the wind. Bruin—so he called the animal he rode that night—was better at weight than speed. Six miles an hour, with his master mounted, was all he cared to go. That night Mr. Pacy worried and hustled him until, at times, he rose to eight. The gentleman kept looking back, with his ears well cocked, to catch the first sounds of Sir Will following, like fate, behind.

To cheer the way he thought of his six thousand pounds, and of Mistress Meg in all her gorgeous array. Six thousand pounds! 'Twould make her sweet as honey and gorgeous as the god of day. But Sir Will had his nine thousand. If he were first upon the field Mr. Pacy feared that in the light of Sir Will's nine the glory of his six would fade away. So he did his best to induce Bruin to better his six-mile jog and make it eight.

At the turnpike the keeper, of course, was fast asleep. So fast indeed that Mr. Pacy had serious thoughts of putting Bruin at the gate to take it in his stride. But as Bruin made it clear that his thoughts were all the other way, he contented himself with battering and damning until the fellow was aroused from slumber and let him through. Then a lucky thought occurred to him. He gave the keeper a piece of gold to fall so fast asleep that he would never hear Sir Will until he had hammered at least a good half-hour. Then he rode on, congratulating himself that Sir Will's language would be at least as bad as his had been and worse.

He was nearing the hut in which lived the woman that was reported to be a witch, chuckling to himself, when something happened which drove all the chuckle out of him. All at once there stood a horse in front of him, his rider's hand was laid on Bruin's bridle, and, what was more, there was a pistol whose muzzle was within twelve inches of Mr. Pacy's nose. He had come so suddenly, this stranger, that Mr. Pacy did not understand whence he came, nor how. He was all bewildered.

"Stand and deliver!"

That was all the stranger said. He had a piece of crape before his face, and seemed indeed a most determined fellow.

"I have not a shilling," Mr. Pacy said. "I have lost it all at play tonight, and am journeying homewards to my wife."

Bang! whiz-z-z! The stranger had fired. The bullet grazed Mr. Pacy's cheek. Congratulating himself on what he supposed was his escape, he raised his hand to strike the other down. But, hey, presto! the pistol was dropped and there was another in the fellow's hand. It was like a conjurer's trick.

"That was for warning! This will hit its mark. Do you think that is the only one I carry? See here!"

The stranger undid his coat and disclosed a belt in which, in the dim light, for there was neither moon nor stars, there seemed a dozen pistols stuck at least. Mr. Pacy felt that it was time to treat. "Sir, I do not think I have a guinea in my purse."

"You lie!"

The stranger's tones were clear and cold, and struck unpleasantly on Mr. Pacy's ears.

"You have won six thousand pounds this night at play. Such as I do not attack a bird if we are not sure he will be worth our plucking. Hand over the six thousand! And, because of the lie that you have told, every ha'porth that you have besides."

"I'll give you half."

"Nor yet three-quarters! I'll have the whole."

"'Tis very hard!" Mr. Pacy said. And "'Tis very hard!" he said again, when the stranger had bidden him a courteous goodnight, and he was left to pursue his way alone. He hesitated as to what, in his sorry plight, it were best to do. To proceed to Mistress Meg without a stiver in his purse would be absurd. With the widow love meant money.

"Is there nothing left for me?"

As Mr. Pacy mused, all at once these words were spoken in his ears. He started as he had been struck. Then turned, and lo! there was another fellow with crape before his face and a pistol in his hand.

"'Fore God!" he cried, with a great oath. "This is a pleasant journeying."

496

This newcomer was of a different make to him who just now had gone. A small, mean man, that wore a hang-dog air.

"Sir," he inquired, "is there nothing left for me?"

"And that there's not! Not the value of a brass farthing's worth! Your friend has plucked me clean! It will hardly pay the cost of powder were you to put a bullet in my head."

"The greedy rogue!" exclaimed this second honest man.

"It was the devil!—or his friend!"

"Sir, it was a gentleman."

'A gentleman! By my life, but he is one now! It is with a good deal more than six thousand pounds that he rides away."

The stranger threw his hands up to the skies. There came from him a sound which was between and betwixt a gasp and a sigh.

"Ye saints in paradise! Sir, I have been upon the road these seven years! In all that time I have not earned the half of that. Yet here comes a gentleman who, just for a frolic, takes to the road but for a single night, and in one sweep doubles the earnings of my seven years. It is hard upon a persevering man. Sir, I have children and a wife to keep. It is not a thing I often do, but under the circumstances I entreat you will forgive me if I relieve you of your coat. 'Twill mean a morning's meal for my children, sir."

"My coat!" Mr. Pacy was aghast. "God's truth, it is a pleasant company one meets!"

And so he told himself again when the stranger, bearing his children's morning meal before him on his horse, had rode away. It was with a heavy heart that Mr. Pacy turned Bruin's head and, in his shirt sleeves, retraced his way. *Adieu* his dreams of gentle dalliance with Mistress Meg! *Adieu* his coat as well! As for the six thousand pounds,—God's curse go with the rogue who plundered him!

He hammered and hammered at the gatekeeper's house. It was with an added bitterness that he thought of the gold piece he had given him, and how he had paid the fellow to sleep sound. To think that he had paid a guinea to be kept shivering in his shirt sleeves all night!

"If I'd a match I'd set the place a-blaze!" *Bang! Bang! Crash!* He hammered with all his might upon the shuttered window-frame. "You fool! 'Tis not the other man! 'Tis I!"

But this was a deserving fellow that desired to earn his wage both faithfully and well. It was the full half-hour before he waked. When he showed his sleepy head, Mr. Pacy was well-nigh spent with rage. It must have warmed the cockles of the keeper's heart, the flood of oaths that poured from the belated traveller's scalding tongue.

They parted with a mutual malediction. Each felt himself aggrieved; though it is doubtless true that the coatless gentleman felt his grievance most. Because of his affliction Bruin suffered wrong. He pounded the poor beast until the creature felt that instead of fifteen stone it must be fifty which he bore upon his back. But still greater wrong awaited him before he saw his crib that night.

As Bruin toiled painfully, and Mr. Pacy furiously, on, suddenly a voice was heard from the roadside. It was a voice Mr. Pacy knew full well,—none other than that belonging to Sir Will. A figure rose from the bank that bordered the road. It was the gay young baronet. But in what a plight! Hatless, without his wig, as though he had been rolled in the mire and dust. Mr. Pacy was amazed. "God's truth! It's Will Pettifer!" he cried.

"What's left of him." The baronet seemed quite sober now. Then he perceived that it was Mr. Pacy, and that it was in his shirt lie rode. "Jack! Without a coat! Riding from Hammersmith, instead of to! What's happened now!"

With many curses Mr. Pacy told of the parting with the six thousand pounds, and then of the coat that went to provide the children's morning meal. The baronet was like a man who has heard the strangest thing that ever yet he heard.

"What! You too! Of all the pretty games that ever yet was played! Jack, as he came from robbing you, he robbed me too!"

"What! The rogue that took the coat?"

"No! He with the six thousand pounds!"

"God's truth!" was all that Mr. Pacy said. Then he added, as though lost in thought, "Not the whole nine thousand, Will?"

"The whole nine thousand! And not that alone. There was another thousand, and more, besides. Jack, between us he has rode off with seventeen thousand pounds!"

"If I knew the fellow I'd treat with him to marry Susan Anne." Susan Anne was Mr. Pacy's sister, a damsel that was past her prime. "It would be a great thing for the girl to get a husband with seventeen thousand pounds."

"You fool! Who was it told us he had lost seventeen thousand pounds tonight?"

"Where are you driving now? Why, 'tis just the sum that Gerard Lovell lost!"

"And won! He has lost and won seventeen thousand pounds all in a single night! Why do you stare? It is as plain as Jack of diamonds. 'Tis Lovell was the thief!"

"Will! God's truth! You don't mean that!"

"Upon my soul I do! 'Tis his revenge he's had. Mine is still to come. It was his voice!"

Mr. Pacy scratched his head.

"I thought that I had heard the voice before!"

"It was his horse!"

"I did not mind his horse."

"It was him, every inch! Besides, how came he to know I carried nine, and you six thousand pounds? How came he to name the very sum? Did he not know we rode to Hammersmith? Did he himself not warn us of the gentlemen upon the road? 'Tis he has done the riding, and, faith! he's ridden well; but I will cry him evens yet before the dawn."

Mr. Pacy still scratched his head.

"The fellow that took my coat said it was a gentleman that did the trick! But Lovell! God's truth! To think 'twas he!"

"What sort of beast is it you ride? I had my screw from Spavin, and when that villain threw me—'fore God, it was the nearest thing! I know 'twas he from that; I've seen him do it in the wrestling ring—the three-legged brute went tearing off. Before now he's at home with Spavin in the yard. I am so sprained

I could not walk to save my life. Let me get up behind. He'll take us both home, I'll swear."

And so it chanced that still greater wrong was done to Bruin. Before he understood that such villainy was even in the air, the baronet was on his back. And so he had to bear a double load. Of a surety that was the greatest wrong of all.

2

Mr. Lovell lived in Rider Street. It was very early in the morning when there came a clamouring at the street door. On the ground floor there lived a Captain Philip Ashton, that had fought in William's wars, and had left a leg in the Low Countries. When Anne came in, he came into a fortune, God alone knows how— unless he stole it, which was the most likely thing to happen with a Whig.

Since then he had set up as a gentleman that kept two rooms, and had increased in the art, to swear, since he had of necessity decreased in the art, to fight. Mr. Lovell had his rooms above the captain's, so, as was natural, 'twas the captain heard the clamour first. He put his head out of the window, all in his bedgown as he was.

"Who knocks so late?" And then came that eloquence of oaths for which he was famed almost more than any man in town. "Ods cannons rot you! 'Tis more than an hour ere the first cock shall crow!"

Then came an answer from the street.

"Sir, 'tis Mr. Lovell we desire to see. 'Tis a matter, sir, of life and death."

The captain saw there were two men and but one horse. And one of the men was without a coat, and the other was without a hat and wig. He that was hatless sang out—

"You know me, Captain Ashton, I'm Will Pettifer, and Mr. Pacy here is my good friend."

The captain strapped on his wooden peg and then stumped to the street door.

"Mr. Lovell is above," began Sir Will. "Captain Ashton, I desire that you will go up with us and be witness of what we have to say unto this gentleman."

So they all three went upstairs, a motley crew. Clatter, clatter went their steps upon the stairs, yet when they reached Mr. Lovell's room it would seem that the din had not awaked that gentleman from sleep. It was twice they knocked before from within there came a voice inquiring who was here.

"The scoundrel!" exclaimed Sir Will. "He pretends he is in bed! Was ever such hypocrisy before!"

Yet when Mr. Lovell undid the door it seemed indeed as though he were but just aroused from sleep, for his eyes were heavy and he was all undressed.

"Sir Will!—Mr. Pacy!—Ashton!—What frolic brings you here?" His surprise, it seemed quite natural, and indeed his whole manner was of a man who is not yet quite wide awake. But Sir Will, with a certain roughness, pushed him aside and strode into the room, with Mr. Pacy and the captain following hard upon his heels.

"Thou prince of actors! Thou damned hypocrite!" Sir Will stretched out his hand towards him with an unusual bitterness.

"Will!" he cried, like one amazed.

"Captain Ashton, you see this gentleman, you see the state his room is in, like one who has slept here honestly the whole night through. He does not look like one who has just returned from robbing of his friends! And that on the high road! And yet 'tis so! He has played the part of highwayman this very night, and robbed Mr. Pacy and myself of seventeen thousand pounds."

"Will!" cried Mr. Lovell, still as one amazed.

Sir Will was so enraged he sprang at Mr. Lovell and caught him by the throat.

"You thief! You gallows spawn! That was a scurvy trick you played! Had you not thrown me from my horse even now my sword had been sticking in your heart!" He threw Mr. Lovell from him with much force. "Jack, go fetch the constables. We should have brought them with us at the first. 'Tis only they can deal with such a knave."

Mr. Pacy turned to go. But Mr. Lovell stepped between the door and him.

"One moment, Mr. Pacy, if you please.—Sir William Pettifer, when I last saw you you were drunk. Am I to understand you are drunk still?"

"You thief!" Sir Will exclaimed. He would have been at Mr. Lovell's throat again had not the captain interposed. Mr. Lovell, in the face of all the other's rage, was both calm and cool, and the dignity of conscious rectitude was in his air in spite of his undress.

"Mr. Pacy, you seem calmer than your friend. What is it you charge me with?"

"You robbed me of six thousand pounds."

"I robbed you of six thousand pounds! How came I to do that?"

"That's what I want to know, whence you came and how. I know that you all at once were there, upon that barb of yours, with a piece of crape before your face and a dozen pistols in your belt, with one of which you scored my cheek—here is the place—where it touched me now—and that you rode away leaving me without so much as a button that I might pawn."

"Captain Ashton, do I dream? or am I in fact awake?"

"You seem to me to be awake, that is if I'm not dreaming too, for it is the strangest tale that ever yet I heard, 'fore God it is."

"Sir William Pettifer, have I robbed you too?"

"Of ten thousand pounds, you knave! But I see plainly you would outbrazen hell,—I'll not contend! Jack, who'll fetch the constables? Is it you or I must go?"

Mr. Lovell drew himself straight up. He was very quiet and very stern.

"Gentlemen, in the presence of that God before whom we stand I do declare that I have never left the house this night— that is, since I parted with these gentlemen at the Cocoa Tree hard by. I am guiltless of this foul crime which, in my innocence, it seems to me that only madness can lay to my charge. I am willing to submit myself to the minions of the law whenever it shall please these gentlemen. But I would advise Sir William Pettifer of this, that sooner or later he shall render me satisfaction with his own right arm. And I would suggest to him that since he uses such bold words he should carry his boldness one small step farther, and submit this matter to the ordeal of the Most High God. Afterwards, there will still be at his service all the terrors of the law."

"Gentlemen do not fight with thieves," replied Sir Will.

"Then, Sir William Pettifer, hear this! While they go fetch the officers I will kill you with my own hands for the cur and coward which you are. That is the only crime with which they ever shall be stained."

"I think that you had better fight him, Will. Or if you shirk it, why then I'll take him on."

Sir Will turned on Mr. Pacy in a rage.

"Shirk it! Do you think I fear?"

"If you can, Sir William Pettifer, look me boldly in the face. Why, I am sure you fear. You dare not meet my eyes. I do believe it is some trick you try, and you yourself have played the thief!"

"That caps it!" cried Sir Will. "I'll fight him now!"

"Captain Ashton," said Mr. Lovell, "have you sufficient faith in the justice of my cause to be my friend?"

The captain was always ready to play the second if he could not be the first, and rather than not have figured on such a scene he would have played the second to Old Nick. So they went out to fight. Mr. Lovell and the captain put on their clothes, but Mr. Pacy and Sir Will went as they were. Sir Will was to have Mr. Pacy's sword, since his own had been snapped in two when he had fallen from his horse.

It was in Hyde Park they fought. In that part of it in which so many suchlike frolic games are played. Sir Will had his back towards the Cake House, and Mr. Lovell had his towards the Ring. It was an uncertain light, since the shimmerings of the dawn were only just beginning to be seen in the sky. Still it was light enough for two serious gentlemen, that meant business, to see the points of their swords.

Before they set to, Mr. Lovell said, and he spoke like a man who is very much in earnest—

"Captain Ashton, I desire you to understand that I am innocent of this crime that is laid to my charge, nor know I any reason why this gentleman should bear me enmity. I submit my cause to God. He shall adjudge the right."

Strangely enough, ere these words could have well ceased fluttering through the bars of heaven's gates, the thing was judged. Although there was no better swordsman in the town than was the gay young baronet, all at once his skill seemed to have deserted him. They all observed the confusion with which he handled his blade. While Mr. Lovell's was like an avenging sword. Hardly had the word been given than he ran Sir William right through the heart, so that he fell stone dead. Withdrawing his sword, Mr. Lovell bent over his fallen foe.

"God has judged!" he said. Then he began to mourn. "Oh, Will, my friend, what madness has overtaken you this night!" Then he stood straight up. "Gentlemen, I call you to witness that this was in fair fight."

Then he put on his clothes and wiped his sword, and went away, leaving the seconds to guard the dead.

It was now getting near the dawn. In the Park there it was light. And there was a fresh breeze that whispered among the grasses and rustled through the leaves. The sky was nearly clear, and there was a suspicion that at any moment, perhaps, the sun might burst in all his glory on the world. It bade fair, in fact, to be a beauteous morn. And Mr. Lovell walked over the grassy slope with his hands behind his back like a man who bears a conscience that is at peace with God and man. And yet there was something of sorrow in his gait—perchance it was sorrow for his friend.

But as he approached the road, more than once he paused, and looked round and stared and listened. And then seeing there was none in sight, went on again. And then again would pause, and go again through the same pantomime as he had done before. It was strange! It seemed to him that he heard footfalls which came close behind him on the grass. Yet when he turned, lo! none was there.

"It is a trick of the imagination!" he declared, and journeyed on. But no sooner had he started than there came the sound again, is of someone who stepped lightly on the grass keeping step with him a few feet behind. Yet when he turned again still none was there.

"It is an echo!" he observed. With his handkerchief he wiped his lips and went his way.

It was the strangest kind of echo that ever was. It kept pace with him all along the grass, seeming to mock his steps. The coolest gentleman was Mr. Lovell, yet this curious echo seemed to trouble him, for he kept giving furtive glances over his shoulder ,is he went. He went upon the gravel, and the echo went with him there. And when he got outside the park there happened the strangest thing of all.

The echo quickened its pace, and came running after. Suddenly a hand was laid upon his shoulder, and Mr. Lovell turned, and behold! a gentleman looked in his face who had come God knows from where. And when he saw this gentleman all at once Mr. Lovell looked like a man who has received his death. God alone wots why! So for some moments they stood, face to face, neither speaking. It seemed as though Mr. Lovell had lost the power of speech. But at last there came, as it might be, a sort of frenzied convulsion of all the muscles in his face, which was horrible to see, and then he spake. But not in his usual clear, soft tones, but in a voice which had the hollow sound of a voice from the grave.

"Who are you that dogs my steps and intercepts me on the public way? I believe I do not know you, sir."

The strange gentleman smiled. That was all he did. Yet Mr. Lovell sank down on his knees, and covered his face with his hands, and was seized with a convulsive agony—there in the highway. The stranger stood and looked at the strong man trembling as with palsy at his feet. He touched him with his finger's tip and said—"Rise up!"

It was as though he had weaved a spell. Mr. Lovell rose to his feet. The stranger passed his right arm through Mr. Lovell's left. A shudder went all over him, and then it was as though he were carved in stone.

"Home!" the stranger said.

Mechanically Mr. Lovell moved his feet, and looking neither to the right nor to the left he went straight on. The sun had just begun to rise. They met no passers-by on the way, yet all the air seemed filled with cries of pain. If Mr. Lovell heard he paid no heed, and for the stranger, he bore continually upon his countenance a smile of wondrous beauty, and yet one which in some strange way seemed filled with the intensest agony of pain,— pain which nothing human shall bear yet live.

When they reached Rider Street there still stood the patient Bruin where his master had tethered him in front of Mr. Lovell's door. But when he saw the stranger that came on Mr. Lovell's arm he gave the oddest cry that ever issued from a horse's throat, and broke his tether and tore off as for his life. He broke even his eight miles an hour record then. But neither Mr. Lovell nor the stranger paid the slightest heed. It might have been the commonest of things for a staid quadruped to go stark mad with fear.

They went up to Mr. Lovell's room. The stranger shut the door. Both were still. Mr. Lovell stood in the centre of the floor like, it might be, the husk of a man. The stranger held out his hand. It was the fairest, sweetest, daintiest hand that ever yet was seen. "Friend!"

And like the sweetest music was the voice in which he spoke the word. And yet it was a music in which there were a thousand things. For in spite of its exceeding sweetness there was in it an unutterable agony of pain. Mr. Lovell covered his face with his hands. He was seized with the ague fit which had overtaken him at first. But he gave no heed to the outstretched hand. So the stranger spoke again.

"You know me, friend!"

With a frantic effort Mr. Lovell managed to get out the one

word—

"No!"

It was a gasp, rather than a voice he said it in.

"Lies! To their father!"

That was all the stranger said. Yet Mr. Lovell fell flat upon the floor. The stranger advanced and stood right over him, looking down upon the quivering man.

"There is truth in the stories that are told. I come at times to men and women. To such as are after my own heart."

He paused. It was horrible to see how Mr. Lovell continued to quiver in every limb as the stranger with his wondrous smile, his wondrous voice, stood looking down. And it was all the time as though the whole air was filled with cries of pain.

"Friend, I bid you rise."

Mr. Lovell rose, mechanically, as he had done before.

"Give me your hand."

Mr. Lovell gave him his hand. As he did so he looked as we may conceive the lost spirits look in hell.

"You are my very child. Fair son! Thou dearest of them all!"

There was a silence. The sweat poured from Mr. Lovell's cheeks as in a sort of frenzy he kept his gaze upon the stranger's face. As if impelled by a fascination which he could not resist, he kept his eyes upon the stranger's eyes. And something that he saw in them he seemed gradually to be drinking in. Of a surety 'twas something strange, for he became transfigured as he gazed.

He lost first that look of a man who was stricken to his death. Then passed from him that look of anguished woe. Then fled from him that appearance of great pain. And last there vanished all signs of fear. It seemed, indeed, that he all at once began to find a pleasure in the presence of the stranger that stood there, and held him by the hand. He stood straight up, all bold, ay, bolder even than before. The transfiguration became indeed most wonderful, as wonderful as the transfiguration which had come on Mr. Lovell when he met the stranger first. And when at last the stranger said—

"It is a pact, thou son of my own heart?"

Mr. Lovell answered out both bold and clear—

"Use me as you will! Make me all yours! Give me the keys of the inner chambers of all sin!"

And the stranger answered, and it seemed as though the unutterable ecstasy of pain which, as it were, was hidden in his voice, acted on Mr. Lovell's veins as though it were the strongest wine—a stranger wine than ever yet was brewed by man.

"You shall be all mine! In my hands are not the keys of life and death, but I will be ever at your side. You shall know all the feverish delight of sin, and after all the mad delirium of unending pain."

Then Mr. Lovell cried, in a strange, wild voice—

"Father! Make me your son!"

And he leaped upon the stranger's breast. And the stranger folded him about with both his arms. And, behold! they kissed. And the effect of the stranger's kiss was to make Mr. Lovell drunker than ever man was made who had drunk more than his full, and that of the fiercest liquor.

3

It was the next night in the house that stood close by the Cocoa Tree. Mr. Pacy was there, and Captain Ashton, and many more besides. And though to be there meant to play, yet it was not play alone which occupied their thoughts that night. There had been strange tales told in town all day, and it was these tales they spoke of now. Here were the two men that knew the truth, and it was the truth that the town was all agog to hear.

The Honourable Cleveland Sprague, that was a son of the Earl of Staines, drew his white buckskin gloves right up his arm. He had sworn to his maiden aunt, the last time she paid his debts, that he never more would touch a dice-box or a card. And so, to keep his vow, he always donned a pair of gloves that went right up his arm. It was they that touched the dice-box and the cards. 'Twas never he.

"So Will Pettifer is dead!" he cried. "Run to the heart! 'Twas not the first time his heart was touched. And I always told him that he-had never caught the trick of the right counter-guard. Phew! How hot these gloves do make my hands! I think I might in honour wear a thinner pair."

"What is this tale they tell," asked Mr. Twentyman, that had killed his partner in a dozen duels, so they say, "of robbery and I know not what? Come, Mr. Pacy, all friends here—treat us to the tale."

But Mr. Pacy seemed not himself. He never had the clearest head even at the best of times. Now he seemed all muddled and bemused. The truth is, he had drunk half a dozen pots or so of good strong ale to sweep the tangle from his brain, and if they had swept it out they certainly had swept it in again.

"It is a sacred subject, Mr. Twentyman." And Mr. Pacy laid his hand upon his heart, and looked more solemn than a sexton's clerk. The dearest friend I ever had is dead, slain by my other dearest friend, that robbed me of six thousand pounds. God's curse light on the rogue that robbed me of my coat besides! 'Twas my cherry coat that I'd had made to show myself to Mistress Margaret in."

"Lovell rob you of your coat! Good lack-a-day! Sure he has coats enough that he can call his own."

"Mr. Twentyman, it was not Mr. Lovell that robbed me of my coat,—it was his friend."

"His friend! Faith! it is fine company he keeps!"

"At least, I do not know it was his friend. It was the fellow that came after." Mr. Pacy leaned against the board, and raised his voice exceeding loud. "Mr. Twentyman, the fellow took my coat for his children's morning meal."

A sound that was very like a titter went round the room. Hut when they saw how fierce Mr. Pacy looked, the sound was hushed.

"Then it was Lovell robbed you of six thousand pounds?"

"Sir, I do not say 'twas he. I have no desire, sir, to affront a trusty friend. If I said 'twas he, he would feel affronted, Mr. Twentyman. God forbid that I should so affront the meanest

rogue that breathes! I was thus—'twas my dear friend, Will Pettifer, that said 'twas he."

"Did Will Pettifer then see it done?"

"Do you think Will Pettifer'd stand by and see me robbed?
God forbid that I should so affront the dead! Sir, Will Pettifer
was a good two miles away."

"As you tell the tale, Mr. Pacy, 'tis like a puzzle, as I live. Let
me ask you, was it Will Pettifer that Mr. Lovell robbed?"

"Sir, he said it was,—it was for that he died. It has misgiven
me a dozen times that Sir Will was wrong."

"Because he died?"

"Yes, sir, because he died. For, sir, 'twas thus. Mr. Lovell declared his innocence with as fine an air as ever yet I saw,—
Captain Ashton will bear me witness that he spoke as would an
honest man. And further he declared that he left his cause unto
the God of battles,—Captain Ashton will proclaim if they were
not solemn words. Sure, had he been guilty 'twas Mr. Lovell, sir,
had died."

Mr. Twentyman snuffed, and then the box went round. Only
Captain Ashton had a mixture of his own, which made him
sneeze.

"Hum! How much had this *incognito* from you, and how
much from Will?"

"More than six thousand pounds from me, and more than
ten from Will. Together, the villain rode away the richer for seventeen thousand pounds."

"Seventeen thousand pounds! Odd! The sum which Mr.
Lovell, standing there where you are standing now, declared that
he had lost."

There was silence. Each man occupied himself with his own
thoughts. Then they began to play. But Mr. Pacy, he stood out.

"I am drained dry. Until my rents come in I shall have to be
in debt even for the things I eat. And but this morning Mistress
Meg writes entreating the loan of a hundred pounds. It is, I think
she says, to pay her glover's bill. It goes to my heart to say her nay,
but when one has to go in debt for the ale one drinks!—Sandy,

bring me a jug of wine!"

"Why don't you go upon the road?" asked Mr. Sprague. "'Fore God, I have a mind to challenge fate myself. 'Tis a good haul, seventeen thousand pounds. If I but saw a chance of it I'd rob a hundred men, and still swear black was white. 'Twould pay my debts, or some of them, and still there'd be a trifle left for my true love besides."

"Ay but he that took my coat said that he had not gained the half of it in seven years. It is not every night one pouches seventeen thousand pounds."

"It is not every night one meets so prime a pair of fools." This, or something like it, was what Mr. Sprague observed beneath his breath.

"Sir, I desire to be informed, sir, what it is you say beneath your breath. It is not a seemly trick to whisper in good company."

"Sir, I will tell you straight. Mr. Pacy, you are my dearest friend; I had rather I had lost these six thousand pounds than you. I beg that I may drink with you."

"Sandy" Mr. Pacy cried, "another jug of wine." It was a good hour after that Mr. Lovell came. By that time the most of the company were too busy with the dice to concern themselves with other things. Yet when he came you might have sworn a little breeze blew through the room so that each man shivered as with cold. With one accord they all looked up, even to the croupiers and the men that served, and there was Mr. Lovell at the door.

It was strange to see how all that company so suddenly was still. Yea, and how all stared. It was as though Mr. Lovell had the power of the loadstone to draw their eyes to him like magnets, as it were. They paused, and he. For the space of thirty seconds there was such silence that it seemed that none there breathed. Then, with that grace which was notoriously his, he took off his hat and made to them the fairest sweeping bow that ever was.

"Unto all this gallant company,—service!"

When he spoke a curious expression flitted across the countenance of each one that heard. For it seemed to them that his voice was not the voice of the Mr. Lovell they had known. It had a bolder, richer, acuter tone. It seemed to ring out through the room until the very lustres were set tinkling. And this rare gentleman was scarce the ruined gambler of yesternight. That was cool and easy yet, withal, a trifle stern. This held himself more bravely than a king. He had grown taller, as it were. On his face there was a radiance that made it strangely beautiful. Yet, as you regarded it, it seemed as though it had the power of communicating to your heart a quaint consciousness of pain.

None returned his salutation. All, as it seemed, even unconsciously to themselves, refrained from speech. With one accord they kept their eyes fastened upon his radiant countenance. But he seemed in no way concerned at the strangeness of their bearing. He came into the room with a buoyant lightness that was glorious to see.

"Jack!" he cried, when he perceived Mr. Pacy standing at his side, "I hope fortune has used you well since yesternight!"

But Mr. Pacy was in a solemn humour still.

"Mr. Lovell, God give you a good greeting."

It was curious to observe how Mr. Lovell was affected when Mr. Pacy spoke those simple words. He grasped the back of a chair with both his hands. A sort of convulsion passed all over him. His face became hideous all at once with its grins and its grimaces. They stared at him amazed.

"It—it is a spasm—of the heart—that sometimes—overtakes me." The words came out as though they rattled in his throat. "Give me—give me some brandy—a tumbler full."

They brought it him. A good half-pint at least. He drank it at a single draught.

"How long have these spasms troubled you?" asked Mr. Twentyman.

"Oh, ever since I was so high,—not higher than that glass is now." He dashed the glass out of his hand so that it was shivered to fragments on the floor. "But I interrupt your play! It should be a more serious person than I that did that! Who holds the bank, and what's the stake?"

He advanced to the table. He thrust his hands into his pockets and drew them out crammed full with notes and gold. And all this wealth he threw upon the board. At sight of it Mr. Sprague cried out—

"It would seem, Mr. Lovell, that you had come into another fortune since you lost your first last night."

"Nay, this is not mine." And Mr. Lovell chinked perhaps a hundred guineas in his hand. "It's the devil's own."

"Why, then, upon my word, I would the devil were at hand with its fellow one for me."

"What!" And Mr. Lovell drew himself straight up and his voice rang out so that it seemed to shake the very walls. "You wish the devil were at hand!" And he leaned forward on the board, and stretching out his hand, stared at Mr. Sprague with an intensity which made them more and more amazed. "Even at this moment the devil looks you in the face."

"Upon my word, Mr. Lovell, I do protest that there is something in your eyes which makes me feel quite strange."

"In my eyes! Oh, but what is there in his! If you could only see! But come, play! play! Let the game go round! We but stand idly here!"

But though they began to play it was not with the zest with which they were wont to pursue that great business of their lives, but in a nervous, fitful fashion, as though their thoughts— if not their hearts—were otherwise. Mr. Lovell played wildly, with no sort of rare or skill, and kept losing all the time. Suddenly he cried—

"See, here's a guinea piece, it shall be staked alone, it may chance to turn my luck, for you see it is a lucky coin."

"'Fore God! It's mine!"

Mr. Lovell was seized with the same convulsion which had overtaken him before, and he grasped the table as it seemed to help him stand. And, indeed, he needed some support. For Mr. Pacy pushed rudely by him and snatched the guinea piece out of his hand.

"It's mine!" roared Mr. Pacy, with the bellow of a bull. "It's mine!"

Before they knew what it was he would be at, he had begun to overhaul the heap of gold which Mr. Lovell had placed upon the board. From it he drew two guinea pieces which were exactly like the first.

"They're mine!" he roared. "As I breathe, they are my lucky three!" Then he turned on Mr. Lovell like a wild animal. "You damnedest rogue! You were the robber all the time!"

But Mr. Lovell stood straight up as calm and easy as ever yet he was.

"Pray, Mr. Pacy, why do you meddle with my money? And why this sudden rage? Have you gone mad? Or are you only drunk—the sequel of last night?"

"Your money! Sure, Mr. Lovell, since I know you I never will believe that ever a lie blasted the liar's throat or you had died the day that you were born. Sirs, I beseech you to observe these coins. In each of them three holes are drilled with a peculiar tool. I did it when I was a boy. They were fastened to a ribbon which hung out of my fob last night when I was robbed even to the buttons that were in my shirt and sleeves. And now Mr. Lovell, that so lately was a ruined man, throws them upon the board with other wealth of notes and gold that he so rightly calls the devil's own."

They all were still. There stood Mr. Pacy, suddenly clear witted as it seemed, the three curious pieces held in his great open palm. It was Mr. Sprague that spoke first. He took the guineas and examined them closely one by one. The whole company looked on.

"It is certainly a little curious," he said. "One would suppose that the man who made these marks could scarcely mistake his work if he came on it again."

"Perhaps the pieces in very truth are Mr. Pacy's own."

It was Mr. Lovell's voice. He seemed no whit abashed. He still held himself quite straight—more bravely than a king. There was still that strange resonance in his voice which made the lustres ring. There was still that radiance in his eyes and on his face, which made those who regarded him the most, most conscious of a sense of pain.

"Suppose they are his own,—what then?"

As he spoke he seemed to increase in radiance and beauty before their very eyes. And with it, too, increased their consciousness of pain.

"I say—what then?"

His voice increased until it became a very ecstasy of song.

"Because I stole them? Why, yes—I did! I lost my money and regained it with my own hands. You see that I am not ashamed."

They saw it very plain. He held himself as though he were the fabled hero of some glorious deed.

"Still less am I afraid. No, of nothing that may come. Sir Will is dead. I slew him with my own hand. Here is the self-same sword which finished him. Mr. Pacy, are you afraid?"

"I am not afraid," Pacy said, "of you."

And in his stolid bearing there was a certain glory too.

"I think you are. You dare not meet me boldly like Sir Will. After all, there was a man. Although he knew me for what I am, he never feared to meet my sword. But you! oh, you will say you do not fight with thieves! And I believe it too! You would far rather run away."

"I will not run away from you."

"You'll fight me then?"

"Yes, you thief, I'll fight you to the death."

"Now?"

"Ay, and even where you stand."

"Nay, the park will serve—where I fought Sir Will until he died. Captain Ashton, may I again entreat you to be my friend?"

But Captain Ashton turned away, a great oath upon his lips, liven his strong stomach could not swallow that. He might stand for Old Nick, but for this brazen gentleman, not he. Mr. Lovell, still unabashed, but smiled at him.

"Am I then to fly in the face of all rules? To fight without a friend—because I am a thief?"

"You shall always have a friend in me!"

It was the strangest voice that spoke the words, stranger than Mr. Lovell's even—ay, stranger far. A voice of the most wondrous music. You knew that he whose voice that was could keep no company with fear. It was like the clarion note that loves to defy the world. Yet in it there was something that spoke of hopeless pain,—pain which no man shall live and know.

And when they heard it each man there, down to the very croupiers even—they that have no souls—was seized with a strange sort of fear. And the fashion of their faces changed. It was as though each man had suddenly grown old. Only one man there was who was the same, and that was Mr. Lovell. There never was a gladder man than that man then, he held himself so very proudly, and his face was all radiant with such a radiancy of light. But all those that were about him shrank shudderingly away.

And, behold, a gentleman advanced towards Mr. Lovell. They know not to this day whence he came, nor how it was he was found so suddenly amongst them in that room. Sure, there never was one finer yet. He bore himself with a most marvellous grace. He was exquisite in each detail of his dress. He was still young,—a wondrous youth, and withal most beautiful. There was upon his lace a most enchanting smile. Yet when they saw it there broke from each man there a little cry of pain. It was as though he smiled in a wild, mad ecstasy of pain.

He advanced towards Mr. Lovell, and took him by the hand. And as he did so it was as though Mr. Lovell was transfigured. It was as though he became the counterpart of the gentleman who had come to be his friend. They were a wondrous pair. And yet all the company shrank tremblingly away, and the fashions of their faces changed, so that it seemed that they had suddenly grown old.

But Mr. Lovell, with the gentleman's hand still linked in his, turned to them, and said—

"This gentleman will be my friend."

And his voice, albeit it seemed that he spoke low, rang through the room with a resonant power that was indeed most wonderful. And yet—yet there was in it that note of pain! Then, perceiving that Mr. Pacy leaned with one hand against the wall, with something greenish about his face and in his eyes—

"Ah, Mr. Pacy, I think that now you are afraid."

It was with a sort of struggle that Mr. Pacy seemed to get the answering words to issue from his lips. Yet after his fashion he was game.

"I'm not afraid of you. I'll fight you now!" Then, with a supreme effort he broke, as it were, into a spasmodic rage. "Fight!—I'll fight you until you die."

The gentleman that had come to be Mr. Lovell's friend regarded him with his fair smile. And beneath his gaze Mr. Pacy seemed to shrink and shrink, and to become every moment a meaner man. The gentleman said—

"Bravely spoken! I would you also were my friend—even as my friend here. But come! Let us all go out to fight."

Holding Mr. Lovell by the hand he led the way out of the room, and like a flock of sheep all followed him, even to the croupiers and the serving men. Down the stairs went he, and after him went they, and out into the night. It was a strange sight to see that gallant company. All held their peace, and all seemed to wear so curious an air of decrepitude and age. There were there some of the bravest and the prettiest men in the town. Youths, some in the prime of life, and others that were old.

Some of England's purest blood was there, some of the finest fortunes in the land, some of its most glorious names. Yet never was seen such a hang-dog crew! They went like a pack of beaten curs, a set of mongrels in whom either life and spirit had never been, or from whom for certain it was ever gone. And the strangest part was that all at once they all seemed to have grown meanly old.

There was a moon that night. Through the moonlit streets they all went after Mr. Lovell and the gentleman that was come to be his friend. And to see the contrast that there was between those two and the sorry set that followed as their tail! The rich dresses of this mangy crowd made them seem a still sorrier set, their gait was in ill accord with the clothes they wore. And all the way they went the air seemed filled with wails and cries of pain.

Into the park they went, and so across the grass, and still not any spoke a word. They were a silent crew! So that when the strange gentleman stopped short, and turning said to Mr. Lovell, who still had his hand—

"Here is where you killed Sir Will!" His sudden speech woke all the echoes of the night. It was as though they were echoes that they heard—wild cries of anguish from afar. And all the gallant gentlemen shivered, and seemed to grow still older and more mean,—they alone knew why.

"Here I will kill Mr. Pacy too. That is, unless Mr. Pacy is afraid."

And Mr. Lovell turned towards Mr. Pacy with his sweet smile. But it seemed that Mr. Pacy was the only one that had a spark of spirit in all that gallant company. With a sort of dreadful energy he drew his sword out of its sheath, and that as awkwardly as though he had never unsheathed a sword before. Holding the naked blade in his great hand, he went and stood in front of Mr. Lovell, where the moonbeams shone upon his face. He was a great shambling fellow, a man of inches and of breadth, a good head taller than Mr. Lovell, yet now as he stood in front of him he seemed to be a smaller man. Yet, in his own peculiar way, it was plain that he was game.

"Pray, Mr. Pacy, are you in the plight I was—without a friend?" One sneaked out from amidst the crowd. It was Mr. Twentyman, so famed in the *duello*. He never spoke a word, but went and stood by Mr. Pacy's side. 'Tis true he helped him to remove his coat and vest, and clumsy enough they were the pair of them, but beyond that he never raised a hand or did a thing. And he so famed in the laws and niceties of the *duello*! It was Mr. Lovell's friend that did it all. And indeed he did it with the rarest grace, as though he loved the work right well. And all the gallant company, in their rich clothes, like a crowd of toothless, shivering curs, stood by.

When all was ready for the fighting to begin it was very strange in look on the opposing pair. The one in all his radiant strength, hearing himself as in a wild maze of joy. The other in the dogged abandonment of a mean despair. Yet was Mr. Pacy game, as they soon saw when the swords were crossed. Never was a more awkward fencer seen. Yet it seemed as though he were consumed with a sullen internal rage, and he had so strong a wrist that it was not easy to turn aside either his defence or his attack.

More than once he thrust nearly home, and followed up his thrust with such fierce determination, that had not Mr. Lovell's agility and skill been marvellous alike, it had gone hard with him that night. And, in truth, it was wonderful to see him fence. In the moonlight his blade moved with the speed of a flash of lightning, here, there, and everywhere at once. Soon it was evident that Mr. Pacy saw that it was vain to fence against this wondrous man. Such skill was never seen. Although it was plain that he perceived that the thing was vain, his determination became more dogged even than before, and he rushed on Mr. Lovell with the rage of a wild beast.

And that instant he was killed. With a most exquisite grace Mr. Lovell thrust him through the breast right to the heart. And with a dreadful suddenness he fell back upon the ground stone dead.

The gentleman that was Mr. Lovell's friend bent over the dead man as he lay upon the ground, and lightly cried—

"You have killed Mr. Pacy as you killed Sir Will."

And then he stood straight up and stretched out his hand to Mr. Lovell. And Mr. Lovell, still with his bloody blade in his right hand, took it with his left. And then he glided between his arms, drawn as it were by something he drank out of the gentleman's bright eyes, and he was folded to his breast, and their lips met in a long, long kiss. And all that gallant company looked on.

And suddenly was heard a wild, hideous, anguished, ear-splitting scream, the like of which God grant no human ever heard before. And all that gallant company cried out in an extremity of terror and of pain. It was a dreadful sound to hear.

And, when they looked again, the gentleman that was Mr. Lovell's friend had gone, and Mr. Lovell himself had fallen all in a horrid heap upon the ground. And when those that were most courageous went to look at him, they found that he was dead. And there was so awful a look upon his face that they shuddered and turned their eyes away. And one with his handkerchief covered the dead man's face.

The Houseboat

(A tale from *The Seen and the Unseen*)

Chapter 1

"I am sure of it!"

Inglis laid down his knife and fork. He stared round and round the small apartment in a manner which was distinctly strange. My wife caught him up. She laid down her knife and fork.

"You're sure of what?"

Inglis seemed disturbed. He appeared unwilling to give a direct answer. "Perhaps, after all, it's only a coincidence."

But Violet insisted "What is a coincidence?"

Inglis addressed himself to me.

"The fact is, Millen, directly I came on board I thought I had seen this boat before."

"But I thought you said that you had never heard of the *Water Lily*."

"Nor have I. The truth is that when I knew it, it wasn't the *Water Lily*."

"I don't understand."

"They must have changed the name. Unless I am very much mistaken this—this used to be the *Sylph*."

"The *Sylph?*"

"You don't mean to say that you have never heard of the *Sylph?*"

Inglis asked this question in a tone of voice which was peculiar.

"My dear fellow, I'm not a riverain authority. I am not acquainted with every houseboat between Richmond and Oxford. It was only at your special recommendation that I took the *Water Lily!*"

"Excuse me, Millen, I advised a houseboat I didn't specify the *Water Lily!*"

"But," asked my wife, "what was the matter with the *Sylph* that she should so mysteriously have become the *Water Lily?*"

Inglis fenced with this question in a manner which seemed to suggest a state of mental confusion.

"Of course, Millen, I know that that sort of thing would not have the slightest influence on you. It is only people of a very different sort who would allow it to have any effect on them. Then, after all, I may be wrong. And, in any case, I don't see that it matters."

"Mr. Inglis, are you suggesting that the *Sylph* was haunted?"

"Haunted!" Inglis started "I never dropped a hint about its being haunted So far as I remember I never heard a word of anything of the kind." Violet placed her knife and fork together on her plate. She folded her hands upon her lap.

"Mr. Inglis, there is a mystery. Will you this mystery unfold?"

"Didn't you really ever hear about the *Sylph*—two years ago?"

"Two years ago we were out of England"

"So you were. Perhaps that explains it You understand, this mayn't be the *Sylph*. I may be wrong—though I don't think I am." Inglis glanced uncomfortably at the chair on which he was sitting. "Why, I believe this is the very chair on which I sat! I remember noticing what a queer shape it was."

It was rather an odd-shaped chair. For that matter, all the things on board were odd.

"Then have you been on board this boat before?"

"Yes." Inglis positively shuddered. "I was, once; if it is the *Sylph*, that is." He thrust his hands into his trouser pockets. He leaned back in his chair. A curious look came into his face. "It is the *Sylph*, I'll swear to it. It all comes back to me. What an extraordinary coincidence! One might almost think there was something supernatural in the thing."

His manner fairly roused me.

"I wish you would stop speaking in riddles, and tell us what you are driving at"

He became preternaturally solemn.

"Millen, I'm afraid I have made rather an ass of myself; I ought to have held my tongue. But the coincidence is such a strange one that it took me unawares, and since I have said so much I suppose I may as well say more. After dinner I will tell you all there is to tell. I don't think it's a story which Mrs. Millen would like to listen to."

Violet's face was a study.

"I don't understand you, Mr. Inglis, because you are quite well aware it is a principle of mine that what is good for a husband to hear is good for a wife. Come, don't be silly. Let us hear what the fuss is about I daresay it's about nothing after all."

"You think so? Well, Mrs. Millen, you shall hear." He carefully wiped his moustache. He began: "Two years ago there was a houseboat on the river called the *Sylph*. It belonged to a man named Hambro. He lent it to a lady and a gentleman. She was rather a pretty woman, with a lot of fluffy, golden hair. He was a quiet unassuming-looking man, who looked as though he had something to do with horses. I made their acquaintance on the river. One evening he asked me on board to dine. I sat, as I believe, on this very chair, at this very table. Three days afterwards they disappeared."

"Well?" I asked. Inglis had paused.

"So far as I know, he has never been seen or heard of since."

"And the lady?"

"Some of us were getting up a picnic. We wanted them to come with us. We couldn't quite make out their sudden disappearance. So, two days after we had missed them, I and another man tried to rout them out I looked through the window. I saw something lying on the floor. 'Jarvis,' I whispered, 'I believe that Mrs. Bush is lying on the floor dead drunk.' 'She can't have

523

been drunk two days,' he said. He came to my side. 'Why, she's in her nightdress. This is very queer. Inglis, I wonder if the door is locked.' It wasn't. We opened it and went inside."

Inglis emptied his glass of wine.

"The woman we had known as Mrs. Bush lay in her nightdress, dead upon the floor. She had been stabbed to the heart She was lying just about where Mrs. Millen is sitting now."

"Mr. Inglis!" Violet rose suddenly.

"There is reason to believe that, from one point of view, the woman was no better than she ought to have been. That is the story."

"But"—I confess it was not at all the story I had expected it was going to be; I did not altogether like it—"who killed her?"

"That is the question. There was no direct evidence to show. No weapon was discovered The man we had known as Bush had vanished, as it seemed, off the face of the earth. He had not left so much as a pocket-handkerchief behind him. Everything both of his and hers had gone. It turned out that nobody knew anything at all about him. They had no servant. What meals they had on board were sent in from the hotel Hambro had advertised the *Sylph*. Bush had replied to the advertisement He had paid the rent in advance, and Hambro had asked no questions."

"And what became of the *Sylph?*"

"She also vanished. She had become a little too notorious. One doesn't fancy living on board a houseboat on which a murder has been committed; one is at too close quarters. I suppose Hambro sold her for what he could get, and the purchaser painted her, and rechristened her the *Water Lily.*"

"But are you sure this is the *Sylph?*"

"As sure as that I am sitting here. It is impossible that I could be mistaken. I still seem to see that woman lying dead just about where Mrs. Millen is standing now."

"Mr. Inglis!"

Violet was standing up. She moved away—towards me. Inglis left soon afterwards. He did not seem to care to stop. He had scarcely eaten any dinner. In fact, that was the case with all of us. Mason had exerted herself to prepare a decent meal in her cramped little kitchen, and we had been so ungrateful as not even to reach the end of her bill of fare. When Inglis had gone she appeared in her bonnet and cloak. We supposed that, very naturally, she had taken umbrage.

"If you please, ma'am, I'm going."

"Mason! What do you mean?"

"I couldn't think of stopping in no place in which murder was committed, least of all a houseboat. Not to mention that last night I heard ghosts, if ever anyone heard them yet"

"Mason! Don't be absurd. I thought you had more sense."

"All I can say is, ma'am, that last night as I lay awake, listening to the splashing of the water, all at once I heard in here the sound of quarrelling. I couldn't make it out. I thought that you and the master was having words. Yet it didn't sound like your voices. Besides, you went on awful. Still, I didn't like to say nothing, because it might have been, and it wasn't my place to say that I had heard. But now I know that it was ghosts."

She went She was not to be persuaded to stay any more than Inglis. She did not even stay to clear the table. I have seldom seen a woman in a greater hurry. As for wages, there was not a hint of them. Staid, elderly, self-possessed female though she was, she seemed to be in a perfect panic of fear. Nothing would satisfy her but that she should, with the greatest possible expedition, shake from her feet the dust of the *Water Lily*, When we were quit of her I looked at Violet and Violet looked at me. I laughed. I will not go so far as to say that I laughed genially; still, I laughed.

"We seem to be in for a pleasant river holiday."

"Eric, let us get outside."

We went on deck. The sun had already set There was no moon, but there was a cloudless sky. The air was languorous and heavy. Boats were stealing over the waters. Someone in the distance was playing a banjo accompaniment while a clear girlish voice was singing "The Garden of Sleep." The other houseboats were radiant with Chinese lanterns. The *Water Lily* alone was still in shadow. We drew our deckchairs close together. Violet's hand stole into mine.

"Eric, do you know that last night I, too, heard voices?"

"You!" I laughed again. "Violet!"

"I couldn't make it out at all. I was just going to wake you when they were still."

"You were dreaming, child. Inglis's story—confound him and his story!—has recalled your dream to mind. I hope you don't wish to follow Mason's example, and make a bolt of it. I have paid pretty stiffly for the honour of being the *Water Lily* tenant for a month, not to mention the fact of disarranging all our plans."

Violet paused before she answered.

"No; I don't think I want, as you say, to make a bolt of it Indeed," she nestled closer to my side, "it is rather the other way. I should like to see it through. I have sometimes thought that I should like to be with someone I can trust in a situation such as this. Perhaps we may be able to fathom the mystery—who knows?"

This tickled me. "I thought you had done with romance."

"With one sort of romance I hope I shall never have done." She pressed my hand. She looked up archly into my face. I knew it, although we were in shadow. "With another sort of romance I may be only just beginning. I have never yet had dealings with a ghost"

Chapter 2

At first I could not make out what it was that had roused me. Then I felt Violet's hand steal into mine. Her voice whispered in my ear, "Eric!" I turned over towards her on the pillow. "Be still. They're here." I did as she bade me. I was still. I heard no sound but the lazy rippling of the river.

"Who's here?" I asked, when, as I deemed, I had been silent long enough.

"S-sh!" I felt her finger pressed against my lips. I was still again. The silence was broken in rather a peculiar manner.

"I don't think you quite understand me."

The words were spoken in a man's voice, as it seemed to me, close behind my back. I was so startled by the unexpected presence of a third person that I made as if to spring up in bed. My wife caught me by the arm. Before I could remonstrate or shake off her grasp a woman's laughter rang through the little cabin. It was too metallic to be agreeable. And a woman's voice replied—

"I understand you well enough, don't you make any error!"

There was a momentary pause.

"You don't understand me, fool!"

The first four words were spoken with a deliberation which meant volumes, while the final epithet came with a sudden malignant ferocity which took me aback. The speaker, whoever he might be, meant mischief. I sprang up and out of bed.

"What are you doing here?" I cried.

I addressed the inquiry apparently to the vacant air. The moonlight flooded the little cabin. It showed clearly enough that it was empty. My wife sat up in bed.

"Now," she observed, "you've done it."

"Done what? Who was that speaking?"

"The voices."

"The voices! What voices? I'll voice them! Where the dickens have they gone?"

I moved towards the cabin door, with the intention of pursuing my inquiries further. Violet's voice arrested me.

"It is no use your going to look for them. They will not be found by searching. The speakers were Mr. and Mrs. Bush."

"Mr. and Mrs. Bush?"

Violet's voice dropped to an awful whisper. "The murderer and his victim."

I stared at her in the moonlight. Inglis's pleasant little story had momentarily escaped my memory. Suddenly roused from a dreamless slumber, I had not yet had time to recall such trivialities. Now it all came back in a flash.

"Violet," I exclaimed, "have you gone mad?"

"They are the voices which I heard last night They are the voices which Mason heard. Now you have heard them. If you had kept still the mystery might have been unravelled. The crime might have been re-acted before our eyes, or at least within sound of our ears."

I sat down upon the ingenious piece of furniture which did duty as a bed. I seemed to have struck upon a novel phase in my wife's character. It was not altogether a pleasing novelty. She spoke with a degree of judicial calmness which, under all the circumstances, I did not altogether relish.

"Violet, I wish you wouldn't talk like that It makes my blood run cold."

"Why should it? My dear Eric, I have heard you yourself say that in the presence of the seemingly mysterious our attitude should be one of passionless criticism. A mysterious crime has been committed in this very chamber." I shivered. "Surely it is our duty to avail ourselves of any opportunities which may offer, and which may enable us to probe it to the bottom."

I made no answer. I examined the doors. They were locked and bolted. There was no sign that anyone had tampered with the fastenings. I returned to bed. As I was arranging myself between the sheets Violet whispered in my ear. "Perhaps if we are perfectly quiet they may come back again."

I am not a man given to adjectives; but I felt adjectival then. I was about to explain, in language which would not have been wanting in force, that I had no desire that they should come back again, when—

"You had better give it to me."

The words were spoken in a woman's voice, as it seemed, within twelve inches of my back. The voice was not that of a lady. I should have said without hesitation, had I heard the voice under any other circumstances, that the speaker had been born within the sound of Bow Bells.

"Had I?"

It was a man's voice which put the question. There was something about the tone in which the speaker put it which reminded one of the line in the people's ballad, "It ain't exactly what 'e sez, it's the nasty way 'e sez it" The question was put in a very "nasty way" indeed.

"Yes, my boy, you had."

"Indeed?"

"Yes, you may say 'indeed,' but if you don't I tell you what I'll do—I'll spoil you."

"And what, my dear Gertie, am I to understand by the mystic threat of spoiling me?"

"I'll go straight to your wife, and I'll tell her everything."

"Oh, you will, will you?"

There was a movement of a chair. The male speaker was getting up.

"Yes, I will."

There was a slight pause. One could fancy that the speakers were facing each other. One could picture the look of impudent defiance upon the woman's countenance, the suggestion of coming storm upon that of the man. It was the man's voice which broke the silence.

"It is odd, Gertrude, that you should have chosen this evening to threaten me, because I myself had chosen this evening, I won't say to threaten, but to make a communication to you."

"Give me a match." The request came from the woman.

"With pleasure. I will give you anything, my dear Gertrude, within reason." There was another pause. In the silence I seemed to hear my wife holding her breath—as I certainly was holding mine. All at once there came a sound of scratching, a flash of light It came so unexpectedly, and such was the extreme tension of my nerves, that, with a stifled exclamation, I half rose in bed. My wife pressed her hand against my lips. She held me down. She spoke in so attenuated a whisper that it was only because all my senses were so keenly on the alert that I heard her.

"You goose! He's only striking a match."

He might have been, but who? She took things for granted. I wanted to know. The light continued flickering to and fro, as a match does flicker. I would have given much to know who held it, or even what was its position in the room. As luck had it, my face was turned the other way. My wife seemed to understand what was passing in my mind

"There's no one there," she whispered.

No one, I presumed, but the match. I took it for granted that was there. Though I did not venture to inquire, I felt that I might not have such perfect control over my voice as my wife appeared to have.

While the light continued to flicker there came stealing into my nostrils—I sniffed, the thing was unmistakable!—the odour of tobacco. The woman was lighting a cigarette. I knew it was the woman because presently there came this request from the man, "After you with the light, my dear."

I presume that the match was passed. Immediately the smell of tobacco redoubled. The man had lit a cigarette as well. I confess that I resented—silently, but still strongly—the idea of two strangers, whether ghosts or anybody else, smoking, uninvited, in my cabin.

The match went out. The cigarettes were lit The man continued speaking.

"The communication, my dear Gertrude, which I intended to make to you was this. The time has come for us to part"

He paused, possibly for an answer. None came.

"I need not enlarge on the reasons which necessitate our parting. They exist"

Pause again. Then the woman.

"What are you going to give me?"

"One of the reasons which necessitate our parting—a very strong reason, as you, I am sure, will be the first to admit—is that I have nothing left to give you."

"So you say."

"Precisely. So I say and so I mean."

"Do you mean that you are going to give me nothing?"

"I mean, my dear Gertrude, that I have nothing to give you. You have left me nothing."

"Bah!"

The sound which issued from the lady's lips was expressive of the most complete contempt

"Look here, my boy, you give me a hundred sovereigns or I'll spoil you."

Pause again. Probably the gentleman was thinking over the lady's observation.

"What benefit do you think you will do yourself by what you call 'spoiling' me?"

"Never mind about that: I'll do it You think I don't know all about you, but I do. Perhaps I'm not so soft as you think. Your wife's got some money if you haven't. Suppose you go back and ask her for some. You've treated me badly enough. I don't see why you shouldn't go and treat her the same. She wouldn't make things warm for you if she knew a few things I could tell her—not at all! You give me a hundred sovereigns or, I tell you straight, I'll go right to your house and I'll tell her all."

" Oh, no, you won't"

"Won't I? I say I will!"

"Oh, no, you won't"

"I say I will! I've warned you, that's all. I'm not going to stop here, talking stuff to you. I'm going to bed You can go and hang yourself for all I care."

There was a sound, an indubitable sound—the sound of a pair of shoes being thrown upon the floor. There were other sounds, equally capable of explanation: sounds which suggested—I wish the printer would put it in small type—that the lady was undressing. Undressing, too, with scant regard to ceremony. Garments were thrown off and tossed higgledy-piggledy here and there. They appeared to be thrown, with sublime indifference, upon table, chairs, and floor. I even felt something alight upon the bed. Some feminine garment, perhaps, which, although it fell by no means heavily, made me conscious, as it fell, of the most curious sensation I had in all my life—till then—experienced. It seemed that the lady, while she unrobed, continued smoking. From her next words it appeared that the gentleman, also smoking, stood and stared at her.

"Don't stand staring at me like a gawk. I'm going to turn in."

"And I'm going to turn out. Not, as you suggested, to hang myself, but to finish this cigarette upon the roof. Perhaps, when I return, you will be in a more equable frame of mind."

"Don't you flatter yourself. What I say I mean. A hundred sovereigns, or I tell your wife."

He laughed very softly, as though he was determined not to be annoyed. Then we heard his footsteps as he crossed the floor. The door opened, then closed. We heard him ascend the steps. Then, with curious distinctness, his measured tramp, tramp, as he moved to and fro upon the roof. In the cabin for a moment there was silence. Then the woman said, with a curious faltering in her voice—

"I'll do it I don't care what he says." There was a choking in her throat "He don't care for me a bit"

Suddenly she flung herself upon her knees beside the bed She pillowed her head and arms upon the coverlet. I lay near the outer edge of the bed, which was a small one, by the way. As I lay I felt the pressure of her limbs. My sensations, as I did, I am unable to describe. After a momentary interval there came the sound of sobbing. I could feel the woman quivering with the strength of her emotion. Violet and I were speechless. I do not think that, for the instant, we could have spoken even had we tried. The woman's presence was so evident, her grief so real. As she wept disjointed words came from her.

"I've given everything for him! If he only cared for me! If he only did."

All at once, with a rapid movement, she sprang up. The removal of the pressure was altogether unmistakable. I was conscious of her resting her hands upon the coverlet to assist her to her bet. I felt the little jerk; then the withdrawal of the hands. She choked back her sobs when she had gained her feet. Her tone was changed.

"What a fool I am to make a fuss. He don't care for me—not that" We heard her snap her fingers in the air. "He never did. Us women are always fools—we're all the same. I'll go to bed"

Violet clutched my arm. She whispered, in that attenuated fashion she seemed to have caught the trick of—

"She's getting into bed. We must get out."

It certainly was a fact, someone was getting into bed. The bedclothes were moved; not our bedclothes, but some phantom coverings. We heard them rustle, we were conscious of a current of air across our faces as someone caught them open. And then!—then someone stepped upon the bed.

"Let's get out!" gasped Violet

CHAPTER 3

She moved away from me. She squeezed herself against the side of the cabin. She withdrew her limbs from between the sheets. As for me, the person who had stepped upon the bed had actually stepped upon me, and that without seeming at all conscious of my presence. Someone sat down plump upon the sheet beside me. That was enough. I took advantage of my lying on the edge of the bed to slip out upon the floor. I might possess an unsuspected capacity for undergoing strange experiences, but I drew the line at sleeping with a ghost

The moonlight streamed across the room. As I stood, in something very like a state of nature on the floor, I could clearly see Violet cowering on the further side of the bed. I could distinguish all her features. But when I looked upon the bed itself—there was nothing there. The moon's rays fell upon the pillow. They revealed its snowy whiteness. There seemed nothing else it could reveal. It was untenanted. And yet, if one looked closely at it, it seemed to be indented, just as it might have been indented had a human head been lying there. But about one thing there could be no mistake whatever—my ears did not play me false, I heard it too distinctly—the sound made by a person who settles himself between the sheets, and then the measured respiration of one who composes himself to slumber.

I remained there silent. On her hands and knees Violet crept towards the foot of the bed. When she had gained the floor she stole on tiptoe to my side.

"I did not dare to step across her." I felt her, as she nestled to me, give me a little shiver. "I could not do it. Can you see her?"

"What a fool I am!" As Violet asked her question there came this observation from the person in the bed—whom, by the way, I could not see. There was a long-drawn sigh. "What fools all we women are! What fools!"

There was a sincerity of bitterness about the tone, which, coming as it did from an unseen speaker—one so near and yet so far—had on one a most uncomfortable effect Violet pressed closer to my side. The woman in the bed turned over. Overhead there still continued the measured tramp, tramping of the man. We were conscious, in some subtle way, that the woman lay listening to the footsteps. They spoke more audibly to her ears even than to ours.

"Ollie! Ollie!" she repeated the name softly to herself, with a degree of tenderness which was in startling contrast to her previous bitterness.

"I wish you would come to bed."

She was silent There was only the sound of her gentle breathing. Her bitter mood had been but transient She was falling asleep with words of tenderness upon her lips. Above, the footsteps ceased. All was still. There was not even the murmur of the waters. The wife and I, side by side, stood looking down upon what seemed an empty bed.

" She is asleep," said Violet

It seemed to me she was: although I could not see her, it seemed to me she was. I could hear her breathing as softly as a child Violet continued whispering—

"How strange! Eric, what can it mean?"

I muttered a reply—

"A problem for the Psychical Research Society."

"It seems just like a dream."

"I wish it were a dream."

"S-sh! There is someone coming down the stairs."

There was—at least, if we could trust our ears, there was. Apparently the man above had had enough of solitude. We heard him move across the roof, then pause just by the steps, then descend them one by one. It seemed to us that in this step there was something stealthy, that he was endeavouring not to arouse attention, to make as little noise as possible. Half-way down he paused; at the foot he paused again.

"He's listening outside the door." It almost seemed that he was. We stood and listened too. "Let's get away from the bed."

My wife drew me with her. At the opposite end of the cabin was a sort of little alcove, which was screened by a curtain, and behind which were hung one or two of our garments which we were not actually using. Violet drew me within the shadow of this alcove. I say drew me because, offering no resistance, I allowed myself to be completely passive in her hands. The alcove was not large enough to hold us. Still the curtain acted as a partial screen.

The silence endured for some moments. Then we heard without a hand softly turning the handle of the door. While I was wondering whether, after all, I was not the victim of an attack of indigestion, or whether I was about to witness an attempt at effecting a burglarious entry into a houseboat, a strange thing happened, the strangest thing that had happened yet.

As I have already mentioned, the moon's rays flooded the cabin. This was owing to the fact that a long narrow casement, which ran round the walls near the roof of the cabin, had been left open for the sake of admitting air and ventilation; but, save for the moonbeams, the cabin was unlighted. When, however, we heard the handle being softly turned, a singular change occurred. It was like the transformation scene in a theatre. The whole place, all at once, was brilliantly illuminated. The moonbeams disappeared. Instead, a large swinging lamp was hanging from the centre of the cabin. So strong was the light which it shed around that our eyes were dazzled.

It was not our lamp; we used small hand-lamps, which stood upon the table. By its glare we saw that the whole cabin was changed. For an instant we failed to clearly realise in what the change consisted. Then we understood it was a question of decoration. The contents of the cabin, for the most part, were the same, though they looked newer, and the positions of the various articles were altered; but the panels of the cabin of the *Water Lily* were painted blue and white. The panels of this cabin were coloured chocolate and gold.

"Eric, it's the *Sylph!*"

The suggestion conveyed by my wife's whispered words, even as she spoke, occurred to me. I understood where, for Inglis, had lain the difficulty of recognition. The two cabins were the same, and yet were not. It was just as though someone had endeavoured, without spending much cash, to render one as much as possible unlike the other.

In this cabin there were many things which were not ours. In fact, so far as I can see, there was nothing which was ours. Strange articles of costume were scattered about; the table was covered with a curious litter; and on the ingenious article of furniture which did duty as a bed, and which stood where our bed stood, and which, indeed, seemed to be our bed, there was someone sleeping.

As my startled eyes travelled round this amazing transformation scene, at last they reached the door. There they stayed. Mechanically I shrank back nearer to the wall. I felt my wife tighten her grasp upon my hand.

The door was open some few inches. Through the aperture thus formed there peered a man. He seemed to be listening. It was so still that one could hear the gentle breathing of the woman sleeping in the bed. Apparently satisfied, he opened the door sufficiently wide to admit of his entering the cabin. My impression was that he could not fail to perceive us, yet to all appearances he remained entirely unconscious of our neighbourhood. He was a man certainly under five feet six in height He was slight in build, very dark, with face clean shaven; his face was long and narrow. In dress and bearing he seemed a gentleman, yet there was that about him which immediately reminded me of what Inglis had said of the man Bush—"he looked as though he had something to do with horses."

He stood for some seconds in an attitude of listening, so close to me that I had only to stretch out my hand to take him by the throat I did not do it I don't know what restrained me; I think, more than anything, it was the feeling that these things which were passing before me must be passing in a dream. His face was turned away. He looked intently towards the sleeping woman.

After he had had enough of listening he moved towards the bed. His step was soft and cat-like; it was absolutely noiseless. Glancing down, I perceived that he was without boots or shoes. He was in his stockinged feet I had distinctly heard the tramp, tramping of a pair of shoes upon the cabin roof. I had heard them descend the steps. Possibly he had paused outside the door to take them off.

When he reached the bed he stood looking down upon the sleeper. He stooped over her, as if the better to catch her breathing. He whispered softly—

"Gerty!"

He paused for a moment, as if for an answer. None came. Standing up, he put his hand, as it seemed to me, into the bosom of his flannel shirt He took out a leather sheath. From the sheath he drew a knife. It was a long, slender, glittering blade. Quite twelve inches in length, at no part was it broader than my little finger. With the empty sheath in his left hand, the knife behind his back in his right, he again leaned over the sleeper. Again he softly whispered, "Gerty!"

Again there was no answer. Again he stood upright, turning his back towards the bed, so that he looked towards us. His face was not an ugly one, though the expression was somewhat saturnine. On it, at the instant, there was a peculiar look, such a look as I could fancy upon the face of a jockey who, toward the close of a great race, settles himself in the saddle with the determination to "finish" well. The naked blade he placed upon the table, the empty sheath beside it Then he moved towards us. My first thought was that now, at last, we were discovered; but something in the expression of his features told me that this was not so. He approached us with an indifference which was amazing. He passed so close to us that we were conscious of the slight disturbance of the air caused by his passage. There was a Gladstone bag on a chair within two feet of us. Picking it up, he bore it to the table. Opening it out, he commenced to pack it

All manner of things he placed within it, both masculine and feminine belongings, even the garments which the sleeper had taken off, and which lay scattered on the chair and on the floor, even her shoes and stockings! When the bag was filled he took a long brown ulster, which was thrown over the back of a chair. He stuffed the pockets with odds and ends. When he had completed his operations the cabin was stripped of everything except the actual furniture. He satisfied himself that this was so by overhauling every nook and corner, in the process passing and repassing Violet and me with a perfect unconcern which was more and more amazing. Being apparently at last clear in his mind upon that point, he put on the ulster and a dark cloth cap, and began to fasten the Gladstone bag.

While he was doing so, his back being turned to the bed, without the slightest warning, the woman in the bed sat up. The man's movements had been noiseless. He had made no sound which could have roused her. Possibly some sudden intuition had come to her in her sleep. However that might be, she all at once was wide awake. She stared round the apartment with wondering eyes. Her glance fell on the man, dressed as for a journey.

"Where are you going?"

The words fell from her lips as unawares. Then some sudden conception of his purpose seemed to have flown to her brain. She sprang out of bed with a bound.

"You shan't go," she screamed.

She rushed to him. He put his hand on the table. He turned to her. Something flashed in the lamplight It was the knife. As she came he plunged it into her side right to the hilt. For an instant he held her spitted on the blade. He put his hand to her throat He thrust her from him. With the other hand he extricated the blade. He let her fall upon the floor. She had uttered a sort of sigh as the weapon was being driven home. Beyond that she had not made a sound.

All was still. He remained for some seconds looking down at her as she lay. Then he turned away. We saw his face. It was, if possible, paler than before. A smile distorted his lips. He stood for a moment as if listening. Then he glanced round the cabin, as if to make sure that he was unobserved.

His black eyes travelled over our startled features, in evident unconsciousness that we were there. Then he glanced at the blade in his hand. As he did so he perceptibly shuddered. The glittering steel was obscured with blood. As he perceived that this was so he gasped. He seemed to realise for the first time what it was that he had done. Taking an envelope from an inner pocket of his ulster he began to wipe the blood from off the blade. While doing so his wandering glance fell upon the woman lying on the floor.

Some new aspect of the recumbent figure seemed to strike him with a sudden horror. He staggered backwards. I thought he would have fallen. He caught at the wall to help him stand— caught at the wall with the hand which held the blade. At that part of the cabin the wall was doubly panelled half-way to the roof. Between the outer and the inner panel there was evidently a cavity, because, when in his sudden alarm he clutched at the wall, the blade slipped from his relaxing grasp and fell between the panels. Such was his state of panic that he did not appear to perceive what had happened. And at that moment a cry rang out upon the river—possibly it was someone hailing the keeper of the lock—"Ahoy!"

The sound seemed to fill him with unreasoning terror. He rushed to the table. He closed the Gladstone with a hurried snap; he caught it up; he turned to flee. As he did so I stepped out of the alcove. I advanced right in front of him. I cannot say whether he saw me, or whether he didn't. But he seemed to see me. He started back. A look of the most awful terror came on his countenance. And at that same instant the whole scene vanished.

I was standing in the cabin of the *Water Lily*. The moon was stealing through the little narrow casement Violet was creeping to my side. She stole into my arms. I held her to me.

"Eric," she moaned.

For myself, I am not ashamed to own that, temporarily, I had lost the use of my tongue. When, in a measure, the faculty of speech returned to me—

"Was it a dream?" I whispered.

"It was a vision."

"A vision?" I shuddered. "Look!"

As I spoke she turned to look. There, in the moonbeams, we saw a woman in her nightdress, lying on the cabin floor. We saw that she had golden hair. It seemed to us that she was dead. We saw her but a moment—she was gone! It must have been imagination; we know that these things are not, but it belonged to that order of imagination which is stranger than reality.

My wife looked up at me.

"Eric, it is a vision which has been sent to us in order that we may expose in the light of day a crime which was hidden in the night"

I said nothing. I felt for a box of matches on the table. I lit a lamp. I looked round and round the cabin, holding the lamp above my head the better to assist my search. It was with a feeling of the most absurd relief that I perceived that everything was unchanged, that, so far as I could see, there was no one there but my wife and I.

"I think, Violet, if you don't mind, I'll have some whisky."

She offered no objection. She stood and watched me as I poured the stuff into a glass. I am bound to admit that the spirit did me good.

"And what," I asked, "do you make of the performance we have just now witnessed?" She was still. I took another drink. There can be no doubt that, under certain circumstances, whisky is a fluid which is not to be despised. "Have we both suddenly become insane, or do you attribute it to the cucumber we ate at lunch?"

"How strange that Mr. Inglis should have told us the story only this afternoon."

"I wish Mr. Inglis had kept the story to himself entirely."

"They were the voices which I heard last night They were the voices Mason heard. It was all predestined. I understand it now."

"I wish that I could say the same."

"I see it all!"

She pressed her hands against her brow. Her eyes flashed fire.

"I see why it was sent to us, what it is we have to do. Eric, we have to find the knife."

I began to fear, from her frenzied manner, that her brain must in reality be softening.

"What knife?"

"The knife which he dropped between the panels. The boat has only been repainted. We know that in all essentials the *Sylph* and the *Water Lily* are one and the same. Mr. Inglis said that the weapon which did the deed was never found. No adequate search was ever made. It is waiting for us where he dropped it"

"My dear Violet, don't you think you had better have a little whisky? It will calm you."

"Have you a hammer and a chisel?"

"What do you want them for?"

"It was here that he was standing; it was here that he dropped the knife." She had taken up her position against the wall at the foot of the bed Frankly, I did not like her manner at all. It was certainly where, in the latter portion of that nightmare, the fellow had been standing. "I will wrench this panel away." She rapped against a particular panel with her knuckles. "Behind it we shall find the knife."

"My dear Violet, this houseboat isn't mine. We cannot destroy another man's property in that wanton fashion. He will hardly accept as an adequate excuse the fact that at the time we were suffering from a severe attack of indigestion."

"This will do."

She took a large carving-knife out of the knife- basket which was on the shelf close by her. She thrust the blade between the panel and the wood- work. It could scarcely have been securely fastened In a surprisingly short space of time she had forced it loose. Then, grasping it with both her hands, she hauled the panel bodily away.

"Eric, it is there!"

Something was there, resting on a little ledge which had checked its fall on to the floor beneath—something which was covered with paint, and dust, and cobwebs, and Violet all at once grew timid.

"You take it; I dare not touch the thing."

"It is very curious; something is there, and, by George, it is a knife!"

It was a knife—the knife which we had seen in the vision, the dream, the nightmare, call it what you will—the something which had seemed so real. There was no mistaking it, tarnished though it was—the long, slender blade which we had seen the man draw from the leather sheath. Stuck to it by what was afterwards shown to be coagulated blood was an envelope—the envelope which we had seen the fellow take from his pocket to wipe off the crimson stain. It had adhered to the blade. When the knife fell the envelope fell too.

"At least," I murmured as I stared at this grim relic, "this is a singular coincidence."

The blood upon the blade had dried. It required but little to cause the envelope to fall away. As a matter of fact, while I was still holding the weapon in my hand it fell to the floor. I picked it up. It was addressed in a woman's hand, "Francis Joynes, Esq., Fairleigh, Streatham."

I at once recognised the name as that of a well-known owner of racehorses and so-called "gentleman rider."

★★★★★★

Not the least singular part of all that singular story was that the letter inside that envelope, which was afterwards opened and read by the proper authorities, was from Mr. Joynes's wife. It was a loving, tender letter, from a wife who was an invalid abroad to a husband whom she supposed was thinking of her at home.

Mr. Joynes was never arrested, and that for this sufficient reason: that when the agents of the law arrived at his residence Mr. Joynes was dead. He had committed suicide on the very night on which we saw that—call it vision—on board the *Water Lily*. I viewed the corpse against my will. I was not called in evidence. Had I been, I was prepared to swear, as was my wife, that Mr. Joynes was the man whom I had seen in a dream that night. It was shown at the inquest that he had suffered of late from horrid dreams—that he had scarcely dared to sleep. I wonder if, in that last and most awful of his dreams, he had seen my face—seen it as I saw his?

It was afterwards shown, from inquiries which were made, that Mr. Joynes and "Mr. Bush," tenant of the *Sylph*, were, beyond all doubt, one and the same person. On the singular circumstances which caused that discovery to be made I offer no comment.

A Set of Chessmen

(A tale from *Both Sides of the Veil*)

1

"But, *Monsieur*, perceive how magnificent they are! There is not in Finistère, there is not in Brittany, nay, it is certain there is not in France so superb a set of chessmen. And ivory! And the carving—observe, for example, the variety of detail."

They certainly were a curious set of chessmen, magnificent in a way, but curious first of all. As M. Bobineau remarked, holding a rook in one hand and a knight in the other, the care paid to details by the carver really was surprising. But two hundred and fifty *francs!* For a set of chessmen!

"So, so, my friend. I am willing to admit that the work is good—in a kind of a way. But two hundred and fifty *francs!* If it were fifty, now?"

"Fifty!" Up went M. Bobineau's shoulders, and down went M. Bobineau's head between them, in the fashion of those toys which are pulled by a string. '*Ah, mon Dieu! Monsieur* laughs at me!'"

And there came another voluble declaration of their merits. They certainly were a curious set. I really think they were the most curious set I ever saw. I would have preferred them, for instance, to anything they have at South Kensington, and they have some remarkable examples there. And, of course, the price was small—I even admit it was ridiculously small. But when one has only five thousand *francs* a year for everything, two hundred and fifty being taken away—and for a set of chessmen—do leave a vacancy behind.

I asked Bobineau where he got them. Business was slack that sunny afternoon—it seemed to me that I was the only customer he ever had, but that must have been a delusion on my part. Report said he was a warm man, one of Morlaix's warmest men, and his queer old shop in the queer old Grande Rue—Grande Rue! What a name for an alley!—contained many things which were valuable as well as queer. But there, at least, was no other customer in sight just then, so Bobineau told me all the tale.

It seemed there had been a M. Funichon—Auguste Funichon— no, not a Breton, a Parisian, a true Parisian, who had come and settled down in the commune of Plouigneau, over by the *gare*. This M. Funichon was, for example, a little—well, a little—a little *exalted,* let us say. It is true that the country people said he was stark mad, but Bobineau, for his part, said no, no, no! It is not necessary, because one is a little eccentric, that one is mad. Here Bobineau looked at me out of the corner of his eye. Are not the English, of all people, the most eccentric, and yet is it not known to all the world that they are not, necessarily, stark mad? This M. Funichon was not rich, quite the contrary. It was a little place he lived in—the merest cottage, in fact. And in it he lived alone, and, according to report, there was only one thing he did all day and all night long, and that was, play chess. It appears that he was that rarest and most amiable of imbeciles, a chess-maniac. Is there such a word?

"What a life!" said M. Bobineau. "Figure it to yourself! To do nothing—nothing!—but play chess! They say"—M. Bobineau looked round him with an air of mystery—"they say he starved himself to death. He was so besotted by his miserable chess that he forgot—absolutely forgot, this imbecile—to eat."

That was what M. Bobineau said they said. It required a vigorous effort of the imagination to quite take it in. To what a state of forgetfulness must a man arrive before he forgets to eat! But whether M. Funichon forgot to eat, or whether he didn't, at least he died, and being dead they sold his goods—why they sold them was not quite clear, but at the sale M. Bobineau was the chief purchaser. One of the chief lots was the set of ivory chessmen which had caught my eyes. They were the dead man's favourite set, and no wonder! Bobineau was of opinion that if he had had his way he would have had them buried with him in his grave.

"It is said," he whispered, again with the glance of mystery around, "that they found him dead, seated at the table, the chessmen on the board, his hand on the white rook, which was giving mate to the adversary's king."

Either what a vivid imagination had Bobineau, or what odd things the people said! One pictures the old man, seated all alone, with his last breath finishing his game.

Well, I bought the set of ivory chessmen. At this time of day I freely admit that they were cheap at two hundred and fifty *francs*—dirt cheap, indeed; but a hundred was all I paid. I knew Bobineau so well—I daresay he bought them for twenty-five. As I bore them triumphantly away my mind was occupied by thoughts of their original possessor. I was filled by quite a sentimental tenderness as I meditated on the part they had played, according to Bobineau, in that last scene. But St. Servan drove all those thoughts away. Philippe Henri de St. Servan was rather a difficult person to get on with. It was with him I shared at that time my apartment on the *place*.

"Let us see!" I remarked when I got in, "what have I here?" He was seated, his country pipe in his mouth, at the open window, looking down upon the river. The Havre boat was making ready to start—at Morlaix the nautical event of the week. There was quite a bustle on the quay. St. Servan just looked round, and then looked back again. I sat down and untied my purchase.

"I think there have been criticisms—derogatory criticisms—passed by a certain person upon a certain set of chessmen. Perhaps that person will explain what he has to say to these."

St. Servan marched up to the table. He looked at them through his half-closed eyelids. "Toys!" was all he said.

"Perhaps! Yet toys which made a tragedy. Have you ever heard of the name of Funichon?" By a slight movement of his grisly grey eyebrows he intimated that it was possible he had. "These chessmen belonged to him. He had just finished a game with them when they found him dead—the winning piece, a white rook, was in his hand. Suggest an epitaph to be placed over his grave. There's a picture for a painter—eh?"

"Bah! He was a Communist!"

That was all St. Servan said. And so saying, St. Servan turned away to look out of the window at the Havre boat again. There was an end of M. Funichon for him. Not that he meant exactly what he said. He simply meant that M. Funichon was not Legitimist—out of sympathy with the gentlemen who met, and decayed, visibly, before the naked eye, at the club on the other side of the *place*. With St. Servan not to be Legitimist meant to be nothing at all—out of his range of vision absolutely. Seeing that was so, it is strange he should have borne with me as he did. But he was a wonderful old man.

2

We played our first game with the ivory chessmen when St. Servan returned from the club. I am free to confess that it was an occasion for me. I had dusted all the pieces, and had the board all laid when St. Servan entered, and when we drew for choice of moves the dominant feeling in my mind was the thought of the dead man sitting all alone, with the white rook in his hand. There was an odour of sanctity about the affair—a whiff of air from the land of the ghosts.

Nevertheless, my loins were girded up, and I was prepared to bear myself as a man in the strife. We were curiously well matched, St. Servan and I. We had played two hundred and twenty games, and, putting draws aside, each had scored the same number of wins. He had his days, and so had I. At one time I was eleven games ahead, but since that thrice blessed hour I had not scored a single game. He had tracked me steadily, and eventually had made the scores exactly tie. In these latter days it had grown with him to be an article of faith that as a chess-player I was quite played out—and there was a time when I had thought the same of him!

He won the move, and then, as usual, there came an interval for reflection. The worst thing about St. Servan—regarded from a chess-playing point of view—was, that he took such a time to begin. When a man has opened his game it is excusable—laudable, indeed—if he pauses to reflect, a reasonable length of time. But I never knew a man who was so fond of reflection before a move was made. As a rule, that absurd habit of his had quite an irritating effect upon my nerves, but that evening I felt quite cool and prepared to sit him out.

There we sat, both smoking our great pipes, he staring at the board, and I at him. He put out his hand, almost touched a piece, and then, with a start, he drew it back again. An interval—the same pantomime again. Another interval—and a repetition of the pantomime. I puffed a cloud of smoke into the air, and softly sighed. I knew he had been ten minutes by my watch. Possibly the sigh had a stimulating effect, for he suddenly stretched out his hand and moved queen's knight's pawn a single square.

I was startled. He was great at book openings, that was the absurdest part of it. He would lead you to suppose that he was meditating something quite original, and then would perhaps begin with fool's mate after all. He, at least, had never tried queen's knight's pawn a single square before.

I considered a reply. Pray let it be understood—though I would not have confessed it to St. Servan for the world—that I am no player. I am wedded to the game for an hour or two at night, or, peradventure, of an afternoon at times; but I shall never be admitted to its inner mysteries—never! not if I outspan Methuselah. I am not built that way. St. Servan and I were two children who, loving the sea, dabble their feet in the shallows left by the tide. I have no doubt that there are a dozen replies to that opening of his, but I did not know one then.

I had some hazy idea of developing a game of my own, while keeping an eye on his, and for that purpose put out my hand to move the queen's pawn two, when I felt my wrist grasped by—well, by what felt uncommonly like an invisible hand. I was so startled that I almost dropped my pipe. I drew my hand back again, and was conscious of the slight detaining pressure of unseen fingers. Of course it was hallucination, but it seemed so real, and was so expected, that—well, I settled my pipe more firmly between my lips—it had all but fallen from my mouth, and took a whiff or two to calm my nerves. I glanced up, cautiously, to see if St. Servan noticed my unusual behaviour, but his eyes were fixed stonily upon the board.

After a moment's hesitation—it was absurd!—I stretched out my hand again. The hallucination was repeated, and in a very tangible form. I was distinctly conscious of my wrist being wrenched aside and guided to a piece I had never meant to touch, and almost before I was aware of it, instead of the move I had meant to make, I had made a servile copy of St. Servan's opening—I had moved queen's knight's pawn a single square!

To adopt the language of the late Dick Swiveller, that was a staggerer. I own that for an instant I was staggered. I could do nothing else but stare. For at least ten seconds I forgot to smoke. I was conscious that when St. Servan saw my move he knit his brows. Then the usual interval for reflection came again. Half unconsciously I watched him. When, as I supposed, he had decided on his move, he stretched out his hand, as I had done, and also, as I had done, he drew it back again. I was a little startled—he seemed a little startled too. There was a momentary pause; back went his hand again, and, by way of varying the monotony, he moved—king's knight's pawn a single square.

I wondered, and held my peace. There might be a gambit based upon these lines, or there might not; but since I was quite clear that I knew no reply to such an opening I thought I would try a little experiment, and put out my hand, not with the slightest conception of any particular move in my head, but simply to see what happened. Instantly a grasp fastened on my wrist; my hand was guided to—king's knight's pawn a single square.

This was getting, from every point of view, to be distinctly interesting. The chessmen appeared to be possessed of a property of which Bobineau had been unaware. I caught myself wondering if he would have insisted on a higher price if he had known of it. Curiosities nowadays do fetch such fancy sums—and what price for a ghost? They appeared to be automatic chessmen, automatic in a sense entirely their own.

Having made my move, or having had somebody else's move made for me, which is perhaps the more exact way of putting it, I contemplated my antagonist. When he saw what I had done, or what somebody else had done—the things are equal—St. Servan frowned. He belongs to the bony variety, the people who would not loll in a chair to save their lives—his aspect struck me as being even more poker-like than usual. He meditated his reply an unconscionable length of time, the more unconscionable since I strongly doubted if it would be his reply after all. But at last he showed signs of action. He kept his eyes fixed steadily upon the board, his frown became pronounced, and he began to raise his hand. I write "began," because it was a process which took some time. Cautiously he brought it up, inch by inch. But no sooner had he brought it over the board than his behaviour became quite singular. He positively glared, and to my eyes seemed to be having a struggle with his own right hand. A struggle in which he was worsted, for he leant back in his seat with a curiously discomfited air.

He had moved queen's rook's pawn two squares—the automatic principle which impelled these chessmen seemed to have a partiality for pawns.

It was my turn for reflection. I pressed the tobacco down in my pipe, and thought—or tried to think—it out. Was it an hallucination, and was St. Servan the victim of hallucination too? Had I moved those pawns spontaneously, actuated by the impulse of my own free will, or hadn't I? And what was the meaning of the little scene I had just observed? I am a tolerably strong man. It would require no slight exercise of force to compel me to move one piece when I had made up my mind that I would move another piece instead. I have been told, and I believe not altogether untruly told, that the rigidity of my right wrist resembles iron. I have not spent so much time in the tennis-court and fencing-room for nothing. I had tried one experiment. I thought I would try another. I made up my mind that I would move queen's pawn two—stop me who stop can.

I felt that St. Servan in his turn was watching me. Preposterously easy though the feat appeared to be as I resolved on its performance, I was conscious of an unusual degree of cerebral excitement—a sort of feeling of do or die. But as, in spite of the feeling, I didn't do, it was perhaps as well I didn't die. Intending to keep complete control over my own muscles, I raised my right hand, probably to the full as cautiously as St. Servan had done. I approached the queen's pawn. I was just about to seize the piece when that unseen grasp fastened on my wrist. I paused, with something of the feeling which induces the wrestler to pause before entering on the veritable tug of war. For one thing, I was desirous to satisfy myself as to the nature of the grasp—what it was that seemed to grasp me.

It seemed to be a hand. The fingers went over the back of my wrist, and the thumb beneath. The fingers were long and thin—it was altogether a slender hand. But it seemed to be a man's hand, and an old man's hand at that. The skin was tough and wrinkled, clammy and cold. On the little finger there was a ring, and on the first, about the region of the first joint, appeared to be something of the nature of a wart. I should say that it was anything but a beautiful hand, it was altogether too attenuated and clawlike, and I would have betted that it was yellow with age.

At first the pressure was slight, almost as slight as the touch of a baby's hand, with a gentle inclination to one side. But as I kept my own hand firm, stiff, resolved upon my own particular move, with, as it were, a sudden snap, the pressure tightened and, not a little to my discomfiture, I felt my wrist held as in an iron vice. Then, as it must have seemed to St. Servan, who, I was aware, was still keenly watching me, I began to struggle with my own hand. The spectacle might have been fun to him, but the reality was, at that moment, anything but fun to me. I was dragged to one side.

Another hand was fastened upon mine. My fingers were forced open—I had tightly clenched my fist to enable me better to resist—my wrist was forced down, my fingers were closed upon a piece, I was compelled to move it forward, my fingers were unfastened to replace the piece upon the board. The move completed, the unseen grasp instantly relaxed, and I was free, or appeared to be free, again to call my hand my own.

I had moved queen's rook's pawn two squares. This may seem comical enough to read about, but it was anything but comical to feel. When the thing was done I stared at St. Servan, and St. Servan stared at me. We stared at each other, I suppose, a good long minute, then I broke the pause.

'Anything the matter?" I inquired. He put up his hand and curled his moustache, and, if I may say so, he curled his lip as well. "Do you notice anything odd about—about the game?" As I spoke about the game I motioned my hand towards my brand-new set of chessmen. He looked at me with hard suspicious eyes.

"Is it a trick of yours?" he asked.

"Is what a trick of mine?"

"If you do not know, then how should I?"

I drew a whiff or two from my pipe, looking at him keenly all the time, then signed towards the board with my hand.

"It's your move," I said.

He merely inclined his head. There was a momentary pause.

When he stretched out his hand he suddenly snatched it back again, and half started from his seat with a stifled execration.

"Did you feel anything upon your wrist?" I asked.

"*Mon Dieu!* It is not what I feel—see that!"

He was eyeing his wrist as he spoke. He held it out under the glare of the lamp. I bent across and looked at it. For so old a man he had a phenomenally white and delicate skin—under the glare of the lamp the impressions of finger-marks were plainly visible upon his wrist. I whistled as I saw them.

"Is it a trick of yours?" he asked again.

"It is certainly no trick of mine."

"Is there anyone in the room besides us two?"

I shrugged my shoulders and looked round. He too looked round, with something I thought not quite easy in his glance.

"Certainly no one of my acquaintance, and certainly no one who is visible to me!"

With his fair white hand—the left, not the one which had the finger-marks upon the wrist—St. Servan smoothed his huge moustache.

"Someone, or something, has compelled me—yes, from the first—to move, not as I would, but—bah! I know not how."

"Exactly the same thing has occurred to me."

I laughed. St. Servan glared. Evidently the humour of the thing did not occur to him, he being the sort of man who would require a surgical operation to make him see a joke. But the humorous side of the situation struck me forcibly.

"Perhaps we are favoured by the presence of a ghost—perhaps even by the ghost of M. Funichon. Perhaps, after all, he has not yet played his last game with his favourite set. He may have returned—shall we say from—where?—to try just one more set-to with us! If, my dear sir"—I waved my pipe affably, as though addressing an unseen personage—"it is really you, I beg you will reveal yourself—materialise is, I believe, the expression now in vogue—and show us the sort of ghost you are!"

Somewhat to my surprise, and considerably to my amusement, St. Servan rose from his seat and stood by the table, stiff and straight as a scaffold-pole.

"These, *Monsieur*, are subjects on which one does not jest."

"Do you, then, believe in ghosts?" I knew he was a superstitious man—witness his fidelity to the superstition of right divine—but this was the first inkling I had had of how far his superstition carried him.

"Believe!—In ghosts! In what, then, do you believe? I, *Monsieur*, am a religious man."

"Do you believe, then, that a ghost is present with us now—the ghost, for instance, of M. Funichon?"

St. Servan paused. Then he crossed himself—actually crossed

himself before my eyes. When he spoke there was a peculiar dryness in his tone.

"With your permission, *Monsieur*, I will retire to bed."

There was an exasperating thing to say! There must be a large number of men in the world who would give—well, a good round sum, to light even on the trail of a ghost. And here were we in the actual presence of something—let us say apparently curious, at any rate, and here was St. Servan calmly talking about retiring to bed, without making the slightest attempt to examine the thing! It was enough to make the members of the Psychical Research Society turn in their graves. The mere suggestion fired my blood.

"I do beg, St. Servan, that you at least will finish the game." I saw he hesitated, so I drove the nail well home. "Is it possible that you, a brave man, having given proofs of courage upon countless fields, can turn tail at what is doubtless an hallucination after all?"

"Is it that *Monsieur* doubts my courage?"

I knew the tone—if I was not careful I should have an affair upon my hands.

"Come, St. Servan, sit down and finish the game."

Another momentary pause. He sat down, and—it would not be correct to write that we finished the game, but we made another effort to go on. My pipe had gone out. I refilled and lighted it.

"You know, St. Servan, it is really nonsense to talk about ghosts."

"It is a subject on which I never talk."

"If something does compel us to make moves which we do not intend, it is something which is capable of a natural explanation."

"Perhaps *Monsieur* will explain it, then?"

"I will! Before I've finished! If you only won't turn tail and go to bed! I think it very possible, too, that the influence, whatever it is, has gone—it is quite on the cards that our imagination has played us some subtle trick. It is your move, but before you do anything just tell me what move you mean to make."

"I will move"—he hesitated—"I will move queen's pawn."

He put out his hand, and, with what seemed to me hysterical suddenness, he moved king's rook's pawn two squares.

"So! our friend is still here then! I suppose you did not change your mind?"

There was a *very* peculiar look about St. Servan's eyes.

"I did not change my mind."

I noticed, too, that his lips were uncommonly compressed.

"It is my move now. I will move queen's pawn. We are not done yet. When I put out my hand you grasp my wrist—and we shall see what we shall see."

"Shall I come round to you?"

"No, stretch out across the table—now!"

I stretched out my hand; that instant he stretched out his, but spontaneous though the action seemed to be, another, an unseen hand, had fastened on my wrist. He observed it too.

"There appears to be another hand between yours and mine."

"I know there is."

Before I had the words well out my hand had been wrenched aside, my fingers unclosed, and then closed, then unclosed again, and I had moved king's rook's pawn two squares. St. Servan and I sat staring at each other—for my part I felt a little bewildered.

"This is very curious! Very curious indeed! But before we say anything about it we will try another little experiment, if you don't mind. I will come over to you." I went over to him. "Let me grasp your wrist with both my hands." I grasped it, as firmly as I could, as it lay upon his knee. "Now try to move queen's pawn."

He began to raise his hand, I holding on to his wrist with all my strength. Hardly had he raised it to the level of the table when two unseen hands, grasping mine, tore them away as though my strength were of no account. I saw him give a sort of shudder—he had moved queen's bishop's pawn two squares.

"This is a devil of a ghost!" I said.

St. Servan said nothing. But he crossed himself, not once, but half a dozen times.

"There is still one little experiment that I would wish to make."

St. Servan shook his head.

"Not I!" he said.

'Ah but, my friend, this is an experiment which I can make without your aid. I simply want to know if there is nothing tangible about our unseen visitor except his hands. It is my move." I returned to my side of the table. I again addressed myself, as it were, to an unseen auditor. "My good ghost, my good M. Funichon—if it is you—you are at liberty to do as you desire with my hand."

I held it out. It instantly was grasped. With my left hand I made several passes in the air up and down, behind and before, in every direction so far as I could. It met with no resistance. There seemed to be nothing tangible but those invisible fingers which grasped my wrist—and I had moved queen's bishop's pawn two squares.

St. Servan rose from his seat.

"It is enough. Indeed it is too much. This ribaldry must cease. It had been better had *Monsieur* permitted me to retire to bed."

"Then you are sure it is a ghost—the ghost of M. Funichon, we'll say?"

"This time *Monsieur* must permit me to wish him a good night's rest."

He bestowed on me, as his manner was, a stiff inclination of the head, which would have led a stranger to suppose that we had met each other for the first time ten minutes ago, instead of being the acquaintances of twelve good years. He moved across the room.

"St. Servan, one moment before you go! You are surely not going to leave a man alone at the post of peril?"

"It were better that *Monsieur* should come too."

"Half a second, and I will. I have only one remark to make, and that is to the ghost."

I rose from my seat. St. Servan made a half-movement towards the door, then changed his mind and remained quite still.

"If there is any other person with us in the room, may I ask that person to let us hear his voice, or hers? Just to speak one word."

Not a sound.

"It is possible—I am not acquainted with the laws which govern—eh—ghosts—that the faculty of speech is denied to them. If that be so, might I ask for the favour of a sign—for instance, move a piece while my friend and I are standing where we are?"

Not a sign; not a chessman moved.

"Then M. Funichon, if it indeed be you, and you are incapable of speech, or even of moving a piece of your own accord, and are only able to spoil our game, I beg to inform you that you are an exceedingly ill-mannered and foolish person, and had far better have stayed away."

As I said this I was conscious of a current of cold air before my face, as though a swiftly moving hand had shaved my cheek.

"By Jove, St. Servan, something has happened at last. I believe our friend the ghost has tried to box my ears!"

St. Servan's reply came quietly stern.

"I think it were better that *Monsieur* came with me."

For some reason St. Servan's almost contemptuous coldness fired my blood. I became suddenly enraged.

"I shall do nothing of the kind! Do you think I am going to be fooled by a trumpery conjuring trick which would disgrace a shilling *séance*? Driven to bed at this time of day by a ghost! And such a ghost! If it were something like a ghost one wouldn't mind; but a fool of a ghost like this!"

Even as the words passed my lips I felt the touch of fingers against my throat. The touch increased my rage. I snatched at them, only to find that there was nothing there.

"Damn you!" I cried. "Funichon, you old fool, do you think that you can frighten me? You see those chessmen; they are mine, bought and paid for with my money—you dare to try and prevent me doing with them exactly as I please."

Again the touch against my throat. It made my rage the more. "As I live, I will smash them all to pieces, and grind them to powder beneath my heel."

My passion was ridiculous—childish even. But then the circumstances were exasperating—unusually so, one might plead. I was standing three or four feet from the table. I dashed forward. As I did so a hand was fastened on my throat. Instantly it was joined by another. They gripped me tightly. They maddened me. With a madman's fury I still pressed forward. I might as well have fought with fate. They clutched me as with bands of steel, and flung me to the ground.

3

When I recovered consciousness I found St. Servan bending over me.

"What is the matter?" I inquired, when I found that I was lying on the floor.

"I think you must have fainted."

"Fainted! I never did such a thing in my life. It must have been a curious kind of faint, I think."

"It was a curious kind of faint."

With his assistance I staggered to my feet. I felt bewildered. I glanced round. There were the chessmen still upon the board, the hanging lamp above. I tried to speak. I seemed to have lost the use of my tongue. In silence he helped me to the door. He half led, half carried me—for I seemed to have lost the use of my feet as well as that of my tongue—to my bedroom. He even assisted me to undress, never leaving me till I was between the sheets. All the time not a word was spoken. When he went I believe he took the key outside and locked the door.

That was a night of dreams. I know not if I was awake or sleeping, but all sorts of strange things presented themselves to my mental eye. I could not shut them from my sight. One figure was prominent in all I saw—the figure of a man. I knew, or thought I knew, that it was M. Funichon. He was a lean old man, and what I noticed chiefly were his hands. Such ugly hands! In some fantastical way I seemed to be contending with them all through the night.

And yet in the morning when I woke—for I did wake up, and that from as sweet refreshing sleep as one might wish to have—it was all gone. It was bright day. The sun was shining into the great, ill-furnished room. As I got out of bed and began to dress, the humorous side of the thing had returned to me again. The idea of there being anything supernatural about a set of ivory chessmen appeared to me to be extremely funny.

I found St. Servan had gone out. It was actually half-past ten! His *table d'hôte* at the Hotel de Bretagne was at eleven, and before he breakfasted he always took a *petit verre* at the club. If he had locked the door overnight he had not forgotten to unlock it before he started. I went into the rambling, barnlike room which served us for a *salon*.

The chessmen had disappeared. Probably St. Servan had put them away—I wondered if the ghost had interfered with him. I laughed to myself as I went out—fancy St. Servan contending with a ghost.

The proprietor of the Hotel de Bretagne is Legitimist, so all the aristocrats go there—of course, St. Servan with the rest. Presumably the landlord's politics is the point, to his cooking they are apparently indifferent—I never knew a worse table in my life! The landlord of the Hôtel de l'Europe may be a Communist for all I care—*his* cooking is first-rate, so I go there. I went there that morning. After I had breakfasted I strolled off towards the Grande Rue, to M. Bobineau.

When he saw me M. Bobineau was all smirks and smiles— he *must* have got those chessmen for *less* than five-and-twenty *francs!* I asked him if he had any more of the belongings of M. Funichon.

"But certainly! Three other sets of chessmen."

I didn't want to look at those, apparently one set was quite enough for me. Was that all he had?

"But no! There was an ancient bureau, very magnificent, carved"—

I thanked him—nor did I want to look at that. In the Grande Rue at Morlaix old bureaux carved about the beginning of the fifteenth century—if you listen to the vendors—are as plentiful as cobblestones.

"But I have all sorts of things of M. Funichon. It was I who bought them nearly all. Books, papers, and"—

M. Bobineau waved his hands towards a multitude of books and papers which crowded the shelves at the side of his shop. I took a volume down. When I opened it I found it was in manuscript.

"That work is unique!" explained Bobineau. "It was the intention of M. Funichon to give it to the world, but he died before his purpose was complete. It is the record of all the games of chess he ever played—in fifty volumes. *Monsieur* will perceive it is unique."

I should think it was unique! In fifty volumes! The one I held was a large quarto, bound in leather, containing some six or seven hundred pages, and was filled from cover to cover with matter in a fine, clear handwriting, written on both sides of the page. I pictured the face of the publisher to whom it was suggested that *he* should give to the world such a work as that.

I opened the volume at the first page. It was, as Bobineau said, apparently the record, with comments, of an interminable series of games of chess. I glanced at the initial game. Here are the opening moves, just as they were given there:—

White.	Black.
Queen's Knight's Pawn, one square.	Queen's Knight's Pawn, one square.
King's Knight's Pawn, one square.	King's Knight's Pawn, one square.
Queen's Rook's Pawn, two squares.	Queen's Rook's Pawn, two squares.
King's Rook's Pawn, two squares.	King's Rook's Pawn, two squares.

They were exactly the moves of the night before. They were

such peculiar moves, and made under such peculiar circumstances, that I was scarcely likely to mistake them. So far as we had gone, St. Servan and I, assisted by the unseen hand, had reproduced M. Funichon's initial game in the first volume of his fifty—and a very peculiar game it seemed to be. I asked Bobineau what he would take for the volume which I held.

"*Monsieur* perceives that to part them would spoil the set, which is unique. *Monsieur* shall have the whole fifty"—I shuddered. I imagine Bobineau saw I did, he spoke so very quickly— "for a five-*franc* piece, which is less than the value of the paper and the binding."

I knew then that he had probably been paid for carting the rubbish away. However, I paid him his five-*franc* piece, and marched off with the volume under my arm, giving him to understand, to his evident disappointment, that at my leisure I would give him instructions as to the other forty-nine.

As I went along I thought the matter over. M. Funichon seemed to have been a singular kind of man—he appeared to have carried his singularity even beyond the grave. Could it have been the coldblooded intention of his ghost to make us play the whole contents of the fifty volumes through? What a fiend of a ghost his ghost must be!

I opened the volume and studied the initial game. The people were right who had said that the man was mad. None but an imbecile would have played such a game—his right hand against his left!—and none but a raving madman would have recorded his imbecility in black and white, as though it were a thing to be proud of! Certainly none but a criminal lunatic would have endeavoured to foist his puerile travesty of the game and study of chess upon two innocent men.

Still the thing was curious. I flattered myself that St. Servan would be startled when he saw the contents of the book I was carrying home. I resolved that I would instantly get out the chessmen and begin another game—perhaps the ghost of M. Funichon would favour us with a further exposition of his ideas of things. I even made up my mind that I would communicate with the Psychical Research Society. Not at all improbably they might think the case sufficiently remarkable to send down a member of their body to inquire into the thing upon the spot.

I almost began to hug myself on the possession of a ghost, a ghost, too, which might be induced to perform at will—almost on the principle of "drop a coin into the slot and the figures move"! It was cheap at a hundred *francs*. What a stir those chessmen still might make! What vexed problems they might solve! Unless I was much mistaken, the expenditure of those hundred francs had placed me on the royal road to immortality.

Filled with such thoughts I reached our rooms. I found that St. Servan had returned. With him, if I may say so, he had brought his friends. Such friends! Ye Goths! When I opened the door the first thing which greeted me was a strong, not to say suffocating, smell of incense. The room was filled with smoke. A fire was blazing on the hearth. Before it was St. Servan, on his knees, his hands clasped in front of him, in an attitude of prayer. By him stood a priest, in his robes of office. He held what seemed a pestle and mortar, whose contents he was throwing by handfuls on to the flames, muttering some doggerel to himself the while. Behind him were two acolytes,

With nice clean faces, and nice white stoles,

who were swinging censers—hence the odour which filled the room. I was surprised when I beheld all this. They appeared to be holding some sort of religious service—and I had not bargained for that sort of thing when I had arranged with St. Servan to share the rooms with him. In my surprise I unconsciously interrupted the proceedings.

"St. Servan! Whatever is the meaning of this?" St. Servan looked up, and the priest looked round—that was all the attention they paid to me. The acolytes eyed me with what I conceived to be a grin upon their faces. But I was not to be put down like that.

"I must ask you, St. Servan, for an explanation." The priest turned the mortar upside down, and emptied the remainder of its contents into the fire. "It is finished," he said.

St. Servan rose from his knees and crossed himself. "We have exorcised the demon," he observed. "You have what?" I asked.

"We have driven out the evil spirit which possessed the chessmen."

I gasped. A dreadful thought struck me.

"You don't mean to say that you have dared to play tricks with my property?"

"*Monsieur*," said the priest, "I have ground it into dust." He had. That fool of a St. Servan had actually fetched his parish priest and his acolytes and their censers, and between them they had performed a comminatory service made and provided for the driving out of demons. They had ground my ivory chessmen in the pestle and mortar, and then burned them in the fire. And this in the days of the Psychical Research Society! And they had cost me a hundred *francs!* And that idiot of a ghost had never stretched out a hand or said a word!

LEONAUR

ALSO FROM LEONAUR

AVAILABLE IN SOFTCOVER OR HARDCOVER WITH DUST JACKET

THE COLLECTED SUPERNATURAL AND WEIRD FICTION OF J. SHERIDAN LE FANU: VOLUME 1 *by J. Sheridan le Fanu*—Contains Two Novels 'The Haunted Baronet' and 'The Evil Guest', One Novella 'Carmilla',One Novelette and Ten Short Stories of the Ghostly and Gothic.

THE COLLECTED SUPERNATURAL AND WEIRD FICTION OF J. SHERIDAN LE FANU: VOLUME 2 *by J. Sheridan le Fanu*—Contains One Novel 'Uncle Silas', One Novelette 'Green Tea' and Five Short Stories of the Ghostly and Gothic.

THE COLLECTED SUPERNATURAL AND WEIRD FICTION OF J. SHERIDAN LE FANU: VOLUME 3 *by J. Sheridan le Fanu*—Contains One Novel 'The House by the Churchyard', and One Short Story 'Dickon the Devil' of the Ghostly and Gothic.

THE COLLECTED SUPERNATURAL AND WEIRD FICTION OF J. SHERIDAN LE FANU: VOLUME 4 *by J. Sheridan le Fanu*—Contains One Novel 'The Wyvern Mystery', One Novelette 'Mr. Justice Harbottle,' and Nine Short Stories of the Ghostly and Gothic.

THE COLLECTED SUPERNATURAL AND WEIRD FICTION OF J. SHERIDAN LE FANU: VOLUME 5 *by J. Sheridan le Fanu*—Contains One Novel 'The Rose and the Key', One Novelette 'Spalatro, From the Notes of Fra Giacomo', and Two Short Stories of the Ghostly and Gothic

THE COLLECTED SUPERNATURAL AND WEIRD FICTION OF J. SHERIDAN LE FANU: VOLUME 6 *by J. Sheridan le Fanu*—Contains One Novel 'Checkmate', and Six Short Stories of the Ghostly and Gothic

THE COLLECTED SUPERNATURAL AND WEIRD FICTION OF J. SHERIDAN LE FANU: VOLUME 7 *by J. Sheridan le Fanu*—Contains Two Novels 'All in the Dark' and 'The Room in the Dragon Volant', Two Novelettes 'The Mysterious Lodger' and 'The Watcher' and Four Short Stories of the Ghostly and Gothic

THE COLLECTED SUPERNATURAL AND WEIRD FICTION OF J. SHERIDAN LE FANU: VOLUME 8 *by J. Sheridan le Fanu*—Contains One Novel 'A Lost Name', One Novelette 'The Last Heir of Castle Connor', and Six Short Stoies of the Ghostly and Gothic

LEONAUR

ALSO FROM LEONAUR
AVAILABLE IN SOFTCOVER OR HARDCOVER WITH DUST JACKET

THE COMPLETE FOUR JUST MEN: VOLUME 2 *by Edgar Wallace—The Law of the Four Just Men* & *The Three Just Men*—disillusioned with a world where the wicked and the abusers of power perpetually go unpunished, the Just Men set about to rectify matters according to their own standards, and retribution is dispensed on swift and deadly wings.

THE COMPLETE RAFFLES: 1 *by E. W. Hornung—The Amateur Cracksman* & *The Black Mask*—By turns urbane gentleman about town and accomplished cricketer, life is just too ordinary for Raffles and that sets him on a series of adventures that have long been treasured as a real antidote to the 'white knights' who are the usual heroes of the crime fiction of this period.

THE COMPLETE RAFFLES: 2 *by E. W. Hornung—A Thief in the Night* & *Mr Justice Raffles*—By turns urbane gentleman about town and accomplished cricketer, life is just too ordinary for Raffles and that sets him on a series of adventures that have long been treasured as a real antidote to the 'white knights' who are the usual heroes of the crime fiction of this period.

THE COLLECTED SUPERNATURAL AND WEIRD FICTION OF WILKIE COLLINS: VOLUME 1 *by Wilkie Collins*—Contains one novel 'The Haunted Hotel', one novella 'Mad Monkton', three novelettes 'Mr Percy and the Prophet', 'The Biter Bit' and 'The Dead Alive' and eight short stories to chill the blood.

THE COLLECTED SUPERNATURAL AND WEIRD FICTION OF WILKIE COLLINS: VOLUME 2 *by Wilkie Collins*—Contains one novel 'The Two Destinies', three novellas 'The Frozen deep', 'Sister Rose' and 'The Yellow Mask' and two short stories to chill the blood.

THE COLLECTED SUPERNATURAL AND WEIRD FICTION OF WILKIE COLLINS: VOLUME 3 *by Wilkie Collins*—Contains one novel 'Dead Secret,' two novelettes 'Mrs Zant and the Ghost' and 'The Nun's Story of Gabriel's Marriage' and five short stories to chill the blood.

FUNNY BONES *selected by Dorothy Scarborough*—An Anthology of Humorous Ghost Stories.

MONTEZUMA'S CASTLE AND OTHER WEIRD TALES *by Charles B. Cory*—Cory has written a superb collection of eighteen ghostly and weird stories to chill and thrill the avid enthusiast of supernatural fiction.

SUPERNATURAL BUCHAN *by John Buchan*—Stories of Ancient Spirits, Uncanny Places & Strange Creatures.

LEONAUR

ALSO FROM LEONAUR
AVAILABLE IN SOFTCOVER OR HARDCOVER WITH DUST JACKET

MR MUKERJI'S GHOSTS *by S. Mukerji*—Supernatural tales from the British Raj period by India's Ghost story collector.

KIPLINGS GHOSTS *by Rudyard Kipling*—Twelve stories of Ghosts, Hauntings, Curses, Werewolves & Magic.

THE COLLECTED SUPERNATURAL AND WEIRD FICTION OF WASHINGTON IRVING: VOLUME 1 *by Washington Irving*—Including one novel 'A History of New York', and nine short stories of the Strange and Unusual.

THE COLLECTED SUPERNATURAL AND WEIRD FICTION OF WASHINGTON IRVING: VOLUME 2 *by Washington Irving*—Including three novelettes 'The Legend of the Sleepy Hollow', 'Dolph Heyliger', 'The Adventure of the Black Fisherman' and thirty-two short stories of the Strange and Unusual.

THE COLLECTED SUPERNATURAL AND WEIRD FICTION OF JOHN KENDRICK BANGS: VOLUME 1 *by John Kendrick Bangs*—Including one novel 'Toppleton's Client or A Spirit in Exile', and ten short stories of the Strange and Unusual.

THE COLLECTED SUPERNATURAL AND WEIRD FICTION OF JOHN KENDRICK BANGS: VOLUME 2 *by John Kendrick Bangs*—Including four novellas 'A House-Boat on the Styx', 'The Pursuit of the House-Boat', 'The Enchanted Typewriter' and 'Mr. Munchausen' of the Strange and Unusual.

THE COLLECTED SUPERNATURAL AND WEIRD FICTION OF JOHN KENDRICK BANGS: VOLUME 3 *by John Kendrick Bangs*—Including twor novellas 'Olympian Nights', 'Roger Camerden: A Strange Story', and ten short stories of the Strange and Unusual.

THE COLLECTED SUPERNATURAL AND WEIRD FICTION OF MARY SHELLEY: VOLUME 1 *by Mary Shelley*—Including one novel 'Frankenstein or the Modern Prometheus', and fourteen short stories of the Strange and Unusual.

THE COLLECTED SUPERNATURAL AND WEIRD FICTION OF MARY SHELLEY: VOLUME 2 *by Mary Shelley*—Including one novel 'The Last Man', and three short stories of the Strange and Unusual.

THE COLLECTED SUPERNATURAL AND WEIRD FICTION OF AMELIA B. EDWARDS *by Amelia B. Edwards*—Contains two novelettes 'Monsieur Maurice', and 'The Discovery of the Treasure Isles', one ballad 'A Legend of Boisguilbert' and seventeen short stories to cill the blood.